Wilbur Smith

Wilbur Smith

GOLD MINE

THE DARK OF THE SUN

THE EYE OF THE TIGER

Sundial

Gold Mine first published in Great Britain in 1970 by
    William Heinemann Ltd ©Wilbur A. Smith 1970

The Dark of the Sun first published in Great Britain in 1965 by
    William Heinemann Ltd © Wilbur A. Smith 1965

The Eye of the Tiger first published in Great Britain in 1975 by
    William Heinemann Ltd © Wilbur A. Smith 1975

This edition first published in Great Britain in 1979 by

Sundial Publications Limited
59 Grosvenor Street
London W.1.

in collaboration with

William Heinemann Limited
15–16 Queen Street
London W.1.

and

Martin Secker & Warburg Limited
54 Poland Street
London W.1.

ISBN 0 906320 00 3

Printed and bound in Great Britain at
William Clowes & Sons Limited
Beccles and London

Contents

GOLD MINE

This book is for
Danielle

CHAPTER I

It began in the time when the world was young, in the time before man, in the time before life itself had evolved upon this planet.

The crust of the earth was still thin and soft, distorted and riven by the enormous pressures from within.

What is now the flat, compacted shield of the African continent, stable and unchanging, was a series of alps. It was range upon range of mountains, thrown up and tumbled down by the movements of the magma at great depth. These were mountains such as man has never seen, so massive as to dwarf the Himalayas, mountains of steaming rock from whose clefts and gaping wounds the molten magma trickled.

It came up from the earth's centre along the fissures and weak places in the crust, bubbling and boiling, yet cooling steadily as it neared the surface so that the least volatile minerals were deposited deeper down, but those with a lower melting point were carried to the surface.

At one point in the measureless passage of time, another series of these fissures opened upon one of the nameless mountain ranges, but from them gushed rivers of molten gold. Some natural freak of temperature and chemical change had resulted in a crude but effective process of refinement during the journey to the earth's surface. The gold was in high concentration in the matrix, and it cooled and solidified at the surface.

If the mountains of that time were so massive as to challenge the imagination of man, then the storms of wind and rain that blew around them were of equal magnitude.

It was a hellish landscape in which the gold field was conceived, cruel mountains reaching stark and sheer into the clouds. Cloud banks dark with the sulphurous gases of the belching earth, so thick that the rays of the sun never penetrated them.

The atmosphere was laden with all the moisture that was to become the seas, so heavy with it that it rained in one perpetual wind-lashed storm upon the hot rock of the cooling earth, then the moisture rose in steam to condense and fall again.

As the years passed by their millions, so the wind and the rain whittled away at the nameless mountain range with its coating of gold-rich ore, grinding it loose and carrying it down in freshets and rivers and rushes of mud and rock into the valley between this range and the next.

Now as the country rock cooled, so the waters lay longer upon the earth before evaporating, and they accumulated in this valley to form a lake the size of an inland sea.

Into this lake poured the storm waters from the golden mountains, carrying with them tiny particles of the yellow metal which settled with other sand and quartz gravel upon the lake bed, to be compacted into a solid sheet.

In time all the gold was scoured from the mountains, transported and laid down upon the lake beds.

Then, as happened every ten million years or so, the earth entered another period of intense seismic activity. The earth shuddered and heaved as earthquake after mammoth earthquake convulsed it.

One fearsome paroxysm cracked the bed of the lake from end to end draining it and fracturing the sedimentary beds, scattering fragments haphazardly so that great sheets of rock many miles across tilted and reared on end.

Again and again the earthquakes gripped and shook the earth. The mountains tottered and collapsed, filling the valley where the lake had stood, burying some of the sheets of gold-rich rock, pulverizing others.

That cycle of seismic activity passed, and the ages wheeled on in their majesty. The floods and the great droughts came and receded. The miraculous spark of life was struck and burned up brightly, through the time of the monstrous reptiles, on through countless twists and turns of evolution until near the middle of the Pleistocene age a man-ape—Australopithecus—picked up the thigh bone of a buffalo from beside an outcrop of rock to use it as a weapon, a tool.

Australopithecus stood at the centre of a flat, sun-seared plateau that reached five hundred miles in each direction to the sea, for the mountains and the lake beds had long ago been flattened and buried.

Eight hundred thousand years later, one of Australopithecus' distant but direct line stood at the same spot with a tool in his hand. The man's name was Harrison and the tool was more sophisticated than that of his ancestor: it was a prospector's pick of wood and metal.

Harrison stooped and chipped at the outcrop of rock that protruded from the dry brown African earth. He freed a piece of the stone and straightened with it in his hand.

He held it to catch the sun and grunted with disgust. It was a most uninteresting piece of stone, conglomerate, marbled black and grey. Without hope he held it to his mouth and licked it, wetting the surface before again holding it to the sun, an old prospector's trick to highlight the metal in the ore.

His eyes narrowed in surprise as the tiny golden flecks in the rock sparkled back at him.

History remembers only his name, not his age nor his antecedents, not the colour of his eyes nor how he died, for within a month he had sold his claim for £10 and disappeared—in search, perhaps, of a really big strike.

He might have done better to retain his title to those claims.

In the eighty years since then an estimated five hundred million ounces of fine gold have been recovered from the fields of the Transvaal and Orange Free State. This is a fraction of that which remains, and which in time will be taken from the earth. For the men who mine the South African fields are the most patiently persistent, inventive and pig-headed of all Vulcan's brood.

This mass of precious metal is the foundation on which the prosperity of a vigorous young nation of eighteen million souls is based.

Yet the earth yields her treasure reluctantly—the men must coax and wrest it from her.

CHAPTER 2

Even with the electric fan blowing up a gale from the corner, it was stinking hot in Rod Ironsides' office.

He reached for the silver Thermos of iced water at the edge of his desk, and arrested the movement as the jug began to dance before his finger tips touched it. The metal bottle skittered across the polished wooden surface; the desk itself shuddered, rustling the papers upon it. The walls of the room shook, so that the windows rattled in their frames. Four seconds the tremor lasted, and then it was still again.

'Christ!' said Rod, and snatched up one of the three telephones on his desk.

'This is the Underground Manager. Get me the rock mechanic's lab, honey, and snap it up, please.'

He drummed his fingers on the desk impatiently as he waited to be connected. The interleading door of his office opened and Dimitri put his head around the jamb.

'You feel that one, Rod? That was a bad one.'

'I felt it.' Then the telephone spoke into his ear.

'Dr Wessels here.'

'Peter, it's Rod. Did you read that one?'

'I haven't got a fix on it yet—can you hold on a minute?'

'I'll wait.' Rod curbed his impatience. He knew that Peter Wessels was the only person who could read the mass of complicated electronic equipment that filled the instrument room of the rock mechanic's laboratory. The laboratory was a joint research project by four of the major gold-mining companies; between them they had put up a quarter of a million Rand to finance an authoritative investigation of rock and seismic activity under stress. They had selected the Sonder Ditch Gold Mining Company's lease area as the site for the laboratory. Now Peter Wessels had his microphones sited thousands of feet down in the earth, and his tape recorders and stylus graphs ready to pin-point any underground disturbance.

Another minute ticked by, and Rod swivelled his chair and stared out of the plate glass window at the monstrous head gear of No. 1 shaft, tall as a ten-storey building.

'Come on, Peter, come on, boy,' he muttered to himself. 'I've got twelve thousand of my boys down there.'

With the telephone still pressed to his ear, he glanced at his watch.

'Two-thirty,' he muttered. 'The worst possible time. They'll still be in the stopes.'

He heard the receiver picked up on the other end, and Peter Wessels' voice was almost apologetic.

'Rod?'

'Yes.'

'I'm sorry, Rod, you've had a force seven pressure burst at 9,500 feet in sector Sugar seven Charlie two.'

'Christ!' said Rod and slammed down the receiver. He was up from his desk in one movement, his face set and angry.

'Dimitri,' he snapped at his assistant still in the doorway. 'We won't wait for them to call us, it's a top sequence emergency. That was a force seven bump, with its source plumb in the middle of our eastern longwall at 95 level.'

'Sweet Mary Mother,' said Dimitri, and darted back into his own office. He bent his glossy black head of curls over the telephone and Rod heard him start his top sequence calls.

'Mine hospital . . . emergency team . . . Chief Ventilation Officer . . . General Manager's office.'

Rod turned away, as the outer door of his office opened and Jimmy Paterson, his electrical engineer, came in.

'I felt it, Rod. How's it look?'

'Bad,' said Rod, then there were the other line managers crowding into his office talking quietly, lighting cigarettes, coughing and shuffling their feet, but all of them watching the white telephone on Rod's desk. The minutes crawled by like crippled insects.

'Dimitri,' Rod called out to break the tension. 'Have you got a cage held at the shaft head?'

'They're holding the Mary Anne for us.'

'I've got five men checking the high tension cable on 95 level,' said Jimmy Paterson, and they ignored him. They were watching the white phone.

'Have you located the boss yet, Dimitri?' Rod asked again. He was pacing in front of his desk. It was only when he stood close to other men that you saw how tall he was.

'He's underground, Rod. He went down at twelve-thirty.'

'Put in an all-stations call for him to contact me here.'

'I've done that already.'

The white phone rang.

Only once, a shrill note that ripped along Rod's nerve ends. Then he had the receiver up to his ear.

'Underground Manager,' he said. There was a long silence and he could hear the man breathing on the other end.

'Speak, man, what is it?'

'The whole bloody thing has come down,' said the voice. It was husky, rough with fear and dust.

'Where are you speaking from?' Rod asked.

'They're still in there,' said the voice. 'They're screaming in there. Under the rock. They're screaming.'

'What is your station?' Rod made his voice cold, hard, trying to reach the man through his shock.

'The whole stope fell in on them. The whole bloody thing.'

'God damn you! You stupid bastard!' Rod bellowed into the phone. 'Give me your station!'

There was stunned silence for a moment. Then the man's voice came back, steadier now, angry from the insult.

'95 level main haulage. Section 43. Eastern longwall.'

'We're coming.' Rod hung up, picked up his yellow fibreglass hard helmet and lamp from the desk.

'43 section. The hanging wall has come down,' he said to Dimitri.

'Fatals?' the little Greek asked.

'For sure. They've got squealers under the rock.'

Rod clapped on his hat.

'Take over on surface, Dimitri.'

CHAPTER 3

Rod was still buttoning the front of his white overalls as he reached the shaft head. Automatically he read the sign above the entrance:

STAY ALERT.   STAY ALIVE.
WITH YOUR CO-OPERATION THIS MINE HAS WORKED
16 FATALITY FREE DAYS.

'We'll have to change the number again,' Rod thought with grim humour.

The Mary Anne was waiting. Into its heavily wired confines were crowded the first aid team and emergency squad. The Mary Anne was the small cage used for lowering and hoisting personnel; there were two much larger cages that could carry one hundred and twenty men at one trip, while the Mary Anne could handle only forty. But that was sufficient for now.

'Let's go,' said Rod as he stepped into the cage, and the onsetter slammed the steel roller doors closed. The bell rang once, twice, and the floor dropped away from under him as the Mary Anne started down. Rod's belly came up to press against his ribs. They went down in one long continuous rush in the darkness. The cage jarring and racketing, the air changing in smell and taste, becoming chemical and processed, the heat building up rapidly.

Rod stood hunch-shouldered, leaning against the metal screen of the cage. The head room was a mere six foot three, and with his helmet on Rod stood taller than that. *So today we get another butcher's bill*, he thought angrily.

He was always angry when the earth took its payment in mangled flesh and snapping bones. All the ingenuity of man and the experience gained in sixty years of deep mining on the Witwatersrand were used in trying to keep the price in blood as low as possible. But when you go down into the ultra-deep levels below eight thousand feet and from those depths you remove a quarter of a million tons of rock each month, mining on an inclined sheet of reef that leaves a vast low-roofed chamber thousands of feet across, then you must pay, for the stress builds up in the rock as the focal points of pressure change until the moment when it reaches breaking point and she bumps. That is when men die.

Rod's knees flexed under him as the cage braked and then yo-yoed to a halt at the brightly lit station on 66 level.

Here they must trans-ship to the sub-main shaft. The door rattled up and Rod left the cage, striding out down the main haulage the size of a railway tunnel; concreted and whitewashed, brightly lit by the bulbs that lined the roof, it curved gently away.

The emergency team followed Rod. Not running, but walking with the suppressed nervous energy of men going into danger. Rod led them towards the sub-main shaft.

There is a limit to the depth which you can sink a shaft into the earth and then equip it to carry men suspended on a steel cable in a tiny wire cage. The limit is about seven thousand feet.

At this depth you must start again, blast out a new headgear chamber from the living rock and below it sink your new shaft, the sub-main.

The sub-main Mary Anne was waiting for them, and Rod led them into it. They stood shoulder to shoulder, and the door rattled shut and again the stomach-swooping rush down into darkness.

Down, down, down.

Rod switched on his head lamp. Now there were tiny motes in the air—air that had been sterilely clean before.

Dust! One of the deadly enemies of the miner. Dust from the burst. As yet the ventilation system had been unable to clear it.

Endlessly they fell in darkness and now it was very hot, the humidity building up so the faces about him, both black and white, were shiny with sweat in the light of his head lamp.

The dust was thicker now, someone coughed. The brightly lit stations flashed past them—76, 77, 78—down, down. The dust was a fine mist now. 85, 86, 87. No one had spoken since entering the cage. 93, 94, 95. The deceleration and stop.

The door rattled up. They were 9,500 feet below the surface of the earth.

'Come on,' said Rod.

CHAPTER 4

There were men cluttering the lobby of 95 station, a hundred and fifty, perhaps two hundred of them. Still filthy from their work in the stopes, clothing sodden with sweat, they were laughing and chattering with the abandon of men freshly released from frightful danger.

In a clear space in the centre of the lobby lay five stretchers, on two of them the bright red blankets were pulled up to cover the faces of the men upon them. The faces of the other three men looked as though they had been dusted with flour.

'Two'—grunted Rod—'so far.'

The station was a shambles, with men milling aimlessly. Each minute more of them came back down the haulages as they were pulled out of the undamaged stopes, which were now suspect.

Quickly Rod looked about him, recognizing the face of one of his mine captains.

'McGee,' he shouted. 'Take over here. Get them sitting down in lines ready to load. We'll start hauling the shift out immediately. Get onto the hoist room, tell them I want the stretcher cases out first.'

He paused long enough to watch McGee take control. He glanced at his watch. Two fifty-six. He realized with astonishment that only twenty-six minutes had passed since he felt the pressure burst in his office.

McGee had the station under a semblance of control. He was shouting into the hoist room telephone, on Rod's authority demanding priority to clear 95 station.

'Right,' said Rod. 'Come on.' And he led into the haulage.

The dust was thick. He coughed. The hanging wall was lower here. As he trudged on once more, Rod pondered the unfortunate choice of mining terminology that had named the roof of an excavation 'the hanging wall'. It made one think of a gallows, or at the best it emphasized the fact that there were millions of tons of rock *hanging* overhead.

The haulage branched, and unerringly Rod took the right fork. In his head he carried an accurate three-dimensional map of the entire 176 miles of tunnels that comprised the Sonder Ditch's workings. The haulage came to a 'T' junction and the arms were lower and narrower. Right to 42 section, left to 43 section. The dust was so thick that visibility was down to ten feet. The dust hung in the air, sinking almost imperceptibly.

'Ventilations knocked out here,' he called over his shoulder. 'Van den Bergh!'

'Yes, sir.' The leader of the emergency squad came up behind him.
'I want air in this drive. Get it on. Use canvas piping if you have to.'
'Right.'
'Then I want pressure on the water hoses to lay this dust.'
'Right.'

Rod turned into the drive. Here the foot wall—the floor—was rough
and the going slower. They came upon a line of steel trolleys filled with
gold reef abandoned in the centre of the drive.

'Get these the hell out of the way,' ordered Rod, and went on.

Fifty paces and he stopped abruptly. He felt the hair on his forearms
stand on end. He could never accustom himself to the sound, no matter
how often he heard it.

In the deliberately callous slang of the miner they called them
'squealers'. It was the sound of a grown man, with his legs crushed
under hundreds of tons of rock, perhaps his spine broken, dust suffocating him, his mind unhinged by the mortal horror of the situation in
which he was trapped, calling for help, calling to his God, calling for
his wife, his children, or his mother.

Rod started forward again, with the sound of it becoming louder, a
terrifying sound, hardly human, sobbing and babbling into silence,
only to start again with a blood-chilling scream.

Suddenly there were men ahead of Rod in the tunnel, dark shapes
looming in the dust mist, their head lamps throwing shafts of yellow
light, grotesque, distorted.

'Who is that?' Rod called, and they recognized his voice.

'Thank God. Thank God you've come, Mr Ironsides.'

'Who is that?'

'Barnard.' The 43 section shift boss.

'What's the damage?'

'The whole hanging wall of the stope came down.'

'How many men in the stope?'

'Forty-two.'

'How many still in?'

'So far we've got out sixteen unhurt, twelve slightly hurt, three
stretcher cases and two dead 'uns.'

The squealer started again, but his voice was much weaker.

'Him?' asked Rod.

'He's got twenty ton of rock lying across his pelvis. I've hit him with
two shots of morphine, but it won't stop him.'

'Can you get into the stope?'

'Yes, there is a crawling hole.' Barnard flashed his lamp over the pile
of fractured blue quartzite that jammed the drive like a collapsed

garden wall. On it was an aperture big enough for a fox terrier to run through. Reflected light showed from the hole, and faintly from within came the grating sounds of movement over loose rock and the muffled voices of men.

'How many men have you got working in there, Barnard?'

'I'—Barnard hesitated, 'I think about ten or twelve.'

And Rod grabbed a handful of his overall front and jerked him almost off his feet.

'You think!' In the head lamps Rod's face was white with fury. 'You've put men in there without recording their numbers? You've put twelve of my boys against the wall to try and save nine?' With a heave Rod lifted the shift boss off his feet and swung him against the side wall of the drive, pinning him there.

'You bastard, you know that most of those nine are chopped already. You know that stope is a bloody killing ground, and you send in *twelve* more to get the chop *and* you don't record their numbers. How the hell would we ever know who to look for if the hanging fell again?' He let the shift boss free, and stood back. 'Get them out of there, clear that stope.'

'But, Mr Ironsides, the General Manager is in there, Mr Lemmer is in there. He was doing an inspection in the stope.'

For a moment Rod was taken aback, then he snarled. 'I don't give a good damn if the State President is in there, clear the stope. We'll start again and this time we'll do it properly.'

Within minutes the rescuers had been recalled; they came squirming out of the aperture, white with dust like maggots wriggling from rotten cheese.

'Right,' said Rod, 'I'll risk four men at a time.'

Quickly he picked four of the floury figures, among them an enormous man on whose right shoulder was the brass badge of a boss boy.

'Big King—you here?' Rod spoke in fanikalo, the lingua franca of the mines which enabled men from a dozen ethnic groups to communicate.

'I am here,' answered Big King.

'You looking for more awards?' A month before, Big King had been lowered on a rope two hundred feet down a vertical orepass to retrieve the body of a white miner. The bravery award by the company had been 100 Rand.

'Who speaks of awards when the earth has eaten the flesh of men?' Big King rebuked Rod softly. 'But today is children's play only. Is the Nkosi coming into the stope?' It was a challenge.

Rod's place was not in the stope. He was the organizer, the co-ordinater. Yet, he could not ignore the challenge, no Bantu would believe that he had not stood back in fear and sent other men into die.

'Yes,' said Rod, 'I'm coming into the stope.'

He led them in. The hole was only just big enough to admit the bulk of Rod's body. He found himself in a chamber, the size of an average room, but the roof was only three and a half feet high. He played his lamp quickly across the hanging wall, and it was wicked. The rock was cracked and ugly, 'a bunch of grapes' was the term.

'Very pretty,' he said, and dropped the beam of his lamp.

The squealer was within an arm's length of Rod. His body from the waist up protruded from under a piece of rock the size of a Cadillac. Someone had wrapped a red blanket around his upper body. He was quiet now, lying still. But as the beam of Rod's lamp fell upon him, he lifted his head. His eyes were crazed, unseeing, his face running with the sweat of terror and insanity. His mouth snapped open, wide and pink in the shiny blackness of his face. He began to scream, but suddenly the sound was drowned by a great red-black gout of blood that came gushing up his throat, and spurted from his mouth.

As Rod watched in horror, the Bantu posed like that, his head thrown back, his mouth gaping as though he were a gargoyle, the life blood pouring from him. Then slowly the head sagged forwards, and flopped face downwards. Rod crawled to him, lifted his head and pillowed it on the red blanket.

There was blood on his hands and he wiped it on the front of his overalls.

'Three,' he said, 'so far.' And leaving the dying man he crawled on towards the broken face of the fall.

Big King crawled up beside him with two pinch bars. He handed one to Rod.

Within an hour it had become a contest, a trial of strength between the two men. Behind them the other three men were shoring up and passing back the rock that Rod and Big King loosened from the face. Rod knew he was being childish, he should have been back in the main haulage, not only directing the rescue, but also making all the other decisions and alternative arrangements that were needed now. The company paid him for his brains and his experience, not for his muscle.

'The hell with it,' he thought. 'Even if we miss the blast this evening, I'm staying here.' He glanced at Big King, and reached forward to get his hands onto a bigger piece of rock in the jam. He strained, using his arms first, then bringing the power of his whole body into it. The rock was solid. Big King placed huge black hands on the rock, and they pulled together. In a rush of smaller rock it came away, and they shoved it back between them, grinning at each other.

At seven o'clock Rod and Big King withdrew from the stope to rest and eat sandwiches, and drink Thermos coffee while Rod spoke to Dimitri over the field telephone that had been laid up to the face.

'We've pulled shift on both shafts, Rod, the workings are clear to blast. Except for your lot, there are fifty-eight men in your 43 section.' Dimitri's voice was reedy over the field telephone.

'Hold on.' Rod revolved the situation in his mind. He worked it out slower than usual, for he was tired, emotionally and physically drained. If he stopped the blast on both shafts for fear of bringing down more rock in 43 section, it would cost the Company a day's production, ten thousand tons of gold reef worth sixteen Rand a ton, the formidable sum of R160,000 or £80,000 or $200,000 whichever way you looked at it.

It was highly probable that every man in the stope was already dead, and the original pressure burst had de-stressed the rock above and around the 95 level, so there was little danger of further bumps.

And yet there might be someone alive in there, someone lying pinned in the womb-warm darkness of the stope with a bunch of loose grapes hanging over his unprotected body. When they hit all the blast buttons on the Sonder Ditch Mine, they fired eighteen tons of Dynagel. The kick was considerable, it would bring down those grapes.

'Dimitri,' Rod made his decision, 'burn all longwalls on No. 2 shaft at seven-thirty exactly.' No. 2 shaft was three miles away. That would save the Company R80,000. 'Then at precisely five minute intervals burn south, north and west longwalls here on No. 1 shaft.' Spreading the blast would reduce the disturbance, and that put another R60,000 in the shareholders' pockets. The total monetary loss inflicted by the disaster was around R20,000. Not too bad really, Rod thought sardonically, blood was cheap. You could buy it at three Rand a pint from the Central Blood Transfusion Service.

'All right,' he stood up, and flexed his aching shoulders, 'I'm pulling everybody back into the safety of the shaft pillar while we blast.'

CHAPTER 5

After the successive earth tremors of the blast, Rod put them back into the stope, and at nine o'clock they uncovered the bodies of two machine boys crushed against the metal of their own rock drill. Ten feet further on they found the white miner; his body was unmarked, but his head was flattened.

At eleven o'clock they found two more machine boys. Rod was in the haulage when they dragged them out through the small opening. Neither of them was recognizable as human, they looked more like lumps of raw meat that had been rubbed in dirt.

A little after midnight Rod and Big King went into the stope again to take over from the team at the face, and twenty minutes later they holed through the wall of loose rock into another chamber that had been miraculously left standing.

The air in here was steamy with heat. Rod recoiled instinctively from the filthy moist gush of it against his face. Then he forced himself to crawl forward and peer into the opening.

Ten feet away lay Frank Lemmer, the General Manager of the Sonder Ditch Mine. He lay on his back. His helmet had been knocked from his head, and a deep gash split the skin above his eye. Blood from the gash had run back into his silver hair and clotted black. He opened his eyes and blinked owlishly in the dazzle of Rod's lamp. Quickly Rod averted the beam.

'Mr Lemmer,' he said.

'What the bloody hell are you doing with the rescue team?' growled Frank Lemmer. 'It's not your job. Haven't you learned a single god-damned thing in twenty years of mining?'

'Are you all right, sir?'

'Get a doctor in here,' replied Frank Lemmer. 'You're going to have to cut me loose from this lot.'

Rod wriggled up to where he lay, and then he saw what Frank Lemmer meant. From the elbow his arm was pinned under a solid slab of rock. Rod ran his hands over the slab, feeling it. Only explosive would shift that rock. As always Frank Lemmer was right.

Rod wriggled out of the opening and called over his shoulder. 'Get the telephone up here.'

After a few minutes delay he had the receiver, and was through to the station at 95 level which had been set up as an advance aid post and rest station for the rescuers.

'This is Ironsides, get me Dr Stander.'

'Hold on.'
Then moments later, 'Hello, Rod, it's Dan.'
'Dan, we've found the old man.'
'How is he, conscious?'
'Yes, but he's pinned—you'll have to cut.'
'Are you sure?' Dan Stander asked.
'Of course I'm bloody well sure,' snapped Rod.
'Whoa, boy!' admonished Dan.
'Sorry.'
'Okay, where's he caught?'
'Arm. You'll have to cut above the elbow.'
'Charming!' said Dan.
I'll wait here for you.'
'Right. I'll be up in five minutes.'

CHAPTER 6

'It's funny, you see them chopped time and again, but you know it will
never happen to you.' Frank Lemmer's voice was steady and even.
The arm must be numb, Rod thought as he lay beside him in the stope.
    Frank Lemmer rolled his head towards Rod. 'Why don't you go
farming, boy?'
    'You know why,' said Rod.
    'Yes.' Lemmer smiled a little, just a twitching of the lips. With his
free hand he wiped his mouth. 'You know, I had just three months more
before I went on pension. I nearly made it. You'll end like this, boy, in
the dirt with your bones crunched up.'
    'It's not the end,' said Rod.
    'Isn't it?' asked Frank Lemmer, and this time he chuckled. 'Isn't it?'
    'What's the joke?' asked Dan Stander, poking his head into the tiny
chamber.
    'Christ, it took you long enough to get here,' growled Frank Lemmer.
    'Give me a hand, Rod.' Dan passed his bag through, then as he
crawled forward he spoke to Frank Lemmer.
    'Union Steel closed at 98 cents tonight. I told you to buy.'
    'Over-priced, over-capitalized,' snorted Frank Lemmer. Dan lay on
his side in the dirt and laid out his instruments, and they argued stocks
and shares. When Dan had the syringe full of pentathol and was
swabbing Frank Lemmer's stringy old arm, Lemmer rolled his head
towards Rod again.

'We made a good dig here, Rodney, you and I. I wish they'd give it to you now, but they won't. You're still too young. But whoever they put in my place, you keep an eye on him, you know the ground—don't let him balls it up.'

And the needle went in.

Dan cut through the arm in four and a half minutes, and twenty-seven minutes later Frank Lemmer died of shock and exposure in the Mary Anne on his way to the surface.

CHAPTER 7

Once he had paid Patti's alimony there was not too much of Rod's salary left for extravagances, but one of these was the big cream Maserati. Although it was a 1967 model, and had done nearly thirty thousand miles when he bought it, the instalments still took a healthy bite out of his monthly pay cheque.

On mornings like this he reckoned the expense worthwhile. He came twisting down from the Kraalkop ridge, and when the national road flattened and straightened for the final run into Johannesburg he let the Maserati go. The car seemed to flatten against the ground like a running lion, and the exhaust note changed subtly, becoming deeper, more urgent.

Ordinarily, it was an hour's run from the Sonder Ditch Mine into the city of Johannesburg, but Rod could clip twenty minutes off that time.

It was Saturday morning, and Rod's mood was light and expectant.

Since the divorce Rod had lived a Jekyll and Hyde existence. Five days of the week he was the company man in top-line management, but on the last two days of the week he went into Johannesburg with his golf clubs in the boot of the Maserati, the keys to his luxury Hillbrow apartment in his pocket, and a chuckle on his lips.

Today the anticipation was keener than ever for, in addition to the twenty-two-year-old blonde model who was prepared to devote her evening to entertaining Rodney Ironsides, there was the mysterious summons from Dr Manfred Steyner to answer.

The summons had been delivered by a nameless female caller describing herself as 'Dr Steyner's Secretary'. It had come the day after Frank Lemmer's funeral, and was for Saturday at eleven o'clock.

Rod had never met Manfred Steyner, but he had, of course, heard of him. Anyone who worked for any of the fifty or sixty companies that comprised the Central Rand Consolidated Group must have heard of

Manfred Steyner, and the Sonder Ditch Gold Company was just one of the Group.

Manfred Steyner had a bachelor's degree in Economics from Berlin University, and a Doctor's degree in Business Administration from Cornell. He had joined C.R.C. a mere twelve years previously at the age of thirty, and now he was the front runner. Hurry Hirschfeld could not live for ever, although he gave indications of doing so, and when he went down to make a takeover bid on Hades, the word was that Manfred Steyner would succeed him as Chairman of C.R.C.

Chairmanship of C.R.C. was an enviable position; the incumbent automatically became one of the five most powerful men in Africa, and that included heads of state.

The betting favoured Dr Steyner for a number of good reasons. He had a brain that had earned him the nickname of 'The Computer'; no one had yet been able to detect in him the slightest evidence of a human weakness, and more than this he had taken the trouble ten years previously to catch Hurry Hirschfeld's only grand-daughter as she emerged from Cape Town University and marry her.

Dr Steyner was in a strong position, and Rod was intrigued with the prospect of meeting him.

The Maserati was registering 125 miles an hour as he went under the over-pass of the Kloof Gold Mining Company property.

'Johannesburg, here I come!' Rod laughed aloud.

It was ten minutes before eleven o'clock when Rod found the brass plaque reading 'Dr M. K. Steyner' in a secluded lane of the lush Johannesburg suburb of Sandown. The house was not visible from the road, and Rod let the Maserati roll gently in through the tall white gates, with their imitation Cape Dutch gables.

The gates, he decided, were a display of shocking taste but the gardens beyond them were paradise. Rod knew rock, but flowers were his weak suit. He recognized the massed banks of red and yellow against the green lawns as cannas, but after that he had no names for the blazing beauty spread about him.

'Wow!' he muttered in awe. 'Someone has done a hell of a lot of work around here.'

Around a curve in the macadamized drive lay the house. It also was Cape Dutch and Rod forgave Dr Steyner his gates.

'Wow!' he said again, and involuntarily braked the Maserati to a standstill.

Cape Dutch is one of the most difficult styles to copy effectively, where one line in a hundred out of place could spoil the effect; this particular example worked perfectly. It gave the feel of timelessness, of solidarity, and mixed it subtly with a grace and finesse of line. He guessed that the shutters and beams were genuine yellow wood and the windows hand-leaded.

Rod looked at it, and felt envy prickle and burn within him. He loved fine things, like his Maserati, but this was another concept in material possessions. He was jealous of the man that owned it, knowing that his own entire year's income would not be sufficient for a down payment on the land alone.

'So I've got my flat,' he grinned ruefully, and coasted down to park in front of the line of garages.

It was not clear which was the correct entrance to use, and he chose at random from a number of paved paths that all led in the general direction of the house.

Around a bend in this path he came on another spectacle. Though smaller it had, if anything, a more profound effect on Rod than the house had. It was a feminine posterior of equal grace and finesse of line, clad in Helanka stretch ski-pants, and protruding from a large and exotic bush.

Rod was captivated. He stood and watched as the bush shook and rustled, and the bottom wriggled and heaved.

Suddenly, in ladylike tones there issued from the bush a most unladylike oath and the bottom shot backwards and its owner straightened up with her forefinger in her mouth, sucking noisily.

'It bit me!' she mumbled around the finger. 'Damned stinkbug bit me!'

'Well, you shouldn't tease them,' said Rod.

And she spun round to face him. The first thing Rod noticed were her eyes—they were enormous, completely out of proportion to the rest of her face.

'I wasn't—' she started, and then stopped. The finger came out of her mouth. Instinctively one hand went to her hair, and the other began straightening her blouse and brushing off bits of vegetation that were clinging to her.

'Who are you?' she asked, and those huge eyes swept over him. This was fairly standard reaction for any woman between the ages of sixteen and sixty viewing Rodney Ironsides for the first time, and Rodney accepted it gracefully.

'My name is Rodney Ironsides. I've an appointment to see Dr Steyner.'

'Oh.' She was hurriedly tucking her shirt-tails into her slacks. 'My husband will be in his study.'

He had known who she was. He had seen her photographs fifty times in the Group newspaper; but in them she was usually in full-length evening dress and diamonds, not in a blouse with a tear in one sleeve nor pig-tails that were coming down. In the pictures her make-up was immaculate; now she had none at all and her face was flushed and dewed with perspiration.

'I must look a mess. I've been gardening,' said Theresa Steyner unnecessarily.

'Did you do this garden yourself?'

'Only a very little of the muscle work, but I planned it,' she answered. She decided he was big and ugly—no, not really ugly, but battered-looking.

'It's beautiful,' said Rod.

'Thank you.' No, not battered-looking, she changed her mind, tough-looking, and the chest hair curled out of the vee of his open neck shirt.

'This is a protea, isn't it?' He indicated the bush from which she had recently emerged. He was guessing.

'Nutans,' she said; he must be in his late thirties, there was greying at his temples.

'Oh, I thought it was a protea.'

'It is. "Nutans" is its proper name. There are over two hundred different varieties of proteas,' she answered seriously. His voice didn't fit his appearance at all, she decided. He looked like a prize fighter but spoke like a lawyer, probably was one. It was usually lawyers or business consultants who came calling on Manfred.

'Is that so? It's very pretty.' Rod touched one of the blooms.

'Yes, isn't it? I've got over fifty varieties growing here.'

And suddenly they were smiling at each other.

'I'll take you up to the house,' said Theresa Steyner.

CHAPTER 8

'Mr Ironsides is here, Manfred.'

'Thank you.' He sat at the stinkwood desk in a room that smelled of wax polish. He made no effort to rise from his seat.

'Would you like a cup of coffee?' Theresa asked from the doorway. 'Or tea?'

'No, thank you,' answered Manfred Steyner without consulting Rod who stood beside her.

'I'll leave you to it, then,' she said.

'Thank you, Theresa.' And she turned away. Rod went on standing where he was; he was studying this man of whom he had heard so much.

Manfred Steyner appeared younger than his forty-two years. His hair was light brown, almost blond, and brushed straight back. He wore spectacles with heavy black frames, and his face was smooth and silky-looking, soft as a girl's with no beard shadow on his chin. His hands that lay on the polished desk top were hairless, smooth, so that Rod wondered if he had used a depilatory on them.

'Come in,' he said, and Rod moved to the desk. Steyner wore a white silk shirt in which the ironing creases still showed. The cloth was snowy white and over it he wore a Royal Johannesburg Golf Club tie, with onyx cuff links. Suddenly Rod realized that neither shirt nor tie had ever been worn before—that much was true of what he had heard then. Steyner ordered his shirts hand-made by the gross and wore each once only.

'Sit down, Ironsides.' Steyner slurred his vowels slightly, just a trace of a Teutonic accent.

'Dr Steyner,' said Rod softly, 'you have a choice. You may call me Rodney or *Mr* Ironsides.'

There was no change in Steyner's voice nor expression.

'I would like to go over your background, please, Mr Ironsides, as a preliminary to our discussion. You have no objection?'

'No, Dr Steyner.'

'You were born October 16th 1931, at Butterworth in the Transkei. Your father was a native trader, your mother died January 1939. Your father was commissioned Captain in the Durban Light Infantry and died of wounds on the Po River in Italy during the winter of 1944. You were raised by your maternal uncle in East London. Matriculating from Queen's College, Grahamstown, in 1947, you were unsuccessful in obtaining a Chamber of Mines scholarship to Witwatersrand University for a B.Sc. (Mining Engineering) degree. You enrolled in the

G.M.T.S. (Government Mining Training School) and obtained your blasting ticket during 1949. At which time you joined the Blyvooruit-zicht Gold Mining Company Ltd as a learner miner.'

Dr Steyner stood up from his desk and crossing to the panelled wall he pressed a concealed switch and a portion of the panelling slid back to reveal a wash basin and towel rack. As he went on talking he began very meticulously to soap and wash his hands.

'In the same year you were promoted to miner and in 1952 to shift boss, 1954 to mine captain. You successfully completed the examination for the Mine Manager's ticket in 1959, and in 1962 you came to us as an Assistant Section Manager; in 1963, Section Manager, 1965, Assist-ant Underground Manager, and in 1968 you achieved your present position as Underground Manager.'

Dr Steyner began drying his hands on a snowy white towel.

'You've memorized my company record pretty thoroughly.' Rod admitted.

Dr Steyner crumpled the towel and dropped it into a bin below the wash basin. He pressed the button and the panelling slid closed, then he came back to the desk stepping precisely over the glossy polished wooden floor, and Rod realized that he was a small man, not more than five and a half feet tall, about the same height as his wife.

'This is something of an achievement,' Steyner went on. 'The next youngest Underground Manager in the entire Group is forty-six years of age, whereas you are not yet thirty-nine.'

Rod inclined his head in acknowledgement.

'Now,' said Dr Steyner as he reseated himself and laid his freshly washed hands on the desk top. 'I would like briefly to touch on your private life—you have no objections?'

Again Rod inclined his head.

'The reason that your application for the Chamber of Mines scholar-ship was refused, despite your straight A matriculation, was the recom-mendation of your headmaster to the selection board in effect that you were of unstable and violent disposition.'

'How the hell did you know that?' ejaculated Rod.

'I have access to the board's records. It seems that once you had received your matric you immediately assaulted your former headmaster.'

'I beat the hell out of the bastard,' Rod agreed happily.

'An expensive indulgence, Mr Ironsides. It cost you a university degree.'

And Rod was silent.

'To continue. In 1959 you married Patricia Anne Harvey. Of the union was born a girl child in the same year, to be precise, seven and a half months after the wedding.'

Rod squirmed slightly in his chair, and Dr Steyner went on quietly.

'This marriage terminated in divorce in 1964, your wife suing you on the grounds of adultery, and receiving custody of the child, alimony and maintenance in the sum of R450.00 monthly.'

'What's all this about?' demanded Rod.

'I am attempting to establish an accurate picture of your present circumstances. It is necessary, I assure you.' Dr Steyner removed his spectacles and began polishing the lens on a clean white handkerchief. There were the marks of the frames on the bridge of his nose.

'Go on, then.' Despite himself, Rod was fascinated to learn just how much Steyner knew about him.

'In 1968 there was a paternity suit brought against you by a Miss Diane Johnson and judgement for R150.00 per month.'

Rod blinked, and was silent.

'I should mention two further actions against you for assault, both unsuccessful on the grounds of justification or self-defence.'

'Is that all?' asked Rod sarcastically.

'Almost,' admitted Dr Steyner. 'It is only necessary to note further recurrent expenditure in the form of a monthly payment of R150.00 on a continental sports car, and a further R100.00 per month rental on the premises 596 Glen Alpine Heights, Corner Lane, Hillbrow.'

Rod was furious; he had believed that no one in C.R.C. knew about the flat.

'Damn you! You've been prying into my affairs!'

'Yes,' agreed Dr Steyner levelly. 'I am guilty, but in good cause. If you bear with me, you'll see why.'

Suddenly Dr Steyner stood up from the desk, crossed the room to the concealed wash basin, and again began to wash his hands. As he dried them, he spoke again.

'Your monthly commitments are R850. Your salary, after deduction of tax, is less than one thousand Rand. You have no mining degree, and the chances of your taking the next step upwards to General Manager without it are remote. You are at your ceiling, Mr Ironsides. On your own ability you can go no further. In thirty years' time you will not be the youngest Underground Manager in the C.R.C. Group, but the oldest.' Dr Steyner paused. 'That is, provided that your rather expensive tastes have not landed you in a debtors' prison, and that neither the quickness and heat of your temper, nor the matching speed and temperature of your genitalia have gotten you into really serious trouble.'

Steyner dropped the towel in the bin and returned to his seat. They sat in absolute silence, regarding each other for a full minute.

'You got me all the way up here to tell me this?' asked Rod. His whole body was tense, his voice slightly husky, it needed only one ounce more of provocation to launch him across the desk at Steyner's throat.

'No.' Steyner shook his head. 'I got you up here to tell you that I will use all my influence, which I flatter myself is considerable, to secure your appointment—and I mean immediate appointment—to the position of General Manager of the Sonder Ditch Gold Mining Company Ltd.'

Rod recoiled in his chair as though Steyner had spat in his face. He stared at him aghast.

'Why?' he asked at last. 'What do you want in exchange?'

'Neither your friendship, nor your gratitude,' Dr Steyner told him. 'But your unquestioning obedience to my instructions. You will be my man—completely.'

Rod went on staring at him while his mind raced. Without Steyner's intervention he would wait at the very least ten years for this promotion, if it ever came. He wanted it, my God, how he wanted it. The achievement, the increase in income, the power that went with the job. His own mine! His own mine at the age of thirty-eight—and an additional ten thousand Rand per annum.

Yet Rod was not gullible enough to believe that Manfred Steyner's price would be cheap. When the instruction came that he was to follow with unquestioning obedience, he knew it would stink like a ten-day corpse. But once he had the job he could refuse the instruction. Get the job first, then decide once he received the instruction whether to follow it or not.

'I accept,' he said.

Manfred Steyner stood up from the desk.

'You will hear from me,' he said. 'Now you may go.'

CHAPTER 9

Rod crossed the wide-flagged stoep without seeing or hearing; vaguely he wandered down across the lawns towards his car. His mind was harrying the recent conversation, tearing it to pieces like a pack of wild dogs on a carcass. He almost bumped into Theresa Steyner before he saw her, and abruptly his mind dropped the subject of the General Managership.

Theresa had changed her clothing, made up her face and eyes, and the pig-tails were concealed under a lime-coloured silk scarf, all this in the half hour since their last meeting. She was hovering over a flower bed with a flower basket on one arm, as bright and pleasing as a hummingbird.

Rod was amused and flattered, vain enough to realize that the change was in his honour, and connoisseur enough to appreciate the improvement. 'Hello.' She looked up, contriving successfully to look both surprised and artless. Her eyes were really enormous, and the make-up was designed to enhance their size.

'You are a busy little bee.' Rod ran a knowledgeable appraisal over the floral slack suit she wore, and saw the colour start in her cheeks as she felt his eyes.

'Did you have a successful meeting?'

'Very.'

'Are you a lawyer?'

'No. I work for your grandfather.'

'Doing what?'

'Mining his gold.'

'Which mine?'

'Sonder Ditch.'

'What's your position?'

'Well, if your husband is as good as his word, I'm the new General Manager.'

'You're too young,' she said.

'That's what I thought.'

'Pops will have something to say on the subject.'

'Pops?' he asked.

'My grandfather.' And Rod laughed before he could stop himself.

'What's so funny?'

'The Chairman of C.R.C. being called "Pops".'

'I'm the only one who calls him that.'

'I bet you are.' Rod laughed again. 'In fact, I'd bet you'd get away with a lot of things no one else would dare.'

Suddenly the underlying sexuality of his last remark occurred to them both and they fell silent. Theresa looked down and carefully snipped the head off a flower.

'I didn't mean it that way,' apologized Rod.

'What way, Mr Ironsides?' She looked up and inquired with mischievous innocence, and they laughed together with the awkwardness gone again.

She walked beside him to the car, making it seem a completely natural thing to do, and as he slipped behind the steering-wheel she remarked:

'Manfred and I will be coming out to the Sonder Ditch next week. Manfred is to present long service and bravery awards to some of your men.' She had already refused the invitation to accompany Manfred, she must now see to it that she was re-invited. 'I shall probably see you then.'

'I look forward to it.' said Rod, and let in the clutch.

Rod glanced in the rear view mirror. She was a remarkably provocative and attractive woman. A careless man could drown in those eyes.

'Dr Manfred Steyner has got himself a big fat problem there,' he decided. 'Our Manfred is probably so busy soaping and scrubbing his equipment, that he never gets round to using it.'

CHAPTER 10

Through the leaded windows Dr Steyner caught a glimpse of the Maserati as it disappeared around the curve in the driveway, and he listened as the throb of the engine dwindled into silence.

He lifted the receiver of the telephone and wiped it with the white handkerchief before putting it to his ear. He dialled and while it rang he inspected the nails of his free hand minutely.

'Steyner,' he said into the mouthpiece. 'Yes—yes.' He listened.

'Yes . . . He has just left . . . Yes, it is arranged . . .No, there will be no difficulty there, I am sure.' As he spoke he was looking at the palm of his hand. He saw the tiny beads of perspiration appear on his skin and an expression of disgust tightened his lips.

'I am fully aware of the consequences. I tell you, I know.'

He closed his eyes and listened for another minute without moving as the receiver squawked and clacked, then he opened his eyes.

'It will be done in good time, I assure you. Goodbye.'

He hung up and went to wash his hands. Now, he thought, as he worked up lather, to get it past the old man.

CHAPTER 11

He was old now, seventy-eight long hard years old. His hair and his eyebrows were creamy white. His skin was folded and creased, freckled and spotted, hanging in unexpected little pouches under his chin and eyes.

His body had dried out, so he stood gaunt and stooped like a tree that has taken a set before the prevailing winds; but there was still the underlying urgency in the way he held himself, the same urgency that had earned him the name of 'Hurry' Hirschfeld when first he bustled into the gold fields sixty years ago.

On this Monday morning he was standing before the full length windows of his penthouse office, looking down on the city of Johannesburg. Reef House stood shoulder to massive shoulder with the Schlesinger Building on the Braamfontein ridge above the city proper. From this height it seemed that Johannesburg cowered at Hurry Hirschfeld's feet, as well it should.

Long ago, even before the great depression of the thirties, he had ceased to measure his wealth in terms of money. He owned outright a little over a quarter of the issued share capital of Central Rand Consolidated. At the present market price of R120 per share, this was a staggering sum. In addition, through a complicated arrangement of trusts, proxy rights and interlocking directorates, he had control of a further massive block of twenty per cent of the company's voting rights.

The overhead intercom pinged softly into this room of soft fabrics and muted colours, and Hurry started slightly.

'Yes,' he said, without turning away from the window.

'Dr Steyner is here, Mr Hirschfeld,' his secretary's voice whispered, ghostly and disembodied into the luscious room.

'Send him in,' snapped Hurry. That goddamned intercom always gave him the creeps. The whole goddamned room gave him the creeps. It was, as Hurry had said often and loudly, like a fairy brothel.

For fifty-five years he had worked in a bleak uncarpeted office with a few yellowing photographs of men and machinery on its walls. Then they had moved him in here—he glanced around the room with the distaste that five years had not lulled. What did they think he was, a bloody ladies' hairdresser?

The panelling door slid noiselessly aside and Dr Manfred Steyner stepped neatly into the room.

'Good morning, Grandfather,' he said. For ten years, ever since

Terry had been bird-brained enough to marry him, Manfred Steyner
had called Hurry Hirschfeld that, and Hurry hated it. He remembered
now that Manfred Steyner was also responsible for the design and decor
of Reef House, and therefore the author of his recent irritation.

'What ever it is you want—No!' he said, and he moved across to the
air-conditioning controls. The thermostat was already set at 'high',
now Hurry turned it to 'highest'. Within minutes the room would be
at the correct temperature for growing orchids.

'How are you this morning, Grandfather?' Manfred seemed not to
have heard; his expression was bland and neutral as he moved to the
desk and laid out his papers.

'Bloody awful,' said Hurry. It was impossible to disconcert the little
prig, he thought, you might as well shout insults at an efficiently functioning piece of machinery.

'I am sorry to hear that.' Manfred took out his handkerchief and
touched his chin and forehead. 'I have the weekly reports.'

Hurry capitulated and went across to the desk. This was business.
He sat down and read quickly. His questions were abrupt, cutting and
instantly answered, but Manfred's handkerchief was busy now, swabbing and dabbing. Twice he removed his spectacles and wiped steam
from the lens.

'Can I turn the air-conditioning down a little, Grandfather?'

'You touch it and I'll kick your arse,' said Hurry without looking up.

Another five minutes and Manfred Steyner stood up suddenly.

'Excuse me, Grandfather.' And he shot across the office and disappeared into the adjoining bathroom suite. Hurry cocked his head to
listen, and when he heard the taps hiss he grinned happily. The air-
conditioning was the only method he had discovered of disconcerting
Manfred Steyner, and for ten years he had been experimenting with
various techniques.

'Don't use all the soap,' he shouted gleefully. 'You are the one always
on about office expenses!'

It did not seem ludicrous to Hurry that one of the richest and most
influential men in Africa should devote so much time and energy to
baiting his personal assistant.

At eleven o'clock Manfred Steyner gathered his papers and began
packing them carefully in his monogrammed pigskin briefcase.

'About the appointment of a new General Manager for the Sonder
Ditch to replace Mr Lemmer. You will recall my memo regarding the
appointment of younger men to key positions—'

'Never read the bloody thing,' lied Hurry Hirschfeld. They both
knew he read everything, and remembered it.

'Well—' Manfred went on to enlarge his thesis for a minute, then ended, 'In view of this, my department, myself concurring entirely, urges the appointment of Rodney Barry Ironsides, the present Underground Manager, to the position. I hoped that you would initial the recommendation and we can put it through at Friday's meeting.'

Dextrously Manfred slid the yellow memo in front of Hurry Hirschfeld, unscrewed the cap of his pen and offered it to him. Hurry picked the memo up between thumb and forefinger as though it were someone's dirty handkerchief and dropped it into the waste-paper bin.

'Do you wish me to tell you in detail what you and your planning department can do?' he asked.

'Grandfather,' Manfred admonished him mildly, 'you cannot run the company as though you were a robber baron. You cannot ignore the team of highly trained men who are your advisers.'

'I've run it that way for fifty years. You show me who's going to change that.' Hurry leaned back in his chair with vast satisfaction and fished a powerful-looking cigar out of his inner pocket.

'Grandfather, that cigar! The doctor said—'

'And I said Fred Plummer gets the job as Manager of the Sonder Ditch.'

'He goes on pension next year,' protested Manfred Steyner.

'Yes,' Hurry nodded. 'But how does that alter the position?'

'He's an old dodderer,' Manfred tried again. There was a desperate edge to his voice. He had not anticipated one of the old man's whims cutting across his plans.

'He's twelve years younger than I am,' growled Hurry ominously. 'How's that make him an old dodderer?'

CHAPTER 12

Now that the weekend was over, Rod found the apartment oppressive, and he longed to get out of it.

He shaved, standing naked before the mirror, and he caught a whiff of the reeking ashtrays and half-empty glasses in the lounge. The char would have her customary Monday-morning greeting when she came in later today. From Louis Botha Avenue the traffic noise was starting to build up and he glanced at his watch—six o'clock in the morning. A good time to examine your soul, he decided, and leaned forward to watch his own eyes in the mirror.

'You're too old for this type of living,' he told himself seriously.

'You've had four years of it now, four years since the divorce, and that's about enough. It would be nice now to go to bed with the same woman on two consecutive nights.'

He rinsed his razor, and turned on the taps in the shower cabinet.

'Might even be able to afford it, if our boy Manfred delivers the goods.' Rod had not allowed himself to believe too implicitly in Manfred Steyner's promise; but during the whole of these last two days the excitement had been there beneath the cynicism.

He stepped into the shower and soaped himself, then turned the cold tap full on. Gasping he shut it off and reached for his towel. Still drying himself, he went through and stood at the foot of the bed; as he towelled himself he examined the girl who lay among the tousled sheets.

She was tanned dark toffee brown so she appeared to be dressed in white transparent bra and panties where the skin was untouched by the sun. Her hair was a blonde-gold flurry across her face and the pillow, at odds with the jet black triangle of body hair. Her lips in sleep were fixed in a soft pink pout, and she looked disquietingly young. Rod had to make a conscious effort to remember her name—she was not the companion with whom he had begun the weekend.

'Lucille,' he said, sitting down beside her. 'Wake up. Time to roll.'

She opened her eyes.

'Good morning,' he said and kissed her gently.

'Mmm.' She blinked. 'What time is it? I don't want to get fired.'

'Six,' he told her.

'Oh, good. Plenty of time.' And she rolled over and snuggled down into the sheets.

'Like hell.' He slapped her bottom lightly. 'Move, girl. Can you cook?'

'No—' She lifted her head. 'What's your name again?' she asked.

'Rod,' he told her.

'That's right—Piston Rod,' she giggled. 'What a way to die! Are you sure you aren't powered by steam?'

'How old are you?' he asked.

'Nineteen. How old are you?'

'Thirty-eight.'

'Daddy, you're vintage!' she told him vehemently.

'Yes, sometimes I feel that way.' He stood up. 'Let's go.'

'You go. I'll lock up when I leave.'

'No sale,' he said. The last one he had left in the flat had cleaned it out—groceries, liquor, glasses, towels, even the ashtrays. 'Five minutes to dress.'

Fortunately she lived on his way. She directed him to a rundown block of flats under the mine dumps at Booysens.

'I'm putting three blind sisters through school. You want to help?' she asked as he parked the Maserati.

'Sure.' He eased a five-Rand note out of his wallet and handed it to her.

'Ta muchly.' And she slipped out of the red leather seat, closed the door and walked away. She did not look back before she disappeared into the block, and Rod felt an unaccountable wave of loneliness wash over him. It was no intense that he sat quiescent for a full minute before he could throw it off, then he hit the gears and screeched away from the kerb.

'My little five-Rand friend,' he said. 'She really cares!'

He drove fast, so that as he topped the Kraalkop ridge the shadows were still long, and the dew lay silver on the grass. He pulled the Maserati into a layby and climbed out. Leaning against the bonnet he lit a cigarette, grimacing at the taste, and looked down at the valley.

There was no natural surface indication of the immense treasure house that lay below. It was like any of the other countless grassy plains of the Transvaal. In the centre stood the town of Kitchenerville, which for half a century had rejoiced in the fact that Lord Kitchener had camped one night here in pursuit of the wily Boer: a collection of three dozen buildings which had expanded miraculously into three thousand, around a magnificent town hall and shopping complex. Dressed in public lawns and gardens, wide streets and bright new houses, all of it was paid for by the mining houses whose lease areas converged on the town.

Out of the bleak veld surrounding the town their headgears stood like colossal monuments to the gold hunger of man. Around the headgears clustered the plants and workshops. There were fourteen headgears in the valley. The field was divided into five lease areas, following the original farm titles, and was mined by five separate companies. Thornfontein Gold Mining, Blaauberg Gold Mining, West Tweefontein Mining, Deep Gold Levels, and the Sonder Ditch Gold Mining Company.

It was to this last that Rod naturally directed his attention.

'You beauty,' he whispered, for in his eyes the mountainous dumps of blue rock beside the shafts were truly beautiful. The complex but carefully thought out pattern of the works buildings, even the sulphur-yellow acres of the slimes dam, had a functional beauty.

'Get it for me, Manfred,' he spoke aloud. 'I want it. I want it badly.'

On the twenty-eight square miles of the Sonder Ditch's property lived fourteen thousand human beings; twelve thousand of them were

Bantu who had been recruited from all over Southern Africa. They lived in the multi-storied hostels near the shaft heads, and each day they went down through two small holes in the ground to depths that were scarcely credible, and came up again out of those same two holes. Twelve thousand men down, twelve thousand up. That was not all: out of those two same holes came ten thousand tons of rock daily, and down them went timber and tools and piping and explosive, ton upon ton of material and equipment. It was an undertaking that must evoke pride in the men who accomplished it.

Rod glanced at his watch, 7.35 a.m. They were down already, all twelve thousand of them. They had started going down at three-thirty that morning and now it was accomplished. The shift was in. The Sonder Ditch was breaking rock, and bringing the stuff out.

Rod grinned happily. His loneliness and depression of an hour ago were gone, swallowed up in the immensity of his involvement. He watched the massive wheels of the headgears spinning, stopping briefly, and then spinning again.

Each of those shafts had cost fifty million Rand, the surface plant and works another fifty million. The Sonder Ditch represented an investment of one hundred and fifty million Rand, two hundred and twenty million dollars. It was big, and it would be his.

Rod flicked away the butt of his cigarette. As he drove down the ridge, his eyes moved eastward down the valley. All mining activity ceased abruptly along an imaginary north-south line, drawn arbitrarily across the open grassland. There was no surface indication why this should be so, but the reason was deep down.

On that line ran a geological freak, a dyke, a wall of hard serpentine rock that had been named 'the Big Dipper'. It cut through the field like an axe stroke, and beyond it was bad ground. The gold reef existed in the bad ground, they knew this; but not one of the five companies had gone after it. They had prospected it tentatively and then shied away from it, for the boreholes that they sank were frightening in their inconsistency.

A big percentage of the Sonder Ditch lease area lay on the far side of the Dipper, and there was a diamond-drilling team working there now. They had already completed five holes.

Rod could remember accurately the results:-

Borehole S.D. No. 1.   Abandoned in water at 4,000 ft.
         S.D. No. 2.   Abandoned in dry hole at 5,250 ft.
         S.D. No. 3.   Intersected carbon leader reef at 6,600 ft.
         Assay valve   27,323 inch penny-weights.

First deflection	6,212 inch penny-weights.
Second deflection	2,114 inch penny-weights.
S.D. No. 4.	Abandoned in artesian water at 3,500 ft.
S.D. No. 5.	Intersected carbon leader at 8,116 ft.
Assay valve	562 inch penny-weights.

And they were drilling the deflections on that one now.

The problem was to build up a picture from results like that. It looked like a mess of faulted and water-logged ground with the gold reef fragmented and fluky, showing unbelievably high values at one spot, and then more than likely pinching out fifty feet away.

They may mine it one day, thought Rod, but I hope to hell I'm on pension by the time they do.

In the distance beyond the slimes dam he could just make out the spidery triangle of the drilling rig against the grown grass.

'Go to it, boys,' he muttered. 'Whatever you find there won't make much difference to me.'

And he went in through the imposing gates at the entrance to the mine property, halting carefully at the stop sign where the railway line crossed the road and forking two fingers at the traffic policeman lurking behind the gates.

The traffic cop grinned and waved; he had caught Rod the previous week, so he was still one up.

Rod drove down to his office.

CHAPTER 13

That Monday morning Allen 'Popeye' Worth was preparing to drill his first deflection on the S.D. No. 5 borehole. Allen was a Texan—not a typical Texan. He stood five feet four inches tall, but was as tough as the steel drill with which he worked. Thirty years before he had started learning his trade on the oilfields around Odessa and he had learned it well.

Now he could start at the surface and drill a four-inch hole down thirteen thousand feet through the earth's crust, keeping the hole straight all the way, an almost impossible task if you took into account the whippiness and torque in a jointed rod of steel that long.

If, as happened occasionally, the steel snapped and broke off thousands of feet down, Allen could fit a fishing tool on the end of his rig, and patiently grope for the stump, find it, grapple it and pull it out of the borehole. When he hit the reef down there, he could purposely kick his drill off the line and pierce the reef again and again to sample it over an area of hundreds of feet. This was what was meant by deflecting.

Allen was one of the best. He could command his own salary and behave like a prima donna, and his bosses would still fawn on him, for the things he could do with a diamond drill were almost magical.

Now he was assessing the angle of his first deflection. The previous day he had lowered a long brass bottle to the end of his borehole and left it overnight. The bottle was half filled with concentrated sulphuric acid, and it had etched the brass of the bottle. By measuring the angle of the etching he knew just how his drill was branching off from his original hole.

In the tiny wood and iron building beside the drilling rig he finished his measurements and stood back from the work bench, grunting with satisfaction.

From his hip pocket he drew a corncob pipe and pouch. Once he had stuffed tobacco into the pipe and lit it, it became very clear as to why his nickname was 'Popeye'. He was a dead ringer for the cartoon character, aggressive jaw, button eyes, battered maritime cap and all.

He puffed contentedly, watching through the single window of the shack as his gang went about the tedious business of lowering the drilling bit down into the earth. Then he took the pipe from his mouth and spat accurately through the window, replaced the pipe and stooped to minutely check his measurements.

His foreman driller interrupted him from the doorway.

'On bottom, and ready to turn, boss.'

'Huh!' Popeye checked his watch. 'Two hours forty to get down—you don't reckon to rupture a gut, do you?'

'That's not bad,' protested the foreman.

'And it sure as hell isn't good either! Okay, okay, cut the cackle and let's get her turning.' He bounced out of the shed and set off for the rig, darting quick beady little glances about him. The rig was a fifty-foot high tower of steel girders and within it the drill rod hung down until it disappeared into the collar. The twin two hundred-horsepower diesel engines throbbed expectantly, waiting to provide the power, their exhausts smoking blue in the early morning sunlight. Beside the rig lay a mountainous heap of drilling rods, beyond them the ten thousand-gallon puddling reservoir to provide water for the hole. Water was pumped into the hole continuously to cool and lubricate the tool as it cut into the rock.

'Stand by to turn her,' Popeye called to his gang, and they moved to their stations. Dressed in blue overalls, coloured fibreglass helmets, and leather gloves, they stood ready and tensed. This was an anxious moment for the whole team; power had to be applied with a lover's touch to the mile and a half length of rod, or it would buckle and snap.

Popeye climbed nimbly up onto the collar, and glanced about him to make sure all was in readiness. The foreman driller was at the controls, watching Popeye with complete absorption, his hands resting on the levers.

'Power up!' shouted Popeye and made the circular motion with his right hand. The diesels bellowed harshly, and Popeye reached out to lay his left hand on the drilling rod. This was how he did it, feeling the rod with his bare hand as he brought in the power, judging the tension by ear and eye and touch.

His right hand gestured and the foreman delicately let in the clutch, the rod moved under Popeye's hand, he gestured again and it revolved slowly. He could feel it was near breaking point and he cut down the power instantly, then let it in again. His right hand moved eloquently, expressively as an orchestral conductor, and the foreman followed it, the junior member of a highly skilled team.

Slowly the tension of the gang relaxed as the revolutions of the drill built up steadily, until Popeye gave the clenched fist 'okay' and jumped down from the collar. They scattered casually to their other duties, while Popeye and the foreman strolled back to the shed, leaving the drill to grind away at a steady four hundred revolutions a minute.

'Got something for you,' said the foreman, as they entered the shed.

'What?' demanded Popeye.

'The latest *Playboy*.'

'You're kidding!' Popeye accused him delightedly, but the foreman fished the rolled magazine out of his lunch box.

'Hey there!' Popeye snatched it from him and turned immediately to the coloured foldout.

'Isn't that something!' He whistled. 'This dolly could get a job in a stockyard beating the oxen to death with her boo-boos!'

The foreman joined the discussion of the young lady's anatomy, and so neither of them noticed the change in the sound of the drill until two minutes had passed. Then Popeye heard it through an erotic haze. He flung the magazine from him, and went through the door of the shed white-faced.

It was fifty yards from the shed to the rig, but even at that distance Popeye could see the vibration in the drilling rod. He could hear the labouring note of the diesels as they carried increased load, and he ran like a fox terrier, trying to reach the controls and shut off the engines before it happened.

He knew what it was. His drill had cut into one of the many fissures with which this badly faulted ground was criss-crossed. The puddling water from his borehole had drained away leaving the bit to run dry against dry rock. The friction heat had built up, the dust from the cut was not being washed away—and in consequence the rod had jammed. It was being held tightly at one end while at the other the two big diesels were straining to turn it. The whole rig was seconds away from a twist-off.

There should have been an operator at the controls to meet just such an emergency, but he was a hundred yards away, just emerging from the wood and iron latrine beyond the puddling dam. He was desperately trying to hoist his pants, clinch the buckle of his belt and run all at the same time.

'You whore's chamberpot!' roared Popeye, as he ran. 'What the hell you goofing off—'

The words choked off in his throat, for as he reached the door of the engine room there was a report like a cannon shot as the rod snapped, and immediately the diesels screamed into over-rev as they were relieved of the load. Just too late, Popeye punched the earth buttons on the magnetos, and the engines spluttered into silence.

In that silence Popeye was sobbing with exertion and frustration and anger.

'A twist-off,' he sobbed. 'A deep one. Oh no! God, no!' It might take two weeks to fish out the broken rod, pump cement into the fissure to seal it, and then start again.

He removed the cap from his head, and with all his strength hurled it on the engine room floor. He then proceeded to jump on it with both feet. This was standard procedure. Popeye jumped on his cap at least once a week, and the foreman knew that when he had finished doing that he would then assault anybody within range.

Quietly the foreman slipped behind the wheel of the Ford truck, and the rest of the gang scrambled aboard. They all bumped away down the rutted track. There was a roadhouse on the main road where they went for coffee at times like this. When the mists of rage had dispersed sufficiently from his mind for Popeye to start seeking a human sacrifice, he looked about to find the drilling area strangely still and deserted.

'Stupid bunch of yellow-bellied baboons!' he bellowed in frustration after the retreating truck, and, as the next best thing, went into the shed to phone his Managing Director.

This gentleman sitting in the air-conditioned offices of 'Hart Drilling and Cementation' high above Rissik Street in Johannesburg was a little taken aback to learn from Popeye Worth that he, the Managing Director, was directly responsible for the twist-off of an expensive diamond drill at the Sonder Ditch No. 5 hole.

'If you used that sack of custard that passes for a brain, you'd fight shy of trying to sink holes into this bunch of knitting,' Popeye yelled into the mouthpiece. 'I'd prefer to stick my old man into a meat grinder than put a drill into this ground. It stinks, I tell you! It's really ugly down there. God help the poor son of a bitch who tries to mine it!'

He slammed down the phone and stuffed his pipe with trembling fingers. Ten minutes later his breathing had returned to normal and his hands were steady. He picked up the phone again and dialled the number of the roadhouse. The proprietor answered.

'José, tell my boys it's okay, they can come home now,' said Popeye.

CHAPTER 14

For Rod Ironsides there was more excitement than usual in meeting and solving the dozen paper problems that lay on his desk to welcome him back to the office. As he worked he kept remembering that Manfred Steyner might be able to do it, might just be able to do it.

The Sonder Ditch might really belong to him soon. He dispatched the last problem and lay back in his swivel chair. His mind was clear of the last cobwebs of dissipation and, as always, he felt purged and cleansed.

If I get her, I'll make her the star performer in the whole field, he thought greedily; they'll talk about the Sonder Ditch from Wall Street to the Bourse, and about the man who is running her. I know how to do it too. I'll cut the costs to the bone, I'll tighten her up solid. Frank Lemmer was a good man, he could get the stuff out of the ground, but he let it creep up on him. It cost him almost nine Rand a ton to mill it.

Well, I'll get it out as well as he did *and* I'll get it out cheaper. An operation takes its temperament from the man at the head. Frank Lemmer would talk about costs every now and then, but he didn't mean it and we knew he didn't mean it. We have become a wasteful operation because we are on a rich reef, we have become big spenders. Well, I'm going to talk costs, and I'll skin the arse of anybody who thinks I'm joking.

Last year Hamilton at Western Holdings kept his working costs per ton milled down to just a touch over six Rand. I could do the same here!

I could jump our profits twelve million Rand in one year. If only they give me the job I'll shout the Sonder Ditch's name across the financial markets of the world.

The problem that Rod was pondering was the nightmare of the gold mining industry. Since the 1930s the price of gold had been fixed at $35 a fine ounce. Each year since then the cost of mining had crept up steadily. In those days they reckoned four penny-weights of gold in a ton of ore was payable value. Now around eight penny-weights was the marginal value.

So in the interim all those millions of tons of ore whose values fell between four and eight penny-weights had been placed beyond the reach of man until such time as they increased the price of gold.

There were many mines with vast reserves of gold-bearing ore, millions in bullion, whose values lay just below the magical number eight. Those mines stood deserted and forlorn, rust reddening their headgears, and the corrugated iron roofs of the buildings collapsing wearily. Rising costs had shot the guts out of them; they were condemned by the single word 'UNPAY'.

The Sonder Ditch was running twenty to twenty-five penny-weights per ton. She was fat, but she could be fatter, Rod decided.

There was a knock at the door.

'Come in!' called Rod, and looked at his watch. It was nine o'clock already. Time for the Monday meeting of his mine captains.

They came in singly and in pairs, twelve of them. These were Rod's front-line men, his combat officers. They went down there each day, each to his own section and directed the actual assault on the rock.

While they chatted idly, waiting for the meeting to begin, Rod looked them over surreptitiously and was reminded of a remark that Herman Koch of Anglo American had made to him once.

'Mining is a hard game, and it attracts a hard breed of men.'

These were men of the hard breed, physically and mentally tough, and Rod realized with a start that he was one of them. No, more than one of them. He was their leader, and with a fierce affection and pride he opened the meeting.

'Right, let's hear your gripes. Who is going to be first to break my heart?'

There are some men with a talent for controlling, and getting the very best results out of other men. Rod was one of them. It was more than his physical size, his compelling voice and hearty chuckle. It was a special magnetism, a personal charm and unerring sense of timing. Under his Chairmanship the meeting would erupt, voices crackle and snap, then subside into chuckles and nods as Rod spoke.

They knew he was as tough as they were, and they respected that. They knew that when he spoke it made sense, so they listened. They knew that when he promised, he delivered, so they were placated. And they knew that when he made a decision or judgement, he acted upon it, so every man knew exactly where he stood.

If asked, any one of these mine captains would have admitted grudgingly that 'there was no bulldust in Ironsides'. This was the equivalent of a presidential citation.

'Very well then.' Rod terminated the meeting. 'You have spent a good two hours of the company's time beating your gums. Now, will you kindly haul arse, go down there and start sending the stuff out.'

CHAPTER 15

As these men planned the week's operation, so their men were at work in the earth below them.

On 87 level, Kowalski moved like a great bear down the dimly-lit drive. He had switched off the lamp on his helmet, and he moved without sound, lightly for a man of such bulk. He heard their voices ahead of him in the dimly-lit tunnel, and he paused, listening intently. There was no sound of shovel crunching into loose rock, and Kowalski's Neanderthal features convulsed into a fearsome scowl.

'Bastards!' he muttered softly. 'They think I am in stopes, hey? They think it all right if they sit on fat black bum, no move da bloody rock, hey?'

He started forward again, a bear on cat's feet.

'They find plenty different from what they bloody think, soon!' he threatened.

He stepped round the angle of the drive and flashed his lamp. There were the three men Kowalski had put on lashing, shovelling the loose stuff from the footwall into waiting cocopans. Two of them sat against the cocopan, smoking contentedly, while the third regaled them with an account of a beer drink he had attended the previous Christmas. Their shovels and sledge hammers leaned unemployed against the side wall of the drive.

All three of them froze into rigidity as the beam of Kowalski's lamp played over them.

'So!' The word burst explosively from Kowalski, and he snatched up a fourteen-pound hammer in one massive fist, reversed it and struck the butt of the handle against the foot wall. The steel head of the hammer fell off and Kowalski was left with a four foot length of selected hickory in his hand.

'You, boss boy!' he bellowed, and his free hand shot out and fastened on the throat of the nearest Bantu. With one heave he jerked him off his feet onto his knees and began dragging him away up the drive. Even in his rage, Kowalski was making sure there were no witnesses. The other two men sat where they were, too horrified to move, while their companion's wails and cries receded into the darkness.

Then the first blow reverberated in the confined space of the drive, followed immediately by a shriek of pain.

The next blow, and another shriek.

The crack, thud, crack, thud, went on repeatedly, but the accompanying shrieks dwindled into moans and soft whimperings, then into complete silence.

Kowalski came back down the drive alone, he was sweating heavily in the lamp light, and the handle of the hammer in his hand was black and glistening with wet blood.

He threw it at their feet.

'Work!' he growled, and was gone, big and bearlike, into the shadows.

CHAPTER 16

On 100 level, Joseph M'Kati was hosing down and sweeping the spillings from under the giant conveyor belt. Joseph had been on this job for five years, and he was a contented and happy man.

Joseph was a Shangaan approaching sixty years of age; the first frost was touching his hair. There were laughter lines around his eyes and at the corner of his mouth. He wore his helmet pushed to the back of his head, his overalls were hand-embroidered and ornamentally patched in blue and red, and he moved with a jaunty bounce and strut.

The conveyor was many hundreds of yards long. From all the levels above the shattered gold reef was scraped from the stopes and trammed back down the haulages in the cocopans. Then from the cocopans it was tipped into the mouths of the ore-passes. These were vertical shafts that dropped down to 100 level, hundreds of feet through the living rock to spew the reef out onto the conveyor belt. A system of steel doors regulated the flow of rock onto the conveyor, and the moving belt carried it down to the shaft and dumped it into enormous storage bins. From there it was fed automatically into the ore cage in fifteen-ton loads and carried at four-minute intervals to the surface.

Joseph worked on happily beneath the whining conveyor. The spillings were small, but important. Gold is strange in its behaviour, it moves downwards. Carried by its own high specific gravity it works its way down through almost any other material. It would find any crack or irregularity in the floor and work its way into it. It would disappear into the solid earth itself if left long enough.

It was this behaviour of gold that accounted in some measure for Joseph M'Kati's contentment. He had worked his way to the end of the conveyor, washing and sweeping, and now he straightened, laid his bast broom aside and rubbed his kidneys with both hands, looking quickly around to make certain that there was no one else in the conveyor tunnel. Beside him was the ore storage bin into which the conveyor was emptying its load. The bin could hold many thousands of tons.

Satisfied that he was alone, Joseph dropped onto his hands and knees and crawled under the storage bin, ignoring the continuous roar of rock into the bin above him, working his way in until he reached the holes.

It had taken Joseph many months to chisel the heads off four of the rivets that held the seam in the bottom of the bin, but once he had done it, he had succeeded in constructing a simple but highly effective heavy media separator.

Free gold in the ore that was dumped into the storage bin immediately and rapidly worked its way down through the underlying rock, its journey accelerated by the vibration of the conveyor and bin as more reef was dropped. When the gold reached the floor of the bin, it sought an avenue through which to continue its downward journey, and it found Joseph's four rivet holes, beneath which he had spread a square of polythene sheet.

The gold-rich fines made four conical piles on the sheet of polythene, looking exactly like powdered black soot.

Crouched beneath the bin, Joseph carefully transferred the black powder to his tobacco pouch, replaced the polythene to catch the next filtering, stuffed the pouch into his hip pocket, and scrambled out from under the bin. Whistling a tribal planting tune Joseph picked up his broom and returned to the endless job of sweeping and hosing.

CHAPTER 17

Johnny Delange was marking his shot holes. Lying on his side in the low stope of 27 section he was calculating by eye the angle and depth of a side cutter blast to straighten a slight bulge in his longwall.

In the Sonder Ditch they were on single blast. One daily, centrally fired, blast. Johnny was paid on *fathomage*, the cubic measure of rock broken and taken out of his stope. He must, therefore, position his shot holes to achieve the maximum disruption and blow-out from the face.

'So,' he grunted, and marked the position of the hole in red paint. 'And so.' With one bold stroke of the paint brush he set the angle on which his machine boy was to drill.

'Shaya, madoda!' Johnny clapped the shoulder of the black man beside him. 'Hit it, man.'

Machine boys were selected for stamina and physique—this one was a Greek sculpture in glistening ebony.

'Nkosi!' The machine boy grinned an acknowledgement, and with his assistant lugged his rock drill into position. The drill looked like a gargantuan version of a heavy calibre machine gun.

The noise as the big Bantu opened the drill was shattering in the low-roofed, constricted space of the stope. The compressed air roared and fluttered into the drill, buffeting the eardrums. Johnny made the clenched-fist gesture of approval, and for a second they smiled at each other in the companionship of shared labour. Then Johnny crawled on up the stope to mark the next shot hole.

Johnny Delange was twenty-seven years old, and he was top rock breaker on the Sonder Ditch. His gang of forty-eight men were a tightly-knit team of specialists. Men fought each other for a place on 27 section, for that's where the money was. Johnny could pick and choose, so each month when the surveyors came in and measured up, Johnny Delange was way out ahead in fathomage.

Here was the remarkable position where the man at the lowest point of authority earned more than the man at the top. Johnny Delange earned more than the General Manager of the Sonder Ditch. Last year he had paid super-tax on an income of twenty-two thousand Rand. Even a miner like Kowalski, who brutalized and bullied his gang until he was left with the dregs of the mine, would earn eight or nine thousand Rand a year, about the same salary as an official of Rod Ironsides' rank.

Johnny reached the top of his longwall and painted in the last shot holes. Down the inclined floor of the stope below him all his drills were roaring, his machine boys lying or crouching behind them. He lay there on one elbow, removed his helmet and wiped his face, resting a moment.

Johnny was an extraordinary-looking young man. His long jet black hair was swept back and tied with a leather thong at the back of his head in a curlicue. His features were those of an American Indian, gaunt and bony. He had cut the sleeves out of his overalls to expose his arms—arms as muscular and sinuous as pythons, tattooed below the elbows, immensely powerful but supple. His body was the same, long and sinewy and powerful.

On his right hand he wore eight rings, two on each finger, and it was clear from the design of the rings that they were not merely ornamental. They were heavy gold rings with skull and cross-bones, wolves' heads and other irregularities worked into them, a mass of metal that formed a permanent knuckle-duster. Of the big eyes in the one skull's head Rod Ironsides had once asked: 'Are those real rubies, Johnny?' And Johnny had replied seriously:

'If they aren't, then I've sure as hell been gypped out of three Rand fifty, Mr Ironsides.'

Johnny Delange had been a really wild youngster, until eight months ago. It was then he had met and married Hettie, courtship and marriage occupying the space of one week. Now he was settling down very well. It was all of ten days since he had last fought anybody.

Lying in the stope he allowed himself five minutes to think about Hettie. She was almost as tall as he was, with a wondrously buxom body and chestnut red hair. Johnny adored her. He was not the best speech-maker in Kitchenerville when it came to expressing his affection, so he bought her things.

He bought her dresses and jewellery, he bought her a deep freeze *and* a fifteen cubic foot Frigidaire, he bought her a Chrysler Monaco with leopard-skin upholstery and a Kenwood Chef. In fact, it was becoming difficult to enter the Delange household without tripping over at least one of Johnny's gifts to Hettie. The congestion was made more acute by the fact that living with them was Johnny's brother, Davy.

'Hell, man!' Happily Johnny shook his head. 'She's a bit of all-right, hey!'

There was an eye-level oven he had spotted in a furniture store in Kitchenerville the previous Saturday.

'She'll love that, man,' he muttered, 'and it's only four hundred Rand. I'll get it for her on pay day.'

The decision made, he clapped his helmet onto his head and began crawling out of the stope. It was time now to go up to the station and collect the explosives for the day's blast.

His boss boy should have been waiting for him in the drive, and Johnny was furious to find no sign of him nor the piccanin who was his assistant.

'Bastard!' he grunted, playing the beam of his lamp up and down the drive. 'He's been acting up like hell.'

The boss boy was a pock-marked Swazi, not a big man, but powerful for his size and highly intelligent. He was also a man of mean disposition. Johnny had never seen him smile, and for an extrovert like Johnny it was galling to work with someone so sullen and taciturn. He tolerated the Swazi because of his drive and reliability, but he was the only man in the gang that Johnny disliked.

'Bastard!' The drive was deserted, the roar of the rock drills was muted.

'Where the hell is he?' Johnny scowled impatiently. 'I'll skin him when I find him.'

Then he remembered the latrine.

'That's where he is!' Johnny set off down the drive. The latrine was a rock chamber cut into the side of the drive, a flap of canvas serving as a door; beyond was a regular four-holer over sanitary buckets.

Johnny pulled the canvas aside and stepped into the cubicle. The boss boy and his assistant were there. Johnny stared in surprise for a moment, not understanding what they were doing. They were so absorbed they were unaware of Johnny's presence.

Suddenly realization dawned, and Johnny's face tightened with revulsion and disgust.

'You filthy—' Johnny snarled, and catching the boss boy by the shoulders pulled him backwards and pinned him against the wall. He lifted his heavily metalled fist and drew it back ready to hurl it into the boss boy's face.

'Strike me and you know what happens,' said the boss boy softly, his expression flat and neutral, looking steadily into Johnny's eyes. Johnny hesitated. He knew the Company rules, he knew the Government labour officers' attitude, he knew what the police would do. If he hit him, they would crucify him.

'You are a pig!' Johnny hissed at him.

'You have a wife,' said the boss boy. 'My wife is in Swaziland. Two years I have not seen her.'

Johnny lowered his fist. Twelve thousand men, and no women. It was a fact. The actuality sickened him, but he understood why it happened.

'Get dressed.' He stepped back, releasing the boss boy. 'Get dressed both of you. Come to the station. I will meet you there.'

CHAPTER 18

For a week now, since the fall of hanging in 43 section, Big King had been out of the stopes.

Rod had ordered it that way. The excuse was that Big King's white miner had been killed in the fall and now he must await an allocation to another section. In reality Rod wanted to rest him. He had seen the strain both physical and emotional that Big King had undergone during the rescue. When together they had unearthed the miner's corpse, the man with whom Big King had worked and laughed, Rod had seen the tears roll unashamedly down Big King's cheeks as he picked up the body and held it easily against his chest.

'Hamba gahle, madoda,' Big King had muttered. 'Go in peace, man.'

Big King was a legend on the Sonder Ditch. They boasted about him; how much Bantu beer he could drink in a sitting, how much rock he could lash single-handed in a shift, how he could dance any other man off his feet. He had been awarded a total of over a thousand Rand in bravery awards. Big King set the pace, others tried to equal him.

Rod had put him in charge of a transport team. For the first few days Big King had enjoyed the opportunity of showing off his strength and socializing, for the transport team moved about the workings allowing Big King to visit most of his numerous friends during a shift. But now Big King was becoming bored. He wanted to get back into the stopes.

'This,' he told his transport team contemptuously, 'is work for old men and young women.' And with one snatch and lift he picked up a forty-four gallon drum of dieseline and unaided placed it on the platform of the loco.

A forty-four gallon drum of dieseline weighs a little over eight hundred pounds avoirdupois.

CHAPTER 19

All this fuss for that. Davy Delange paused in his labour of tamping the Dynagel into the shot holes. He leaned forward to inspect the reef. In the face of the stope it was a black line, drawn against the blue quartz rock.

The Carbon Leader Reef, it was called. A thin layer of carbon never more than a few inches thick, more often half an inch. Black soot, that's what it was. Davy shook his head thoughtfully. You could not even see the gold in it.

Davy was two years older than his brother Johnny, and there was no physical or mental resemblance between the two of them. Davy's sandy hair was cropped into a conventional 'short back and sides'. He wore no personal jewellery, and his manner was quiet and reserved.

Johnny was tall and lean, Davy squat and muscular. Johnny was extravagant, Davy careful beyond the point of meanness. Their only common trait was that they were both first-class miners. If Johnny broke more rock than Davy, it was only because Davy was more careful than Johnny; he did not take the same chances, he observed all the safety procedures which Johnny frequently flouted.

Davy earned less money than Johnny, but saved every penny he could. It was for his farm. Davy was going to buy a farm one day. Already he had saved a little over forty-nine thousand Rand towards it. In five more years he would have enough. Then he could get himself a farm and a wife to help run it. Johnny, on the other hand, spent every penny he earned. He was usually in debt to Davy by the end of each month.

'Lend us a hundred till pay day, Davy.' Disapprovingly, Davy lent him the money. Davy disapproved of Johnny, his appearance, attire and habits.

Abandoning his microscopic inspection of the Carbon Leader Reef, Davy resumed tamping in the explosive, working carefully and precisely on this highly dangerous procedure. The sticks of explosive were charged with detonators and ready to burn. By law, nobody but the miner-in-charge could perform this operation, but Davy did it automatically while he thought about Johnny's latest trespass. He had raised Davy's rent.

'A hundred Rand a month!' Davy protested aloud. 'I've got a good mind to move out and find my own digs.'

But he knew he would do no such thing. Hettie's cooking was too good, and her presence too feminine and alluring. Davy would stay on with them.

CHAPTER 20

'Rod.' Dan Stander's voice was serious and low. 'I've got a nasty one
for you.'

'Thanks for nothing.' Rod made his own voice weary and resigned
as he spoke into the telephone. 'I'm just going on my underground
tour. Can't it wait?'

'No,' Dan assured him. 'Anyway, it's on your way. I'm speaking
from the first-aid station at the shaft head. Come across.'

'What is it?'

'Assault. White on Bantu.'

'Christ.' Rod jerked upright in his chair. 'Bad?'

'Ugly. Worked him over with the handle of a fourteen-pound hammer. I've put in forty-seven stitches, but I'm worried about a fracture
of the skull.'

'Who did it?'

'Miner by the name of Kowalski.'

'Him!' Rod was breathing heavily. 'All right, Dan. Can he make a
statement?'

'No. Not for a day or two.'

'I'll be there in a few minutes.'

Rod hung up the phone and crossed the office.

'Dimitri.'

'Boss?'

'Pull Kowalski out of the stopes. I want him in my office soonest. Put
someone in to finish his shift.'

'Okay, Rod, what's the trouble?'

'He beat up one of his boys.'

Dimitri whistled softly, and Rod went on.

'Call personnel, get them onto the police.'

'Okay, Rod.'

'Have Kowalski here when I get back from my tour.'

Dan was waiting for him in the first-aid room.

'Take a look.' He indicated the figure on the stretcher. Rod knelt
beside him, his mouth tightening into a thin pale line.

The catgut stitches lay neatly across the dark swollen gashes in the
man's flesh. His one ear had been torn off, and Dan had sewn it back
on. There was a black gap where teeth had been behind the swollen
purple lips.

'You will be all right now.' Rod spoke gently, and the Bantu's eyes
swivelled towards him. 'The man who did this will be punished.'

Rod stood up. 'Let me have a written report on his injuries, Dan.'
'I'll fix it. See you for a drink at the Club after work?'

'Sure,' said Rod, but underneath he was seething with anger, and it
stayed with him during the whole of his underground tour.

CHAPTER 21

Rod dropped straight down to 100 level. His first duty was to get the
stuff out, and he wanted to check the reserve in the ore storage bins. He
came into the long brightly-lit tunnel beneath the ore passes, and
paused. The loaded conveyor belt whined monotonously, speeding the
broken reef towards the bins.

The tunnel was deserted, except for the lonely figure of the sweeper
at the far end. It was one of the phenomena of a well-run gold mine
that in a tour through the workings you encountered so few human
beings. Mile after mile of haulage and drive were silent and devoid of
life, and yet there were twelve thousand men down here.

Rod set off towards the bins at the shaft end of the tunnel.

'Joseph,' he greeted the old sweeper with a smile.

'Nkosi.' Joseph ducked and bobbed with shy pleasure.

'All is well?' Rod asked. Joseph was one of Rod's favourites, he was
always so cheerful, so uncomplaining, so patently honest and without
guile. Rod always made a point of stopping to chat to him.

'It is well with me, Nkosi. Is it well with you?'

Rod's smile died suddenly. He had noticed the fine white powdering
of dust on Joseph's upper lip.

'You old rogue!' he scolded him. 'How often must I tell you to hose
down before you sweep? Water! You must use water!'

This was part of the ceaseless battle of the miner to keep down the
dust.

'The dust will eat your lungs!'

Phthisis, the dread incurable occupational disease of the miner, caused
by silica particles being drawn into the lungs and there solidifying.

Joseph grinned shamefaced, shifting from one foot to the other. He
was always embarrassed by Rod's childish obsession with dust. In
Joseph's opinion this was one of the few flaws in Rod Ironsides' character. Apart from this weird delusion that dust could hurt a man, he was
a good boss.

'It is much harder to sweep wet dirt than dry dirt,' Joseph explained
patiently. Rod never seemed to understand this self-evident fact—

Joseph had to point it out to him every time they had this particular discussion.

'Listen to me, old man, without water the dust will enter your body.' Rod was exasperated. 'The dust will kill you!'

Joseph bobbed again, grinning at Rod to placate him.

'Very well, I will use plenty water.'

To prove it he picked up the hose and began spraying the floor with enthusiasm.

'That is good!' Rod encouraged him. 'Use plenty of water.' And Rod went on down to the storage bins.

When Rod was out of sight, Joseph turned off the hose and leaned on his broom.

'The dust will kill you!' he mimicked Rod, and chuckled merrily, shaking his head in wonder at the childishness of it.

'The dust will kill you!' he repeated, and burst into delighted laughter, slapping his thigh.

He did a few shuffling dance steps, it was so funny.

The dance steps were awkward, for under his trousers, strapped to the calves of both legs, were heavy polythene bags filled with gold fines from under the bins.

CHAPTER 22

Rod stepped out of the Mary Anne at 85 level, and paused to watch Big King loading a baulk of timber onto the loco while his transport team stood back respectfully and watched him. Turning from his task Big King saw Rod standing on the station landing and marched up to him.

'I see you,' he greeted Rod. Big King was not one to make hasty judgements; it was only after the rescue operations in 43 section that he had decided Rod was a man. He was now ready to accept him as an equal.

'I see you also, King Nkulu.' Rod returned the greeting.

'Find me work with men. I sicken of this.'

'You will be back in the stopes before the week is ended,' Rod promised.

'You are my father,' Big King thanked him and went back to the transport team.

CHAPTER 23

Johnny Delange saw the Underground Manager coming up the haul-age towards him. There was no mistaking that tall wide-shouldered silhouette, nor the man's free swinging stride.

'Whee!' Johnny whistled with relief, grateful for the premonition that had warned him to pack the fifty-pound cardboard cartons of Dynagel into the explosives locker of the railway truck, rather than, as he usually did, pile them haphazard onto the platform in defiance of safety standards.

'Stop!' Johnny commanded the boss boy and his assistant who were pushing the truck, and it trundled to a halt beside Rod.

'Morning, Johnny.'

'Hello, Mr Ironsides.'

'How's it going?'

Johnny hesitated before replying, and immediately Rod was aware of the tension between the three men. He glanced at the two Swazis—they were sullen and apprehensive.

'There's been trouble,' he thought. 'Not like Johnny, he's too clever to let tension cut down his fathomage.'

'Well—' Johnny paused again. 'Look, Mr Ironsides, get rid of this bastard for me.' He jerked his thumb at the boss boy. 'Give me someone else.'

'What's the trouble?'

'No trouble, I just can't work with him.'

Rod raised an eyebrow in disbelief, but turned to the boss boy.

'Are you happy in this section, or do you want transfer?'

'I want transfer!' growled the boss boy.

'Right.' Rod was relieved. Sometimes in a case like this the Swazi would refuse transfer. 'Tomorrow you will be told your new section.'

'Nkosi!' The boss boy glanced sideways at his assistant. 'It is the wish of my friend that he transfers with me.'

So that's it, Rod thought, the ever-present spectre which we must ignore because we can find no way to lay it. Johnny had probably caught them at it.

'Your friend shall go with you,' Rod nodded, telling himself that this was not condonation, but merely practical politics. If he separated them, the boss boy would pick on someone else who might not be recep-tive. Then there would be more trouble, stabbings, faction fighting.

'I'll get you a replacement,' he told Johnny, and then suddenly a thought occurred to him. My God, yes! What a team they would make!

'Johnny, how would you like Big King?'

'Big King!' Johnny's gaunt bony features split into a wide smile. 'Now you're talking, boss!'

CHAPTER 24

At three o'clock Rod had finished his tour and was in the cage on the way to the surface. The cage was crowded, men pressed shoulder to shoulder, the stench of sweat almost overpowering. They were hauling shift now, the day's work was over, the stopes were scraped and washed down, the shot holes drilled and charged, the fuses connected into the electrical circuit.

The men were out of the stopes now, falling back in orderly companies and battalions along the haulages to the stations, there to wait patiently for their turn to enter the cages and be whisked to the surface.

Rod was mulling over the myriad problems he had encountered during the day, and the solutions he had dreamed up. He had opened a new section in the back pages of his notebook and headed it simply 'COSTS'.

Already there were two entries there. Let them give me the job, he thought fervently, just let me have it one month and I'll move the world.

'Mr Ironsides.' The man beside him spoke. Rod glanced down at him, recognizing him.

'Hello, Davy.' It was remarkable how dissimilar the two brothers were.

'Mr Ironsides, my boss boy has worked his ticket. He's going home at the end of the month. Can you see that I get a good man to replace him?'

'Your brother's boss boy has asked for transfer. Will you take him?'

'Ja!' Davy Delange nodded. 'I know him, he's a good boy.'

And that takes care of one more detail, thought Rod, as he stepped out of the cage into a bright summer's afternoon and tasted the fresh sweet air with pleasure. Now there are only the butt ends of the day's work to tidy up. Then I can go and fetch the drink that Dan promised me.

Dimitri met him in the passage outside the office.

'I've got Kowalski in my office.'

'Good,' said Rod grimly. He went into his own office and sat on the edge of his desk.

'Send him in,' he called through to Dimitri.

Kowalski came through the door and stopped. He stood very still, his long arms hanging slackly at his side, his belly bulging out over his belt.

'You call me,' he muttered thickly, his English hardly intelligible. It was a peasant's face, coarse-featured, dull-eyed. He had not shaved, dirt from the stopes clung in the thick black stubble of beard.

'You beat a man today?' Rod asked softly.

'He no work,' Kowalski nodded. 'I beat him. Maybe next time his brothers they work. No bloody nonsense!'

'You're fired,' said Rod. 'Pull your time and get the hell off this property.'

'You fire?' Kowalski blinked in surprise.

'There will be criminal charges pressed against you by the company.' Rod went on. 'But in the meantime I want you off the property.'

'Police?' Kowalski growled. There was expression on his face now.

'Yes,' said Rod, 'police.'

The spade-sized hands at the end of Kowalski's arms balled slowly into massive fists.

'You call da bloody police!' He took a step towards the desk, big, menacing.

'Dimitri,' Rod called sharply, 'close the door.'

Dimitri had been listening intently, now he jumped up from his desk and closed the interleading door. He stood with his ear pressed to the panelling. For thirty seconds more there was the growl and mutter of voices, then suddenly a thud, a bellow, another thud and a shattering crash.

Dimitri winced theatrically.

'Dimitri!' Rod's voice, and he pushed the door open.

Rod sat on the edge of his desk, swinging one leg casually, he was sucking the knuckle of his right hand.

'Dimitri, tell them not to put so much polish on the floor. Our friend slipped and hit his jaw on the desk.'

Dimitri clucked sympathetically as he stood over the reclining hulk of the big Pole. Kowalski was snoring loudly through his mouth.

'Gave himself a nasty bump,' said Dimitri. 'Shame!'

CHAPTER 25

Dr Steyner worked on quietly for the remainder of Monday morning. He favoured the use of a tape recorder, for this cut out human contact which Manfred found vaguely repellent. He disliked having to speak his thoughts to a female who sat opposite him with skirts up around her thighs, squirming her bottom and touching her hair. However, what he really could not abide was the odour. Manfred was very sensitive to smells, even his own body smell of perspiration disgusted him. Women, he found, had a peculiar cloying odour that he could detect beneath their perfume and cosmetics. It nauseated him. This was why he had insisted on separate bedrooms for Theresa and himself. Naturally he had not told her the reason, but had insisted instead that he was such a light sleeper that he could not share a room with another person.

His office was in white and ice-blue, the air clean and cold from the air-conditioning unit, his voice was crisp and impersonal, the whirr of the recorder subdued, and with the conscious portion of his mind Manfred was happily absorbed in his conjuring tricks with figures and money, past performance and future estimates, a three-dimensional structure of variables and contingencies which only a super-normal brain could visualize. But beneath it was a sense of disquiet; he was waiting, hanging in time, and the outward sign of his agitation was the way the fingers of his right hand ran up and down his thigh as he worked, a caressing narcissistic gesture.

A few minutes before noon the unlisted direct telephone on his desk rang, and the movement of his hand stilled. Only one caller could reach him here, only one caller had that number. For a few seconds he sat unmoving, delaying the moment, then deliberately he switched off the recorder and lifted the telephone.

'Dr Manfred Steyner.' He identified himself.

'You have got our man in?' the voice inquired.

'Not yet, Andrew.'

There was silence from the other end, a dangerous crackling silence.

'But there is no cause for alarm. It is nothing. A delay merely, not a setback.'

'How long?'

'Two days—at the latest by the end of the week.'

'You will be in Paris next week?'

'Yes.' Manfred was an adviser to the Government team which was to meet the French for gold price talks.

'He will meet you there. It would be best for you that your side of the bargain were completed by then. You understand?'

'I understand, Andrew.'

The discussion was ended, but Manfred interjected to prevent the caller from hanging up.

'Andrew!'

'Yes.'

'Will you ask him if—' Manfred's tone had changed almost imperceptively, there was an obsequious edge in it. 'Ask him if I may play tonight, please, Andrew.'

'Wait.'

The minutes drifted by, and then the voice came back on the line.

'Yes, you may play. Simon will inform you of your limits.'

'Thank you. Tell him, thank you.'

Manfred made no effort to conceal his relief as he cradled the receiver. He sat beaming at the ice-blue paper on the far wall of his office—even his spectacles seemed to sparkle.

CHAPTER 26

There were five men in the opulently furnished room. One of the men was subservient to the others; he was younger than they, attentive to their moods and wishes. Clearly he was a servant. Of the remaining four, one was just as obviously the host. He was seated at the focus of all their attention. He was fat, but not excessively so, the fat of good living not of gluttony. He was speaking, addressing himself to his three guests.

'You have expressed doubts as to reliability of the tool I intend using in the coming venture. I have arranged a demonstration which I hope will convince you that your concern is groundless. That is the reason for the invitation that Andrew here conveyed to you this afternoon.'

The host turned to the younger man. 'Andrew, would you be good enough to go through and wait for Dr Steyner to arrive. As soon as that happens, please let Simon seat him while you come through and inform us.' He gave his orders with dignity and courtesy, a man accustomed to command.

'Now, gentlemen, while we wait may I offer you a drink?'

The conversation that sprang up between the four of them as they sipped their drinks was knowledgeable, and extraordinarily well informed. At its root was one subject: wealth. Mineral wealth, industrial wealth, the harvest of the land and the sea. Oil, steel, coal, fish, wheat and—gold.

There were clues to the stature of these men in the cut and quality of the cloth they wore, the sparkle of a stone on a finger, the tone of authority in a voice, the casual unaffected use of a high name.

'He is here, sir,' Andrew interrupted them from the doorway.

'Oh! Thank you, my boy.' The host stood up. 'Would you mind stepping this way, please, gentlemen.'

He crossed the room and drew aside one of the gold and maroon drapes. Behind it was a window.

The four men clustered about the window and looked through into the room beyond. It was a gaming room of an expensive gambling establishment. There were men and women sitting about a baccarat table, and none of them so much as glanced up at the window overlooking them.

'This is a one-way glass, gentlemen,' the host explained. 'So you need not worry about being seen in such a den of iniquity.'

They chuckled politely.

'What kind of profit does this place show you?' one of them asked.

'My dear Robert!' The host feigned shock. 'You don't for a moment believe that I would be in any way associated with an illegal undertaking?'

This time they chuckled with genuine amusement.

'Ha!' explained the host. 'Here he is.'

Across the gaming room Dr Manfred Steyner was being ushered to a seat at the table by a tall sallow-faced young man, who in his evening dress looked like an undertaker.

'I have asked Simon to place him so that you may watch his face as he plays.'

They were intent now, leaning forward slightly, scrutinizing the man as he arranged the plaques that Simon had stacked at his elbow.

Dr Manfred Steyner began to play. His face was completely devoid of expression, but the pallor was startling. Every few seconds the pink tip of his tongue slipped out between his lips, then disappeared again. In the intervals between each coup, there was a reptilian stillness about him, the stillness of a lizard or an iguana. Only a pulse beat steadily in his throat and his spectacles glittered like a snake's eyes.

'May I direct your attention to his right hand during the play of this coup,' the host murmured, and all their eyes flicked downwards.

Manfred's right hand lay open beside the pile of his chips, but as his card was laid before him so his fingers closed.

'*Carte.*' Soundlessly he mouthed the word, and now his hand was a fist, the knuckles whitened, the tension was so fierce that his fist trembled. Yet, still his face was neutral.

The banker flipped his card.

'*Sept!*' The croupier's mouth formed the number. He faced Manfred's card, then he swept Manfred's stake away. Manfred's hand flopped open and lay soft and hairless as a dead fish on the green baize.

'Let us leave him to his pleasures,' suggested the host and drew the curtains across the window. They returned to their chairs, and they were strangely subdued.

'Jesus,' muttered one of the guests. 'That was ugly. I felt like a peeping tom, like watching someone, you know, pulling his pudding.'

The host glanced at him quickly, surprised at his perception.

'In effect, that is exactly what you were watching,' he told him. 'You will excuse me playing the role of lecturer, but I know a little about this man. It cost me nearly four hundred Rand for an analytical report on him by one of our leading psychiatrists.'

The host paused, assuring himself of their complete attention.

'The reasons are obscure, probably arising from an event or series of events during the period in which Dr Steyner was an orphan wandering through the smoking ruins of war-torn Europe.' The host coughed, deprecating his own flight of oratory. 'Be that as it may. The results are there for all to see. Dr Manfred Kurt Steyner's intelligence quotient is a genius rating of 158. He neither smokes nor drinks. He has no hobbies, plays no sport, has never made so much as an improper remark to any woman other than his wife, and there is some doubt as to just how often or to what extent she is favoured by his attentions.' The host sipped his drink conscious of their intense interest. 'Mechanically, if that is the correct term, Dr Steyner is neither impotent nor deficient in his manhood. However, he finds all bodily contact, and especially the secretions that may arise from such contact, to be utterly loathsome. For arousal he relies on the baccarat cards, for release he might endure a brief contact with a member of the opposite sex, but more likely he would —oh, what was the expression you used, Robert?'

They absorbed this in silence.

'He is, to be precise, a compulsive gambler. He is also a compulsive loser.'

They stirred with disbelief.

'You mean he tries to lose?' demanded Robert incredulously.

'No.' The host shook his head. 'Not on the conscious level. He believes he is trying to win, but he lays bets against odds that, with his magnificent brain, he must realize are suicidal. It is a deep-seated subconscious need to lose, to be humiliated. A form of masochism.'

The host opened a black leather notebook and checked its contents.

'During the period from 1958 to 1963 Dr Steyner lost the total sum of R227,000 at this table. In 1964 he was able to arrive at an arrangement with his sole creditor to discharge the debt plus the accumulated interest.'

You could see the faces change as they rapidly searched their memories for a set of circumstances which would fit the dates and principals. Robert reached the correct deduction first. In 1964 their host had sold his majority holding in the North Maun Copper Co. to C.R.C. at a price that could only be considered advantageous. Just prior to this Dr Steyner had been made head of finance and planning at C.R.C.

'North Maun Copper,' said Robert with admiration. That is how he had done it, the cunning old fox! He had forced Steyner to buy well above market value.

The host smiled softly, deferentially, neither confirming nor denying.

'Since 1964 to the present Dr Steyner has continued to patronize this establishment. His gambling losses for this further period amount to—' he consulted his notebook again, pretending surprise at the figure, 'to a touch over R300,000.'

They sighed and moved restlessly. Even to these men it was a very large sum of money.

'I think we can rely on him.' The host closed his notebook with a snap, and smiled around at them.

CHAPTER 27

Theresa lay in the dark. The night was warm, the stillness spoiled only by the klonking of a frog down at the fishpond. The moonlight came in through the window, playing shadow pictures through the branches of the Pride of India tree onto the wall of her bedroom.

She threw back the single sheet and swung her legs off the bed. She could not sleep, it was too warm, her nightdress kept binding under her armpits. She stood up and on a sudden reckless impulse she drew the nightdress off over her head and tossed it through the open door of her dressing-room, then, naked, she walked out onto the wide veranda. Into the moonlight, with the cool stone flags under her bare feet, and the warm night air moving like the touch of fairy hands on her skin.

She felt suddenly devilish and daring; she wanted to run down across the lawns and to have someone catch her doing it. She giggled, uncertain of this mood. It was so far removed from Manfred's conception of a good German Hausfrau's behaviour.

'He'd be furious,' she whispered with wicked delight, and then she heard the motor of the car.

She froze with horror. The headlights flicked through the trees as the car came up the driveway and she darted back into her room. In panic she dropped to her knees and searched for her nightdress, found it and ran to the bed as she dragged it on over her head.

She lay in the darkness and listened to the car door slam. There was silence until she heard him pass her door. His heels clacked on the yellow wood floor, he was almost running. Theresa knew the symptoms, the late night return, the suppressed urgency, and she lay rigid in her bed, waiting.

The minutes passed slowly, and then the interleading door from Manfred's suite swung open silently.

'Manfred, is that you?' She sat up and reached for the switch of the bedside lamp.

'Don't put the light on.' His voice was breathless, slurred as though he had been drinking, but there was no trace of liquor on his breath as he stooped over her and kissed her. His lips were dry and tightly closed as he slipped off his dressing-gown.

Two and a half minutes later he stood up from the bed, turning his back to Theresa as he quickly shrugged into the silk dressing-gown.

'Excuse me a minute, Theresa.' The breathlessness was gone from his voice. He went through the door of his own suite, and seconds later she heard the hiss of the shower and the tinkling splash of water.

She lay on her back and her fingernails cut into the palms of her hands. Her body was trembling with a mixture of revulsion and desire, it had been so fleeting a contact—enough to stir her, but so swift as to leave her with a feeling of having been used and sullied. She knew that the rest of the night would pass infinitely slowly, with restless burning tension, remorse and self-pity alternating with wild elation and half-crazed erotic fantasy.

'Damn him,' she screamed silently within her skull. 'Damn him! Damn him!'

She heard the shower stop, and then Manfred returned to her room. He smelt of 4711 Eau de Cologne, and he sat down carefully on the end of the bed.

'You may turn on the light, Theresa.'

It required a conscious effort for her to unclench her hand and reach out for the lamp switch. Manfred blinked behind his spectacles at the flood of light. His hair was damp and freshly combed, his cheeks shone like ripe apples.

'I hope you had an enjoyable day?' he asked, and listened seriously to her reply. Despite her tension, Theresa found herself falling under the almost hypnotic influence he wielded over her. His voice precise, almost monotonous. The glitter of his spectacles, the reptilian stillness of his body and features.

As she had so many times before, she thought of herself as a warm fluffy rabbit sitting tense and fascinated before the cobra.

'It is late,' he said at last and he stood up.

Looking down at her as she lay cuddled into the white silk sheets, he asked with as little emphasis as if he were requesting her to pass the sugar: 'Theresa, could you raise three hundred thousand Rand without your grandfather knowing?'

'Three hundred thousand!' She sat up startled.

'Yes. Could you?'

'Good Lord, Manfred, that's a small fortune.' She truly saw nothing unusual in her choice of adjective. 'You know it's all in the Trust Fund, well, most of it. There is the farm and the—no, I couldn't find half of that without Pops knowing.'

'Pity,' murmured Manfred.

'Manfred, you aren't in—difficulties?'

'No. Good Lord, no. It was just a thought. Forget that I asked. Good night, Theresa, I hope you sleep well.'

Involuntarily she lifted her hands towards him in invitation.

'Good night, Manfred.'

He turned and left the room, she let her hands fall to her sides. For Theresa Steyner the long night had begun.

CHAPTER 28

'Ladies and Gentlemen, it is customary for the General Manager to introduce the distinguished guest who presents our special service awards. Last week, in tragic circumstances our General Manager, Mr Frank Lemmer, was killed in the Company's service, a loss which we all bitterly regret, and I am sure you all join me in sincere condolence to Mrs Eileen Lemmer.' Rod paused for the acknowledging murmur from his audience. There were two hundred of them packed into the mine club hall. 'It falls upon me, therefore, as Acting General Manager, to introduce to you Dr Manfred Steyner who is a senior Director of Central Rand Consolidated, our parent company. He is also head of the Departments of Finance and Planning.'

Sitting beside her husband, Theresa Steyner had noticed Manfred's irritation at Rod's mention of Frank Lemmer. It was company policy not to draw public attention to accidental death or injury inflicted on employees by the Company's operation. She liked Rod the better for his small tribute to Frank Lemmer.

Theresa was wearing sunglasses, for her eyes were swollen and red. In the dawning, after a sleepless night, she had succumbed suddenly to a fit of bitter weeping. The tears were without cause, or reason, and had left her feeling strangely light-headed and with a brittle sense of well-being. However, her enormous eyes always showed up badly for hours after she had wept.

She sat with her legs demurely crossed, immaculate in a suit of cream shantung, a black silk scarf catching her hair and then letting it fall in a dark glossy brown cascade onto her shoulders. She leaned forward in polite attention to the speaker, one elbow on her knee, her chin cupped in her palm, one long tapered finger lying against her cheek. A lady with diamonds on her fingers and pearls at her throat, smiling an acknowledgement at Rod's reference to 'the lovely grand-daughter of our Chairman'.

Except for the slight incongruity of the sunglasses, she was the perfect image of the young matron. Polished, poised, cosseted, secure in her unassailable virtue and duty.

However, the thoughts that were running through Theresa Steyner's head, and the flutterings and sensations that were prickling and tickling her, had they been known, would have broken up the assembly in disorder. All the formless fantasy and emotional disturbance of the previous night were now directed at one target—Rodney Ironsides. Suddenly, with a start of amusement and alarm, she was aware of a phenomenon that she had last experienced many years ago. She moved quickly, shifting her seat, for the cream shantung marked so easily with any moisture.

'Terry Styner!' she thought, deliciously shocked at herself, and found with relief that Rod had finished speaking and Manfred was standing up to reply. She joined in the applause enthusiastically to distract her errant fancy.

Manfred briefly mentioned the six gentlemen sitting in the front row of seats whose courage and devotion to duty they had come to honour; he then went on into an exploration of the prospects of an increase in the price of gold. In measured, carefully considered terms, he set out the advantages and benefits that would accrue to the industry, the nation and the world at large. It was an erudite and convincing dissertation, and there was a large contingent of newspaper men to record it. The press had been alerted by the public relations department of C.R.C. to the text of Dr Steyner's speech and all the leading dailies, weeklies, financial gazettes and journals were represented.

At intervals a photographer would come to crouch below the platform and pop a flash bulb up at Dr Steyner. On the eve of the gold price talks with France this would make good copy, for Steyner was the boy genius in the South African team.

The six heroes sat uncomfortably, forlorn in their best suits, scrubbed like schoolboys at a prize-giving ceremony, staring up at the speaker, not understanding a single word of the foreign language, but maintaining expressions of grave dignity.

Rod caught Big King's eye and winked at him. Solemnly Big King's right eyelid drooped and rose in reply, and quickly Rod averted his gaze to prevent himself laughing out loud.

He looked straight into Theresa Steyner's face, taking her completely off her guard. Not even the dark glasses could conceal her thoughts, they were as clear as if she had spoken them aloud. Before she could drop her eyes to examine the hem of her skirt, Rod knew with a stomach swoop of excitement how it could be if he chose.

With a new awareness he examined her from the corner of his eye, seeing her for the first time as an accessible woman, a highly desirable woman, but nevertheless still the grand-daughter of Hurry Hirschfeld and the wife of Manfred Steyner. This made her as dangerous as a force ten pressure burst, he knew, but the desire and temptation were hard to deny, inflamed perhaps rather than dampened by the danger.

He saw that she was blushing now, her fingers picking nervously at the hem of her skirt. She was as agitated as a schoolgirl, she knew he was watching her. Rod Ironsides, who until five minutes before had been thinking of nothing but his speech, now found himself impelled into a completely new and exciting dimension.

After the awards had been made, tea had been drunk, biscuits consumed and the crowd had dispersed, Rod escorted the Steyners down across the vivid green lawns of Kikuyu grass to where the chauffeur was holding the Daimler.

'What a magnificent physique that Shangaan has, what was his name—King?' Terry was walking between the two men.

'King Nkulu. Big King, we call him.'

Rod found his speech unsteady, he had stuttered slightly. This thing between the two of them was suddenly overpowering, it hummed like a turbine, making the space between them crackle with tension. Unless he were deaf, Manfred Steyner must be aware of it.

'He is pretty special. There is nothing he can't do, and do it far and away better than his nearest rival. My God, you should see him dance.'

'Dance?' inquired Terry with interest.

'Tribal dancing, you know.'

'Of course.' Terry hoped the relief in her voice was not obvious. She had been racking her badly flustered brains for an excuse to visit the Sonder Ditch again or have Rod Ironsides come to Johannesburg. 'I have a friend who is absolutely mad keen on seeing the dances. She pesters me every time I see her.'

Quickly she selected a name from her list of friends—she must have one ready should Manfred ask.

'They dance every Saturday afternoon, bring her out any time.' Rod fielded the ball neatly.

'What about this Saturday?' Terry turned to her husband. 'Would that be all right, Manfred?'

'What's that?' Manfred looked at her vaguely, he had not been following the conversation. Manfred Steyner was a worried man; he was pondering his obligation to gain control of the management of the Sonder Ditch within two days.

'May we come out here on Saturday afternoon to watch the tribal dancing?' Terry repeated her request.

'Have you forgotten that I fly to Paris on Saturday morning, Theresa?'

'Oh, dear.' Terry bit her lip thoughtfully. 'It *had* slipped my mind. What a pity, I would have enjoyed it.'

Manfred frowned slightly, irritated.

'My dear Theresa, there is no reason why you shouldn't come out to the Sonder Ditch without me. I am sure you will be safe enough in Mr Ironsides' hands.'

His choice of words brought the colour to Terry's cheeks again.

CHAPTER 29

After the award ceremony, Big King's first stop was the Recruiting Agency Office at the entrance to the No. 1 shaft hostel. There were men clustered about the counter, but they stood aside for Big King and he acknowledged the courtesy by slapping their backs indiscriminately and greeting them with:

'Kunjane, madoda. How is it, men?'

The clerk behind the counter hurried to serve him. Up at the Mine Club Big King might be a little out of his depth, but here he was treated like a reigning monarch.

In two neat bundles Big King placed the award money on the counter.

'Twenty-five Rand you will send to my senior wife.' He instructed the clerk. 'And twenty-five Rand you will put to my book.'

Big King was scrupulously fair. Half of all his earnings was remitted to the senior of his four wives, and half was added to the substantial sum already credited in his savings bank passbook.

The agency was the procurer of labour for the insatiably man-hungry gold mines of the Witwatersrand and Orange Free State. Its representatives operated across the southern half of the continent. From the swamps and fever lagoons along the great Zambesi, from among the palm groves fringing the Indian Ocean, out of those simmering plains that the bushmen called 'the big dry', down from the mountains of Basutoland and the grasslands of Swaziland and Zululand they gathered the Bantu, the men themselves completing the first fifty or sixty miles of the journey on foot. Individuals meeting on a footpath to become pairs, arriving at a little general dealer's store in the bleak scrub desert to find three or four others already waiting, the arrival of the recruiting truck with a dozen men and the luggage aboard, the long bumping grinding progress through the bush. The stops at which more men scrambled aboard, until a full truck load of fifty or sixty disembarked at a railway siding in the wilderness.

Here the tiny trickle of humanity joined a stream, and at the first major centre they trans-shipped and became part of the great flood that washed towards 'Goldi'.

However, once they had reached Johannesburg and been allocated to one of the sixty major gold mines, the Agency's obligations towards its recruits were not yet discharged. Between them the employing mine and the Agency must provide each man with employment, training, advice and comfort, maintain contact between him and his family, for very few of them could write, reassure him when he worried that his goats were sick or his wife unfaithful. They must provide a banking and savings service with a personal involvement unknown to any commercial banking institute. They had, in short, to make certain that a man taken from an environment that had not changed in a thousand years and deposited into the midst of a sophisticated and technological society would retain his health, happiness and sanity, so that at the end of his contract he would return to the place from which he had come and tell them all how wonderful it was at 'Goldi'. He would show them his hard helmet, and his new suitcase crammed with clothes, his transistor radio and the little blue book with its printed figures, inflaming them also with the desire to make the pilgrimage, and keep the flood washing towards 'Goldi'.

Big King completed his business transactions and went in through the gates of the hostel. He was going to take advantage of the fact that he had missed the shift and would be among the first at the ablutions and dining-hall.

He went down across the lawns to his block. Despite the size of an establishment that housed six thousand men, the Company had tried to make it as attractive as possible. The result was an unusual design, half-way between a motel and an advanced penitentiary.

As a senior boss boy, Big King rated a room of his own. An ordinary labourer would share with five others.

Carefully Big King brushed down his suit and hung it in the built-in cupboard, wiped down his glossy shoes and racked them, then with a towel around his waist he set off for the ablution block and was irritated to find it already filled with new recruits up from the acclimatization centre.

Big King ran an appraising eye over their naked bodies and judged that this batch must be nearing the completion of their eight-day acclimatization. They were sleek and shiny, the muscle definition showing clearly through the skin.

You could not take a man straight out of his village, probably suffering from malnutrition, and put him down a gold mine to lash and bar and drill in a dry bulb heat of 91° Fahrenheit and 84 per cent relative humidity, without running a serious risk of killing him with heat stroke or exhaustion.

Every recruit judged medically fit to work underground went into acclimatization. For eight days, eight hours a day, he and hundreds of others stood with only a loin cloth about his middle in a vast barn-like hall stepping up onto and down from a platform. The height of the platform was carefully matched to the man's height and body weight, the speed of his movements was regulated by a flashing panel of lights, the temperature and humidity were controlled at 91° and 84 per cent, every ten minutes he was given water and his body temperature was registered by the half dozen trained medical assistants in charge of the room.

At the end of the eighth day he emerged as fit as an olympic athlete, and quite able to perform heavy physical labour in conditions of high temperature and humidity without discomfort or danger.

'Gwedeni!' growled Big King, and the nearest recruit, still white with soap suds, hurriedly vacated his shower with a respectful 'Keshle!' in deference to Big King's rank and standing. Big King removed his towel and stepped under the shower, revelling as always in the rush of hot water over his skin, flexing the great muscles of his arms and chest.

The messenger found him there.

'King Nkulu, I have word for thee.' The man used Shangaan, not the bastard Fanikalo.

'Speak,' Big King invited, soaping his belly and buttocks.

'The Induna bids you call at his house after you have eaten the evening meal.'

'Tell him I will attend his wishes,' said Big King and held his face up into the rush of steaming water.

Dressed in a white open-neck shirt and blue slacks, Big King sauntered down to the kitchens. Again the recruits were ahead of him, queueing with bowls in hand outside the serving hatches. Big King walked past them through the door marked 'No Admittance—Staff only.'

The kitchens were cavernous, glistening with white porcelain tiles and stainless steel cookers and bins that could serve eighteen thousand hot meals a day.

When Big King entered a room, even one as large as this, no one was unaware of his presence. One of the assistant cooks snatched up a bowl not much smaller than a baby's bath, and hurried across to the nearest stainless steel bin. He opened the lid and looked expectantly at Big King. Big King nodded and the cook ladled about two litres of steaming sugar beans into the bowl, before passing on to the next bin where he again looked for and obtained Big King's approval. He added an equal quantity of mixed vegetables to the bowl, slammed down the lid and scampered across to where a second assistant waited with a spade beside yet another bin.

The spade was the same as those used for lashing gold reef underground, but the blade of this one had been polished to gleaming cleanliness. The second cook dug into the bin and came up with a spadeful of white maize porridge, cooked stiff as cake, the smell of it as saliva-making as the smell of new bread. This was the staple of Bantu diet. He deposited the spadeful in the bowl.

'I am hungry.' Big King spoke for the first time, and the second cook dug out another spadeful and added it to the bowl. They passed on to the end of the kitchens, and at their approach another cook lifted the lid on a pressure cooker the size of a washing machine. From it rose a cloud of fragrant steam.

Apologetically the cook held out his hand and Big King produced his meat ticket. Meat was the only food that was rationed. Each man was limited to one pound of meat a day; the Company had long ago discovered to its astonishment and cost that a Bantu, offered unlimited supplies of fresh meat, was quite capable of eating his own weight of it monthly.

Having ascertained that Big King was entitled to his daily pound, the book proceeded to ladle at least five pounds of it into the bowl.

'You are my brother,' Big King thanked him, and the little procession moved on to where yet another cook was filling a half-gallon jug of thick, gruel-like, mildly alcoholic Bantu beer from one of the multiple spiggots beneath the thousand-gallon tank.

The bowl and jug were ceremonially handed to Big King and he went out onto the covered terraces where benches and tables were set out for alfresco dining in mild weather.

While he ate, the terrace began to fill, for the shift was out of the mine now. Every man who passed his table greeted Big King, but only a few privileged persons took the liberty of seating themselves at the same table. One of them was Joseph M'Kati, the little old sweeper from 100 level.

'It has been a good week, King Nkulu.'

'You say so.' Big King was non-committal. 'I go now to a meeting with the Old One. Then we shall see.'

The Old One, the Shangaan Induna, lived in a Company house. A self-contained residence with lounge and dining-room, kitchen and bathroom. He was handsomely paid by the Company, provided with servants, food, furniture and all the other appurtenances of his rank and station.

He was the head of the Shangaan community on the Sonder Ditch. A chief of the blood, a greybeard and member of the tribal councils. In similar houses and with the same privileges and in·equal style lived the Indunas of the other tribal groups that made up the labour force of the Sonder Ditch. They were the paternal figureheads, the tribal jurists, ruling and judging within the framework of law and custom. The Company could not hope to maintain harmony and order without the assistance of these men.

'Baba!' Big King greeted his Induna from the doorway of his house, touching the forehead in respect not only for the man but also for what he represented.

'My son.' The Induna smiled his greeting. 'Come and sit by me.' He gestured for his servants to leave the room, and Big King went to squat at the feet of the old man. 'Is it true you go now to work with the mad one?' That was Johnny Delange's nickname.

They talked, the Induna questioning him on fifty matters that affected the welfare of his people. For Big King this was a comforting and nostalgic experience, for the Induna stood in the place of his father.

At last, satisfied, the Induna went on to other matters.

'There is a parcel ready tonight. Crooked Leg waits for you.'

'I shall go for it.'

'Go in peace then, my son.'

On his way through the gates of the hostel Big King stopped to chat with the guards. These men had the right of search over any person entering or leaving the hostel. Particularly they were concerned with preventing either women disguised as men or bottles of spirits entering the premises, both of which tended to have a disruptive effect on the community. As an after-thought they were also instructed to look out for stolen property entering or leaving. Big King had to ensure that none of them would ever, under any circumstances, take it into his head to search Big King.

While he stood at the gates, the last glow of the sunset faded and the lights began to come on across the valley. The clusters of red aerial warning lights atop the headgears, the massed yellow squares of the hotels, the strings of street lamps and the isolated pinpricks of the residential areas up on the ridge.

When it was truly dark, Big King left the guards and sauntered down the main road, until a bend in the road took him out of their sight. Then Big King left the road and started up the slope. He moved like a night animal, swiftly and with certainty of the path he followed.

He passed the ranch-type split-levels of the line management officials with their wide lawns and swimming-pools, pausing only once when a dog yapped near-by, then moving on again until he was into the broken rock and rank grass of the upper ridge; he crossed the skyline and started down the far side until he made out the grass-covered mound of rubble in the moonlight. He slowed and moved cautiously forward until he found the rusty barbed wire fence that guarded the entrance. He vaulted it easily and went on into the black mouth of the tunnel.

Fifty years before, a long-defunct mining company had suspected the existence of a gold reef in this area and had driven prospecting addits into the side of the ridge, exhausting its funds in the process, and finally abandoning the network of tunnels in despair.

Big King paused long enough to draw an electric torch from his pocket before going on into the tunnel, flashing the beam ahead of him. Soon the air stank of bats and their wings swished about his head. Unperturbed, Big King went on deeper and deeper into the side of the hill, taking a turning and fork in the tunnel without hesitation. At last there was a faint glow of yellow light ahead and Big King switched off his torch.

'Crooked Leg!' he called. His voice bounced and boomed along the tunnel. There was no reply.

'It is I, Big King!' he shouted again, and immediately a shadow detached itself from the sidewall and limped towards him, sheathing a wicked-looking knife as it came.

'All is ready.' The little cripple came to greet him. 'Come, I have it here.'

Crooked Leg had earned his limp and his nickname in a rockfall a dozen years ago. Now he owned and operated the concession photographic studio on the mine property, a flourishing enterprise, for dearly the Bantu love their own image on film. Not, however, as profitable as his nocturnal activities in the abandoned workings beyond the ridge.

He led Big King into a small rock chamber lit by a suspended hurricane lantern. Mingled with the bat stench was the acrid reek of sulphuric acid in high concentration.

On a wooden trestle table that occupied most of the chamber were earthernware jars, heavy glass bowls, polythene bags, and a variety of shoddy and very obviously second-hand laboratory equipment. In a clear space among all this clutter stood a large screw-topped bottle. The bottle was filled with a dirty yellow powder.

'Ha!' Big King exclaimed his pleasure. 'Plenty!'

'Yes. It has been a good week,' Crooked Leg agreed.

Big King picked up the bottle, marvelling once again at the unbelievable weight of it. This was not pure gold, for Crooked Leg's acid reduction methods were crude, but it was at least sixteen carats fine.

The bottle represented the week's collection of fines and concentrates by men like Joseph M'Kati from a dozen vulnerable points along the line of production; in some cases carried out from the Company reduction works itself under the noses of the heavily armed guards.

All the men involved in this surreptitious milking-off of the Company's gold were Shangaans. There was only one man in whom was vested sufficient authority and prestige to prevent the greed and hostility which gold breeds from destroying the whole operation. That was the Shangaan Induna. There was only one man with the physical presence and necessary command of the Portuguese language to negotiate the disposal of the gold. That was Big King.

Big King placed the bottle in his pocket. The weight pulled his clothing out of shape.

'Run like a gazelle, Crooked Leg.' He turned back into the dark tunnel.

'Hunt like a leopard, King Nkulu,' chuckled the little cripple, as he disappeared into the moving shadows.

CHAPTER 30

'A packet of Boxer tobacco,' said Big King. The eyes of José Almeida, the Portuguese owner of the mine concession store and the local road-house, narrowed slightly. He took down the yellow four-ounce packet from the shelves and handed it across the counter, accepted Big King's payment and counted the change into his palm.

He watched as the giant Bantu wandered down between the loaded shelves and racks of merchandise to disappear through the front door of the store into the night.

'Take charge,' he muttered in Portuguese to his plump little wife with her silky dark moustache, and she nodded in understanding, moving into José's place in front of the cash register. José went through into his storerooms and living quarters behind the store.

Big King was waiting in the shadows. When the back door opened he slipped through and José closed the door behind him. José led him through into a cubicle of an office, and from a cupboard he took down a jeweller's balance. Under Big King's watchful eye he began to weigh the gold.

José Almeida purchased the gold from the unofficial outlets of each of the five major mines on the Kitchenerville field, paying five Rands an ounce and selling again for sixteen. He justified the large profit margin he allowed himself by the fact that mere possession of un-registered gold was a criminal offence in South Africa, punishable by up to five years' imprisonment.

Almeida was a man in his middle thirties with lank black hair that he continually pushed back from his forehead, bright brown inquisitive eyes and dirty fingernails. Despite his grubby and well-worn clothing and unkempt hair style, he was a man of substance.

He had been able to pay in cash the forty thousand Rand demanded by the Company for the monopoly concession to trade on the mine property. He had, therefore, an exclusive clientele of twelve thousand well-paid Bantu, and had recovered his forty thousand during his first year of trading. He did not really need to run the risk of illicit gold buying, but gold is strange material. It infects most men who touch it with a reckless greed.

'Two hundred and sixteen ounces,' said José. His scale was set to record a twenty per cent error—in José's favour.

'One thousand and eighty Rand,' agreed Big King in Portuguese, and José went to the big green safe in the corner.

CHAPTER 31

Terry Steyner entered the 'Grape and Gable' bar of the President Hotel at 1.14 p.m. precisely, and as Hurry Hirschfeld stood to greet her he reflected that fourteen minutes was hardly late at all for a beautiful woman. Terry's grandmother would have considered herself to be early if she was only that late.

'You're late,' growled Hurry. No sense in letting her get away with it unscathed.

'And you are a big, cuddly, growly, lovable old bear,' said Terry and kissed him on the tip of his nose before he could duck. Hurry sat down quickly, scowling thunderously with pleasure. He decided he didn't give a good damn if Marais and Hardy, who further down the bar were listening and trying to cover their grins, repeated the incident to the entire membership of the Rand Club.

'Good day, Mrs Steyner.' The scarlet-jacketed barman smiled his greeting. 'Can I mix you a Manhattan?'

'Don't tempt me, Thomas. I'm on a diet. I'll just have a glass of soda water.'

'Diet,' snorted Hurry. 'You're skinny enough as it is. Give her a Manhattan, Thomas, and put a cherry in it. Never was a Hirschfeld woman that looked like a boy, and you'll not be the first of them.' As an afterthought, he added, 'I've ordered your lunch also, you'll not starve yourself in my company.'

'You are a shocker, Pops,' said Terry fondly.

'Now, young lady, let's hear what you've been up to since I last saw you.'

They talked together as friends, very dear and trusted friends. The affection they felt for each other went beyond the natural duty of their blood tie. There was a kinship of the spirit as well as the flesh. They sat close, heads together, watching each other's face as they talked, completely lost in the pleasure of each other's company, the murmur of their voices interrupted by a tinkling burst of laughter or a deep chuckle.

They were so absorbed that Peter, the head waiter, came through from the Transvaal Room to find them.

'Mr Hirschfeld, the chef is in tears.'

'Good Lord.' Hurry looked at the antique clock above the bar. 'It's almost two o'clock. Why didn't someone tell me?'

The oysters had been flown up from Mossel Bay that morning, and Terry sighed with pleasure after each of them.

'I was out at the Sonder Ditch with Manfred on Wednesday.'

'Yes, I saw the photograph in the paper.' Hurry engulfed his twelfth and final oyster.

'I must say I like your new General Manager.'

Hurry laid down his forks and a little flush of anger started in his withered old cheeks.

'You mean Fred Plummer?'

'Don't be silly, Pops, I mean Rodney Ironsides.'

'Has that cold fish of yours been briefing you?' Hurry demanded.

'Manfred?' She was genuinely puzzled by the question, Hurry could see that. 'What's he got to do with it?'

'All right, forget it.' Hurry dismissed Manfred with a shake of his head. 'Why do you like Ironsides?'

'Have you heard him speak?'

'No.'

'He's very good. I'm sure he must be a first-class mining man.'

'He is.' Hurry nodded, watchful and non-committal.

Peter whisked Terry's plate away, giving her the respite she needed to gather her resources. In the previous few seconds she had realized that Rodney Ironsides was not, as she had believed, a certainty for the job. In fact, Pops had already chosen old plum-faced Plummer for the General Managership. It took another moment for her to decide that she would use even the dirtiest in-fighting to see that Rod was not overlooked.

Peter laid plates of cold rock lobster in front of them, and when he had withdrawn Terry looked up at Hurry. She had perfected the trick of enlarging her already enormous eyes. By holding them open like this she could flood them with tears. The effect was devastating.

'Do you know, Pops, he reminds me so much of the photographs of Daddy.'

Colonel Bernard Hirschfeld, Terry's father, had burned to death in his tank at Sidi Rezegh. She saw Hurry Hirschfeld's expression crack with pain, and Terry felt a sick little flutter of guilt. Had it been necessary to use such a vicious weapon to achieve her ends?

Hurry pushed at the rock lobster with his fork, his head was bowed so she could not see his face. She reached out to touch his hand.

'Pops—' she whispered, and he looked up. There was a restrained excitement in Hurry's manner.

'You know, you're bloody well right! He does look a bit like Bernie. Did I ever tell you about the time when your father and I—'

Terry felt dizzy with relief. I didn't hurt him, she told herself, he likes the idea, he really does. With a woman's instinct she had chosen the only form of persuasion that could have moved Hurry Hirschfeld from his decision.

CHAPTER 32

Manfred Steyner fastened his safety belt and lay back in the seat of the Boeing 707, feeling slightly nauseated with relief.

Ironsides was in, and he was safe. Hurry Hirschfeld had sent for him two hours before to wish him farewell and good luck with the talks. Manfred had stood before him, trying desperately to think of some way in which he could bring up the subject naturally. Hurry saved him the trouble.

'By the way, I'm giving Ironsides the Sonder Ditch. Reckon it's about time we had some young blood in top management.'

It was as easy as that. Manfred had difficulty in persuading himself that those threats which had kept him lying awake during the past four nights were no longer of consequence. Ironsides was in. He could go to Paris and tell them. *Ironsides is in. We are ready to go.*

The note of the jets changed, and the Boeing began to roll forward. Manfred twisted his head against the neck rest and peered through the perspex porthole. He could not distinguish Terry's figure among the crowd on the observation balcony of Jan Smuts Airport. They taxied past a Pan Am Boeing which cut off his view and Manfred looked straight ahead. Instantly his nostrils flared, he looked around quickly.

The passenger in the seat beside him had stripped to his shirtsleeves. He was a big beefy individual who very obviously did not use deodorant. Almost in desperation Manfred looked about. The aircraft was full, there would be little chance of changing seats and beside him the beefy individual produced a pack of cigarettes.

'You can't smoke,' cried Manfred. 'The light's on.' The combination of body odour and cigarette smoke would be unbearable.

'I'm not smoking,' said the man, 'yet.' And placed a cigarette between his lips, his lighter ready in the other hand.

Nearly two thousand miles to Nairobi, thought Manfred, with his stomach starting to heave.

CHAPTER 33

'Terry darling, why on earth should I go all the way out to Kitchener-ville to watch a lot of savages prancing around?'

'As a favour to me, Joy,' Terry pleaded into the telephone.

'It means mucking up my whole weekend. I've got rid of the kids to their grandmother, I've got a copy of *A Small Town in Germany* and I was going to have a lovely time reading and—'

'Please, Joy, you're my last hope.'

'What time will we be home?' Joy was weakening. Terry sensed her advantage and pressed forward ruthlessly.

'You might meet a lovely man out at the mine, and he'll sweep you—'

'No, thanks.' Joy had been divorced a little over a year ago—some people took longer than others to recover. 'I've had lovely men in big fat chunks.'

'Oh, Joy, you can't sit around moping for ever. Come on, I'll pick you up in half an hour.'

Joy sighed with resignation. 'Damn you, Terry Steyner.'

'Half an hour,' said Terry and hung up before she could change her mind.

'I'm playing golf. It's Saturday, and I'm playing golf,' said Dr Daniel Stander stubbornly.

'You remember when I drove all the way to Bloemfontein to—' Rod began, and Dan interrupted quickly.

'All right, all right, I remember. You don't have to bring that up again.'

'You owe me plenty, Stander,' Rod reminded him. 'All I am asking is one of your lousy Saturday afternoons. Is that so much?'

'I can't let the boys down. It's a long-standing date.' Dan wriggled to escape.

'I've already phoned Ben. It will be a pleasure for him to take your place.'

There was a long gloomy silence, then Dan asked, 'What's this bird like?'

'She's a beautiful, rich nymphomaniac, and she owns a brewery.'

'Yeah! Yeah!' said Dan sarcastically. 'All right, I'll do it. But I hereby declare all my obligation and debts to you fully discharged.'

'I'll give you a written receipt,' Rod agreed.

Dan was still sulking when the Daimler came up the drive and parked at the front of the Mine Club. He and Rod were standing at the Ladies' Bar, watching for the arrival of their guests.

Dan had just ordered his third beer.

'Here they come,' said Rod.

'Is that them?' Dan's depression lifted magically as he peered through the coloured-glass windows. The chauffeur was letting the two ladies out of the Daimler. They were both in floral slack suits and dark glasses.

'That's them.'

'Jesus!' said Dan with rare approval. 'Which one is mine?'

'The blonde.'

'Ha!' Dan grinned for the first time since their meeting. 'Why the hell are we standing here?'

'Why indeed?' asked Rod, his stomach was tied up in knots that twisted tighter as he went down the front steps towards Terry.

'Mrs Steyner. I'm so glad you could come.' With a wild lift of elation he saw it was still there, he had not imagined it, it was there in her eyes and her smile.

'Thank you, Mr Ironsides.' She was like a schoolgirl again, uncertain of herself, flustered.

'I'd like you to meet Mrs Albright. Joy, this is Rodney Ironsides.'

'Hello.' He smiled at her as he clasped her hand. 'It's gin time, I think.'

Dan was waiting at the bar for them, and Rod made the introductions.

'Joy is so excited at the chance of watching the dancing,' said Terry as they sat down on the bar stools. 'She's been looking forward to it for days.' And for an instant Joy looked stunned.

'You'll love it,' agreed Dan, moving in to take up a position at Joy's elbow. 'I wouldn't miss it for anything.'

Joy was a tall slim girl with long straight golden hair that hung to her shoulders; her eyes were cool green but her mouth when she smiled was soft and warm. She smiled now full into Dan's eyes.

'Nor would I,' she said, and with relief Rod knew he could devote all his attention to Terry Steyner. Joy Albright would be more than adequately looked after. He ordered drinks, and all four of them promptly lost further interest in tribal dancing.

At one stage Rod told Terry Steyner, 'I am going up to Johannesburg this evening. There is no point in having your unfortunate chauffeur sit around all afternoon. Let him go, and I'll take you home.'

'Good,' Terry agreed immediately. 'Would you tell him, please?'

The next time Rod looked at his watch it was half past three.

'Good Lord!' he exclaimed. 'If we don't hurry, it will be all over.'
Reluctantly Joy and Dan, who had their heads close together, drew
apart.

The overflow from the amphitheatre pressed about them, a merry
jostling throng, all inhibitions long since evaporated in the primeval
excitement of the dance, much like the crowd at a bull ring.

Rod and Dan ran interference for the girls, ploughing a path through
the main gateway and down to their reserved seats in the front row. All
four of them were laughing and flushed by the time they were seated—
the excitement about them was infectious and the liquor had heightened
their sensibilities.

An expectant hum of voices.

'The Shangaans!' And the audience craned towards the entrance
from which pranced a dozen drummers, their long wooden drums
hung on rawhide straps about their necks. They took up stations around
the circular earthen stage.

Tap, tap. Tap, tap—from one of the drummers, and silence gripped
the amphitheatre.

Tap, tap. Tap, tap. Naked, except for their brief loin cloths, stooped
over the drums that they clasped between their knees, they began to
lay down the rhythm of the dance. It was a broken, disturbing beat, that
jerked and twitched like a severed nerve. A compelling, demanding
sound, the pulse of a continent and a people.

Then came the dancers, shuffling, row upon row, head-dresses
dipping and rustling, the animal tail kilts swirling, war rattles at the
wrists and ankles, black muscles already oiled with the sweat of excitement, coming in slowly, rank upon majestic rank, moving as though
the drums were pumping life into them.

A shrill blast on a duiker horn and the ranks whirled like dry leaves
in a wind, they fell again into a new pattern, and through the opening
in their midst came a single gigantic figure.

'Big King!' The name blew like a sigh through the audience, and
immediately the drums changed their rhythm. Faster, demanding, and
the dancers hissed in their throats a sound like storm surf rushing up a
stony beach.

Big King flung his arms wide, braced on legs like black marble
columns, his head thrown back. He sang a single word of command,
shrilling it, and in instantaneous response every right knee was brought
up to the level of the chest. Half a second's pause and then two hundred
horny bare feet stamped down simultaneously with a crash that shook

the amphitheatre to its foundations. The Shangaans began to dance, and reality was gone in the moving, charging, swirling, retreating ranks.

Once Rod tore his eyes from the spectacle. Terry Steyner was sitting forward on the bench, eyes sparkling, lips slightly parted, completely lost in the erotic turmoil and barbaric splendour of it.

Joy and Dan had a firm hold on each others' hands, their shoulders and the outside of their thighs were pressed tightly together, and Rod was stabbed by a painful thrust of envy.

Afterwards, back in the Ladies' Bar of the Club, there was very little conversation but they were all of them tensed up, restless, moved by strange undercurrents and interplays of primitive desires and social restraints.

'Well,' said Rod at last, 'if I am to get you two ladies back to Johannesburg at a decent hour—'

Dan and Joy spoke together.

'Don't worry, Rod, I'll—'

'Dan says he will—' Then they stopped and grinned at each other sheepishly.

'I take it that Dan has suddenly remembered that he has to go to Johannesburg this evening also, and he has offered to give you a lift?' asked Rod dryly, and they laughed in confirmation.

'It looks as though we are on our own, Mrs Steyner.' Rod turned to Terry.

'I'll trust you,' said Terry.

'If you do that, you're crazy,' said Dan.

Outside the Maserati, darkness was falling swiftly, the horizon blending into the black sky, isolated lights winking at them out of the surrounding veld.

Rod switched on the headlights, and the instrument panel glowed softly, turning the interior into a warm secluded place, isolating them from the world. The wind whispered, and the tyres and the engine hummed a gentle intimate refrain.

Terry Steyner sat with her legs curled up under her, cuddled into the soft maroon leather of the bucket seat. She was staring ahead down the path of the headlights, and she seemed withdrawn and yet very close. Every few minutes Rod would take his eyes from the road and study her profile briefly. He did so again, and this time she met his gaze frankly.

'You realize what is happening?' she asked.

'Yes,' he answered as frankly.

'You know how dangerous it could be for you?'

'And you.'

'No, not me. I am invulnerable. I am a Hirschfeld—but you, it could destroy you.'

Rod shrugged.

'If we counted the consequences before every action, nobody would do anything.'

'Have you thought that I might be a spoiled little rich girl amusing myself? I might do this all the time.'

'You might,' Rod agreed. They were silent for a long while, then Terry spoke again.

'Rod?' she used his given name for the first time.

'Yes?'

'I don't, you know. I really don't.'

'I guessed that.'

'Thank you.' She opened her bag. 'I need a cigarette. I feel as though I'm standing poised on the edge of a cliff and I've got this terrible compulsion to hurl myself over the edge.'

'Light me one, Terry.'

'You need one also?'

'Badly.'

They smoked in silence again, both of them staring ahead, then Terry rolled down the window and flicked the cigarette butt away.

'You've got the job, you know.' All day she had wanted to tell him, it had been bubbling inside her. Watching his face, she saw his lips stiffen, his eyes crease into slits.

'Did you hear me?' she asked at last, and he braked the Maserati, swinging it off onto the shoulder of the road. He pulled on the hand brake and turned to face her.

'Terry, what did you say?'

'I said, you've got the job.'

'What job?' he demanded harshly.

'Pops signed the instruction this morning. You'll receive it on Monday. You're the new General Manager of the Sonder Ditch.' She wanted to go on and say—*and I got it for you. I made Pops give it to you.*

I never will, she promised, I will never spoil it for him. He must believe he won it fairly, not as my gift.

CHAPTER 34

It was Saturday night, the big night in Dump City.

The Blaauberg Mine was the oldest producer on the Kitchenerville field. There were sections of its property which had been worked out completely, and the old waste dumps were now abandoned and overgrown. Among the scrub and head-high weed in the valleys between these man-made hills had grown up a shanty town. Dump City, the inhabitants had named it. The buildings were made of discarded galvanized iron sheets and flattened oil drums, there was no sanitation or running water.

Remote from the main roads, the residential communities of the neighbouring mines or the town of Kitchenerville, hidden among the dumps, accessible only to a man on foot, never visited by members of the South African Constabulary, it was ideally suited to the purposes for which its three hundred permanent inhabitants had chosen it.

Every one of the shacks was a shebeen, a clip joint where watered liquor was sold at inflated prices, where dagga* was freely obtainable and where men from the surrounding mines gathered to carouse.

They came not so much for the liquor. Each of the mine hostels had a bar where a full range of liquor was on sale at club prices. Very few of them came for the dagga. There was little addiction amongst these well-fed, hard-worked and contented men. What they came for were the women.

Five mines in the area, each employing ten or twelve thousand men. Here at Dump City were two hundred women, the only available women within twenty miles. It was not necessary for the young ladies of Dump City to solicit custom, even the fat, the withered, the toothless, could behave like queens.

Big King came down the path that skirted the mine dump. With him were two dozen of his fellow tribesmen, big Shangaans wearing their regalia, carrying their fighting sticks and still tensed up from the dancing. They came at a trot, Big King leading them. They were singing, not the gentle planting or courting melodies, not the work chant nor the song of welcome.

They were singing the fighting songs, those their forefathers had sung when they carried the spear in search of cattle and slaves. The driving inflammatory rhythm, the fiercely patriotic words wrought so mightily on the delicate susceptibilities of the average Shangaan that the company had found it necessary to ban the singing of these songs.

*Marijuana.

Like a Scot hearing the pipes, when a Shangaan began singing these warlike chants, he was ready for violence.

The song ended as Big King led them down to the nearest shanty, and pushed aside the sacking that acted as a door. He stooped through the opening, and his comrades crowded in behind him.

A brittle electric silence fell on the large room. The air was so thick with smoke, and the light from the suspended hurricane lamps so feeble, that it was impossible to see the far wall. The room was filled with men, forty or fifty of them, the smell of humanity and bad liquor was solid. Among this press of men were half a dozen bright spots of girls' dresses, but with their curiosity aroused by the singing more girls were coming through from the interleading doorways at the back. Some of them had men with them and were still shrugging into their clothing. When they saw Big King and his warriors in full war kit, they fell silent and watchful.

At Big King's shoulder one of his Shangaans whispered:

'Basutos! They are all Basutos!' He was right, Big King saw that they were all men of that mountainous little independent state.

Big King started forward, swaggering just enough to make his leopard tail kilt swing and swirl and the heron feathers of his head-dress rustle. He reached the primitive bar counter.

'Flying Bird,' he told the crone who owned the house, and she placed a bottle of Eagle Brandy on the counter.

Big King half filled a tumbler, conscious that every eye was on him, and drained it.

Slowly he turned and surveyed the room.

'What is it,' he asked in a voice that carried to every corner, 'that sits on top of a mountain and scratches its fleas. Is it a baboon, or a Basuto?'

A roar of delight went up from his Shangaans.

'A Basuto!' they shouted, crowding forward to the bar, while a growl and mutter went up from the rest of the room.

'What is it,' shouted a Basuto jumping to his feet, 'that has feathers on its head and crows from a dungheap? Is it a rooster, or a Shangaan?'

Without seeming to move, Big King picked up the bottle of Eagle Brandy and hurled it. With a crack it burst against the Basuto's forehead and he went over backwards, taking two of his companions with him.

The old crone snatched up her cash register and ran as the room exploded into violent movement.

There was not enough space in which to use the fighting sticks, Big King realized, so he lifted a section of the bar counter off its trestles and holding it in front of him like the blade of a bulldozer, he charged across the room, flattening all and everything before him.

The crash of breaking furniture and the yelp and squeal of men being struck down drove Big King beyond the frontiers of sanity into the red atavistic fury of the berserker.

Basuto is also one of the fighting tribes of the N'guni group. These wiry mountaineers rushed into the conflict with the same savage joy as the Shangaans, a conflict that raged and roared out of the single room to engulf the entire population of Dump City.

One of the girls, her dress ripped from her back so she was left with only a tattered pair of bloomers, had climbed on top of the remains of the bar counter from where, with her big melon breasts swinging in the lamp light, she shrilled that peculiar ululation that Bantu women used to goad their menfolk into battle frenzy. A dozen of the other girls joined in, trilling, squealing, and the sound was too much for Big King.

With the bar top held ahead of him he charged straight through the flimsy wall of the shack, bursting it open like a paper bag; the roof sagged down wearily, and Big King raged on unchecked down the narrow dirt street, striking down any man who crossed his path, scattering chickens and yelping dogs, roaring like a bull gorilla.

He turned at the end of the encampment and came back, his frustration mounting as he found the street deserted except for a few prostrate bodies. Through the gaping hole in the wall he entered the Shebeen once more to find that here also the fighting had died down. A few of the participants were crawling, or moaning as they ley on a carpet of broken glass.

Big King glared about him, seeking a further outlet for his wrath.

'King Nkulu!' The girl was still on the trestle table, her eyes bright with excitement, her legs trembling with it.

Big King let out another roar, and hurled the bar top from him. It clattered against the far wall and Big King started towards her.

'You are a lion!' She shrieked encouragement at him, and she took one of her big black velvety breasts in each hand and pointed them at him, squeezing them together, shaking with excitement.

'Eat me!' she screamed, as Big King swept her off the table and lifting her high, ran with her out into the night. Carrying her into the scrub below the mine dumps, holding her easily with one arm, ripping the leopard-tail kilt from his own waist as he ran.

CHAPTER 35

It was Saturday night in Paris also, but there were men who were still working, for there were lights burning in the upstairs rooms of one of the big Embassies in the rue Royale.

The fat man who had been the host in the gambling establishment in Johannesburg was now the guest. He sat at ease in a leather club easy, his corpulence and the steel-grey hair at his temples giving him dignity. His face heavy, tanned, intelligent. His eyes glittery and hard as the diamond on his finger.

He was listening intently to a man of about the same age as himself who stood before a projected image on a screen that covered one wall of the room. There was that in the man's bearing and manner that marked him as a scholar. He was speaking now, addressing himself directly to the listener in the easy chair, pointing with a marker to the screen beside him.

'You see here a plan of the working of the five producing gold mines of the Kitchenerville fields in relation to each other.' He touched the screen with a marker. 'Thornfontein, Blaauberg, Tweefontein, Deep Gold Levels and Sonder Ditch.'

The man in the chair nodded. 'I have seen and studied this diagram before.'

'Good, then you will know that the Sonder Ditch property sits in the centre of the field. It has common boundaries with the other four mines and here,' he tapped the screen again, 'it is intersected by the massive serpentine dyke which they call the Big Dipper.'

Again the fat man nodded.

'It is for these reasons we have selected the Sonder Ditch as the trigger point.' The lecturer touched a button on the wall panel and the image on the screen changed.

'Now, here is something you have not seen before.'

The man in the chair crouched forward.

'What is it?'

'It is an underground map based on the borehole results of the five companies who have been exploring the ground to the east of the Big Dipper. These results have been pooled and interpreted by some of the finest brains in the fields of geology and hydrophysics. You have here a carefully considered representation of exactly what lies on the far side of the Big Dipper fault.'

The big man moved uncomfortably in his chair.

'It's a monster!'

'Yes, a monster. Lying just beyond the fault is an underground lake, no, that is not the correct word. Let us call it an underground sea, the size of, say, Lake Eyrie. The water is held in a vast sponge of porous dolomite rock.'

'My God.' For the first time the fat man had lost his poise. 'If this is right, why don't the mining companies arrive at the same conclusion and keep well away from it?'

'Because,' the lecturer switched off the image and the overhead lights came on, 'because in their highly competitive attitudes none of them has access to the findings of the others. It is only when all the results are studied that the picture becomes clear.'

'How did your Government come to be in possession of *all* the results?' demanded the fat man.

'That is not important.' The lecturer was brusque, impatient of the interruption. 'We are also in possession of the findings of a certain Dr Peter Wessels who is at present head of a research team in Rock Mechanics based on the Sonder Ditch mine property. It is Company classified information and consists of a paper that Dr Wessels has written on the shatter patterns and stresses of rock. His researches are directly related to the Ventersdorp quartzites which comprise the country rock of the Sonder Ditch workings.'

The lecturer picked up a pamphlet from his desk.

'I will not weary you by asking you to wade through its highly technical findings. Instead I will give it to you in capsule form. Dr Wessels arrives at the conclusion that a column of Ventersdorp quartzite 120 feet thick would shatter under a side pressure of 4,000 pounds per square inch.'

The lecturer dropped the pamphlet back on the desk.

'As you know, by law, the gold mining companies are bound to leave a barrier of solid rock 120 feet thick along their boundaries. That is all that separates one mine's workings from another, just that wall of rock. You understand?'

'Of course. It is very simple.'

'Simple? Yes, it is simple! This Dr Steyner, over whom you have control, will instruct the new General Manager of the Sonder Ditch to drive a tunnel through the Big Dipper dyke. The drive will puncture the vast underground reservoir and the water will run back and flood the entire Sonder Ditch workings. Once they are flooded, the pressure delivered by a 6,000-foot head of water at the lower levels will be in excess of 4,000 pounds per square inch. That is sufficient to burst the rock walls, and flood the Thornfontein, the Blaauberg, Deep Gold Levels and Tweefontein gold mines.

'The entire Kitchenerville gold fields would be effectively and permanently put out of production. The consequences for the economy of the Republic of South Africa would be catastrophic.'

The fat man was visibly shaken.

'Why do you want to do it?' he asked, shaking his head in awe.

'My colleague here,' the lecturer indicated a man who was sitting quietly in one corner, 'will explain that to you presently.'

'But—people!' the fat man protested. 'There will be people down there when it bursts, thousands of them.'

The lecturer smiled, raising one eyebrow. 'If I were to tell you that six thousand men would drown, would you refuse to proceed, and forfeit the million-dollar payment my Government has offered you?'

The fat man looked down, embarrassed, and muttered barely audibly, 'No.'

The lecturer chuckled. 'Good! Good! However, you may salve your aching conscience by assuring yourself that we do not expect more than forty or fifty fatalities from the flooding. Naturally, those men actually working on the face will be killed. But that tremendous volume of water under immense pressure should make it a merciful death. For the rest of them, the mine can be evacuated swiftly enough to allow them excellent chances of survival. The surrounding mines will have days to evacuate before the water pressure builds up sufficiently to burst through the boundary walls.'

There was silence then in the room for nearly a minute.

'Have you any questions?'

The fat man shook his head.

'Very well, in that case I will leave it to my colleague to complete the briefing. He will explain the necessity for this operation, will arrange the terms of payment and conditions upon which you will proceed.' The lecturer gathered up the pamphlet and other papers from the desk. 'It remains only for me to wish you good luck.' He chuckled again and left the room quickly.

The little man who up until then had remained silent, suddenly bounced out of his chair and began pacing up and down the wall-to-wall carpeting. He spoke rapidly, shooting occasional sideways glances at his audience, his bald head shining in the fluorescent lighting, wriggling his moustache like rabbit whiskers, puffing nervously at his cigarette.

'Reasons first. I'll make it short and sweet, right? The South Africans and the Frogs have got together. They're here in Paris now cooking up mischief. We know what they're up to, they're going to launch an all-out attack on my Government's currency. Gold price increase, you know. Very complicated and very nasty for us, right? They might just be able to do it, South Africa is the world's biggest gold producer. With the Frogs helping her, they might just be able to force an increase.'

He stopped in front of the fat man and thrust out an accusing finger.

'Are we going to sit back and let them have a free run? No, sir! We are going to throw down our own curve ball! In three months time the Syndicate will be ready to attack. At that precise moment we will kick the chair out from under the South Africans by cutting their gold production in half. We will flood the Kitchenerville gold fields and the attack will fizzle out like a damp squib, right?'

'As simple as that?' asked the fat man.

'As simple as that!' The bald head nodded vigorously. 'Now, my next duty is to make clear to you that the agreed million dollars is *all* the reward you receive. Neither you nor your agents may indulge in any financial transactions that might, in retrospect, show that this was a planned operation, right?'

'Right.' The fat man nodded.

'You give your assurance that you will not deal in any of the shares of the companies involved?'

'You have my solemn word.' The fat man told him earnestly, and not for the first time in his life reflected how easily and painlessly a promise could be given.

With the assistance of the three men who had watched Manfred Steyner that night at the gambling club in Johannesburg, he intended launching a bear offensive on the stock exchanges of the world.

On the day that they drilled into the Big Dipper dyke he and his partners would sell millions of the shares of the five mining companies for one of the biggest financial killings in the history of money.

'We are agreed then.' The bald head bobbed. 'Now, as for this Dr Steyner, we have had a screening and personality analysis and we believe that, despite the secure hold you have on his loyalties, he would jib at giving the order to drive on the Big Dipper if he were aware of the consequences. Therefore we have prepared a second geological report,' he produced from his brief case a thick manila folder, 'incorporating those figures which he will recognize. In other words the drilling results of the C.R.C. exploration teams, but the other figures are fictitious. This report purports to prove the existence of a fabulously rich gold reef beyond the fault.' He crossed to the fat man and handed him the folder. 'Take it. It will help you convince Dr Steyner, and he in turn to convince the new General Manager of the Sonder Ditch gold mine.'

'You have been thorough,' said the fat man.

'We try to give a satisfactory service to customers,' said the bald man.

CHAPTER 36

The game was five card stud poker, and there were two big winners at
the table, Manfred Steyner and the Algerian.

Manfred had timed his arrival in Paris to ensure himself an uninterrupted weekend before the rest of the delegates came in on the
Monday morning flight.

He had checked in at the Hotel George Cinq on Saturday afternoon,
bathed and rested for three hours until eight in the evening, then he
had set out for the Club Chat Noir by taxi.

He had been playing now for five hours, and a steady succession of
strong cards had pushed his winnings up to a formidable sum. It lay
piled in front of him, a fruit salad of garish French bank notes. Across
the table sat the Algerian, a slim dark-skinned Arab with toffee eyes
and a silky black moustache. His teeth were very white against the
creamy brown skin. He wore a turtle-neck shirt in pink silk, and a linen
jacket of baby blue. With long brown fingers he kept smoothing and
stacking his own pile of bank notes.

A girl sat on the arm of his chair, an Arab girl in a skin-tight gold
trouser suit. Her hair was shiny black and hung onto her shoulders. Her
eyes were disconcertingly level as she watched Manfred.

'Ten thousand.' Manfred's voice was explosive, like that of a teutonic
drillmaster. He was betting on his fourth card which had just been
dealt to him. He and the Algerian were the remaining players in the
game. The others had folded their hands and were sitting back watching
with the casual interest of men no longer involved.

The Algerian's eyes narrowed slightly and the girl leaned down to
whisper softly in his ear. He shook his head, annoyed, and drew on his
cigarette. He had a pair of queens and a six showing and he leaned
forward to study Manfred's cards.

The dealer's voice prodded. 'The bet is ten thousand francs, from
four, five, seven of clubs. Possible straight flush.'

'Bet or drop,' said one of the uncommitted players. 'You're wasting
time.'

The Algerian flashed him a venomous glance.

'Bet,' he said, and counted out ten thousand-franc notes into the
pool.

'Carte.' The dealer slid a card face down in front of each of them.
Quickly the Algerian lifted one corner of his card with his thumb,
glanced at it and then closed the face.

Manfred sat very still, the card lying inches from his right hand. His face was pale, calm, but he was seething internally. Far from a possible straight flush, Manfred was holding four, five, seven of clubs and the eight of hearts. A six was the only card that could improve his hand and one six was already showing among the Algerian's cards. His chances were remote.

His lower belly and loins were tight and hot with excitement, his chest constricted. He drew out the sensation, wanting it to last for ever.

'Pair of queens to bet,' murmured the dealer.

'Ten thousand.' The Algerian pushed the notes forward.

'He has found another queen,' thought Manfred, 'but he is uncertain of my flush or straight.'

Manfred placed his smooth white hand over his fifth card, cupping it. He lifted it.

'Table,' said Manfred calmly, and there was a gasp and rustle from the watchers. The girl's hand tightened on the Algerian's sleeve, she stared with hatred into Manfred's face.

'The gentleman has made a table bet,' intoned the croupier. 'House rules. Any player may bet the entire stake he has upon the table.' He reached across and began to count the notes in front of Manfred.

Minutes later he announced the total. 'Two hundred and twelve thousand francs.' He looked across at the Algerian. 'It is now up to you to bet against the possible straight flush.'

The girl whispered urgently into the Arab's ear, but he snapped a single word at her and she recoiled. He looked about the room, as if seeking guidance, then he lifted and examined his cards again.

Suddenly his face hardened, and he looked steadily across at Manfred.

'Call!' he blurted, and Manfred's clenched right hand fell open upon the table.

The Arab faced his hand. Three queens. The whole room looked expectantly at Manfred.

He flicked over his last card. Two of diamonds. His hand was worthless.

With a birdlike cry of triumph the Algerian leaped from his seat and reaching across the table began raking Manfred's stake with both arms towards him.

Manfred stood up from the table, and the Arab girl grinned maliciously at him, taunting him in Arabic. He turned quickly away and almost ran down the steps that led to the cloakrooms. Twenty minutes later, feeling weak and slightly dizzy, Manfred slipped into the back seat of a Citroen taxi cab.

'George Cinq,' he told the driver. As he entered the lobby of the hotel he saw a tall figure rise from one of the leather armchairs and follow him across to the lifts. Shoulder to shoulder they stepped into the lift and as the doors slid closed the tall man spoke.

'Welcome to Paris, Dr Steyner.'

'Thank you, Andrew. I presume you have come to give me my instructions?'

'That is correct. He wishes to see you tomorrow at ten o'clock. I will call for you.'

CHAPTER 37

It was Saturday night in Kitchenerville and in the men's bar of the Lord Kitchener Hotel the daily-paid men from the five gold mines were bellying up to the counter three deep.

The public dance had been in progress for three hours. At tables along the veranda the women-folk sat primly sipping their port and lemonade. Although they all were admirably ignoring the absence of the men, yet a constant and merciless vigil was kept on the door to the men's bar. Most of the wives already had the automobile keys safely in their handbags.

In the dining-hall, cleared of its furniture and sprinkled liberally with french chalk, the local four-piece band who played under the unlikely name of the 'Wind Dogs' launched without preliminaries into a lively rendition of 'Die Ou Kraal Liedjie', and from the men's bar, in various stages of inebriation, answering the call to arms came the troops.

Many of them had shed their jackets, the knots of their ties had slipped, their voices were boisterous and legs were a little unsteady as they led their women onto the dance floor and immediately showed to which school of the dance they belonged.

There was the cavalry squadron which tucked partner under one arm, very much like a lance, and charged. At the other end of the scale were those who plodded grimly around the perimeter, looking neither left nor right, speaking to no one, not even their partners. Then there were the sociables who reeled about the floor, red in the face, their movements completely unrelated to the music, shouting to their friends and attempting to pinch any feminine posterior that came within range. Their unpredictable progress interfered with the evolutions of the dedicated.

The dedicated took up their positions in the centre of the floor and twisted. A half dozen years previously the twist had swept like an Asian flu epidemic through the world and then faded out. Gone, forgotten, except in places like Kitchenerville. Here it had been taken and firmly entrenched into the social culture of the community.

Even in this stronghold of the twist, there was one master. 'Johnny Delange? Gott man, but he can twist, hey!' they murmured with awe.

With the sinuous erotic movements of an erect cobra, Johnny was twisting with Hettie. His shiny rayon suit caught the light and the lace ruffles of his shirt fluttered at his throat. There was a fierce grin of pleasure on his hawk features, and the jewelled buckles of his pointed Italian shoes twinkled as he danced.

A big girl with copper hair and creamy skin, Hettie was light on her feet. She had a tiny waist and a swelling regal bottom under the emerald-green skirt. She laughed as she danced, a full healthy laugh to match her body.

The two of them moved with the expertise of a couple who have danced together often. Hettie anticipated each of Johnny's movements, and he grinned his approval at her.

From the veranda Davy Delange watched them. He stood in the shadows, clutching a tankard of beer, a squat, lonely figure. When another dancing couple cut off his view of Hettie's luscious revolving buttocks he would exclaim with irritation and move restlessly.

The music ended and the dancers spilled out onto the veranda, laughing and breathless, mopping streaming faces; girls squealing and giggling as the men led them to their seats, deposited them and then headed for the bar.

'See you.' Johnny left Hettie reluctantly. He would have liked to stay with her, but he was sensitive about what the boys would say if he spent the whole evening with his wife.

He was absorbed into the masculine crowd, to join their banter and loud laughter. He was deeply involved in a discussion of the merits of the new Ford Mustang, which he was considering buying, when Davy nudged him.

'It's Constantine!' he whispered, and Johnny looked up quickly. Constantine was a Greek immigrant, a stoper on the Blaauberg Mine. He was a big strong black-haired individual with a broken nose. Johnny had broken his nose for him about ten months previously. As a bachelor Johnny would fight him on the average of once a month, nothing serious, just a semi-friendly punch-up.

However, Constantine could not understand that nowadays Johnny was forbidden by his brand new wife from indulging in casual exchanges of fisticuffs. He had developed the erroneous theory that Johnny Delange was afraid of him.

He was coming down the bar room now, holding his glass in his massive hairy right hand with the little finger extended genteely. On his hip rested his other hand and he minced along with a simpering smile on his blue-jowled granite-textured features. Stopping in front of the mirror to pat his hair into place, he winked at his cronies and then came on down to where Johnny stood. He paused and ogled Johnny heavily, fluttering his eyelids and wriggling his hips. His colleagues from the Blaauberg Mine were weak with laughter, gurgling merrily, hanging onto each other's shoulders.

Then with a bump and grind that raised another howl of laughter Constantine disappeared into the lavatories, to emerge minutes later and blow Johnny a kiss as he went back to join his friends. They plied liquor on the Greek in appreciation of his act. Johnny's smile was a little strained as he resumed the discussion on the Mustang's virtues.

Twenty minutes and half a dozen brandies later, Constantine repeated his little act again on the way to the latrine. His repertoire was limited.

'Hold it, Johnny,' whispered Davy. 'Let's go and sit on the veranda.'

'He's asking for it. I'm telling you!' Johnny's smile had disappeared.

'Come on, Johnny, man.'

'No, hell, they'll think I'm running. I can't go now.'

'You know what Hettie will say,' Davy warned him. For a moment longer Johnny hesitated.

'The hell with what Hettie says.' Johnny bunched his right fist with its array of gold rings as he moved down to Constantine and leaned beside him on the counter.

'Herby,' he called the barman, and when he had his attention he indicated the Greek. 'Please give the lady a port and lemonade.'

And the bystanders scattered for cover. Davy shot out of the door onto the veranda to report to Hettie.

'Johnny!' he gasped. 'He's fighting again.'

'Is he!' Hettie came to her feet like a red-headed Valkyrie. But her progress to the men's bar was delayed by the crowd of spectators that jammed the doorway and all the windows. The crowd was tiptoeing and climbing onto the chairs and tables for a better view, every thud or crash of breaking furniture was greeted with a roar of delight.

Hettie had her handbag clutched in her right hand, and like a jungle explorer hacking his way through the undergrowth with a machete, she opened a path for herself to the bar room door.

At the door she paused. The conflict had reached a critical stage. Among the litter of broken glass and shattered stools, Johnny and the Greek were circling each other warily, weaving and feinting, all their wits concentrated upon each other. Both of them were marked. The

Greek was bleeding from his lip, a thin red ribbon of blood down his chin that dripped onto his shirt. Johnny had a shiny red swelling closing one eye. The crowd was silent, waiting.

'Johnny Delange!' Hettie's voice cracked like a mauser rifle fired from ambush. Johnny started guiltily, dropping his hands, half turning towards her as the Greek's fist crashed into the side of his head. Johnny spun from the blow, hit the wall and slid down quietly.

With a roar of triumph Constantine rushed forward to put the boots into Johnny's prostrate form, but he pitched forward to sprawl unconscious beside Johnny. Hettie had hit him with the water bottle snatched up from one of the table tops.

'Please help me get my husband to the car,' she appealed to the men around her, suddenly helpless and little-girlish.

She sat beside Davy in the front of the Monaco, fuming with anger. Johnny lay at ease upon the back seat. He was snoring softly.

'Don't be angry, Hettie.' Davy was driving sedately.

'I've told him, not once, a hundred times.' Hettie's voice crackled like static. 'I told him I wouldn't put up with it.'

'It wasn't his fault. The Greek started it,' Davy explained softly and placed his hand on her leg.

'You stick up for him, just because he's your brother.'

'That's not true,' Davy soothed her, stroking her leg. 'You know how I feel about you, Hettie.'

'I don't believe you.' His hand was moving higher. 'You men are all the same. You all stick together.'

Her anger was fast solidifying into a burning resentment of Johnny Delange, one in which she was willing to take a calculated revenge. She knew that Davy's hand was no longer trying to comfort her and quench her anger. Before she married Johnny Delange, Hettie had had every opportunity to learn about men, and she had been an enthusiastic and receptive pupil. She placed no special importance on an act of the flesh, dispensing her favours as casually as someone might offer a cigarette-case around.

'Why not?' she thought. 'That will fix Mr Johnny Delange! Not all the way, of course, but just enough to get my own back on him.'

'No, Hettie. It's true—I tell you.' Davy's voice was husky, as he felt her knees fall apart under his hand. He touched the silky-smooth skin above her stocking top.

The Monaco slowed to almost walking pace, and it was ten minutes more before they reached the company-owned house on the outskirts of Kitchenerville.

In the back seat Johnny groaned. Immediately Davy's hand jerked back to the steering-wheel, and Hettie sat up in the seat, straightening her skirt.

'Help me get him inside,' she said, and her voice was shaky and her cheeks flushed. She was no longer angry.

CHAPTER 38

They were both a little tipsy. They had stopped to celebrate Rod's promotion at the Sunnyside Hotel. They had sat side by side in one of the booths, drinking quickly, excitedly, laughing together, sitting close but not touching.

Terry Steyner could not remember when she had last behaved this way. It must have been all of ten years ago, her last term at Cape Town varsity, swigging draught beer in the 'Pig and Whistle' at Randall's Hotel and talking the most inane rubbish. All the matronly dignity that Manfred insisted she maintain was gone, she felt like a freshette on a first date with the captain of the rugby team.

'Let's get out of here,' Rod said suddenly, and she stood up unquestioningly. He took her arm down the stairs, and the light touch of his fingers tingled on her bare skin.

In the Maserati again she experienced the feeling of isolation from reality.

'How often do you see your daughter, Rod?' she asked as he settled into the seat beside her, and he glanced at her, surprised.

'Every Sunday.'

'Tomorrow?'

'Yes.'

'How old is she?'

'Nine next birthday.'

'What do you do with her?'

Rod pressed the starter.

'How do you mean?'

'Where do you take her, what do you do together?'

'We go rowing on Zoo Lake, or eat ice cream sundaes. If it's cold or raining we sit in the apartment and we play mah-jong.' He let in the clutch, and as they pulled away he added, 'She cheats.'

'The apartment?'

'I keep a hideaway in town.'

'Where?'

'I'll show you,' said Rod quietly.

She sat on the studio couch and looked about her with interest. She had not expected the obvious care that he had taken in furnishing the apartment. It was in wheatfield gold, chocolate brown and copper. There was a glorious glowing autumn landscape on the far wall that she recognized as a Dino Paravano.

She noticed a little ruefully how Rod stage-managed the lighting for full romantic effect, and then moved automatically to the liquor cabinet.

'Where is the bathroom?' Terry asked.

'Second left, down the passage.'

She lingered in the bathroom, opening the medicine cabinet like a thief. There were three toothbrushes hanging in the slots, and below them an aerosol can of 'Bidex'. Quickly she shut the cabinet, feeling disturbed, not sure if it was jealousy or guilt at her own prying.

The bedroom door was open and so she could not help seeing the double bed as she went back to the lounge. She stood in front of the painting.

'I love his work,' she said.

'Not too photographic for your taste?'

'No. I love it.'

He gave her the drink and stood beside her, studying the painting. She tinkled the ice in her glass, and he turned towards her. The feeling of unreality was still holding Terry as she felt him take the glass from her hand.

She was conscious of his hands only, they were strong and very prac-tised. They touched her shoulders, and then moved onto her back calmly. She felt a voluptuous shudder shake her whole body, and then his mouth came down over hers and the sense of unreality was com-plete. It was all warm and misty, and she let him take control.

She never knew how long afterwards she jerked back to complete, chilling reality. They were on the couch. She lay in his arms. The front of her slack suit was open to the waist and her bra was unhooked. His head was bowed over her and with a handful of his thick springy hair she was directing his lips in their quest. His mouth was warm and sucky on her breast.

'I must be mad!' she gasped, and struggled violently from his arms. She was trembling with fright, horrified with herself. Nothing like this had ever happened to her before.

'This is madness!' Her eyes were great dark pools in her pale face, and her fingers were frantic as she buttoned her blouse. As the last button slipped into its hole, anger replaced her fright.

'How many women have you seduced on that couch, Rodney Ironsides?'

Rod stood up, reaching out a hand to reassure her.

'Don't touch me!' She stepped back. 'I want to go home!'

'I'll take you home, Terry. Just calm down. Nothing happened.'

'That's not your fault,' she blazed.

'No, it's not,' he agreed.

'If you had your way, you'd have—' she bit it off.

'Yes, I would have.' Rod nodded. 'But only if you wanted the same thing.'

She stared at him, starting to recover her temper and her control.

'I shouldn't have come up here, I know. It was asking for trouble, but please take me home now.'

CHAPTER 39

The telephone woke Rod. He checked his wrist watch as he tottered naked and half asleep through to the lounge. Eight o'clock.

'Ironsides!' He yawned into the mouthpiece, and then came fully awake as he recognized her voice.

'Good morning, Rodney. How's your hangover?'

He had not expected to hear from her again.

'Just bearable.'

'I called to thank you for an amusing and—instructive evening.'

'Hark at the girl!' He grinned and scratched his chest. 'She changes with the wind. Last night I expected a bullet between the eyes.'

'Last night I got one big fright,' she admitted. 'It comes as a bit of a shock to discover suddenly that you are quite capable of acting the wanton. Not all the names I called you were meant.'

'I am sorry for my contribution to your distress,' Rod said.

'Don't be, you were very impressive.' Then quickly, changing the subject, 'You are picking up your daughter today?'

'Yes.'

'I'd like to meet her.'

'That could be arranged.' Rod was cautious.

'Does she like horses?'

'She's crazy about them.'

'Would you like to take her and me out to my stud farm on the Vaal river?'

Rod hesitated. 'Is it safe? I mean, being seen together?'

'It's my reputation, I'll look after it.'

'Fine!' Rod agreed. 'We'd love to visit your farm.'

'I'll meet you at your apartment. When?'
'Half past nine!'

Patti was still in her dressing-gown and she offered Rod her cheek
casually to be pecked. There were curlers in her hair and from her eyes
he could tell she'd had a late night.

'Hello, you're getting thin. Melly is dressing. Do you want some
coffee? Your maintenance cheque was late again this month.' And she
took a swipe at the spaniel pup as it squatted on the carpet. 'Damn dog
pees all over the place. *Melanie*.' She raised her voice. 'Hurry up!
Your Papa is here.'

'Hello, Daddy!' Melanie's voice shrieked delightedly from the interior of the apartment.

'Hello, baby.'

'You can't come in, Daddy, I haven't got any clothes on.'

'Well hurry up! I've come a million miles to see you.'

'Not a *million*!' You couldn't fool Melanie Ironsides.

'Did you say you wanted coffee? It's no trouble, it's made already.'
Pattie led him through into the sitting-room.

'Thanks.'

'How are things?' she asked as she filled a cup and gave it to him.

'They've made me General Manager of the Sonder Ditch.' He could
not prevent himself, it was too good. He had to boast.

Patti looked at him, startled.

'You're joking!' she accused, and then he saw her mind beginning
to work like a cash register.

He almost laughed out loud. 'No. It's true.'

'God!' She sat down limply. 'It will nearly *double* your salary.'

He looked at her dispassionately, and not for the first time felt a great
wash of relief as he realized he was no longer shackled to her.

'It's usual to offer congratulations,' he prompted her.

'You don't deserve it.' She was angry now. 'You are a selfish, phil-
andering bastard, Rodney Ironsides, you don't deserve the good things
that keep happening to you.' He had cheated her. She could have been
the General Manager's wife, first lady of the gold fields. Now she was
a divorcee, stuck with a miserable four fifty a month. It had seemed
good before, but not now.

'I hope you will have enough conscience to make a suitable adjustment for Melanie and me. We are entitled to a share.'

The door burst open and Melanie Ironsides arrived at a gallop to wrap herself around Rod's neck. She had long blonde hair and green eyes.

'I got nine out of ten for spelling!'

'You're not clever, you're a genius. Also you're beautiful.'

'Will you carry me down to the car, Daddy?'

'What's wrong? Your legs in plaster?'

'Please, please, pretty please times three.'

Patti interrupted the love feast.

'Have you got your jersey, young lady?' And Melanie flew.

'I'll have her back before seven,' said Rod.

'You haven't answered my question.' Patti was surly. 'Do we get a share?'

'Yes, of course,' said Rod. 'The same big juicy four fifty you've had all along.'

They had been in Rod's apartment ten minutes when the doorbell announced Terry's arrival. She was in jeans and a checked shirt with her hair in a plait, and she greeted Rod self-consciously. When he introduced her to Melanie, she did not look much older than his daughter.

The two girls summed each other up solemnly. Melanie was suddenly very demure and refined, and Rod was relieved to see that Terry had the good sense not to gush over the child.

They were in the Maserati and half way to the village of Parys on the Vaal River before Melanie had completed her microscopic scrutiny of Terry.

'Can I come up front and sit on your lap?' she asked at last.

'Yes, of course.' Terry was hard put to conceal her relief and pleasure. Melanie scrambled over the seat and settled on Terry's lap.

'You are pretty,' Melanie gave her considered opinion.

'Thank you. So are you.'

'Are you Daddy's girl friend?' Melanie demanded. Terry glanced across at Rod, then burst out laughing.

'Almost,' she gurgled, and then all three of them were laughing.

They laughed often that day. It was a day of sunshine and laughter.

Terry and Rod walked together with fingers almost touching through the green paddocks along the willow-lined bank of the Vaal. Melanie ran ahead of them shrieking with glee at the antics of the foals.

They went up to the stables where Melanie fed sugar lumps to a winner of the Cape Metropolitan Handicap and then kissed his velvety muzzle.

They swam in the pool beside the elegant white-washed homestead, laughter mingling with the splashes, and when they drove back to Johannesburg in the evening Melanie curled in exhausted slumber on Terry's lap, her head cushioned on Terry's bosom.

Terry waited in the Maserati while Rod carried the sleeping child up to her mother, and when he returned and slipped into the driver's seat, Terry murmured, 'My car is at your apartment. You'll have to take me with you.'

Neither of them spoke until they were back in Rod's sitting-room. Then he said, 'Thank you for a wonderful day.' And he took her to his chest and kissed her.

In the darkness she lay pressed to his sleeping body, clinging to him, as though he might be taken from her. She had never felt such intensity of emotion before, it was a compound of awed wonder and gratitude. She had just been admitted to a new level of human experience she had never suspected existed.

The sheets were still damp. She felt bruised internally, aching, a slow voluptuous pulse of pain that she cherished.

Lightly she touched his body, not wanting to wake him, running her fingertips through the coarse curls that covered his chest, marvelling still at the infinity that separated this from what she had known before.

She shuddered with almost unbearable pleasure as she remembered his voice describing her body to her, making her proud of it for the first time in her life. She remembered the words he had used to tell her exactly what they were doing together, and the feel of his hands, so gentle, sure, so lovingly possessive upon her.

He was so unashamed, taking such obvious joy in her, that the reserves which the barren years of her marriage had placed in her mind were swept away and she was able to go with Rodney Ironsides beyond the storm into that tranquil state where mind and body are completely at peace.

She became aware of him awakening beside her, and she touched his face, his lips and his eyes with her fingertips.

'Thank you,' she whispered, and he seemed to understand, for he took her head and drew it gently down into the hollow of his shoulder.

'Sleep now,' he told her softly, and she closed her eyes and lay very still and quiet beside him, but she did not sleep. She would not miss one moment of this experience.

CHAPTER 40

Rod's letter of appointment lay on his desk when he arrived at his office at seven-thirty on the Monday morning.

He sat down and lit a cigarette. Then he began to read it slowly, savouring each word.

'Duly instructed by the Board of Directors,' it began, and ended, 'it remains only to tender the congratulations of the Board, and to voice their confidence in your ability.'

Dimitri came through from his office, distracted.

'Hey! Rod! Christ what a start to the week! We've got a fault in the main high voltage cable on 90 level, and—'

'Don't come squealing to me,' Rod cut him short. 'I'm not the Underground Manager.'

Dimitri gaped at him, taken by surprise.

'What the hell, have they fired you?'

'Next best thing,' said Rod and flipped the letter across the desk. 'Look what the bastards have done to me.'

Dimitri read and then whooped;

'My God, Rod! My God!' He shot down the passage to carry the news to the other line managers. Then they were all in his office, shaking his hand. He judged most of their reactions as favourable, though occasionally he detected a false note. A twinge of envy here, one there who had recently had his ears burned by the Ironsides tongue, and an incompetent who knew his job was now in danger. The phone rang. Rod answered it, his expression changed and he cleared his office with a peremptory wave.

'Hirschfeld here.'

'Morning, Mr Hirschfeld.'

'Well, you've got your chance, Ironsides.'

'I'm grateful for it.'

'I want to see you. I'll give you today to sort yourself out. Tomorrow morning at nine o'clock, my office at Reef Buildings.'

'I'll be there.'

'Good.'

Rod hung up, and the day dissolved into a welter of activity and reorganization, constantly interrupted by a stream of wellwishers. He was still running the Underground Manager's job in addition to the General Manager's. It would be some considerable time before a new Underground Manager was transferred in from one of the other group mines. He was trying to arrange his move to the big office in the main

Administrative Block up on the ridge, when he had another visitor, Frank Lemmer's secretary: Miss Lily Jordan, in a severe grey flannel suit looking like a wardress from Ravensbruck.

'Mr Ironsides, you and I have not seen eye to eye in the past.' This was the understatement of the year. 'It is unlikely that we will in the future. Therefore, I have come to tender my resignation. I have made arrangements.'

The phone rang. Dan Stander's voice, breezy and carefree.

'Rod, I'm in love.'

'Oh Christ, no!' Rod groaned. 'Not this morning.'

'I've got to thank you for introducing me to her. She's the most wonderful—'

'Yeah, yeah!' Rod cut him short. 'Look, Dan, I'm rather busy. Some other time, all right?'

'Oh yes, I forgot. You are the new General Manager they tell me. Congratulations. You can buy me a drink at the Club. Six o'clock.'

'Right. By then I'll need one.' Rod hung up, and faced the hanging-judge expression of Miss Lily Jordan.

'Miss Jordan, in the past our interests have conflicted. In future they will not. You are the best private secretary within a hundred miles of the Sonder Ditch. I need you, the Company needs you.'

That was the magic word. Miss Jordan had twenty-five years' service with the Company. She wavered visibly.

'Please, Miss Jordan, give me a chance.' Shamelessly Rod switched on his most engaging smile. Miss Jordan's femininity was not so completely atrophied that she could resist that smile.

'Very well, then, Mr Ironsides. I'll stay on initially until the end of the month. We'll see after that.' She stood up. 'Now, I'll get your things moved up to the new office.'

'Thank you, Miss Jordan.' With relief he let her take over, and tackled the problems that were piling up on his desk. One man, two jobs. Now he was responsible for surface operation as well as underground. The phone rang, men queued up in the passage, memos kept coming through from Dimitri's office. There was no lunch hour, and by the time she rang he was exhausted.

'Hello,' she said. 'Do I see you tonight?' Her voice was as refreshing as a wet cloth on the brow of a prizefighter between rounds.

'Terry.' He simply spoke her name in reply.

'Yes or no. If it's *no*, I intend jumping off the top of Reef Building.'

'Yes,' he said. 'Pops has summoned me to a meeting at nine tomorrow morning, so I'll be staying overnight at the apartment. I'll call you as soon as I get in.'

'Goody! Goody!' said she.

At five-thirty Dimitri stuck his head around the door.

'I'm going down to No. 1 shaft to supervise the shoot, Rod.'

'My God, what time is it?' Rod checked his watch. 'So late already.'

'It gets late early around here,' Dimitri agreed. 'I'm off.'

'Wait!' Rod stopped him. 'I'll shoot her.'

'No trouble.' Dimitri demurred. Company standard procedure laid down that each day's blast must be supervised by either the Underground Manager or his Assistant.

'I'll do it,' Rod repeated. Dimitri opened his mouth to protest further, then he saw that expression on Rod's face and changed his mind quickly.

'Okay then. See you tomorrow.' And he was gone.

Rod grinned at his own sentimentality. The Sonder Ditch was his now and, by God, he was going to shoot his own first blast on her.

They were waiting for him at the steel door of the blast control room at the shaft head. It was a small concrete room like a wartime pillbox, and there were only two keys to the door. Dimitri had one, Rod the other.

The duty mine captain and the foreman electrician added their congratulations to the hundreds he had received during the day, and Rod opened the door and they went into the tiny room.

'Check her out,' Rod instructed, and the mine captain began his calls to the shaft overseers at both No. 1 and No. 2 for their confirmation that the workings of the Sonder Ditch were deserted, that every human being who had gone down that morning had come out again this evening.

Meanwhile, the foreman electrician was busy at the electrical control board. He looked up at Rod.

'Ready to close the circuits, Mr Ironsides.'

'Go ahead,' Rod nodded and the man touched a switch. A green light showed up on the board.

'No. 1 north longwall closed and green.'

'Lock her in,' Rod instructed and the electrician touched another switch.

'No. 1 east longwall closed and green.'

'Lock her in.'

The green light showed that the firing circuit was intact. A red light would indicate a fault and the faulty circuit would not be locked into the blast pattern.

Circuit after circuit was readied until finally the foreman stood back from the control board.

'All green and locked in.'

Rod glanced at the mine captain.

'All levels clear, Mr Ironsides. She's ready to burn.'

'Cheesa!' said Rod, the traditional command that had come down from the days when each fuse had been individually lit by a hand-held igniter stick.

'Cheesa' was the Bantu word for 'burn'.

The mine captain crossed to the control board and opened the cage that guarded a large red button.

'Cheesa!' echoed the mine captain and hit the button with the heel of his hand.

Immediately the row of green lights on the control board was extinguished, and in their place showed a row of red lights. Every circuit had been broken by the explosions.

The ground under their feet began to tremble. Throughout the workings the shots were firing. In the stopes the head charges fired at the top of the inclines, then in succession the other shots went off behind them, each charge taking a ten-ton bite of rock and reef out of the face.

At the end of the development drives, a more complicated pattern was shooting. First a row of *cutters* went off down the middle of the oval face. Then the *shoulder charges* at the top corners, followed by the *knee charges* at the bottom corners. A moment's respite with the dust and nitrous fumes swirling back down the drive, then a roar as the *easers* on each side shaped the hole. Another respite and then the *lifters* along the bottom picked up the heap of broken rock and threw it back from the face.

Rod could imagine it clearly. Though no human eye had ever witnessed the blast, he knew exactly what was taking place down there.

The last tremor died away.

'That's it. A full blast,' said the mine captain.

'Thank you.' Rod felt tired suddenly. He wanted that drink, even though their brief exchange that morning had warned him that Dan would probably be insufferable. He could guess the conversation would revolve around Dan's new-found love.

Then he smiled as he thought about what waited for him in Johannesburg later that night, and suddenly he wasn't all that tired.

CHAPTER 41

They sat facing each other.

'Only three things worry me,' Terry told Rod.

'What are they?' Rod rubbed soap into the face flannel.

'Firstly, your legs are too long for this bath.'

Rod rearranged his limbs, and Terry shot half out of the water with a squeak.

'Rodney Ironsides, would you be good enough to take a bit more care where you put your toes!'

'Forgive me.' He leaned forward to kiss her. 'Tell me what else worries you.'

'Well, the second thing that worries me is that I'm not worried.'

'What part of Ireland did you say you were from?' Rod asked. 'County Cork?'

'I mean, it's terrible but I'm not even a little conscience-stricken. Once I believed that if it ever happened to me I would never be able to look another human being in the eyes, I'd be so ashamed.' She took the flannel from his hands and began soaping his chest and shoulders. 'But, far from being ashamed, I'd like to stand in the middle of Eloff Street at rush hour and shout "Rodney Ironsides is my lover".'

'Let's drink to that.' Rodney rinsed the soap from his hands and reached over the side of the bath to pick up the two wine glasses from the floor. He gave one to Terry and they clinked them together, the sparkling Cape Burgundy glowing ruby red.

'Rodney Ironsides is my lover!' she toasted him.

'Rodney Ironsides is your lover,' he agreed and they drank.

'Now, I give *you* a toast,' he said.

'What is it?' She held her glass ready, and Rod leaned forward and poured the red wine from the crystal glass between her breasts. It ran like blood down her white skin and he intoned solemnly:

'Bless this ship and all who sail in her!'

Terry gurgled with delight.

'To her Captain. May he keep a firm hand on the rudder!'

'May her bottom never hit the reef!'

'May she be torpedoed regularly!'

'Terry Steyner, you are terrible.'

'Yes, aren't I?' And they drained their glasses.

'Now,' Rod asked, 'what is your third worry?'

'Manfred will be home on Saturday.'

They stopped laughing, Rod reached down for the Burgundy bottle and refilled the glasses.

'We still have five days,' he said.

CHAPTER 42

It had been a week of personal triumph for Manfred Steyner. His address to the conference had been the foundation of the entire talks, all discussion had revolved upon it. He had been called upon to speak at the closing banquet which General de Gaulle had attended in person, and afterwards the General had asked Manfred to take coffee and brandy with him in one of the anterooms. The General had been gracious, had asked questions and listened attentively to the answers. Twice he had called his finance minister's attention to Manfred's replies.

Their farewells had been cordial, with a hint of state recognition for Manfred, a decoration. In common with most Germans, Manfred had a weakness for uniforms and decorations. He imagined how a star and ribbon might look on the snowy front of his dress shirt.

There had been a wonderful press both in France and at home. Even a bad-tempered quarter column in *Time* Magazine, with a picture, De Gaulle stooping over the diminutive Manfred solicitously, one hand on his shoulder. The caption read:

'The huntsman and the hawk. To catch a dollar?'

Now standing in the tiny cloakroom in the tail of the South African Airways Boeing, Manfred was whistling softly as he stripped off his shirt and vest, crumpled them into a ball and dropped them into the bin.

Naked to the waist, he wiped his upper body with a wet cloth and then rubbed 4711 Eau de Cologne into his skin. From the briefcase he took an electric razor. The whistling stopped as he contorted his face for the razor.

Through his mind ran page after page of the report that Andrew had delivered that morning to his hotel room. Manfred had total recall when it came to written material. Although the report was in the briefcase beside him, in his mind's eye he could review it word for word, figure for figure.

It was a stupendous piece of work. How the authors had gained access to the drilling and exploration reports of the five Kitchenerville field companies he could not even guess, for the gold mining companies' security was as tight as that of any national intelligence agency. But the figures were genuine. He had checked those purporting to be from C.R.C. carefully. They were correct. So therefore the other four must also be genuine.

The names of the authors of the report were legend. They were the top men in the field. Their opinions were the best in Harley Street. The conclusion that they reached was completely convincing. In effect it was this:

If a haulage was driven from 66 level of the Sonder Ditch No. 1 shaft through the Big Dipper dyke, it would pass *under* the limestone water-bearing formations, and just beyond the fault it would intersect a reef of almost unbelievable value.

It had not needed the lecture that Manfred had received from his corpulent creditor to show him the possibilities. The man who gave the order to drive through the Big Dipper would receive the credit. He would certainly be elected to the Chairmanship of the Group when that office fell vacant.

There was another possibility. A person who purchased a big packet of Sonder Ditch shares immediately before the reef was intersected would be a very rich man when he came to sell those shares later. He would be so rich that he would no longer be dependent on his wife for the means to live the kind of life he wanted, and indulge his own special tastes.

Manfred blew the hairs from his razor and returned it to his brief case. Then as he took out a fresh shirt and vest, he began to sing the words to the tune:

> *'Heute ist der schönste Tag*
> *In meinem Leben.'*

He would telephone Ironsides from Jan Smuts Airport as soon as he had passed through customs. Ironsides would come up to the house on Sunday morning and receive his orders.

As he knotted the silk of his tie Manfred knew that he stood at the threshold of a whole new world, the events of the next few months would lift him high above the level of ordinary men.

It was the chance for which he had worked and waited all these years.

CHAPTER 43

Circumstances had changed completely since his last visit, Rod reflected, as he took the Maserati up the drive towards the Dutch gabled house.

He parked the car and switched off the ignition, sitting a while, reluctant to face the man who had sponsored his career and whom Rod in return had presented with a fine pair of horns.

'Courage, Ironsides!' he muttered and climbed out of the Maserati and went up the path across the lawns.

Terry was on the veranda in a gay print dress, with her hair loose, sprawled in a canvas chair with the Sunday papers scattered about her.

'Good morning, Mr Ironsides,' she greeted him as he came up the steps. 'My husband is in his study. You know the way, don't you?'

'Thank you, Mrs Steyner.' Rod kept his voice friendly but disinterested, then as he passed her chair he growled softly, 'I could eat you without salt.'

'Don't waste it, you gorgeous beast,' Terry murmured and ran the tip of her tongue over her lips.

Fifteen minutes later, Rod sat stony-faced and internally chilled before Manfred Steyner's desk. When at last he forced himself to speak, it felt as though the skin on his lips would tear with the effort.

'You want me to drive through the Big Dipper,' he croaked.

'More than that, Mr Ironsides. I want you to complete the drive within three months, and I want a complete security blanket on the development,' Manfred told him primly. Despite the fact that it was Sunday he was formally dressed, white shirt and dark suit. 'You will commence the drive from No. 1 shaft 66 level and make an intersect on reef at 6,600 feet with the S.D. No. 3 borehole 250 feet beyond the calculated extremity of the serpentine intrusion of the Big Dipper.'

'No,' Rod shook his head. 'You can't go through that. No one can take the chance. God alone knows what is on the other side, we only know that it is bad ground. Stinking rotten ground.'

'How do you know that?' Manfred asked softly.

'Everybody on the Kitchenerville field knows it.'

'How?'

'Little things.' Rod found it hard to put into words. 'You get a feeling, the signs are there and when you've been in the game long enough you have a sixth sense that warns you when—'

'Nonsense,' Manfred interrupted brusquely. 'We no longer live in the days of witchcraft.'

'Not witchcraft, experience,' Rod snapped angrily. 'You've seen the drilling results from the other side of the fault?'

'Of course,' Manfred nodded. 'S.D. No. 3 found values of thousands of penny-weights.'

'And the other holes went dry and twisted off, or had water squirting out of them like a pissing horse!'

Manfred flushed fiercely. 'You will be good enough not to employ bar-room terminology in this house.'

Rod was taken off balance, and before he could answer Manfred went on.

'Would you put the considered opinions of,' Manfred named three men, 'before your own vague intuitions?'

'They are the best in the business,' Rod conceded reluctantly.

'Read that,' snapped Manfred. He tossed a manila folder onto the desk top, then stood up and went to wash his hands at the concealed basin.

Rod picked up the folder, opened it and was immediately engrossed. Ten minutes later, without looking up from the report, he fumbled a pack of cigarettes from his pocket.

'Please do not smoke!' Manfred stopped him sharply.

Three-quarters of an hour later, Rod closed the folder. During that time Manfred Stenyer had sat with reptilian stillness behind his desk, with the glitter of his eyes the only signs of life.

'How the hell did you get hold of those figures and reports?' Rod asked with wonder.

'That does not concern you.' Manfred retrieved the folder from him, his first movement in forty-five minutes.

'So that's it!' muttered Rod. 'The water is in the lime stone near the surface. We go in under it!' He stood up from the chair abruptly and began to pace up and down in front of Manfred's desk.

'Are you convinced?' Manfred asked, and Rod did not answer.

'I have promoted you above older and more experienced men,' said Manfred softly. 'If I tear you down again, and tell the world you were not man enough for the job, then, Rodney Ironsides, you are finished. No one else would take a chance on you again, ever!'

It was true. Rod knew it.

'However, if you were to follow my instructions and we intersected this highly enriched reef, then part of the glory would rub off on you.'

That was also true. Rod stopped pacing, he stood with shoulders hunched, in an agony of indecision. Could he trust that report beyond his own deep intuition? When he thought about that ground beyond the dyke, his skin tickled with gooseflesh. He almost had the stink of it in his nostrils. Yet he could be wrong, and the weight of the opposition was heavy. The eminent names on the report, the threats which he knew Manfred would not hesitate to put into effect.

'Will you give me a written instruction?' Rod demanded harshly.

'What effect would that have?' Manfred asked mildly. 'As General Manager, the decision to work certain ground or not to work it is technically yours. In the very unlikely event that you encountered trouble beyond the fault, it would be no defence to produce a written instruction from me. Just as if you murdered my wife you could not defend yourself by producing a written instruction from me to do so.'

This again was true. Rod knew he was trapped. He could refuse, and wreck his career. Or he could comply and take the consequences whatever they may be.

'No,' said Manfred, 'I will not give you a written instruction.'

'You bastard,' Rod said softly.

Manfred answered as gently. 'I warned you that you would not be able to refuse to obey me.'

And the last twinge of remorse that Rod felt for his association with Terry Steyner faded and was gone.

'You've given me three months to hit the Big Dipper. All right, Steyner. You've got it!'

Rod turned on his heel and walked out of the room.

Terry was waiting for him among the protea plants on the bottom lawn. She saw his face and dropped all pretence. She went to meet him.

'Rod, what is it?' Her hand on his arm, looking up into his eyes.

'Careful!' he warned her, and she dropped her hand and stood back. 'What is it?'

'That bloody Gestapo bastard,' Rod snarled, and then, 'I'm sorry, Terry, he's your husband.'

'What has he done?'

'I can't tell you here. When can I see you?'

'I'll find an excuse to get away later today. Wait for me at your apartment.'

Later she sat on the couch below the Paravano painting and listened while he told her about it. All of it, the report, the threat and the order to pierce the Big Dipper.

She listened but expressed neither approval nor disapproval of his decision.

Manfred turned away from the window and went back to his desk.

Even at that distance there had been no doubt about his wife's gesture. The hand outstretched, the face turned up, the lips parted in anxious inquiry, and then the guilty start and withdrawal.

He sat down at his desk, and laid his hands neatly in front of him. For the first time he was thinking of Rodney Ironsides as a man and not a tool.

He thought how big he was, tall and as wide across the shoulders as a gallow. Any reprisal on Ironsides could not be physical, and it could not be immediate. It must be after the drive to the Big Dipper.

I can wait, he thought coldly, there is time for everything in this life.

CHAPTER 44

Johnny and Davy Delange sat in the two chairs before Rod's desk. They were both awkward and uncomfortable up here in the big office with picture windows looking out over the Kitchenerville valley.

I don't blame them, Rod thought, even I am not accustomed to it yet. Wall-to-wall carpeting, air-conditioning, original paintings on the wood-panelled walls.

'I have sent for you because you two are the best rock breakers on the Sonder Ditch,' Rod began.

'Tin ribs wants something,' thought Davy, with all the suspicion of the union man for management.

'We will now have a few words from our sponsor,' Johnny grinned to himself. 'Before we start the programme.'

Rod looked at their faces and knew exactly what they were thinking. He had been on daily pay himself once. Cut out the compliments, Ironsides—he advised himself—these are two tough cookies and they are not impressed.

'I am pulling you out of the stopes and putting you onto a special development end. You will take it in turns to work day and night shift. You will be directly responsible to me and there will be a security blanket on your activity.'

They watched him without reaction, their expressions guarded. Johnny broke the short silence.

'One end, one blast a day?' He was thinking of his pay. Calculated on the amount of rock broken, he would earn little more than basic salary with a blast on one small face daily.

'No.' Rod shook his head. 'Ultra-fast, multi-blast, and shaft sinkers' rates.'

And both the Delange brothers sat forward in their chairs.

'Multi-blast?' Davy asked. That meant that they could shoot just as soon as they were ready. A good team could blast three—maybe four times a shift.

'Ultra-fast?' Johnny demanded. That was language Johnny understood. It was a term employed only in emergency, as when driving in to rescue trapped men after a fall. It was tacit approval from management to waive standard safety procedure in favour of speed. Christ, Johnny exulted, I can shoot her four—maybe five times a shift.

'Shaft sinkers' rates?' they asked together. That was a twenty per cent bonus on stopers' rates. It was a fortune they were being offered.

Rod nodded affirmative to their questions, and waited for the reaction which he knew would follow. It came immediately.

The Delange brothers now began to look for the catch. They sat stolidly turning the deal over in their minds, like two cautious housewives examining a tomato for blemishes because the price was too cheap.

'How long is this drive?' Johnny asked. If the drive was short, a few hundred feet, then it was worth nothing. They would hardly get into their stride before it was completed.

'Close on six thousand feet,' Rod assured him. They looked relieved.

'Where is it headed?' Davy discovered the rub.

'We are going to drive through the Big Dipper to intersect on reef at 6,000 feet.'

'Jesus!' said Johnny. 'The Big Dipper!' He was awed but unafraid. It excited him, the danger, the challenge. Had he been born earlier, Johnny Delange would have made a fine spitfire pilot.

'The Big Dipper,' Davy murmured. His mind was racing. Nothing in this world or beyond would entice Davy Delange to drive through the Big Dipper. He had an almost religious fear of it. The name alone conjured up all sorts of hidden menace and unspeakable horror. Water. Gas. Friable ground, faults. Mud-rushes. All a miner's nightmare.

There was no question of him doing it, yet the money was too good to pass up. He could net ten or eleven thousand Rand on those terms.

'All right, Mr Ironsides,' he said. 'I'll take the first night shifts. Johnny can start the day shifts.'

Davy Delange had made his decision. He would work until his drills hit the greenish-black serpentine rock of the dyke. He would then walk out of the drive and quit. He would go up to, but not beyond the dyke.

Afterwards, any of the other mines would snap him up, he had an impeccable record and he would force Johnny to follow him.

'Hey, Davy!' Johnny was delighted, he had expected Davy to turn the deal down flat.

Now he would be able to buy the Mustang for certain—and perhaps an MGB GT for Hettie—and take a holiday to Durban over Christmas, and . . .

Rod was puzzled by Davy's easy agreement. He studied him a moment and decided that he had ferrety eyes. He's a sneaky little bastard, Rod decided, I'll have to watch him.

CHAPTER 45

It took one shift only to prepare for the development. Rod selected the starting point. The main haulage curved away from the shaft on 66 level. Three hundred feet along this tunnel there was a chamber that had been cut out as a loco repair station but which was now out of use. Two large batwing ventilation doors were fitted to the opening of the chamber to provide privacy and behind them the chief underground surveyor set up his instruments and marked out the head of the tunnel that would fly arrow straight a mile and more through the living rock to strike through the Big Dipper into the unknown.

The area surrounding the head chamber was roped off and signposted with warnings.

'DANGER
INDEPENDENT BLASTING'

The mine captains were instructed to keep their men well away, and all loco traffic was rerouted through a secondary haulage.

On the doors of the chamber another notice was fixed.

'FIERY MINE PROCEDURE IN FORCE
NO NAKED LIGHTS BEYOND THIS POINT'

Owing to small deposits of coal and other organic substance in the upper stratas of rock, the Sonder Ditch was classed as a fiery mine and subject to the Government legislation covering this subject. No matches, lighters or other spark-generating devices were allowed into a new development end, because the presence of methane gas was always suspected.

Colourless, odourless, tasteless, detectable only by test with a safety lamp, it was a real and terrifying danger. A nine per cent concentration in air was highly explosive. Stringent precautions were taken against accidental triggering of methane that may have oozed out of a fissure or cavity in the rock.

From the main compressed air-pipes running down the corners of the shaft were taken leads to air tanks in the haulage, ensuring that sixty pounds per square inch of pressure was available for the rock drills. Then drills, pinchbars, hammers, shovels, and the other tools were unloaded from the cage at 66 level and stored at the shaft head.

Lastly, explosive was placed in the red lockers at the head of the development, and on the evening of October 23rd 1968, thirty minutes after the main blast, Davy Delange and his gang disembarked from the cage and went to the disused loco shop.

Davy, with the surly little Swazi boss boy beside him, stood before the rock wall on which the surveyor had marked the outline of the tunnel. Behind him his gang had fallen unbidden to their labour, each man knowing exactly what was expected of him.

Already the machine boys and their assistants were lugging their ungainly tools forward.

'You! You! You! You!' Davy indicated to each of them the hole on which he was to begin and then stepped back.

'Shaya!' he commanded. 'Hit it!' And with a fluttering bellow that buffeted the eardrums the drive began.

The drilling ceased and Davy charged the holes. The fuses hung like the tails of white mice from their holes. Each length carefully cut to ensure correct firing sequence.

'Clear the drive!' The boss boy's whistle shrilled, the tramp of heavy boots receded until silence hung heavy in the chemically cleaned air.

'Cheesa!' Davy and the boss boy, with the igniters burning like children's fireworks in their right hands, touched them to the hanging tails until the chamber was lit by the fierce blue light of the burning fuses. The shadows of the two men flickered gigantic and distorted upon the walls.

'All burning. Let's go!' And the two men walked quickly back to where the gang waited along the haulage.

The detonations sucked at their ears, and thrust against their lungs, so that afterwards the silence was stunning.

Davy checked his wristwatch. By law there was a mandatory thirty minutes' wait before anyone could go back to the face. There may be a hang-fire waiting to blow the eyes out of someone's head. Even if there were not, there was still the cloud of poisonous nitrous fumes that would destroy the hair follicles in a man's nostrils and render him still more vulnerable to the fine particles of rock dust that would seek to enter his lungs.

Davy waited those thirty minutes, by which time the ventilation had sucked away the fumes and dust.

Then, alone, he went up the haulage. With him he carried his safety lamp, its tiny blue flame burning behind the screen of fine brass wire mesh. That mesh was flash proof and insulated the flame from any methane in the air.

Standing before the raw circular wound in the rock wall, Davy tested for methane gas, watching the blue flame for the tell-tale cap. There was no sign of it, and satisfied he extinguished the lamp.

'Boss boy!' he yelled, and the Swazi came up uncoiling the hose behind him.

'Water down!'

Only when the rock face and all the loose rubble below it was glistening and dripping with water was Davy satisfied that the dust was laid sufficiently to bring up his gang.

'Bar boys!' he yelled, and they came up, carrying the twelve-foot long pinchbars, a tool like a giant crowbar.

'Bar down. Make safe!' And the bar boys attacked the bunches of loose rock that were flaking and crumbling from the hanging wall, two of them manipulating one bar between them, with the steel point striking sparks from the rock. The dislodged fragments rained down, heavily at first and then less and less until the rock above their heads was solid and clean.

Only then did Davy scramble over the pile of rubble to reach the face and begin marking in the shot holes.

Behind him his gang was lashing the stuff into the waiting coco pans, and his machine boys were dragging the drills up to the face.

Davy's gang made three blasts that first night. As he rode up in the cage into a pink, sweet-smelling dawn, Davy was satisfied.

'Perhaps tonight we will get in four blasts,' he thought.

In the Company change house he showered, running the water steaming hot so his skin turned dull angry red, and he worked up a fat white lather of soap suds over his head and at his armpits and crotch.

He rubbed down with a rough thick towel and dressed quickly. Crossing the parking lot to his battered old Ford Anglia he felt happy and good-tired; hungry and ready for bed.

He drove into Kitchenerville at a steady forty miles an hour, and by this time the sun was just showing over the Kraalkop ridge. The dawn was misty rose, with long shadows against the earth, and he thought that this was how it would be in the early mornings on the farm.

On the outskirts of the town Johnny's Monaco roared past him going in the opposite direction. Johnny waved and blew the horn, shouting something that was lost in the howl of wind and motor.

'They'll catch him yet.' Davy shook his head in disapproval. 'The speed limit is forty-five along here.'

He parked the Anglia in the garage and let himself in through the kitchen door. The Bantu maid was busy over the stove.

'Three eggs,' he told her and went through to his bedroom. He shrugged off his jacket and threw it on the bed. Then he returned to the door and glanced quickly up and down the passage. It was deserted, and there was no sound besides the clatter of the maid in the kitchen.

Davy sidled into the passage. The door to Johnny's bedroom was ajar, and Davy moved quietly down to it. His heart was pounding in his throat, his breathing was stifled by his guilt and excitement.

He peered around the edge of the door and gasped aloud. This morning it was better than usual.

Hettie was a sound sleeper. Johnny always maintained it would take a shot of Dynagel to wake her. She never wore night clothes and she never rose before ten-thirty in the morning. She lay on her stomach, hugging a pillow to her chest, her hair a joyous tangle of flaming red against the green sheets. The morning was warm and her blankets had been kicked aside.

Davy stood in the passage. A nerve in his eyelid began to twitch, and under his shirt a drop of perspiration slid from his armpit down along his flank.

On the bed Hettie mumbled unintelligibly in her sleep, drew her knees up and rolled slowly onto her back. One arm came up and flopped limply over her face, her eyes were covered by the crook of her elbow.

She sighed deeply. The twin mounds of her bosom were pulled out of shape by their own weight and the angle of her arm. The hair in her armpit and at the base of her belly was bright shiny red-gold. She was long and smooth and silky white, crowned and tipped with flame.

She moved her body languorously, voluptuously, and then settled once more into slumber.

'Breakfast ready, master,' the maid called from the kitchen. Davy started guiltily, then retreated down the passage.

He found with surprise that he was panting, as though he had run a long way.

CHAPTER 46

Johnny Delange leaned against the sidewall of the haulage, his hard helmet tilted at a jaunty angle and a cigarette dangling from his lips.

Down at the face the shots began to fire. Johnny recognized each detonation, and when the last dull jar disrupted the air about them, he pushed himself away from the wall with his shoulder.

'That was the *lifters*,' he announced. 'Come on, Big King!'

Not for Johnny Delange a thirty-minute waste of time. As he and Big King set off down the haulage together they were binding scarves over their noses and mouths. Ahead of them a bluey-white fog of dust and fumes filled the tunnel, and Big King had the hose going, using a fine mist spray to absorb the fumes and particles.

They pushed on up to the face, Johnny stooping over the safety lamp. Even he had a healthy respect for methane gas.

'Bar boys!' he bellowed, not waiting for Big King to finish watering down. They came up like ghosts in the fog. Hard behind them the machine boys hovered with their drills.

Taking calculated risks, Johnny had his drills roaring forty-five minutes sooner than Davy Delange would have in the same circumstances.

When he came back to the face from cutting fuses and priming his explosives, he found his lashing gang struggling with a massive slab of rock that had been blown intact from the face. Five of them were beating on it with fourteen-pound hammers in an attempt to crack it into manageable pieces. As Johnny reached them, Big King was berating them mercilessly.

'You look like a bunch of virgins grinding millet.'

The hammers clanged and struck sparks from the slab. Sweat oozed from every pore of the hammer boys' skin, greasing their bodies, flying from their heads in sparkling droplets with each blow.

'Shaya!' Big King goaded them on. 'Between you all you wouldn't crack the shell of an egg. Hit it, man! Hit it!'

One by one the men fell back exhausted, their chests heaving, gulping air through gaping mouths, blinded by their own sweat.

'All right,' Johnny intervened. The rock was holding up the whole blast. It warranted drastic measures to break it up.

'I'll pop her,' he said, and any government inspector or mine safety officer would have paled at those words.

'Stand far back and turn your faces away,' Big King instructed his gang. From the forehead of one of his men he took a pair of wire mesh goggles, designed to shield the eyes from flying splinters and rock fragments. He handed them to Johnny who placed them over his eyes.

From the canvas carrying bag he took out a stick of Dynagel. It looked like a candle wrapped in yellow greased paper.

'Give me your knife.' Big King opened a large clasp knife and handed it to Johnny.

Carefully Johnny cut a coin-shaped sliver of explosive from one end of the stick, a piece twice as thick as a penny. He returned the remains of the stick to the bag and handed it to Big King.

'Get back,' he said and Big King moved away.

Johnny eyed the slab of rock thoughtfully and then placed the fragment of Dynagel in the centre of it. He adjusted the goggles over his eyes, and picked up one of the fourteen-pound hammers.

'Turn your eyes away,' he warned and took deliberate aim. Then with a smooth overhead two-handed swing he brought the hammer down on the Dynagel.

The explosion was painful in the confined space of the drive, and afterwards Johnny's ears hummed with it. A tiny drop of blood ran down his cheek from the scratch inflicted by a flying splinter. His wrists ached from the jolt of the hammer in his hands.

'Gwenyama!' grunted Big King in admiration. 'The man is a lion.'

The explosion had cracked the slab into three wedge-shaped segments. Johnny pushed the goggles onto his forehead and wiped the blood from his cheek with the back of his hand.

'Get it the hell out of here,' he grinned, then he turned to Big King.

'Come.' He jerked his head towards the end of the tunnel. 'Help me charge the holes.'

The two of them worked quickly, sliding the sticks of Dynagel into the shot holes and tamping them home with the charging sticks.

For anyone who was not in possession of a blasting licence, to charge up was an offence punishable by a fine of one hundred Rand or two months' imprisonment, or both. Big King had no licence, but his assistance saved fifteen minutes on the operation.

Johnny and his gang blew the face five times that day, but as they rode up in the cage into the cool evening air he was not satisfied.

'Tomorrow we'll shoot her six times,' he told Big King.

'Maybe seven,' said Big King.

———————

Hettie was waiting for him in the lounge when he got home. She flew to him and threw her arms about his neck.

'Did you bring me a present?' she asked with her lips against his ear, and Johnny laughed tantalizingly. It was very seldom that he did not have a gift for her.

'You did!' she exclaimed, and began to run her hands over his pockets.

'There!' She thrust her hand into the inside pocket of his jacket, and brought out the little white jeweller's box.

'Oh!' She opened it, and then her expression changed slightly.

'You don't like them?' Johnny asked anxiously.

'How much did they cost?' she inquired as she examined the porcelain and lacquer earrings, representing two vividly coloured parrots.

'Well,' Johnny looked shamefaced, 'you see, Hettie, it's the end of the month, you see, and well, like I'm a bit short till pay day, you see, so I couldn't—'

'How much?'

'Well, you see,' he took a breath, 'two Rand fifty.'

'Oh,' said Hettie, 'they're nice.' And she promptly lost interest in them. She tossed the box carelessly onto the crowded mantelpiece and set off for the kitchen.

'Hey, Hettie,' Johnny called after her. 'How about we go across to Fochville? There's a dance there tonight. We go and twist, hey?'

Hettie turned back, her expression alive again.

'Gee, yes, man!' she enthused. 'Let's do that. I'll go and change, hey!' And she ran up the passage.

Davy came out of his bedroom, on his way to work.

'Hey, Davy.' Johnny stopped him. 'You got any money on you?'

'Are you broke again?'

'Just 'till pay day.'

'Hell, man, Johnny, you got a cheque for eleven hundred the beginning of the month. You spent it all?'

'Next month,' Johnny winked, 'I'm going to get a cheque for two or three thousand. Then watch me go! Come, Davy, lend me fifty. I'm taking Hettie dancing.'

CHAPTER 47

For Rod the days flicked past like telegraph poles viewed from a speeding automobile. Each day he gained confidence in his own ability. He had never doubted that he could handle the underground operation and now he found that he had a firm grasp on the surface as well. He knew that his campaign to reduce working costs was having effect, but its full harvest would only be apparent when the quarterly reports were drafted.

Yet he lay awake in the big Manager's residence on the ridge in which he and his few sticks of furniture seemed lost and lonely, and he worried. There were always myriad nagging little problems, but there were others more serious.

This morning Lily Jordan had come through into his office.

'Mr Innes is coming up to see you at nine.'

'What's he want?' Herbert Innes was the Manager of the Sonder Ditch Reduction works.

'He wouldn't tell me,' Lily answered. The end of the month had come and gone and Lily was still with him. Rod presumed that he had been approved.

Herby Innes, burly and red-faced, sat down and drank the cup of tea that Lily provided, while he regaled Rod with a stroke by stroke account of his Sunday afternoon golf round. Rod interrupted him after he had hit a nine-iron short at the third, and shanked his chip.

'Okay, Herby. What's the problem?'

'We've got a leak, Rod.'

'Bad?'

'Bad enough,' Herby grunted. To him the loss of a single ounce of gold during the process of recovery and refinement was catastrophic.

'What do you reckon?'

'Between the wash and the pour we are losing a couple of hundred ounces a week.'

'Yes,' Rod agreed. 'That is bad enough.'

Twenty thousand Rand a month, one hundred twenty thousand a year.

'Have you any ideas?'

'It's been going on for some time, even in Frank Lemmer's day. We've tried everything.'

Rod was a little hazy about the workings of the reduction plant, not that he would admit that, but he was. He knew that the ore was weighed and sampled when it reached the surface, and from this a fairly accurate estimate of gold content was made and compared with actual recovery. Any discrepancy had to be investigated and traced.

'What is your recovery rate for the last quarter?'

'Ninety-six point seven-three.'

'That's pretty good,' Rod admitted. It was impossible to recover all the gold in the ore that was surfaced but Herby was getting most of it out. 96.73 per cent of it, to be precise. Which meant that very little of the missing two hundred ounces was being lost into the dumps and the slimes dam.

'I tell you what, Herby,' Rod decided. 'I'll come down to the plant this afternoon. We'll go over it together, perhaps a fresh eye may be able to spot the trouble.'

'May do.' Herby was sceptical. 'We've tried everything else. We're pouring this afternoon. What time shall I expect you?'

'Two o'clock.'

They started at the shaft head, where the ore cage, the copie, arrived at the surface every four minutes with its cargo of rock which it dumped into a concrete chute. Each load was classified as either 'reef' or 'waste'.

The reef was dropped into the massive storage bins, while the waste was carried off on a conveyor to the wash house to be sluiced down before going to the dump. Tiny particles of gold sticking to the waste rock were gathered in this way.

Herby put his lips close to Rod's ear to make himself heard above the rumbling roar of rock rolling down the chute.

'I'm not worried about this end. It's all bulk here and very little shine.' Herby used the reduction plant slang for gold. 'The closer we get to the end, the more dangerous it is.'

Rod nodded and followed Herby down the steel ladder until they reached a door below the storage bins. They went through into a long underground tunnel very similar to the ore tunnel on 100 level.

Again there was a massive conveyor belt moving steadily along the tunnel while ore from the bins above was fed onto it. Rod and Herby walked along beside the belt until it passed under a massive electro magnet. Here they paused for a while. The magnet was extracting from the ore all those pieces of metal which had found their way into the ore passes and bins.

'How much you picking up?' Rod asked.

'Last week fourteen tons,' Herby answered, and taking Rod's arm led him through the door beside them. They were in an open yard that looked like a scrap-metal merchant's premises. A mountain of pinch bars, jumper bits, shovels, steel wire rope, snatch blocks, chain, spanners, fourteen-pound hammers, and other twisted and unrecognizable pieces of metal filled the yard. All of it was rusted, much of it unusable. It had been separated from the ore by the magnet.

Rod's mouth tightened. Here he was presented with indisputable evidence of the carelessness and it-belongs-to-the-Company attitude of his men. This pile of scrap represented a waste that would total hundreds of thousands of Rand annually.

'We will see about that!' he muttered.

'If one of those hammers got into my jaw mills it would smash it to pieces,' Herby told him dolefully and led him back into the conveyor tunnel.

The belt angled upwards sharply and they followed the cat-walk beside it. They climbed steadily for five minutes and Herby was puffing like a steam engine. Through the holes in the honeycomb steel plate under his feet, Rod could see that they were now a few hundred feet above ground level.

The conveyor reached the head of a tall tower and dumped its load of ore into the gaping mouths of the screeners. As the rock fell down the tower to ground level again it was sorted for size, and the larger pieces diverted to the jaw crushers which chewed it into fist-size bites.

'See anything?' Herby asked, barely concealing the sarcasm.

Rod grinned at him.

They climbed down the steel ladders that seemed endless, the screeners rattling and the crushers hammering, until Rod's eardrums pleaded for mercy.

At last they reached ground level and went through into the mill room. This was a cavernous galvanized-iron shed the size of a large air-craft hangar. At least one hundred yards long and fifty feet high, it was filled with long rows of the cylindrical tube mills.

Forty of them in all, they were as thick as the boiler of a steam loco-motive and about twice as long. Into one end of them was fed the ore which had been reduced in size by the jaw crushers. The tube mills re-volved and the loose steel balls within them pounded the rock to powder.

If the noise before had been bad, it was hideous in the mill room. Rod and Herby made no effort to speak to each other until they had walked through into the comparative quiet of the first heavy-media separator room.

'Now,' Herby explained. 'This is where we start worrying.' He indi-cated the rows of pale blue six-inch piping that came through the wall from the mill room.

'In there is the powdered rock mixed with water to a smooth flowing paste. About forty per cent of the gold is free.'

'No one can get into those pipes and you've checked for any possible leak?' Rod asked. Herby nodded.

'But,' he said, 'have a look here!'

Along the far wall was a series of cages. They were made of heavy steel mesh, the perforations would not allow a man's finger through. The heavy steel doors were barred and locked. Outside each battery of cages stood a Bantu attendant in clean white overalls. They were all concentrating on the manipulation of the turncock that obviously regulated the flow of the powdered ore through the pipes.

Herby stopped at one of the cages.

'Shine!' he pointed. Beyond the heavy guard screen the grey paste of rock powder was flowing from a series of nozzles over an inclined black rubber sheet. The surface of the rubber sheet was deeply corrugated, and in each corrugation the free gold was collecting, held there by its own weight. The gold was thick as butter in a Dagwood sandwich, greasy yellow-looking in the folds of rubber.

Rod laid hold of the steel screen and shook it.

'No,' Herby laughed. 'No one will get in that way.'

'How do you clean the gold off that sheet? Does someone have access to the separator?' Rod asked.

'The separator cleans itself automatically,' Herby answered. 'Look!'

Rod noticed for the first time that the rubber sheet was moving very slowly; it was also an endless belt running round two rollers. As the belt inverted, so fine jets of water washed the gold from the corrugations into a collection tank.

'I'm the only one who has access. We change the collection tanks daily,' said Herby.

It looked foolproof, Rod had to admit.

Rod turned and glanced down the row of four Bantu attendants. They were all intent on their duties, and Rod knew that each of them had a high security rating. They had been carefully selected and screened before being allowed into the reduction works.

'Satisfied?' Herby asked.

'Okay,' Rod nodded, and the two of them went out through the door in the far wall, locking it behind them.

Immediately they had gone the four Bantu attendants reacted. They straightened up, the scowls of concentration smoothed out to be replaced by grins of relief. One made a remark and they all laughed, and opened the waist bands of their tunics. From inside each trouser leg they drew a length of quarter-inch copper wire and began probing them through the steel screen.

It had taken Crooked Leg, the photographer, almost a year to work out a means of milking gold from the heavily screened and guarded separators. The method which he had discovered was, like all workable plans, extremely simple.

Mercury, quicksilver, absorbs gold the way blotting paper sucks up moisture. It will suck in any speck of gold that comes in contact with it. Mercury has a further property: it can be made to spread on copper like butter on bread. This layer of mercury on copper retains its powers of absorbing gold.

Crooked Leg had devised the idea of coating lengths of copper wire with mercury. The wire could be inserted through the apertures in the steel mesh and the wire laid across the corrugated rubber sheet, where it set about mopping up every speck of gold that flowed over it. The lengths of wire could be quickly slipped down the trouser leg at the approach of an official, and they could be smuggled in and out of the reduction works the same way.

Every evening Crooked Leg retrieved the gold-thickened wire, and issued his four accomplices with newly coated lengths. Every night in the abandoned workings beyond the ridge he boiled the mercury to make it release its gold.

'Now,' Herby could speak normally in the blessed quiet of the cyanide plant, 'we have skimmed off the free gold—and we are left with the sulphide gold.' He offered Rod a cigarette as they made their way between the massive steel tanks that spread over many acres. 'We pump this into the tanks and add cyanide. The cyanide dissolves the gold and takes it into solution. We tap it off and run it through zinc powder. The gold is deposited on the zinc, we burn away the zinc and we are left with the gold.'

Rod lit his cigarette. He knew all this but Herby was giving him a Cook's tour for visiting V.I.P.s. He flicked his lighter for Herby. 'There is no way anyone could swipe it when it's in solution.'

Herby shook his head, exaling smoke. 'Apart from anything else, cyanide is a deadly poison.' He glanced at his watch. 'Three-twenty, they'll be pouring now. Shall we go across to the smelt house?'

The smelt house was the only brick building among all the galvanized iron. It stood a little isolated. Its windows were high up and heavily barred.

At the steel door Herby buzzed, and a peep-hole opened in the door. He and Rod were immediately recognized and the door swung open. They were in a cage of bars which could only be opened once the door was closed behind them.

'Afternoon, Mr Ironsides, Mr Innes.' The guard was apologetic. 'Would you sign, please?' He was a retired policeman with a paunch and a holstered revolver on his hip.

They signed and the guard signalled to his mate on the steel catwalk high above the smelt room floor. This guard tucked his pump action shotgun under one arm, and threw the switch on the walk beside him.

The cage door opened and they went through.

Along the far wall the electric furnaces were set into the brickwork. They resembled the doors of the bread ovens in a bakery.

The concrete floor of the room was uncluttered, except for the mechanical loader that carried the gold crucible in its steel arms, and the moulds before it. The half dozen personnel of the smelt house barely looked up as Rod and Herby approached.

The pour was well advanced, the arms of the loader tilted and a thin stream of molten gold issued from the spout of the crucible, and fell into the mould. The gold hissed and smoked and crackled, and tiny red and blue sparks twinkled on its surface as it cooled.

Already forty or fifty bars were laid out on the rubber-wheeled trolley beside the mould. Each bar was a little smaller than a cigar box. It had the knobby bumpy look of roughly cast metal.

Rod stopped and touched one of the bars. It was still hot and it had the slightly greasy feeling that new gold always has.

'How much?' he asked Herby, and Herby shrugged.

'About a million Rand's worth, perhaps a little more.'

So that's what a million Rand looks like, Rod mused, it's not very impressive.

'What's the procedure now?' Rod asked.

'We weigh it, and stamp the weight and batch number into each bar.' He pointed to a massive circular safe deposit door in the near wall. 'It's stored there over-night, and tomorrow a refinery armoured car will come out from Johannesburg and pick it up.' Herby led the way out of the smelt house. 'Anyway, that's not the trouble. Our leak is sucking off the shine before it ever reaches the smelt house.'

'Let me think about it for a few days,' Rod said. 'Then we'll get together again, try and find the solution.'

He was still thinking about it now. Lying in the darkness and smoking cigarette after cigarette.

There seemed to be only one solution. They would have to plant Bantu police in the reduction works.

It was an endless game involving all the mining companies and their reduction plant personnel. An inventive mind would devise a new system of sucking off the shine. The Company would become aware of the activity by comparison of estimated and actual recovery and they would work on the leak for a week, a month, sometimes a year. Then they would break the system. There would be prosecutions, stiff gaol sentences, and the Company would circularize its neighbours, and they would all settle back and wait for the next customer to appear.

Gold has many remarkable properties, its weight, its non-corruptibility and, not least, the greed and lust it conjures up in the hearts of men.

Rod stubbed his cigarette, rolled onto his side and pulled the bed-clothes up over his shoulders. His last thought before sleep was for the major problem that, these days, was never very far from the surface of his mind.

The Delange brothers had driven almost fifteen hundred feet in two weeks. At this rate they would hit the Big Dipper seven weeks from now, then even the theft of gold would pale into insignificance.

CHAPTER 48

At the time that Rod Ironsides was composing himself for sleep, Big King was taking a little wine with his business associate and tribal brother Philemon N'gabai, alias Crooked Leg.

They sat facing each other in a pair of dilapidated cane chairs with a lantern and a gallon jug of Jeripigo set between them. The bat stench of the abandoned workings did little to bring out the bouquet of the wine, which was of small concern to either man, for they were drinking not for taste but for effect.

Crooked Leg refilled the cheap glass tumbler that Big King proffered, and as the wine glug-glugged from the jar he continued his attack on the character and moral fibre of José Almeida, the Portuguese.

'For many months now I have had it in my heart to speak to you of these matters,' he told Big King, 'but I have waited until I could set a deadfall for the man. He is like a lion that preys upon our herds, we hear him roar in the night and in the dawn we see his spoor in the earth about the carcasses of our animals, but we cannot meet him face to face.'

Big King enjoyed listening to the oratory of Crooked Leg and while he listened he drank the Jeripigo as though it were water, and Crooked Leg kept refilling the tumbler for him.

'In counsel with myself I spoke thus: "Philemon N'gabai, it is not enough that thou should suspect this white man. It is necessary also that you see with your own eyes that he is eating your substance".'

'How, Crooked Leg?' Big King's voice was thickening, the level of the jug had fallen steadily and now showed less than half. 'Tell me how we shall take this man.' Big King showed a fist the size of a bunch of bananas. 'I will . . .'

'No, Big King.' Crooked Leg was scandalized. 'You must not hurt the man. How then would we sell our gold? We must prove he is cheating us and show him we know it. Then we will proceed as ever, but he will give us full measure in the future.'

Big King thought about that for some time, then at last he sighed regretfully. 'You are right, Crooked Leg. Still, I would have liked to . . .' He showed that fist again, and Crooked Leg went on hurriedly.

'Therefore, I have sent to my brother who drives a delivery van for S.A. Scale Company in Johannesburg, and he has taken from his Company a carefully measured weight of eight ounces.' Crooked Leg produced the cylindrical metal weight from his pocket and handed it to Big King who examined it with interest. 'Tonight, after the Portuguese has weighed the gold you take to him, you will say, "Now, my friend, please weigh this for me on your scale," and you will watch to see that his scale reads the correct number. Each time in the future he will weigh this on his scale before we sell our gold.'

'Hau!' Big King chuckled. 'You are a crafty one, Crooked Leg.'

Big King's eyes were smoky and blood-shot. The Jeripigo was a raw rough fortified wine, and he had drunk very nearly a gallon of it. He sat opposite the Portuguese store-keeper in the back room behind the concession store, and watched while he poured the gold dust into the pan of the jeweller's scale. It made a yellow pyramid that shone dully in the light from the single bare bulb above their heads.

'One hundred and twenty-three ounces.' Almeida looked up at Big King for confirmation. A strand of greasy black hair hung on his forehead. His face was pale from lack of sun so that the blue stubble of beard was in heavy contrast.

'That is right,' Big King nodded. He could taste the liquor fumes in the back of his throat, and they were as strong as his distaste for the man who sat opposite him. He belched.

Almeida removed the pan from the scale and carefully poured the dust back into the screw-top bottle.

'I will get the money.' He half rose from his chair.

'Wait!' said Big King, and the Portuguese looked at him in mild surprise.

Big King took the weight from the pocket of his jacket. He placed it on the desk.

'Weigh that on your scale,' he said in Portuguese.

Almeida's eyes flicked down to the weight, and then back to Big King's face. He sank back into his seat, and pushed the strand of hair off his forehead. He began to speak, but his voice cracked and he cleared his throat.

'Why? Is there something wrong?' Suddenly he was aware of the size of the man opposite him. He could smell the liquor on his breath.

'Weigh it!' Big King's voice was flat, without rancour. His face was expressionless, but the smoky red glare of his eyes was murderous.

Suddenly Almeida was afraid, deadly, coldly afraid. He could guess what would happen once the error in his balance was disclosed.

'Very well,' he said, and his voice was forced and off key. The pistol was in the drawer beside his right knee. It was loaded, with a cartridge under the hammer. The safety-catch was on, but that would only delay him an instant. He knew it would not be necessary to fire—once he had the weapon in his hand he would have control of the situation again.

If he did have to fire, the calibre was .45 and the heavy slug would stop even a giant like this Bantu. *Self defence*, he was working it out feverishly. *A burglar*, I surprised him and he attacked. *Self defence*. It would work. They'd believe it.

But how to get the pistol? Try and sneak it out of the drawer, or make a grab for it?

There was a desk between them, it would take a few seconds for the Bantu to realize what he was doing, a few more for him to get around the desk. He would have plenty of time.

He snatched the handle of the drawer, and it flew open. His finger-nails scrabbled against the wood work as he clawed for the big black U.S. Navy automatic, and with a surge of triumph his hand closed over the butt.

Big King came over the top of the desk like a black avalanche. The scale and the jar of gold dust was swept aside to clatter and shatter against the floor.

Still seated in his chair, with the pistol in his hand, Almeida was borne over backwards with Big King on top of him. Many years before, Big King had worked with a safari outfit in Portuguese East Africa, and he had seen the effect of gunshot wounds in the flesh of dead animals.

In the instant that he had recognized the weapon in Almeida's hand, he had been as afraid as the Portuguese. Fear had triggered the speed of his reaction, it was responsible for the savagery of his attack as he lay over the struggling body of the Portuguese.

He had Almeida's pistol hand held by the wrist and he was shaking it to force him to drop the firearm. With his right hand he had the Portuguese by the throat, and instinctively he was applying the full strength of his arms to both grips. He felt something break under his right hand, cracking like the kernel of a nut, and his fingers locked deeper into the quivering flesh. The pistol flew from fingers that were suddenly without strength, and skittered across the floor to come up against the far wall with a thump.

Only then did Big King begin to regain the sanity that fear had scattered. Suddenly he realized that the Portuguese was lying quietly under him. He realised his grip and scrambled to his knees. The Portuguese was dead. His neck was twisted away from his shoulders at an impossible angle. His eyes were wide and surprised, and a smear of blood issued from one nostril over his upper lip.

Big King backed away towards the door, his gaze fixed in horror on the sprawling corpse. When he reached the door, he hesitated, fighting down the urge to run. He subdued it, and went back to kneel beside the desk. First he picked up the controversial cylindrical weight and placed it in his pocket, then he began sweeping up the scattered gold dust and the shattered fragments of the screw-topped container. He placed them in separate envelopes that he found among the papers on the desk. Ten minutes later he slipped out through the back door of the concession store, into the night.

CHAPTER 49

At the time Big King was hurrying back towards the mine hostel, Rod Ironsides thrashed restlessly in a bed in which the sheets were already bunched and damp with sweat. He was imprisoned in his own fantasy, locked in a nightmare from which he could not break away. The nightmare was infinite and green, quivering, unearthly, translucent. He knew it was held back only by a transparent barrier of glass. He cowered before it, and he knew it was icy cold, he could see light shining through it, and he was deadly afraid.

Suddenly there was a crack in the glass wall, a hairline crack, and through it oozed a single drop. A large, pear-shaped drop, as perfect as though it had been painted by Tretchikoff. It glittered like a gemstone.

It was the most terrifying thing that Rod had ever seen in his life. He cried out in his sleep, trying to warn them, but the crack starred further, and the drop slid down the glass, to be followed by another and another.

Suddenly a jagged slab of glass exploded out of the wall, and Rod screamed as the water burst through, in a frothing jet.

With a roar the entire glass wall collapsed, and a mountain high wave of green water hissed down upon him, carrying a white plume of spray at its crest.

He awoke sitting upright in his bed, a cry of horror on his lips and his body bathed in sweat. It took minutes for him to steady the wild racing of his heart. Then he went through to the bathroom. He ran a glass of water and held it up to the light. 'Water. It's there!' he muttered. 'I know it's there!' He drank from the tumbler.

Standing naked, with his sweat drying cold on his body, the tumbler held to his lips, the idea came to him. He had never heard of anyone trying it before, but then nobody he knew would be crazy enough to drive into a death trap like the Big Dipper.

'I'll drill and charge a matt of explosive into the hanging wall of the drive. I'll get the Delange boys on to it right away. Then at any time I choose I can blast the whole bloody roof in and seal off the tunnel.'

Rod was surprised at the strength of the relief that flooded over him. He knew then how it had been worrying him. He went back to the bedroom and straightened out his bedclothes. However, sleep would not come easily to him. His imagination was overheated, and a series of events and ideas kept playing through his mind, until abruptly he was presented with the image of Terry Steyner.

He had not seen her for almost two weeks, not since Manfred Steyner's return from Europe. He had spoken to her twice on the telephone, hasty, confused conversations that left him feeling dissatisfied. He was increasingly aware that he was missing her. His one attempt to find solace elsewhere had been a miserable failure. He had lost interest half way through the approach manoeuvres and had returned the young lady to the bosom of her family at the unheard of hour of eleven o'clock on a Saturday night.

Only the unremitting demands of his new job had prevented him from slipping away to Johannesburg and taking a risk.

'You know, Ironsides, you'd better start bracing up a little, don't lose your head over this woman. Remember our vow—*Never Again*!'

He punched the pillow into shape and settled into it.

Terry lay quietly, waiting for it. It was after one o'clock in the morning. It was one of those nights. He would come soon now. As never before she was filled with dread. A cold slimy feeling in the pit of her stomach. Yet she had been fortunate. He had not been near her since his return from Paris. Over two weeks, but it could not last. Tonight.

She heard the sound of the car coming up the drive and she felt physically ill. I can't do it, she decided, not any more, not ever again. It wasn't meant to be like this, I know that now. It's not dirty and furtive and horrible, it's like . . . like . . . it's the way Rod makes it.

She heard him in his bedroom, suddenly she sat up in bed. She felt desperate, hunted.

The door of her room opened softly.

'Manfred?' she asked sharply.

'It's me. Don't worry.' He came briskly towards her bed, a dark impersonal shape and he was undoing the cord of his dressing-gown.

'Manfred,' Terry blurted, 'I'm early this month, I'm sorry.'

He stopped. She saw his hands fall back to his sides, and he stood completely still.

'Oh!' he said at last, and she heard him shuffle his feet into the thick pile of the carpet. 'I just came to tell you,' he hesitated, seeking an excuse for his visit, 'that . . . that I'll be going away for five days. Leaving on Friday. I have to go to Durban and Cape Town.'

'I'll pack for you,' she said.

'What? Oh, yes—thank you.' He shuffled his feet again. 'Well, then.' He hesitated, then stooped quickly and brushed her cheek with his lips. 'Good night, Theresa.'

'Good night, Manfred.'

Five days, she lay alone in the darkness and gloated. *Five whole days alone with Rod.*

CHAPTER 50

Detective Inspector Hannes Grobbelaar of the South African Criminal Investigation Department sat on the edge of the office chair with his hat tipped onto the back of his head and spoke into the telephone, which he held in a handkerchief-covered hand. He was a tall man with a long sad face and a mournful looking moustache that was streaked with grey.

'Gold buying,' he said into the receiver, and then in reply to the obvious question. 'There's gold dust spilled all over the place and a jeweller's scale, and a .45 automatic with a full magazine and the safety-catch still on, dead man's prints on it.' He listened. 'Ja. Ja. All right, ja. Broken neck, looks like.' Inspector Grobbelaar swivelled his chair and looked down at the corpse that lay on the floor beside him. 'Bit of blood on his lip, but nothing else.'

One of the finger-print men came to the desk and Grobbelaar stood up to give him room to work, the receiver still held to his ear.

'Prints?' he asked in disgust. 'There are finger prints on everything, we have isolated at least forty separate sets so far.' He listened a few seconds. 'No, we will get him, all right. It must be a Bantu mine worker and we have got all the finger prints of the men from outside the Republic. It's just a matter of checking them all out and then questioning. Ja, we'll have him within a month, that's for sure! I'll be back at John Vorster Square about five o'clock, just as soon as we finish up here.' He hung up the receiver, and stood looking down at the murdered man.

'Ugly bastard,' said Sergeant Hugo beside him. 'Asked for it, buying gold. It's as bad as diamonds.' He drew attention to the large envelope he carried in his hand. 'I've got a whole lot of glass fragments. Looks like the container the gold was in. The murderer tried to clean up, but he didn't make a very good job. These were under the desk.'

'Prints?'

'Only one piece big enough. It's got a smeary print on it. Might be of use.'

'Good,' Grobbelaar nodded. 'Get cracking on that, then.'

There was a feminine wail from somewhere in the interior of the building, and Hugo grimaced.

'There she starts again. Hell, I thought she'd exhausted herself. Bloody Portuguese women are the end.'

'You should hear them having a baby,' grunted Grobbelaar.

'Where did you hear one?'

'There was one in the ward next door to my old girl at the maternity home. She nearly brought the bloody roof down.'

Grobbelaar's moustache took on a more melancholy droop as he thought about the work that lay ahead. Hours, days, weeks of questioning and checking and cross-checking, with a succession of sullen and unco-operative suspects.

He sighed and jerked a thumb at the corpse. 'All right, we've finished with him. Tell the butcher boys to come and fetch him.'

CHAPTER 51

It had taken Rod almost two days to design his drop-blast matt. The angle and depth of the shot holes were carefully placed to achieve maximum disruption of the hanging wall. In addition he had decided to drill and charge the side walls of the drive with charges timed to explode *after* the hanging wall had collapsed. This would kick in on the rubble filling the tunnel and jam it solid.

Rod was fully aware of the power of water under pressures of 2,000 pounds per square inch and more and he had decided it was necessary to block at least three hundred feet of the tunnel. His matt blast was designed to do so, and yet he knew that this would not seal off the water completely. It would, however, reduce the flow sufficiently to allow cementation crews to get in and plug the drive solid.

The Delange brothers did not share Rod's enthusiasm for the project.

'Hey man, that's going to take three or four days to drill and charge,' Johnny protested when Rod showed him his carefully drawn plan.

'Like hell it will,' Rod growled at him. 'I want it done properly. It will take at least a week.'

'You said ultra-fast. You didn't say nothing about drilling the hanging wall with more holes than a cheese!'

'Well, I'm saying it now,' Rod told him grimly. 'And I'm also saying that you will drill, but you won't charge the holes until I come down and make sure that you've gone in as deep as I want them.'

He didn't trust either Johnny or Davy to spend time drilling in twenty feet, when he could go in six feet, charge up and nobody would know the difference. Not until it was too late.

Davy Delange spoke for the first time.

'Will you credit us bonus fathomage while we fiddle around with this?' he asked.

'Four fathoms a shift.' Rod agreed to pay them for the removal of fictitious rock.

'Eight?' said Davy.

'Hell, no!' Rod exclaimed. That was robbery.

'I don't know,' Davy murmured, watching Rod with sly ferrety little eyes. 'Maybe I should talk to Brother Duivenhage, you know, ask his advice.'

Duivenhage was No. 1 shaft shop steward for the Mine Workers' Union. He had driven Frank Lemmer to the edge of a nervous breakdown and was now starting on Rodney Ironsides. Rod was pleading with Head Office to offer Duivenhage a fat job in management to get him out of the way. The last thing in the world that Rod wanted was Brother Duivenhage snooping around his drive on the Big Dipper.

'Six,' he said.

'Well . . .' Davy hesitated.

'Six is fair, Davy,' Johnny interrupted, and Davy glared at him. Johnny had snatched complete victory from his grasp.

'Good, that's agreed.' Quickly Rod closed the negotiations. 'You'll start drilling the matt right away.'

———————

Rod's design demanded nearly twelve hundred shot holes to be filled with two and a half tons of explosive. It was a thousand feet down the drive from the main haulage on 66 level to where the matt began.

The drive now was a spacious, well lit and freshly ventilated tunnel, with the vent piping, the compressed air pipe, and the electrical cable bolted into the hanging wall, and a set of steel railway tracks laid along the floor.

All work on the face ceased while the Delange brothers set about drilling the matt. It was light work that demanded little from the men. As each hole was drilled, Davy would insert his charging rod to check the depth and then plug the entrance with a wad of paper. There was much time for drinking Thermos coffee and for thinking.

There were three subjects that endlessly occupied Davy's mind as he sat at ease, waiting for the completion of the next shot hole. Sometimes for half an hour at a time Davy would hold the image of that fifty thousand Rand in his mind. It was his, tax paid, painstakingly accumulated over the years and lovingly deposited with the local branch of the Johannesburg Building Society. He imagined it bundled and stacked in neat green piles in the Society's vault. Each bundle was labelled 'David Delange'.

Then his imagination would pass automatically onto the farm that the money would buy. He saw how it would be in the evenings when he sat on the wide stoep, with the setting sun striking the peaks of the Swart Berg across the valley, and the cattle coming in from the paddocks towards the homestead.

Always there was a woman sitting beside him on the stoep. The woman had red hair.

———————

On the fifth morning Davy drove home in the dawn. He was not tired—the night's labours had been easy and unexacting.

The door of Johnny and Hettie's bedroom was closed. Davy read the newspapers with his breakfast, as always the cartoon strip adventures of Modesty Blaise and Willie Garvin intrigued him completely. This morning Modesty was depicted in a bikini and Davy studied her comparing her to the big healthy body of his brother's wife. The thought of her stayed with him as he rolled into his bed, and he lay unsleeping, daydreaming an adventure in which Modesty Blaise had become Hettie, and Willie Garvin was Davy.

An hour later he was still awake. He sat up and reached for the towel which lay across the foot of his bed. He wrapped the towel around his waist as he went down the passage to the bathroom. As he reached for the handle of the bathroom door, it opened under his hand and he was face to face with Hettie Delange.

She wore a white lace dressing-gown with ostrich-feather mules on her feet. Her face was innocent of make-up and she had brushed her hair and tied it with a ribbon.

'Oh!' she gasped with surprise. 'You gave me a fright, man.'

'I'm sorry, hey.' Davy grinned at her, holding the towel with one hand. Hettie let her eyes run quickly over his naked upper body.

Davy was muscled like a prize fighter. His chest hair was crisp and curly. On both arms the tattoos drew attention to the thickness and weight of muscle.

'Gee, you *are* built,' Hettie murmured in admiration, and Davy sucked in his belly reflexively.

'You think so?' His grin was self-conscious now.

'Yes.' Hettie leaned forward and touched his arm. 'It's hard too!'

The movement had allowed the front of her dressing-gown to gape open. Davy's face flushed as he looked down into the opening. He started to say something, but his voice had dried up on him. Hettie's fingers stroked down his arm, and she was watching the direction of his eyes. Slowly she moved closer to him.

'Do you like me, Davy?' she asked, her voice throaty and low, and with an animal cry Davy attacked her.

His hands ripping at the opening of her gown, pinning her to the wall of the bathroom with his mouth frantically hunting hers. His body pressing hard and urgent, his eyes wild, his breathing ragged.

Hettie was laughing, a breathless gasping laugh.

This was what she loved. When they lost their heads, when they went mad for her.

'Davy,' she said, jerking loose his towel. 'Davy.'

She kept wriggling away from his thrusting hips, knowing that it would inflame him further. His hands were tearing at her body, his eyes were maniacal.

'Yes!' she hissed into his mouth. He threw her off balance and she slid down the wall onto the floor.

'Wait,' she panted. 'Not here—the bedroom.'

But it was too late.

Davy had spent the afternoon locked in his bedroom, lying on his bed in an agony of black all-pervading remorse and guilt.

'My brother,' he kept repeating. 'Johnny is my brother.'

Once he wept, each sob tearing something in his chest. The tears squeezed out between burning eyelids, leaving him feeling exhausted and weak.

'My *own* brother,' he shook his head slowly in horrified disbelief. 'I cannot stay here,' he decided miserably. 'I'll have to go.'

He went to the washbasin and washed his eyes. Stooping over the basin, water still dripping from his face, he decided.

'I will have to tell him.' The burden of guilt was too heavy. 'I'll write to Johnny. I'll write it all, and then I'll go away.'

Frantically he searched for pen and paper, it was almost as though he could wipe away the deed by writing it down. He sat at the table by the window and wrote slowly and laboriously. When he had finished it was three o'clock. He felt better.

He sealed the four closely written pages into an envelope and slipped it into the inside pocket of his jacket. He dressed quickly, and crept out of the house, fearful of meeting Hettie, but she was nowhere about. Her big white Monaco was not in the garage, and with relief he turned out of the driveway and took the road out to the Sonder Ditch. He wanted to reach the mine before Johnny came off shift.

Davy listened to his brother's voice, as he kidded and laughed with the other off-duty miners in the company change house. He had locked himself in one of the lavatory closets to avoid meeting his brother, and he sat disconsolately on the toilet seat. The sound of Johnny's voice brought his guilt flooding back in its full strength. His letter of confession was buttoned into the top pocket of his overalls, and he took it out, broke open the flap and reread the contents.

'So long, then.' Johnny's voice sang out gaily from the change room. 'See you bastards tomorrow.'

There was an answering chorus from the other miners, then the door slammed.

Davy went on sitting alone for another twenty minutes in the stench of stale bodies and urine, dirty socks and rank disinfections from the foot baths. At last he tucked the letter away in his pocket and opened the closet door.

Davy's gang were at their waiting place at the head of the drive. They were sitting along the bench laughing and chatting. There was a holiday spirit amongst them for they knew it would be another shift of easy going.

They greeted Davy cheerfully as he came down the haulage. Both the Delange brothers were popular with their gangs and it was unusual that Davy did not reply to the chorused greeting. He did not even smile.

The Swazi boss boy handed him the safety lamp, and Davy grunted an acknowledgement. He set off alone down the tunnel, trudging heavily, not conscious of his surroundings, his mind encased in a padding of guilt and self-pity.

A thousand feet along the drive he reached the day's work area. Johnny's shift had left the rock drills in place, still connected to the compressed air system, ready for use. Davy came to a halt in the centre of the work area, and without a conscious command from his brain his hands began the routine process of striking the wick of the safety lamp.

The little blue flame came alight behind the protective screen of wire mesh, and Davy held the lamp at eye level before him and walked slowly along the drive. His eyes were watching the flame without seeing it.

The air in the tunnel was cool and refrigerated, scrubbed and filtered, there was no odour nor taste to it. Davy walked on somnambulantly. He was wallowing in self-pity now. He saw himself in a semi-heroic role, one of the great lovers of history caught up in tragic circumstances. His brain was fully occupied with the picture. His eyes were unseeing. Blindly he performed the ritual that a thousand times before had begun the day's shift.

Slowly in its wire mesh cage the blue flame of the safety lamp changed shape. Its crest flattened, and there formed above it a ghostly pale line. Davy's eyes saw it, but his brain refused to accept the message. He walked on in a stupor of guilt and self-pity.

That line above the flame was called 'the cap'; it signified that there was at least a five per cent concentration of methane gas in the air. The last shot hole that Johnny Delange's gang had drilled before going off shift had bored into a methane-filled fissure. For the previous three hours, gas had been blowing out of that hole. The ventilation system was unable to wash the air fast enough and now the gas had spread slowly down the drive. The air surrounding Davy's body was heavy with gas, he had breathed it into his lungs. It needed just one spark to ignite it.

Davy reached the end of the drive and snapped the snuffer over the wick, estinguishing the flame in the lamp.

'All safe,' he muttered, not realizing that he had spoken. He went back to his waiting men.

'All safe,' he repeated, and with the Swazi boss boy leading them the forty men of Davy Delange's gang trooped gaily into the mouth of the drive.

Moodily Davy followed them. As he walked he reached into his hip pocket and took out a pack of Lexington filter tips. He put one between his lips, returned the pack and began patting his pockets to locate his lighter.

Davy went from team to team of his machine boys, directing them in the line and spot to be drilled. Every time he spoke, the unlit cigarette waggled between his lips. He gesticulated with the hand that held his cigarette-lighter.

It took twenty minutes for him to set all his drills to work. And he stood and looked back along the tunnel. Each machine boy and his assistant formed a separate sculpture. Most of them were stripped to the waist. Their bodies appeared to be carved and polished in oiled ebony, as they braced themselves behind the massive rock drills.

Davy lifted his cupped hands, holding the cigarette-lighter near his face and he flicked the cog wheel.

The air in the tunnel turned to flame. In a flash explosion, the flame reached the temperature of a welding torch. It seared the skin from the faces and exposed bodies of the machine boys, it burned the hair from their scalps. It turned their ears to charred stumps. It roasted their eyeballs in their sockets. It scorched their clothing, so as they fell the cloth smouldered and burned against their flesh.

In that instant, as the skin was licked from his face and hands, Davy Delange opened his mouth in a great gasp of agony. The flame shot down his throat into his gas-drenched lungs. Within the confines of his body the gas exploded and his chest popped like a paper bag, his ribs fanning outward about the massive wound like the petals of a sunflower.

Forty-one men died at the same moment. In the silence after that whooshing, sucking detonation, they lay like scorched insects along the floor of the drive. One or two of them were moving still, an arched spine relaxing, a leg straightening, charred fingers unclenching, but within a minute all was absolutely still.

Half an hour later Dr Dan Stander and Rodney Ironsides were the first men into the drive. The smell of burned flesh was overpowering. Both of them had to swallow down their nausea as they went forward.

CHAPTER 52

Dan Stander sat at his desk and looked out over the car park in front of the mine hospital. He appeared to have aged ten years since the previous evening. Dan envied his colleagues the detachment they could bring to their work. He had never been able to perfect the trick. He had just completed forty-one examinations for issue of death certificates.

For fifteen years he had been a mine doctor, so he was accustomed to dealing with death in its more hideous forms. This, however, was the worst he had ever encountered. Forty-one of them, all victims of severe burning and massive explosion trauma.

He felt washed out, exhausted with ugliness. He massaged his temples as he examined the tray of pathetic possessions that lay on the desk before him. These were the contents of the pockets of the man Delange. Extracting them from the scorched clothing had been a filthy business in itself. Cloth had burned into the flesh. The man had been wearing a cheap nylon shirt under his overalls. The fabric had melted in the heat and had become part of his blistered skin.

There was a bunch of keys on a brass ring, a Joseph Rogers pen-knife with a bone handle, a Ronson cigarette-lighter which had been clutched in the man's clawed and charred right hand, a springbok skin wallet, and a loose envelope with one corner burned away.

Dan had already passed on the effects of the Bantu victims to the agent of the Bantu Recruiting Agency, who would send them on to the men's families. Now he sighed with distaste and picked up the wallet. He opened it.

In one compartment there were half a dozen postage stamps, and five Rands in notes. The other flap bulged with paper. Dan glanced through salesmen's cards, dry-cleaning receipts, newspaper cuttings offering farms for sale, a folded page from the *Farmers' Weekly* on the planning of a dairy herd, a J.B.S. Savings Book.

Dan opened the Savings Book and whistled when he saw the total. He fanned the remaining pages.

There was a much-fingered envelope, unsealed and tucked behind the cardboard cover of the Savings Book. Dan opened it, and pulled a face. It contained a selection of photographs of the type which one found offered for sale in the dock area of the Mozambique port of Lourenço Marques. It was for this type of material that Dan was searching.

When the man's possessions were returned to his grieving relatives, Dan wanted to spare them this evidence of human frailty. He burned the photographs and the envelope in his ashtray and then crushed the blackened sheets to powder before spilling it into his waste-paper bin.

He went across to the window and opened it to let the smell of smoke escape. He stood at the window and searched the car park for Joy's Alfa Romeo. She had not arrived as yet and Dan returned to his desk.

The remaining envelope caught his eye and he picked it up. There was a smear of blood upon it, and the corner was burned away. Dan removed the four sheets of paper and spread them on the desk:

> *Dear Johnny,*
>   *When Pa died you were still little—and I always reckoned you were more like my son, you know, than my brother.*
>   *Well, Johnny, I reckon now I've got to tell you something . . .*

Dan read slowly, and he did not hear Joy come into the room. She stood at the door watching him. Her expression fond, a small smile on her lips, shiny blonde hair hanging straight to her shoulders. Then she moved up quietly behind his chair and kissed his ear. Dan started and turned to face her.

'Darling,' Joy said and kissed him on the mouth. 'What is so interesting that you ignore my arrival?'

Dan hesitated a moment before telling her.

'There was a man killed last night in a ghastly accident. This was in his pocket.'

He handed her the letter and she read it slowly.

'He was going to send this to his brother? she asked, and Dan nodded.

'The bitch,' Joy whispered, and Dan looked surprised.

'Who?'

'The girl—it's her fault, you know.' Joy opened her purse and took out a tissue to dab her eyes. 'Damn it, now I'm messing my make-up.' She sniffed, and then went on, 'It would serve her right if you gave that letter to her husband.'

'You mean I shouldn't give it to him?' Dan asked. 'We have no right to play God.'

'Haven't we?' asked Joy, and Dan watched quietly as she tore the letter to tiny shreds, screwed them into a ball, then dropped them into the waste bin.

'You are wonderful,' he said. 'Will you marry me?'

'I've already answered that question, Dr Stander.' And she kissed him again.

CHAPTER 53

Hettie Delange was in a turmoil.

It had started with the phone call that had roused Johnny from their bed. He had said something about trouble at the shaft as he pulled on his clothes, but she had come only briefly awake and then drifted off again as Johnny hurried out into the night.

He had come in hours later and sat on the edge of the bed, his hands clasped between his knees and his head bowed.

'What's wrong, man,' she had snapped at him. 'Come to bed. Don't just sit there.'

'Davy's dead.' His voice had been listless.

There was a moment's shock that had convulsed the muscles of her belly, and brought her fully awake. Then, immediately, she had felt a swift cleansing rush of relief.

He was dead. It was as easy as that! All day she had worried. She had been stupid to let it happen. Just that moment of weakness, that self-indulgent slip and she had been dreading the consequences all that day. She had imagined Davy trailing after her with puppy eyes, trying to touch her, making it so obvious that even Johnny would see it. She had enjoyed it but just the once was enough. She wanted no repeat performance and certainly no complications to follow the original deed.

Now it was all taken care of. He was dead.

'Are you sure?' she had asked anxiously, and Johnny heard the tone as concern.

'I saw him!' Johnny had shuddered, and wiped the back of his hand across his mouth.

'Gee, that's terrible.' Hettie had remembered her role, and sat up to put her arms about Johnny. 'That's terrible for you.'

She had not slept again that night. Somehow the thought of Davy going directly from her to his violent death was exciting. It was like in the movies, or a book, or something. Like he was an airman and he had been shot down, and she was his girl. Perhaps she was pregnant and all alone in the world, and she would have to go to Buckingham Palace to get his medal for him. And the Queen would say . . .

The fantasies had played out in her mind until the dawn, with Johnny tossing and muttering beside her.

She woke him when it was first light in the room.

'How was he?' she asked softly. 'What did he look like, Johnny?'

Johnny shuddered again, and then he started to tell her. His voice was husky, and the sentences broken and disconnected. When he stumbled into silence, Hettie found herself trembling with excitement.

'How terrible,' she kept repeating. 'Oh, how awful!' And she pressed against him. After a while Johnny made love to her, and for Hettie it was better than she had ever known it to be.

All that morning there were phone calls, and four of her friends came over to drink coffee with her. A reporter and photographer from the *Johannesburg Star* called and asked questions. Hettie was the centre of attraction, and again and again she repeated the story with all its grisly details.

After lunch Johnny came home with a little dark-haired man in a charcoal suit and black Italian shoes, with a matching black briefcase.

'Hettie, this is Mr Boart. He was Davy's lawyer. He's got something to tell you.'

'Mrs Delange. May I convey to you my sincere condolences in the tragic bereavement you and your husband have suffered.'

'Yes, it's terrible, isn't it?' Hettie was apprehensive. Had Davy told this lawyer about them? Had this man come to make trouble?

'You brother-in-law made a will of which I am the executor. Your brother-in-law was a wealthy man. His estate is in excess of fifty thousand Rand.' Boart paused portentously. 'And you and your husband are the sole beneficiaries.'

Hettie looked dubiously from Boart to Johnny.

'I don't—what's that mean? Beneficiary?'

'It means that you and your husband share the estate between you.'

'I get half of fifty thousand Rand?' Hettie asked in delighted disbelief.

'That's right.'

'Gee,' exulted Hettie. 'That's fabulous!' She could hardly wait for Johnny and the lawyer to go before she phoned her friends again. All four of them returned to drink more coffee, to thrill again and to envy Hettie the glamour and excitement of it.

'Twenty-five thousand,' they kept repeating the sum with relish.

'Hell, man, he must really have liked you a lot, Hettie,' one of the girls commented with heavy emphasis, and Hettie lowered her eyes and contrived to look bereft and mysterious.

Johnny came home after six, unsteady on his feet and reeking of liquor. Reluctantly Hettie's four friends left to rejoin their waiting families, and almost immediately after that a big white sports car pulled up in the driveway and Hettie's day of triumph was complete. Not one of her friends had ever had the General Manager of the Sonder Ditch Gold Mining Company call at their home.

She had the front door open the instant the doorbell rang. Her greeting had been shamelessly plagiarized from a period movie that had recently played at the local cinema.

'Mr Ironsides, how good of you to come.'

When she led Rod through into the over-furnished lounge, Johnny looked up but did not get to his feet.

'Hello, Johnny,' said Rod. 'I have come to tell you that I'm sorry about Davy, and to . . .'

'Don't give me that bull dust, Tin Ribs,' said Johnny Delange.

'Johnny,' gasped Hettie, 'you can't talk to Mr Ironsides like that.' And she turned to Rod, laying a hand on his sleeve. 'He doesn't mean it, Mr Ironsides. He has been drinking.'

'Get out of here,' said Johnny. 'Get into the bloody kitchen where you belong.'

'Johnny!'

'Get out!' roared Johnny, rising from his chair, and Hettie fled from the room.

Johnny lurched across to the chrome and glass liquor cabinet that filled one corner. He sloshed whisky into two glasses and handed one to Rod.

'God speed to my brother,' he said.

'To Davy Delange, one of the best rock hounds on the Kitchenerville field,' said Rod, and tossed the drink back in one gulp.

'The best!' Johnny corrected him, and emptied his own glass. He gasped at the sting of the whisky, then leaned forward to speak into Rod's face.

'You've come to find out if I'm game to finish your bloody drive for you, or if I'm going to quit. Davy didn't mean nothing to you and I don't mean nothing to you. Only one thing worrying you—you want to know about your bloody drive.' Johnny refilled his glass. 'Well, hear this, friend, and hear it well. Johnny Delange don't quit. That drive ate my brother but I'll beat the bastard, so you got nothing to worry about. You go home and get a good night's sleep, 'cos Johnny Delange will be on shift and breaking rock tomorrow morning first thing.'

CHAPTER 54

A Silver Cloud Rolls Royce was parked amongst the trees in the misty morning. Ahead was the practice track with the white-painted railings curving away towards the willow-lined river. The mist was heavier along the river and the grass was very green against it.

The uniformed chauffeur stood away from the Rolls, leaving its two occupants in privacy. They sat on the back seat with an angora wool travelling rug spread over their knees. On the folding table in front of them was a silver Thermos of coffee, shell-thin porcelain cups, and a plate of ham sandwiches.

The fat man was eating steadily, washing each mouthful down with coffee. The little bald-headed man was not eating, instead he puffed quickly and nervously at his cigarette and looked out of the window at the horses. The grooms were walking the horses in circles, nostrils steaming in the morning chill, blankets flapping. The jockeys stood looking up at the trainer. They wore hard caps and polo-necked jerseys. All of them carried whips. The trainer was speaking urgently, his hands thrust deep into the pockets of his overcoat.

'It's a very fine service,' said the little man. 'I particularly enjoyed the stop in Rio. My first visit there.'

The fat man grunted. He was annoyed. They shouldn't have sent this agent out. It was a mark of suspicion, distrust, and it would seriously hamper his market operation.

The conference between trainer and jockeys had ended. The diminutive riders scattered to their mounts, and the trainer came towards the Rolls.

'Good morning, sir.' He spoke through the open window, and the fat man grunted again.

'I'm giving him a full run,' the trainer went on. 'Emerald Isle will make pace for him to the five, Pater Noster will take over and push him to the mile, I've Tiger Shark to pace him for the run in.'

'Very well.'

'Perhaps you'd like to keep time, sir.' The trainer proffered a stop-watch, and the fat man seemed to recover his urbanity and charm.

'Thank you, Henry.' He smiled. 'He looks good, I'll say that.'

The trainer was pleased by the condescension.

'Oh! He's red hot! By Saturday I'll have him sharpened down to razor edge.' He stood back from the window. 'I'll get them off, then.' He walked away.

'You have a message for me?' asked the fat man.

'Of course.' The other wriggled his moustache like a rabbit's whiskers. It was an annoying habit. 'I didn't fly all this way out here to watch a couple of mokes trotting around a race-track.'

'Would you like to give me the message?' The fat man hid his affront. What the agent had called a moke was some of the finest horseflesh in Africa.

'They want to know about this gas explosion.'

'Nothing.' The fat man dismissed the question with a wave of his hand. 'A flash explosion. Killed a few men. No damage to the workings. Negligence on the part of the miner in charge.'

'Will it affect our plans?'

'Not one iota.'

The two horses had jumped away from the start, shoulder to shoulder, with the wreaths of mists swirling in their wake. The glossy bay horse on the rails ran with an easy floating action while the grey plunged along beside it.

'My principals are very concerned.'

'Well, they have no need to be,' snapped the fat man. 'I tell you it makes no difference.'

'Was the explosion due to an error of judgement on the part of this man Ironsides?'

'No.' The fat man shook his head. 'It was negligence of the miner in charge. He should have detected the gas.'

'Pity.' The bald man shook his head regretfully. 'We had hoped it was a flaw in the Ironsides character.'

The grey horse was tiring, while the bay ran on smoothly, drawing away from him. From the side rail a third horse came in to replace the grey, and ran shoulder to shoulder with the bay.

'Why should the character of Ironsides concern you?'

'We have heard disturbing reports. This is no pawn to be moved at will. He is taking the job of general manager by the throat. Already our sources indicate that he has reduced running costs on the Sonder Ditch by a scarcely believable two per cent. He seems to be tireless, inventive —a man, in short, to reckon with.'

'Well and good,' the fat man conceded. 'But I still fail to see why your —ah, principals—are alarmed. Do they expect that this man will hold back the flood waters by the sheer force of his personality?'

The second pacemaker was faltering, but still the big bay ran on alone, a far figure in the mist, passing the mile post, joined at last by the third pacemaker.

'I know nothing about horses,' said the bald man watching the two flying forms. 'But I've just seen that one,' he pointed with his cigarette at the far-off bay. 'I've just seen him run the guts out of the other two. One after the other he has broken their hearts and left them staggering along behind him. We would call him an imponderable, one who cannot be judged by normal standards.' He puffed at his cigarette before going on. 'There are men like that also, imponderable. It seems to us that Ironsides is one of them, and we don't like it. We don't like them on the opposing team. It is just possible that he could upset the entire operation, not, as you put it, by sheer force of personality, but by suddenly doing the unexpected, by behaving in a manner for which we have not allowed.'

Both men fell silent watching the galloping horses come round the last bend and hit the straight.

'Watch this.' The fat man spoke softly, and as though in response to his words the big bay lengthened his stride, reaching out, driving strongly away from the other horses. His head was going like a hammer, twin jets of steam shot from wide flaring nostrils, and thrown turf and dirt flew from his hooves. Five lengths clear of the following horse he went slashing past the finish line and the fat man clicked his stop watch.

He scrutinized the dial of the watch anxiously and then chuckled like a healthy baby.

'And he wasn't really being extended!'

He rapped on the window beside him, and immediately the uniformed chauffeur opened the driving door and slid in behind the wheel.

'To my office,' instructed the fat man, 'and close the partition.'

When the sound-proof glass panel had slid closed between driver and passengers, the fat man turned to his guest.

'And so, my friend, you consider Ironsides to be an imponderable. What do you want me to do about him?'

'Get rid of him.'

'Do you mean what I think you mean?' The fat man lifted an eyebrow.

'No. Nothing that drastic.' The bald head bobbed agitatedly. 'You have been reading too much James Bond. Simply arrange it that Ironsides is far away and well occupied when the drive holes through the Big Dipper Dyke, otherwise there is an excellent chance that he will do something to frustrate our good intentions.'

'I think we can arrange that,' said the fat man, and helped himself to another ham sandwich.

CHAPTER 55

As he had promised, Manfred caught the Friday evening flight for Cape Town. On the Saturday night Rod and Terry took a wild chance on not being recognized and spent the evening at the Kyalami Ranch Hotel. They danced and dined in the Africa Room, but were on their way back to the apartment before midnight.

In the dawn a playful slap with the rolled-up Sunday papers which Rod delivered to Terry's naked posterior as she slept triggered off a noisy brawl in which a picture was knocked off the wall by a flying pillow, a coffee table overturned and the shrieking and laughter reached such a pitch that it called down a storm of indignant thumping from the apartment above them.

Terry made a defiant gesture at the ceiling, but they both subsided gasping with laughter back onto the bed to indulge in activity every bit as strenuous if not nearly so noisy.

Later, much later, they collected Melanie and once again spent the Sunday at the stud farm on the Vaal. Melanie actually *rode* a horse, a traumatic experience which bade fair to alter her whole existence. After lunch they launched the speedboat from the boat house on the bank of the river and water-skied down as far as the barrage, Terry and Rod taking turns at the wheel and on the skis. It occurred to Rod that Terry Steyner looked good in a white bikini. It was dark before Rod delivered his sleeping daughter to her mother.

'Who is this *Terry* that Melanie talks about all the time?' demanded Patti. She was still sulking about Rod's promotion. Patti had a memory like a tax collector.

'Terry?' Tod feigned surprise. 'I thought you knew.' And he left Patti glaring after him as he went back down the stairs.

Terry was curled up in the leather bucket seat of the Maserati, just the tip of her nose protruding from the voluminous fur coat she wore.

'I love your daughter, Mr Ironsides,' she murmured.

'It would appear that the feeling is reciprocated.'

Rod drove slowly towards the hillbrow ridge, and Terry's hand came out of the wide fur sleeve and lay on his knee.

'Wouldn't it be nice if we had a daughter of our own one day?'

'Wouldn't it,' Rod agreed dutifully, and then found to his intense amazement that he really meant it.

He was still investigating this remarkable phenomenon as he parked the Maserati in the basement garage of his apartment and went round to open Terry's door.

Manfred Steyner watched Terry climb out of the Maserati and lift her face towards Rodney Ironsides. Ironsides stooped over her and kissed her, then he slammed and locked the door of the Maserati, and arm in arm the two of them crossed to the lift.

'Peterson Investigations always delivers the goods,' said the man at the wheel of the black Ford parked in the shadows of the garage. 'We will give them half an hour to get settled in comfortably, then we will go up and knock on the door of his apartment.'

Manfred Steyner sat very still and unblinking on the seat beside the private detective. He had arrived back in Johannesburg three hours previously in answer to the summons from the investigation bureau.

'You will leave me here. Drive the Ford out and park at the corner of Clarendon Circle. Wait for me there,' said Manfred.

'Hey? Aren't you going to . . . ?' The detective was taken aback.

'Do as I tell you.' Manfred's voice stung like thrown vitriol, but the detective persisted.

'You will need evidence for the court, you need me as a witness . . .'

'Get out,' Manfred snapped, and opening the door of the Ford he climbed out and closed the door behind him. The detective hesitated a moment longer, then started the engine and drove out of the garage leaving Manfred alone.

Manfred moved slowly towards the big shiny sports car. From his pocket he took a gold-plated penknife and opened the large blade.

He had recognized that the car was of special significance to the man. It was the only form of retaliation he could make at the moment. Until Rodney Ironsides completed the drive on the Big Dipper Dyke, he could not confront him nor Theresa Steyner. He could not let them know he even suspected them.

Such human emotions as love and hate and jealousy Manfred Steyner seldom experienced, except in their mildest manifestations. Theresa Hirschfeld he had never loved, as he had never loved any woman. He had married her for her wealth and station in life. The emotion that gripped him was neither hatred nor jealousy. It was affront. He was affronted that these two insignificant persons should conspire to cheat him.

He would not rush in blindly now with threats of physical violence and divorce. No, he would administer an anonymous punishment that would hurt the man deeply. This would be part payment. Later, when he had served his purpose, Manfred would crush him as coldly as though he were stepping on an ant.

As for the woman, he was aware of a mild relief. Her irresponsible behaviour had placed her completely at his mercy, both legally and morally. As soon as the strike beyond the Big Dipper had made him financially secure and independent, he could throw her aside. She would have served her purpose admirably.

The journey which he had interrupted by this hurried return to Johannesburg was connected with the purchase of Sonder Ditch shares. He was touring the major centres arranging with various firms of stock brokers that on a given date they would commence to purchase every available scrap of Sonder Ditch script.

As soon as he had completed this business he would tell the private detective to drive him out to Jan Smuts Airport where he had a reservation on the night plane to Durban, where he would continue his preparations.

It had all worked out very well, he thought, as he slipped the knife blade through the rubber buffer of the triangular side window of the Maserati. With a quick twist he lifted the window catch, and pushed the window open. He reached through and turned the door handle. The door clicked open and Manfred climbed into the driver's seat.

The blade of the penknife was razor sharp. He started on the passenger seat and then the driver's seat, ripping the leather upholstery to shreds before moving to the back seat and repeating the process there. He slid the panel that concealed the tray of tools each in their separate foam rubber padded compartment, and selected a tyre lever.

With this he smashed all the dials on the dashboard, broken glass tinkling and falling to the carpeted floor. With the point of the tyre lever he dug into the rosewood panelling and tore out a section, splintering and cracking the woodwork into complete ruin.

He climbed out of the Maserati and struck the wind-shield with the tyre lever. The glass starred. He rained blows on it, unable to shatter it but reducing it to a sagging opaque sheet.

Then he dropped the tyre lever and groped for his penknife again. On his knees he slashed at the front offside tyre. The rubber was tougher than he had allowed. Annoyed, he slashed again. The knife turned in his hand, the blade folding against the blow. It sliced the ball of his thumb, a deep stinging cut. Manfred came to his feet with a cry, clutching his injured jumb. Blood spurted from the wound.

'Mein Gott! Mein Gott!' Manfred gasped, horrified by his own blood. As he staggered wildly from the basement garage, he was wrapping a handkerchief around his thumb.

He reached the waiting Ford, hauled the door open and fell into the front seat beside the detective.

'A doctor! For God's sake, get me to a doctor. I'm badly hurt. Quickly! Drive quickly!'

CHAPTER 56

Terry's husband is due back in town today, Rod thought, as he sat down at his desk. It was not a thought that gave him strength to work through a day he knew would be filled with hectic activity.

The quarterly reports were due at Head Office tomorrow morning. In consequence the entire administration was in its usual last-minute panic. Already there was a mob in the waiting-room outside his office that Lily Jordan would soon need a stock whip to control. At three o'clock he was due at a consultants' meeting at Head Office, but before that he wanted to go underground to check the drop-blast matt that Johnny Delange had now completed and charged up.

The phone went as Lily led in his first visitor, a tall, thin, sorrowful-looking man with a droopy moustache.

'Mr Ironsides?' said the voice on the phone.

'Yes.'

'Porters Motors here. I've got an estimate on the repairs to your Maserati.'

'How much?' Rod crossed his fingers.

'Twelve hundred Rand.'

'Wow!' Rod gasped.

'Do you want us to go ahead?'

'No, I'll have to contact my insurance company first. I'll call you.'

He hung up. That act of unaccountable vandalism still irked him terribly. He realized that he would be reduced to the Company Volkswagen for a further indefinite period.

He turned his attention to his visitor.

'Detective Inspector Grobbelaar,' the tall man introduced himself. 'I am investigating officer in the murder of José Almeida, the concession store proprietor on this mine.'

They shook hands.

'Have you any ideas on who did it?' Rod asked.

'We have always got ideas,' said the Inspector, so sadly that for a moment Rod had the impression that his name was on the list of suspects. 'We believe that the murderer is employed by one of the mines in the district, probably the Sonder Ditch. I have called on you to ask for your co-operation in the investigation.'

'Of course.'

'I will be conducting a great number of interrogations among your Bantu employees. I hoped you might find a room for me to use on the premises.'

Rod lifted his phone and while he dialled he told Grobbelaar, 'I'm calling our Compound Manager.' Then he transferred his attention to the mouthpiece. 'Ironsides here. I am sending an Inspector Grobbelaar down to see you. Please see that an office is placed at his disposal and that he receives full co-operation.'

Grobbelaar stood up and extended his hand.

'I won't take up more of your time. Thank you, Mr Ironsides.'

His next visitor was Van der Bergh, his Personal Officer, brandishing his departmental reports as though they were a winning lottery ticket.

'All finished,' he announced triumphantly. 'All we need is your signature.'

As Rod uncapped his pen, the telephone squealed again.

'My God,' he muttered with pen in one hand and telephone in the other. 'Is it worth it?'

It was well after one o'clock when Rod fled his office, leaving Lily Jordan to hold back the tide. He went directly to No. 1 shaft where he was welcomed like the prodigal son by Dimitri and his old Line Managers. They were all anxious to know who would be replacing him as Underground Manager. Rod promised to find out that afternoon when he visited Head Office, and changed into his overalls and helmet.

At the spot where Davy Delange had died, Rod found a gang fixing a screen of wire mesh over the hanging wall to protect the fuses of his drop-blast. The electric cable that carried the blasting circuit to the surface was covered with a distinctive green plastic coating and securely pegged to the roof of the drive.

In the concrete blast room at the shaft head, his electrician had already set up a separate control for this circuit. It would be in readiness at all times. He could fire it within minutes. Rod felt as though a great weight had been lifted from his shoulders as he passed through the swinging ventilation doors and tramped on up the drive to speak to Johnny Delange.

Half-way to the face he met the gigantic figure of Big King coming back towards him with a small gang of lashing boys under his command. Rod greeted him, and Big King stopped and let his gang go on out of earshot before he spoke.

'I wish to speak.'

'Speak then.' Rod noticed suddenly that Big King's face was gaunt, his eyes appeared sunken and his skin had the dusty greyish look of sickness so evident in an ailing Bantu.

'I wish to return to my wives in Portuguese Mozambique,' said Big King.

'Why?' Rod was dismayed at the prospect of losing such a valuable boss boy.

'My blood is thin.' This was as non-committal an answer as any man has ever received. In essence it meant, 'My reasons are my own, and I have no intention of disclosing them.'

'When your blood is thick again, will you return to work here?' Rod asked.

'That is with the gods.' An answer signifying no more than the one preceding it.

'I cannot stop you if you wish to go, Big King, you know that,' Rod told him. 'Report to the Compound Manager and he will mark your notice.'

'I have told the Compound Manager. He wants me to work out my ticket, thirty-three more days.'

'Of course,' Rod nodded. 'You know that it is a contract. You must work it out.'

'I wish to leave at once,' Big King replied stubbornly.

'Then you must give me your reason. I cannot let you break contract unless there is some good reason.' Rod knew better than to set a dangerous precedent like that.

'There is no reason.' Big King admitted defeat. 'I will work out the ticket.'

He left Rod and followed his gang down the drive. Since the night he killed the Portuguese, Big King had slept little and eaten less. Worry had kept his stomach in a turmoil of dysentry, he had neither danced nor sung. Nothing that Crooked Leg nor the Shangaan Induna could say comforted him. He waited for the police to come. As the days passed, so the flesh melted from his body; he knew that they would come before the thirty-three days of his contract expired.

His approach to Rod had been a last despairing effort. Now he was resigned. He knew that the police were inexorable. One day soon they would come. They would lock the silver chains on his wrists and lead him to the closed van. He had seen many men led away like that and he had heard what happened to them after that. The white man's law was the same as the tribal law of the Shangaans. The taking of life must be paid for with life.

They would break his neck with the rope. His ancestors would have crushed his skull with a war club, it was the same in the end.

Rod found Johnny Delange drinking cold tea from his canteen while his gang barred down the face.

'How's it going?' he asked.

'Now we have finished messing about, it has started moving again.' Johnny wiped cold tea from his lips and recorked the canteen. 'We have broken almost fifteen hundred feet since Davy died.'

'That's good going.' Rod ignored the reference to the methane explosion and the drop-blast matt.

'Would have been better if Davy were still alive.' Johnny disliked Campbell, the miner who had replaced Davy on the night shift. 'The night shift aren't breaking their fair ground.'

'I'll chase them up,' Rod promised.

'You do that.' Johnny turned away to shout an order at his gang.

Rod stood and stared at the end of the drive. Less than a thousand feet ahead lay the dark hard rock of the Big Dipper—and beyond it...? Rod felt his skin creep as he remembered his nightmare. That cold green translucent thing waiting for them beyond the dyke.

'All right, Johnny, you are getting close now.' Rod tore his imagination away from that green horror. 'As soon as you hit the Serpentine rock you are to stop work immediately and report to me. Is that understood?'

'You'd better tell that to Campbell also,' said Johnny. 'The night shift may hit the Big Dipper.'

'I'll tell him,' Rod agreed. 'But you make sure you remember. I want to be down here when we hole through the dyke.'

Rod glanced at his watch. It was almost two o'clock. He had an hour to get to the consultants' meeting at Head Office.

'You are late, Mr Ironsides.' Dr Manfred Steyner looked up from the head of the board-room table.

'My apologies, gentlemen.' Rod took his seat at the long oak table. 'Just one of those days.'

The men about the table murmured sympathetic acknowledgement, and Dr Steyner studied him for a moment without expression before speaking.

'I would be obliged for a few minutes of your time after this meeting, Mr Ironsides.'

'Of course, Dr Steyner.'

'Good.' Manfred nodded. 'Now that Mr Ironsides has graced the table with his presence, the meeting can come to order.' It was the closest any of them had ever heard Dr Steyner come to making a joke.

It was dark outside when the meeting ended. The participants shrugged on their coats, made their farewells and left Manfred and Rod sitting at the table with its overflowing ash trays and littered pencils and note pads.

Manfred Steyner waited for fully three minutes after the door had closed on the last person to leave. Rod was accustomed to these long intent silences, yet he was uneasy. He sensed a new hostility in the man's attitude. He covered his awkwardness by lighting another cigarette and blowing a series of smoke rings at the portrait of Norman Hradsky, the original chairman of the Company. Flanking Hradsky's portrait were two others. One of a slim blond man, with ravaged good looks and laughing blue eyes. The caption read: 'Dufford Charleywood. Director of C.R.C. from 1867–1872.' The other portrait in its heavy gilt frame depicted an impressively built man with mutton-chop whiskers and black Irish features. 'Sean Courtney' said the caption, and the dates were the same as Charleywood's.

These three had founded the Company, and Rod knew a little of their story. They had been as pretty a bunch of rogues as would be found in any convict settlement. Hradsky had ruined the other two in an ingenious bear raid on the stock exchange, and had virtually stolen their shares in the Company.*

We have become a lot more sophisticated since then, thought Rod. He looked instinctively towards the head of the long table and met Dr Steyner's level, unblinking stare. *Or have we?* he wondered. Just what devilment has our friend in mind?

Manfred Steyner was examining Rod with detached curiosity. So remote from any emotional rancour was Manfred, that he intended using the relationship that had developed between this man and his wife to further the instructions he had received that morning.

'How far is the end of the drive from the dyke?' he asked.

'Less than a thousand feet.'

'How much longer before you reach it?'

'Ten days. No more, possibly less.'

'As soon as the dyke is reached, all work on it must cease immediately. The timing of this is important, do you understand?'

'I have already instructed my miners not to hole through without my specific orders.'

'Good.' Manfred lapsed into silence for another full minute. Andrew had called him that morning with instructions from the man. Ironsides

* Read *When the Lion Feeds*

was to be well away from the Sonder Ditch when they pierced the dyke. It was left to Manfred to engineer his absence.

'I must inform you, Mr Ironsides, that it will be at least three weeks before I give the order to drill through. When you reach the dyke, it will be necessary for me to proceed to Europe to make certain arrangements there. I will be away for at least ten days during which time no work of any type must be allowed in the drive to the Big Dipper.'

'You will be away over Christmas?' Rod asked with surprise.

'Yes,' Manfred nodded, and could read Rod's mind.

Terry will be alone, Rod thought quickly, she will be alone over Christmas. The Sonder Ditch goes onto *essential services only* for a full seven days over Christmas. Just a skeleton crew to keep her going. I could get away for a week, a whole week away together.

Manfred waited until he knew that Rod had reached the decision to which he had been steered, then he asked: 'You understand? You will await my order to hole through. You need not expect that order until the middle of January.'

'I understand.'

'You may go.' Manfred dismissed him.

'Thanks,' Rod acknowledged drily.

There was a coffee bar in the ground-floor shopping centre of Reef Building. Rod beat a bearded hippie to the telephone booth, and dialled the Sandown number. It was safe enough, he had just left Manfred upstairs.

'Theresa Steyner,' she answered his call.

'We've got a week to ourselves,' he told her. 'One whole glorious week.'

'When?' she demanded joyously.

And he told her.

'Where shall we go?' she asked.

'We'll think of somewhere.'

CHAPTER 57

At 11.26 a.m. on December 16th, Johnny Delange blasted the face of the drive, and went forward in the fumes and dust.

In the beam of his lantern, the new rock blown from the face was completely different from the bluish Ventersdorp quartzite. It was a glassy, blackish green, veined with tiny white lines, more like marble than country rock.

'We are on the dyke.' He spoke to Big King, and stooped to pick up a lump of the Serpentine rock. He weighed it in his hand.

'We've done it, we've beaten the bastard!'

Big King stood silently beside him. He did not share Johnny's elation.

'Right!' Johnny tossed the lump of rock back onto the pile. 'Bar down, and make safe. Then pull them out of the drive. We are finished here until further orders.'

'Well done, Johnny,' applauded Rod. 'Clean her up and pull out of the drive. I don't know how much longer it will be till we get the order to hole through the dyke. But take a holiday in the meantime. I'll pay you four fathoms of bonus a day while you are waiting.' He broke the connection with his finger, keeping the receiver to his ear. He dialled and spoke to the switchboard girl at Head Office. 'Get me Dr Steyner, please. This is Rodney Ironsides.' He waited a few seconds and then Manfred came on the line.

'We've hit the Big Dipper,' Rod told him.

'I will leave for Europe on tomorrow morning's Boeing,' said Manfred. 'You are to do nothing until I return.' Manfred cradled the receiver and depressed the button on his intercom.

'Cancel all my appointments,' he told his secretary. 'I am unavailable.'

'Very well, Dr Steyner.'

Manfred picked up the receiver of his unlisted, direct-line telephone. He dialled.

'Hello, Andrew. Will you tell him that I am ready to discharge my obligations. We have intersected the Big Dipper.' He listened for a few seconds, then spoke again. 'Very well, I will wait for your reply.'

Andrew replaced the telephone and went out through the sliding glass doors onto the terrace. It was a lazy summer's day, hushed with heat, and the sun sparkled on the crystal clear waters of the swimming-pool. Insects murmured languidly in the massed banks of blooms that surrounded the terrace.

The fat man stood before an artist's easel. He wore a blue beret and a white smock that hung like a maternity dress over his jutting stomach.

His model lay face down on an air mattress by the edge of the pool. She was a dainty, dark-haired girl with a pixy face and a doll-like body. Her discarded bikini lay in a damp bundle on the flags of the terrace. Drops of water caught the sun and bejewelled her creamy buttocks, giving her a paradoxical air of innocence and oriental eroticism.

'That was Steyner,' said Andrew. 'He reports that they have hit the Big Dipper.'

The fat man did not look up. He went on laying paint upon the canvas with complete concentration.

'Please lift your right shoulder, my dear, you are covering that utterly delightful bosom of yours,' he instructed, and the girl obeyed him immediately.

Finally he stepped back and regarded his own work critically.

'You may have a break now.' He wiped his brushes while the naked girl stood up, stretched like a cat and then dived into the pool. She surfaced with the water slicking her short dark hair against her head like the pelt of an otter, and swam slowly to the far end of the pool.

'Cable New York, Paris, London, Tokyo and Berlin the code word "Gothic",' he instructed Andrew. This was the word which would unleash the bear offensive on the financial markets of the world. On receipt of those cables, agents in the major cities would begin to sell the shares of the companies mining the Kitchenerville field, sell them by the millions.

'Then instruct Steyner to get Ironsides out of the way, and hole through the dyke.'

Manfred answered Andrew's return call on the unlisted line. He listened to, and acknowledged, his instructions. Afterwards he sat still as a lizard, running over his preparations. Reviewing them minutely, examining them for flaws. There were none.

It was time to begin the purchase of Sonder Ditch shares. He called his secretary on the intercom and instructed her to place calls to numbers in Cape Town, Durban and Johannesburg itself. He wanted the purchase orders to come through a number of different brokers, so that it would not be obvious that there was only one buyer in the market. There was also the question of credit; he was not covering his purchase orders with Bankers' guarantees. The stock brokers were buying for him simply on his name and reputation and position with C.R.C. Manfred could not place too large a buying order with any one firm lest they ask him to provide surety. Dr Manfred Steyner had no surety to offer.

So, instead, he placed moderate orders with dozens of different firms. By three o'clock that afternoon Manfred had ordered the purchase of three quarters of a million Rands' worth of shares. He had no means of paying for those shares but he knew he would never be called upon to do so. When he sold them again in a few weeks' time they would have doubled in value.

A few minutes after his final conversation with the firm of Swerling and Wright in Cape Town, his secretary came through on the intercom.

'S.A.A. have confirmed your reservation on the Boeing to Salisbury. Flight 126 at nine o'clock tomorrow morning. You are booked to return to Johannesburg on the Rhodesian Airways Viking at six o'clock tomorrow evening.'

'Thank you.' Manfred grudged this wasted day but it was imperative that Theresa believed he had left for Europe. She must see him depart on the S.A.A. flight. 'Please get my wife on the phone for me.'

'Theresa,' he told her, 'something important has come up. I have to fly to London tomorrow morning. I am afraid I will be away over Christmas.'

Her display of surprise and regret was unconvincing. She and Ironsides had made their own arrangements for the time he was away, Manfred was convinced of this.

It was all working out very well, he thought, as he cradled the receiver, very well indeed.

CHAPTER 58

The Daimler drew up under the portico of Jan Smuts Airport and the chauffeur opened the door for Terry and then for Manfred.

While the porter removed his luggage from the boot of the Daimler, Manfred swept the car park with a quick scrutiny. So early in the morning it was less than half filled. There was a cream Volkswagen with a Kitchenerville number plate parked near the far end. All the line and senior managers of the Sonder Ditch had cream Volkswagens as their official vehicles.

'The bee has come to the honeypot,' thought Manfred, and smiled bleakly. He took Terry's elbow and they followed the porter with the crocodile-skin luggage into the main concourse of the airport.

Terry waited while Manfred went through his ticket and immigration formalities. On the outside she was a demure and dutiful wife, but she also had seen the Volkswagen and inside she was itching and bubbling with excitement, darting surreptitious glances from behind her sunglasses, looking for that tall broad-shouldered figure among the crowds.

It seemed a lifetime until she stood alone on the observation balcony with the wind whipping her piebald calf-skin coat around her legs, and blowing her hair into a snapping, dancing tangle. The long shark-like shape of the Boeing jet crouched at the far end of the runway and as it started forward Terry turned from the balcony rail and ran back into the main building.

Rod was waiting for her just inside the doors, and he swung her off her feet.

'Gottcha!'

With her feet dangling, she put her arms around his neck and kissed him.

The watchers paused and smiled, and there was a minor traffic jam at the head of the stairs.

'Come on,' she entreated, 'let's not waste a minute of it.'

He put her on her feet, and they ran down the staircase hand in hand. Terry paused only to dismiss the chauffeur, and then they ran through the car park like children let out of school, and clambered into the Volkswagen. Their luggage was on the back seat.

'Go,' she said, 'go as fast as you can!'

Twenty minutes later Rod pulled the Volkswagen to a tyre-squealing halt in front of the hangars at the private airfield.

The twin-engined Cessna stood on the tarmac. Both engines were ticking over in readiness, and the mechanic climbed down from the cockpit when he recognized Terry.

'Hello, Terry, right on time,' he greeted her.

'Hello, Hank. You've got her warmed up already. You are a sweety!'

'Filed your flight plan also. Nothing too good for my most favourite customer.' The mechanic was a chunky grizzled little man, and he looked at Rod curiously.

'Give you a hand with the bags,' he said.

By the time they had the luggage stowed away in its compartment, Terry was in the cockpit speaking to the control tower.

Rod climbed up into the passenger seat beside her.

Terry switched off her radio and leaned over Rod's lap to speak to Hank.

'Thanks, Hank.' She paused delicately, and then went on with a rush. 'Hank, if anyone asks you, I was on my own today, okay?'

'Okay.' Hank grinned at her. 'Happy landings.' And he closed the cockpit door, and Terry taxied out onto the runway.

'Is this yours?' Rod asked. It was a hundred thousand Rands' worth of aircraft.

'Pops gave it to me for my birthday,' Terry replied. 'Do you like it?'

'Not bad,' Rod admitted.

Terry turned upwind and applied the wheel brakes while she ran the engines up to peak revs, testing their response.

Suddenly Rod realized that he was in the hands of a woman pilot. He fell silent and his nerves began to tighten up.

'Let's go,' said Terry and kicked off the brakes. The Cessna surged forward, and Rod gripped the arm rests and froze with his gaze fixed dead ahead.

'Relax, Ironsides,' Terry advised him without taking her eyes off the runway, 'I've been flying since I was sixteen.'

At three thousand feet she levelled out and banked gently onto an easterly heading.

'Now that didn't hurt too much did it?' She smiled sideways at him.

'You are quite a girl,' he told her. 'You can do all sorts of tricks.'

'You just wait,' she warned him. 'You ain't seen nothing yet!'

They flew in silence until the Highveld had fallen away behind them, and they were over the dense green mattress of the Bushveld.

'I'm going to divorce him.' She broke the silence, and Rod was not surprised that they were experiencing the mental telepathy of closely attuned minds. He had been thinking about her husband also.

'Good,' he said.

'You think I'd have a chance with you if I did?'

'If you played your cards right, you might get that lucky.'

'Conceited swine,' she said. 'I don't know why I love you.'

'Do you?' he asked.

'Yes.'

'And I you.'

They relapsed into a contented silence, until Terry put the Cessna in a shallow dive.

'What's wrong?' Rod asked with alarm.

'Going down to have a look for game.'

They flew low over thick olive-green bush broken by vleis of golden brown grass.

'There,' said Rod, pointing ahead. A line of fat black bugs was moving across one of the open places. 'Buffalo!'

'And over there.' Terry pointed left.

'Zebra and wildebeeste,' Rod identified them. 'And there is a giraffe.' Its long stalk of a neck stuck up like a periscope. It broke into an awkward stiff-legged run as the aircraft roared overhead.

'We have arrived.' Terry indicated a pair of round granite koppies on the horizon ahead. They were as symmetrical as a young girl's breasts, and as they drew nearer Rod made out the thatched roof of a large building standing in the hollow between the koppies. Beyond it a long straight landing-strip had been cut from the trees, and the fat white sausage of a wind sock flew from its pole.

Terry throttled back and circled the homestead. On the lawns half a dozen tiny figures waved up at the Cessna, and as they watched, two of the figures climbed into a toy Landrover and set off for the landing-strip. A ribbon of white dust blew out from behind it.

'That's Hans,' Terry explained. 'We can go down now.'

She lined the Cessna up for its approach, and then let it sink down with the motors rumbling softly. The ground came up and jarred the undercarriage, then they were taxiing to meet the racing Landrover.

The man who piled out of the Landrover was white-haired, and sunburned like old leather.

'Mrs Steyner!' He was making no attempt to conceal his pleasure. 'It's been much too long. Where have you been?'

'I've been busy, Hans.'

'New York? What the hell for?' said Hans surprisingly.

'This is Mr Ironsides.' Terry introduced them. 'Rod, this is Hans Kruger.'

'Van Breda?' asked Hans as they shook hands. 'You related to the van Bredas from Caledon?'

'I don't think so,' Rod muttered, looking at Terry appealingly.

'He is stone deaf,' Terry explained. 'Both his ear drums blown out by a hangfire in the 1930s. He won't admit it though.'

'I'm glad to hear it,' Hans nodded, happily. 'You always were a healthy girl. I remember when you were a little piccanin.'

'He is an absolute darling though, so is his wife. They look after the shooting lodge for Pops,' Terry told Rod.

'Good idea!' Hans agreed heartily. 'Let's get your bags into the Land-rover and go up to the house. I bet Mr van Breda could use a drink also.' And he winked at Rod.

The lodge had thatch and rough-hewn timber roofing, stone-flagged floors covered with cured animal skins and Kelim rugs. There was a walk-in fireplace flanked by gun racks on which were displayed fifty fine examples of the gunsmith's art. The furniture was massive and masculine, leather-cushioned and low. The Spanish plaster walls were hung with trophies, horned heads and native weapons.

A vast wooden staircase led up to the bedrooms that opened off the gallery above the main room. The bedrooms were air-conditioned and after they had got rid of Hans and his fat wife, Rod and Terry tested the bed to see if it was suitable.

An hour and a half later the bed had been judged eminently satis-factory, and as they went down to pass further judgement on the gar-gantuan lunch that fat Mrs Hans had spread for them, Terry remarked, 'Has it ever occurred to you, Mr Ironsides, that there are parts of your anatomy other than your flanks which are ferrous in character?' Then she giggled and added softly, 'And thank the Lord for that!'

Lunch was an exhausting experience and Terry pointed out that there was little sense in going out before four o'clock as the game would still be in thick cover avoiding the midday heat, so they went back upstairs.

After four o'clock Rod selected a .375 magnum Holland and Holland rifle from the rack, filled a cartridge belt with ammunition from one of the drawers, and they went out to the Landrover.

'How big is this place?' Rod asked as he turned the Landrover away from the gardens and took the track out into the virgin bush.

'You can drive for twenty miles in any direction and it's all ours. Over there our boundary runs against the Kruger National Park,' Terry answered.

They drove along the banks of the river, skirting sandbanks on which grew fluffy-headed reeds. The water ran fast between glistening black rocks, then spread into slow lazy pools.

They saw a dozen varieties of big game, stopping every few hundred yards to watch some lovely animal.

'Pops obviously doesn't allow shooting here,' Rod remarked, as a kudu bull with long spiral horns and trumpet-shaped ears studied them with big wet eyes from a range of thirty feet. 'The game is as tame as domestic cattle.'

'Only family are allowed to shoot,' Terry agreed. 'You qualify as family, however.'

Rod shook his head. 'It would be murder.' Rod indicated the kudu. 'That old fellow would eat out of your hand.'

'I'm glad you feel like that,' Terry said, and they drove on slowly.

The evening was not cool enough to warrant a log fire in the cavernous fireplace of the lodge. They lit one anyway because Rod decided it would be pleasant to sit in front of a big, leaping fire, drink whisky and hold the girl you love.

CHAPTER 59

When Inspector Grobbelaar lowered his teacup, there was a white scum of cream on the tips of his moustache. He licked it off carefully, and looked across at Sergeant Hugo.

'Who have we got next?' he asked.

Hugo consulted his notebook.

'Philemon N'gabai.' He read out the name, and Grobbelaar sighed.

'Number forty-eight, only sixteen more.' The single smeary fingerprint on the fragment of glass from the gold container had been examined by the fingerprint department. They had provided a list of sixty-four names, any one of which might be the owner of that print. Each of them had to be interrogated; it was a lengthy and so far unrewarding labour.

'What do we know about friend Philemon?' Grobbelaar asked.

'He is approximately forty years old. A Shangaan from Mozambique. Height 5' 7½", weight 146 lb. Crippled right leg. Two previous convictions. 1956: sixty days for bicycle theft. 1962: ninety days for stealing a camera from a parked car,' Hugo read from the file.

'At 146 lb. I don't see him breaking many necks. But send him in, let's talk to him,' Grobbelaar suggested, and dunked his moustache in the tea cup again. Hugo nodded to the African Sergeant and he opened the door to admit Crooked Leg and his escort of an African constable.

They advanced to the desk at which the two detectives sat in their shirt sleeves. No one spoke. The two interrogators subjected him to a calculated and silent scrutiny to set him at as great a disadvantage as possible.

Grobbelaar prided himself on being able to sniff out a guilty conscience at fifty paces, and Philemon N'gabai reeked of guilt. He could not stand still, he was sweating heavily, and his eyes darted from floor to ceiling. He was guilty as hell, but not necessarily of murder. Grobbelaar did not feel the slightest confidence as he shook his head sorrowfully and asked, 'Why did you do it, Philemon? We have found the marks of your hand on the gold bottle.'

The effect on Crooked Leg was instantaneous and dramatic. His lips parted and began to tremble, saliva dribbled onto his chin. His eyes for the first time fixed on Grobbelaar's face, wide and staring.

'Hello! Hello!' Grobbelaar thought, straightening in his chair, coming completely alert. He sensed Hugo's quickening interest beside him.

'You know what they do to people who kill, Philemon? They take them away to . . .' Grobbelaar did not have an opportunity to finish.

With a howl Crooked Leg darted for the door. His crippled gait was deceptive, he was fast as a ferret. He had the door open before the Bantu Sergeant collared him and dragged him gibbering and struggling back into the room.

'The gold, but not the man! I did not kill the Portuguese,' he babbled, and Grobbelaar and Hugo exchanged glances.

'Pay dirt!' Hugo exclaimed with deep satisfaction.

'Bull's eye!' agreed Grobbelaar, and smiled, a rare and fleeting occurrence.

CHAPTER 60

'You see it has a little light that comes on to show you where the keyhole is,' said the salesman, pointing to the ignition switch on the dashboard.

'Ooh! Johnny, see that!' Hettie gushed, but Johnny Delange had his head under the bonnet of the big glossy Ford Mustang.

'Why don't you sit in her?' the salesman suggested. He was very cute really, Hettie decided, with dreamy eyes and the most *fabulous* side burns.

'Ooh! Yes, I'd love to.' She manoeuvred her bottom into the leather bucket seat of the sports car. Her skirt pulled up, and the salesman's dreamy eyes followed the hem all the way.

'Can you adjust the seat?' Hettie asked innocently looking up at him.

'Here, I'll show you.' He leaned into the interior of the Mustang and reached across Hettie's lap. His hand brushed over her thigh, and Hettie pretended not to notice his touch. He smelled of Old Spice after-shave lotion.

'That's better!' Hettie murmured, and wriggled into a more comfortable position, contriving to make the movement provocative and revealing.

The salesman was encouraged, he lingered with his wrist just touching a sleek thigh.

'What's the compression ratio on this model?' Johnny Delange demanded as he emerged from the engine, and the salesman straightened up quickly and hurried to join him.

An hour later Johnny signed the purchase contract, and both he and Hettie shook the salesman's hand.

'Let me give you my card,' the salesman insisted, but Johnny had returned to his new toy, and Hettie took the cardboard business card.

'Call me if you need anything, anything at all,' said the salesman with heavy significance.

'Dennis Langley. Sales Manager,' Hettie read out aloud. 'My! You're very young to be Sales Manager.'

'Not all that young!'

'I'll bet,' Hettie murmured, and her eyes were suddenly bold. She ran the tip of a pink tongue over her lips. 'I won't lose it,' she promised, and placing the card in her handbag, walked to the Mustang, leaving him with a tantalizing promise and a memory of swaying hips and clicking heels.

They raced the new Mustang as far as Potchefstroom, Hettie encouraging Johnny to overtake slower vehicles with inches to spare for oncoming traffic. With horn blaring he tore over blind rises, forking ringed fingers at the protesting toots of other drivers. They had the speedometer registering 120 m.p.h. on the return run, and it was dark as they pulled into the driveway and Johnny hit the brakes hard to avoid running into the back of a big black Daimler that was parked outside their front door.

'Jesus,' gasped Johnny. 'That's Dr Steyner's bus!'

'Who is Dr Steyner?' Hettie demanded.

'Hell, he's one of the big shots from Head Office.'

'You're kidding!' Hettie challenged him.

'Truth!' Johnny affirmed. 'One of the real big shots.'

'Bigger than Mr Ironsides?' The General Manager of the Sonder Ditch was as high up the social ladder as Hettie had ever looked.

'Tin Ribs is chicken feed compared to this joker. Just look at his bus, it's five times better than Tin Ribs' clapped-out old Maserati.'

'Gee!' Hettie could follow the logic of this line of argument. 'What's he want with us?'

'I don't know,' Johnny admitted with a twinge of anxiety. 'Let's go and find out.'

The lounge of the Delange home was not the setting which showed Dr Manfred Steyner to best advantage.

He sat on the edge of a scarlet and gold plastic-covered armchair as stiff and awkward as the packs of china dogs that stood on every table and shelf of the show cabinet, or the porcelain wild ducks which flew in diminishing perspective along the pale pink painted wall. In contrast to the tinsel Christmas decorations that festooned the ceiling and the gay greeting cards that Hettie had pinned to strips of green ribbon, Manfred's black homburg and Astrakhan-collared overcoat were unnecessarily severe.

'You will forgive my presumption,' he greeted them without rising. 'You were not at home and your maid let me in.'

'You're welcome, I'm sure,' Hettie simpered.

'Of course you are, Dr Steyner,' Johnny supported her.

'Ah! So you know who I am?' Manfred asked with satisfaction. This would make his task much easier.

'Of course we do.' Hettie went to him and offered her hand. 'I am Hettie Delange, how do you do?'

With horror Manfred saw that her armpit was unshaven, filled with damp ginger curls. Hettie had not bathed since the previous evening. Manfred's nostrils twitched and he fought down a queasy wave of nausea.

'Delange, I want to speak to you alone.' He cowered away from Hettie's overwhelming physical presence.

'Sure.' Johnny was eager to please. 'How about you making us some coffee, honey,' he asked Hettie.

Ten minutes later Manfred sank with relief into the lush upholstery of the Daimler's rear seat. He ignored the two Delanges waving their farewells, and closed his eyes. It was done. Tomorrow morning Johnny Delange would be on shift and drilling into the glassy green rock of the Big Dipper.

By noon Manfred would own quarter of a million shares in the Sonder Ditch.

In a week he would be a rich man.

In a month he would be divorced from Theresa Steyner. He would sue with all possible notoriety on the grounds of adultery. He no longer needed her.

The chauffeur drove him back to Johannesburg.

CHAPTER 61

It began on the floor of the Johannesburg Stock Exchange.

For some months nearly all the activity had been in the industrial counters, centring about the Alex Sagov group of companies and their merger negotiations.

The only spark of life in the mining and mining financials had been Anglo American Corporation and De Beers Deferred rights issues, but this was now old news and the prices had settled at their new levels. So it was that nobody was expecting fireworks when the call over of the gold mining counters began. The brokers' clerks crowding the floor were quietly spoken and behaved, when the first squib popped.

'Buy Sonder Ditch,' from one end of the hall.

'Buy Sonder Ditch,' a voice raised.

'Buy!' The throng stirred, heads turned.

'Buy.' The brokers suddenly agitated swirled in little knots, broke and reformed as transactions were completed. The price jumped fifty cents, and a broker ran from the floor to confer with his principal.

Here a broker thumped another on the back to gain his attention, and his urgency was infectious.

'Buy! Buy!'

'What the hell's happening?'

'Where is the buying coming from?'

'It's local!'

The price hit ten Rand a share, and then the panic began in earnest.

'It's overseas buying.'

'Eleven Rand!'

Brokers rushed to telephone warnings to favoured clients that a bull run was developing.

'Twelve fifty. It's only local buying.'

'Buy at best. Buy five thousand.'

Clerks raced back onto the floor carrying the hastily telephoned instructions, and plunged into the hysterical trading.

'Jesus Christ! Thirteen Rand, sell now. Take your profit! It can't go much higher.'

'Thirteen seventy five, it's overseas buying. Buy at best.'

In fifty brokers' offices around the country, the professionals who spent their lives hovering over the tickers regained their balance and, cursing themselves for having been taken unawares, they scrambled onto the bull wagon. Others, the more canny ones, recognized the makings of a sick run and off-loaded their holdings, selling industrial shares as well as mining shares. Prices ran amok.

At ten-fifteen there was a priority call from the offices of the Minister of Finance in Pretoria to the office of the President of the Johannesburg Stock Exchange.

'What are you going to do?'

'We haven't decided. We won't close the floor if we can possibly help it.'

'Don't let it go too far. Keep me informed.'

Sixteen Rand and still spiralling when at eleven o'clock South African time, the London Stock Exchange came in. For the first fifteen wild minutes the price of Sonder Ditch gold mining rocketed in sympathy with the Johannesburg market.

Then suddenly and unexpectedly the Sonder Ditch shares ran head-on into massive selling pressure. Not only the Sonder Ditch, but all the Kitchenerville gold mining companies staggered as the pressure increased. The prices wavered, rallied a few shillings and then fell back, wavered again, and then crashed downwards, plummeting far below their opening prices.

'Sell!' was the cry. 'Sell at best!' Within minutes freshly-made paper fortunes were wiped away.

When the price of the Sonder Ditch gold mining shares fell to five Rand seventy-five cents, the committee of the Johannesburg Stock Exchange closed the floor in the interests of the national welfare, preventing further trading.

But in New York, Paris and London the investing public continued to beat South African gold mining shares to death.

In the air-conditioned office of a skyscraper building, the little bald-headed man was smashing his balled fist onto the desk top of his superior officer.

'I told you not to trust him,' he was almost sobbing with anger. 'The fat greedy slug. One million dollars wasn't enough for him! No, he had to blow the whole deal!'

'Please, Colonel,' his chief intervened. 'Control yourself. Let us make a fair and objective appraisal of this financial activity.'

The bald-headed man sank back into his chair, and tried to light a cigarette with hands that trembled so violently as to extinguish the flame of his lighter.

'It sticks out a mile.' He flicked the lighter again, and puffed quickly. 'The first activity on the Johannesburg Exchange was Dr Steyner being clever. Buying up shares on the strength of our dummy report. That was quite natural and we expected it, in fact we wanted that to happen. It took suspicion away from us.' His cigarette had gone out, the tip was wet with spit. He threw it away and lit another.

'Fine! Everything was fine up to then. Dr Steyner had committed financial suicide, and we were on the pig's back.' He sucked at his new cigarette. 'Then! Then our fat friend pulls the big double-cross and starts selling the Kitchenerville shares short. He must have gone into the market for millions.'

'Can we abort the operation at this late date?' his chief asked.

'Not a chance.' The bald head shook vigorously. 'I have sent a cable to our fat friend, ordering him to freeze the work on the tunnel but can you imagine him obeying that order? He is financially committed for millions of dollars and he will protect that investment with every means at his disposal.'

'Could we not warn the management of the Sonder Ditch company?'

'That would put the finger squarely on us, would it not?'

'Hmm!' the chief nodded. 'We could send them an anonymous warning.'

'Who would put any credence on that?'

'You're right,' the chief sighed. 'We will just have to batten down our hatches and ride out the storm. Sit tight and deny everything.'

'That is all we can do.' The cigarette had gone out again, and there were bits of wet tobacco in his moustache. The little man flicked his lighter.

'The bastard, the fat, greedy bastard!' he muttered.

172

CHAPTER 62

Johnny and Big King rode up shoulder to shoulder in the cage. It had been a good shift. Despite the hardness of the Serpentine rock that cut down the drilling rate by fifty per cent, they had been able to get in five blasts that day. Johnny reckoned they had driven more than half-way through the Big Dipper. There was no night shift working now. Campbell had gone back to the stopes, so the honour of holing through would be Johnny's. He was excited at the prospect. Tomorrow he would be through into the unknown.

'Until tomorrow, Big King,' he said as they reached the surface and stepped out of the cage.

They separated, Big King heading for the Bantu hostel, Johnny to the glistening new Mustang in the car park.

Big King went straight to the Shangaan Induna's cottage without changing from his working clothes. He stood in the doorway and the Induna looked up from the letter he was writing.

'What news, my father?' Big King asked.

'The worst,' the Induna told him softly. 'The police have taken Crooked Leg.'

'Crooked Leg would not betray me,' Big King declared, but without conviction.

'Would you expect him to die in your place?' asked the Induna. 'He must protect himself.'

'I did not mean to kill him,' Big King explained miserably. 'I did not mean to kill the Portuguese, it was the gun.'

'I know, my son.' The Induna's voice was husky with helpless pity.

Big King turned from the doorway and walked down across the lawns to the ablution block. The spring and swagger had gone from his step. He walked listlessly, slouching, dragging his feet.

CHAPTER 63

Manfred Steyner sat at his desk. His hands lay on the blotter before him, one thumb wearing a turban of crisp white bandage. His only movement was the steady beat of a pulse in his throat and a nerve that fluttered in one eyelid. He was deathly pale, and a light sheen of perspiration gave his features the look of having been sculptured from washed marble.

The volume of the radio was turned high, so the voice of the announcer boomed and reverberated from the panelled walls.

'The climax of the drama was reached at eleven forty-five South African time when the President of the Johannesburg Stock Exchange declared the floor closed and all further trading suspended.

'Latest reports from the Tokyo Stock Exchange are that Sonder Ditch gold mining shares were being traded at the equivalent of four Rand forty cents. This compares with the morning's opening price of the same share on the Johannesburg Stock Exchange of nine Rand forty-five cents.

'A spokesman for the South African Government stated that although no reason for these extraordinary price fluctuations was apparent, the Minister of Mines, Dr Carel De Wet, had ordered a full-scale commission of enquiry.'

Manfred Steyner stood up from his desk and went through into the bathroom. With his flair for figures he did not need pen and paper to compute that the shares he had purchased that morning had depreciated in value by well over one million Rand at the close of business that evening.

He knelt on the tiled floor in front of the toilet bowl and vomited.

CHAPTER 64

The sky was darkening rapidly, for the sun had long ago sunk below a blazing horizon.

Rod heard the whisper of wings, and strained his eyes upwards into the gloom. They came in fast, in vee-formation, slanting down towards the pool of the river. He stood up from the blind and swung the shotgun on them, leading well ahead of the line of flight.

He squeezed off both barrels, Wham! Wham! And the duck broke formation and rocketed upwards, whirring aloft on noisy wings.

'Damn it!' said Rod.

'What's wrong, dead-eye Dick, did you miss?' asked Terry.

'The light's too bad.'

'Excuses! Excuses!' Terry stood up beside him, and Rod pushed a balled fist lightly against her cheek.

'That's enough from you, woman. Let's go home.'

Carrying the shotguns and bunches of dead duck, they trudged along the bank in the dusk to the waiting Landrover.

It was completely dark as they drove back to the lodge.

'What a wonderful day it's been,' Terry murmured dreamily. 'If for nothing else, I will always be grateful to you for teaching me how to enjoy my life.'

Back at the lodge, they bathed and changed into fresh clothes. For dinner they had wild duck and pineapple, with salads from Mrs Fat Hans' vegetable garden. Afterwards, they sprawled on the leopard-skin rugs in front of the fireplace and watched the log fire without talking, relaxed and happy and tired.

'My God, it's almost nine o'clock,' Terry checked her wristwatch. 'I fancy a bit of bed myself, how about you, Mr Ironsides?'

'Let's hear the nine o'clock news first.'

'Oh Rod! Nobody ever listens to the news here. This is fairyland!'

Rod switched on the radio and the first word froze them both. It was 'Sonder Ditch'.

In horrified silence they listened to the full report. Rod's expression was granite hard, his mouth a tight grim line. When the news report ended, Rod switched off the radio set and lit a cigarette.

'There is trouble,' he said. 'Big trouble. I'm sorry, Terry, we must go back. As soon as possible. I have to get back to the mine.'

'I know,' Terry agreed immediately. 'But Rod, I can't take off from this landing-strip in the dark. There is no flare path.'

'We'll leave at first light.'

Rod slept very little that night. Whenever she woke, Terry sensed him lying unsleeping, worrying. Twice she heard him get up and go to the bathroom.

In the very early hours of the morning she woke from her own troubled sleep and saw him silhouetted against the starlit window. He was smoking a cigarette and staring out into the darkness. It was the first night they had spent together without making love. In the dawn Rod was haggard and puffy-eyed.

They were airborne at eight o'clock and they landed in Johannesburg a little after ten.

Rod went straight to the telephone in Hank's office and Lily Jordan answered his call.

'Miss Jordan, what the hell is happening? Is everything all right?'

'Is that you, Mr Ironsides. Oh! Thank God! Thank God you've come, something terrible has happened!'

CHAPTER 65

Johnny Delange blew the face of the drive twice before nine o'clock, cutting thirty feet further into the glassy green dyke.

He had found that by drilling his cutter blast holes an additional three feet deeper, he could achieve a shatter effect on the serpentine rock which more than compensated for the additional drilling time. This next blast he was going to flout standard regulations and experiment with double charging his cutter holes. He would need additional explosives.

'Big King,' he shouted to make himself heard above the roar of drills. 'Take a gang back to the shaft station. Pick up six cases of Dynagel.'

He watched Big King and his gang retreat back down the drive, and then he lit a cigarette and turned his attention to his machine boys. They were poised before the rock face, sweating behind their drills. The dark rock of the dyke absorbed the light from the overhead electric bulbs. It made the end of the drive a gloomy place, filled with a sense of foreboding.

Johnny began to think about Davy. He was aware suddenly of a sense of disquiet, and he moved restlessly. He felt the hair on his forearms come slowly erect, each on a separate goose pimple. *Davy is here.* He knew it suddenly, and surely. His flesh crawled and he went cold with dread. He turned quickly and looked over his shoulder. The tunnel behind him was deserted, and Johnny gave a sickly grin.

'Shaya, madoda,' he called loudly and unnecessarily to his gang. They could not hear him above the roar of the drills, but the sound of his own voice helped reassure him.

Yet the creepy sensation was still with him. He felt that Davy was still there, trying to tell him something.

Johnny fought the sensation. He walked quickly forward, standing close to his machine boys, as though to draw comfort from their physical presence. It did not help. His nerves were shrieking now, and he felt himself beginning to sweat.

Suddenly the machine boy who was drilling the cutter hole in the centre of the face staggered backwards.

'Hey!' Johnny shouted at him, then he saw that water was spurting in fine needle jets from around the drill steel. Something was squeezing the drill steel out of its hole, like toothpaste out of a tube. It was pushing the machine boy backwards.

'Hey!' Johnny started forward and at that instant the heavy metal drill was fired out of the rock with the force of a cannon ball. It decapitated the machine boy, tearing his head from his body with such savagery that his carcass was thrown far back down the drive, his blood spraying the dark rock walls.

From the drill hole shot a solid jet of water. It came out under such pressure that when it caught the machine boy's assistant in the chest it stove in his ribs as though he had been hit by a speeding automobile.

'Out!' yelled Johnny. 'Get out!' And the rock face exploded. It blew outwards with greater force than if it had been blasted with Dynagel. It killed Johnny Delange instantly. He was smashed to a bloody pulp by the flying rock. It killed every man in his gang with him, and immediately afterwards the monstrous burst of water that poured from the face picked up their mutilated remains and swept them down the drive.

Big King was at the shaft station when they heard the water coming. It sounded like an express train in a tunnel, a dull bellow of irresistible power. The water was pushing the air from the drive ahead of it, so that a hurricane of wind came roaring from the mouth of the drive, blowing out a cloud of dust and loose rubbish.

Big King and his gang stood and stared in uncomprehending terror until the head of the column of water shot from the drive, frothing solid, carrying with it a plug of debris and human remains.

Bursting into the T-junction of the main 66 level haulage, the strength of the flood was reduced, yet still it swept down towards the lift station in a waist deep wall.

'This way!' Big King was the first to move. He leapt for the steel emergency ladder that led up to the level above. The rest of his gang were not fast enough, the water picked them up and crushed them against the steel-mesh barrier that guarded the shaft. The crest of the wave burst around Big King's legs, sucking at him, but he tore himself from its grip and climbed to safety.

Beneath him the water poured into the shaft like bath water into a plug hole, forming a spinning whirlpool about the collar as it roared down to flood the workings below 66 level.

CHAPTER 66

Leaving Terry at the airfield to solicit transport from Hank, the mechanic, Rod drove directly to the head of No. 1 shaft of the Sonder Ditch. He jumped from the Volkswagen into the clamouring crowd clustered above the shaft head.

Dimitri was wide-eyed and distracted, beside him Big King towered like a black colossus.

'What happened?' Rod demanded.

'Tell him,' Dimitri instructed Big King.

'I was at the shaft with my gang. A river leaped from the mouth of the drive, a great river of water running faster than the Zambesi in flood; roaring like a lion the water ate all the men with me. I alone climbed above it.'

'We've hit a big one, Rod,' Dimitri interrupted. 'It's pouring in fast. We calculate it will flood the entire workings up to 66 level in four hours from now.'

'Have you cleared the mine?' Rod demanded.

'All the men are out except Delange and his gang. They were in the drive. They've been chopped, I'm afraid,' Dimitri answered.

'Have you warned the other mines we could have a burst through into their workings?'

'Yes, they are pulling all their shifts out.'

'Right.' Rod set off for the blast control room with Dimitri trotting to keep up with him. 'Give me your keys, and find the foreman electrician.'

Within minutes the three of them were crowded into the tiny concrete control room.

'Check in the special circuit,' Rod instructed. 'I'm going to shoot the drop-blast matt and seal off the drive.'

The foreman electrician worked quickly at the control panel. He looked up at Rod.

'Ready!' he said.

'Check her in,' Rod nodded.

The foreman threw the switch. The three of them caught their breath together.

Dimitri said it for them: 'Red!'

On the control panel of the special circuit the red bulb glared balefully at them, the Cyclops eye of the god of despair.

'Christ!' swore the foreman. 'The circuit is shot. The water must have torn the wires out.'

'It may be a fault in the board.'

'No.' The foreman shook his head with certainty.

'We've had it,' whispered Dimitri. 'Goodbye the Sonder Ditch!'

Rod burst out of the blast control room into the expectant crowd outside.

'Johnson!' He singled out one of his mine captains. 'Go down to the Yacht Club at the dam, get me the rubber rescue dinghy. Quick as you can, man.'

The man scurried away, and Rod turned on the electrician foreman as he emerged from the control room.

'Get me a battery hand-operated blaster, a reel of wire, pliers, gloves, two coils of nylon rope. Hurry!'

The foreman went.

'Rod.' Dimitri caught his arm. 'What are you going to do?'

'I'm going down there. I'm going to find the break in the circuit and I'm going to blast her by hand.'

'Jesus!' Dimitri gasped. 'You are crazy, Rod. You'll kill yourself for sure!'

Rod completely ignored his protest.

'I want one man with me. A strong man. The strongest there is. We will have to drag the dinghy against the flood.' Rod looked about him. Big King was standing by the banksman's office. The two of them were tall enough to face each other over the heads of the men between them.

'Will you come with me, Big King?' Rod asked.

'Yes,' said Big King.

CHAPTER 67

In less than twenty minutes they were ready. Rod and Big King were stripped down to singlets and bathing-trunks. They wore canvas tennis shoes to protect their feet, and the hard helmets on their heads were incongruous against the rest of their attire.

The rubber dinghy was ex-naval disposal. A nine-foot air-filled mattress, so light that a man could lift it with one hand. Into it was packed the equipment they would need for the task ahead. A water-proof bag contained the battery blaster, the reel of insulated wire, the pliers, gloves and a spare lantern. Lashed to the eyelets along the sides of the dinghy were two coils of light nylon rope, a small crowbar, an axe and a razor-sharp machete in a leather sheath. To the bows of the dinghy were fastened a pair of looped nylon towing lines.

'What else will you need, Rod?' Dimitri asked.

Rod shook his head thoughtfully. 'That's it, Dimitri. That should do it.'

'Right!' Dimitri beckoned and four men came forward and carried the dinghy into the waiting cage.

'Let's go,' said Dimitri and followed the dinghy into the cage. Big King went next and Rod paused a second to look up at the sky. It was very blue and bright.

Before the onsetter could close the shutter door, a Silver Cloud Rolls Royce came gliding onto the bank. From the rear door emerged first Hurry Hirschfeld and then Terry Steyner.

'Ironsides!' roared Hurry. 'What the hell is going on?'

'We've hit water,' Rod answered him from the cage.

'Water? Where did it come from?'

'Beyond the Big Dipper.'

'You drove through the Big Dipper?'

'Yes.'

'You bastard, you've drowned the Sonder Ditch,' roared Hurry, advancing on the cage.

'Not yet, I haven't,' Rod contradicted.

'Rod.' Terry was white-faced beside her grandfather. 'You can't go down there.' She started forward.

Rod pushed the onsetter aside and pulled down the steel shutter door of the cage. Terry threw herself against the steel mesh of the guard barrier, but the cage was gone into the earth.

'Rod,' she whispered, and Hurry Hirschfeld put his arm around her shoulders and led her to the Rolls Royce.

From the back seat of the Rolls, Hurry Hirschfeld was conducting a Kangaroo Court Trial of Rodney Ironsides. One by one he called for the line managers of the Sonder Ditch and questioned them. Even those who were loyal to Rod could say little in his defence, and there were others who took the opportunity to level scores with Rodney Ironsides.

Sitting beside her grandfather, Terry heard such a condemnation of the man she loved as to chill her to the depths of her soul. There was no doubt that Rodney Ironsides, without Head Office sanction, had instituted a new development so risky and contrary to Company policy as to be criminal in concept.

'Why did he do it?' muttered Hurry Hirschfeld. He seemed bewildered. 'What could he possibly achieve by driving through the Big Dipper. It looks like a deliberate attempt to sabotage the Sonder Ditch.' Hurry's anger began to seethe within him. 'The bastard! He has drowned the Sonder Ditch and killed dozens of men.' He punched his fist into the palm of his hand. 'I'll make him pay for this. I'll break him, so help me God, I'll smash him! I'll bring criminal charges against him. Malicious damage to property. Manslaughter. Culpable homicide! By Jesus, I'll have his guts for this!'

Listening to Hurry ranting and threatening, Terry could keep silent no longer.

'It wasn't his fault, Pops. Truly it wasn't. He was forced to do it.'

'Ha!' snorted Hurry. 'I heard you at the pithead a few minutes ago. Just what is this man to you, Missy, that you spring to his defence so nobly?'

'Pops, please believe me.' Her eyes were enormous in her pale face.

'Why should I believe you? The two of you are obviously up to mischief together. Naturally you will try and protect him.'

'Listen to me at least,' she pleaded, and Hurry checked the run of his tongue and breathing heavily he turned to face her.

'This better be good, young lady,' he warned her.

In her agitation she told it badly, and half-way through she realized that she wan't even convincing herself. Hurry's expression became more and more bleak, until he interrupted her impatiently.

'Good God, Theresa, this isn't like you. To try and put the blame for this onto your own husband! That's despicable! To try and switch the blame for this . . .'

'It's true! As God is my witness.' Terry was almost in tears, she was tugging at Hurry's sleeve in her agitation. 'Rod was forced to do it. He had no option.'

'You have proof of this?' Hurry asked drily, and Terry fell silent, staring at him dumbly. What proof was there?

CHAPTER 68

The cage checked and slowed as it approached 65 level. The lights were still burning, but the workings were deserted. They lugged the dinghy out onto the station.

They could hear the dull waterfall roar of the flood on the level below them. The displacement of huge volumes of water disturbed the air so that a strong cool breeze was blowing up the shaft.

'Big King and I will go down the emergency ladder. You will lower the dinghy to us afterwards,' Rod told Dimitri. 'Make sure all the equipment is tied into it.'

'Right.' Dimitri nodded.

All was in readiness. The men who had come down with them in the cage were waiting expectantly. Rod could find no reason for further delay. He felt something cold and heavy settle in his guts.

'Come on, Big King.' And he went to the steel ladder.

'Good luck, Rod.' Dimitri's voice floated down to him, but Rod saved his breath for that cold dark climb downwards.

All the lights had fused on 66 level, and in the beam of his lamp the water below him was black and agitated. It poured into the mouth of the shaft, bending the mesh barrier inwards. The mesh acted as a gigantic sieve, straining the floating rubbish from the flood. Among the timber and planking, the sodden sacking and unrecognizable objects, Rod made out the waterlogged corpses of the dead pressed against the wire.

He climbed down and gingerly lowered himself into the water. Instantly it dragged at his lower body, shocking in its power. It was waist deep here, but he found that by bracing his body against the steel ladder he could maintain his footing.

Big King climbed down beside him, and Rod had to raise his voice above the hissing thunder of water.

'All right?'

'Yes. Let them send down the boat.'

Rod flashed his lamp up the shaft, and within minutes the dinghy was swaying slowly down to them. They reached up and guided it right side up to the surface of the water, before untying the rope.

The dinghy was sucked firmly against the wire mesh, and Rod checked its contents quickly. All was secure.

'Right.' Rod tied a bight of the nylon rope around his waist, and climbed up the wire mesh barrier until he could reach the roof of the tunnel. Behind him Big King was paying out the nylon line.

Rod leaned out until he could get his hands on the compressed air pipes that ran along the roof of the tunnel. The pipes were as thick as a man's wrist, bolted securely into the hanging wall of the drive and they would support a man's weight with ease. Rod settled his grip firmly on the piping and then kicked his feet free from the barrier. He hung above the rushing waters, his feet just brushing the surface.

Hand over hand, swinging forward with his feet dangling, he started up the tunnel. The nylon rope hung down behind him like a long white tail. It was three hundred feet to where the water boiled from the drive into the main haulage, and Rod's shoulder muscles were shrieking in protest before he reached it. It seemed that his arms were being wrenched from their sockets, for the weight of the nylon rope that was dragging in the water was fast becoming intolerable.

There was a back eddy in the angle formed by the drive and the haulage. Here the flood swirled in a vortex, and Rod lowered himself slowly into it. The water buffeted him, but again he was able to cower against the side wall of the haulage and hold his footing. Quickly he began tying the rope onto the rawlbolts that were driven into the side-wall to consolidate the rock. Within minutes he had established a secure base from which to operate, and when he flashed his lamp back down the haulage he saw Big King following him along the compressed air piping.

Big King dropped into the waist deep water beside Rod, and they gripped the nylon rope and rested their burning arm muscles.

'Ready?' asked Rod at last, and Big King nodded.

They laid hold of the rope that led back to the dinghy and hauled upon it. For a moment nothing happened, the other end might just as well have been anchored to a mountain.

'Together!' grunted Rod, and they recovered a foot of rope.

'Again!' And they drew the dinghy inch by inch up the haulage against the rush of water.

Their hands were bleeding when they at last pulled the laden dinghy up to their own position and anchored it to the rawlbolts beside them. It bounced and bobbed with the water drumming against its underside.

Neither Rod nor Big King could talk. They hung exhausted on the body lines with the water ripping at their skin and gasped for breath.

At last Rod looked up at Big King, and in the lamp light he saw his own doubts reflected in Big King's eyes. The drop-blast matt was a thousand feet up the drive. The strength and speed of the water in the drive was almost double what it was in the haulage. Could they ever fight their way against such primeval forces as these that were now unleashed about them?

'I will go next,' Big King said and Rod nodded his agreement.

The huge Bantu drew himself up the rope until he could reach the compressed air pipe. His skin in the lamplight glistened like that of a porpoise. Hand over hand he disappeared into the gaping black maw of the drive. His lamp threw deformed and monstrous shadows upon the walls of rock.

When Big King's lamp flashed the signal to him, Rod climbed up to the pipe and followed him into the drive. Three hundred feet later he found Big King had established another base. But here they were exposed to the full force of the flood, and they were pulled so violently against the body lines that the harsh nylon seared the skin from their bodies. Together they dragged the dinghy up to them and anchored it.

Rod was sobbing softly as he held his torn hands to his chest and wondered if he could do it again.

Ready?' Big King asked beside him, and Rod nodded. He reached up and placed the raw flesh of his palms onto the metal piping, and felt the tears of pain flood his eyes. He blinked them back and dragged himself forward.

Vaguely he realized that should he fall, he was a dead man. The flood would sweep him away, dragging him along the jagged side walls of the drive, ripping his flesh from the bone, and finally hurling him against the mesh surrounding the shaft to crush the life from his body.

He went on until he knew he could go no farther. Then he selected a rawlbolt in the side wall and looped the rope through it. And they repeated the whole heart-breaking procedure. Twice as he strained against the dinghy rope Rod saw his vision explode into stars and pinwheels. Each time he dragged himself back from the drink of unconsciousness by sheer force of will.

The example that Big King was setting was the inspiration which kept Rod from failing. Big King worked without change of expression, but his eyes were bloodshot with exertion. Only once Rod heard him grunt like a gut-shot lion, and there was bright blood on the rope where he touched it.

Rod knew he could not give in while Big King held on.

Reality dissolved slowly into a dark roaring nightmare of pain, wherein muscles and bone were loaded beyond all endurance, and yet continued to function. It seemed that for all time Rod had hung on arms that were leadened and slow with exhaustion. He was inching his way along the compressed air pipe for yet another advance up the drive. Sweat running into his eyes was blurring his vision, so at first he did not credit what he saw ahead of him in the darkness.

He shook his head to clear his eyes, and then squinted along the beam of his lamp. A heavy timber structure was hanging drunkenly from the roof of the drive. The bolts that held it were resisting the efforts of the water to tear it loose.

Rod realized abruptly that this was what remained of the frame which had held the ventilation doors. The doors were gone, ripped away, but the frame was still in position. He knew that just beyond the ventilation doors the drop-blast matt began. They had reached it!

New strength flowed into his body and he swung forward along the pipe. The timber frame made a fine anchor point and Rod secured the rope to it, and flashed back the signal to Big King. He hung in the loop of rope and rested awhile, then he forced himself to take an interest in his surroundings. He played the beam over the distorted timber frame and saw instantly why the blasting circuit had been broken.

In the lamp light the distinctive green plastic-coated blasting cable hung in festoons from the roof of the drive; clearly it had become entangled in the ventilation doors and been severed when they were ripped away. The loose end of the cable dangled to the surface of the racing water. Rod fastened his eyes on it, drawing comfort and strength from the knowledge that they would not have to continue their agonized journey down the drive.

When Big King came up out of the gloom, Rod indicated the dangling cable.

'There!' he gasped, and Big King narrowed his eyes in acknowledgement; he was unable to speak.

It was five minutes before they could commence the excruciating business of hauling the dinghy up and securing it to the door frame.

Again they rested. Their movements were slowing up drastically. Neither of them had much strength left to draw upon.

'Get hold of the end of the cable,' Rod instructed Big King, and he dragged himself over the side of the dinghy and lay sprawled full-length on the floor boards.

His weight forced the dinghy deeper, increasing its resistance to the racing water, and the rope strained against the wooden frame. Rod began clumsily to unpack the battery blaster. Big King stood waist-deep clinging with one arm to the wooden frame, reaching forward with the other towards the end of the green-coated cable. It danced just beyond his finger tips, and he edged forward against the current, steadying himself against the timber frame, placing a greater strain on the retaining bolts.

His fingers closed on the cable and with a grunt of satisfaction he passed it back to Rod.

Working with painstaking deliberation, Rod connected the crocodile clips from the reel of wire to the loose end of the green cable. Rod's plan was for both he and Big King to climb aboard the dinghy and, paying out the nylon rope, let themselves be carried back down the drive. At the same time they would be letting the wire run from its reel. At a safe distance they would fire the drop-blast matt.

Rod's fingers were swollen and numbed. The minutes passed as he completed his preparations and all that while the strain on the wooden frame was heavy and consistent.

Rod looked up from his task, and crawled to his knees.

'All right, Big King,' he wheezed as he knelt in the bows of the dinghy and gripped the wooden frame to steady the dinghy. 'Come aboard. We are ready.'

Big King waded forward and at that instant the retaining bolts on one side of the heavy timber frame gave way. With a rending, tearing sound the frame slewed across the tunnel. The beams of timber crossed each other like the blades of a pair of gigantic scissors. Both Rod's arms were between the beams. The bones in his forearms snapped with the loud crackle of breaking sticks.

With a scream of pain Rod collapsed onto the floorboards of the dinghy, his arms useless, sticking out at absurd angles from their shattered bones. Three feet away Big King was still in the water. His mouth was wide open, but no sound issued from his throat. He stood still as a black statue and his eyes bulged from their sockets. Even through his own suffering Rod was horrified by the expression on Big King's contorted features.

Below the surface of the water the bottom timber beams had performed the same scissor movement, but this time they had caught Big King's lower body between them. They had closed across his pelvis and crushed it. Now they held him in a vicelike grip from which it was not possible to shake them.

The white face and the black face were but a few feet apart. The two stricken companions in disaster, looked into each other's eyes and knew that there was no escape. They were doomed.

'My arms,' whispered Rod huskily. 'I cannot use them.' Big King's bulging eyes held Rod's gaze.

'Can you reach the blaster?' Rod whispered urgently. 'Take it and turn the handle. Burn it, Big King, burn it!'

Slow comprehension showed in Big King's pain-glazed eyes.

'We are finished, Big King. Let us go like men. Burn it, bring down the rock!'

Above them the rock was sown with explosive. The blaster was connected. In his agitation Rod tried to reach out for the blaster. His forearm swung loosely, the fingers hanging open like the petals of a dead flower, and the pain checked him.

'Get it, Big King,' Rod urged him, and Big King picked up the blaster and held it against his chest with one arm.

'The handle!' Rod encouraged him. 'Turn the handle!'

But instead Big King reached into the dinghy once more and drew the machete from its sheath.

'What are you doing?' Rod demanded, and in reply Big King swung the blade back over his shoulder and then brought it forward in a gleaming arc aimed at the nylon rope that held the dinghy anchored to the wooden frame. Clunk! The blade bit into the wood, severing the rope that was bound around it.

Freed by the stroke of the machete, the dinghy was whisked away by the current. Lying in the dancing rubber dinghy, Rod heard a bull voice bellow above the rush of the water.

'Go in peace, my friend.'

Then Rod was careening back along the drive, a hell ride during which the dinghy spun like a top and in the beam of his lamp the roof and walls melted into a dark racing blue as Rod lay maimed on the floor of the dinghy.

Then suddenly the air jarred against his ear drums, a long rolling concussion in the confines of the drive and he knew that Big King had fired the drop-blast matt. Rodney Ironsides slipped over the edge of consciousness into a soft warm dark place from which he hoped never to return.

CHAPTER 69

Dimitri squatted on his haunches above the shaft at 65 level. He was smoking his tenth cigarette. The rest of his men waited as impatiently as he did. Every few minutes Dimitri would cross to the shaft and flash his lamp down the hundred foot hole to 66 level.

'How long have they been gone,' he asked, and they all glanced at their watches.

'An hour and ten minutes.'

'No, an hour and fourteen minutes.'

'Christ, call me a liar for four minutes!'

And they lapsed into silence once more. Suddenly the station telephone shrilled, and Dimitri jumped up and ran to it.

'No, Mr Hirschfeld, nothing yet!'

He listened a moment.

'All right, send him down then.'

He hung up the telephone, and his men looked at him inquiringly.

'They are sending down a policeman,' he explained.

'What the hell for?'

'They want Big King.'

'Why?'

'Warrant of arrest for murder.'

'Murder?'

'Ja, they reckon he murdered that Portuguese storekeeper.'

'Jeez!'

'Big King, is that so!' Delighted to have found something to pass the time, they fell into an animated debate.

The police inspector arrived in the cage at 65 level, but he was disappointing. He looked like a down-at-heel undertaker, and he replied to their eager questions with a sorrowful stare that left them stuttering.

For the fifteenth time Dimitri went to the shaft and peered down into it. The blast shook the earth around them, a long rumbling that persisted for many seconds.

'They've done it!' yelled Dimitri, and began to caper wildly. His men leapt to their feet and began beating each other on the back, shouting and laughing. The police inspector alone took no part in the celebrations.

'Wait,' yelled Dimitri at last. 'Shut up all of you! Shut up! Damn it! Listen!'

They fell silent.

'What is it?' someone asked. 'I can't hear anything.'

'That's just it!' exulted Dimitri. 'The water! It has stopped!'

Only then did they become aware that the dull roar of water to which their ears had become resigned was now ended. It was quiet; a cathedral hush lay upon the workings. They began to cheer, their voices thin in the silence, and Dimitri ran to the steel ladder and swarmed down it like a monkey.

From thirty feet up Dimitri saw the dinghy marooned among the filth and debris around the shaft. He recognized the crumpled figure lying in the bottom of it.

'Rod!' he was shouting before he reached the station at 66 level. 'Rod, are you all right?'

The floor of the haulage was wet, and here and there a trickle of water still snaked towards the shaft. Dimitri ran to the stranded dinghy and started to turn Rod onto his back. Then he saw his arms.

'Oh, Christ!' he gasped in horror, then he was yelling up the ladder. 'Get a stretcher down here.'

Rod regained consciousness to find himself covered with blankets and strapped securely into a mine stretcher. His arms were splinted and bandaged, and from the familiar rattle and rush of air he knew he was in the cage on the way to the surface.

He recognized Dimitri's voice raised argumentatively.

'Damn it! The man is unconscious and badly injured, can't you leave him alone?'

'I have my duty to perform,' a strange voice answered.

'What's he want, Dimitri?' Rod croaked.

'Rod, how are you?' At the sound of his voice Dimitri was kneeling beside the stretcher anxiously.

'Bloody awful,' Rod whispered. 'What does this joker want?'

'He's a police officer. He wants to arrest Big King for murder,' Dimitri explained.

'Well, he's a bit bloody late,' whispered Rod, and even through his pain this seemed to Rod to be terribly funny. He began to laugh. He sobbed with laughter, each convulsion sending bright bursts of pain along his arms. He was shaking uncontrollably with shock, sweat pouring from his face, and he was laughing wildly.

'He's a bit bloody late,' he repeated through his hysterical laughter as Dr Dan Stander pushed the hypodermic needle into his arm and shot him full of morphine.

CHAPTER 70

Hurry Hirschfeld stood in the main haulage on 66 level. There was bustle all around him. Already the crews from the cementation company were manhandling their equipment up towards the blocked drive.

These were specialists from an independent contracting company. They were about to begin pumping thousands of tons of liquid cement into the rock jam that sealed the drive. They would pump it in at pressures in excess of 3,000 pounds per square inch, and when that concrete set it would form a plug that would effectively seal off the drive for all time. It would also form a burial vault for the body of Big King, thought Hurry, a fitting monument to the man who had saved the Sonder Ditch.

He would arrange to have a commemorative plaque placed on the outer wall of the cement plug with a suitable inscription describing the man and the deed.

The man's dependants must be properly taken care of, perhaps they could be flown down for the unveiling of the plaque. Anyway he could leave that to Public Relations and Personnel.

The haulage stank of wetness and mud. It was dank and clammy cool, and it would not improve his lumbago. Hurry had seen enough; he started back towards the shaft. Faintly he was aware of the muted clangour of the mighty pumps which in a few days would free the Sonder Ditch of the water that filled her lower levels.

The laden stretchers with their grisly blanket-covered burdens stood in a row under the hastily rigged electric lights along one wall of the tunnel. Hurry's expression hardened as he passed them.

'I'll have the guts of the man responsible for this,' he vowed silently as he waited for the cage.

———————————

Terry Steyner rode in the rear of the ambulance with Rod. She wiped the mud from his face.

'How bad is it, Dan?' she asked.

'Hell, Terry, he'll be up and about in a few days. The arms of course are not very pretty, that's why I'm taking him directly to Johannesburg. I want a specialist orthopaedic surgeon to set them. Apart from that he is suffering from shock pretty badly and his hands are superficially lacerated. But he will be fine.'

Dan watched curiously as Terry fussed ineffectually with the damp hair of the drugged man.

'You want a smoke?' he asked.

'Light me one, please, Dan.'

He passed her the cigarette.

'I didn't know that you and Rod were so friendly,' he ventured.

Terry looked up at him quickly.

'How very delicate you are, Dr Stander,' she mocked him.

'None of my business, of course.' Hurriedly Dan withdrew.

'Don't be silly, Dan. You're a good friend of Rod's and Joy is of mine. You two are entitled to know. I am desperately, crazily in love with this big hunk. I intend divorcing Manfred just as soon as possible.'

'Is Rod going to marry you?'

'He hasn't said anything about marriage but I'll sure as hell start working on him,' Terry grinned, and Dan laughed.

'Good luck to you both, then. I'm sure Rod will be able to get another job.'

'What do you mean?' Terry demanded.

'They say your grandfather is threatening to fire him so high he'll be the first man on the moon.'

Terry relapsed into silence. Proof was what Pops had asked for, but what proof was there?

'They'll be waiting on the X-Ray reports.' Joy Allbright gave her opinion. Since her engagement to Dan, Joy had suddenly become something of a medical expert. She had rushed down to the Johannesburg Central Hospital at Dan's hurried telephonic request. Dan wanted her to keep Terry company while she waited for Rod to come out of emergency. They sat together in the waiting-room.

'I expect so,' Terry agreed. Something Joy had just said had jolted in her mind, something she must remember.

'It takes them twenty minutes or so to expose the plates and develop them. Then the radiologist has to examine the plates and make his report to the surgeon.'

There, Joy had said it again. Terry sat up straight and concentrated on what Joy had said. Which word had disturbed her?

Suddenly she had it.

'The report!' she exclaimed. 'That's it! The report, that's the proof.'

She leapt out of her chair.

'Joy! Give me the keys of your car,' she demanded.

'What on earth?' Joy looked startled.

'I can't explain now. I have to get home to Sandown urgently, give me your keys. I'll explain later.'

Joy fished in her handbag and produced a leather key folder. Terry snatched it from her.

'Where are you parked?' Terry demanded.

'In the car park, near the main gate.'

'Thanks, Joy.' Terry dashed from the waiting-room, her high heels clattering down the passage.

'Crazy woman.' Joy looked after her, bewildered.

Ten minutes later Dan looked into the waiting-room.

'Rod's fine now. Where's Terry?'

'She went mad—' And Joy explained her abrupt departure. Dan looked grave.

'I think we'd better follow her, Joy.'

'I think you're right, darling.'
'I'll just grab my coat,' said Dan.

————————————

There was only one place where Manfred would keep the geological report on the Big Dipper that Rod had told her about. That was in the safe deposit behind the panelling in his study. Because her jewellery was kept in the same safe, Terry had a key and the combination to the lock.

Even in Joy's Alfa Romeo, taking liberties with the traffic regulations, it was a thirty-five minute drive out to Sandown. It was after five in the evening when Terry coasted down the long driveway and parked before the garages.

The extensive grounds were deserted, for the gardeners finished at five, and there was no sign of life from the house. This was as it should be, for she knew Manfred was still in Europe. He was not due back for at least another four days.

Leaving the ignition keys in the Alfa, Terry ran up the pathway and onto the stoep. She fumbled in her handbag and found the keys to the front door. She let herself in, and went directly to Manfred's study. She slid the concealing panel aside and set about the lengthy business of opening the steel safe. It required both key and combination to activate the mechanism, and Terry had never developed much expertise at tumbling the combination.

Finally, however, the door swung open and she was confronted by the voluminous contents. Terry began removing the various documents and files, examining each one and then stacking them neatly on the floor beside her.

She had no idea of the shape, size nor colour of the report for which she was searching, and it was ten minutes before she selected an unmarked folder and flicked open the cover. 'Confidential Report on the geological formations of the Kitchenerville gold fields, with special reference to those areas lying to the east of the Big Dipper Dyke.'

Terry felt a wonderful lift of relief as she read the titling, for she had begun doubting that the report was here. Quickly she thumbed through the pages and began reading at random. There was no doubt.

'This is it!' she exclaimed aloud.

'*I'll take that, thank you.*' The dreaded familiar voice cut into her preoccupation, and Terry spun around and came to her feet in one movement, clutching the file protectively to her breast. She backed away from the man who stood in the doorway.

She hardly recognized her own husband. She had never seen him like this. Manfred was coatless, and his shirt was without collar or stud. He appeared to have slept in his trousers, for they were rumpled and baggy. There was a yellow stain down the front of his white shirt.

His scanty brown hair was dishevelled, hanging forward wispily onto his forehead. He had not shaved, and the skin around his eyes was discoloured and puffy.

'Give that to me.' He came towards her with hand outstretched.

'Manfred.' She kept moving away from him. 'What are you doing here? When did you get back?'

'Give it to me, you slut.'

'Why do you call me that?' She asked, trying for time.

'Slut!' he repeated, and lunged towards her. Terry whirled away from him lightly.

She ran for the study door, with Manfred close behind her. She beat him into the passage and raced for the front door. Her heel caught in one of the Persian carpets that covered the floor of the passage, and she staggered and fell against the wall.

'Whore!' He was on her instantly trying to wrestle the report out of her hands, but she clung to it with all her strength. Face to face they were almost of a height, and she saw the madness in his eyes.

Suddenly Manfred released her. He stepped back, bunched his fist and swung it round-armed into her cheek. Her head jerked back and cracked against the wall. He drew back his fist and hit her again. She felt the quick warm burst of blood spurt from her nose, and staggered through the door beside her into the dining-room. She was dizzy from the blows and she fell against the heavy stinkwood table.

Manfred was close behind her. He charged her, sending her sprawling backwards onto the table. He was on top of her, both his hands at her throat.

'I'm going to kill you, you whore,' he wheezed. His thumbs hooked and pressed deep into the flesh of her throat. With the frenzied strength of despair, Terry clawed at his eyes with both hands. Her nails scored his face, raking long red lines into his flesh. With a cry Manfred released her, and backed away holding both hands to his injured face, leaving Terry lying gasping across the table.

He stood for a moment, then uncovered his face and inspected the blood on his hands.

'I'll kill you for that!'

But as he advanced towards her, Terry rolled over the table.

'Whore! Slut! Bitch!' he screamed at her, following her around the table. Terry kept ahead of him.

There were a matched pair of heavy Stuart crystal decanters on the sideboard, one containing port, the other sherry. Terry snatched up one of them and turned to face Manfred. She hurled the decanter with all her remaining strength at his head.

Manfred did not have time to duck. The decanter cracked against his forehead, and he fell backwards, stunned. Terry snatched up the report and ran out of the dining-room, down the passage, out of the front door and into the garden. She was running weakly, following the driveway towards the main road.

Then behind her she heard the engine of an automobile roar into life. Panting wildly, holding the report, she stopped and looked back. Manfred had followed her out of the house. He was behind the steering wheel of Joy's Alfa Romeo. As she watched he threw the car into gear and howled towards her, blue smoke burning from the rear tyres with the speed of the acceleration. His face behind the windscreen was white and streaked with the marks of her nails, his eyes were staring, insane, and she knew he was going to ride her down.

She kicked off her shoes and ran off the driveway onto the lawns.

Crouched forward in the driver's seat of the Alfa, Manfred watched the fleeing figure ahead of him.

Terry ran with the full-hipped sway of the mature woman; her long legs were tanned and her hair flew out loosely behind her.

Manfred was not concerned with the return of the geological report— its existence was no longer of significance to him. What he wanted was to destroy this woman completely. In his crazed state, she had become the symbol and the figurehead of all his woes. His humiliation and fall were all linked to her. He could exact his vengeance by destroying her, crushing that revolting warm and clinging body, bruising it, ripping it with the steel of the Alfa Romeo's chassis.

He hit second gear and spun the steering-wheel. The Alfa swerved from the driveway, and as its rear wheels left the tarmac, they skidded on the thick grass. Deftly Manfred checked the skid and lined up on Terry's running back.

Already she was among the protea bushes on the lower terrace. The Alfa buck-jumped the slope, flying bird-free before crashing down heavily on its suspension. Wheels spun and bit, and the sleek vehicle shot forward again.

Terry looked back over her shoulder; her face was white and her eyes very big and fear-filled. Manfred giggled. He was aware of a sense of power, the ability to dispense life or death. He steered for her, reckless of all consequences, intent on destroying her.

There was a six-foot tall protea bush ahead of him, and Manfred roared through it, bursting it asunder. Scattering branches and leaves, giggling again, he saw Terry directly ahead of him. She was still looking back at him, and at that moment she stumbled and fell onto her knees.

She was helpless, her face streaked with tears and blood, her hair falling forward in wild disorder, kneeling as though for the headsman's stroke. Manfred felt a flood of disappointment. He did not want it to end so soon, he wanted to savour this sadistic elation, this sense of power.

At the last possible moment he yanked the wheel over and the car slewed violently. It shot past Terry with six inches to spare, and its rear wheels pelted her with clods of turf and thrown dirt.

Laughing aloud, wild-eyed, Manfred held the wheel hard over, bringing the Alfa around in a tight skidding circle, crackling sideways through another protea bush.

Terry was up and running again. He saw immediately that she was heading for the changing rooms of the swimming-pool among the trees on the bottom lawn and she was far enough ahead to elude him, perhaps.

'Bitch!' he snarled, and crash-changed into third gear, with engine revs peaking. The Alfa howled in pursuit of the running girl.

Had Terry thrown the bulky report aside, she might have reached the brick changing rooms ahead of the racing sports car, but the report hampered and slowed her. She still had twenty yards to cover, she was running along the paved edge of the swimming-pool, and she sensed that the car was right on top of her.

Terry dived sideways, hitting the water flat on her side, and the Alfa roared past. Manfred trod heavily on the brakes, the Michelin metallic tyres screeched against the paving stones, and Manfred was out of the driver's seat the moment the Alfa stopped.

He ran back to the pool side. Terry was floundering towards the far steps. She was exhausted, weak with exertion and terror. Her sodden hair streamed down over her face, and she was gasping open-mouthed for air.

Manfred laughed again, a high-pitched, almost girlish giggle, and he dived after her, landing squarely between Terry's shoulder blades with his full weight. She went under, sucking water agonizingly into already aching lungs, and when she surfaced she was coughing and gagging, blinded with water and her own wet hair.

Almost immediately she felt herself seized from behind and forced face down into the water. For half a minute she struggled fiercely, then her movements slowed and became weaker.

Manfred stood over her, chest deep in the clear water, gripping her around the waist and by a handful of her sodden hair, forcing her face deep below the surface. He had lost his spectacles, and he blinked owlishly. The wet silk of his shirt clung to his upper body, and the water had slicked his hair down.

As he felt the life going out of her, and her movements becoming sluggish and slow, he began to laugh again. The broken, incoherent laughter of a madman.

'Dan!' Joy pointed through the trees. 'That's my car down there, parked by the swimming-pool!'

'What the hell is it doing there?'

'There's something wrong, Terry wouldn't drive through her beloved garden, unless there was!'

Dan braked sharply and pulled his Jaguar to the side of the driveway.

'I'm going to take a look.' He slid out of the car and started off across the lawns. Joy opened her own door and trotted after him.

Dan saw the man in the water, fully dressed, intent on what he was doing. He recognized Manfred Steyner.

'What the hell is he up to?' Dan started running. He reached the edge of the pool, and suddenly he realized what was happening.

'Christ! He's drowning her,' he shouted aloud, and he sprang into the water.

He did not waste time struggling with Manfred. He hit him a great open-handed, round-armed blow, that cracked against the side of Manfred's head like a pistol shot and sent him lurching sideways, releasing his grip on Terry.

Ignoring Manfred, Dan picked Terry from the water like a drowned kitten and waded to the steps. He carried her out and laid her face down on the paving. He knelt over her and began applying artificial respiration. He felt Terry stir under his hands, then cough and retch weakly.

Joy came up at the run and dropped on her knees beside him.

'My God, Dan, what happened?'

'That little bastard was trying to drown her.'

Dan looked up from his labours without interrupting the rhythm of his movement over Terry. She spluttered and retched again.

On the far side of the pool Manfred Steyner had dragged himself from the pool. He was sitting on the edge with his feet still dangling in the water, his head was hanging, and he was fingering the side of his face where Dan had hit him. On his lap he held a wet pulpy mess that had been the geological report.

'Joy, can you take over here? Terry's not too far gone, and I want to get my hands on that little Hun.'

Joy took Dan's place over Terry's prostrate form, and Dan stood up. 'What are you going to do to him?' Joy asked.

'I'm going to beat him to a pulp.'

'Good show!' Joy encouraged him. 'Give him one for me.'

Manfred had heard the exchange and as Dan ran around the edge of the pool he scrambled to his feet, and staggered to the parked Alfa. He slammed the door and whirred the engine to life. Dan was just too late to stop him. The car shot forward across the lawns, leaving Dan running, futile, behind it.

'Look after her, Joy!' Dan shouted back.

By the time Dan had run up the terrace to his Jaguar and reversed it to point in the opposite direction, the Alfa had disappeared through the white gates with a musical flutter of its exhaust.

'Come on, girlie,' Dan spoke to his Jaguar. 'Let's go get him.'

The rear wheels spun as he pulled away.

Without his spectacles Manfred Steyner's vision was blurred and milky. The outlines of all objects on which he looked were softened and indistinct.

He instinctively checked the Alfa at the stop street at the bottom of the lane. He sat undecided, water still streaming from his clothing, squelching in his shoes. Beside him on the passenger seat lay the sodden report, its pages beginning to disintegrate from its soaking and the rough handling it had received.

He had to get rid of it. It was the shred of incriminating evidence. That was the only clear thought Manfred had. For the first time in his life the crystalline clarity of his thought processes was interrupted. He was confused, his mind jerking abruptly from one subject to another, the intense pleasure of inflicting hurt on Terry mingled with the sting and smart of his own injuries. He could not concentrate on either sensation for overlying it all was a sense of fear, of uncertainty. He felt vulnerable, hunted, hurt and shaken. His brain flickered and wavered as though a computer had developed an electrical fault. The answers it produced were nonsensical.

He looked in the rear view mirror, saw the Jaguar glide out between the white gates and turn towards him.

'Christ!' he panicked. He rammed his foot down on the accelerator and engaged the clutch. The Alfa screeched out into the main highway, swerved into the path of a heavy truck, bounded over the far kerb and swung back onto the road.

Dan watched it tear away towards Kyalami.

He let the truck pass and then swung into the traffic behind it. He had to wait until the road was clear ahead before he could overtake the truck, and by that time the Alfa was a dwindling cream speck ahead of him.

Dan settled back in the leather bucket seat, and gave the Jaguar its head. He was furious, outraged by the treatment he had seen Manfred meting out to Terry. Her swollen and bruised face had shocked him and his feet were firmly set upon the path of vengeance.

His hands gripped the steering-wheel fiercely, he was muttering threats of violence as the speedometer moved up over the hundred mile per hour mark and he began relentlessly overhauling the cream sports car.

Steadily he moved up behind the Alfa until he was driving almost on its rear bumper. The Alfa was held up by a green school bus. Dan could not pass, however, for there was a steady stream of traffic coming in the opposite direction.

He fastened his attention on the back of Manfred's head, still fuming with anger.

Dan dropped down a gear, ready to pull out and overtake the Alfa when the opportunity arose. At that moment Manfred looked up into his rear view mirror. Dan saw the reflection of his white face with disordered damp hair hanging onto the forehead, saw his expression change immediately he recognized Dan and the Alfa shot out into the face of the approaching traffic.

There was the howl and blare of horns, vehicles swerved to make way for Manfred's wild rush. Dan glimpsed frightened faces flicking past, but the Alfa had squeezed around the green bus and was speeding away.

Dan dropped back, then sent the Jaguar like a thrown javelin through the gap between bus and kerb, overtaking on the wrong side and ignoring the bus driver's yell of protest.

The Jaguar had a higher top speed, and on the long straight Pretoria highway Dan crept up steadily on the cream Alfa.

He could see Manfred glancing repeatedly into his driving-mirror, and he grinned mirthlessly.

Ahead of them the highway rose and then dipped over a low rounded ridge. A double avenue of tall blue gum trees flanked each side of the road.

Travelling in the same direction as the two high performance sports cars was a mini of a good vintage year. Its elderly driver was triumphantly about to overtake an overloaded vegetable truck. Neck and neck they approached the blind rise at twenty-five miles per hour, between them they effectively blocked half the road.

The horn of the Alfa wailed a high-pitched warning, and Manfred pulled out to overtake both slower vehicles. He was level with them, well out over the white dividing line, when a cement truck popped up over the blind rise.

Dan stood on his brake pedal with all the strength of his right leg, and watched it happen.

The cement truck and the Alfa came head on towards each other at a combined speed of well over a hundred miles per hour. At the last moment the Alfa began to turn away but it was too late by many seconds.

It caught the heavy cement truck a glancing blow and was hurled across the path of the two slower vehicles, miraculously touching neither of them; it skidded sideways leaving reeking black smears of rubber on the tarmac, and hurdled the low bank. It struck one of the blue gums full on, with a force that shivered the giant tree trunk and brought down a rain of leaves.

Dan pulled the Jaguar into the side of the road, parked it, and walked back.

He knew there was no hurry. The drivers of the mini and the vegetable truck were there before him. They were attempting to talk each other down, both of them excited and relieved by their own escapes.

'I'm a doctor,' said Dan, and they fell back respectfully.

'He doesn't need a doctor,' said one of them. 'He needs an undertaker.'

One look was sufficient. Dr Manfred Steyner was as dead as Dan had ever seen anybody. His crushed head was thrust through the windscreen. Dan picked up the sodden bundle of paper from the seat beside the huddled body. He was aware that some particular importance was attached to it.

Dan's anger had evaporated entirely, and he felt a twinge of pity as he looked into the wreckage at the corpse. It appeared so frail and small —of such little consequence.

CHAPTER 71

The sunlight was sparkling bright, broken into a myriad eye-stinging fragments by the rippling surface of the bay.

The breeze was strong enough for the Arrow class yachts to fly their spinnakers as they came down on the wind. The sails bulged out blue and yellow and bright scarlet against the sombre green of the great whale-back fluff above Durban Bay.

Under the awning on the afterdeck of the motor yacht it was cool, but the fat man wore only a pair of white linen slacks with his feet thrust into dark blue cloth espadrilles.

Sprawled in a deck-chair, his belly bulged smooth and hard over the waistband of his slacks; he was tanned a dark mahogany colour and his body-hair grew thick and curly from chest to navel.

'Thank you, Andrew.' He extended his empty glass, and the younger man carried it to the open-air bar. The fat man watched him as he mixed another Pimms No. 1 cup.

A white-clad crew member clambered down the companion way from the bridge. He touched his cap respectfully to the fat man.

'Captain's respects, sir, and we are ready to sail when you give the order.'

'Thank you. Please tell the captain we will sail as soon as Miss du Maine comes aboard.' And the crew man ran back to the bridge.

'Ah!' The fat man sighed happily as Andrew placed the Pimms in his out-stretched hand. 'I have really earned this break. The last few weeks have been nerve-racking, to say the least.'

'Yes, sir,' Andrew agreed dutifully. 'But, as usual, you snatched victory from the ashes.'

'It was close,' the fat man agreed. 'Young Ironsides gave us all a nasty fright with his drop-blast matt. I was only just able to make good my personal commitments before the price shot up again. The profit was not as high as I had anticipated, but then I have never made a habit of peering into the mouths of gift-horses.'

'It was a pity that our associates lost all that money,' Andrew ventured.

'Yes, yes. A great pity. But rather them than us, Andrew.'

'Indeed, sir.'

'In a way I am glad it worked out as it did. I am a patriotic man, at heart. I am relieved that it was not necessary to disrupt the economy of the country to make our little profit.'

He stood up suddenly, his interest quickening as a taxi cab came

down onto the Yacht Club jetty. The cabby opened a rear door and
from it emerged a very beautiful young lady.

'Ah, Andrew! Our guest has arrived. You may warn the captain that
we will be sailing within minutes; and send a man to fetch her luggage.'

He went to the entry port to welcome the young lady.

CHAPTER 72

In mid-summer in the Zambesi Valley the heat is a solid white shimmering thing. In the noon day nothing moves in the merciless sunlight.

At the centre of the native village grew a baobab tree, a monstrous
bloated trunk with malformed branches like the limbs of a polio victim.
The carrion crows sat in it, black and shiny as cockroaches. A score of
grass huts ringed the tree, and beyond them lay the tilled fields. The
millet stood tall and green in the sun.

Along the rude track towards the village came a Landrover. It came
slowly, lurching and jolting over the rough ground, its motor growling
in low gear. Printed in black on its sides were the letters A.R.C.,
African Recruiting Corporation.

The children heard it first, and crawled from the grass huts. Naked
black bodies, and shrill excited voices in the sunlight.

They ran to meet the Landrover and danced beside it, shrieking and
laughing. The Landrover came to a halt in the meagre shade under the
baobab tree. An elderly white man climbed from the cab. He wore
khaki safari clothes and a wide-brimmed hat. Complete silence fell,
and one of the oldest boys fetched a carved stool and placed it in
the shade.

The white man sat on the stool. A girl came forward, knelt before
him and offered a gourd of millet beer. The white man drank from the
gourd. No one spoke, none would disturb an honoured guest until he
had taken refreshment, but from the grass huts the adult members of
the village came. Blinking into the sunlight, winding their loin clothes
about their waists, they came and squatted in a semi-circle before the
white man on his stool.

He lowered the gourd and set it aside. He looked at them.

'I see you, my friends,' he greeted them, and the response was warm.

'We see you, old one,' they chorused, but the expression of their
visitor remained grave.

'Let the wives of King Nkulu come forward,' he called. 'Let them
bring each their first-born son with them.'

Four women and four adolescent boys left the crowd and came shyly into the open. For a moment the white man studied them compassionately, then he stood and stepped forward. He placed a hand on the shoulder of each of the two eldest lads.

'Your father has gone to *his* fathers,' he told them. There was a stirring, an intake of breath, a startled cry, and then, as was proper, the eldest wife let out the first sobbing wail of mourning.

One by one each wife sank down onto the dry dusty earth and covered her head with her shawl.

'He is dead,' the white man repeated against the background of their keening lament. 'But he died in such honour as to let his name live on forever. So great was his dying that for all their lives money will each month be paid to his wives, and for each of his sons there is already set aside a place at the University, that each may grow as strong in learning as his father was in body. Of Big King there will be raised up an image in stone.

'The wives of Big King and his sons will travel in a flying machine to I'Goldi, that their eyes also may look upon the stone image of the man who was their husband and their father.' The white man paused for breath, it was a lengthy speech in the midday heat of the valley. He wiped his face and then tucked the handkerchief into his pocket.

'He was a lion!'

'Ngwenyama!' whispered the sturdy twelve-year-old boy standing beside the white man. The tears started from his eyes and greased down his cheeks. He turned away and ran alone into the millet fields.

CHAPTER 73

Dennis Langley, the Sales Manager of Kitchenerville Motors who were the local Ford agents, stretched his arms over his head luxuriously. He sighed with deep contentment. What a lovely way to spend a working day morning.

'Happy?' asked Hettie Delange beside him in the double bed. In reply Dennis grinned and sighed again.

Hettie sat up and let the sheet fall to her waist. Her breasts were big and white, and damp with perspiration. She looked down on his naked chest and arm muscles approvingly.

'Gee, you're built nicely.'

'So are you,' Dennis smiled up at her.

'You're different from the other chaps I've gone out with,' Hettie told him. 'You speak so nicely—like a gentleman, you know.'

Before Dennis Langley could decide on a suitable reply, the front door bell shrilled, the sound of it echoing through the house. Dennis shot into an upright position with a fearful expression on his face.

'Who's that?' he demanded.

'It's probably the butcher delivering the meat.'

'It may be my wife!' Dennis cautioned her. 'Don't answer it.'

'Of course I've got to answer it, silly.' Hettie threw back the sheet, and rose in her white and golden glory to find her dressing-gown. The sight was enough momentarily to quiet Dennis Langley's misgivings, but as she belted her gown and hid it from view he urged her again.

'Be careful! Make sure it's not her before you open the door.'

Hettie opened the front door, and immediately drew her gown more closely around her with one hand, while with the other she tried to pat her hair into a semblance of order.

'Hello,' she breathed.

The tall young man in the doorway was really rather dreamy. He wore a dark business suit and carried an expensive leather briefcase.

'Mrs Delange?' he enquired. He had a nice soft dreamy voice.

'Yes, I'm Mrs Delange.' Hettie fluttered her eyelashes. 'Won't you come in?'

She led him through to the lounge, and she was pleasantly aware of his eyes on the opening of her gown.

'What can I do for you?' she asked archly.

'I am your local representative of the Sanlam Insurance Company, Mrs Delange. I have come to express my Company's condolences on your recent sad bereavement. I would have called sooner, but I did not wish to intrude on your sorrow.'

'Oh!' Hettie dropped her eyes, immediately adopting the role of the widow.

'However, we hope we can bring a little light to disperse the darkness that surrounds you. You may know that your husband was a policy-holder with our Company?'

Hettie shook her head, but watched with interest while the visitor opened his briefcase.

'Yes, he was. Two months ago he took out a straight life policy with double indemnity. The policy was ceded to you.' The insurance man extracted a sheaf of papers from his case. 'I have here my Company's cheque in full settlement of all claims under the policy. If you will just sign for it, please.'

'How much?' Hettie abandoned the role of the bereaved.

'With the double indemnity, the cheque is for forty-eight thousand Rand.'

Hettie's eyes flew wide with delight.
'Gee!' she gasped. 'That's *fabulous*!'

CHAPTER 74

Hurry's original intentions had expanded considerably. Instead of a plaque on the cement plug at 66 level, the monument to Big King had become a life-sized statue in bronze. He sited it on the lawns in front of the Administrative offices of the Sonder Ditch on a base of black marble.

It was effective. The artist had captured a sense of urgency, of vibrant power. The inscription was simple, just the name of the man— 'King Nkulu'—and the date of his death.

Hurry attended the unveiling in person, even though he hated ceremonies and avoided them whenever possible. In the front row of guests facing him his grand-daughter sat beside Dr Stander and his very new blonde wife. She winked at him and Hurry frowned lovingly back at her.

From the seat beside Hurry, young Ironsides stood up to introduce the Chairman. Hurry noted the expression on his grand-daughter's face as she transferred all her attention to the tall young man with both his arms encased in plaster of Paris and supported by slings.

'Perhaps I should have fired him, after all,' thought Hurry. 'He is going to cut one out of my herd.'

Hurry glanced sideways at his General Manager, and decided with resignation, 'Too late'. Then went on to cheer himself. 'Anyway, he looks like good breeding stock.'

His line of thought switched again. 'Better start making arrangements to transfer him up to Head Office. He will need a lot of grooming and polishing.'

Without thinking he fished a powerful-looking cigar from his breast pocket. He had it half-way to his mouth when he caught Terry's scandalized glare. Silently her lips formed the words: 'Your doctor!'

Guiltily Hurry Hirschfeld stuffed the cigar back into his pocket.

THE DARK OF THE SUN

CHAPTER 1

'I don't like the idea,' announced Wally Hendry, and belched. He moved his tongue round his mouth, getting the taste of it before he went on. 'I think the whole idea stinks like a ten-day corpse.' He lay sprawled on one of the beds with a glass balanced on his naked chest and he was sweating heavily in the Congo heat.

'Unfortunately your opinion doesn't alter the fact that we are going.' Bruce Curry went on laying out his shaving tackle without looking up.

'You should-a told them to keep it, told them we were staying here in Elisabethville—why didn't you tell them that, hey?' Hendry picked up his glass and swallowed the contents.

'Because they pay me not to argue.' Bruce spoke without interest and looked at himself in the fly-spotted mirror above the wash-basin. The face that looked back was sun-darkened with a cap of close-cropped black hair; soft hair that would be unruly and inclined to curl if it were longer. Black eyebrows slanting upwards at the corners, green eyes with a heavy fringe of lashes and a mouth which could smile as readily as it could sulk. Bruce regarded his good looks without pleasure. It was a long time since he had felt that emotion, a long time since his mouth had either smiled or sulked. He did not feel the old tolerant affection for his nose, the large slightly hooked nose that rescued his face from prettiness and gave him the air of a genteel pirate.

'Jesus!' growled Wally Hendry from the bed. 'I've had just about a gutsful of this nigger army. I don't mind fighting—but I don't fancy going hundreds of miles out into the bush to play nursemaid to a bunch of bloody refugees.'

'It's a hell of a life,' agreed Bruce absently and spread shaving-soap on his face. The lather was very white against his tan. Under a skin that glowed so healthily that it appeared to have been freshly oiled, the muscles of his shoulders and chest changed shape as he moved. He was in good condition, fitter than he had been for many years, but this fact gave him no more pleasure than had his face.

'Get me another drink, André.' Wally Hendry thrust his empty glass into the hand of the man who sat on the edge of the bed.

The Belgian stood up and went across to the table obediently.

'More whisky and less beer in this one,' Wally instructed, turned once more to Bruce and belched again. 'That's what I think of the idea.'

As André poured Scotch whisky into the glass and filled it with beer, Wally hitched around the pistol in its webbing holster until it hung between his legs.

'When are we leaving?' he asked.

'There'll be an engine and five coaches at the goods yard first thing tomorrow morning. We'll load up and get going as soon as possible.' Bruce started to shave, drawing the razor down from temple to chin and leaving the skin smooth and brown behind it.

'After three months of fighting a bunch of greasy little Gurkhas I was looking forward to a bit of fun—I haven't even had a pretty in all that time—now the second day after the cease-fire and they ship us out again.'

'C'est la guerre,' muttered Bruce, his face twisted in the act of shaving.

'What's that mean?' demanded Wally suspiciously.

'That's war,' Bruce translated.

'Talk English, Bucko.'

It was the measure of Wally Hendry that after six months in the Belgian Congo he could neither speak nor understand a single word of French.

There was silence again, broken only by the scraping of Bruce's razor and the small metallic sounds as the fourth man in the hotel room stripped and cleaned his FN rifle.

'Have a drink, Haig,' Wally invited him.

'No, thanks.' Michael Haig glanced up, not trying to conceal his distaste as he looked at Wally.

'You're another snotty bastard—don't you want to drink with me, hey? Even the high-class Captain Curry is drinking with me. What makes you so goddam special?'

'You know that I don't drink.' Haig turned his attention back to his weapon, handling it with easy familiarity. For all of them the ugly automatic rifles had become an extension of their own bodies. Even while shaving Bruce had only only to drop his hand to reach the rifle propped against the wall, and the two men on the bed had theirs on the floor beside them.

'You don't drink!' chuckled Wally. 'Then how did you get that complexion, Bucko? How come your nose looks like a ripe plum?'

Haig's mouth tightened and the hands on his rifle stilled.

'Cut it out, Wally,' said Bruce without heat.

'Haig don't drink,' crowed Wally, and dug the little Belgian in the ribs with his thumb, 'get that, André! He's a tee-bloody-total! My old man was a teetotal also; sometimes for two, three months at a time he was a teetotal, and then he'd come home one night and sock the old lady in the clock so you could hear her teeth rattle from across the street.'

His laughter choked him and he had to wait for it to clear before he went on.

'My bet is that you're that kind of teetotal, Haig. One drink and you wake up ten days later; that's it, isn't it? One drink and—pow!— the old girl gets it in the chops and the kids don't eat for a couple of weeks.'

Haig laid the rifle down carefully on the bed and looked at Wally with his jaws clenched, but Wally had not noticed. He went on happily.

'André, take the whisky bottle and hold it under Old Teetotal Haig's nose. Let's watch him slobber at the mouth and his eyes stand out like a pair of dog's balls.'

Haig stood up. Twice the age of Wally—a man in his middle fifties, with grey in his hair and the refinement of his features not completely obliterated by the marks that life had left upon them. He had arms like a boxer and a powerful set to his shoulders. 'It's about time you learned a few manners, Hendry. Get on your feet.'

'You wanta dance or something? I don't waltz—ask André. He'll dance with you—won't you, André?'

Haig was balanced on the balls of his feet, his hands closed and raised slightly. Bruce Curry placed his razor on the shelf above the basin, and moved quietly round the table with soap still on his face to take up a position from which he could intervene. There he waited, watching the two men.

'Get up, you filthy guttersnipe.'

'Hey, André, get that. He talks pretty, hey? He talks real pretty.'

'I'm going to smash that ugly face of yours right into the middle of the place where your brain should have been.'

'Jokes! This boy is a natural comic.' Wally laughed, but there was something wrong with the sound of it. Bruce knew then that Wally was not going to fight. Big arms and swollen chest covered with ginger hair, belly flat and hard-looking, thick-necked below the wide flat-featured face with its little Mongolian eyes; but Wally wasn't going to fight. Bruce was puzzled: he remembered the night at the road bridge and he knew that Hendry was no coward, and yet now he was not going to take up Haig's challenge.

Mike Haig moved towards the bed.

'Leave him, Mike.' André spoke for the first time, his voice soft as a girl's. 'He was only joking. He didn't mean it.'

'Hendry, don't think I'm too much of a gentleman to hit you because you're on your back. Don't make that mistake.'

'Big deal,' muttered Wally. 'This boy's not only a comic, he's a bloody hero also.'

Haig stood over him and lifted his right hand with the fist, bunched like a hammer, aimed at Wally's face.

'Haig!' Bruce hadn't raised his voice but its tone checked the older man.

'That's enough,' said Bruce.

'But this filthy little—'

'Yes, I know,' said Bruce. 'Leave him!' With his fist still up Mike Haig hesitated, and there was no movement in the room. Above them the corrugated iron roof popped loudly as it expanded in the heat of the Congo midday, and the only other sound was Haig's breathing. He was panting and his face was congested with blood.

'Please, Mike,' whispered André. 'He didn't mean it.'

Slowly Haig's anger changed to disgust and he dropped his hand, turned away and picked up his rifle from the other bed.

'I can't stand the smell in this room another minute. I'll wait for you in the truck downstairs, Bruce.'

'I won't be long,' agreed Bruce as Mike went to the door.

'Don't push your luck, Haig,' Wally called after him. 'Next time you won't get off so easily.'

In the doorway Mike Haig swung quickly, but, with a hand on his shoulder, Bruce turned him again.

'Forget it, Mike,' he said, and closed the door after him.

'He's just bloody lucky that he's an old man,' growled Wally. 'Otherwise I'd have fixed him good.'

'Sure,' said Bruce. 'It was decent of you to let him go.' The soap had dried on his face and he wet his brush to lather again.

'Yeah, I couldn't hit an old bloke like that, could I?'

'No.' Bruce smiled a little. 'But don't worry, you frightened the hell out of him. He won't try it again.'

'He'd better not!' warned Hendry. 'Next time I'll kill the old bugger.'

No, you won't, thought Bruce, you'll back down again as you have just done, as you've done a dozen times before. Mike and I are the only ones who can make you do it; in the same way as an animal will growl at its trainer but cringe away when he cracks the whip. He began shaving again.

The heat in the room was unpleasant to breathe; it drew the perspiration out of them and the smell of their bodies blended sourly with stale cigarette smoke and liquor fumes.

'Where are you and Mike going?' André ended the long silence.

'We're going to see if we can draw the supplies for this trip. If we have any luck we'll take them down to the goods yard and have Ruffy put an armed guard on them overnight,' Bruce answered him, leaning over the basin and splashing water up into his face.

'How long will we be away?'

Bruce shrugged. 'A week—ten days.' He sat on his bed and pulled on one of his jungle boots. 'That is, if we don't have any trouble.'

'Trouble, Bruce?' asked André

'From Msapa Junction we'll have to go two hundred miles through country crawling with Baluba.'

'But we'll be in a train,' protested André. 'They've only got bows and arrows, they can't touch us.'

'André, there are seven rivers to cross—one big one—and bridges are easily destroyed. Rails can be torn up.' Bruce began to lace the boot. 'I don't think it's going to be a Sunday school picnic.'

'Christ. I think the whole thing stinks,' repeated Wally moodily. 'Why are we going anyway?'

'Because,' Bruce began patiently, 'for the last three months the entire population of Port Reprieve has been cut off from the rest of the world. There are women and children with them. They are fast running out of food and the other necessities of life.' Bruce paused to light a cigarette, and then went on talking as he exhaled. 'All around them the Baluba tribe is in open revolt, burning, raping and killing indiscriminately. As yet they haven't attacked the town but it won't be very long until they do. Added to which there are rumours that rebel groups of Central Congolese troops and of our own forces have formed themselves into bands of heavily-armed *shufta*. They also are running amok through the northern part of the territory. Nobody knows for certain what is happening out there, but whatever it is you can be sure it's not very pretty. We are going to fetch those people in to safety.'

'Why don't the U.N. people send out a plane?' asked André.

'No landing field.'

'Helicopters?'

'Out of range.'

'For my money the bastards can stay there,' grunted Wally. 'If the Balubas fancy a little man steak, who are we to do them out of a meal? Every man's entitled to eat and as long as it's not me they're eating, more power to their teeth, say I.' He placed his foot against André's back and straightened his leg suddenly, throwing the Belgian off the bed on to his knees.

'Go and get me a pretty.'

'There aren't any, Wally. I'll get you another drink.' André scrambled to his feet and reached for Wally's empty glass, but Wally's hand dropped onto his wrist.

'I said *pretty*, André, not *drink*.'

'I don't know where to find them, Wally.' André's voice was desperate. 'I don't know what to say to them even.'

'You're being stupid, Bucko. I might have to break your arm.' Wally
twisted the wrist slowly. 'You know as well as I do that the bar downstairs is full of them. You know that, don't you?'

'But what do I say to them?' André's face was contorted with the
pain of his twisted wrist.

'Oh, for Christ's sake, you stupid bloody frog-eater—just go down
and flash a banknote. You don't have to say a dicky bird.'

'You're hurting me, Wally.'

'No? You're kidding!' Wally smiled at him, twisting harder, his
slitty eyes smoky from the liquor, and Bruce could see he was enjoying
it. 'Are you going, Bucko? Make up your mind—get me a pretty or
get yourself a broken arm.'

'All right, if that's what you want. I'll go. Please leave me, I'll go,'
mumbled André.

'That's what I want.' Wally released him, and he straightened up
massaging his wrist.

'See that she's clean and not too old. You hear me?'

'Yes, Wally. I'll get one.' André went to the door and Bruce noticed
his expression. It was stricken beyond the pain of a bruised wrist. What
lovely creatures they are, thought Bruce, and I am one of them and yet
apart from them. I am the watcher, stirred by them as much as I would
be by a bad play. André went out.

'Another drink, Bucko?' said Wally expansively. 'I'll even pour you
one.'

'Thanks,' said Bruce, and started on the other boot. Wally brought
the glass to him and he tasted it. It was strong, and the mustiness of
the whisky was ill-matched with the sweetness of the beer, but he drank
it.

'You and I,' said Wally, 'we're the shrewd ones. We drink 'cause
we want to, not 'cause we have to. We live like we want to live, not
like other people think we should. You and I got a lot in common,
Bruce. We should be friends, you and I. I mean, us being so much
alike.' The drink was working in him now, blurring his speech a little.

'Of course we are friends—I count you as one of my very dearest,
Wally.' Bruce spoke solemnly, no trace of sarcasm showing.

'No kidding?' Wally asked earnestly. 'How's that, hey? Christ, I
always thought you didn't like me. Christ, you never can tell, isn't that
right? You just never can tell,' shaking his head in wonder, suddenly
sentimental with the whisky. 'That's really true? You like me. Yeah,
we could be buddies. How's that, Bruce? Every guy needs a buddy.
Every guy needs a back stop.'

'Sure,' said Bruce. 'We're buddies. How's that, hey?'

'That's on, Bucko!' agreed Wally with deep feeling, *and I feel nothing*, thought Bruce, *no disgust, no pity—nothing. That way you are secure; they cannot disappoint you, they cannot disgust you, they cannot sicken you, they cannot smash you up again.*

They both looked up as André ushered the girl into the room. She had a sexy little pug face, painted lips—ruby on amber.

'Well done, André,' applauded Wally, looking at the girl's body. She wore high heels and a short pink dress that flared into a skirt from her waist but did not cover her knees.

'Come here, cookie.' Wally held out his hand to her and she crossed the room without hesitation, smiling a bright professional smile. Wally drew her down beside him onto the bed.

André went on standing in the doorway. Bruce got up and shrugged into his camouflage battle-jacket, buckled on his webbing belt and adjusted the holstered pistol until it hung comfortably on his outer thigh.

'Are you going?' Wally was feeding the girl from his glass.

'Yes.' Bruce put his slouch hat on his head; the red, green and white Katangese sideflash gave him an air of artificial gaiety.

'Stay a little—come on, Bruce.'

'Mike is waiting for me.' Bruce picked up his rifle.

'Muck him. Stay a little, we'll have some fun.'

'No, thanks.' Bruce went to the door.

'Hey, Bruce. Take a look at this.' Wally tipped the girl backwards over the bed, he pinned her with one arm across her chest while she struggled playfully and with the other hand he swept her skirt up above her waist.

'Take a good look at this and tell me you still want to go!'

The girl was naked under the skirt, her lower body shaven so that her plump little sex pouted sulkily.

'Come on, Bruce,' laughed Wally. 'You first. Don't say I'm not your buddy.'

Bruce glanced at the girl, her legs scissored and her body wriggled as she fought with Wally. She was giggling.

'Mike and I will be back before curfew. I want this woman out of here by then,' said Bruce.

There is no desire, he thought as he looked at her, *that is all finished.* He opened the door.

'Curry!' shouted Wally. 'You're a bloody nut also. Christ, I thought you were a man. Jesus Christ! You're as bad as the others. André, the doll boy. Haig, the rummy. What's with you, Bucko? It's women with you, isn't it? You're a bloody nut-case also!'

Bruce closed the door and stood alone in the passage. The taunt had gone through a chink in his armour and he clamped his mind down on the sting of it, smothering it.

It's all over. She can't hurt me any more. He thought with determination, remembering her, the woman, not the one in the room he had just left but the other one who had been his wife.

'The bitch,' he whispered, and then quickly, almost guiltily, 'I do not hate her. There is no hatred and there is no desire.'

CHAPTER 2

The lobby of the Hotel Grand Leopold II was crowded. There were gendarmes carrying their weapons ostentatiously, talking loudly, lolling against walls and over the bar; women with them, varying in colour from black through to pastel brown, some already drunk; a few Belgians still with the stunned disbelieving eyes of the refugee, one of the women crying as she rocked her child on her lap; other white men in civilian clothes but with the alertness about them and the quick restless eyes of the adventurer, talking quietly with Africans in business suits; a group of journalists at one table in damp shirtsleeves, waiting and watching with the patience of vultures. And everybody sweated in the heat.

Two South African charter pilots hailed Bruce from across the room.

'Hi, Bruce. How about a snort?'

'Dave. Carl.' Bruce waved. 'Big hurry now—tonight perhaps.'

'We're flying out this afternoon.' Carl Engelbrecht shook his head. 'Back next week.'

'We'll make it then,' Bruce agreed, and went out of the front door into the Avenue du Kasai. As he stopped on the sidewalk the white-washed buildings bounced the glare into his face. The naked heat made him wince and he felt fresh sweat start out of his body beneath his battle-suit. He took the dark glasses from his top pocket and put them on as he crossed the street to the Chev three-tonner in which Mike Haig waited.

'I'll drive, Mike.'

'Okay.' Mike slid across the seat and Bruce stepped up into the cab. He started the truck north down the Avenue du Kasai.

'Sorry about that scene, Bruce.'

'No harm done.'

'I shouldn't have lost my temper like that.'

Bruce did not answer, he was looking at the deserted buildings on either side. Most of them had been looted and all of them were pock-marked with shrapnel from the mortar bursts. At intervals along the sidewalk were parked the burnt-out bodies of automobiles looking like the carapaces of long-dead beetles.

'I shouldn't have let him get through to me, and yet the truth hurts like hell.'

Bruce was silent but he trod down harder on the accelerator and the truck picked up speed. *I don't want to hear*, he thought, *I am not your confessor—I just don't want to hear.* He turned into the Avenue l'Etoile, headed towards the zoo.

'He was right, he had me measured to the inch,' persisted Mike.

'We've all got troubles, otherwise we wouldn't be here.' And then, to change Mike's mood, 'We few, we happy few. We band of brothers.'

Mike grinned and his face was suddenly boyish. 'At least we have the distinction of following the second oldest profession—we, the mercenaries.'

'The oldest profession is better paid and much more fun,' said Bruce and swung the truck into the driveway of a double-storied residence, parked outside the front door and switched off the engine.

Not long ago the house had been the home of the chief accountant of Union Minière du Haut; now it was the billet of 'D' section, Special Striker Force, commanded by Captain Bruce Curry.

Half a dozen of his black gendarmes were sitting on the low wall of the veranda, and as Bruce came up the front steps they shouted the greeting that had become traditional since the United Nations intervention.

'U.N.—Merde!'

'Ah!' Bruce grinned at them in the sense of companionship that had grown up between them in the past months. 'The cream of the Army of Katanga!'

He offered his cigarettes around and stood chatting idly for a few minutes before asking, 'Where's Sergeant Major?' One of the gendarmes jerked a thumb at the glass doors that led into the lounge and Bruce went through with Mike behind him.

Equipment was piled haphazardly on the expensive furniture, the stone fireplace was half filled with empty bottles, a gendarme lay snoring on the Persian carpet, one of the oil paintings on the wall had been ripped by a bayonet and the frame hung askew, the imbuia-wood coffee table tilted drunkenly towards its broken leg, and the whole lounge smelled of men and cheap tobacco.

'Hello, Ruffy,' said Bruce.

'Just in time, boss.' Sergeant Major Ruffararo grinned delightedly from the armchair which he was overflowing. 'These goddam Arabs have run fresh out of folding stuff.' He gestured at the gendarmes that crowded about the table in front of him. 'Arab' was Ruffy's word of censure or contempt, and bore no relation to a man's nationality.

Ruffy's accent was always a shock to Bruce. You never expected to hear pure Americanese come rumbling out of that huge black frame. But three years previously Ruffy had returned from a scholarship tour of the United States with a command of the idiom, a diploma in land husbandry, a prodigious thirst for bottled beer (preferably Schlitz, but any other was acceptable) and a raving dose of the Old Joe.

The memory of this last, which had been a farewell gift from a high yellow sophomore of U.C.L.A., returned most painfully to Raffararo when he was in his cups; so painfully that it could be assuaged only by throwing the nearest citizen of the United States.

Fortunately, it was only on rare occasions that an American and the necessary five or six gallons of beer were assembled in the same vicinity so that Ruffy's latent race antipathy could find expression. A throwing by Ruffy was an unforgettable experience, both for the victim and the spectators. Bruce vividly recalled that night at the Hotel Lido when he had been a witness at one of Ruffy's most spectacular throwings.

The victims, three of them, were journalists representing publications of repute. As the evening wore on they talked louder; an American accent has a carry like a well-hit golf ball and Ruffy recognized it from across the terrace. He became silent, and in his silence drank the last gallon which was necessary to tip the balance. He wiped the froth from his upper lip and stood up with his eyes fastened on the party of Americans.

'Ruffy, hold it. Hey!'—Bruce might not have spoken. Ruffy started across the terrace. They saw him coming and fell into an uneasy silence.

The first was in the nature of a practice throw; besides, the man was not aerodynamically constructed and his stomach had too much wind resistance. A middling distance of twenty feet.

'Ruffy, leave them!' shouted Bruce.

On the next throw Ruffy was getting warmed up, but he put excessive loft into it. Thirty feet; the journalist cleared the terrace and landed on the lawn below with his empty glass still clutched in his hand.

'Run, you fool!' Bruce warned the third victim, but he was paralysed.

And this was Ruffy's best ever, he took a good grip—neck and seat of the pants—and put his whole weight into it. Ruffy must have known that he had executed the perfect throw, for his shout of 'Gonorrhoea!' as he launched his man had a ring of triumph to it.

Afterwards, when Bruce had soothed the three Americans, and they had recovered sufficiently to appreciate the fact that they were privileged by being party to a record throwing session, they all paced out the distances. The three journalists developed an almost proprietary affection for Ruffy and spent the rest of the evening buying him beers and boasting to every newcomer in the bar. One of them, he who had been thrown last and farthest, wanted to do an article on Ruffy—with pictures. Towards the end of the evening he was talking wildly of whipping up sufficient international enthusiasm to have a man-throwing event included in the Olympic Games.

Ruffy accepted both their praise and their beer with modest gratitude; and when the third American offered to let Ruffy throw him again, he declined the offer on the grounds that he never threw the same man twice. All in all, it had been a memorable evening.

Apart from these occasional lapses, Ruffy had a more powerful body and happier mind than any man Bruce had ever known, and Bruce could not help liking him. He could not prevent himself smiling as he tried to reject Ruffy's invitation to play cards.

'We've got work to do now, Ruffy. Some other time.'

'Sit down, boss. We'll play just a couple of tricks, then we talk about work.' He shuffled the three cards back and forth between his hands.

'Sit down, boss,' Ruffy repeated, and Bruce grimaced resignedly and took the chair opposite him.

'How much you going to bet?' Ruffy leaned forward.

'Un mille.' Bruce laid a thousand-franc note on the table; 'when that's gone, then we go.'

'No hurry,' Ruffy soothed him. 'We got all day.' He dealt the three cards face down. 'The old Christian monarch is in there somewhere; all you got to do is find him and it's the easiest mille you ever made.'

'In the middle,' whispered the gendarme standing beside Bruce's chair. 'That's him in the middle.'

'Take no notice of that mad Arab—he's lost five mille already this morning,' Ruffy advised.

Bruce turned over the right-hand card.

'Mis-luck,' crowed Ruffy. 'You got yourself the queen of hearts.' He picked up the banknote and stuffed it into his breast pocket. 'She'll see you wrong every time, that sweet-faced little bitch.' Grinning, he turned over the middle card to expose the Jack of spades with his sly eyes and curly little moustache. 'She's been shacked up there with the Jack right under the ole King's nose.' He turned the king face up. 'Look you at that dozy old guy—he's not even facing in the right direction.'

Bruce stared at the three cards and he felt that sickness in his stomach again. The whole story was there; even the man's name was right, but the Jack should have worn a beard and driven a red Jaguar and his queen of hearts never had such innocent eyes. Bruce spoke abruptly. 'That's it, Ruffy. I want you and ten men to come with me.'

'Where we going?'

'Down to Ordnance—we're drawing special supplies.'

Ruffy nodded and buttoned the playing cards into his top pocket while he selected the gendarmes to accompany them; then he asked Bruce. 'We might need some oil; what you think, boss?'

Bruce hesitated; they had only two cases of whisky left of the dozen they had looted in August. The purchasing power of a bottle of genuine Scotch was enormous and Bruce was loath to use them except in extraordinary circumstances. But now he realized that his chances of getting the supplies he needed were remote, unless he took along a substantial bribe for the quartermaster.

'Okay, Ruffy. Bring a case.'

Ruffy came up out of the chair and clapped his steel helmet on his head. The chin straps hung down on each side of his round black face.

'A full case?' He grinned at Bruce. 'You want to buy a battleship?'

'Almost,' agreed Bruce; 'go and get it.'

Ruffy disappeared into the back area of the house and returned almost immediately with a case of Grant's Standfast under one arm and half a dozen bottles of Simba beer held by their necks between the fingers of his other hand.

'We might get thirsty,' he explained.

The gendarmes climbed into the back of the truck with a clatter of weapons and shouted cheerful abuse at their fellows on the veranda. Bruce, Mike and Ruffy crowded into the cab and Ruffy set the whisky on the floor and placed two large booted feet upon it.

'What's this all about, boss?' he asked as Bruce trundled the truck down the drive and turned into the Avenue l'Etoile. Bruce told him and when he had finished Ruffy grunted non-committally and opened a bottle of beer with his big white chisel-blade teeth; the gas hissed softly and a little froth ran down the bottle and dripped onto his lap.

'My boys aren't going to like it,' he commented as he offered the open bottle to Mike Haig. Mike shook his head and Ruffy passed the bottle to Bruce.

Ruffy opened a bottle for himself and spoke again. 'They going to hate it like hell.' He shook his head. 'And there'll be even bigger trouble when we got to Port Reprieve and pick up the diamonds.'

Bruce glanced sideways at him, startled. 'What diamonds?'

'From the dredgers,' said Ruffy. 'You don't think they're sending us all that way just to bring in these other guys. They're worried about the diamonds, that's for sure!'

Suddenly, for Bruce, much which had puzzled him was explained. A half-forgotten conversation that he had held earlier in the year with an engineer from Union Minière jumped back into his memory. They had discussed the three diamond dredgers that worked the gravel from the bed of the Lufira swamps. The boats were based on Port Reprieve and clearly they would have returned there at the beginning of the emergency; they must still be there with three or four months' recovery of diamonds on board. Something like half a million sterling in uncut stones. That was the reason why the Katangese Government placed such priority on this expedition, the reason why such a powerful force was being used, the reason why no approaches had been made to the U.N. authorities to conduct the rescue.

Bruce smiled sardonically as he remembered the humanitarian arguments that had been given to him by the Minister of the Interior.

'It is our duty, Captain Curry. We cannot leave these people to the not-so-tender mercy of the tribesmen. It is our duty as civilized human beings.'

There were others cut off in remote mission stations and government outposts throughout southern Kasai and Katanga; nothing had been heard of them for months, but their welfare was secondary to that of the settlement at Port Reprieve.

Bruce lifted the bottle to his lips again, steering with one hand and squinting ahead through the windscreen as he drank. All right, we'll fetch them in and afterwards an ammunition box will be loaded onto a chartered aircraft, and later still there will be another deposit to a numbered account in Zurich. Why should I worry? They're paying me for it.

'I don't think we should mention the diamonds to my boys.' Ruffy spoke sadly. 'I don't think that would be a good idea at all.'

Bruce slowed the truck as they ran into the industrial area beyond the railway line. He watched the buildings as they passed, until he recognized the one he wanted and swung off the road to stop in front of the gate. He blew a blast on the hooter and a gendarme came out and inspected his pass minutely. Satisfied, he shouted out to someone beyond the gate and it swung open. Bruce drove the truck through into the yard and switched off the engine.

There were half a dozen other trucks parked in the yard, all emblazoned with the Katangese shield and surrounded by gendarmes in

uniforms patchy with sweat. A white lieutenant leaned from the cab of
one of the trucks and shouted.

'Ciao, Bruce!'

'How things, Sergio?' Bruce answered him.

'Crazy! Crazy!' Bruce smiled. For the Italian everything was crazy.
Bruce remembered that in July, during the fighting at the road bridge,
he had bent him over the bonnet of a Landrover and with a bayonet
dug a piece of shrapnel out of his hairy buttocks—that also had been
crazy.

'See you around,' Bruce dismissed him and led Mike and Ruffy
across the yard to the warehouse. There was a sign on the large double
doors *Dépôt Ordinance—Armée du Katanga* and beyond them at a desk in
a glass cubicle sat a major with a pair of Gandhi-type steel-rimmed
spectacles perched on a face like that of a jovial black toad. He looked
up at Bruce.

'Non,' he said with finality. 'Non, non.' Bruce produced his
requisition form and laid it before him. The major brushed it aside
contemptuously.

'We have not got these items, we are destitute. I cannot do it. No!
I cannot do it. There are priorities. There are circumstances to consider. No, I am sorry.' He snatched a sheaf of papers from the side of
his desk and turned his whole attention to them, ignoring Bruce.

'This requisition is signed by Monsieur le Président,' Bruce pointed
out mildly, and the major laid down his papers and came round from
behind the desk. He stood close to Bruce with the top of his head on a
level with Bruce's chin.

'Had it been signed by the Almighty himself, it would be of no use.
I am sorry, I am truly sorry.'

Bruce lifted his eyes and for a second allowed them to wander over
the mountains of stores which packed the interior of the warehouse.
From where he stood he could identify at least twenty items that he
needed. The major noticed the gesture and his French became so
excited that Bruce could make out only the repeated use of the word
'Non'. He glanced significantly at Ruffy and the sergeant major stepped
forward and placed an arm soothingly about the major's shoulders;
then very gently he led him, still protesting, out into the yard and
across the truck. He opened the door of the cab and the major saw
the case of whisky.

A few minutes later, after Ruffy had prised open the lid with his
bayonet and allowed the major to inspect the seals on the caps, they
returned to the office with Ruffy carrying the case.

'Captain,' said the major as he picked up the requisition from the desk. 'I see now that I was mistaken. This is indeed signed by Monsieur le Président. It is my duty to afford you the most urgent priority.'

Bruce murmured his thanks and the major beamed at him. 'I will give you men to help you.'

'You are too kind. It would disrupt your routine. I have my own men.'

'Excellent,' agreed the major and waved a podgy hand around the warehouse. 'Take what you need.'

CHAPTER 3

Again Bruce glanced at his wrist watch. It was still twenty minutes before the curfew ended at 06.00 hours. Until then he must fret away the time watching Wally Hendry finishing his breakfast. This was a spectacle without much appeal, for Hendry was a methodical but untidy eater.

'Why don't you keep your mouth closed?' snapped Bruce irritably, unable to stand it any longer.

'Do I ask you your business?' Hendry looked up from his plate. His jowls were covered with a ginger stubble of beard and his eyes were inflamed and puffy from the previous evening's debauchery. Bruce looked away from him and checked his watch again.

The suicidal temptation to ignore the curfew and set off immediately for the railway station was very strong. It required an effort to resist it. The least he could expect if he followed that course was an arrest by one of the patrols and a delay of twelve hours while he cleared himself; the worst would be a shooting incident.

He poured himself another cup of coffee and sipped it slowly. Impatience has always been one of my weaknesses, he reflected; nearly every mistake I have ever made stems from that cause. But I have improved a little over the years—at twenty I wanted to live my whole life in a week. Now I'll settle for a year.

He finished his coffee and checked the time again. Five minutes before six, he could risk it now. It would take almost that long to get out to the truck.

'If you are ready, gentlemen.' He pushed back his chair and picked up his pack, slung it over his shoulder and led the way out.

Ruffy was waiting for them, sitting on a pile of stores in one of the corrugated iron goods sheds. His men squatted round a dozen small fires on the concrete floor cooking breakfast.

'Where's the train?'

'That's a good question, boss,' Ruffy congratulated him, and Bruce groaned.

'It should have been here long ago,' Bruce protested, and Ruffy shrugged.

'*Should have been* is a lot different from *is.*'

'Goddammit! We've still got to load up. We'll be lucky if we get away before noon,' snapped Bruce. 'I'll go up to the station master.'

'You'd better take him a present, boss. We've still got a case left.'

'No, hell!' Bruce growled. 'Come with me, Mike.'

With Mike beside him they crossed the tracks to the main platform and clambered up onto it. At the far end a group of railway officials stood chatting and Bruce fell upon them furiously.

Two hours later Bruce stood beside the coloured engine driver on the footplate and they puffed slowly down towards the goods yard.

The driver was a roly-poly little man with a skin too dark for mere sunburn and a set of teeth with bright red plastic gums.

'Monsieur, you do not wish to proceed to Port Reprieve?' he asked anxiously.

'Yes.'

'There is no way of telling the condition of the permanent way. No traffic has used it these last four months.'

'I know. You'll have to proceed with caution.'

'There is a United Nations barrier across the lines near the old aerodrome,' protested the man.

'We have a pass.' Bruce smiled to soothe him; his bad temper was abating now that he had his transport. 'Stop next to the first shed.'

With a hiss of steam brakes the train pulled up beside the concrete platform and Bruce jumped down.

'All right, Ruffy,' he shouted. 'Let's get cracking.'

Bruce had placed the three steel-sided open trucks in the van, for they were the easiest to defend. From behind the breast-high sides the Bren guns could sweep ahead and on both flanks. Then followed the two passenger coaches, to be used as store rooms and officers' quarters; also for the accommodation of the refugees on the return journey. Finally, the locomotive in the rear, where it would be least vulnerable and would not spew smoke and soot back over the train.

The stores were loaded into four of the compartments, the windows shuttered and the doors locked. Then Bruce set about laying out his defences. In a low circle of sandbags on the roof of the leading coach he sited one of the Brens and made this his own post. From here he could look down over the open trucks, back at the locomotive, and also command an excellent view of the surrounding country.

The other Brens he placed in the leading truck and put Hendry in command there. He had obtained from the major at Ordnance three of the new walkie-talkie sets; one he gave to the engine driver, another to Hendry up front, and the third he retained in his emplacement; and his system of communication was satisfactory.

It was almost twelve o'clock before these preparations were complete and Bruce turned to Ruffy who sat on the sandbags beside him.

'All set?'

'All set, boss.'

'How many missing?' Bruce had learned from experience never to expect his entire command to be in any one place at any one time.

'Eight, boss.'

'That's three more than yesterday; leaves us only fifty-two men. Do you think they've taken off into the bush also?' Five of his men had deserted with their weapons on the day of the cease-fire. Obviously they had gone out into the bush to join one of the bands of *shufta* that were already playing havoc along the main roads: ambushing all unprotected traffic, beating up lucky travellers and murdering those less fortunate, raping when they had the opportunity, and generally enjoying themselves.

'No, boss. I don't think so, those three are good boys. They'll be down in the cité indigène having themselves some fun; guess they just forgot the time.' Ruffy shook his head. 'Take us about half an hour to find them; all we do is go down and visit all the knock-shops. You want to try?'

'No, we haven't time to mess around if we are going to make Msapa Junction before dark. We'll pick them up again when we get back.' Was there ever an army since the Boer War that treated desertion so lightly, Bruce wondered.

He turned to the radio set beside him and depressed the transmit button.

'Driver.'

'Oui, Monsieur.'

'Proceed—very slowly until we approach the United Nations barrier. Stop well this side of it.'

'Oui, monsieur.'

They rolled out of the goods yard, clicking over the points; leaving the industrial quarter on their right with the Katangese guard posts on the Avenue du Cimetière intersection; out through the suburbs until ahead of them Bruce saw the U.N. positions and he felt the first stirring of anxiety. The pass he carried in the breast pocket of his jacket was signed by General Rhee Singh, but before in this war the orders of an Indian general had not been passed by a Sudanese captain to an Irish sergeant. The reception that awaited them could be exciting.

'I hope they know about us.' Mike Haig lit his cigarette with a show of nonchalance, but he peered over it anxiously at the piles of fresh earth on each side of the tracks that marked the position of the emplacements.

'These boys have got bazookas, and they're Irish Arabs,' muttered Ruffy. 'I reckon that's the maddest kind of Arab there is—Irish. How would you like a bazooka bomb up the throat, boss?'

'No, thanks, Ruffy,' Bruce declined, and pressed the button of the radio.

'Hendry!'

In the leading truck Wally Hendry picked up his set and, holding it against his chest, looked back at Bruce.

'Curry?'

'Tell your gunners to stand away from the Brens, and the rest of them to lay down their rifles.'

'Right.'

Bruce watched him relaying the order, pushing them back, moving among the gendarmes who crowded the forward trucks. Bruce could sense the air of tension that had fallen over the whole train, watched as his gendarmes reluctantly laid down their weapons and stood empty-handed staring sullenly ahead at the U.N. barrier.

'Driver!' Bruce spoke again into the radio. 'Slow down. Stop fifty yards this side of the barrier. But if there is any shooting open the throttle and take us straight through.'

'Oui, monsieur.'

Ahead of them there was no sign of a reception committee, only the hostile barrier of poles and petrol drums across the line.

Bruce stood upon the roof and lifted his arms above his head in a gesture of neutrality. It was a mistake; the movement changed the passive mood of the gendarmes in the trucks below him. One of them lifted his arms also, but his fists were clenched.

'U.N.—merde!' he shouted, and immediately the cry was taken up.

'U.N.—merde! U.N.—merde!' They chanted the war cry—laughing at first, but then no longer laughing, their voices rising sharply.

'Shut up, damn you,' Bruce roared and swung his open hand against the head of the gendarme beside him, but the man hardly noticed it. His eyes were glazing with the infectious hysteria to which the African is so susceptible; he had snatched up his rifle and was holding it across his chest; already his body was beginning to jerk convulsively as he chanted.

Bruce hooked his fingers under the rim of the man's steel helmet and yanked it forward over his eyes so that the back of his neck was exposed; he chopped him with a judo blow and the gendarme slumped forward over the sandbags, his rifle slipping from his hands.

Bruce looked up desperately; in the trucks below him the hysteria was spreading.

'Stop them—Hendry, de Surrier! Stop them for God's sake.' But his voice was lost in the chanting.

A gendarme snatched up his rifle from where it lay at his feet; Bruce saw him elbow his way towards the side of the truck to begin firing; he was working the slide to lever a round into the breech.

'Mwembe!' Bruce shouted the gendarme's name, but his voice could not penetrate the uproar.

In two seconds the whole situation would dissolve into a pandemonium of tracer and bazooka fire.

Poised on the forward edge of the roof, Bruce checked for an instant to judge the distance, and then he jumped. He landed squarely on the gendarme's shoulders, his weight throwing the man forward so his face hit the steel edge of the truck, and they went down together onto the floor.

The gendarme's finger was resting on the trigger and the rifle fired as it spun from his hands. A complete hush followed the roar of the rifle and in it Bruce scrambled to his feet, drawing his pistol from the canvas holster on his hip.

'All right,' he panted, menacing the men around him. 'Come on, give me a chance to use this!' He picked out one of his sergeants and held his eyes. 'You! I'm waiting for you—start shooting!'

At the sight of the revolver the man relaxed slowly and the madness faded from his face. He dropped his eyes and shuffled awkwardly.

Bruce glanced up at Ruffy and Haig on the roof, and raised his voice. 'Watch them. Shoot the first one who starts it again.'

'Okay, boss.' Ruffy thrust forward the automatic rifle in his hands. 'Who's it going to be?' he asked cheerfully, looking down at them. But the mood had changed. Their attitudes of defiance gave way to sheepish embarrassment and a small buzz of conversation filled the silence.

'Mike,' Bruce yelled, urgent again. 'Call the driver, he's trying to take us through!'

The noise of their passage had risen, the driver accelerating at the sound of the shot, and now they were racing down towards the U.N. barrier.

Mike Haig grabbed the set, shouted an order into it, and immediately the brakes swooshed and the train jolted to a halt not a hundred yards short of the barrier.

Slowly Bruce clambered back onto the roof of the coach.

'Close?' asked Mike.

'My God!' Bruce shook his head, and lit a cigarette with slightly unsteady hands. 'Another fifty yards—!' Then he turned and stared coldly down at this gendarmes.

'Canaille! Next time you try to commit suicide don't take me with you.' The gendarme he had knocked down was now sitting up, fingering the ugly black swelling above his eye. 'My friend,' Bruce turned on him, 'later I will have something for your further discomfort!' Then to the other man in the emplacement beside him who was massaging his neck, 'And for you also! Take their names, Sergeant Major.'

'Sir!' growled Ruffy.

'Mike.' Bruce's voice changed, soft again. 'I'm going ahead to toss the blarney with our friends behind the bazookas. When I give you the signal bring the train through.'

'You don't want me to come with you?' asked Mike.

'No, stay here.' Bruce picked up his rifle, slung it over his shoulder, dropped down the ladder onto the path beside the tracks, and walked forward with the gravel crunching beneath his boots.

An auspicious beginning to the expedition, he decided grimly, tragedy averted by the wink of an eye before they had even passed the outskirts of the city.

At least the Mickies hadn't added a few bazooka bombs to the altercation. Bruce peered ahead, and could make out the shape of helmets behind the earthworks.

Without the breeze of the train's passage it was hot again, and Bruce felt himself starting to sweat.

'Stay where you are, Mister.' A deep brogue from the emplacement nearest the tracks; Bruce stopped, standing on the wooden crossties in the sun. Now he could see the faces of the men beneath the helmets: unfriendly, not smiling.

'What was the shooting for?' the voice questioned.

'We had an accident.'

'Don't have any more or we might have one also.'

'I'd not be wanting that, Paddy.' Bruce smiled thinly, and the Irishman's voice had an edge to it as he went on. 'What's your mission?'

'I have a pass, do you want to see it?' Bruce took the folded sheet of paper from his breast pocket.

'What's your mission?' repeated the Irishman.

'Proceed to Port Reprieve and relieve the town.'

'We know about you.' The Irishman nodded. 'Let me see the pass.'

Bruce left the tracks, climbed the earth wall and handed the pink slip to the Irishman. He wore the three pips of a captain, and he glanced briefly at the pass before speaking to the man beside him.

'Very well, Sergeant, you can be clearing the barrier now.'

'I'll call the train through?' Bruce asked, and the captain nodded again.

'But make sure there are no more accidents—we don't like hired killers.'

'Sure and begorrah now, Paddy, it's not your war you're a-fighting either,' snapped Bruce and abruptly turned his back on the man, jumped down onto the tracks and waved to Mike Haig on the roof of the coach.

The Irish sergeant and his party had cleared the tracks and while the train rumbled slowly down to him Bruce struggled to control his irritation—the Irish captain's taunt had reached him. Hired killer, and of course that was what he was. Could a man sink any lower?

As the coach drew level with where he stood, Bruce caught the hand rail and swung himself aboard, waved an ironical farewell to the Irish captain and climbed up onto the roof.

'No trouble?' asked Mike.

'A bit of lip, delivered in music-hall brogue,' Bruce answered, 'but nothing serious.' He picked up the radio set.

'Driver.'

'Monsieur?'

'Do not forget my instructions.'

'I will not exceed forty miles the hour, and I shall at all times be prepared for an emergency stop.'

'Good!' Bruce switched off the set and sat down on the sand-bags between Ruffy and Mike.

Well, he thought, here we go at last. Six hours' run to Msapa Junction. That should be easy. And then—God knows, God alone knows.

The tracks curved, and Bruce looked back to see the last white-washed buildings of Elisabethville disappear among the trees. They were out into the open savannah forest.

Behind them the black smoke from the loco rolled sideways into the trees; beneath them the crossties clattered in strict rhythm, and ahead the line ran arrow straight for miles, dwindling with perspective until it merged into the olive-green mass of the forest.

Bruce lifted his eyes. Half the sky was clear and tropical blue, but in the north it was bruised with cloud, and beneath the cloud grey rain drifted down to meet the earth. The sunlight through the rain spun a rainbow, and the cloud shadow moved across the land as slowly and as darkly as a herd of grazing buffalo.

He loosened the chin strap of his helmet and laid his rifle on the roof beside him.

'You'd like a beer, boss?'

'Have you any?'

'Sure.' Ruffy called to one of the gendarmes and the man climbed down into the coach and came back with half a dozen bottles. Ruffy opened two with his teeth. Each time half the contents frothed out and splattered back along the wooden side of the coach.

'This beer's as wild as an angry woman,' he grunted as he passed a bottle to Bruce.

'It's wet anyway,' Bruce tasted it, warm and gassy and too sweet.

'Here's how!' said Ruffy.

Bruce looked down into the open trucks at the gendarmes who were settling in for the journey. Apart from the gunners at the Brens, they were lying or squatting in attitudes of complete relaxation and most of them had stripped down to their underwear. One skinny little fellow was already asleep on his back with his helmet as a pillow and the tropical sun beating full into his face.

Bruce finished his beer and threw the bottle overboard. Ruffy opened another and placed it in his hand without comment.

'Why we going so slowly, boss?'

'I told the driver to keep the speed down—give us a chance to stop if the tracks have been torn up.'

'Yeah. Them Balubas might have done that—they're mad Arabs all of them.'

The warm beer drunk in the sun was having a soothing effect on Bruce. He felt at peace now, withdrawn from the need to make decisions, to participate in the life around him.

'Listen to that train-talk,' said Ruffy, and Bruce focused his hearing on the clickety-click of the crossties.

'Yes, I know. You can make it say anything you want it to,' agreed Bruce.

'And it can sing,' Ruffy went on. 'It's got real music in it, like this.' He inflated the great barrel of his chest, lifted his head and let it come.

His voice was deep but with a resonance that caught the attention of the men in the open trucks below them. Those who had been sprawled in the amorphous shapes of sleep stirred and sat up. Another voice joined in humming the tune, hesitantly at first, then more confidently; then others took it up, the words were unimportant, it was the rhythm that they could not resist. They had sung together many times before and like a well-trained choir each voice found its place, the star performers leading, changing the pace, improvising, quickening until the original tune lost its identity and became one of the tribal chants. Bruce recognized it as a planting song. It was one of his favourites and he sat drinking his lukewarm beer and letting the singing wash round him, build up into the chorus like storm waves, then fall back into a tenor solo before rising once more. And the train ran on through the sunlight towards the rain clouds in the north.

Presently André came out of the coach below him and picked his way forward through the men in the trucks until he reached Hendry. The two of them stood together, André's face turned up towards the taller man and deadly earnest as he talked.

'*Doll boy*,' Hendry had called him, and it was an accurate description of the effeminately pretty face with the big toffee eyes; the steel helmet he wore seemed too large for his shoulders to carry.

I wonder how old he is; Bruce watched him laugh suddenly, his face still turned upwards to Hendry; not much over twenty and I have never seen anything less like a hired killer.

'How the hell did anyone like de Surrier get mixed up in this?' His voice echoed the thought, and beside him Mike answered.

'He was working in Elisabethville when it started, and he couldn't return to Belgium. I don't know the reason but I guess it was something personal. When it started his firm closed down. I suppose this was the only employment he could find.'

'That Irishman, the one at the barrier, he called me a hired killer.' Thinking of André's position in the scheme of things had turned Bruce's thoughts back to his own status. 'I hadn't thought about it that way before, but I suppose he's right. That is what we are.'

Mike Haig was silent for a moment, but when he spoke there was a stark quality in his voice.

'Look at these hands!' Involuntarily Bruce glanced down at them, and for the first time noticed that they were narrow with long moulded fingers, possessed of a functional beauty, the hands of an artist.

'Look at them,' Mike repeated, flexing them slightly; 'they were fashioned for a purpose, they were made to hold a scalpel, they were made to save life.' Then he relaxed them and let them drop on to the rifle across his lap, the long delicate fingers incongruous upon the blue metal. 'But look what they hold now!'

Bruce stirred irritably. He had not wanted to provoke another bout of Mike Haig's soul-searching. Damn the old fool—why must he always start this, he knew as well as anyone that in the mercenary army of Katanga there was a taboo upon the past. It did not exist.

'Ruffy,' Bruce snapped, 'aren't you going to feed your boys.'

'Right now, boss.' Ruffy opened another beer and handed it to Bruce. 'Hold that—it will keep your mind off food while I rustle it up.' He lumbered off along the roof of the coach still singing.

'Three years ago, it seems like all eternity,' Mike went on as though Bruce had not interrupted. 'Three years ago I was a surgeon and now this—' The desolation had spread to his eyes, and Bruce felt his pity for the man deep down where he kept it imprisoned with all his other emotions. 'I was good. I was one of the best. Royal College. Harley Street. Guy's.' Mike laughed without humour, with bitterness. 'Can you imagine me being driven in my Rolls to address the College on my advanced technique of cholecystectomy?'

'What happened?' The question was out before he could stop it, and Bruce realized how near to the surface he had let his pity rise. 'No, don't tell me. It's your business. I don't want to know.'

'But I'll tell you, Bruce. I want to. It helps somehow, talking about it.'

At first, thought Bruce, I wanted to talk also, to try and wash the pain away with words.

Mike was silent for a few seconds. Below them the singing rose and fell, and the train ran on through the forest.

'It had taken me ten hard years to get there, but at last I had done it. A fine practice; doing the work I loved with skill, earning the rewards I deserved. A wife that any man would have been proud of, a lovely home, many friends, too many friends perhaps; for success breeds friends the way a dirty kitchen breeds cockroaches.'

Mike pulled out a handkerchief and dried the back of his neck where the wind could not reach.

'Those sort of friends mean parties,' he went on. 'Parties when you've worked all day and you're tired; when you need the lift that you can get so easily from a bottle. You don't know if you have the weakness for the stuff until it's too late; until you have a bottle in the drawer of your desk; until suddenly your practice isn't so good any more.'

Mike twisted the handkerchief around his fingers as he ploughed doggedly on. 'Then you know it suddenly. You know it when your hands dance in the morning and all you want for breakfast is *that*, when you can't wait until lunch time because you have to operate and that's the only way you can keep your hands steady. But you know it finally and utterly when the knife turns in your hand and the artery starts to spurt and you watch it paralysed—you watch it hosing red over your gown and forming pools on the theatre floor.' Mike's voice dried up then and he tapped a cigarette from his pack and lit it. His shoulders were hunched forward and his eyes were full of the shadows of his guilt. Then he straightened up and his voice was stronger.

'You must have read about it. I was headlines for a few days, all the papers. But my name wasn't Haig in those days. I got that name off a label on a bottle in a bar-room.

'Gladys stayed with me, of course, she was that type. We came out to Africa. I had enough saved from the wreck for a down payment on a tobacco farm in the Centenary block outside Salisbury. Two good seasons and I was off the bottle. Gladys was having our first baby, we had both wanted one so badly. It was all coming right again.'

Mike stuffed the handkerchief back in his pocket, and his voice lost its strength again, turned dry and husky.

'Then one day I took the truck into the village and on the way home I stopped at the club. I had been there often before, but this time it was different. Instead of half an hour, I stayed there until they threw me out at closing time and when I got back to the farm I had a case of Scotch on the seat beside me.'

Bruce wanted to stop him; he knew what was coming and he didn't want to hear it.

'The first rains started that night and the rivers came down in flood. The telephone lines were knocked out and we were cut off. In the morning—' Mike stopped again and turned to Bruce.

'I suppose it was the shock of seeing me like that again, but in the morning Gladys went into labour. It was her first and she wasn't so young any more. She was still in labour the next day, but by then she was too weak to scream. I remember how peaceful it was without her screaming and pleading with me to help. You see, she knew I had all the instruments I needed. She begged me to help. I can remember that; her voice through the fog of whisky. I think I hated her then. I think I remember hating her, it was all so confused, so mixed up with the screaming and the liquor. But at last she was quiet. I don't think I realized she was dead. I was simply glad she was quiet and I could have peace.'

He dropped his eyes from Bruce's face.

'I was too drunk to go to the funeral. Then I met a man in a bar-room, I can't remember how long after it was, I can't even remember where. It must have been on the Copperbelt. He was recruiting for Tshombe's army and I signed up; there didn't seem anything else to do.'

Neither of them spoke again until a gendarme brought food to them, hunks of brown bread spread with tinned butter and filled with bully beef and pickled onions. They ate in silence listening to the singing, and Bruce said at last:

'You needn't have told me.'

'I know.'

'Mike—' Bruce paused.

'Yes?'

'I'm sorry, if that's any comfort.'

'It is,' Mike said. 'It helps to have—not to be completely alone. I like you, Bruce.' He blurted out the last sentence and Bruce recoiled as though Mike had spat in his face.

You fool, he rebuked himself savagely, *you were wide open then. You nearly let one of them in again.*

Remorselessly he crushed down his sympathy, shocked at the effort it required, and when he picked up the radio the gentleness had gone from his eyes.

'Hendry,' he spoke into the set, 'don't talk so much. I put you up front to watch the tracks.'

From the leading truck Wally Hendry looked round and forked two fingers at Bruce in a casual obscenity, but he turned back and faced ahead.

'You'd better go and take over from Hendry,' Bruce told Mike. 'Send him back here.'

Mike Haig stood up and looked down at Bruce.

'What are you afraid of?' his voice softly puzzled.

'I gave you an order, Haig.'

'Yes, I'm on my way.'

CHAPTER 4

The aircraft found them in the late afternoon. It was a Vampire jet of the Indian Air Force and it came from the north.

They heard the soft rumble of it across the sky and then saw it glint like a speck of mica in the sunlight above the storm clouds ahead of them.

'I bet you a thousand francs to a handful of dung that this Bucko don't know about us,' said Hendry with anticipation, watching the jet turn off its course towards them.

'Well, he does now,' said Bruce.

Swiftly he surveyed the rain clouds in front of them. They were close; another ten minutes' run and they would be under them, and once there they were safe from air attack for the belly of the clouds pressed close against the earth and the rain was a thick blue-grey mist that would reduce visibility to a few hundred feet. He switched on the radio.

'Driver, give us all the speed you have—get us into that rain.'

'Oui, monsieur,' came the acknowledgement and almost immediately the puffing of the loco quickened and the clatter of the crossties changed its rhythm.

'Look at him come,' growled Hendry. The jet fell fast against the back-drop of cloud, still in sunlight, still a silver point of light, but growing.

Bruce clicked over the band selector of the radio, searching the ether for the pilot's voice. He tried four wavelengths and each time found only the crackle and drone of static, but with the fifth came the gentle sing-song of Hindustani. Bruce could not understand it, but he could hear that the tone was puzzled. There was a short silence on the radio while the pilot listened to an instruction from the Kamina base which was beyond the power of their small set to receive, then a curt affirmative.

'He's coming in for a closer look,' said Bruce, then raising his voice, 'Everybody under cover—and stay there.' He was not prepared to risk another demonstration of friendship.

The jet came cruising in towards them under half power, yet incredibly fast, leaving the sound of its engine far behind it, sharklike above the forest. Then Bruce could see the pilot's head through the canopy; now he could make out his features. His face was very brown beneath the silver crash helmet and he had a little moustache, the same as the Jack of Spades. He was so close that Bruce saw the exact moment that he recognized them as Katangese; his eyes showed white and his mouth puckered as he swore. Beside Bruce the radio relayed the oath with metallic harshness, and then the jet was banking away steeply, its engine howling in full throttle, rising, showing its swollen silver belly and the racks of rockets beneath its wings.

'That frightened seven years' growth out of him,' laughed Hendry. 'You should have let me blast him. He was close enough for me to hit him in the left eyeball.'

'You'll get another chance in a moment,' Bruce assured him grimly.

The radio was gabbling with consternation as the jet dwindled back into the sky. Bruce switched quickly to their own channel.

'Driver, can't you get this thing moving?'

'Monsieur, never before has she moved as she does now.'

Once more he switched back to the jet's frequency and listened to the pilot's excited voice. The jet was turning in a wide circle, perhaps fifteen miles away. Bruce glanced at the piled mass of cloud and rain ahead of them; it was moving down to meet them, but with ponderous dignity.

'If he comes back,' Bruce shouted down at his gendarmes, 'we can be sure that it's not just to look at us again. Open fire as soon as he's in range. Give him everything you've got, we must try and spoil his aim.'

Their faces were turned up towards him, subdued by the awful inferiority of the earth-bound to the hunter in the sky. Only André did not look at Bruce; he was staring at the aircraft with his jaws clenching nervously and his eyes too large for his face.

Again there was silence on the radio, and every head turned back to watch the jet.

'Come on, Bucko, come on!' grunted Hendry impatiently. He spat into the palm of his right hand and then wiped it down the front of his jacket. 'Come on, we want you.' With his thumb he flicked the safety catch of his rifle on and off, on and off.

Suddenly the radio spoke again. Two words, obviously acknowledging an order, and one of the words Bruce recognized. He had heard it before in circumstances that had burned it into his memory. The Hindustani word 'Attack!'

'All right,' he said and stood up. 'He's coming!'

The wind fluttered his shirt against his chest. He settled his helmet firmly and pumped a round into the chamber of his FN.

'Get down into the truck, Hendry,' he ordered.

'I can see better from here.' Hendry was standing beside him, legs planted wide to brace himself against the violent motion of the train.

'As you like,' said Bruce. 'Ruffy, you get under cover.'

'Too damn hot down there in that box,' grinned the huge Negro.

'You're a mad Arab too,' said Bruce.

'Sure, we're all mad Arabs.'

The jet wheeled sharply and stooped towards the forest, levelling, still miles out on their flank.

'This Bucko is a real apprentice. He's going to take us from the side, so we can all shoot at him. If he was half awake he'd give it us up the bum, hit the loco and make sure that we were all shooting over the top of each other,' gloated Hendry.

Silently, swiftly it closed with them, almost touching the tops of the trees. Then suddenly the cannon fire sparkled lemon-pale on its nose and all around them the air was filled with the sound of a thousand whips. Immediately every gun on the train opened up in reply. The tracers from the Brens chased each other out to meet the plane and the rifles joined their voices in a clamour that drowned the cannon fire.

Bruce aimed carefully, the jet unsteady in his sights from the lurching of the coach; then he pressed the trigger and the rifle juddered against his shoulder. From the corner of his eye he saw the empty cartridge cases spray from the breech in a bright bronze stream, and the stench of cordite stung his nostrils.

The aircraft slewed slightly, flinching from the torrent of fire.

'He's yellow!' howled Hendry. 'The bastard's yellow!'

'Hit him!' roared Ruffy. 'Keep hitting him.'

The jet twisted, lifted its nose so that the fire from its cannons passed harmlessly over their heads. Then its nose dropped again and it fired its rockets, two from under each wing. The gunfire from the train stopped abruptly as everybody ducked for safety; only the three of them on the roof kept shooting.

Shrieking like four demons in harness, leaving parallel lines of white smoke behind them, the rockets came from about four hundred yards out and they covered the distance in the time it takes to draw a deep breath, but the pilot had dropped his nose too sharply and fired too late. The rockets exploded in the embankment of the tracks below them.

The blast threw Bruce over backwards. He fell and rolled, clutching desperately at the smooth roof, but as he went over the edge his fingers caught in the guttering and he hung there. He was dazed with the concussion, the guttering cutting into his fingers, the shoulder-strap of his rifle round his neck strangling him, and the gravel of the embankment rushing past beneath him.

Ruffy reached over, caught him by the front of his jacket and lifted him back like a child.

'You going somewhere, boss?' The great round face was coated with dust from the explosions, but he was grinning happily. Bruce had a confused conviction that it would take at least a case of dynamite to make any impression on that mountain of black flesh.

Kneeling on the roof Bruce tried to rally himself. He saw that the wooden side of the coach nearest the explosions was splintered and torn and the roof was covered with earth and pebbles. Hendry was sitting beside him, shaking his head slowly from side to side; a small trickle of blood ran down from a scratch on his cheek and dripped from his chin. In the open trucks the men stood or sat with stunned expressions on their faces, but the train still raced on towards the rain storm and the dust of the explosions hung in a dense brown cloud above the forest far behind them.

Bruce scrambled to his feet, searched frantically for the aircraft and found its tiny shape far off above the mass of cloud.

The radio was undamaged, protected by the sandbags from the blast. Bruce reached for it and pressed the transmit button.

'Driver, are you all right?'

'Monsieur, I am greatly perturbed. Is there—'

'Not you alone,' Bruce assured him. 'Keep this train going.'

'Oui, monsieur.'

Then he switched to the aircraft's frequency. Although his ears were singing shrilly from the explosions, he could hear that the voice of the pilot had changed its tone. There was a slowness in it, a breathless catch on some of the words. He's frightened or he's hurt, thought Bruce, but he still has time to make another pass at us before we reach the storm front.

His mind was clearing fast now, and he became aware of the complete lack of readiness in his men.

'Ruffy!' he shouted. 'Get them on their feet. Get them ready. That plane will be back any second now.'

Ruffy jumped down into the truck and Bruce heard his palm slap against flesh as he began to bully them into activity. Bruce followed him down, then climbed over into the second truck and began the same process there.

'Haig, give me a hand, help me get the lead out of them.'

Further removed from the shock of the explosion, the men in this truck reacted readily and crowded to the side, starting to reload, checking their weapons, swearing, faces losing their dull dazed expressions.

Bruce turned and shouted back, 'Ruffy, are any of your lot hurt?'

'Couple of scratches, nothing bad.'

On the roof of the coach Hendry was standing again, watching the aircraft, blood on his face and his rifle in his hands.

'Where's André?' Bruce asked Haig as they met in the middle of the truck.

'Up front. I think he's been hit.'

Bruce went forward and found André doubled up, crouching in a corner of the truck, his rifle lying beside him and both hands covering his face. His shoulders heaved as though he were in pain.

Eyes, thought Bruce, he's been hit in the eyes. He reached him and stooped over him, pulling his hands from his face, expecting to see blood.

André was crying, his cheeks wet with tears and his eyelashes gummed together. For a second Bruce stared at him and then he caught the front of his jacket and pulled him to his feet. He picked up André's rifle and the barrel was cold, not a single shot had been fired out of it.

He dragged the Belgian to the side and thrust the rifle into his hands.

'De Surrier,' he snarled, 'I'm going to be standing beside you. If you do that again I'll shoot you. Do you understand?'

'I'm sorry, Bruce.' André's lips were swollen where he had bitten them; his face was smeared with tears and slack with fear. 'I'm sorry. I couldn't help it.'

Bruce ignored him and turned his attention back to the aircraft. It was turning in for its next run.

He's going to come from the side again, Bruce thought; this time he'll get us. He can't miss twice in a row.

In silence once more they watched the jet slide down the valley between two vast white mountains of cloud and level off above the forest. Small and dainty and deadly it raced in towards them.

One of the Bren gunners opened up, rattling raucously, sending out tracers like bright beads on a string.

'Too soon,' muttered Bruce. 'Much too soon; he must be all of a mile out of range.'

But the effect was instantaneous. The jet swerved, almost hit the tree tops and then over-corrected, losing its line of approach.

A howl of derision went up from the train and was immediately lost in the roar as every gun opened fire. The jet loosed its remaining rockets, blindly, hopelessly, without a chance of a hit. Then it climbed steeply, turning away into the cloud ahead of them. The sound of its engines receded, was muted by the cloud and then was gone.

Ruffy was performing a dance of triumph, waving his rifle over his head. Hendry on the roof was shouting abuse at the clouds into which the jet had vanished, one of the Brens was still firing short ecstatic bursts, someone else was chanting the Katangese war cry and others were taking it up. And then the driver in the locomotive came in with his whistle, spurting steam with each shriek.

Bruce slung his rifle over his shoulder, pushed his helmet on to the back of his head, took out a cigarette and lit it, then stood watching them sing and laugh and chatter with the relief from danger.

Next to him André leaned out and vomited over the side; a little of it came out of his nose and dribbled down the front of his battle-jacket. He wiped his mouth with the back of his hand.

'I'm sorry, Bruce. I'm sorry, truly I am sorry,' he whispered.

And they were under the cloud, its coolness slumped over them like air from an open refrigerator. The first heavy drops stung Bruce's cheek and then rolled down heavily, washing away the smell of cordite, melting the dust from Ruffy's face until it shone again like washed coal.

Bruce felt his jacket cling wetly to his back.

'Ruffy, two men at each Bren. The rest of them can get back into the covered coaches. We'll relieve every hour.' He reversed his rifle so the muzzle pointed downwards. 'De Surrier, you can go, and you as well, Haig.'

'I'll stay with you, Bruce.'

'All right then.'

The gendarmes clambered back into the covered coaches still laughing and chattering, and Ruffy came forward with a groundsheet and handed it to Bruce.

'The radios are all covered. If you don't need me, boss, I got some business with one of those Arabs in the coach. He's got near twenty thousand francs on him; so I'd better go and give him a couple of tricks with the cards.'

'One of these days I'm going to explain your Christian monarchs to the boys. Show them that the odds are three to one against them,' Bruce threatened.

'I wouldn't do that, boss,' Ruffy advised seriously. 'All that money isn't good for them, just gets them into trouble.'

'Off you go then. I'll call you later,' said Bruce. 'Tell them I said "well done", I'm proud of them.'

'Yeah. I'll tell them,' promised Ruffy.

Bruce lifted the tarpaulin that covered the set.

'Driver, desist before you burst the boiler!'

The abandoned flight of the train steadied to a more sedate pace, and Bruce tilted his helmet over his eyes and pulled the groundsheet up around his mouth before he leaned out over the side of the truck to inspect the rocket damage.

'All the windows blown out on this side and the woodwork torn a little,' he muttered. 'But a lucky escape all the same.'

'What a miserable comic-opera war this is,' grunted Mike Haig. 'That pilot had the right idea: why risk your life when it's none of your business.'

'He was wounded,' Bruce guessed. 'I think we hit him on his first run.'

Then they were silent, with the rain driving into their faces, slitting their eyes to peer ahead along the tracks. The men at the Brens huddled into their brown and green camouflage groundsheets, all their jubilation of ten minutes earlier completely gone. They are like cats, thought Bruce as he noticed their dejection, they can't stand being wet.

'It's half past five already.' Mike spoke at last. 'Do you think we'll make Msapa Junction before nightfall?'

'With this weather it will be dark by six.' Bruce looked up at the low cloud that was prematurely bringing on the night. 'I'm not going to risk travelling in the dark. This is the edge of Baluba country and we can't use the headlight of the loco.'

'You going to stop then?'

Bruce nodded. What a stupid bloody question, he thought irritably. Then he recognized his irritation as reaction from the danger they had just experienced, and he spoke to make amends.

'We can't be far now—if we start again at first light we'll reach Msapa before sun-up.'

'My God, it's cold,' complained Mike and he shivered briefly.

'Either too hot or too cold,' Bruce agreed; he knew that it was also the reaction that was making him garrulous. But he did not attempt to stop himself. 'That's one of the things about this happy little planet of ours; nothing is in moderation. Too hot or too cold, either you are hungry or you've overeaten, you are in love or you hate the world—'

'Like you?' asked Mike.

'Dammit, Mike, you're as bad as a woman. Can't you conduct an objective discussion without introducing personalities?' Bruce demanded. He could feel his temper rising to the surface; he was cold and edgy, and he wanted to smoke.

'Objective theories must have subjective application to prove their worth,' Mike pointed out. There was just a trace of an amused smile on his broad ravaged old face.

'Let's forget it then. I don't want to talk personalities,' snapped Bruce; then immediately went on to do so. 'Humanity sickens me if I think about it too much. De Surrier puking his heart out with fear, that animal Hendry, you trying to keep off the liquor, Joan—' He stopped himself abruptly.

'Who is Joan?'

'Do I ask you your business?' Bruce flashed the standard reply to all personal questions in the mercenary army of Katanga.

'No. But I'm asking you yours—who is Joan?'

All right. I'll tell him. If he wants to know, I'll tell him. Anger had made Bruce reckless.

'Joan was the bitch I married.'

'So, that's it then!'

'Yes—that's it! Now you know. So you can leave me alone.'

'Kids?'

'Two—a boy and a girl.' The anger was gone from Bruce's voice, and the raw naked pain was back for an instant. Then he rallied and his voice was neutral once more.

'And none of it matters a damn. As far as I'm concerned the whole

human race—all of it—can go and lose itself. I don't want any part
of it.'

'How old are you, Bruce?'

'Leave me alone, damn you!'

'How old are you?'

'I'm thirty.'

'You talk like a teenager.'

'And I feel like an old, old man.'

The amusement was no longer on Mike's face as he asked, 'What
did you do before this?'

'I slept and breathed and ate—and got trodden on.'

'What did you do for a living?'

'Law.'

'Were you successful?'

'How do you measure success? If you mean, did I make money, the
answer is yes.'

I made enough to pay off the house and the car, he thought bitterly,
and to contest custody of my children, and finally to meet the divorce
settlement. I had enough for that, but, of course, I had to sell my
partnership.

'Then you'll be all right,' Mike told him. 'If you've succeeded once
you'll be able to do it again when you've recovered from the shock;
when you've rearranged your life and taken other people into it to
make you strong again.'

'I'm strong now, Haig. I'm strong *because* there is no one in my life.
That's the only way you can be secure, on your own. Completely free
and on your own.'

'Strong!' Anger flared in Mike's voice for the first time. 'On your
own you're *nothing*, Curry. On your own you're so weak I could piss on
you and wash you away!' Then the anger evaporated and Mike went
on softly, 'But you'll find out—you're one of the lucky ones. You attract
people to you. You don't have to be alone.'

'Well, that's the way I'm going to be from now on.'

'We'll see,' murmured Mike.

'Yes, we'll see,' Bruce agreed, and lifted the tarpaulin over the radio.

'Driver, we are going to halt for the night. It's too dark to proceed
with safety.'

CHAPTER 5

Brazzaville Radio came through weakly on the set and the static was bad, for outside the rain still fell and thunder rolled around the sky like an unsecured cargo in a high sea.

'—Our Elisabethville correspondent reports that elements of the Katangese Army in the South Kasai province today violated the cease-fire agreement by firing upon a low-flying aircraft of the United Nations command. The aircraft, a Vampire jet fighter of the Indian Air Force, returned safely to its base at Kamina airfield. The pilot, however, was wounded by small arms fire. His condition is reported as satisfactory.

'The United Nations Commander in Katanga, General Rhee, has lodged a strong protest with the Katangese government—' The announcer's voice was overlaid by the electric crackle of static.

'We winged him!' rejoiced Wally Hendry. The scab on his cheek had dried black, with angry red edges.

'Shut up,' snapped Bruce, 'we're trying to hear what's happening.'

'You can't hear a bloody thing now. André, there's a bottle in my pack. Get it! I'm going to drink to that coolie with a bullet up his—'

Then the radio cleared and the announcer's voice came through loudly.

'—at Senwati Mission fifty miles from the river harbour of Port Reprieve. A spokesman for the Central Congolese Government denied that Congolese troops were operating in this area, and it is feared that a large body of armed bandits is taking advantage of the unsettled conditions to—' Again the static drowned it out.

'Damn this set,' muttered Bruce as he tried to tune it.

'—stated today that the removal of missile equipment from the Russian bases in Cuba had been confirmed by aerial reconnaissance—'

'That's all that we are interested in.' Bruce switched off the radio. 'What a shambles! Ruffy, where is Senwati Mission?'

'Top end of the swamp, near the Rhodesian border.'

'Fifty miles from Port Reprieve,' muttered Bruce, not attempting to conceal his anxiety.

'It's more than that by road, boss, more like a hundred.'

'That should take them three or four days in this weather, with time off for looting along the way,' Bruce calculated. 'It will be cutting it fairly fine. We must get through to Port Reprieve by tomorrow evening and pull out again at dawn the next day.'

'Why not keep going tonight?' Hendry removed the bottle from his lips to ask. 'Better than sitting here being eaten by mosquitoes.'

'We'll stay,' Bruce answered. 'It won't do anybody much good to
derail this lot in the dark.' He turned back to Ruffy. 'Three-hour
watches tonight, Sergeant Major. Lieutenant Haig will take the first,
then Lieutenant Hendry, then Lieutenant de Surrier, and I'll do the
dawn spell.'

'Okay, boss. I'd better make sure my boys aren't sleeping.' He left
the compartment and the broken glass from the corridor windows
crunched under his boots.

'I'll be on my way also.' Mike stood up and pulled the groundsheet
over his shoulders.

'Don't waste the batteries of the searchlights, Mike. Sweep every ten
minutes or so.'

'Okay, Bruce.' Mike looked across at Hendry. 'I'll call you at nine
o'clock.'

'Jolly good show, old fruit.' Wally exaggerated Mike's accent. 'Good
hunting, what!' and then as Mike left the compartment, 'Silly old
bugger, why does he have to talk like that?'

No one answered him, and he pulled up his shirt behind.

'André, what's this on my back?'

'It's a pimple.'

'Well, squeeze it then.'

Bruce woke in the night, sweating, with the mosquitoes whining
about his face. Outside it was still raining and occasionally the reflected
light from the searchlight on the roof of the coach lit the interior dimly.

On one of the bottom bunks Mike Haig lay on his back. His face
was shining with sweat and he rolled his head from side to side on the
pillow. He was grinding his teeth—a sound to which Bruce had become
accustomed, and he preferred it to Hendry's snores.

'You poor old bugger,' whispered Bruce.

From the bunk opposite, André de Surrier whimpered. In sleep he
looked like a child with dark soft hair falling over his forehead.

CHAPTER 6

The rain petered out in the dawn and the sun was hot before it cleared the horizon. It lifted a warm mist from the dripping forest. As they ran north the forest thickened, the trees grew closer together and the under-growth beneath them was coarser than it had been around Elisabethville.

Through the warm misty dawn Bruce saw the water tower as Msapa Junction rising like a lighthouse above the forest, its silver paint streaked with brown rust. Then they came round the last curve in the tracks and the little settlement huddled before them.

It was small, half a dozen buildings in all, and there was about it the desolate aspect of human habitation reverting to jungle.

Beside the tracks stood the water tower and the raised concrete coal bins. Then the station buildings of wood and iron, with the large sign above the veranda:

'MSAPA JUNCTION. Elevation 963m.'

An avenue of casia flora trees with very dark green foliage and orange flowers; and beyond that, on the edge of the forest, a row of cottages.

One of the cottages had been burned, its ruins were fire blackened and tumbled; and the gardens had lost all sense of discipline with three months' neglect.

'Driver, stop beside the water tower. You have fifteen minutes to fill your boiler.'

'Thank you, monsieur.'

With a heavy sigh of steam the loco pulled up beside the tower.

'Haig, take four men and go back to give the driver a hand.'

'Okay, Bruce.'

Bruce turned once more to the radio.

'Hendry.'

'Hello there.'

'Get a patrol together, six men, and search those cottages. Then take a look at the edge of the bush—we don't want any unexpected visitors.'

Wally Hendry waved an acknowledgement from the leading truck, and Bruce went on:

'Put de Surrier on.' He watched Hendry pass the set to André. 'De Surrier, you are in charge of the leading trucks in Hendry's absence. Keep Hendry covered, but watch the bush behind you also. They could come from there.'

Bruce switched off the set and turned to Ruffy. 'Stay up here on the roof, Ruffy. I'm going to chase them up with the watering. If you see anything, don't write me a postcard, start popping off.'

Ruffy nodded. 'Have some breakfast to take with you.' He proffered an open bottle of beer.

'Better than bacon and eggs.' Bruce accepted the bottle and climbed down onto the platform. Sipping the beer he walked back along the train and looked up at Mike and the engine driver in the tower.

'Is it empty?' he called up at them.

'Half full, enough for a bath if you want one,' answered Mike.

'Don't tempt me.' The idea was suddenly very attractive, for he could smell his own stale body odour and his eyelids were itchy and swollen from mosquito bites. 'My kingdom for a bath.' He ran his fingers over his jowls and they rasped over stiff beard.

He watched them swing the canvas hose out over the loco. The chubby little engine driver clambered up and sat astride the boiler as he fitted the hose.

A shout from behind him made Bruce turn quickly, and he saw Hendry's patrol coming back from the cottages. They were dragging two small prisoners with them.

'Hiding in the first cottage,' shouted Hendry. 'They tried to leg it into the bush.' He prodded one of them with his bayonet. The child cried out and twisted in the hands of the gendarme who held her.

'Enough of that.' Bruce stopped him from using the bayonet again and went to meet them. He looked at the two children.

The girl was close to puberty with breasts like insect bites just starting to show, thin-legged with enlarged knee-caps out of proportion to her thighs and calves. She wore only a dirty piece of trade cloth drawn up between her legs and secured round her waist by a length of bark string, and the tribal tattoo marks across her chest and cheeks and forehead stood proud in ridges of scar tissue.

'Ruffy,' Bruce called him down from the coach. 'Can you speak to them?'

Ruffy picked up the boy and held him on his hip. He was younger than the girl—seven, perhaps eight years old. Very dark skinned and completely naked, as naked as the terror on his face.

Ruffy grunted sharply and the gendarme released the girl. She stood trembling, making no attempt to escape.

Then in a soothing rumble Ruffy began talking to the boy on his hip; he smiled as he spoke and stroked the child's head. Slowly a little of the fear melted and the boy answered in a piping treble that Bruce could not understand.

'What does he say?' urged Bruce.

'He thinks we're going to eat them,' laughed Ruffy. 'Not enough here for a decent breakfast.' He patted the skinny little arm, grey with crushed filth, then he gave an order to one of the gendarmes. The man disappeared into the coach and came back with a handful of chocolate bars. Still talking, Ruffy peeled one of them and placed it in the boy's mouth. The child's eyes widened appreciatively at the taste and he chewed quickly, his eyes on Ruffy's face, his answers now muffled with chocolate.

At last Ruffy turned to Bruce.

'No trouble here, boss. They come from a small village about an hour's walk away. Just five or six families, and no war party. These kids sneaked across to have a look at the houses, pinch what they could perhaps, but that's all.'

'How many men at this village?' asked Bruce, and Ruffy turned back to the boy. In reply to the question he held up the fingers of both hands, without interrupting his chewing.

'Does he know if the line is clear through to Port Reprieve? Have they burnt the bridges or torn up the tracks?' Both children were dumb to this question. The boy swallowed the last of his chocolate and looked hungrily at Ruffy, who filled his mouth again.

'Jesus,' muttered Hendry with deep disgust. 'Is this a crèche or something. Let's all play ring around the roses.'

'Shut up,' snapped Bruce, and then to Ruffy, 'Have they seen any soldiers?'

Two heads shaken in solemn unison.

'Have they seen any war parties of their own people?'

Again solemn negative.

'All right, give them the rest of the chocolate,' instructed Bruce. That was all he could get out of them, and time was wasting. He glanced back at the tower and saw that Haig and the engine driver had finished watering. For a further second he studied the boy. His own son would be about the same age now; it was twelve months since—Bruce stopped himself hurriedly. That way lay madness.

'Hendry, take them back to the edge of the bush and turn them loose. Hurry up. We've wasted long enough.'

You're telling me!' grunted Hendry and beckoned to the two children. With Hendry leading and a gendarme on each side they trotted away obediently and disappeared behind the station building.

'Driver, are your preparations complete?'

'Yes, monsieur, we are ready to depart.'

'Shovel all the coal in, we've gotta keep her rolling.' Bruce smiled, he liked the little man and their stilted exchanges gave him pleasure.

'Pardon, monsieur.'

'It was an imbecility, a joke—forgive me.'

'Ah, a joke!' The roly-poly stomach wobbled merrily.

'Okay, Mike,' Bruce shouted, 'get your men aboard. We are—'

A burst of automatic gunfire cut his voice short. It came from behind the station buildings, and it battered into the heat-muted morning with such startling violence that for an instant Bruce stood paralysed.

'Haig,' he yelled, 'get up front and take over from de Surrier.' That was the weak point, and Mike's party ran down the train.

'You men.' Bruce stopped the six gendarmes. 'Come with me.' They fell in behind him, and with a quick glance Bruce assured himself that the train was safe. All along its length rifle barrels were poking out protectively, while on the roof Ruffy was dragging the Bren round to cover the flank. A charge by even a thousand Baluba must fail before the fire power that was ready now to receive it.

'Come on,' said Bruce and ran, with the gendarmes behind him, to the sheltering wall of the station building. There had been no shot fired since that initial burst, which could mean either that it was a false alarm or that Hendry's party had been overwhelmed by the first rush.

The door of the station master's office was locked. Bruce kicked and it crashed open with the weight of his booted foot behind it.

I've always wanted to do that, he thought happily in his excitement, ever since I saw Gable do it in *San Francisco*.

'You four—inside! Cover us from the windows.' They crowded into the room with their rifles held ready. Through the open door Bruce saw the telegraph equipment on a table by the far wall; it was clattering metallically from traffic on the Elisabethville–Jadotville line. Why is it that under the stimulus of excitement my mind always registers irrelevances? Which thought is another irrelevancy, he decided.

'Come on, you two, stay with me.' He led them down the outside wall, keeping in close to its sheltering bulk, pausing at the corner to check the load of his rifle and slip the selector on to rapid fire.

A further moment he hesitated. What will I find around this corner? A hundred naked savages crowded round the mutilated bodies of Hendry and his gendarmes, or?

Crouching, ready to jump back behind the wall, rifle held at high port across his chest, every muscle and nerve of his body cocked like a hair-trigger, Bruce stepped sideways into the open.

Hendry and the two gendarmes stood in the dusty road beyond the first cottage. They were relaxed, talking together, Hendry reloading his rifle, cramming the magazine with big red hands on which the gingery hair caught the sunlight. A cigarette dangled from his lower lip and he laughed suddenly, throwing his head back as he did so and the cigarette ash dropped down his jacket front. Bruce noticed the long dark sweat stain across his shoulders.

The two children lay in the road fifty yards farther on.

Bruce was suddenly cold, it came from inside, a cramping coldness of the guts and chest. Slowly he straightened up and began to walk towards the children. His feet fell silently in the powder dust and the only sound was his own breathing, hoarse, as though a wounded beast followed close behind him. He walked past Hendry and the two gendarmes without looking at them; but they stopped talking, watching him uneasily.

He reached the girl first and went down on one knee beside her, laying his rifle aside and turning her gently onto her back.

'This isn't true,' he whispered. 'This can't be true.'

The bullet had taken half her chest out with it, a hole the size of a coffee cup, with the blood still moving in it, but slowly, oozing, welling up into it with the viscosity of new honey.

Bruce moved across to the boy; he felt an almost dreamlike sense of unreality.

'No, this isn't true.' He spoke louder, trying to undo it with words.

Three bullets had hit the boy; one had torn his arm loose at the shoulder and the sharp white end of the bone pointed accusingly out of the wound. The other bullets had severed his trunk almost in two.

It came from far away, like the rising roar of a train along a tunnel. Bruce could feel his whole being shaken by the strength of it, he shut his eyes and listened to the roaring in his head, and with his eyes tight closed his vision was filled with the colour of blood.

'Hold on!' a tiny voice screamed in his roaring head. 'Don't let go, fight it. Fight it as you've fought before.'

And he clung like a flood victim to the straw of his sanity while the great roaring was all around him. Then the roar was muted, rumbling away, gone past, a whisper, now nothing.

The coldness came back to him, a coldness more vast than the flood had been.

He opened his eyes and breathed again, stood up and walked back to where Hendry stood with the two gendarmes.

'Corporal,' Bruce addressed one of the men beside Hendry; and with a shock he heard that his own voice was calm, without any trace of the fury that had so nearly carried him away on its flood.

'Corporal, go back to the train. Tell Lieutenant Haig and Sergeant Major Ruffararo that I want them here.'

Thankfully the man went, and Bruce spoke to Wally Hendry in the same dispassionate tone.

'I told you to turn them loose,' he said.

'So they could run home and call the whole pack down on us—is that what you wanted, Bucko?' Hendry had recovered now, he was defiant, grinning.

'So instead you murdered them?'

'Murdered! You crazy or something, Bruce? They're Baluba, aren't they? Bloody man-eating Baluba!' shouted Hendry angrily, no longer grinning. 'What's wrong with you, man? This is war, Bucko, war. C'est la guerre, like the man said, c'est la guerre!' Then suddenly his voice moderated again. 'Let's forget it. I did what was right, now let's forget it; what's two more bloody Baluba after all the killing that's been going on. Let's forget it.'

Bruce did not answer, he lit a cigarette and looked beyond Hendry for the others to come.

'How's that, Bruce? You willing we just forget it?' persisted Hendry.

'On the contrary, Hendry, I make you a sacred oath, and I call upon God to witness it.' Bruce was not looking at him, he couldn't trust himself to look at Hendry without killing him. 'This is my promise to you: I will have you hanged for this, not shot, hanged on good hemp rope. I have sent for Haig and Ruffararo so we'll have plenty of witnesses. The first thing I do once we get back to Elisabethville will be to turn you over to the proper authorities.'

'You don't mean that!'

'I have never meant anything so seriously in my life.'

'Jesus, Bruce—!'

Then Haig and Ruffy came; they came running until they saw, and then they stopped suddenly and stood uncertainly in the bright sun, looking from Bruce to the two frail little corpses lying in the road.

'What happened?' asked Mike.

'Hendry shot them,' answered Bruce.

'What for?'

'Only he knows.'

'You mean he—he just killed them, just shot them down?'

'Yes.'

'My God,' said Mike, and then again, his voice dull with shock, 'my God.'

'Go and look at them, Haig. I want you to look closely so you remember.'

Haig walked across to the children.

'You too, Ruffy. You'll be a witness at the trial.'

Mike Haig and Ruffy walked side by side to where the children lay, and stood staring down at them. Hendry shuffled his feet in the dust awkwardly and then went on loading the magazine of his rifle.

'Oh, for Chrissake!' he blustered. 'What's all the fuss. They're just a couple of Baluba.'

Wheeling slowly to face him Mike Haig's face was a yellowish colour with only his cheeks and his nose still flushed with the tiny burst veins beneath the surface of the skin, but there was no colour in his lips. Each breath he drew sobbed in his throat. He started back towards Hendry, still breathing that way, and his mouth was working as he tried to force it to speak. As he came on he unslung the rifle from his shoulder.

'Haig!' said Bruce sharply.

'This time—you—you bloody—this is the last—' mouthed Haig.

'Watch it, Bucko!' Hendry warned him. He stepped back, clumsily trying to fit the loaded magazine onto his rifle.

Mike Haig dropped the point of his bayonet to the level of Hendry's stomach.

'Haig!' shouted Bruce, and Haig charged surprisingly fast for a man of his age, leaning forward, leading with the bayonet at Hendry's stomach, the incoherent mouthings reaching their climax in a formless bellow.

'Come on, then!' Hendry answered him and stepped forward. As they came together Hendry swept the bayonet to one side with the butt of his own rifle. The point went under his armpit and they collided chest to chest, staggering as Haig's weight carried them backwards. Hendry dropped his rifle and locked both arms round Haig's neck, forcing his head back so that his face was tilted up at the right angle.

'Look out, Mike, he's going to butt!' Bruce had recognized the move, but his warning came too late. Hendry's head jerked forward and Mike gasped as the front of Hendry's steel helmet caught him across the bridge of the nose. The rifle slipped from Mike's grip and fell into the road; he lifted his hands and covered his face with spread fingers and the redness oozed out between them.

Again Hendry's head jerked forward like a hammer and again Mike gasped as the steel smashed into his face and fingers.

'Knee him, Mike!' Bruce yelled as he tried to take up a position from which to intervene, but they were staggering in a circle, turning like a wheel and Bruce could not get in.

Hendry's legs were braced apart as he drew his head back to strike again, and Mike's knee went up between them, all the way up with power into the fork of Hendry's crotch.

Breaking from the clinch, his mouth open in a silent scream of agony, Hendry doubled up with both hands holding his lower stomach, and sagged slowly on to his knees in the dust.

Dazed, with blood running into his mouth, Mike fumbled with the canvas flap of his holster.

'I'll kill you, you murdering swine.'

The pistol came out into his right hand; short-barrelled, blue and ugly.

Bruce stepped up behind him, his thumb found the nerve centre below the elbow and as he dug in the pistol dropped from Mike's paralysed hand and dangled on its lanyard against his knee.

'Ruffy, stop him,' Bruce shouted, for Hendry was clawing painfully at the rifle that lay in the dust beside him.

'Got it, boss!' Ruffy's huge boot trod down heavily on the rifle and Hendry struggled ineffectually to pull it out from under him.

'Take his pistol,' Bruce ordered.

'Got that too!' Ruffy stooped quickly over the crawling body at his feet, in one swift movement opened the flap of the holster, drew the revolver and the lanyard snapped like cotton as he jerked on it.

They stood like that: Bruce holding Haig from behind, and Hendry crouched at Ruffy's feet. The only sound for several seconds was the hoarse rasping of breath.

Bruce felt Mike Haig relaxing in his grip as the madness left him; he unclipped his pistol from its lanyard and let it drop.

'Leave me, Bruce. I'm all right now.'

'Are you sure? I don't want to shoot you.'

'No, I'm all right.'

'If you start it again, I'll have to shoot you. Do you understand?'

'Yes, I'll be all right now. I lost my senses for a moment.'

'You certainly did,' Bruce agreed, and released him.

They formed a circle round the kneeling Hendry, and Bruce spoke.

'If either you or Haig start it again you'll answer to me, do you hear me?'

Hendry looked up, his small eyes slitted with pain. He did not answer.

'Do you hear me?' Bruce repeated the question and Hendry nodded.

'Good! From now on, Hendry, you are under open arrest. I can't spare men to guard you, and you're welcome to escape if you'd like to try. The local gentry would certainly entertain you most handsomely, they'd probably arrange a special banquet in your honour.'

Hendry's lips drew back in a snarl that exposed teeth with green slimy stains on them.

'But remember my promise, Hendry, as soon as we get back to—'

'Wally, Wally, are you hurt?' André came running from the direction of the station. He knelt beside Hendry.

'Get away, leave me alone.' Hendry struck out at him impatiently and André recoiled.

'De Surrier, who gave you permission to leave your post? Get back to the train.'

André looked up uncertainly, and then back to Hendry.

'De Surrier, you heard me. Get going. And you also, Haig.'

He watched them disappear behind the station building before he glanced once more at the two children. There was a smear of blood and melted chocolate across the boy's cheek and his eyes were wide open in an expression of surprise. Already the flies were settling, crawling delightedly over the two small corpses.

'Ruffy, get spades. Bury them under those trees.' He pointed at the avenue of casia flora. 'But do it quickly.' He spoke brusquely so that how he felt would not show in his voice.

'Okay, boss. I'll fix it.'

'Come on, Hendry,' Bruce snapped, and Wally Hendry heaved to his feet and followed him meekly back to the train.

CHAPTER 7

Slowly from Msapa Junction they travelled northwards through the forest. Each tree seemed to have been cast from the same mould, tall and graceful in itself, but when multiplied countless million times the effect was that of numbing monotony. Above them was a lane of open sky with the clouds scattered, but slowly regrouping for the next assault, and the forest shut in the moist heat so they sweated even in the wind of the train's movement.

'How is your face?' asked Bruce and Mike Haig touched the parallel swellings across his forehead where the skin was broken and discoloured.

'It will do,' he decided; then he lifted his eyes and looked across the open trucks at Wally Hendry. 'You shouldn't have stopped me, Bruce.'

Bruce did not answer, but he also watched Hendry as he leaned uncomfortably against the side of the leading truck, obviously favouring his injuries, his face turned half away from them, talking to André.

'You should have let me kill him,' Mike went on. 'A man who can shoot down two small children in cold blood and then laugh about it afterwards—!' Mike left the rest unsaid, but his hands were opening and closing in his lap.

'It's none of your business,' said Bruce, sensitive to the implied rebuke. 'What are you? One of God's avenging angels?'

'None of my business, you say?' Mike turned quickly to face Bruce. 'My God, what kind of man are you? I hope for your sake that you don't mean that!'

'I'll tell you in words of one syllable what kind of man I am, Haig,' Bruce answered flatly. 'I'm the kind that minds my own bloody business, that lets other people lead their own lives. I am ready to take reasonable measures to prevent others flouting the code which society has drawn up for us, but that's all. Hendry has committed murder; this I agree is a bad thing, and when we get back to Elisabethville I will bring it to the attention of the people whose business it is. But I am not going to wave banners and quote from the Bible and froth at the mouth.'

'That's all?'

'That's all.'

'You don't feel sorry for those two kids?'

'Yes I do. But pity doesn't heal bullet wounds; all it does is distress me. So I switch off the pity—they can't use it.'

'You don't feel anger or disgust or horror at Hendry?'

'The same thing applies,' explained Bruce, starting to lose patience again. 'I could work up a sweat about it if I let myself loose on an emotional orgy, as you are doing.'

'So instead you treat something as evil as Hendry with an indifferent tolerance?' asked Mike.

'Jesus Christ!' grated Bruce. 'What the hell do you want me to do?'

'I want you to stop playing dead. I want you to be able to recognize evil and to destroy it.' Mike was starting to lose his temper also; his nerves were taut.

'That's great! Do you know where I can buy a secondhand crusader outfit and a white horse, then single-handed I will ride out to wage war on cruelty and ignorance, lust and greed and hatred and poverty—'

'That's not what I—' Mike tried to interrupt, but Bruce overrode him, his handsome face flushed darkly with anger and the sun. 'You want me to destroy evil wherever I find it. You old fool, don't you know that it has a hundred heads and that for each one you cut off another hundred grow in its place? Don't you know that it's in you also, so to destroy it you have to destroy yourself?'

'You're a coward, Curry! The first time you burn a finger you run away and build yourself an asbestos shelter—'

'I don't like being called names, Haig. Put a leash on your tongue.'

Mike paused and his expression changed, softening into a grin.

'I'm sorry, Bruce. I was just trying to teach you—'

'Thank you,' scoffed Bruce, his voice still harsh; he had not been placated by the apology. 'You are going to teach me, thanks very much! But what are you going to teach me, Haig? What are you qualified to teach? "How to find success and happiness" by Laughing Lad Haig who worked his way down to a lieutenancy in the black army of Katanga—how's that as a title for your lecture, or do you prefer something more technical like: "The applications of alcohol to spiritual research—"'

'All right, Bruce. Drop it, I'll shut up,' and Bruce saw how deeply he had wounded Mike. He regretted it then, he would have liked to unsay it. But that's one thing you can never do.

Beside him Mike Haig was suddenly much older and more tired looking, the pouched wrinkles below his eyes seemed to have deepened in the last few seconds, and a little more of the twinkle had gone from his eyes. His short laughter had a bitter humourless ring to it.

'When you put it that way it's really quite funny.'

'I punched a little low,' admitted Bruce, and then, 'perhaps I should let you shoot Hendry. A waste of ammunition really, but seeing that you want to so badly,' Bruce drew his pistol and offered it to Mike butt first, 'use mine'. He grinned disarmingly at Mike and his grin was almost impossible to resist; Mike started to laugh. It wasn't a very good joke, but somehow it caught fire between them and suddenly they were laughing together.

Mike Haig's battered features spread like warm butter and twenty years dropped from his face. Bruce leaned back against the sandbags with his mouth wide open, the pistol still in his hand and his long lean body throbbing uncontrollably with laughter.

There was something feverish in it, as though they were trying with laughter to gargle away the taste of blood and hatred. It was the laughter of despair.

Below them the men in the trucks turned to watch them, puzzled at first, and then beginning to chuckle in sympathy, not recognizing the sickness of that sound.

'Hey, boss,' called Ruffy. 'First time I ever seen you laugh like you meant it.'

And the epidemic spread, everyone was laughing, even André de Surrier was smiling.

Only Wally Hendry was untouched by it, silent and sullen, watching them with small expressionless eyes.

They came to the bridge over the Cheke in the middle afternoon.
Both the road and the railway line crossed it side by side, but after this
brief meeting they diverged and the road twisted away to the left. The
river was padded on each bank by dense dark green bush, three
hundred yards thick, a matted tangle of thorn and tree fern with the
big trees growing up through it and bursting into flower as they
reached the sunlight.

'Good place for an ambush,' muttered Mike Haig, eyeing the solid
green walls of vegetation on each side of the lines.

'Charming, isn't it,' agreed Bruce, and by the uneasy air of alertness
that had settled on his gendarmes it was clear that they agreed with
him.

The train nosed its way carefully into the river bush like a steel snake
along a rabbit run, and they came to the river. Bruce switched on the
set.

'Driver, stop this side of the bridge. I wish to inspect it before
entrusting our precious cargo to it.'

'Oui, monsieur.'

The Cheke river at this point was fifty yards wide, deep, quick-
flowing and angry with flood water which had almost covered the
white sand beaches along each bank. Its bottle-green colour was
smoked with mud and there were whirlpools round the stone columns
of the bridge.

'Looks all right,' Haig gave his opinion. 'How far are we from Port
Reprieve now?'

Bruce spread his field map on the roof of the coach between his legs
and found the brackets that straddled the convoluted ribbon of the
river.

'Here we are.' He touched it and then ran his finger along the
stitched line of the railway until it reached the red circle that marked
Port Reprieve. 'About thirty miles to go, another hour's run. We'll be
there before dark.'

'Those are the Lufira hills.' Mike Haig pointed to the blue smudge
that only just showed above the forest ahead of them.

'We'll be able to see the town from the top,' agreed Bruce. 'The
river runs parallel to them on the other side, and the swamp is off to
the right; the swamp is the source of the river.'

He rolled the map and passed it back to Ruffy who slid it into the
plastic map case.

'Ruffy, Lieutenant Haig and I are going ahead to have a look at
the bridge. Keep an eye on the bush.'

'Okay, boss. You want a beer to take with you?'

'Thanks.' Bruce was thirsty and he emptied half the bottle before climbing down to join Mike on the gravel embankment. Rifles unslung, watching the bush on each side uneasily, they hurried forward and with relief reached the bridge and went out into the centre of it.

'Seems solid enough,' commented Mike. 'No one has tampered with it.'

'It's wood.' Bruce stamped on the heavy wild mahogany timbers. They were three feet thick and stained with a dark chemical to inhibit rotting.

'So, it's wood?' enquired Mike.

'Wood burns,' explained Bruce. 'It would be easy to burn it down.' He leaned his elbows on the guard rail, drained the beer bottle and dropped it to the surface of the river twenty feet below. There was a thoughtful expression on his face.

'Very probably there are Baluba in the bush'—he pointed at the banks—'watching us at this moment. They might get the same idea. I wonder if I should leave a guard here?'

Mike leaned on the rail beside him and they both stared out to where the river took a bend two hundred yards downstream; in the crook of the bend grew a tree twice as tall as any of its neighbours. The trunk was straight and covered with smooth silvery bark and its foliage piled to a high green steeple against the clouds. It was the natural point of focus for their eyes as they weighed the problem.

'I wonder what kind of tree that is. I've never seen one like it before.' Bruce was momentarily diverted by the grandeur of it. 'It looks like a giant blue gum.'

'It's quite a sight,' Mike concurred. 'I'd like to go down and have a closer—'

Then suddenly he stiffened and there was an edge of alarm in his voice as he pointed.

'Bruce, there! What's that in the lower branches.'

'Where?'

'Just above the first fork, on the left—' Mike was pointing and suddenly Bruce saw it. For a second he thought it was a leopard, then he realized it was too dark and long.

'It's a man,' exclaimed Mike.

'Baluba,' snapped Bruce; he could see the shape now and the sheen of naked black flesh, the kilt of animal tails and the headdress of feathers. A long bow stood up behind the man's shoulder as he balanced on the branch and steadied himself with one hand against the trunk. He was watching them.

Bruce glanced round at the train. Hendry had noticed their agitation and, following the direction of Mike's raised arm, he had spotted the Baluba. Bruce realized what Hendry was going to do and he opened his mouth to shout, but before he could do so Hendry had snatched his rifle off his shoulder, swung it up and fired a long, rushing, hammering burst.

'The trigger-happy idiot,' snarled Bruce and looked back at the tree. Slabs of white bark were flying from the trunk and the bullets reaped leaves that fluttered down like crippled insects, but the Baluba had disappeared.

The gunfire ceased abruptly and in its place Hendry was shouting with hoarse excitement.

'I got him, I got the bastard.'

'Hendry!' Bruce's voice was also hoarse, but with anger. 'Who ordered you to fire?'

'He was a bloody Baluba, a mucking big bloody Baluba. Didn't you see him, hey? Didn't you see him, man?'

'Come here, Hendry.'

'I got the bastard,' rejoiced Hendry.

'Are you deaf? Come here!'

While Hendry climbed down from the truck and came towards them Bruce asked Haig:

'Did he hit him?'

'I'm not sure. I don't think so, I think he jumped. If he had been hit he'd have been thrown backwards, you know how it knocks them over.'

'Yes,' said Bruce, 'I know.' A .300 bullet from an FN struck with a force of well over a ton. When you hit a man there was no doubt about it. All right, so the Baluba was still in there.

Hendry came up, swaggering, laughing with excitement.

'So you killed, hey?' Bruce asked.

'Stone dead, stone bloody dead!'

'Can you see him?'

'No, he's down in the bush.'

'Do you want to go and have a look at him, Hendry? Do you want to go and get his ears?'

Ears are the best trophy you can take from a man, not as good as the skin of a black-maned lion or the great bossed horns of a buffalo, but better than a scalp. The woolly cap of an African scalp is a drab thing, messy to take and difficult to cure. You have to salt it and stretch it inside out over a helmet; even then it smells badly. Ears are much less trouble and Hendry was an avid collector. He was not the only one in the army of Katanga; the taking of ears was common practice.

'Yeah, I want them.' Hendry detached the bayonet from the muzzle of his rifle. 'I'll nip down and get them.'

'You can't let anyone go in there, Bruce. Not even him,' protested Haig quietly.

'Why not? He deserves it, he worked hard for it.'

'Only take a minute.' Hendry ran his thumb along the bayonet to test the edge. My God! he really means it, thought Bruce; he'd go into that tangled stuff for a pair of ears—he's not brave he's just stupendously lacking in imagination.

'Wait for me, Bruce, it won't take long.' Hendry started back.

'You're not serious, Bruce?' Mike asked.

'No,' agreed Bruce, 'I'm not serious,' and his voice was cold and hard as he caught hold of Hendry's shoulder and stopped him.

'Listen to me! You have no more chances—that was it. I'm waiting for you now, Hendry. Just once more, that's all. Just once more.'

Hendry's face turned sullen again.

'Don't push me, Bucko.'

'Get back to the train and bring it across,' said Bruce contemptuously and turned to Haig.

'Now we'll have to leave a guard here. They know we've gone across and they'll burn it for a certainty, especially after that little fiasco.'

'Who are you going to leave?'

'Ten men, say, under a sergeant. We'll be back by nightfall or tomorrow morning at the latest. They should be safe enough. I doubt there is a big war party here, a few strays perhaps, but the main force will be closer to the town.'

'I hope you're right.'

'So do I,' said Bruce absently, his mind busy with the problem of defending the bridge. 'We'll strip all the sandbags off the coaches and build an emplacement here in the middle of the roadway, leave two of the battery-operated searchlights and a case of flares with them, one of the Brens and a couple of cases of grenades. Food and water for a week. No, they'll be all right.'

The train was rolling down slowly towards them—and a single arrow rose from the edge of the jungle. Slowly it rose, curving in flight and falling towards the train, dropping faster now, silently into the mass of men in the leading truck.

So Hendry had missed and the Baluba had come upstream through the thick bush to launch his arrow in retaliation. Bruce sprang to the guard rail and, using it as a rest for his rifle, opened up in short bursts, searching the edge of the jungle blindly, firing into the green mass and seeing it tremble with his bullets. Haig was shooting also, hunting the area from which the arrow had come.

The train was up to them now and Bruce slung his rifle over his shoulder and scrambled up the side of the truck. He pushed his way to the radio set.

'Driver, stop the covered coaches in the middle of the bridge,' he snapped, and then he switched it off and looked for Ruffy.

'Sergeant Major, get all those sandbags off the roof into the roadway.' While they worked, the gendarmes would be protected from further arrows by the body of the train.

'Okay, boss.'

'Kanaki.' Bruce picked his most reliable sergeant. 'I am leaving you here with ten men to hold the bridge for us. Take one of the Brens, and two of the lights—' Quickly Bruce issued his orders and then he had time to ask André:

'What happened to that arrow? Was anyone hit?'

'No, missed by a few inches. Here it is.'

'That was a bit of luck.' Bruce took the arrow from André and inspected it quickly. A light reed, crudely fletched with green leaves and with the iron head bound into it with a strip of rawhide. It looked fragile and ineffectual, but the barbs of the head were smeared thickly with a dark paste that had dried like toffee.

'Pleasant,' murmured Bruce, and then he shuddered slightly. He could imagine it embedded in his body with the poison purple-staining the flesh beneath the skin. He had heard that it was not a comfortable death, and the iron-tipped reed was suddenly malignant and repulsive. He snapped it in half and threw it out over the side of the bridge before he jumped down from the truck to supervise the building of the guard post.

'Not enough sandbags, boss.'

'Take the mattresses off all the bunks, Ruffy.' Bruce solved that quickly. The leather-covered coir pallets would stop an arrow with ease.

Fifteen minutes later the post was completed, a shoulder-high ring of sandbags and mattresses large enough to accommodate ten men and their equipment, with embrasures sited to command both ends of the bridge.

'We'll be back early tomorrow, Kanaki. Let none of your men leave this post for any purpose; the gaps between the timbers are sufficient for purposes of sanitation.'

'We shall enjoy enviable comfort, Captain. But we will lack that which soothes.' Kanaki grinned meaningly at Bruce.

'Ruffy, leave them a case of beer.'

'A whole case?' Ruffy made no attempt to hide his shocked disapproval of such a prodigal order.

'Is my credit not good?'

'Your credit is okay, boss,' and then he changed to French to make his protest formal. 'My concern is the replacement of such a valuable commodity.'

'You're wasting time, Ruffy!'

CHAPTER 8

From the bridge it was thirty miles to Port Reprieve. They met the road again six miles outside the town; it crossed under them and disappeared into the forest again to circle out round the high ground taking the easier route into Port Reprieve. But the railroad climbed up the hills in a series of traverses and came out at the top six hundred feet above the town. On the stony slopes the forest found meagre purchase and the vegetation was sparser; it did not obscure the view.

Standing on the roof Bruce looked out across the Lufira swamps to the north, a vastness of poisonous green swamp grass and open water, disappearing into the blue heat haze without any sign of ending. From its southerly extremity it was drained by the Lufira river. The river was half a mile wide, deep olive-green, ruffled darker by eddies of wind across its surface, fenced into the very edge of the water by a solid barrier of dense river bush. In the angle formed by the swamp and the river was a headland which protected the natural harbour of Port Reprieve. The town was on a spit of land, the harbour on one side and a smaller swamp on the other. The road came round the right-hand side of the hills, crossed a causeway over the swamp and entered the single street of the town from the far side.

There were three large buildings in the centre of the town opposite the railway yard, their iron roofs bright beacons in the sunlight; and clustered round them were perhaps fifty smaller thatched dwellings.

Down on the edge of the harbour was a long shed, obviously a workshop, and two jetties ran out into the water. The diamond dredgers were moored alongside; three of them, ungainly black hulks with high superstructures and blunt ends.

It was a place of heat and fever and swamp smells, an ugly little village by a green reptile river.

'Nice place to retire,' Mike Haig grunted.

'Or open a health resort,' said Bruce.

Beyond the causeway, on the main headland, there was another cluster of buildings, just the tops showing above the forest. Among them rose the copper-clad spire of a church.

'Mission station,' guessed Bruce.

'St Augustine's,' agreed Ruffy. 'My first wife's little brudder got himself educated there. He's an attaché to the ministry of something or other in Elisabethville now, doing damn good for himself.' Boasting a little.

'Bully for him,' said Bruce.

The train had started angling down the hills towards the town.

'Well, I reckon we've made it, boss.'

'I reckon also; all we have to do is get back again.'

'Yessir, I reckon that's all.'

And they ran into the town.

There were more than forty people in the crowd that lined the platform to welcome them.

We'll have a heavy load on the way home, thought Bruce as he ran his eye over them. He saw the bright spots of women's dresses in the throng. Bruce counted four of them. That's another complication; one day I hope I find something in this life that turns out exactly as expected, something that will run smoothly and evenly through to its right and logical conclusion. Some hope, he decided, some bloody hope.

The joy and relief of the men and women on the platform was pathetically apparent in their greetings. Most of the women were crying and the men ran beside the train like small boys as it slid in along the raised concrete platform. All of them were of mixed blood, Bruce noted. They varied in colour from creamy yellow to charcoal. The Belgians had certainly left much to be remembered by.

Standing back from the throng, a little aloof from the general jollification, was a half-blooded Belgian. There was an air of authority about him that was unmistakeable. On one side of him stood a large bosomy woman of his own advanced age, darker skinned than he was; but Bruce saw immediately that she was his wife. At his other hand stood a figure dressed in a white open-necked shirt and blue jeans that Bruce at first thought was a boy, until the head turned and he saw the long plume of dark hair that hung down her back, and the unmanly double pressure beneath the white shirt.

The train stopped and Bruce jumped down onto the platform and laughingly pushed his way through the crowds towards the Belgian. Despite a year in the Congo, Bruce had not grown accustomed to being kissed by someone who had not shaved for two or three days and who smelled strongly of garlic and cheap tobacco. This atrocity was committed upon him a dozen times or more before he arrived before the Belgian.

'The Good Lord bless you for coming to our aid, Monsieur Captain.' The Belgian recognized the twin bars on the front of Bruce's helmet and held out his hand. Bruce had expected another kiss, so he accepted the handshake with relief.

'I am only glad that we are in time,' he answered.

'May I introduce myself—Martin Boussier, district manager of Union Minière Corporation, and this is my wife, Madame Boussier.' He was a tall man but, unlike his wife, sparsely fleshed. His hair was completely silver and his skin folded, toughened and browned by a life under the equatorial sun. Bruce took an instant liking to him. Madame Boussier pressed her bulk against Bruce and kissed him heartily. Her moustache was too soft to cause him discomfort and she smelled of toilet soap, which was a distinct improvement, decided Bruce.

'May I also present Madame Cartier,' and for the first time Bruce looked squarely at the girl. A number of things registered in his mind simultaneously: the paleness of her skin which was not unhealthy but had an opaque coolness which he wanted to touch, the size of her eyes which seemed to fill half her face, the unconscious provocation of her lips, and the use of the word *Madame* before her name.

'Captain Curry—of the Katanga Army,' said Bruce. She's too young to be married, can't be more than seventeen. She's still got that little girl freshness about her and I bet she smells like an unweaned puppy.

'Thank you for coming, monsieur.' She had a throatiness in her voice as though she were just about to laugh or to make love, and Bruce added three years to his estimate of her age. That was not a little girl's voice, nor were those little girl's legs in the jeans, and little girls had less under their shirt fronts.

His eyes came back to her face and he saw that there was colour in her cheeks now and sparks of annoyance in her eyes.

My God, he thought, I'm ogling her like a matelot on shore leave. He hurriedly transferred his attention back to Boussier, but his throat felt constricted as he asked:

'How many are you?'

'There are forty-two of us, of which five are women and two are children.'

Bruce nodded, it was what he had expected. The women could ride in one of the covered coaches. He turned and surveyed the railway yard.

'Is there a turn-table on which we can revolve the locomotive?' he asked Boussier.

'No, Captain.'

They would have to reverse all the way back to Msapa Junction, another complication. It would be more difficult to keep a watch on the tracks ahead, and it would mean a sooty and uncomfortable journey.

'What precautions have you taken against attack, monsieur?'

'They are inadequate, Captain,' Boussier admitted. 'I have not sufficient men to defend the town—most of the population left before the emergency. Instead I have posted sentries on all the approaches and I have fortified the hotel to the best of my ability. It was there we intended to stand in the event of attack.'

Bruce nodded again and glanced up at the sun. It was already reddening as it dropped towards the horizon, perhaps another hour or two of daylight.

'Monsieur, it is too late to entrain all your people and leave before nightfall. I intend to load their possessions this evening. We will stay overnight and leave in the early morning.'

'We are all anxious to be away from this place; we have twice seen large parties of Baluba on the edge of the jungle.'

'I understand,' said Bruce. 'But the dangers of travelling by night exceed those of waiting another twelve hours.'

'The decision is yours,' Boussier agreed. 'What do you wish us to do now.'

'Please see to the embarkation of your people. I regret that only the most essential possessions may be entrained. We will be almost a hundred persons.'

'I shall see to that myself,' Boussier assured him, 'and then?'

'Is that the hotel?' Bruce pointed across the street at one of the large double-storied buildings. It was only two hundred yards from where they stood.

'Yes, Captain.'

'Good,' said Bruce. 'It is close enough. Your people can spend the night there in more comfort than aboard the train.'

He looked at the girl again; she was watching him with a small smile on her face. It was a smile of almost maternal amusement, as though she were watching a little boy playing at soldiers. Now it was Bruce's turn to feel annoyed. He was suddenly embarrassed by his uniform and epaulettes, by the pistol at his hip, the automatic rifle across his shoulder and the heavy helmet on his head.

'I will require someone who is familiar with the area to accompany me, I want to inspect your defences,' he said to Boussier.

'Madame Cartier could show you,' suggested Boussier's wife artlessly. I wonder if she noticed our little exchange, thought Bruce. Of course she did. All women have a most sensitive nose for that sort of thing.

'Will you go with the captain, Shermaine?' asked Madame Boussier.

'As the captain wishes.' She was still smiling.

'That is settled then,' said Bruce gruffly. 'I will meet you at the hotel in ten minutes, after I have made arrangements here.' He turned back to Boussier. 'You may proceed with the embarkation, monsieur.' Bruce left them and went back to the train.

'Hendry,' he shouted, 'you and de Surrier will stay on board. We are not leaving until the morning but these people are going to load their stuff now. In the meantime rig the searchlights to sweep both sides of the track and make sure the Brens are properly sited.'

Hendry grunted an acknowledgement without looking at Bruce.

'Mike, take ten men with you and go to the hotel. I want you there in case of trouble during the night.'

'Okay, Bruce.'

'Ruffy.'

'Sa!'

'Take a gang and help the driver refuel.'

'Okay, boss. Hey, boss!'

'Yes.' Bruce turned to him.

'When you go to the hotel, have a look-see maybe they got some beer up there. We're just about fresh out.'

'I'll keep it in mind.'

'Thanks, boss.' Ruffy looked relieved. 'I'd hate like hell to die of thirst in this hole.'

The townsfolk were streaming back towards the hotel. The girl Shermaine walked with the Boussiers, and Bruce heard Hendry's voice above him.

'Jesus, look what that pretty has got in her pants. What ever it is, one thing is sure: it's round and it's in two pieces, and those pieces move like they don't belong to each other.'

'You haven't any work to do, Hendry?' Bruce asked harshly.

'What's wrong, Curry,' Hendry jeered down at him. 'You got plans yourself. Is that it, Bucko?'

'She's married,' said Bruce, and immediately was surprised that he had said it.

'Sure,' laughed Hendry. 'All the best ones are married; that don't mean a thing, not a bloody thing.'

'Get on with your work,' snapped Bruce, and then to Haig, 'Are you ready? Come with me then.'

CHAPTER 9

When they reached the hotel Boussier was waiting for them on the open veranda. He led Bruce aside and spoke quietly.

'Monsieur, I don't wish to be an alarmist but I have received some most disturbing news. There are brigands armed with modern weapons raiding down from the north. The last reports state that they have sacked Senwati Mission, about three hundred miles north of here.'

'Yes,' Bruce nodded, 'I know about them. We heard on the radio.'

'Then you will have realized that they can be expected to arrive here very soon.'

'I don't see them arriving before tomorrow afternoon; by then we should be well on our way to Msapa Junction.'

'I hope you are right, monsieur. The atrocities committed by this General Moses at Senwati are beyond the conception of any normal mind. He appears to bear an almost pathological hatred for all people of European descent.' Boussier hesitated before going on. 'There were a dozen white nuns at Senwati. I have heard that they—'

'Yes,' Bruce interrupted him quickly; he did not want to listen to it. 'I can imagine. Try and prevent these stories circulating among your people. I don't want to have them panic.'

'Of course,' Boussier nodded.

'Do you know what force this General Moses commands?'

'It is not more than a hundred men but, as I have said, they are all armed with modern weapons. I have even heard that they have with them a cannon of some description, though I think this unlikely. They are travelling in a convoy of stolen vehicles and at Senwati they captured a gasoline tanker belonging to the commercial oil companies.'

'I see,' mused Bruce. 'But it doesn't alter my decision to remain here overnight. However, we must leave at first light tomorrow.'

'As you wish, Captain.'

'Now, monsieur,' Bruce changed the subject, 'I require some form of transport. Is that car in running order?' He pointed at a pale green Ford Ranchero station wagon parked beside the veranda wall.

'It is. It belongs to my Company.' Boussier took a key ring from his pocket and handed it to Bruce. 'Here are the keys. The tank is full of gasoline.'

'Good,' said Bruce. 'Now if we can find Madame Cartier—'

She was waiting in the hotel lounge and she stood up as Bruce and Boussier came in.

'Are you ready, madame?'

'I await your pleasure,' she answered, and Bruce looked at her sharply. Just a trace of a twinkle in her dark blue eyes suggested that she was aware of the double meaning.

They walked out to the Ford and Bruce opened the door for her.

'You are gracious, monsieur.' She thanked him and slid into the seat. Bruce went round to the driver's side and climbed in beside her.

'It's nearly dark,' he said.

'Turn right on to the Msapa Junction road, there is one post there.'

Bruce drove out along the dirt road through the town until they came to the last house before the causeway. 'Here,' said the girl and Bruce stopped the car. There were two men there, both armed with sporting rifles. Bruce spoke to them. They had seen no sign of Baluba, but they were both very nervous. Bruce made a decision.

'I want you to go back to the hotel. The Baluba will have seen the train arrive; they won't attack in force, we'll be safe tonight. But they may try and cut a few throats if we leave you out here.'

The two half-breeds gathered together their belongings and set off towards the centre of town, obviously with lighter hearts.

'Where are the others?' Bruce asked the girl.

'The next post is at the pumping station down by the river—there are three men there.'

Bruce followed her directions. Once or twice as he drove he glanced surreptitiously at her. She sat in her corner of the seat with her legs drawn up sideways under her. She sat very still, Bruce noticed. I like a woman who doesn't fidget; it's soothing. Then he smiled; this one isn't soothing. She is as disturbing as hell! She turned suddenly and caught him looking again, but this time she smiled.

'You are English, aren't you, Captain?'

'No, I am a Rhodesian,' Bruce answered.

'It's the same,' said the girl. 'You speak French so very badly that you had to be English.'

Bruce laughed. 'Perhaps your English is better than my French,' he challenged her.

'It couldn't be much worse,' she answered him in his own language. 'You are different when you laugh, not so grim, not so heroic. Take the next road to your right.'

Bruce turned the Ford down towards the harbour.

'You are very frank,' he said. 'Also your English is excellent.'

'Do you smoke?' she asked, and when he nodded she lit two cigarettes and passed one to him.

'You are also very young to smoke, and very young to be married.'

She stopped smiling and swung her legs off the seat.

'Here is the pumping station,' she said.

'I beg your pardon. I shouldn't have said that.'

'It's of no importance.'

'It was an impertinence,' Bruce demurred.

'It doesn't matter.'

Bruce stopped the car and opened his door. He walked out on to the wooden jetty towards the pump house, and the boards rang dully under his boots. There was a mist coming up out of the reeds round the harbour and the frogs were piping in fifty different keys. He spoke to the men in the single room of the pump station.

'You can get back to the hotel by dark if you hurry.'

'Oui, monsieur,' they agreed. Bruce watched them set off up the road before he went to the car. He spun the starter motor and above the noise of it the girl asked:

'What is your given name, Captain Curry?'

'Bruce.'

She repeated it, pronouncing it 'Bruise', and then asked, 'Why are you a soldier?'

'For many reasons.' His tone was flippant.

'You do not look like a soldier, for all your badges and your guns, for all the grimness and the frequent giving of orders.'

'Perhaps I am not a very good soldier.' He smiled at her.

'You are very efficient and very grim except when you laugh. But I am glad you do not look like one,' she said.

'Where is the next post?'

'On the railway line. There are two men there. Turn to your right again at the top, Bruce.'

'You are also very efficient, Shermaine.' They were silent again, having used each other's names. Bruce could feel it between them, a good feeling, warm like new bread. But what of her husband, he thought, I wonder where he is, and what he is like. Why isn't he here with her?

'He is dead,' she said quietly. 'He died four months ago of malaria.'

With the shock of it, Shermaine answering his unspoken question and also the answer itself, Bruce could say nothing for a moment, then, 'I'm sorry.'

'There is the post,' she said, 'in the cottage with the thatched roof.'

Bruce stopped the car and switched off the engine. In the silence she spoke again.

'He was a good man, so very gentle. I only knew him for a few months but he was a good man.'

She looked very small sitting beside him in the gathering dark with the sadness on her, and Bruce felt a great wave of tenderness wash over him. He wanted to put his arm around her and hold her, to shield her from the sadness. He searched for the words, but before he found them, she roused herself and spoke in a matter of fact tone.

'We must hurry, it's dark already.'

At the hotel the lounge was filled with Boussier's employees; Haig had mounted a Bren in one of the upstairs windows to cover the main street and posted two men in the kitchens to cover the back. The civilians were in little groups, talking quietly, and their expressions of complete doglike trust as they looked at Bruce disconcerted him.

'Everything under control, Mike?' he asked brusquely.

'Yes, Bruce. We should be able to hold this building against a sneak attack. De Surrier and Hendry, down at the station yard, shouldn't have any trouble either.'

'Have these people,' Bruce pointed at the civilians, 'loaded their luggage?'

'Yes, it's all aboard. I have told Ruffy to issue them with food from our stores.'

'Good.' Bruce felt relief; no further complications so far.

'Where is old man Boussier?'

'He is across at his office.'

'I'm going to have a chat with him.'

Unbidden, Shermaine fell in beside Bruce as he walked out into the street, but he liked having her there.

Boussier looked up as Bruce and Shermaine walked into his office. The merciless glare of the petromax lamp accentuated the lines at the corners of his eyes and mouth, and showed up the streaks of pink scalp beneath his neatly combed hair.

'Martin, you are not still working!' exclaimed Shermaine, and he smiled at her, the calm smile of his years.

'Not really, my dear, just tidying up a few things. Please be seated, Captain.'

He came round and cleared a pile of heavy leather-bound ledgers off the chair and packed them into a wooden case on the floor, went back to his own chair, opened a drawer in the desk, brought out a box of cheroots and offered one to Bruce.

'I cannot tell you how relieved I am that you are here, Captain. These last few months have been very trying. The doubt. The anxiety.' He struck a match and held it out to Bruce who leaned forward across the desk and lit his cheroot. 'But now it is all at an end; I feel as though a great weight has been lifted from my shoulders.' Then his voice sharpened. 'But you were not too soon. I have heard within the last

hour that this General Moses and his column have left Senwati and
are on the road south, only two hundred miles north of here. They will
arrive tomorrow at their present rate of advance.'

'Where did you hear this?' Bruce demanded.

'From one of my men, and do not ask me how he knows. There is
a system of communication in this country which even after all these
years I do not understand. Perhaps it is the drums, I heard them
this evening, I do not know. However, their information is usually
reliable.'

'I had not placed them so close,' muttered Bruce. 'Had I known this
I might have risked travelling tonight, at least as far as the bridge.'

'I think your decision to stay over the night was correct. General
Moses will not travel during darkness—none of his men would risk that
—and the condition of the road from Senwati after three months'
neglect is such that he will need ten or twelve hours to cover the
distance.'

'I hope you're right.' Bruce was worried. 'I'm not sure that we
shouldn't pull out now.'

'That involves a risk also, Captain,' Boussier pointed out. 'We know
there are tribesmen in close proximity to the town. They have been
seen. They must be aware of your arrival, and might easily have
wrecked the lines to prevent our departure. I think your original
decision is still good.'

'I know.' Bruce was hunched forward in his chair, frowning, sucking
on the cheroot. At last he sat back and the frown evaporated. 'I can't
risk it. I'll place a guard on the causeway, and if this Moses gentleman arrives we can hold him there long enough to embark your
people.'

'That is probably the best course,' agreed Boussier. He paused,
glanced towards the open windows and lowered his voice. 'There is
another point, Captain, which I wish to bring to your attention.'

'Yes?'

'As you know, the activity of my company in Port Reprieve is
centred on the recovery of diamonds from the Lufira swamps.'

Bruce nodded.

'I have in my safe'—Boussier jerked his thumb at the heavy steel
door built into the wall behind his desk—'nine and a half thousand
carats of gem-quality diamonds and some twenty-six thousand carats
of industrial diamonds.'

'I had expected that.' Bruce kept his tone non-committal.

'It may be as well if we could agree on the disposition and handling
of these stones.'

'How are they packaged?' asked Bruce.

'A single wooden case.'

'Of what size and weight?'

'I will show you.'

Boussier went to the safe, turned his back to them and they heard the tumblers whirr and click. While he waited Bruce realized suddenly that Shermaine had not spoken since her initial greeting to Boussier. He glanced at her now and she smiled at him. I like a woman who knows when to keep her mouth shut.

Boussier swung the door of the safe open and carried a small wooden case across to the desk.

'There,' he said.

Bruce examined it. Eighteen inches long, nine deep and twelve wide. He lifted it experimentally.

'About twenty pounds weight,' he decided. 'The lid is sealed.'

'Yes,' agreed Boussier, touching the four wax imprints.

'Good,' Bruce nodded. 'I don't want to draw unnecessary attention to it by placing a guard upon it.'

'No, I agree.'

Bruce studied the case a few seconds longer and then he asked, 'What is the value of these stones?'

Boussier shrugged. 'Possibly five hundred million francs.' And Bruce was impressed; half a million sterling. Worth stealing, worth killing for.

'I suggest, monsieur, that you secrete this case in your luggage. In your blankets, say. I doubt there will be any danger of theft until we reach Msapa Junction. A thief will have no avenue of escape. Once we reach Msapa Junction I will make other arrangements for its safety.'

'Very well, Captain.'

Bruce stood up and glanced at his watch. 'Seven o'clock, as near as dammit. I will leave you and see to the guard on the causeway. Please make sure that your people are ready to entrain before dawn tomorrow morning.'

'Of course.'

Bruce looked at Shermaine and she stood up quickly. Bruce held the door open for her and was just about to follow her when a thought struck him.

'That mission station—St Augustine's, is it? I suppose it's deserted now?'

'No, it's not.' Boussier looked a little shamefaced. 'Father Ignatius is still there, and of course the patients at the hospital.'

'Thanks for telling me.' Bruce was bitter.

'I'm sorry, Captain. It slipped my mind, there are so many things to think of.'

'Do you know the road out to the mission?' he snapped at Shermaine. *She* should have told him.

'Yes, Bruce.'

'Well, perhaps you'd be good enough to direct me.'

'Of course.' She also looked guilty.

Bruce slammed the door of Boussier's office and strode off towards the hotel with Shermaine trotting to keep pace with him. You can't rely on anyone, he thought, not anybody!

And then he saw Ruffy coming up from the station, looking like a big bear in the dusk. With a few exceptions, Bruce corrected himself.

'Sergeant Major.'

'Hello, boss.'

'This General Moses is closer to us than we reckoned. He's reported two hundred miles north of here on the Senwati road.'

Ruffy whistled through his teeth. 'Are you going to take off now, Boss?'

'No, I want a machine-gun post on this end of the causeway. If they come we can hold them there long enough to get away. I want you to take command.'

'I'll see to it now.'

'I'm going out to the mission—there's a white priest there. Lieutenant Haig is in command while I'm away.'

'Okay, boss.'

CHAPTER 10

'I'm sorry, Bruce. I should have told you.' Shermaine sat small and repentant at her end of the Ranchero.

'Don't worry about it,' said Bruce, not meaning it.

'We have tried to make Father Ignatius come in to town. Martin has spoken to him many times, but he refuses to move.'

Bruce did not answer. He took the car down on to the causeway, driving carefully. There were shreds of mist lifting out of the swamp and drifting across the concrete ramp. Small insects, bright as tracer in the headlights, zoomed in to squash against the windscreen. The froggy chorus from the swamp honked and clinked and boomed deafeningly.

'I have apologized,' she murmured.

'Yes, I heard you,' said Bruce. 'You don't have to do it again.'

She was silent, and then:

'Are you always so bad-tempered?' she asked in English.

'*Always*,' snapped Bruce, 'is one of the words which should be eliminated from the language.'

'Since it has not been, I will continue to use it. You haven't answered my question: are you always so bad tempered?'

'I just don't like balls-ups.'

'What is *balls-ups*, please?'

'What has just happened: a mistake, a situation precipitated by inefficiency, or by somebody not using his head.'

'You never make balls-up, Bruce?'

'It is not a polite expression, Shermaine. Young ladies of refinement do not use it.' Bruce changed into French.

'You never make mistakes?' she corrected herself. Bruce did not answer. That's quite funny, he thought—never make mistakes! Bruce Curry, the original balls-up.

Shermaine held one hand across her middle and sat up straight.

'Bonaparte,' she said. 'Cold, silent, efficient.'

'I didn't say that—' Bruce started to defend himself. Then in the glow from the dash light he saw her impish expression and he could not stop himself; he had to grin.

'All right, I'm acting like a child.'

'You would like a cigarette?' she asked.

'Yes, please.'

She lit it and passed it to him.

'You do not like—' she hesitated, 'mistakes. Is there anything you do like?'

'Many things,' said Bruce.

'Tell me some.'

They bumped off the end of the causeway and Bruce accelerated up the far bank.

'I like being on a mountain when the wind blows, and the taste of the sea. I like Sinatra, crayfish thermidor, the weight and balance of a Purdey Royal, and the sound of a little girl's laughter. I like the first draw of a cigarette lit from a wood fire, the scent of jasmine, the feel of silk; I also enjoy sleeping late in the morning, and the thrill of forking a queen with my knight. Shadows on the floor of a forest please me. And, of course, money. But especially I like women who do not ask too many questions.'

'Is that all?'

'No, but it's a start.'

'And apart from—mistakes, what are the things you do not like.'

'Women who ask too many questions,' and he saw her smile. 'Selfishness except my own, turnip soup, politics, blond pubic hairs, Scotch whisky, classical music and hangovers.'

'I'm sure that is not all.'

'No, not nearly.'

'You are very sensual. All these things are of the senses.'

'Agreed.'

'You do not mention other people. Why?'

'Is this the turn off to the mission?'

'Yes, go slowly, the road is bad. Why do you not mention your relationship to other people?'

'Why do you ask so many questions? Perhaps I'll tell you some day.'

She was silent a while and then softly, 'And what do you want from life—just those things you have spoken of? Is that all you want?'

'No. Not even them. I want nothing, expect nothing; that way I cannot be disappointed.'

Suddenly she was angry. 'You not only act like a child, you talk like one.'

'Another thing I don't like: criticism.'

'You are young. You have brains, good looks—'

'Thank you, that's better.'

'—and you are a fool.'

'That's not so good. But don't fret about it.'

'I won't, don't worry,' she flamed at him. 'You can—' she searched for something devastating. 'You can go jump out of the lake.'

'Don't you mean into?'

'Into, out of, backwards, sideways. I don't care!'

'Good, I'm glad we've got that settled. There's the mission, I can see a light.'

She did not answer but sat in her corner, breathing heavily, drawing so hard on her cigarette that the glowing tip lit the interior of the Ford.

The church was in darkness, but beyond it and to one side was a long low building. Bruce saw a shadow move across one of the windows.

'Is that the hospital?'

'Yes.' Abruptly.

Bruce stopped the Ford beside the small front veranda and switched off the headlights and the ignition.

'Are you coming in?'

'No.'

'I'd like you to present me to Father Ignatius.'

For a moment she did not move, then she threw open her door and
marched up the steps of the veranda without looking back at Bruce.

He followed her through the front office, down the passage, past the
clinic and small operating theatre, into the ward.

'Ah, Madame Cartier.' Father Ignatius left the bed over which he
was stooping and came towards her.

'I heard that the relief train had arrived at Port Reprieve. I thought
you would have left by now.'

'Not yet, Father. Tomorrow morning.'

Ignatius was tall, six foot three or four, Bruce estimated, and thin.
The sleeves of his brown cassock had been cut short as a concession to
the climate and his exposed arms appeared to be all bone, hairless,
with the veins blue and prominent. Big bony hands, and big bony feet
in brown open sandals.

Like most tall, thin men he was round-shouldered. His face was not
one that you would remember, an ordinary face with steel-rimmed
spectacles perched on a rather shapeless nose, neither young nor old,
nondescript hair without grey in it, but there was about him that
unhurried serenity you often find in a man of God. He turned his
attention to Bruce, scrutinizing him gently through his spectacles.

'Good evening, my son.'

'Good evening, Father.' Bruce felt uncomfortable; they always made
him feel that way. If only, he wished with envy, I could be as certain
of one thing in my life as this man is certain of everything in his.

'Father, this is Captain Curry.' Shermaine's tone was cold, and then
suddenly she smiled again. 'He does not care for people, that is why
he has come to take you to safety.'

Father Ignatius held out his hand and Bruce found the skin was
cool and dry, making him conscious of the moistness of his own.

'That is most thoughtful of you,' he said smiling, sensing the tension
between them. 'I don't want to seem ungrateful, but I regret I cannot
accept your offer.'

'We have received reports that a column of armed bandits is only
two hundred miles or so north of here. They will arrive within a day
or two. You are in great danger, these people are completely merciless,'
Bruce urged him.

'Yes,' Father Ignatius nodded. 'I have also heard, and I am taking
the steps I consider necessary. I shall take all my staff and patients into
the bush.'

'They'll follow you,' said Bruce.

'I think not.' Ignatius shook his head. 'They will not waste their time.
They are after loot, not sick people.'

'They'll burn your mission.'

'If they do, then we shall have to rebuild it when they leave.'

'The bush is crawling with Baluba, you'll end up in the cooking pot.' Bruce tried another approach.

'No.' Ignatius shook his head. 'Nearly every member of the tribe has at one time or another been a patient in this hospital. I have nothing to fear there, they are my friends.'

'Look here, Father. Don't let us argue. My orders are to bring you back to Elisabethville. I must insist.'

'And my orders are to stay here. You do agree that mine come from a higher authority than yours?' Ignatius smiled mildly. Bruce opened his mouth to argue further; then, instead, he laughed.

'No, I won't dispute that. Is there anything you need that I might be able to supply?'

'Medicines?' asked Ignatius.

'Acriflavine, morphia, field dressings, not much I'm afraid.'

'They would help, and food?'

'Yes, I will let you have as much as I can spare,' promised Bruce.

One of the patients, a woman at the end of the ward, screamed so suddenly that Bruce started.

'She will be dead before morning,' Ignatius explained softly. 'There is nothing I can do.'

'What's wrong with her?'

'She has been in labour these past two days; there is some complication.'

'Can't you operate?'

'I am not a doctor, my son. We had one here before the trouble began, but he is here no longer—he has gone back to Elisabethville. No,' his voice seemed to carry helpless regret for all the suffering of mankind, 'No, she will die.'

'Haig!' said Bruce.

'Pardon?'

'Father, you have a theatre here. Is it fully equipped?'

'Yes, I believe so.'

'Anesthetic?'

'We have chloroform and pentothal.'

'Good,' said Bruce. 'I'll get you a doctor. Come on, Shermaine.'

CHAPTER 11

'This heat, this stinking heat!' Wally Hendry mopped at his face with a grubby handkerchief and threw himself down on the green leather bunk. 'You notice how Curry leaves me and you here on the train while he puts Haig up at the hotel and he goes off with that little French bit. It doesn't matter that me and you must cook in this box, long as he and his buddy Haig are all right. You notice that, hey?'

'Somebody's got to stay aboard, Wally,' André said.

'Yeah, but you notice who it is? Always you and me—those high society boys stick together, you've got to give them that, they look after each other.' He transferred his attention back to the open window of the compartment. 'Sun's down already, and still hot enough to boil eggs. I could use a drink.' He unlaced his jungle boots, peeled off his socks and regarded his large white feet with distaste. 'This stinking heat's got my athlete's foot going again.'

He separated two of his toes and picked at the loose scaly skin between. 'You got any of that ointment left, André?'

'Yes, I'll get it for you.' André opened a flap of his pack, took out the tube and crossed to Wally's bunk.

'Put it on,' instructed Wally and lay back offering his feet. André took them in his lap as he sat down on the bunk and went to work. Wally lit a cigarette and blew smoke towards the roof, watching it disperse.

'Hell, I could use a drink. A beer with dew on the glass and a head that thick.' He held up four fingers, then he lifted himself on one elbow and studied André as he spread ointment between the long prehensile toes.

'How's it going?'

'Nearly finished, Wally.'

'Is it bad?'

'Not as bad as last time, it hasn't started weeping yet.'

'It itches like you wouldn't believe it,' said Wally.

André did not answer and Wally kicked him in the ribs with the flat of his free foot.

'Did you hear what I said?'

'Yes, you said it itches.'

'Well, answer me when I talk to you. I ain't talking to myself.'

'I'm sorry, Wally.'

Wally grunted and was silent a while, then, 'Do you like me, André?'

'You know I do, Wally.'

'We're friends, aren't we, André?'

'Of course, you know that, Wally.'

An expression of cunning had replaced Wally's boredom. 'You don't mind when I ask you to do things for me, like putting stuff on my feet?'

'I don't mind—it's a pleasure, Wally.'

'It's a pleasure, is it?' There was an edge in Wally's voice now. 'You like doing it?'

André looked up at him apprehensively. 'I don't mind it.' His molten toffee eyes clung to the narrow Mongolian ones in Wally's face.

'You like touching me, André?'

André stopped working with the ointment and nervously wiped his fingers on his towel.

'I said, do you like touching me, André? Do you sometimes wish I'd touch you?'

André tried to stand up, but Wally's right arm shot out and his hand fastened on André's neck, forcing him down onto the bunk. 'Answer me, damn you, do you like it?'

'You're hurting me, Wally,' whispered André.

'Shame, now ain't that a shame!'

Wally was grinning. He shifted his grip to the ridge of muscle above André's collar bone and dug his fingers in until they almost met through the flesh.

'Please, Wally, please,' whimpered André, wriggling face down on the bunk.

'You love it, don't you? Come on, answer me.'

'Yes, all right, yes. Please don't hurt me, Wally.'

'Now, tell me truly, doll boy, have you ever had it before? I mean for real.' Wally put his knee in the small of André's back, bearing down with all his weight.

'No!' shrieked André. 'I haven't. Please, Wally, don't hurt me.'

'You're lying to me, André. Don't do it.'

'All right. I was lying.' André tried to twist his head round, but Wally pushed his face into the bunk.

'Tell me all about it—come on, doll boy.'

'It was only once, in Brussels.'

'Who was this beef bandit?'

'My employer, I worked for him. He had an export agency.'

'Did he throw you out, doll boy? Did he throw you out when he was tired of you?'

'No, you don't understand!' André denied with sudden vehemence. 'You don't understand. He looked after me. I had my own apartment, my own car, everything. He wouldn't have abandoned me if it hadn't been for—for what happened. He couldn't help it, he was true to me. I swear to you—he loved me!'

Wally snorted with laughter, he was enjoying himself now. 'Loved you! Jesus wept!' He threw his head back, for the laughter was almost strangling him, and it was ten seconds before he could ask, 'Then what happened between you and your true blue lover? Why didn't you get married and settle down to raise a family, hey?' At the improbability of his own sense of humour Wally convulsed with laughter once more.

'There was an investigation. The police—ooh! you're hurting me, Wally.'

'Keep talking, mamselle!'

'The police—he had no alternative. He was a man of position, he couldn't afford the scandal. There was no other way out—there never is for us. It's hopeless, there is no happiness.'

'Cut the crap, doll boy. Just give me the story.'

'He arranged employment for me in Elisabethville, gave me money, paid for my air fare, everything. He did everything, he looked after me, he still writes to me.'

'That's beautiful, real true love. You make we want to cry.' Then Wally's laughter changed its tone, harsher now. 'Well, get this, doll boy, and get it good. I don't like queers!' He dug his fingers in again and André squealed.

'I'll tell you a story. When I was in reform school there was a queer there that tried to touch me up. One day I got him in the shower rooms with a razor, just an ordinary Gillette razor. There were twenty guys singing and shouting in the other cubicles. He screamed just like they were all screaming when the cold water hit them. No one took any notice of him. He wanted to be a woman, so I helped him.' Hendry's voice went hoarse and gloating with the memory. 'Jesus!' he whispered. 'Jesus, the blood!' André was sobbing now, his whole body shaking.

'I won't—please, Wally. I can't help it. It was just that one time. Please leave me.'

'How would you like me to help you, André?'

'No,' shrieked André. And Hendry lost interest; he released him, left him lying on the bunk and reached for his socks.

'I'm going to find me a beer.' He laced on his boots and stood up.

'Just you remember,' he said darkly, standing over the boy on the bunk. 'Don't get any ideas with me, Bucko.' He picked up his rifle and went out into the corridor.

Wally found Boussier on the veranda of the hotel talking with a group of his men.

'Where's Captain Curry?' he demanded.

'He has gone out to the mission station.'

'When did he leave?'

'About ten minutes ago.'

'Good,' said Wally. 'Who's got the key to the bar?'

Boussier hesitated.

'The captain has ordered that the bar is to remain locked.'

Wally unslung his rifle.

'Don't give me a hard time, friend.'

'I regret, monsieur, that I must obey the captain's instructions.'

For a minute they stared at each other, and there was no sign of weakening in the older man.

'Have it your way then,' said Wally and swaggered through the lounge to the bar-room door. He put his foot against the lock and the flimsy mechanism yielded to the pressure. The door flew open and Wally marched across to the counter, laid his rifle on it and reached underneath to the shelves loaded with Simba beer.

The first bottle he emptied without taking it from his lips. He belched luxuriously and reached for the second, hooked the cap off with the opener and inspected the bubble of froth that appeared at its mouth.

'Hendry!' Wally looked up at Mike Haig in the doorway.

'Hello, Mike.' He grinned.

'What do you think you're doing?' Mike demanded.

'What does it look like?' Wally raised the bottle in salutation and then sipped delicately at the froth.

'Bruce has given strict orders that no one is allowed in here.'

'Oh, for Chrissake, Haig. Stop acting like an old woman.'

'Out you get, Hendry. I'm in charge here.'

'Mike,' Wally grinned at him, 'you want me to die of thirst or something?' He leaned his elbows on the counter. 'Give me a couple more minutes. Let me finish my drink.'

Mike Haig glanced behind him into the lounge and saw the interested group of civilians who were craning to see into the bar-room. He closed the door and walked across to stand opposite Hendry.

'Two minutes, Hendry,' he agreed in an unfriendly tone, 'then out with you.'

'You're not a bad guy, Mike. You and I rubbed each other up wrong. I tell you something, I'm sorry about us.'

'Drink up!' said Mike. Without turning Wally reached backwards and took a bottle of Remy Martin cognac off the shelf. He pulled the cork with his teeth, selected a brandy balloon with his free hand and poured a little of the oily amber fluid into it.

'Keep me company, Mike,' he said and slid the glass across the counter towards Haig. First without expression, and then with his face seeming to crumble, Mike Haig stared at the glass. He moistened his lips, again older and tired-looking. With a physical wrench he pulled his eyes away from the glass.

'Damn you, Hendry.' His voice was unnaturally low. 'God damn you to hell.' He hit out at the glass, spinning it off the counter to shatter against the far wall.

'Did I do something wrong, Mike?' asked Hendry softly. 'Just offered you a drink, that's all.'

The smell of spilt brandy, sharp, fruity with the warmth of the grape, and Mike moistened his lips again, the saliva jetting from under his tongue, and the deep yearning aching want in his stomach spreading outwards slowly, numbing him.

'Damn you,' he whispered. 'Oh, damn you, damn you,' pleading now as Hendry filled another glass.

'How long has it been, Mike? A year, two years? Try a little, just a mouthful. Remember the lift it gives you. Come on, boy. You're tired, you've worked hard. Just one—there you are. Just have this one with me.'

Mike wiped his mouth with the back of his hand, sweating now across the forehead and on his upper lip, tiny jewels of sweat squeezed out of the skin by the craving of his body.

'Come on, boy.' Wally's voice was hoarse with excitement, teasing, wheedling, tempting.

Mike's hand closed round the tumbler, moving of its own volition, lifting it towards lips that were suddenly slack and trembling, his eyes filled with mingled loathing and desire.

'Just this one,' whispered Hendry. 'Just this one.'

Mike gulped it with a sudden savage flick of his arm, one swallow and the glass was empty. He held it with both hands, his head bowed over it.

'I hate you. My God, I hate you.' He spoke to Hendry, and to himself, and to the empty glass.

'That's my boy!' crowed Wally. 'That's the lad! Come on, let me fill you up.'

CHAPTER 12

Bruce went in through the front door of the hotel with Shermaine trying to keep pace with him. There were a dozen or so people in the lobby, and an air of tension among them. Boussier was one of them and he came quickly to Bruce.

'I'm sorry, Captain, I could not stop them. That one, that one with the red hair, he was violent. He had his gun and I think he was ready to use it.'

'What are you talking about?' Bruce asked him, but before Boussier could answer there was the bellow of Hendry's laughter from behind the door at the far end of the lobby; the door to the bar-room.

'They are in there,' Boussier told him. 'They have been there for the past hour.'

'Goddam it to hell,' swore Bruce. 'Now of all times. Oh, goddam that bloody animal.'

He almost ran across the room and threw open the double doors. Hendry was standing against the far wall with a tumbler in one hand and his rifle in the other. He was holding the rifle by the pistol grip and waving vague circles in the air with it.

Mike Haig was building a pyramid of glasses on the bar counter. He was just placing the final glass on the pile.

'Hello, Bruce, old cock, old man, old fruit,' he greeted Bruce, and waved in an exaggerated manner. 'Just in time, you can have a couple of shots as well. But Wally's first, he gets first shot. Must abide by the rules, no cheating, strictly democratic affair, everyone has equal rights. Rank doesn't count. That's right, isn't it, Wally?' Haig's features had blurred; it was as though he were melting, losing his shape. His lips were loose and flabby, his jowls hung pendulously as an old woman's breasts, and his eyes were moist.

He picked up a glass from beside the pyramid, but this glass was nearly full and a bottle of Remy Martin cognac stood beside it.

'A very fine old brandy, absolutely exquisite.' The last two words didn't come out right, so he repeated them carefully. Then he grinned loosely at Bruce and his eyes weren't quite in focus.

'Get out of the way, Mike,' said Hendry, and raised the rifle one-handed, aiming at the pile of glasses.

'Every time she bucks, she bounces,' hooted Haig, 'and every time she bounces you win a coconut. Let her tip, old fruit.'

'Hendry, stop that,' snapped Bruce.

'Go and get mucked,' answered Hendry and fired. The rifle kicked back over his shoulder and he fell against the wall. The pyramid of glasses exploded in a shower of fragments and the room was filled with the roar of the rifle.

'Give the gentleman a coconut!' crowed Mike.

Bruce crossed the room with three quick strides and pulled the rifle out of Hendry's hand.

'All right, you drunken ape. That's enough.'

'Go and muck yourself,' growled Hendry. He was massaging his wrist; the rifle had twisted it.

'Captain Curry,' said Haig from behind the bar, 'you heard what my friend said. You go and muck yourself sideways to sleep.'

'Shut up, Haig.'

'This time I'll fix you, Curry,' Hendry growled. 'You've been on my back too long—now I'm going to shake you off!'

'Kindly descend from my friend's back, Captain Curry,' chimed in Mike Haig. 'He's not a howdah elephant, he's my blood brother. I will not allow you to persecute him.'

'Come on, Curry. Come on then!' said Wally.

'That's it, Wally. Muck him up.' Haig filled his glass again as he spoke. 'Don't let him ride you.'

'Come on then, Curry.'

'You're drunk,' said Bruce.

'Come on then; don't talk, man. Or do I have to start it?'

'No, you don't have to start it,' Bruce assured him, and lifted the rifle butt-first under his chin, swinging it up hard. Hendry's head jerked and he staggered back against the wall. Bruce looked at his eyes; they were glazed over. That will hold him, he decided; that's taken the fight out of him. He caught Hendry by the shoulder and threw him into one of the chairs. I must get to Haig before he absorbs any more of that liquor, he thought, I can't waste time sending for Ruffy and I can't leave this thing behind me while I work on Haig.

'Shermaine,' he called. She was standing in the doorway and she came to his side. 'Can you use a pistol?'

She nodded. Bruce unclipped his Smith & Wesson from its lanyard and handed it to her.

'Shoot this man if he tries to leave that chair. Stand here where he cannot reach you.'

'Bruce—' she started.

'He is a dangerous animal. Yesterday he murdered two small children and, if you let him, he'll do the same to you. You must keep him here while I get the other one.'

She lifted the pistol, holding it with both hands and her face was even paler than was usual.

'Can you do it?' Bruce asked.

'Now I can,' she said and cocked the action.

'Hear me, Hendry.' Bruce took a handful of his hair and twisted his face up. 'She'll kill you if you leave this chair. Do you understand. She'll shoot you.'

'Muck you and your little French whore, muck you both. I bet that's what you two have been doing all evening in that car—playing "hide the sausage" down by the river side.'

Anger flashed through Bruce so violently that it startled him. He twisted Hendry's hair until he could feel it coming away in his hand. Hendry squirmed with pain.

'Shut that foul mouth—or I'll kill you.'

He meant it, and suddenly Hendry knew he meant it.

'Okay, for Chrissake, okay. Just leave me.'

Bruce loosened his grip and straightened up.

'I'm sorry, Shermaine,' he said.

'That's all right—go to the other one.'

Bruce went to the bar counter, and Haig watched him come.

'What do you want, Bruce? Have a drink.' He was nervous. 'Have a drink, we are all having a little drink. All good clean fun, Bruce. Don't get excited.'

'You're not having any more; in fact, just the opposite,' Bruce told him as he came round the counter. Haig backed away in front of him.

'What are you going to do?'

'I'll show you,' said Bruce and caught him by the wrist, turning him quickly and lifting his arm up between his shoulder-blades.

'Hey, Bruce. Cut it out, you've made me spill my drink.'

'Good,' said Bruce and slapped the empty glass out of his hand. Haig started to struggle. He was still a powerful man but the liquor had weakened him and Bruce lifted his wrist higher, forcing him onto his toes.

'Come along, buddy boy,' instructed Bruce and marched him towards the back door of the bar-room. He reached round Haig with his free hand, turned the key in the lock and opened the door.

'Through here,' he said and pushed Mike into the kitchens. He kicked the door shut behind him and went to the sink, dragging Haig with him.

'All right, Haig, let's have it up,' he said and changed his grip quickly, thrusting Haig's head down over the sink. There was a dishtowel hanging beside it which Bruce screwed into a ball; then he used his thumbs to open Haig's jaws and wedged the towel between his back teeth.

'Let's have all of it.' He probed his finger down into Haig's throat. It came up hot and gushing over his hand, and he fought down his own nausea as he worked. When he had finished he turned on the cold tap and held Haig's head under it, washing his face and his own hand.

'Now I've got a little job for you, Haig.'

'Leave me alone, damn you,' groaned Haig, his voice indistinct beneath the rushing tap. Bruce pulled him up and held him against the wall.

'There's a woman in childbirth at the mission. She's going to die, Haig. She's going to die if you don't do something about it.'

'No,' whispered Haig. 'No, not that. Not that again.'

'I'm taking you there.'

'No, please not that. I can't—don't you see that I can't.' The little red and purple veins in his nose and cheeks stood out in vivid contrast to his pallor. Bruce hit him open-handed across the face and the water flew in drops from his hair at the shock.

'No,' he mumbled, 'please, Bruce, please.'

Bruce hit him twice more, hard, watching him carefully, and at last he saw the first flickering of anger.

'Damn you, Bruce Curry, damn you to hell.'

'You'll do,' rejoiced Bruce. 'Thank God for that.'

He hustled Haig back through the bar-room. Shermaine still stood over Hendry, holding the pistol.

'Come on, Shermaine. You can leave that thing now. I'll attend to him when we get back.'

As they crossed the lobby Bruce asked Shermaine, 'Can you drive the Ford?'

'Yes.'

'Good,' said Bruce. 'Here are the keys. I'll sit with Haig in the back. Take us out to the mission.'

Haig lost his balance on the front steps of the hotel and nearly fell, but Bruce caught him and half carried him to the car. He pushed him into the back seat and climbed in beside him. Shermaine slid in behind the wheel, started the engine and U-turned neatly across the street.

'You can't force me to do this, Bruce. I can't, I just can't,' Haig pleaded.

'We'll see,' said Bruce.

'You don't know what it's like. You can't know. She'll die on the table.' He held out his hands palms down. 'Look at that, look at them. How can I do it with these?' His hands were trembling violently.

'She's going to die anyway,' said Bruce, his voice hard. 'So you might as well do it for her quickly and get it over with.'

Haig brought his hands up to his mouth and wiped his lips.

'Can I have a drink, Bruce? That'll help. I'll try then, if you give me a drink.'

'No,' said Bruce, and Haig began to swear. The filth poured from his lips and his face twisted with the effort. He cursed Bruce, he cursed himself, and God in a torrent of the most obscene language that Bruce had ever heard. Then suddenly he snatched at the door handle and tried to twist it open. Bruce had been waiting for this and he caught the back of Haig's collar, pulled him backwards across the seat and held him there. Haig's struggles ceased abruptly and he began to sob softly.

Shermaine drove fast; across the causeway, up the slope and into the side road. The headlights cut into the darkness and the wind drummed softly round the car. Haig was still sobbing on the back seat.

Then the lights of the mission were ahead of them through the trees and Shermaine slowed the car, turned in past the church and pulled up next to the hospital block.

Bruce helped Haig out of the car, and while he was doing so the side door of the building opened and Father Ignatius came out with a petromax lantern in his hand. The harsh white glare of the lantern lit them all and threw grotesque shadows behind them. It fell with special cruelty on Haig's face.

'Here's your doctor, Father,' Bruce announced.

Ignatius lifted the lantern and peered through his spectacles at Haig. 'Is he sick?'

'No, Father,' said Bruce. 'He's drunk.'

'Drunk? Then he can't operate?'

'Yes, he damn well can!'

Bruce took Haig through the door and along the passage to the little theatre. Ignatius and Shermaine followed them.

'Shermaine, go with the Father and help him bring the woman,' Bruce ordered, and they went; then he turned his attention back to Haig.

'Are you so far down there in the slime that you can't understand me?'

'I can't do it, Bruce. It's no good.'

'Then she'll die. But this much is certain: you are going to make the attempt.'

'I've got to have a drink, Bruce.' Haig licked his lips. 'It's burning me up inside, you've got to give me one.'

'Finish the job and I'll give you a whole case.'

'I've got to have one now.'

'No.' Bruce spoke with finality. 'Have a look at what they've got here in the way of instruments. Can you do it with these?' Bruce crossed to the sterilizer and lifted the lid; the steam came up out of it in a cloud. Haig looked in also.

'That's all I need, but there's not enough light in here, and I need a drink.'

'I'll get you more light. Start cleaning up.'

'Bruce, please let me—'

'Shut up,' snarled Bruce. 'There's the basin. Start getting ready.'

Haig crossed to the hand basin; he was more steady on his feet and his features had firmed a little. *You poor old bastard*, thought Bruce, *I hope you can do it. My God, how much I hope you can.*

'Get a move on, Haig, we haven't got all night.'

Bruce left the room and went quickly down the passage to the ward. The windows of the theatre were fixed and Haig could escape only into the passage. Bruce knew that he could catch him if he tried to run for it.

He looked into the ward. Shermaine and Ignatius, with the help of an African orderly, had lifted the woman onto the theatre trolley.

'Father, we need more light.'

'I can get you another lantern, that's all.'

'Good, do that then. I'll take the woman through.'

Father Ignatius disappeared with the orderly and Bruce helped Shermaine manoeuvre the trolley down the length of the ward and into the passage. The woman was whimpering with pain, and her face was grey, waxy grey. They only go like that when they are very frightened, or when they are dying.

'She hasn't much longer,' he said.

'I know,' agreed Shermaine. 'We must hurry.'

The woman moved restlessly on the trolley and gabbled a few words; then she sighed so that the great blanket-covered mound of her belly rose and fell, and she started to whimper again.

Haig was still in the theatre. He had stripped off his battle-jacket and, in his vest, he stooped over the basin washing. He did not look round as they wheeled the woman in.

'Get her on the table,' he said, working the soap into suds up to his elbows.

The trolley was of a height with the table and, using the blanket to lift her, it was easy to slide the woman across.

'She's ready, Haig,' said Bruce. Haig dried his arms on a clean towel and turned. He came to the woman and stood over her. She did not know he was there; her eyes were open but unseeing. Haig drew a deep breath; he was sweating a little across his forehead and the stubble of beard on the lower part of his face was stippled with grey.

He pulled back the blanket. The woman wore a short white jacket, open-fronted, that did not cover her stomach. Her stomach was swollen out, hard-looking, with the navel inverted, knees raised slightly and the thick peasant's thighs spread wide in the act of labour. As Bruce watched, her whole body arched in another contraction. He saw the stress of the muscles beneath the dark greyish skin as they struggled to expel the trapped foetus.

'Hurry, Mike!' Bruce was appalled by the anguish of birth. *I didn't know it was like this; in sorrow thou shalt bring forth children—but this!* Through the woman's dry grey swollen lips burst another of those moaning little cries, and Bruce swung towards Mike Haig.

'Hurry, goddam you!'

And Mike Haig began his examination, his hands very pale as they groped over the dark skin. At last he was satisfied and he stood back from the table.

Ignatius and the orderly came in with two more lanterns. Ignatius started to say something, but instantly he sensed the tension in the room and he fell silent. They all watched Mike Haig's face.

His eyes were tight closed, and his face was hard angles and harsh planes in the lantern light. His breathing was shallow and laboured.

I must not push him now, Bruce knew instinctively, *I have dragged him to the lip of the precipice and now I must let him go over the edge on his own.*

Mike opened his eyes again, and he spoke.

'Caesarian section,' he said, as though he had pronounced his own death sentence. Then his breathing stopped. They waited, and at last the breath came out of him in a sigh.

'I'll do it,' he said.

'Gowns and gloves?' Bruce fired the question at Ignatius.

'In the cupboard.'

'Get them!'

'You'll have to help me, Bruce. And you also, Shermaine.'

'Yes, show me.'

Quickly they scrubbed and dressed. Ignatius held the pale green theatre gowns while they dived into them and flapped and struggled through.

'That tray, bring it here,' Mike ordered as he opened the sterilizer. With a pair of long-nosed forceps he lifted the instruments out of the steaming box and laid them on the tray naming each one as he did so.

'Scalpel, retractors, clamps.'

In the meantime the orderly was swabbing the woman's belly with alcohol and arranging the sheets.

Mike filled the syringe with pentothal and held it up to the light. He was an unfamiliar figure now; his face masked, the green skull cap covering his hair, and the flowing gown falling to his ankles. He pressed the plunge and a few drops of the pale fluid dribbled down the needle.

He looked at Bruce, only his haunted eyes showing above the mask. 'Ready?'

'Yes,' Bruce nodded. Mike stooped over the woman, took her arm and sent the needle searching under the soft black skin on the inside of her elbow. The fluid in the syringe was suddenly discoloured with drawn blood as Mike tested for the vein, and then the plunger slid slowly down the glass barrel.

The woman stopped whimpering, the tension went out of her body and her breathing slowed and became deep and unhurried.

'Come here.' Mike ordered Shermaine to the head of the table, and she took up the chloroform mask and soaked the gauze that filled the cone.

'Wait until I tell you.'

She nodded. *Christ, what lovely eyes she has*, thought Bruce, before he turned back to the job in hand.

'Scalpel,' said Mike from across the table, pointing to it on the tray, and Bruce handed it to him.

Afterwards the details were confused and lacking reality in Bruce's mind.

The wound opening behind the knife, the tight stretched skin parting and the tiny blood vessels starting to squirt.

Pink muscle laced with white; butter-yellow layers of subcutaneous fat, and then through to the massed bluish coils of the gut. Human tissue, soft and pulsing, glistening in the flat glare of the petromax.

Clamps and retractors, like silver insects crowding into the wound as though it were a flower.

Mike's hands, inhuman in yellow rubber, moving in the open pit of the belly. Swabbing, cutting, clamping, tying off.

Then the swollen purple bag of the womb, suddenly unzipped by the knife.

And at last, unbelievably, the child curled in a dark grey ball of legs and tiny arms, head too big for its size, and the fat pink snake of the placenta enfolding it.

Lifted out, the infant hung by its heels from Mike's hand like a small grey bat, still joined to its mother.

Scissors snipped and it was free. Mike worked a little longer, and the infant cried.

It cried with minute fury, indignant and alive. From the head of the table Shermaine laughed with spontaneous delight, and clapped her hands like a child at a Punch and Judy show. Suddenly Bruce was

laughing also. It was a laugh from long ago, coming out from deep
inside him.

'Take it,' said Haig and Shermaine cradled it, wet and feebly wriggling in her arms. She stood with it while Haig sewed up. Watching her
face and the way she stood, Bruce suddenly and unaccountably felt the
laughter snag his throat, and he wanted to cry.

Haig closed the womb, stitching the complicated pattern of knots like
a skilled seamstress, then the external sutures laid neatly across the fat
lips of the wound, and at last the white tape hiding it all. He covered
the woman, jerked the mask from his face and looked up at Shermaine.
'You can help me clean it up,' he said, and his voice was strong again
and proud. The two of them crossed to the basin.

Bruce threw off his gown and left the room, went down the passage
and out into the night. He leaned against the bonnet of the Ford and
lit a cigarette.

Tonight I laughed again, he told himself with wonder, *and then I nearly
cried. And all because of a woman and a child. It is finished now, the pretence.
The withdrawal. The big act. There was more than one birth in there tonight. I
laughed again, I had the need to laugh again, and the desire to cry. A woman and
a child, the whole meaning of life.* The abscess had burst, the poison
drained, and he was ready to heal.

'Bruce, Bruce, where are you?' She came out through the door; he
did not answer her for she had seen the glow of his cigarette and she
came to him. Standing close in the darkness.

'Shermaine—' Bruce said, then he stopped himself. He wanted to
hold her, just hold her tightly.

'Yes, Bruce.' Her face was a pale round in the darkness, very close
to him.

'Shermaine, I want—' said Bruce and stopped again.

'Yes, me too,' she whispered and then, drawing away, 'come, let's
go and see what your doctor is doing now.' She took his hand and led
him back into the building. Her hand was cool and dry, with long
tapered fingers in his.

Mike Haig and Father Ignatius were leaning over the cradle that now
stood next to the table on which lay the blanket-covered body of the
Baluba woman. The woman was breathing softly, and the expression
on her face was of deep peace.

'Bruce, come and have a look. It's a beauty,' called Haig.

Still holding hands Bruce and Shermaine crossed to the cradle.

'He'll go all of eight pounds,' announced Haig proudly. Bruce looked
at the infant; new-born black babies are more handsome than ours—
they have not got that half-boiled look.

'Pity he's not a trout,' murmured Bruce. 'That would be a national record.' Haig stared blankly at him for a second, then he threw back his head and laughed; it was a good sound. There was a different quality in Haig now, a new confidence in the way he held his head, a feeling of completeness about him.

'How about that drink I promised you, Mike?' Bruce tested him.

'You have it for me, Bruce, I'll duck this one.' He isn't just saying it either, thought Bruce, as he looked at his face; he really doesn't need it now.

'I'll make it a double as soon as we get back to town.' Bruce glanced at his watch. 'It's past ten, we'd better get going.'

'I'll have to stay until she comes out from the anaesthetic,' demurred Haig. 'You can come back for me in the morning.'

Bruce hesitated. 'All right then. Come on, Shermaine.'

They drove back to Port Reprieve, sitting close together in the intimate darkness of the car. They did not speak until after they had reached the causeway, then Shermaine said, 'He is a good man, your doctor. He is like Paul.'

'Who is Paul?'

'Paul was my husband.'

'Oh.' Bruce was embarrassed. The mention of that name snapped the silken thread of his mood. Shermaine went on, speaking softly and staring down the path of the headlights.

'Paul was of the same age. Old enough to have learned understanding—young men are so cruel.'

'You loved him.' Bruce spoke flatly, trying to keep any trace of jealousy from his voice.

'Love has many shapes,' she answered. Then, 'Yes, I had begun to love him. Very soon I would have loved him enough to—' She stopped.

'To what?' Bruce's voice had gone rough as a wood rasp. *Now it starts*, he thought, *once again I am vulnerable*.

'We were only married four months before he—before the fever.'

'So?' Still harsh, his eyes on the road ahead.

'I want you to know something. I must explain it all to you. It is very important. Will you be patient with me while I tell you?' There was a pleading in her voice that he could not resist and his expression softened.

'Shermaine, you don't have to tell me.'

'I must. I want you to know.' She hesitated a moment, and when she spoke again her voice had steadied. 'I am an orphan, Bruce. Both my Mama and Papa were killed by the Germans, in the bombing. I was only a few months old when it happened, and I do not remember them. I do not remember anything, not one little thing about them; there is not even a photograph.' For a second her voice had gone shaky but again it firmed. 'The nuns took me, and they were my family. But somehow that is different, not really your own. I have never had anything that has truly belonged to me, something of my very own.'

Bruce reached out and took her hand; it lay very still in his grasp. *You have now,* he thought, *you have me for your very own.*

'Then when the time came the nuns made the arrangements with Paul Cartier. He was an engineer with Union Minière du Haut here in the Congo, a man of position, a suitable man for one of their girls.

'He flew to Brussels and we were married. I was not unhappy, for although he was old—as old as Dr Mike—yet he was very gentle and kind, of great understanding. He did not—' She stopped and turned suddenly to Bruce, gripping his hand with both of hers, leaning towards him with her face serious and pale in the half-darkness, the plume of dark hair falling forward over her shoulder and her voice full of appeal. 'Bruce, do you understand what I am trying to tell you?'

Bruce stopped the car in front of the hotel, deliberately he switched off the ignition and deliberately he spoke.

'Yes, I think so.'

'Thank you,' and she flung the door open and went out of it and up the steps of the hotel with her long jeaned legs flying and her hair bouncing on her back.

Bruce watched her go through the double doors. Then he pressed the lighter on the dashboard and fished a cigarette from his pack. He lit it, exhaled a jet of smoke against the windscreen, and suddenly he was happy. He wanted to laugh again.

He threw the cigarette away only a quarter finished and climbed out of the Ford. He looked at his wrist watch; it was after midnight. *My God, I'm tired. Too much has happened today; rebirth is a severe emotional strain.* And he laughed out loud, savouring the sensation, letting it come slowly shaking up his throat from his chest.

Boussier was waiting for him in the lounge. He wore a towelling dressing-gown, and the creases of sleep were on his face.

'Are all your preparations complete, monsieur?'

'Yes,' the old man answered. 'The women and the two children are asleep upstairs. Madame Cartier has just gone up.'

'I know,' said Bruce, and Boussier went on, 'As you see, I have all the men here.' He gestured at the sleeping bodies that covered the floor of the lounge and bar-room.

'Good,' said Bruce. 'We'll leave as soon as it's light tomorrow.' He yawned, then rubbed his eyes, massaging them with his finger tips.

'Where is my officer, the one with the red hair?'

'He has gone back to the train, very drunk. We had more trouble with him after you had left.' Boussier hesitated delicately. 'He wanted to go upstairs, to the women.'

'Damn him.' Bruce felt his anger coming again. 'What happened?'

'Your sergeant major, the big one, dissuaded him and took him away.'

'Thank God for Ruffy.'

'I have reserved a place for you to sleep.' Boussier pointed to a comfortable leather armchair. 'You must be exhausted.'

'That is kind of you,' Bruce thanked him. 'But first I must inspect our defences.'

CHAPTER 13

Bruce woke with Shermaine leaning over the chair and tickling his nose. He was fully dressed with his helmet and rifle on the floor beside him and only his boots unlaced.

'You do not snore, Bruce,' she congratulated him, laughing her small husky laugh. 'That is a good thing.'

He struggled up, dopey with sleep.

'What time is it?'

'Nearly five o'clock. I have breakfast for you in the kitchen.'

'Where is Boussier?'

'He is dressing; then he will start moving them down to the train.'

'My mouth tastes as though a goat slept in it.' Bruce moved his tongue across his teeth, feeling the fur on them.

'Then I shall not kiss you good morning, mon capitaine.' She straightened up with the laughter still in her eyes. 'But your toilet requisites are in the kitchen. I sent one of your gendarmes to fetch them from the train. You can wash in the sink.'

Bruce laced up his boots and followed her through into the kitchen, stepping over sleeping bodies on the way.

'There is no hot water,' Shermaine apologized.

'That is the least of my worries.' Bruce crossed to the table and opened his small personal pack, taking out his razor and soap and comb.

'I raided the chicken coop for you,' Shermaine confessed. 'There were only two eggs. How shall I cook them?'

'Soft boiled, one minute.' Bruce stripped off his jacket and shirt, went to the sink and filled it. He sluiced his face and lifted handfuls of water over his head, snorting with pleasure.

Then he propped his shaving mirror above the taps and spread soap on his face. Shermaine came to sit on the draining board beside him and watched with frank interest.

'I will be sorry to see the beard go,' she said. 'It looked like the pelt of an otter, I liked it.'

'Perhaps I will grow it for you one day.' Bruce smiled at her. 'Your eyes are blue, Shermaine.'

'It has taken you a long time to find that out,' she said and pouted dramatically. Her skin was silky and cool-looking, lips pale pink without make-up. Her dark hair, drawn back, emphasized the high cheek bones and the size of her eyes.

'In India "sher" means "tiger",' Bruce told her, watching her from the corner of his eye. Immediately she abandoned the pout and drew her lips up into a snarl. Her teeth were small and very white and only slightly uneven. Her eyes rolled wide and then crossed at an alarming angle. She growled. Taken by surprise, Bruce laughed and nearly cut himself.

'I cannot abide a woman who clowns before breakfast. It ruins my digestion,' he laughed at her.

'Breakfast!' said Shermaine and uncrossed her eyes, jumped off the draining board and ran to the stove.

'Only just in time.' She checked her watch. 'One minute and twenty seconds—will you forgive me?'

'This once only, never again.' Bruce washed the soap off his face, dried and combed his hair and came to the table. She had a chair ready for him.

'How much sugar in your coffee?'

'Three, please.' Bruce chopped the top off his egg, and she brought the mug and placed it in front of him.

'I like making breakfast for you.' Bruce didn't answer her. This was dangerous talk. She sat down opposite him, leaning forward on her elbows with her chin in her hands.

'You eat too fast,' she announced and Bruce raised an eyebrow. 'But at least you keep your mouth closed.'

Bruce started on his second egg.

'How old are you?

'Thirty,' said Bruce.

'I'm twenty—nearly twenty-one.'

'A ripe old age.'

'What do you do?'

'I'm a soldier,' he answered.

'No, you're not.'

'All right, I'm a lawyer.'

'You must be clever,' she said solemnly.

'A genius, that's why I'm here.'

'Are you married?'

'No—I was. What is this, a formal interrogation?'

'Is she dead?'

'No.' He prevented the hurt from showing in his face, it was easier to do now.

'Oh!' said Shermaine. She picked up the teaspoon and concentrated on stirring his coffee.

'Is she pretty?'

'No—yes, I suppose so.'

'Where is she?' Then quickly, 'I'm sorry it's none of my business.'

Bruce took the coffee from her and drank it. Then he looked at his watch.

'It's nearly five-fifteen. I must go out and get Mike Haig.'

Shermaine stood up quickly.

'I'm ready.'

'I know the way—you had better get down to the station.'

'I want to come with you.'

'Why?'

'Just because, that's why.' Searching for a reason. 'I want to see the baby again.'

'You win.' Bruce picked up his pack and they went through into the lounge. Boussier was there, dressed and efficient. His men were nearly ready to move.

'Madame Cartier and I are going out to the mission to fetch the doctor. We will be back in half an hour or so. I want all your people aboard by then.'

'Very well, Captain.'

Bruce called to Ruffy, who was standing on the veranda. 'Did you load those supplies for the mission?'

'They're in the back of the Ford, boss.'

'Good. Bring all your sentries in and take them down to the station. Tell the engine driver to get steam up and keep his hand on the throttle. We'll shove off as soon as I get back with Lieutenant Haig.'

'Okay, boss.'

Bruce handed him his pack. 'Take this down for me, Ruffy.' Then his eyes fell on the large heap of cardboard cartons at Ruffy's feet. 'What's that?'

Ruffy looked a little embarrassed. 'Coupla bottles of beer, boss. Thought we might get thirsty going home.'

'Good for you!' grinned Bruce. 'Put them in a safe place and don't drink them all before I get back.'

'I'll save you one or two,' promised Ruffy.

'Come along, tiger girl,' and Bruce led Shermaine out to the Ford. She sat closer to him than the previous day, but with her legs curled up under her, as before. As they crossed the causeway she lit two cigarettes and passed one to him.

'I'll be glad to leave this place,' she said, looking out across the swamp with the mist lifting sluggishly off it in the dawn, hanging in grey shreds from the fluffy tops of the papyrus grass. 'I've hated it here since Paul died. I hate the swamp and the mosquitoes and the jungle all around. I'm glad we're going.'

'Where will you go?' Bruce asked.

'I haven't thought about it. Back to Belgium, I suppose. Anywhere away from the Congo. Away from this heat to a country where you can breathe. Away from the disease and the fear. Somewhere so that I know tomorrow I will not have to run. Where human life has meaning, away from the killing and the burning and the rape.' She drew on her cigarette almost fiercely, staring ahead at the green wall of the forest.

'I was born in Africa,' said Bruce. 'In the time when the judge's gavel was not the butt of an FN rifle, before you registered your vote with a burst of gunfire.' He spoke softly with regret. 'In the time before the hatred. But now I don't know. I haven't thought much about the future either.'

He was silent for a while. They reached the turn-off to the mission and he swung the Ford into it.

'It has all changed so quickly; I hadn't realized how quickly until I came here to the Congo.'

'Are you going to stay here, Bruce? I mean, stay here in the Congo?'

'No,' he said, 'I've had enough. I don't even know what I'm fighting for.'

He threw the butt of his cigarette out of the window.

Ahead of them were the mission buildings.

Bruce parked the car outside the hospital buildings and they sat together quietly.

'There must be some other land,' he whispered, 'and if there is I'll find it.'

He opened the door and stepped out. Shermaine slid across the seat

under the wheel and joined him. They walked side by side to the
hospital; her hand brushed his and he caught it, held it and felt the
pressure of his fingers returned by hers. She was taller than his shoulder,
but not much.

Mike Haig and Father Ignatius were together in the women's ward,
too engrossed to hear the Ford arrive.

'Good morning, Michael,' called Bruce. 'What's the fancy dress for?'

Mike Haig looked up and grinned. 'Morning, Bruce. Hello, Shermaine.' Then he looked down at the faded brown cassock he wore.

'Borrowed it from Ignatius. A bit long in the leg and tight round the
waist, but less out of place in a sick ward than the accoutrements
of war.'

'It suits you, Dr Mike,' said Shermaine.

'Nice to hear someone call me that again.' The smile spread all over
Haig's face. 'I suppose you want to see your baby, Shermaine?'

'Is he well?'

'Mother and child both doing fine,' he assured her and led Shermaine
down between the row of beds, each with a black woolly head on the
pillow and big curious eyes following their progress.

'May I pick him up?'

'He's asleep, Shermaine.'

'Oh, please!'

'I doubt it will kill him. Very well, then.'

'Bruce, come and look. Isn't he a darling?' She held the tiny black
body to her chest and the child snuffled, its mouth automatically starting to search. Bruce leaned forward to peer at it.

'Very nice,' he said and turned to Ignatius. 'I have those supplies I
promised you. Will you send an orderly to get them out of the car?'
Then to Mike Haig, 'You'd better get changed, Mike. We're all ready
to leave.'

Not looking at Bruce, fiddling with the stethoscope round his neck,
Mike shook his head. 'I don't think I'll be going with you, Bruce.'

Surprised, Bruce faced him.

'What?'

'I think I'll stay on here with Ignatius. He has offered me a job.'

'You must be mad, Mike.'

'Perhaps,' agreed Haig and took the infant from Shermaine, placed
it back in the cradle beside its mother and tucked the sheet in round its
tiny body, 'and then again, perhaps not.' He straightened up and
waved a hand down the rows of occupied beds. 'There's plenty to do
here, that you must admit.'

Bruce stared helplessly at him and then appealed to Shermaine.

'Talk him out of it. Perhaps you can make him see the futility of it.'
Shermaine shook her head. 'No, Bruce, I will not.'
'Mike, listen to reason, for God's sake. You can't stay here in this
disease-ridden backwater, you can't—'
'I'll walk out to the car with you, Bruce. I know you're in a hurry—'
He led them out through the side door and stood by the driver's
window of the Ford while they climbed in. Bruce extended his hand
and Mike took it, gripping hard.
'Cheerio, Bruce. Thanks for everything.'
'Cheerio, Mike. I suppose you'll be taking orders and having your-
self made into a fully licensed dispenser of salvation?'
'I don't know about that, Bruce. I doubt it. I just want another
chance to do the only work I know. I just want a last-minute rally to
reduce the formidable score that's been chalked up against me so far.'
'I'll report you "missing, believed killed"—throw your uniform in
the river,' said Bruce.
'I'll do that.' Mike stepped back. 'Look after each other, you two.'
'I don't know what you mean,' Shermaine informed him primly,
trying not to smile.
'I'm an old dog, not easy to fool,' said Mike. 'Go to it with a will.'
Bruce let out the clutch and the Ford slid forward.
'God speed, my children.' That smile spread all over Mike's face as
he waved.
'Au revoir, Dr Michael.'
'So long, Mike.'
Bruce watched him in the rear-view mirror, tall in his ill-fitting
cassock, something proud and worthwhile in his stance. He waved
once more and then turned and hurried back into the hospital.
Neither of them spoke until they had almost reached the main road.
Shermaine nestled softly against Bruce, smiling to herself, looking
ahead down the tree-lined passage of the road.
'He's a good man, Bruce.'
'Light me a cigarette, please, Shermaine.' He didn't want to talk
about it. It was one of those things that can only be made grubby by
words.
Slowing for the intersection, Bruce dropped her into second gear,
automatically glancing to his left to make sure the main road was clear
before turning into it.
'Oh my God!' he gasped.
'What is it, Bruce?' Shermaine looked up with alarm from the
cigarette she was lighting.
'Look!'

A hundred yards up the road, parked close to the edge of the forest, was a convoy of six large vehicles. The first five were heavy canvas-canopied lorries painted dull military olive, the sixth was a gasoline tanker in bright yellow and red with the Shell Company insignia on the barrel-shaped body. Hitched behind the leading lorry was a squat, rubber-tyred 25-pounder anti-tank gun with its long barrel pointed jauntily skywards. Round the vehicles, dressed in an assortment of uniforms and different styled helmets, were at least sixty men. They were all armed, some with automatic weapons and others with obsolete bolt-action rifles. Most of them were urinating carelessly into the grass that lined the road, while the others were standing in small groups smoking and talking.

'General Moses!' said Shermaine, her voice small with the shock.

'Get down,' ordered Bruce and with his free hand thrust her onto the floor. He rammed the accelerator flat and the Ford roared out into the main road, swerving violently, the back end floating free in the loose dust as he held the wheel over. Correcting the skid, meeting it and straightening out, Bruce glanced at the rear-view mirror. Behind them the men had dissolved into a confused pattern of movement; he heard their shouts high and thin above the racing engine of the Ford. Bruce looked ahead; it was another hundred yards to the bend in the road that would hide them and take them down to the causeway across the swamp.

Shermaine was on her knees pulling herself up to look over the back of the seat.

'Keep on the floor, damn you!' shouted Bruce and pushed her head down roughly.

As he spoke the roadside next to them erupted in a rapid series of leaping dust fountains and he heard the high hysterical beat of machine-gun fire.

The bend in the road rushed towards them, just a few more seconds. Then with a succession of jarring crashes that shook the whole body of the car a burst of fire hit them from behind. The windscreen starred into a sheet of opaque diamond lacework, the dashboard clock exploded powdering Shermaine's hair with particles of glass, two bullets tore through the seat, ripping out the stuffing like the entrails of a wounded animal.

'Close your eyes,' shouted Bruce and punched his fist through the windscreen. Slitting his own eyes against the chips of flying glass, he could just see through the hole his fist had made. The corner was right on top of them and he dragged the steering-wheel over, skidding into it, his off-side wheels bumping into the verge, grass and leaves brushing the side of the car.

Then they were through the corner and racing down towards the causeway.

'Are you all right, Shermaine?'

'Yes, are you?' She emerged from under the dashboard, a smear of blood across one cheek where the glass had scratched her, and her eyes bigger than ever with fright.

'I only pray that Boussier and Hendry are ready to pull out. Those bastards won't be five minutes behind us.'

They went across the causeway with the needle of the speedometer touching eighty, up the far side and into the main street of Port Reprieve. Bruce thrust his hand down on the hooter ring, blowing urgent warning blasts.

'Please God, let them be ready,' he muttered. With relief he saw that the street was empty and the hotel seemed deserted. He kept blowing the horn as they roared down towards the station, a great billowing cloud of dust rising behind them. Braking the Ford hard, he turned it in past the station buildings and onto the platform.

Most of Boussier's people were standing next to the train. Boussier himself was beside the last truck with his wife and the small group of women around him. Bruce shouted at them through the open window.

'Get those women into the train, the *shufta* are right behind us, we're leaving immediately.'

Without question or argument old Boussier gathered them together and hurried them up the steel ladder into the truck. Bruce drove down the station platform, shouting as he went.

'Get in! For Chrissake, hurry up! They're coming!'

He braked to a standstill next to the cab of the locomotive and shouted up at the bald head of the driver.

'Get going. Don't waste a second. Give her everything she's got. There's a bunch of *shufta* not five minutes behind us.'

The driver's head disappeared into the cab without even the usual polite, 'Oui, monsieur.'

'Come on, Shermaine.' Bruce grabbed her hand and dragged her from the car. Together they ran to one of the covered coaches and Bruce pushed her half way up the steel steps.

At that moment the train jerked forward so violently that she lost her grip on the hand rails and tumbled backwards on top of Bruce. He was caught off balance and they fell together in a heap on the dusty platform. Above them the train gathered speed, pulling away. He remembered this nightmare from his childhood, running after a train and never catching it. He had to fight down his panic as he and Shermaine scrambled up, both of them panting, clinging to each others, the coaches clackety-clacking past them, the rhythm of their wheels mounting.

'Run!' he gasped, 'run!' and with the panic weakening their legs he just managed to catch the hand rail of the second coach. He clung to it, stumbling along beside the train, one arm round Shermaine's waist. Sergeant Major Ruffararo leaned out, took Shermaine by the scruff of her neck and lifted her in like a lost kitten. Then he reached down for Bruce.

'Boss, some day we going to lose you if you go on playing around like that.'

'I'm sorry, Bruce,' she panted, leaning against him.

'No damage done.' He could grin at her. 'Now I want you to get into that compartment and stay there until I tell you to come out. Do you understand?'

'Yes, Bruce.'

'Off you go.' He turned from her to Ruffy. 'Up onto the roof, Sergeant Major! We're going to have fireworks. Those *shufta* have got a field gun with them and we'll be in full view of the town right up to the top of the hills.'

By the time they reached the roof of the train it had pulled out of Port Reprieve and was making its first angling turn up the slope of the hills. The sun was up now, well clear of the horizon, and the mist from the swamp had lifted so that they could see the whole village spread out beneath them.

General Moses' column had crossed the causeway and was into the main street. As Bruce watched, the leading truck swung sharply across the road and stopped. Men boiled out from under the canopy and swarmed over the field gun, unhitching it, manhandling it into position.

'I hope those Arabs haven't had any drill on that piece,' grunted Ruffy.

'We'll soon find out,' Bruce assured him grimly and looked back along the train. In the last truck Boussier stood protectively over the small group of four women and their children, like an old white-haired collie with its sheep. Crouched against the steel side of the truck, André de Surrier and half a dozen gendarmes were swinging and sighting the two Bren guns. In the second truck also the gendarmes were preparing to open fire.

'What are you waiting for?' roared Ruffy. 'Get me that field gun—start shooting.'

They fired a ragged volley, then the Bren guns joined in. With every burst André's helmet slipped forward over his eyes and he had to stop and push it back. Lying on the roof of the leading coach, Wally Hendry was firing short business-like bursts.

The *shufta* round the field gun scattered, leaving one of their number lying in the road, but there were men behind the armour shield—Bruce could see the tops of their helmets.

Suddenly there was a long gush of white smoke from the barrel, and the shell rushed over the top of the train, with a noise like the wings of a giant pheasant.

'Over!' said Ruffy.

'Under!' to the next shot as it ploughed into the trees below them.

'And the third one right up the throat,' said Bruce. But it hit the rear of the train. They were using armour-piercing projectiles, not high explosive, for there was not the burst of yellow cordite fumes but only the crash and jolt as it struck.

Anxiously Bruce tried to assess the damage. The men and women in the rear trucks looked shaken but unharmed and he started a sigh of relief, which changed quickly to a gasp of horror as he realized what had happened.

'They've hit the coupling,' he said. 'They've sheared the coupling on the last truck.'

Already the gap was widening, as the rear truck started to roll back down the hill, cut off like the tail of a lizard.

'Jump,' screamed Bruce, cupping his hands round his mouth. 'Jump before you gather speed.'

Perhaps they did not hear him, perhaps they were too stunned to obey, but no one moved. The truck rolled back, faster and faster as gravity took it down the hill towards the village and the waiting army of General Moses.

'What can we do, boss?'

'Nothing,' said Bruce.

The firing round Bruce had petered out into silence as every man, even Wally Hendry, stared down the slope at the receding truck. With a constriction of his throat Bruce saw old Boussier stoop and lift his wife to her feet, hold her close to his side and the two of them looking back at Bruce on the roof of the departing train. Boussier raised his right hand in a gesture of farewell and then he dropped it again and stood very still. Behind him, André de Surrier had left the Bren gun and removed his helmet. He also was looking back at Bruce, but he did not wave.

At intervals the field gun in the village punctuated the stillness with its deep boom and gush of smoke, but Bruce hardly heard it. He was watching the *shufta* running down towards the station yard to welcome the truck. Losing speed it ran into the platform and halted abruptly as it hit the buffers at the end of the line. The *shufta* swarmed over it like little black ants over the body of a beetle and faintly Bruce heard the pop, pop, pop of their rifles, saw the low sun glint on their bayonets. He turned away.

They had almost reached the crest of the hills; he could feel the train increasing speed under him. But he felt no relief, only the prickling at the corners of his eyes and the ache of it trapped in his throat.

'The poor bastards,' growled Ruffy beside him. 'The poor bastards.' And then there was another crashing jolt against the train, another hit from the field gun, this time up forward, on the locomotive. There was a shriek of escaping steam, the train checking its pace, losing power. But they were over the crest of the hills, the village was out of sight and gradually the train speeded up again as they started down the back slope. But steam spouted out of it, hissing white jets of it, and Bruce knew they had received a mortal wound. He switched on the radio.

'Driver, can you hear me? How bad is it?'

'I cannot see, Captain. There is too much steam. But the pressure on the gauge is dropping swiftly.'

'Use all you can to take us down the hill. It is imperative that we pass the level crossing before we halt. It is absolutely imperative—if we stop this side of the level crossing they will be able to reach us with their lorries.'

'I will try, Captain.'

They rocketed down the hills but as soon as they reached the level ground their speed began to fall off. Peering through the dwindling clouds of steam Bruce saw the pale brown ribbon of road ahead of them, and they were still travelling at a healthy thirty miles an hour as they passed it. When finally the train trickled to a standstill Bruce estimated that they were three or four miles beyond the level crossing, safely walled in by the forest and hidden from the road by three bends.

'I doubt they'll find us here, but if they do they'll have to come down the line from the level crossing to get at us. We'll go back a mile and lay an ambush in the forest on each side of the line,' said Bruce.

'Those Arabs won't be following us, boss. They've got themselves women and a whole barful of liquor. Be two or three days before old General Moses can sober them up enough to move them on.'

'You're probably right, Ruffy. But we'll take no chances. Get that ambush laid and then we'll try and think up some idea for getting home.'

Suddenly a thought occurred to him: Martin Boussier had the diamonds with him. They would not be too pleased about that in Elisabethville.

Almost immediately Bruce was disgusted with himself. The diamonds were by far the least important thing that they had left behind in Port Reprieve.

CHAPTER 14

André de Surrier held his steel helmet against his chest the way a man holds his hat at a funeral; the wind blew cool and caressing through his dark sweat-damp hair. His hearing was dulled by the strike of the shell that had cut the truck loose from the rear of the train, but he could hear one of the children crying and the crooning, gentling voice of its mother. He stared back up the railway line at the train, saw the great bulk of Ruffy beside Bruce Curry on the roof of the second coach.
'They can't help us now.' Boussier spoke softly. 'There's nothing they can do.' He lifted his hand stiffly in almost a military salute and then dropped it to his side. 'Be brave, *ma chère*,' he said to his wife. 'Please be brave', and she clung to him.

André let the helmet drop from his hands. It clanged onto the metal floor of the truck. He wiped the sweat from his face with nervous fluttering hands and then turned slowly to look down at the village.
'I don't want to die,' he whispered. 'Not like this, not now, please not now.' One of his gendarmes laughed, a sound without mirth, and stepped across to the Bren. He pushed André away from it and started firing at the tiny running figures of the men in the station yard.
'No,' shrilled André. 'Don't do that, no, don't antagonize them. They'll kill us if you do that—'
'They'll kill us anyway,' laughed the gendarme and emptied the magazine in one long despairing burst. André started towards him, perhaps to pull him away from the gun, but his resolve did not carry him that far. His hands dropped to his sides, clenching and unclenching. His lips quivered and then opened to spill out his terror.
'No!' he screamed. 'Please, no! Oh, God have mercy. Oh, save me, don't let this happen to me, please, God. Oh, my God.'
He stumbled to the side of the truck and clambered onto it. The truck was slowing as it ran into the platform. He could see men coming with rifles in their hands, shouting as they ran, black men in dirty tattered uniforms, their faces working with excitement, pink shouting mouths, baying like hounds in a pack.
André jumped and the dusty concrete of the platform grazed his cheek and knocked the wind out of him. He crawled to his knees,

clutching his stomach and trying to scream. A rifle butt hit him between the shoulder-blades and he collapsed. Above him a voice shouted in French.

'He is white, keep him for the general. Don't kill him.' And again the rifle butt hit him, this time across the side of the head. He lay in the dust, dazed, with the taste of blood in his mouth and watched them drag the others from the truck.

They shot the black gendarmes on the platform, without ceremony, laughing as they competed with each other to use their bayonets on the corpses. The two children died quickly, torn from their mothers, held by the feet and swung head first against the steel side of the truck.

Old Boussier tried to prevent them stripping his wife and was bayoneted from behind in anger, and then shot twice with a pistol held to his head as he lay on the platform.

All this happened in the first few minutes before the officers arrived to control them; by that time André and the four women were the only occupants of the truck left alive.

André lay where he had fallen, watching in fascinated skin-crawling horror as they tore the clothing off the women and with a man to each arm and each leg held them down on the platform as though they were calves to be branded, hooting with laughter at their struggling naked bodies, bickering for position, already unbuckling belts, pushing each other, arguing, some of them with fresh blood on their clothing.

But then two men, who by their air of authority and the red sashes across their chests were clearly officers, joined the crowd. One of them fired his pistol in the air to gain their attention and both of them started a harangue that slowly had effect. The women were dragged up and herded off towards the hotel.

One of the officers came across to where André lay, stooped over him and lifted his head by taking a handful of hair.

'Welcome, mon ami. The general will be very pleased to see you. It is a pity that your other white friends have left us, but then, one is better than nothing.'

He pulled André into a sitting position, peered into his face and then spat into his eyes with sudden violence. 'Bring him! The general will talk to him later.'

They tied André to one of the columns on the front veranda of the hotel and left him there. He could have twisted his head and looked through the large windows into the lounge at what they were doing to the women, but he did not. He could hear what was happening; by noon the screams had become groans and sobbing; by mid-afternoon the women were making no sound at all. But the queue of *shufta* was still out of the front door of the lounge. Some of them had been to the head of the line and back to the tail three or four times. All of them were drunk now. One jovial fellow carried a bottle of Parait Amour liqueur in one hand and a bottle of Harpers whisky in the other. Every time he came back to join the queue again he stopped in front of André.

'Will you drink with me, little white boy?' he asked. 'Certainly you will,' he answered himself, filled his mouth from one of the bottles and spat it into André's face. Each time it got a big laugh from the others waiting in the line. Occasionally one of the other *shufta* would stop in front of André, unsling his rifle, back away a few paces, sight along the bayonet at André's face and then charge forward, at the last moment twisting the point aside so that it grazed his cheek. Each time André could not suppress his shriek of terror, and the waiting men nearly collapsed with merriment.

Towards evening they started to burn the houses on the outskirts of town. One group, sad with liquor and rape, sat together at the end of the veranda and started to sing. Their deep beautiful voices carrying all the melancholy savagery of Africa, they kept on singing while an argument between two *shufta* developed into a knife fight in the road outside the hotel.

The sweet bass lilt of singing covered the coarse breathing of the two circling, bare-chested knife fighters and the shuffle, shuffle, quick shuffle of their feet in the dust. When finally they locked together for the kill, the singing rose still deep and strong but with a triumphant note to it. One man stepped back with his rigid right arm holding the knife buried deep in the other's belly and as the loser sank down, sliding slowly off the knife, the singing sank with him, plaintive, regretful and lamenting into silence.

They came for André after dark. Four of them, less drunk than the others. They led him down the street to the Union Minière offices. General Moses was there, sitting alone at the desk in the front office.

There was nothing sinister about him; he looked like an elderly clerk, a small man with the short woollen cap of hair grizzled to grey above the ears and a pair of horn-rimmed spectacles. On his chest he wore three rows of full-dress medals; each of his fingers was encased in rings to the second joint, diamonds, emeralds and the occasional red glow of a ruby; most of them had been designed for women, but the metal had been cut to enlarge them for his stubby black fingers. The face was almost kindly, except the eyes. There was a blankness of expression in them, the lifeless eyes of a madman. On the desk in front of him was a small wooden case made of unvarnished deal which bore the seal of the Union Minière Company stencilled in black upon its side. The lid was open, and as André came in through the door with his escort General Moses lifted a white canvas bag from the case, loosened the draw string and poured a pile of dark grey industrial diamonds onto the blotter in front of him.

He prodded them thoughtfully with his finger, stirring them so they glittered dully in the harsh light of the petromax.

'Was this the only case in the truck?' he asked without looking up.

'Oui, mon général. There was only the one,' answered one of André's escorts.

'You are certain?'

'Oui, mon général. I myself have searched thoroughly.'

General Moses took another of the canvas bags from the case and emptied it onto the blotter. He grunted with disappointment as he saw the drab little stones. He reached for another bag, and another, his anger mounting steadily as each yielded only dirty grey and black industrial diamonds. Soon the pile on the blotter would have filled a pint jug.

'Did you open the case?' he snarled.

'Non, mon général. It was sealed. The seal was not broken, you saw that.'

General Moses grunted again, his dark chocolate face set hard with frustration. Once more he dipped his hand into the wooden case and suddenly he smiled.

'Ah!' he said pleasantly. 'Yes! yes! what is this?' He brought out a cigar box, with the gaudy wrappers still on the cedar wood. A thumb nail prised the lid back and he beamed happily. In a nest of cotton wool, sparkling, breaking the white light of the petromax into all the rainbow colours of the spectrum, were the gem stones. General Moses picked one up and held it between thumb and forefinger.

'Pretty,' he murmured. 'Pretty, so pretty.' He swept the industrial stones to one side and laid the gem in the centre of the blotter. Then one by one he took the others from the cigar box, fondling each and laying it on the blotter, counting them, smiling, once chuckling softly, touching them, arranging them in patterns.

'Pretty,' he kept whispering. 'Bon—forty-one, forty-two. Pretty! My darlings! Forty-three.'

Then suddenly he scooped them up and poured them into one of the canvas bags, tightened the draw string, dropped it into his breast pocket above the medals and buttoned the flap.

He laid his black, bejewelled hands on the desk in front of him and looked up at André.

His eyes were smoky yellow with black centres behind his spectacles. They had an opaque, dreamlike quality.

'Take off his clothes,' he said in a voice that was as expressionless as the eyes.

They stripped André with rough dispatch and General Moses looked at his body.

'So white,' he murmured. 'Why so white?' Suddenly his jaws began chewing nervously and there was a faint shine of sweat on his forehead.

He came round from behind the desk, a small man, yet with an intensity about him that doubled his size.

'White like the maggots that feed in the living body of the elephant.' He brought his face close to André's. 'You should be fatter, my maggot, having fed so long and so well. You should be much fatter.'

He touched André's body, running his hands down his flanks in a caress.

'But now it is too late, little white maggot,' he said, and André cringed from his touch and from his voice. 'For the elephant has shaken you from the wound, shaken you out onto the ground, shaken you out beneath his feet—and will you pop when he crushes you?'

His voice was still soft through the sweat oozed in oily lines down his cheeks and the dreaminess of his eyes had been replaced by a burning black brightness.

'We shall see,' he said and drew back. 'We shall see, my maggot,' he repeated, and brought his knee up into André's crotch with a force that jerked his whole frame and flung his shoulders back.

The agony flared through André's lower body, fierce as the touch of heated steel. It clamped in on his stomach, contracting it in a spasm like childbirth, it rippled up across the muscles of his chest into his head and burst beneath the roof of his skull in a whiteness that blinded him.

'Hold him,' commanded General Moses, his voice suddenly shrill. The two guards took André by the elbows and forced him to his knees, so that his genitals and lower belly were easily accessible to the general's boots. They had done this often.

'For the times you gaoled me!' And General Moses swung his booted foot into André's body. The pain blended with the other pain, and it was too strong for André to scream.

'This, for the insults,' and André could feel his testicles crush beneath it. Still it was too strong—he could not use his voice.

'This, for the times I have grovelled.' The pain had passed its zenith, this time he could scream with it. He opened his mouth and filled his empty lungs.

'This, for the times I have hungered.' Now he must scream. Now he must—the pain, oh, sweet Christ, I must, please let me scream.

'This, for your white man's justice.' Why can't I, please let me. Oh, no! No—please. Oh, God, oh, please.

'This, for your prisons and your Kiboko!'

The kicks so fast now, like the beat of an insane drummer, like rain on a tin roof. In his stomach he felt something tear.

'And this, and this, and this.'

The face before him filled the whole field of his vision. The voice and the sound of boot into him filled his ears.

'This, and this, and this.' The voice high-pitched and within him the sudden warm flood of internal bleeding.

The pain was fading now as his body closed it out in defence, and he had not screamed. The leap of elation as he knew it. *This last thing I can do well, I can die now WITHOUT SCREAMING.* He tried to stand up, but they held him down and his legs were not his own, they were on the other side of the great numb warmth of his belly. He lifted his head and looked at the man who was killing him.

'This for the white filth that bore you, and this, and this—'

The blows were not a part of reality, he could feel the shock of them as though he stood close to a man who was cutting down a tree with an axe. And André smiled.

He was still smiling when they let him fall forward to the floor.

'I think he is dead,' said one of the guards. General Moses turned away and walked back to his seat at the desk. He was shaking as though he had run a long way, and his breathing was deep and fast. The jacket of his uniform was soaked with sweat. He sank into the chair and his body seemed to crumple; slowly the brightness faded from his eyes until once more they were filmed over, opaque and dreamy. The two guards squatted down quietly on each side of André's body; they knew it would be a long wait.

Through the open window there came an occasional shout of drunken laughter, and the red flicker and leap of flames.

CHAPTER 15

Bruce stood in the centre of the tracks and searched the floor of the forest critically. At last he could make out the muzzle of the Bren protruding a few inches from the patch of elephant grass. Despite the fact that he knew exactly where to look for it, it had taken him a full two minutes to find it.

'That'll do, Ruffy,' he decided. 'We can't get it much better than that.'

'I reckon not, boss.'

Bruce raised his voice. 'Can you hear me?' There were muffled affirmatives from the bush on each side, and Bruce continued.

'If they come you must let them reach this spot before you open fire. I will mark it for you.' He went to a small shrub beside the line, broke off a branch and dropped it on the tracks.

'Can you see that?'

Again the affirmatives from the men in ambush. 'You will be relieved before darkness—until then stay where you are.'

The train was hidden beyond a bend in the line, half a mile ahead, and Bruce walked back with Ruffy.

The engine driver was waiting for them, talking with Wally Hendry beside the rear truck.

'Any luck?' Bruce asked him.

'I regret, mon capitaine, that she is irreparably damaged. The boiler is punctured in two places and there is considerable disruption of the copper tubing.'

'Thank you,' Bruce nodded. He was neither surprised nor disappointed. It was precisely what his own judgement had told him after a brief examination of the locomotive.

'Where is Madame Cartier?' he asked Wally.

'*Madame* is preparing the luncheon, *monsir*,' Wally told him with heavy sarcasm. 'Why do you ask, Bucko? Are you feeling randy again so soon, hey? You feel like a slice of veal for lunch, is that it?'

Bruce snuffed out the quick flare of his temper and walked past him. He found Shermaine with four gendarmes in the cab of the locomotive. They had scraped the coals from the furnace into a glowing heap on the steel floor and were chopping potatoes and onions into the five gallon pots.

The gendarmes were all laughing at something Shermaine had said. Her usually pale cheeks were flushed with the heat; there was a sooty smudge on her forehead. She wielded the big knife with professional dexterity. She looked up and saw Bruce, her face lighting instantly and her lips parting.

'We're having a Hungarian goulash for lunch—bully beef, potatoes and onions.'

'As of now I am rating you acting second cook without pay.'

'You are too kind,' and she put her tongue out at him. It was a pink pointed little tongue like a cat's. Bruce felt the old familiar tightening of his legs and the dryness in his throat as he looked at it.

'Shermaine, the locomotive is damaged beyond repair. It is of no further use.' He spoke in English.

'It makes a passable kitchen,' she demurred.

'Be serious.' Bruce's anxiety made him irritable. 'We're stranded here until we think of something.'

'But, Bruce, you are the genius. I have complete faith in you. I'm sure you'll think of some truly beautiful idea.' Her face was solemn but she couldn't keep the banter out of her eyes. 'Why don't you go and ask General Moses to lend you his transportation.'

Bruce's eyes narrowed in thought and the black inverted curves of his eyebrows nearly touched above the bridge of his nose.

'The food better be good or I'll break you to third cook,' he warned, clambered down from the cab to the ground and hurried back along the train.

'Hendry, Sergeant Major, come here, please. I want to discuss something with you.'

They came to join him and he led the way up the ladder into one of the covered coaches. Hendry dropped onto the bunk and placed his feet on the wash basin.

'That was a quick one,' he grinned through the coppery stubble of his beard.

'You're the most uncouth, filthy-mouthed son of a bitch I have ever met, Hendry,' said Bruce coldly. 'When I get you back to Elisabethville I'm going to beat you to pulp before I hand you over to the military authority for murder.'

'My, my,' laughed Hendry. 'Big talker, hey? Curry, big, big talker.'

'Don't make me kill you now—don't do that, please. I still need you.'

'What's with you and that Frenchy, hey? You love it or something? You love it, or you just fancy a bit of that fat little arse? It can't be her titties—she ain't got much there, not even a handful each side.'

Bruce started for him, then changed his mind and swung round to stare out of the window. His voice was strangled when he spoke.

I'll make a bargain with you, Hendry. Until we get out of this you keep off my back and I'll keep off yours. When we reach Msapa

Junction the truce is off. You can do and say whatever you like and, if I don't kill you for it, I'll try my level best to see you hanged for murder.'

'I'm making no bargain with you or nobody, Curry. I play along until it suits me, and I won't give you no warning when it doesn't suit me to play along any more. And let me tell you now, Bucko, I don't need you and I don't need nobody. Not Haig or you, with your fancy too-good-to-kiss-my-arse talk; when the time comes I'm going to trim you down to size—just remember that, Curry. And don't say I didn't warn you.' Hendry was leaning forward, hands on his knees, body braced and his whole face twisted and contorted with the vehemence of his speech.

'Let's make it now, Hendry.' Bruce wheeled away from the window, crouching slightly, his hands stiffening into the flat hard blades of the judo fighter.

Sergeant Major Ruffararo stood up from the opposite bunk with surprising grace and speed for such a big man. He interposed his great body.

'You wanted to tell us something, boss?'

Slowly Bruce straightened out of his crouch, his hands relaxing. Irritably he brushed at the damp lock of dark hair that had fallen onto his forehead, as if to brush Wally Hendry out of his mind with the same movement.

'Yes,' controlling his voice with an effort, 'I wanted to discuss our next move.' He fished the cigarette pack from his top pocket and lit one, sucking the smoke down deep. Then he perched on the lid of the wash basin and studied the ash on the tip of the cigarette. When he spoke again his voice was normal.

'There is no hope of repairing this locomotive, so we have to find alternative transport out of here. Either we can walk two hundred miles back to Msapa Junction with our friends the Baluba ready to dispute our passage, or we can ride back in General Moses' trucks!' He paused to let it sink in.

'You going to pinch those trucks off him?' asked Ruffy. 'That's going to take some doing, boss.'

'No, Ruffy, I don't think we have any chance of getting them out from under his nose. What we will have to do is attack the town and wipe him out.'

'You're bloody crazy,' exclaimed Wally. 'You're raving bloody mad.'

Bruce ignored him. 'I estimate that Moses has about sixty men. With Kanaki and nine men on the bridge, Haig and de Surrier and six others gone, we have thirty-four men left. Correct, Sergeant Major?'

'That's right, boss.'

'Very well,' Bruce nodded. 'We'll have to leave at least ten men here to man that ambush in case Moses sends a patrol after us, or in case of an attack by the Baluba. It's not enough, I know, but we will just have to risk it.'

'Most of these civilians got arms with them, shotguns and sports rifles,' said Ruffy.

'Yes,' agreed Bruce. 'They should be able to look after themselves. So that leaves twenty-four men to carry out the attack, something like three to one.'

'Those *shufta* will be so full of liquor, half of them won't be able to stand up.'

'That's what I am banking on: drunkenness and surprise. We'll hit them and try and finish it before they know what's happened. I don't think they will have realized how badly we were hit; they probably expect us to be a hundred miles away by now.'

'When do you want to leave, boss?'

'We are about twelve miles from Port Reprieve—say, six hours' march in the dark. I want to attack in the early hours of tomorrow morning, but I'd like to be in position around midnight. We'll leave here at six o'clock, just before dark.'

'I'd better go and start sorting the boys out.'

'Okay, Ruffy. Issue an extra hundred rounds to each man and ten grenades. I'll want four extra haversacks of grenades also.' Bruce turned to Hendry and looked at him for the first time. 'Go with the sergeant major, Hendry, and give him a hand.'

'Jesus, this is going to be a ball,' grinned Wally in anticipation. 'With any luck I'll get me a sackful of ears.' He disappeared down the corridor behind Ruffy, and Bruce lay back on the seat and took off his helmet. He closed his eyes and once again he saw Boussier and his wife standing together in the truck as it rolled back down the hill, he saw the huddle of frightened women, and André standing bareheaded staring back at him with big brown gentle eyes. He groaned softly. 'Why is it always the good ones, the harmless, the weak?'

A tap on the door roused him and he sat up quickly.

'Yes?'

'Hello, Bruce.' Shermaine came in with a multiple-decked metal canteen in one hand and two mugs in the other. 'It's lunchtime.'

'Already!' Bruce checked his watch. 'Good Lord, it's after one.'

'Are you hungry?'

'Breakfast was a century ago.'

'Good,' she said, lowered the collapsible table and began serving the food.

'Smells good.'

'I am a chef Cordon Bleu. My bully beef goulash is demanded by the crowned heads of Europe.'

They ate in silence, for both of them were hungry. Once they looked at each other and smiled but returned to the food.

'That was good,' sighed Bruce at last.

'Coffee, Bruce?'

'Please.'

As she poured it she asked, 'So, what happens now?'

'Do you mean what happens now we are alone?'

'You are forward, monsieur. I meant how do we get out of here.'

'I am adopting your suggestion: borrowing General Moses' transportation.'

'You make jokes, Bruce!'

'No,' he said, and explained briefly.

'It will be very dangerous, will it not? You may be hurt?'

'Only the good die young.'

'That is why I worry. Please do not get hurt—I am starting to think I would not like that.' Her face was very serious and pale. Bruce crossed quickly and stooped over her, lifting her to her feet.

'Shermaine, I—'

'No, Bruce. Don't talk. Don't say anything.' Her eyes were closed with thick black lashes interlaced, her chin lifted exposing the long smooth swell of her neck. He touched it with his lips and she made a soft noise in her throat so he could feel the skin vibrate. Her body flattened against his and her fingers closed in the hair at the back of his head.

'Oh, Bruce. My Bruce, please do not get hurt. Do not let them hurt you.'

Wanting now, urgently, his mouth hunted upwards and hers came to meet it, willing prey. Her lips were pink and not greased with make-up, they parted to the pressure of his tongue, he felt the tip of her nose cool upon his cheek and his hand moved up her back and closed round the nape of her neck, slender neck with silky down behind her ears.

'Oh, Bruce—' she said into his mouth. His other hand went down onto the proud round, deeply divided thrust of her buttocks, he pulled her lower body against his and she gasped as she felt him—the arrogant maleness through cloth.

'No,' she gasped and tried to pull away, but he held her until she relaxed against him once more. She shook her head, '*Non, non*', but her mouth was open still and her tongue fluttered against his. Down came his hand from her neck and twitched her shirt tails loose from under her belt, then up again along her back, touching the deep lateral depression of her spine so that she shuddered, clinging to him. Stroking velvet skin stretched tight over rubber-hard flesh, finding the outline of her shoulder-blades, tracing them upwards then back to the armpits, silky-haired armpits that maddened him with excitement, quickly past them to her breasts, small breasts with soft tips hardening to his touch.

Now she struggled in earnest, her fists beating on his shoulders and her mouth breaking from his, and he stopped himself, dropped the hand away to encircle her waist. Holding her loosely within his arms.

'That was not good, Bruce. You get naughty very quick.' Her cheeks flamed with colour and her blue eyes had darkened to royal, her lips were still wet from his, and her voice was unsteady, as unsteady as his when he answered.

'I'm sorry, Shermaine. I don't know what happened then. I did not mean to frighten you.'

'You are very strong, Bruce. But you do not frighten me, only a little bit. Your eyes frighten me when they look at me but do not see.'

You really made a hash of that one, he rebuked himself. Bruce Curry, the gentle sophisticated lover. Bruce Curry, the heavyweight, catch-as-catch-can, two-fisted rape artist.

He felt shaky, his legs wobbly, and there was something seriously wrong with his breathing.

'You do not wear a brassière,' he said without thinking, and immediately regretted it, but she chuckled, soft and husky.

'Do you think I need to, Bruce?'

'No, I didn't mean that,' he protested quickly, remembering the saucy tilt of that small breast. He was silent then, marshalling his words, trying to control his breathing, fighting down the madness of desire.

She studied his eyes. 'You can see again now—perhaps I will let you kiss me.'

'Please,' he said and she came back to him.

Gently now, Bruce me boy. The door of the compartment flew back with a crash and they jumped apart. Wally Hendry stood on the threshold.

'Well, well, well.' His shrewd little eyes took it all in. 'That's nice!'

Shermaine was hurriedly tucking in her shirt tail and trying to smooth her hair at the same time.

Wally grinned. 'Nothing like it after a meal, I always say. Get's the digestion going.'

'What do you want?' snapped Bruce.

'There's no doubt what you want,' said Wally. 'Looks like you're getting it too.' He let his eyes travel up from Shermaine's waist, slowly over her body to her face.

Bruce stepped out into the corridor, pushing Hendry back and slammed the door.

'What do you want?' he repeated.

'Ruffy wants you to check his arrangements, but I'll tell him you're busy. We can put the attack off until tomorrow night if you like.'

Bruce scowled at him. 'Tell him I'll be with him in two minutes.'

Wally leaned against the door. 'Okay, I'll tell him.'

'What are you waiting for?'

'Nothing, just nothing,' grinned Wally.

'Well, bugger off then,' snarled Bruce.

'Okay, okay, don't get your knickers in a knot, Bucko.'

He sauntered off down the corridor.

Shermaine was standing where Bruce had left her, but with her eyes bright with tears of anger.

'He is a pig, that one. A filthy, filthy pig.'

'He's not worth worrying about.' Bruce tried to take her in his arms again, but she shrugged him off.

'I hate him. He makes everything seem so cheap, so dirty.'

'Nothing between you and I could be cheap and dirty,' said Bruce, and instantly her fury abated.

'I know, my Bruce. But he can make it seem that way.' They kissed, gently.

'I must go. They want me.' For a second she clung to him.

'Be careful. Promise me you'll be careful.'

'I promise,' said Bruce and she let him go.

CHAPTER 16

They left before dark, but the clouds had come up during the afternoon and now they hung low over the forest, trapping the heat beneath them.

Bruce led, with Ruffy in the middle of the line and Hendry at the rear.

By the time they reached the level crossing the night was on them and it had started to rain, soft fat drops weeping like a woman exhausted with grief, warm rain in the darkness. And the darkness was complete. Once Bruce touched the top of his nose with his open palm, but he could not see his hand.

He used a staff to keep contact with the steel rail that ran beside him, tapping along it like a blind man, and at each step the gravel of the embankment crunched beneath his feet. The hand of the man behind him was on his shoulder, and he could sense the presence of the others that followed him like the body of a serpent, could hear the crunch of their steps and the muted squeak and rattle of their equipment. A man's voice was raised in protest and immediately quenched by Ruffy's deep rumble.

They crossed the road and the gradient changed beneath Bruce's feet so that he had to lean forward against it. They were starting up the Lufira hills.

I will rest them at the top, he thought, and from there we will be able to see the lights of the town.

The rain stopped abruptly, and the quietness after it was surprising. Now he could distinctly hear the breathing of the man behind him above the small sounds of their advance, and in the forest near by a tree frog clinked as though steel pellets were being dropped into a crystal glass. It was a sound of great purity and beauty.

All Bruce's senses were enhanced to compensate for his lack of sight; his hearing; his sense of smell, so that he could catch the over-sweet perfume of a jungle flower and the heaviness of decaying wet vegeta-tion; his sense of touch, so that he could feel the raindrops on his face and the texture of his clothing against his body; then the other animal sense of danger told him with sickening, stomach-tripping certainty that there was something ahead of him in the darkness.

He stopped, and the man following him bumped into him, throwing him off balance. All along the line there was a ripple of confusion and then silence. They all waited.

Bruce strained his hearing, half crouched with his rifle held ready. There was something there, he could almost feel it.

Please God, let them not have a machine-gun set up here, he thought; *they could cut us into a shambles.*

He turned cautiously and felt for the head of the man behind him, found it and drew it towards him until his mouth was an inch from the ear.

'Lie down very quietly. Tell the one behind you that he may pass it back.'

Bruce waited, poised, listening and trying to see ahead into the utter blackness. He felt a gentle tap on his ankle from the gendarme at his feet. They were all down.

'All right, let's go take a look.' Bruce detached one of the grenades from his webbing belt. He drew the pin and dropped it into the breast pocket of his jacket. Then, feeling for the cross-ties of the rails with each foot, he started forward. Ten paces and he stopped again. Then he heard it, the tiny click of two pebbles just ahead of him. His throat closed so he could not breathe and his stomach was very heavy.

I'm right on top of them. My God, if they open up now— Inch by inch he drew back the hand that held the grenade. *I'll have to lob short and then get down fast. Five-second fuse—too long, they'll hear it and start shooting.*

His hand was right back, he bent his legs and sank slowly onto his knees. *Here we go,* he thought, and at that instant sheet lightning fluttered across the sky and Bruce could see. The hills were outlined black below the pale grey belly of the clouds, and the steel rails glinted in the sudden light. The forest was dark and high at each hand, and—a leopard, a big golden and black leopard, stood facing Bruce. In that brief second they stared at each other and then the night closed down again.

The leopard coughed explosively in the darkness, and Bruce tried desperately to bring his rifle up, but it was in his left hand and his other arm was held back ready to throw.

This time for sure, he thought, *this time they lower the boom on you.*

It was with a feeling of disbelief that he heard the leopard crash sideways into the undergrowth, and the scrambling rush of its run dwindle into the bush.

He subsided onto his backside, with the primed grenade in his hand, the hysterical laughter of relief coming up into his throat.

'You okay, boss?' Ruffy's voice lifted anxiously.

'It was a leopard,' answered Bruce, and was surprised at the squeakiness of his own voice.

There was a buzz of voices from the gendarmes and a rattle and clatter as they started to stand up. Someone laughed.

'That's enough noise,' snapped Bruce and climbed to his feet; he found the pin in his pocket and fitted it back into the grenade. He groped his way back, picked up the staff from where he had dropped it, and took his position at the head of the column again.

'Let's go,' he said.

His mouth was dry, his breathing too quick and he could feel the heat beneath the skin of his cheeks from the shock of the leopard.

I truly squirted myself full of adrenalin that time, Bruce grinned precariously in the dark, *I'm as windy as hell. And before tonight is over I shall find fear again.*

They moved on up the incline of the hills, a serpent of twenty-six men, and the tension was in all of them. Bruce could hear it in the footsteps behind him, feel it in the grip of the hand upon his shoulder and catch it in the occasional whiffs of body smell that came forward to him, the smell of nervous sweat like acid on metal.

Ahead of them the clouds that had crouched low upon the hills lifted slowly, and Bruce could see the silhouette of the crests. It was no longer utterly dark for there was a glow on the belly of the clouds now, a faint orange glow of reflected light that grew in strength, then faded and grew again. It puzzled Bruce for a while, and thinking about it gave his nerves a chance to settle. He plodded steadily on, watching the fluctuations of the light. The ground tilted more sharply upwards beneath his feet and he leaned forward against it, slogging up the last half mile to the pass between the peaks, and at last came out on the top.

'Good God,' Bruce spoke aloud, for from here he could see the reason for that glow on the clouds. They were burning Port Reprieve. The flames were well established in the buildings along the wharf, and as Bruce watched, one of the roofs collapsed slowly in upon itself in a storm of sparks, leaving the walls naked and erect, the wooden sills of the windows burning fiercely. The railway buildings were also on fire, and there was fire in the residential area beyond the Union Minière offices and the hotel. Quickly Bruce looked towards St Augustine's. It was dark, no flames there, no light even; and he felt a small lift of relief.

'Perhaps they have overlooked it, perhaps they're too busy looting,' and as he looked back at Port Reprieve, his mouth hardened. 'The senseless wanton bastards!' His anger started as he watched the meaningless destruction of the town.

'What can they possibly hope to gain by this?' There were new fires nearer the hotel. Bruce turned to the man behind him.

'We will rest here, but there will be no smoking and no talking.'

He heard the order passed back along the line and the careful sounds of equipment being lowered and men settling gratefully down upon the gravel embankment. Bruce unslung the case that contained his binoculars. He focused them on the burning town.

It was bright with the light of fires and through the glasses he could almost discern the features of the men in the streets. They moved in packs, heavily armed and restless. Many carried bottles and already the gait of some of them was unsteady. Bruce tried to estimate their numbers but it was impossible; men kept disappearing into buildings and reappearing, groups met and mingled and dispersed.

He dropped his glasses onto his chest to rest his eyes, and heard movement beside him in the dark. He glanced sideways. It was Ruffy, his bulk exaggerated by the load he carried; his rifle across one shoulder, on the other a full case of ammunition, and round his neck half a dozen haversacks full of grenades.

'Looks like they're having fun, hey, boss?'

'Fifth of November,' agreed Bruce. 'Aren't you going to take a breather?'

'Why not?' Ruffy set down the ammunition case and lowered his great backside onto it. 'Can you see any of those folks we left behind?' he asked.

Bruce lifted the glasses again and searched the area beyond the station buildings. It was darker there but he made out the square shape of the truck standing among the moving shadows.

'The truck's still there,' he murmured, 'but I can't see—'

At that moment the thatched roof of one of the houses exploded upwards in a column of flame, lighting the railway yard, and the truck stood out sharply.

'Yes,' said Bruce, 'I can see them now.' They were littered untidily across the yard, still lying where they had died. Small and fragile, unwanted as broken toys.

'Dead?' askec Ruffy.

'Dead,' confirmed Bruce.

'The women?'

'It's hard to tell.' Bruce strained his eyes. 'I don't think so.'

'No.' Ruffy's voice was soft and very deep. 'They wouldn't waste the women. I'd guess they've got them up at the hotel, taking it in turn to give them the business. Four women only—they won't last till morning. Those bastards down there could shag an elephant to death.' He spat thoughtfully into the gravel at his feet. 'What you going to do, boss?'

Bruce did not answer for a minute; he swung the glasses slowly back across the town. The field gun was still standing where he had last seen it, its barrel pointing accusingly up towards him. The transports were parked before the Union Minière offices; he could see the brilliant yellow and red paint and the Shell sign on the tanker. I hope it's full, Bruce thought, we'll need plenty of gasoline to get us back to Elisabethville.

'Ruffy, you'd better tell your boys to keep their bullets away from that tanker, otherwise it'll be a long walk home.'

'I'll tell them,' grunted Ruffy. 'But you know these mad Arabs—once they start shooting they don't stop till they're out of bullets, and they're not too fussy where those bullets go.'

'We'll split into two groups when we get to the bottom of the hill. You and I will take our lot through the edge of the swamp and cross to the far side of the town. Tell Lieutenant Hendry to come here.' Bruce waited until Wally came forward to join them, and when the three of them crouched together he went on.

'Hendry, I want you to spread your men out at the top of the main street—there in the darkness on this side of the station. Ruffy and I are going to cross the edge of the swamp to the causeway and lay out on the far side. For God's sake keep your boys quiet until Ruffy and I hit them—all we need is for your lot to start popping off before we are ready and we won't need those lorries, we'll need coffins for the rest of our journey. Do you understand me?'

'Okay, okay, I know what I'm doing,' muttered Wally.

'I hope so,' said Bruce, and then went on. 'We'll hit them at four o'clock tomorrow morning, just before first light. Ruffy and I will go into the town and bomb the hotel—that's where most of them will be sleeping. The grenades should force the survivors into the street and as soon as that happens you can open up—but not before. Wait until you get them in the open. Is that clear?'

'Jesus,' growled Hendry. 'Do you think I'm a bloody fool, do you think I can't understand English?'

'The crossfire from the two groups should wipe most of them out.' Bruce ignored Wally's outburst. 'But we mustn't give the remainder a chance to organize. Hit them hard and as soon as they take cover again you must follow them in—close with them and finish them off. If we can't get it over in five to ten minutes then we are going to be in trouble. They outnumber us three to one, so we have to exploit the element of surprise to the full.'

'Exploit the element of surprise to the full!' mimicked Wally. 'What for all the fancy talk—why not just murder the bastards?'

Bruce grinned lightly in the dark. 'All right, murder the bastards,' he agreed. 'But do it as quickly as bloody possible.' He stood up and inclined the luminous dial of his wrist watch to catch the light. 'It's half past ten now—we'll move down on them. Come with me, Hendry, and we'll sort them into two groups.'

Bruce and Wally moved back along the line and talked to each man in turn.

'You will go with Lieutenant Hendry.'

'You come with me.'

Making sure that the two English-speaking corporals were with Wally, they took ten minutes to divide them into two units and to redistribute the haversacks of grenades. Then they moved on down the slope, still in Indian file.

'This is where we leave you, Hendry,' whispered Bruce. 'Don't go jumping the gun—wait until you hear my grenades.'

'Yeah, okay—I know all about it.'

'Good luck,' said Bruce.

'Your bum in a barrel, Captain Curry,' rejoined Wally and moved away.

'Come on, Ruffy.' Bruce led his men off the embankment down into the swamp. Almost immediately the mud and slime was knee deep and as they worked their way out to the right it rose to their waists and then to their armpits, sucking and gurgling sullenly as they stirred it with their passage, belching little evil-smelling gusts of swamp gas.

The mosquitoes closed round Bruce's face in a cloud so dense that he breathed them into his mouth and had to blink them out of his eyes. Sweat dribbled down from under his helmet and clung heavily in his eyebrows and the matted stems of the papyrus grass dragged at his feet. Their progress was tortuously slow and for fifteen minutes at a time Bruce lost sight of the lights of the village through the wall of papyrus; he steered by the glow of the fires and the occasional column of sparks.

It was an hour before they had half completed their circuit of Port Reprieve. Bruce stopped to rest, still waist deep in swamp ooze and with his arms aching numb from holding his rifle above his head.

'I could use a smoke now, boss,' grunted Ruffy.

'Me too,' answered Bruce, and he wiped his face on the sleeve of his jacket. The mosquito bites on his forehead and round his eyes burnt like fire.

'What a way to make a living,' he whispered.

'You go on living and you'll be one of the lucky ones,' answered Ruffy. 'My guess is there'll be some dying before tomorrow.'

But the fear of death was submerged by physical discomfort. Bruce had almost forgotten that they were going into battle; right now he was more worried that the leeches which had worked their way through the openings in his anklets and were busily boring into his lower legs might find their way up to his crotch. There was a lot to be said in favour of a zip fly, he decided.

'Let's get out of this,' he whispered. 'Come on, Ruffy. Tell your boys to keep it quiet.'

He worked in closer to the shore and the level fell to their knees once more. Progress was more noisy now as their legs broke the surface with each step and the papyrus rustled and brushed against them.

It was almost two o'clock when they reached the causeway. Bruce left his men crouched in the papyrus while he made a stealthy reconnaissance along the side of the concrete bridge, keeping in its shadow, moving doubled up until he came to dry land on the edge of the village. There were no sentries posted and except for the crackle of the flames the town was quiet, sunk into a drunken stupor, satiated. Bruce went back to call his men up.

He spread them in pairs along the outskirts of the village. He had learned very early in this campaign not to let his men act singly;

nothing drains an African of courage more than to be on his own, especially in the night when the ghosts are on the walk-about.

To each couple he gave minute instructions.

'When you hear the grenades you shoot at anybody in the streets or at the windows. When the street is empty move in close beside that building there. Use your own grenades on every house and watch out for Lieutenant Hendry's men coming through from the other side. Do you understand?'

'It is understood.'

'Shoot carefully. Aim each shot—not like you did at the road bridge, and in the name of God do not hit the gasoline tanker. We need that to get us home.'

Now it was three o'clock, Bruce saw by the luminous figures on his wrist watch. Eight hours since they had left the train, and twenty-two hours since Bruce had last slept. But he was not tired, although his body ached and there was that gritty feeling under his eyelids, yet his mind was clear and bright as a flame.

He lay beside Ruffy under a low bush on the outskirts of Port Reprieve and the night wind drifted the smoke from the burning town down upon them, and Bruce was not tired. For I am going to another rendezvous with fear.

Fear is a woman, he thought, with all the myriad faces and voices of a woman. Because she is a woman and because I am a man I must keep going back to her. Only this time the appointment is one that I cannot avoid, this time I am not deliberately seeking her out.

I know she is evil, I know that after I have possessed her I will feel sick and shaken. I will say, 'That was the last time, never again.'

But just as certainly I know I will go back to her again, hating her, dreading her, but also needing her.

I have gone to find her on a mountain—on Dutoits Kloof Frontal, on Turret Towers, on the Wailing Wall, and the Devil's Tooth.

And she was there, dressed in a flowing robe of rock, a robe that fell sheer two thousand feet to the scree slope below. And she shrieked with the voice of the wind along the exposed face. Then her voice was soft, tinkling like cooling glass in the Berg ice underfoot, whispering like nylon rope running free, grating as the rotten rock moved in my hand.

I have followed her into the Jessie bush on the banks of the Sabi and the Luangwa, and she was there, waiting, wounded, in a robe of buffalo hide with the blood dripping from her mouth. And her smell was the sour-acid smell of my own sweat, and her taste was like rotten tomatoes in the back of my throat.

I have looked for her beyond the reef in the deep water with the

lemand valve of a scuba repeating my breathing with metallic hoarse-
ness. And she was there with rows of white teeth in the semi-circle of her
mouth, a tall fin on her back, dressed this time in shagreen, and her touch
was cold as the ocean, and her taste was salt and the taint of dying things.

I have looked for her on the highway with my foot pressed to the
floorboards and she was there with her cold arm draped round my
shoulders, her voice the whine of rubber on tarmac and the throaty hum
of the motor.

With Colin Butler at the helm (a man who treated fear not as a lover,
but with tolerant contempt as though she were his little sister) I went to
find her in a small boat. She was dressed in green with plumes of spray
and she wore a necklace of sharp black rock. And her voice was the
roar of water breaking on water.

We met in darkness at the road bridge and her eyes glinted like
bayonets. But that was an enforced meeting not of my choosing, as
tonight will be.

I hate her, he thought, but she is a woman and I am a man.

Bruce lifted his arm and turned his wrist to catch the light of the fires.

'Fifteen minutes to four, Ruffy. Let's go and take a look.'

'That's a good idea, boss.' Ruffy grinned with a show of white teeth in
the darkness.

'Are you afraid, Ruffy?' he asked suddenly, wanting to know, for his
own heart beat like a war drum and there was no saliva in his mouth.

'Boss, some questions you don't ask a man.' Ruffy rose slowly into a
crouch. 'Let's go take a look around.'

So they moved quickly together into the town, along the street,
hugging the hedges and the buildings, trying to keep in shadow, their
eyes moving everywhere, breathing quick and shallow, nerves screwed
up tight until they reached the hotel.

There were no lights in the windows and it seemed deserted until
Bruce made out the untidy mass of humanity strewn in sleep upon the
front veranda.

'How many there, Ruffy?'

'Dunno—perhaps ten, fifteen.' Ruffy breathed an answer. 'Rest of
them will be inside.'

'Where are the women—be careful of them.'

'They're dead long ago, you can believe me.'

'All right then, let's get round the back.' Bruce took a deep breath
and then moved quickly across the twenty yards of open firelit street to
the corner of the hotel. He stopped in the shadow and felt Ruffy close
beside him. 'I want to take a look into the main lounge, my guess is
that most of them will be in there,' he whispered.

'There's only four·bedrooms,' agreed Ruffy. 'Say the officers up-stairs and the rest in the lounge.'

Now Bruce moved quickly round the corner and stumbled over something soft. He felt it move against his foot.

'Ruffy!' he whispered urgently as he teetered off balance. He had trodden on a man, a man sleeping in the dust beside the wall. He could see the firelight on his bare torso and the glint of the bottle clutched in one outflung hand. The man sat up, muttering, and then began to cough, hacking painfully, swearing as he wiped his mouth with his free hand. Bruce regained his balance and swung his rifle up to use the bayonet, but Ruffy was quicker. He put one foot on the man's chest and trod him flat onto his back once more, then standing over him he used his bayoneted rifle the way a gardener uses a spade to lift potatoes, leaning his weight on it suddenly and the blade vanished into the man's throat.

The body stiffened convulsively, legs thrust out straight and arms rigid, there was a puffing of breath from the severed windpipe and then the slow melting relaxation of death. Still with his foot on the chest, Ruffy withdrew the bayonet and stepped over the corpse.

That was very close, thought Bruce, stifling the qualm of horror he felt at the neat execution. The man's eyes were fixed open in almost comic surprise, the bottle still in his hand, his chest bare, the front of his trousers unbuttoned and stiff with dried blood—not his blood, guessed Bruce angrily.

They moved on past the kitchens. Bruce looked in and saw that they were empty, with the white enamel tiles reflecting the vague light and piles of used plates and pots cluttering the tables and the sink. Then they reached the bar-room and there was a hurricane lamp on the counter diffusing a yellow glow; the stench of liquor poured out through the half-open window, the shelves were bare of bottles and men were asleep upon the counter, men lay curled together upon the floor like a pack of dogs, broken glass and rifles and shattered furniture littered about them. Someone had vomited out of the window leaving a yellow streak down the whitewashed wall.

'Stand here,' breathed Bruce into Ruffy's ear. 'I will go round to the front where I can throw onto the veranda and also into the lounge. Wait until you hear my first grenade blow.'

Ruffy nodded and leaned his rifle against the wall; he took a grenade in each fist and pulled the pins.

Bruce slipped quickly round the corner and along the side wall. He reached the windows of the lounge. They were tightly closed and he peered in over the sill. A little of the light from the lamp in the bar-room came through the open doors and showed up the interior. Here again there were men covering the floor and piled upon the sofas along the far wall. Twenty of them at least, he estimated by the volume of their snoring, and he grinned without humour. My God, what a shambles it is going to be.

Then something at the foot of the stairs caught his eye and the grin on his face became fixed, baring his teeth and narrowing his eyes to slits. It was the mound of nude flesh formed by the bodies of the four women; they had been discarded once they had served their purpose, dragged to one side to clear the floor for sleeping space, lying upon each other in a jumble of naked arms and legs and cascading hair.

No mercy now, thought Bruce with hatred replacing his fear as he looked at the women and saw by the attitudes in which they lay that there was no life left in them. *No mercy now!*

He slung his rifle over his left shoulder and filled his hands with grenades, pulled the pins and moved quickly to the corner so that he could look down the length of the covered veranda. He rolled both grenades down among the sleeping figures, hearing clearly the click of the priming and the metallic rattle against the concrete floor. Quickly he ducked back to the lounge window; snatching two more grenades from his haversack and pulling the pins, he hurled them through the closed windows. The crash of breaking glass blended with the double thunder of the explosions on the veranda.

Someone shouted in the room, a cry of surprise and alarm, then the windows above Bruce blew outwards, showering him with broken glass and the noise half deafening him as he tossed two more grenades through the gaping hole of the window. They were screaming and groaning in the lounge. Ruffy's grenades roared in the bar-room, bursting through the double doors, then Bruce's grenades snuffed out the sounds of life in the lounge with violent white flame and thunder. Bruce tossed in two more grenades and ran back to the corner of the veranda, unslinging his rifle.

A man with his hands over his eyes and blood streaming through his fingers fell over the low veranda wall and crawled to his knees. Bruce shot him from so close that the shaft of gun flame joined the muzzle of his rifle and the man's chest, punching him over backwards, throwing him spreadeagled onto the earth.

He looked beyond and saw two more in the road, but before he could raise his rifle the fire from his own gendarmes found them, knocking them down amid spurts of dust.

Bruce hurdled the veranda wall. He shouted, a sound without form or meaning. Exulting, unafraid, eager to get into the building, to get amongst them. He stumbled over the dead men on the veranda. A burst of gunfire from down the street rushed past him, so close he could feel the wind on his face. Fire from his own men.

'You stupid bastards!' Shouting without anger, without fear, with only the need to shout, he burst into the lounge through the main doors. It was half dark but he could see through the darkness and the haze of plaster dust.

A man on the stairs, the bloom of gunfire and the sting of the bullet across Bruce's thigh, fire in return, without aiming from the hip, miss and the man gone up and round the head of the stairs, yelling as he ran.

A grenade in Bruce's right hand, throw it high, watch it hit the wall and bounce sideways round the angle of the stairs. The explosion shocking in the confined space and the flash of it lighting the building and outlining the body of the man as it blew him back into the lounge, lifting him clear of the banisters, shredded and broken by the blast, falling heavily into the room below.

Up the stairs three at a time and into the bedroom passage, another man naked and bewildered staggering through a doorway still drunk or half asleep, chop him down with a single shot in the stomach, jump over him and throw a grenade through the glass skylight of the second bedroom, another through the third and kick open the door of the last room in the bellow and flash of the explosions.

A man was waiting for Bruce across the room with a pistol in his hand, and both of them fired simultaneously, the clang of the bullet glancing off the steel of Bruce's helmet, jerking his head back savagely, throwing him sideways against the wall, but he fired again, rapid fire, hitting with every bullet, so that the man seemed to dance, a jerky grotesque twitching jig, pinned against the far wall by the bullets.

On his knees now Bruce was stunned, ears singing like a million mad mosquitoes, hands clumsy and slow on the reload, back on his feet, legs rubbery but the loaded rifle in his hands making a man of him.

Out into the passage, another one right on top of him, a vast dark shape in the darkness—kill him! kill him!

'Don't shoot, boss!'

Ruffy, thank God, Ruffy.

'Are there any more?'

'All finished, boss—you cleaned them out good.'

'How many?' Bruce shouted above the singing in his ears.

'Forty or so. Jesus, what a mess! There's blood all over the place. Those grenades—'

'There must be more.'

'Yes, but not in here, boss. Let's go and give the boys outside a hand.'

They ran back down the passage, down the stairs, and the floor of the lounge was sodden and sticky, dead men everywhere; it smelt like an abattoir—blood and ripped bowels. One still on his hands and knees, creepy-crawling towards the door. Ruffy shot him twice, flattening him. 'Not the front door, boss. Our boys will get you for sure. Go out the window.'

Bruce dived through the window head first, rolled over behind the cover of the veranda wall and came to his knees in one movement. He felt strong and invulnerable. Ruffy was beside him.

'Here come our boys,' said Ruffy, and Bruce could see them coming down the street, running forward in short bursts, stopping to fire, to throw a grenade, then coming again.

'And there are Lieutenant Hendry's lot.' From the opposite direction but with the same dodging, checking run, Bruce could see Wally with them. He was holding his rifle across his hip when he fired, his whole body shaking with the juddering of the gun.

Like a bird rising in front of the beaters one of the *shufta* broke from the cover of the grocery store and ran into the street unarmed, his head down and his arms pumping in time with his legs. Bruce was close enough to see the panic in his face. He seemed to be moving in slow motion, and the flames lit him harshly, throwing a distorted shadow in front of him. When the bullets hit him he stayed on his feet, staggering in a circle, thrashing at the air with his hands as though he were beating off a swarm of bees, the bullets slapping loudly against his body and lifting little puffs of dust from his clothing. Beside Bruce, Ruffy aimed carefully and shot him in the head, ending it.

'There must be more,' protested Bruce. 'Where are they hiding?'

'In the offices, I'd say.'

And Bruce turned his attention quickly to the block of Union Minière offices. The windows were in darkness and as he stared he thought he saw movement. He glanced quickly back at Wally's men and saw that four of them had bunched up close behind Wally as they ran.

'Hendry, watch out!' he shouted with all his strength. 'On your right, from the offices!'

But it was too late, gunfire sparkled in the dark windows and the little group of running men disintegrated.

Bruce and Ruffy fired together, raking the windows, emptying their automatic rifles into them. As he reloaded, Bruce glanced back at where Wally's men had been hit. With disbelief he saw that Wally was the only one still on his feet; crossing the road, sprinting through an area of bullet-churned earth towards them, he reached the veranda and fell over the low wall.

'Are you wounded?' Bruce asked.

'Not a touch—those bastards couldn't shoot their way out of a French letter,' Wally shouted defiantly, and his voice carried clearly in the sudden hush. He snatched the empty magazine off the bottom of his rifle, threw it aside and clipped on a fresh one. 'Move over,' he growled, 'let me get a crack at those bastards.' He lifted his rifle and rested the stock on top of the wall, knelt behind it, cuddled the butt into his shoulder and began firing short bursts into the windows of the office block.

'This is what I was afraid of.' Bruce lifted his voice above the clamour of the guns. 'Now we've got a pocket of resistance right in the centre of the town. There must be fifteen or twenty of them in there—it might take us days to winkle them out.' He cast a longing look at the canvas-covered trucks lined up outside the station yard. 'They can cover the lorries from there, and as soon as they guess what we're after, as soon as we try and move them, they'll knock out that tanker and destroy the trucks.'

The firelight flickered on the shiny yellow and red paint of the tanker. It looked so big and vulnerable standing there in the open. It needed just one bullet out of the many hundred that had already been fired to end its charmed existence.

We've got to rush them now, he decided. Beyond the office block the remains of Wally's group had taken cover and were keeping up a heated fire. Bruce's group straggled up to the hotel and found positions at the windows.

'Ruffy.' Bruce caught him by the shoulder. 'We'll take four men with us and go round the back of the offices. From that building there we've got only twenty yards or so of open ground to cover. Once we get up against the wall they won't be able to touch us and we can toss grenades in amongst them.'

'That twenty yards looks like twenty miles from here,' rumbled Ruffy, but picked up his sack of grenades and crawled back from the veranda wall.

'Go and pick four men to come with us,' ordered Bruce.

'Okay, boss. We'll wait for you in the kitchen.'

'Hendry. Listen to me.'

'Yeah. What is it?'

'When I reach that corner over there I'll give you a wave. We'll be ready to go then. I want you to give us all the cover you can—keep their heads down.'

'Okay,' agreed Wally and fired another short burst.

'Try not to hit us when we close in.'

Wally turned to look at Bruce and he grinned wickedly.

'Mistakes happen, you know. I can't promise anything. You'd look real grand in my sights.'

'Don't joke,' said Bruce.

'Who's joking?' grinned Wally and Bruce left him. He found Ruffy and four gendarmes waiting in the kitchen.

'Come on,' he said and led them out across the kitchen yard, down the sanitary lane with the steel doors for the buckets behind the out-houses and the smell of them thick and fetid, round the corner and across the road to the buildings beyond the office block. They stopped there and crowded together, as though to draw courage and comfort from each other. Bruce measured the distance with his eye.

'It's not far,' he announced.

'Depends on how you look at it,' grunted Ruffy.

'There are only two windows opening out onto this side.'

'Two's enough—how many do you want?'

'Remember, Ruffy, you can only die once.'

'Once is enough,' said Ruffy. 'Let's cut out the talking, boss. Too much talk gets you in the guts.'

Bruce moved across to the corner of the building out of the shadows. He waved towards the hotel and imagined that he saw an acknowledge-ment from the end of the veranda.

'All together,' he said, sucked in a deep breath, held it a second and then launched himself into the open. He felt small now, no longer brave and invulnerable, and his legs moved so slowly that he seemed to be standing still. The black windows gaped at him.

Now, he thought, *now you die.*

Where, he thought, *not in the stomach, please God, not in the stomach.*

And his legs moved stiffly under him, carrying him half way across.

Only ten more paces, he thought, one more river, just one more river to Jordan. But not in the stomach, please God, not in my stomach. And his flesh cringed in anticipation, his stomach drawn in hard as he ran.

Suddenly the black windows were brightly lit, bright white oblongs in the dark buildings, and the glass sprayed out of them like untidy spittle from an old man's mouth. Then they were dark again, dark with smoke billowing from them and the memory of the explosion echoing in his ears.

'A grenade!' Bruce was bewildered. 'Someone let off a grenade in there!'

He reached the back door without stopping and it burst open before his rush. He was into the room, shooting, coughing in the fumes, firing wildly at the small movements of dying men.

In the half darkness something long and white lay against the far wall. A body, a white man's naked body. He crossed to it and looked down.

'André,' he said, 'it's André—he threw the grenade.' And he knelt beside him.

CHAPTER 17

Curled naked upon the concrete floor, André was alive but dying as the haemorrhage within him leaked his life away. His mind was alive and he heard the crump, crump of Bruce's grenades, then the gunfire in the street, and the sound of running men. The shouts in the night and then the guns very close, they were in the room in which he lay.

He opened his eyes. There were men at each of the windows, crouched below the sills, and the room was thick with cordite fumes and the clamour of the guns as they fired out into the night.

André was cold, the coldness was all through him. Even his hands drawn up against his chest were cold and heavy. His stomach only was warm, warm and immensely bloated.

It was an effort to think, for his mind also was cold and the noise of the guns confused him.

He watched the men at the windows with a detached disinterest, and slowly his body lost its weight. He seemed to float clear of the floor and look down upon the room from the roof. His eyelids sagged and he dragged them up again, and struggled down towards his own body.

There was suddenly a rushing sound in the room and plaster sprayed from the wall above André's head, filling the air with pale floating dust. One of the men at the windows fell backwards, his weapon ringing loudly on the floor as it dropped from his hands; he flopped over twice and lay still, face down within arm's length of André.

Ponderously André's mind analysed the sights his eyes were recording. Someone was firing on the building from outside. The man beside him was dead and from his head wound the blood spread slowly across the floor towards him. André closed his eyes again, he was very tired and very cold.

There was a lull in the sound of gunfire, one of those freak silences in the midst of battle. And in the lull André heard a voice far off, shouting. He could not hear the words but he recognized the voice and his eyelids flew open. There was an excitement in him, a new force, for it was Wally's voice he had heard.

He moved slightly, clenching his hands and his brain started to sing.

Wally has come back for me—he has come to save me. He rolled his head slowly, painfully, and the blood gurgled in his stomach.

I must help him, I must not let him endanger himself—these men are trying to kill him. I must stop them. I mustn't let them kill Wally.

And then he saw the grenades hanging on the belt of the man that lay beside him. He fastened his eyes on the round polished metal bulbs and he began to pray silently.

'Hail, Mary, full of grace, the Lord is with thee.'

He moved again, straightening his body.

'Blessed art though among women, and blessed is the fruit of thy womb, Jesus.'

His hand crept out into the pool of blood, and the sound of the guns filled his head so he could not hear himself pray. Walking on its fingers, his hand crawled through the blood as slowly as a fly through a saucer of treacle.

'Blessed is the fruit of thy womb, Jesus. Oh, Jesus. Pray for me now, and at the hour. Full of grace.'

He touched the smooth, deeply segmented steel of the grenade.

'Us sinners—at the day, at the hour. This day—this day our daily bread.'

He fumbled at the clip, fingers stiff and cold.

'Hallowed be thy—Hallowed be thy—'

The clip clicked open and he held the grenade, curling his fingers round it.

'Hail, Mary, full of grace.'

He drew the grenade to him and held it with both hands against his chest. He lifted it to his mouth and took the pin between his teeth.

'Pray for us sinners,' he whispered and pulled the pin.

'Now and at the hour of our death.'

And he tried to throw it. It rolled from his hand and bumped across the floor. The firing handle flew off and rattled against the wall. General Moses turned from the window and saw it—his lips opened and his spectacles glinted above the rose-pink cave of his mouth. The grenade lay at his feet. Then everything was gone in the flash and roar of the explosion.

Afterwards in the acrid swirl of fumes, in the patter of falling plaster, in the tinkle and crunch of broken glass, in the small scrabbling noises and the murmur and moan of dying men, André was still alive. The body of the man beside him had shielded his head and chest from the full force of the blast.

There was still enough life in him to recognize Bruce Curry's face close to his, though he could not feel the hands that touched him.

'André!' said Bruce. 'It's André—he threw the grenade!'

'Tell him—' whispered André and stopped.

'Yes, André—?' said Bruce.

'I didn't, this day and at the hour. I had to—not this time.' He could feel it going out in him like a candle in a high wind and he tried to cup his hands around it.

'What is it, André? What must I tell him?' Bruce's voice, but so far away.

'Because of him—this time—not of it, I didn't.' He stopped again and gathered all of what was left. His lips quivered as he tried so hard to say it.

'Like a man!' he whispered and the candle went out.

'Yes,' said Bruce softly, holding him. 'This time like a man.'

He lowered André gently until his head touched the floor again; then he stood upright and looked down at the terribly mutilated body. He felt empty inside, a hollowness, the same feeling as after love.

He moved across to the desk near the far wall. Outside the gunfire dwindled like half-hearted applause, flared up again and then ceased. Around him Ruffy and the four gendarmes moved excitedly, inspecting the dead, exclaiming, laughing the awkward embarrassed laughter of men freshly released from mortal danger.

Loosening the chin straps of his helmet with slow steady fingers, Bruce stared across the room at André's body.

'Yes,' he whispered again. 'This time like a man. All the other times are wiped out, the score is levelled.'

His cigarettes were damp from the swamp, but he took one from the centre of the pack and straightened it with calm nerveless fingers. He found his lighter and flicked it open—then, without warning, his hands started to shake. The flame of the lighter fluttered and he had to hold it steady with both hands. There was blood on his hands, new sticky blood. He snapped the lighter closed and breathed in the smoke. It tasted bitter and the saliva flooded into his mouth. He swallowed it down, nausea in his stomach, and his breathing quickened.

It was not like this before, he remembered, even that night at the road bridge when they broke through on the flank and we met them with bayonets in the dark. Before it had no meaning, but now I can feel again. Once more I'm alive.

Suddenly he had to be alone; he stood up.

'Ruffy.'

'Yes, boss?'

'Clean up here. Get blankets from the hotel for de Surrier and the women, also those men down in the station yard.' It was someone else speaking; he could hear the voice as though it were a long way off.
'You okay, boss?'
'Yes.'
'Your head?'
Bruce lifted his hand and touched the long dent in his helmet.
'It's nothing,' he said.
'Your leg?'
'Just a touch, get on with it.'
'Okay, boss. What shall we do with these others?'
'Throw them in the river,' said Bruce and walked out into the street.
Hendry and his gendarmes were still on the veranda of the hotel, but they had started on the corpses there, using their bayonets like butchers' knives, taking the ears, laughing also the strained nervous laughter.
Bruce crossed the street to the station yard. The dawn was coming, drawing out across the sky like a sheet of steel rolled from the mill, purple and lilac at first, then red as it spread above the forest.
The Ford Ranchero stood on the station platform where he had left it. He opened the door, slid in behind the wheel, and watched the dawn become day.

CHAPTER 18

'Captain, the sergeant major asks you to come. There is something he wants to show you.'
Bruce lifted his head from where it was resting on the steering wheel. He had not heard the gendarme approach.
'I'll come,' he said, picked up his helmet and his rifle from the seat beside him and followed the man back to the office block.
His gendarmes were loading a dead man into one of the trucks, swinging him by his arms and legs.
'Un, deux, trois,' and a shout of laughter as the limp body flew over the tailboard onto the gruesome pile already there.
Sergeant Jacque came out of the office dragging a man by his heels. The head bumped loosely down the steps and there was a wet brown drag mark left on the cement veranda.
'Like pork,' Jacque called cheerily. The corpse was that of a small grey-headed man, skinny, with the marks of spectacles on the bridge of

his nose and a double row of decorations on his tunic. Bruce noted that one of them was the purple and white ribbon of the military cross—strange loot for the Congo. Jacque dropped the man's heels, drew his bayonet and stooped over the man. He took one of the ears that lay flat against the grizzled skull, pulled it forward and freed it with a single stroke of the knife. The opened flesh was pink with the dark hole of the eardrum in the centre.

Bruce walked on into the office and his nostrils flared at the abattoir stench.

'Have a look at this lot, boss.' Ruffy stood by the desk.

'Enough to buy you a ranch in Hyde Park,' grinned Hendry beside him. In his hand he held a pencil. Threaded onto it like a kebab were a dozen human ears.

'Yes,' said Bruce as he looked at the pile of industrial and gem diamonds on the blotter. 'I know about those. Better count them, Ruffy, then put them back in the bags.'

'You're not going to turn them in?' protested Hendry. 'Jesus, if we share this lot three ways—you, Ruffy and I—there's enough to make us all rich.'

'Or put us against a wall,' said Bruce grimly. 'What makes you think the gentlemen in Elisabethville don't know about them?' He turned his attention back to Ruffy. 'Count them and pack them. You're in charge of them. Don't lose any.'

Bruce looked across the room at the blanket-wrapped bundle that was André de Surrier.

'Have you detailed a burial squad?'

'Yes, boss. Six of the boys are out back digging.'

'Good,' Bruce nodded. 'Hendry, come with me. We'll go and have a look at the trucks.'

Half an hour later Bruce closed the bonnet of the last vehicle. 'This is the only one that won't run. The carburettor's smashed. We'll take the tyres off it for spares.' He wiped his greasy hands on the sides of his trousers. 'Thank God, the tanker is untouched. We've got six hundred gallons there, more than enough for the return trip.'

'You going to take the Ford?' asked Hendry.

'Yes, it may come in useful.'

'And it will be more comfortable for you and your little French thing.' Heavy sarcasm in Hendry's voice.

'That's right,' Bruce answered evenly. 'Can you drive?'

'What you think? You think I'm a bloody fool?'

'Everyone is always trying to get at you, aren't they? You can't trust anyone, can you?' Bruce asked softly.

'You're so bloody right!' agreed Hendry.

Bruce changed the subject. 'André had a message for you before he died.'

'Old doll boy!'

'He threw that grenade. Did you know that?'

'Yeah. I knew it.'

'Don't you want to hear what he said?'

'Once a queer, always a queer, and the only good queer is a dead queer.'

'All right.' Bruce frowned. 'Get a couple of men to help you. Fill the trucks with gas. We've wasted enough time already.'

They buried their dead in a communal grave, packing them in quickly and covering them just as quickly. Then they stood embarrassed and silent round the mound.

'You going to say anything, boss?' Ruffy asked, and they all looked at Bruce.

'No.' Bruce turned away and started for the trucks.

What the hell can you say, he thought angrily. Death is not someone to make conversation with. All you can say is, 'These were men; weak and strong, evil and good, and a lot in between. But now they're dead— like pork.'

He looked back over his shoulder. 'All right, let's move out.'

The convoy ground slowly over the causeway. Bruce led in the Ford and the air blowing in through the shattered windscreen was too humid and steamy to give relief from the rising heat.

The sun stood high above the forest as they passed the turn-off to the mission.

Bruce looked along it, and he wanted to signal the convoy to continue while he went up to St Augustine's. He wanted to see Mike Haig and Father Ignatius, make sure that they were safe.

Then he put aside the temptation. If there is more horror up there at St Augustine's, if the *shufta* have found them and there are raped women and dead men there, then there is nothing I can do and I don't want to know about it.

It is better to believe that they are safely hidden in the jungle. It is better to believe that out of all this will remain something good.

He led the convoy resolutely past the turn-off and over the hills towards the level crossing.

Suddenly another idea came to him and he thought about it, turning it over with pleasure.

Four men came to Port Reprieve, men without hope, men abandoned by God.

And they learned that it was not too late, perhaps it is never too late

For one of them found the strength to die like a man, although he have lived his whole life with weakness.

Another rediscovered the self-respect he had lost along the way, and with it the chance to start again.

The third found—he hesitated—yes, the third found love.

And the fourth? Bruce's smile faded as he thought of Wally Hendry It was a neat little parable, except for Wally Hendry. What had he found? A dozen human ears threaded on a pencil?

CHAPTER 19

'Can't you get up enough steam to move us back to the crossing—only a few miles.'

'I am desolate, m'sieur. She will not hold even a belch, to say nothing of a head of steam.' The engine driver spread his pudgy little hands in a gesture of helplessness. Bruce studied the rent in the boiler. The metal was torn open like the petals of a flower. He knew it had been a forlorn request.

'Very well. Thank you.' He turned to Ruffy. 'We'll have to carry everything back to the convoy. Another day wasted.'

'It's a long walk,' Ruffy agreed. 'Better get started.'

'How much food have we?'

'Not too much. We've been feeding a lot of extra mouths, and we sent a lot out to the mission.'

'How much?'

'About two more days.'

'That should get us to Elisabethville.'

'Boss, you want to carry everything to the lorries? Searchlights, ammunition, blankets—all of it?'

Bruce paused for a moment. 'I think so. We may need it.'

'It's going to take the rest of the day.'

'Yes,' agreed Bruce. Ruffy walked back along the train but Bruce called after him.

'Ruffy!'

'Boss?'

'Don't forget the beer.'

Ruffy's black moon of a face split laterally into a grin.

'You think we should take it?'

'Why not?' Bruce laughed.

'Man, you talked me right into it!'

And the night was almost on them before the last of the equipment had been carried back from the abandoned train to the convoy and loaded into the trucks.

Time is a slippery thing, even more so than wealth. No bank vault can hold it for you, this precious stuff which we spend in such prodigal fashion on the trivialities. By the time we have slept and eaten and moved from one place to the next there is such a small percentage left for the real business of living.

Bruce felt futile resentment as he always did when he thought about it. And if you discount the time spent at an office desk, then how much is there left? Half of one day a week, that's how much the average man lives! That's how far short of our potential is the actuality of existence.

Take it further than that: we are capable of using only a fraction of our physical and mental strength. Only under hypnosis are we able to exert more than a tenth of what is in us. So divide that half of one day a week by ten, and the rest is waste! Sickening waste!

'Ruffy, have you detailed sentries for tonight?' Bruce barked at him.

'Not yet. I was just—'

'Well, do it, and do it quickly.'

Ruffy looked at Bruce in speculation and through his anger Bruce felt a qualm of regret that he had selected that mountain of energy on which to vent his frustration.

'Where the hell is Hendry?' he snapped.

Without speaking Ruffy pointed to a group of men round one of the trucks at the rear of the convoy and Bruce left him.

Suddenly consumed with impatience Bruce fell upon his men, shouting at them, scattering them to a dozen different tasks. He walked along the convoy making sure that his instructions were being carried out to the letter; checking the siting of the Brens and the searchlights, making sure that the single small cooking fire was screened from Baluba eyes, stopping to watch the refuelling of the trucks and the running maintenance he had ordered. Men avoided catching his eye and bent to their tasks with studied application. There were no raised voices or sounds of laughter in the camp.

Again Bruce had decided against a night journey. The temptation itched within him, but the exhaustion of those gendarmes who had not slept since the previous morning and the danger of travelling in the dark he could not ignore.

'We'll leave as soon as it's light tomorrow,' Bruce told Ruffy.

'Okay, boss,' Ruffy nodded, and then soothingly, 'you're tired. Food's nearly ready, then you get some sleep.'

Bruce glared at him, opening his mouth to snarl a retort, and then closed it again. He turned and strode out of the camp into the forest.

He found a fallen log, sat down and lit a cigarette. It was dark now and there were only a few stars among the rain clouds that blackened the sky. He could hear the faint sounds from the camp but there were no lights—the way he had ordered it.

The fact that his anger had no focal point inflamed it rather than quenched it. It ranged restlessly until at last it found a target—himself.

He recognized the brooding undirected depression that was descending upon him. It was a thing he had not experienced for a long time, nearly two years. Not since the wreck of his marriage and the loss of his children. Not since he had stifled all emotion and trained himself not to participate in the life around him.

But now his barrier was gone, there was no sheltered harbour from the storm surf and he would have to ride it out. Furl all canvas and rig a sea anchor.

The anger was gone now. At least anger had heat but this other thing was cold; icy waves of it broke over him, and he was small and insignificant in the grip of it.

His mind turned to his children and the loneliness howled round him like a winter wind from the south. He closed his eyes and pressed his fingers against the lids. Their faces formed in the eye of his mind.

Christine with pink fat legs under her frilly skirt, and the face of a thoughtful cherub below soft hair cropped like a page boy.

'I love you best of all,' said with much seriousness, holding his face with small hands only a little sticky with ice cream.

Simon, a miniature reproduction of Bruce even to the nose. Scabs on the knees and dirt on the face. No demonstrations of affection from him, but in its place something much better, a companionship far beyond his six years. Long discussions on everything from religion, 'Why didn't Jesus used to shave?' to politics, 'When are you going to be prime minister, Dad?'

And the loneliness was a tangible thing now, like the coils of a reptile squeezing his chest. Bruce ground out the cigarette beneath his heel and tried to find refuge in his hatred for the woman who had been his wife. The woman who had taken them from him.

But his hatred was a cold thing also, dead ash with a stale taste. For he knew that the blame was not all hers. It was another of his failures; perhaps if I had tried harder, perhaps if I had left some of the cruel things unsaid, perhaps—yes, it might have been, and perhaps and maybe. But it was not. It was over and finished and now I am alone.

There is no worse condition; no state beyond loneliness. It is the waste land and the desolation.

Something moved near him in the night, a soft rustle of grass, a presence felt rather than seen. And Bruce stiffened. His right hand closed over his rifle. He brought it up slowly, his eyes straining into the darkness.

The movement again, closer now. A twig popped underfoot. Bruce slowly trained his rifle round to cover it, pressure on the trigger and his thumb on the safety. Stupid to have wandered away from the camp; asking for it, and now he had got it. Baluba tribesmen! He could see the figure now in the dimness of starlight, stealthily moving across his front. How many of them, he wondered. If I hit this one, there could be a dozen others with him. Have to take a chance. One quick burst and then run for it. A hundred yards to the camp, about an even chance. The figure was stationary now, standing listening. Bruce could see the outline of the head—no helmet, can't be one of us. He raised the rifle and pointed it. Too dark to see the sights, but at that range he couldn't miss. Bruce drew his breath softly, filling his lungs, ready to shoot and run.

'Bruce?' Shermaine's voice, frightened, almost a whisper. He threw up the rifle barrel. God, that was close. He had nearly killed her.

'Yes, I'm here.' His own voice was scratchy with the shock of realization.

'Oh, there you are.'

'What the hell are you doing out of the camp?' he demanded furiously as anger replaced his shock.

'I'm sorry, Bruce, I came to see if you were all right. You were gone such a long time.'

'Well, get back to the camp, and don't try any more tricks like that.'

There was a long silence, and then she spoke softly, unable to keep the hurt out of her tone.

'I brought you something to eat. I thought you'd be hungry. I'm sorry if I did wrong.'

She came to him, stooped and placed something on the ground in front of him. Then she turned and was gone.

'Shermaine.' He wanted her back, but the only reply was the fading rustle of the grass and then silence. He was alone again.

He picked up the plate of food.

You fool, he thought. You stupid, ignorant, thoughtless fool. You'll lose her, and you'll have deserved it. You deserve everything you've had, and more.

You never learn, do you, Curry? You never learn that there is a penalty for selfishness and for thoughtlessness.

He looked down at the plate in his hands. Bully beef and sliced onion, bread and cheese.

Yes, I have learned, he answered himself with sudden determination. I will not spoil this, this thing that is between this girl and me. That was the last time; now I am a man I will put away childish things, like temper and self-pity.

He ate the food, suddenly aware of his hunger. He ate quickly, wolfing it. Then he stood up and walked back to the camp.

A sentry challenged him on the perimeter and Bruce answered with alacrity. At night his gendarmes were very quick on the trigger; the challenge was an unusual courtesy.

'It is unwise to go alone into the forest in the darkness,' the sentry reprimanded him.

'Why?' Bruce felt his mood changing. The depression evaporated.

'It is unwise,' repeated the man vaguely.

'The spirits?' Bruce teased him delicately.

'An aunt of my sister's husband disappeared not a short throw of a spear from my hut. There was no trace, no shout, nothing. I was there. It is not a matter for doubt,' said the man with dignity.

'A lion perhaps?' Bruce prodded him.

'If you say so, then it is so. I know what I know. But I say only that there is no wisdom in defying the custom of the land.'

Suddenly touched by the man's concern for him, Bruce dropped a hand onto his shoulder and gripped it in the old expression of affection.

'I will remember. I did it without thinking.'

He walked into the camp. The incident had confirmed something he had vaguely suspected, but in which previously he had felt no interest. The men liked him. A hundred similar indications of this fact he had only half noted, not caring one way or the other. But now it gave him intense pleasure, fully compensating for the loneliness he had just experienced.

He walked past the little group of men round the cooking fire to where the Ford stood at the head of the convoy. Peering through the side window he could make out Shermaine's blanket-wrapped form on the back seat. He tapped on the glass and she sat up and rolled down the window.

'Yes?' she asked coolly.

'Thank you for the food.'

'It is nothing.' The slightest hint of warmth in her voice.

'Shermaine, sometimes I say things I do not mean. You startled me. I nearly shot you.'

'It was my fault. I should not have followed you.'

'I was rude,' he persisted.

'Yes.' She laughed now. That husky little chuckle. 'You were rude but with good reason. We shall forget it.' She placed her hand on his arm. 'You must rest, you haven't slept for two days.'

'Will you ride in the Ford with me tomorrow to show that I am forgiven?'

'Of course,' she nodded.

'Good night, Shermaine.'

'Good night, Bruce.'

No, Bruce decided as he spread his blankets beside the fire, I am not alone. Not any more.

CHAPTER 20

'What about breakfast, boss?'

'They can eat on the road. Give them a tin of bully each—we've wasted enough time on this trip.'

The sky was paling and pinking above the forest. It was light enough to read the dial of his wrist watch. Twenty minutes to five.

'Get them moving, Ruffy. If we make Msapa Junction before dark we can drive through the night. Home for breakfast tomorrow.'

'Now you're talking, boss.' Ruffy clapped his helmet on his head and went off to rouse the men who lay in the road beside the trucks.

Shermaine was asleep. Bruce leaned into the window of the Ford and studied her face. A wisp of hair lay over her mouth, rising and falling with her breathing. It tickled her nose and in her sleep it twitched like a rabbit.

Bruce felt an almost unbearable pang of tenderness towards her. With one finger he lifted the hair off her face. Then he smiled at himself.

If you can feel like this before breakfast, then you've got it in a bad way, he told himself.

Do you know something, he retorted, I like the feeling.

'Hey, you lazy wench!' He pulled the lobe of her ear. 'Time to wake up.'

It was almost half past five before the convoy got under way. It had taken that long to bully and cajole the sleep out of sixty men and get them into the lorries. This morning Bruce did not find the delay unbearable. He had managed to find time for four hours' sleep during the night. Four hours was not nearly enough to make up for the previous two days.

Now he felt light-headed, a certain unreal quality of gaiety overlaying his exhaustion, a carnival spirit. There was no longer the same urgency, for the road to Elisabethville was clear and not too long. Home for breakfast tomorrow!

'We'll be at the bridge in a little under an hour.' He glanced sideways at Shermaine.

'You've left a guard on it?'

'Ten men,' answered Bruce. 'We'll pick them up almost without stopping, and then the next stop, room 201, Grand Hotel Leopold II, Avenue du Kasai.' He grinned in anticipation. 'A bath so deep it will slop over onto the floor, so hot it will take five minutes to get into it. Clean clothes. A steak that thick, with French salad and a bottle of Liebfraumilch.'

'For breakfast!' protested Shermaine.

'For breakfast,' Bruce agreed happily. He was silent for a while, savouring the idea. The road ahead of him was tiger-striped with the shadows of the trees thrown by the low sun. The air that blew in through the missing windscreen was cool and clean-smelling. He felt good. The responsibility of command lay lightly on his shoulders this morning; a pretty girl beside him, a golden morning, the horror of the last few days half-forgotten—they might have been going on a picnic.

'What are you thinking?' he asked suddenly. She was very quiet beside him.

'I was wondering about the future,' she answered softly. 'There is no one I know in Elisabethville, and I do not wish to stay there.'

'Will you return to Brussels?' he asked. The question was without significance, for Bruce Curry had very definite plans for the immediate future, and these included Shermaine.

'Yes, I think so. There is nowhere else.'

'You have relatives there?'

'An aunt.'

'Are you close?'

Shermaine laughed, but there was bitterness in the husky chuckle. 'Oh, very close. She came to see me once at the orphanage. Once in all those years. She brought me a comic book of a religious nature and told me to clean my teeth and brush my hair a hundred strokes a day.'

'There is no one else?' asked Bruce.

'No.'

'Then why go back?'

'What else is there to do?' she asked. 'Where else is there to go?'

'There's a life to live, and the rest of the world to visit.'

'Is that what you are going to do?'

'That is exactly what I'm going to do, starting with a hot bath.'

Bruce could feel it between them. They both knew it was there, but it was too soon to talk about it. *I have only kissed her once, but that was enough. So what will happen? Marriage?* His mind shied away from that word with startling violence, then came hesitantly back to examine it, stalking it as though it were a dangerous beast, ready to take flight again as soon as it showed its teeth.

For some people it is a good thing. It can stiffen the spineless; ease the lonely; give direction to the wanderers; spurt those without ambition—and, of course, there was the final unassailable argument in its favour. Children.

But there are some who can only sicken and shrivel in the colourless cell of matrimony. With no space to fly, your wings must weaken with disuse; turned inwards, your eyes become short-sighted; when all your communication with the rest of the world is through the glass windows of the cell, then your contact is limited.

And I already have children. I have a daughter and I have a son.

Bruce turned his eyes from the road and studied the girl beside him. *There is no fault I can find. She is beautiful in the delicate, almost fragile way that is so much better and longer-lived than blonde hair and big bosoms. She is unspoilt; hardship has long been her travelling companion and from it she has learned kindness and humility.*

She is mature, knowing the ways of this world; knowing death and fear, the evilness of men and their goodness. I do not believe she has ever lived in the fairy-tale cocoon that most young girls spin about themselves.

And yet she has not forgotten how to laugh.

Perhaps, he thought, *perhaps. But it is too soon to talk about it.*

'You are very grim.' Shermaine broke the silence, but the laughter shivered just below the surface of her voice. 'Again you are Bonaparte. And when you are grim your nose is too big and cruel. It is a nose of great brutality and it does not fit the rest of your face. I think that when they had finished you they had only one nose left in stock. "It is too big," they said, "but it is the only nose left, and when he smiles it will not look too bad." So they took a chance and stuck it on anyway.'

'Were you never taught that it is bad manners to poke fun at a man's weakness?' Bruce fingered his nose ruefully.

'Your nose is many things, but not weak. Never weak.' She laughed now and moved a little closer to him.

'You know you can attack me from behind your own perfect nose, and I cannot retaliate.'

'Never trust a man who makes pretty speeches so easily, because he surely makes them to every girl he meets.' She slid an inch further across the seat until they were almost touching. 'You waste your talents, *mon capitaine*. I am immune to your charm.'

'In just one minute I will stop this car and—'

'You cannot.' Shermaine jerked her head to indicate the two gendarmes in the seat behind them. 'What would they think, Bonaparte? It would be very bad for discipline.'

'Discipline or no discipline, in just one minute I will stop this car and spank you soundly before I kiss you.'

'One threat does not frighten me, but because of the other I will leave your poor nose.' She moved away a little and once more Bruce studied her face. Beneath the frank scrutiny she fidgeted and started to blush.

'Do you mind! Were you never taught that it is bad manners to stare?'

So now I am in love again, thought Bruce. This is only the third time, an average of once every ten years or so. It frightens me a little because there is always pain with it. The exquisite pain of loving and the agony of losing.

It starts in the loins and it is very deceptive because you think it is only the old thing, the tightness and tension that any well-rounded stern or cheeky pair of breasts will give you. Scratch it, you think, it's just a small itch. Spread a little of the warm salve on it and it will be gone in no time.

But suddenly it spreads, upwards and downwards, all through you. The pit of your stomach feels hot, then the flutters round the heart. It's dangerous now; once it gets this far it's incurable and you can scratch and scratch but all you do is inflame it.

Then the last stages, when it attacks the brain. No pain there, that's the worst sign. A heightening of the senses: your eyes are sharper, your blood runs too fast, food tastes good, your mouth wants to shout and legs want to run. Then the delusions of grandeur: you are the cleverest, strongest, most masculine male in the universe, and you stand ten feet tall in your socks.

How tall are you now, Curry, he asked himself. About nine feet six and I weigh twenty stone, he answered, and almost laughed aloud.

And how does it end? It ends with words. Words can kill anything. It ends with cold words; words like fire that stick in the structure and take hold and lick it up, blackening and charring it, bringing it down in smoking ruins.

It ends in suspicion of things not done, and in the certainty of things done and remembered. It ends with selfishness and carelessness, and words, always words.

It ends with pain and greyness, and it leaves scar tissue and damage that will never heal.

Or it ends without fuss and fury. It just crumbles and blows away like dust on the wind. But there is still the agony of loss.

Both these endings I know well, for I have loved twice, and now I love again.

Perhaps this time it does not have to be that way. Perhaps this time it will last. Nothing is for ever, he thought. Nothing is for ever, not even life, and perhaps this time if I cherish it and tend it carefully it will last that long, as long as life.

'We are nearly at the bridge,' said Shermaine beside him, and Bruce started. The miles had dropped unseen behind them and now the forest was thickening. It crouched closer to the earth, greener and darker along the river.

Bruce slowed the Ford and the forest became dense bush around them, the road a tunnel through it. They came round one last bend in the track and out of the tunnel of green vegetation into the clearing where the road met the railway line and ran beside it onto the heavy timber platform of the bridge.

Bruce stopped the Ranchero, switched off the engine and they all sat silently, staring out at the solid jungle on the far bank with its screen of creepers and monkey-ropes hanging down, trailing the surface of the deep green swift-flowing river. They stared at the stumps of the bridge thrusting out from each bank towards each other like the arms of parted lovers; at the wide gap between with the timbers still smouldering and the smoke drifting away downstream over the green water.

'It's gone,' said Shermaine. 'It's been burnt.'

'Oh, no,' groaned Bruce. 'Oh, God, no!'

With an effort he pulled his eyes from the charred remains of the bridge and turned them onto the jungle about them, a hundred feet away, ringing them in. Hostile, silent. 'Don't get out of the car,' he snapped as Shermaine reached for the door handle. 'Roll your window up, quickly.'

She obeyed.

'They're waiting in there.' He pointed at the edge of the jungle.

Behind them the first of the convoy came round the bend into the clearing. Bruce jumped from the Ford and ran back towards the leading truck.

'Don't get out, stay inside,' he shouted and ran on down the line, repeating the instruction to each of them as he passed. When he reached Ruffy's cab he jumped onto the running board, jerked the door open, slipped in onto the seat and slammed the door.

'They've burnt the bridge.'

'What's happened to the boys we left to guard it?'

'I don't know but we'll find out. Pull up alongside the others so that I can talk to them.'

Through the half-open window he issued his orders to each of the drivers and within ten minutes all the vehicles had been manoeuvred into the tight defensive circle of the laager, a formation Bruce's ancestors had used a hundred years before.

'Ruffy, get out those tarpaulins and spread them over the top to form a roof. We don't want them dropping arrows in amongst us.'

Ruffy selected half a dozen gendarmes and they went to work, dragging out the heavy folded canvas.

'Hendry, put a couple of men under each truck. Set up the Brens in case they try to rush us.'

In the infectious urgency of defence, Wally did not make his usual retort, but gathered his men. They wriggled on their stomachs under the vehicles, rifles pointed out towards the silent jungle.

'I want the extinguishers here in the middle so we can get them in a hurry. They might use fire again.'

Two gendarmes ran to each of the cabs and unclipped the fire-extinguishers from the dashboards.

'What can I do?' Shermaine was standing beside Bruce.

'Keep quiet and stay out of the way,' said Bruce as he turned and hurried across to help Ruffy's gang with the tarpaulins.

It took them half an hour of desperate endeavour before they completed the fortifications to Bruce's satisfaction.

'That should hold them.' Bruce stood with Ruffy and Hendry in the centre of the laager and surveyed the green canvas roof above them and the closely packed vehicles around them. The Ford was parked beside the tanker, not included in the outer ring for its comparative size would have made it a weak point in the defence.

'It's going to be bloody hot and crowded in here,' grumbled Hendry.

'Yes, I know.' Bruce looked at him. 'Would you like to relieve the congestion by waiting outside?'

'Funny boy, big laugh,' answered Wally.

'What now, boss?' Ruffy put into words the question Bruce had been asking himself.

'You and I will go and take a look at the bridge,' he said.

'You'll look a rare old sight with an arrow sticking out of your jack,' grinned Wally. 'Boy, that's going to kill me!'

'Ruffy, get us half a dozen gas capes each. I doubt their arrows will go through them at a range of a hundred feet, and of course we'll wear helmets.'

'Okay, boss.'

It was like being in a sauna bath beneath the six layers of rubberized canvas. Bruce could feel the sweat squirting from his pores with each pace, and rivulets of it coursing down his back and flanks as he and Ruffy left the laager and walked up the road to the bridge.

Beside him Ruffy's bulk was so enhanced by the gas capes that he reminded Bruce of a prehistoric monster reaching the end of its gestation period.

'Warm enough, Ruffy?' he asked, feeling the need for humour. The ring of jungle made him nervous. Perhaps he had underestimated the carry of a Baluba arrow—despite the light reed shaft, they used iron heads, barbed viciously and ground to a needle point, and poison smeared thickly between the barbs.

'Man, look at me shiver,' grunted Ruffy and the sweat greased down his jowls and dripped from his chin.

Long before they reached the access to the bridge the stench of putrefaction crept out to meet them. In Bruce's mind every smell had its own colour, and this one was green, the same green as the sheen of putrefaction on rotting meat. The stench was so heavy he could almost feel it bearing down on them, choking in his throat and coating his tongue and the roof of his mouth with the oily over-sweetness.

'No doubt what that is!' Ruffy spat, trying to get the taste out of his mouth.

'Where are they?' gagged Bruce, starting to pant from the heat and the effort of breathing the fouled air.

They reached the bank and Bruce's question was answered as they looked down onto the narrow beach.

There were the black remains of a dozen cooking fires along the water's edge, and closer to the high bank were two crude structures of poles. For a moment their purpose puzzled Bruce and then he realized what they were. He had seen those crosspieces suspended between two uprights often before in hunting camps throughout Africa. They were paunching racks! At intervals along the crosspieces were the bark ropes that had been used to string up the game, heels first, with head and forelegs dangling and belly bulging forward so that at the long abdominal stroke of the knife the viscera would drop out easily.

But the game they had butchered on *these* racks were men, his men. He counted the hanging ropes. There were ten of them, so no one had escaped.

'Cover me, Ruffy. I'm going down to have a look.' It was a penance

Bruce was imposing upon himself. They were his men, and he had left them here.

'Okay, boss.'

Bruce clambered down the well-defined path to the beach. Now the smell was almost unbearable and he found the source of it. Between the racks lay a dark shapeless mass. It moved with flies; its surface moved, trembled, crawled with flies. Suddenly, humming, they lifted in a cloud from the pile of human debris, and then settled once more upon it.

A single fly buzzed round Bruce's head and then settled on his hand. Metallic blue body, wings cocked back, it crouched on his skin and gleefully rubbed its front legs together. Bruce's throat and stomach convulsed as he began to retch. He struck at the fly and it darted away.

There were bones scattered round the cooking fires and a skull lay near his feet, split open to yield its contents.

Another spasm took Bruce and this time the vomit came up into his mouth, acid and warm. He swallowed it, turned away and scrambled up the bank to where Ruffy waited. He stood there gasping, suppressing his nausea until at last he could speak.

'All right, that's all I wanted to know,' and he led the way back to the circle of vehicles.

Bruce sat on the bonnet of the Ranchero and sucked hard on his cigarette, trying to get the taste of death from his mouth.

'They probably swam downstream during the night and climbed the supports of the bridge. Kanaki and his boys wouldn't have known anything about it until they came over the sides.' He drew on the cigarette again and trickled the smoke out of his nostrils, fumigating the back of his throat and his nasal passages. 'I should have thought of that. I should have warned Kanaki of that.'

'You mean they ate all ten of them—Jesus!' even Wally Hendry was impressed. 'I'd like to have a look at that beach. It must be quite something.'

'Good!' Bruce's voice was suddenly harsh. 'I'll put you in charge of the burial squad. You can go down there and clean it up before we start work on the bridge.' And Wally did not argue.

'You want me to do it now?' he asked.

'No,' snapped Bruce. 'You and Ruffy are going to take two of the trucks back to Port Reprieve and fetch the materials we need to repair the bridge.'

They both looked at Bruce with rising delight.

'I never thought of that,' said Wally.

'There's plenty of roofing timber in the hotel and the office block,' grinned Ruffy.

'Nails,' said Wally as though he were making a major contribution. 'We'll need nails.'

Bruce cut through their comments. 'It's two o'clock now. You can get back to Port Reprieve by nightfall, collect the material tomorrow morning and return here by the evening. Take those two trucks there— check to see they're full of gas and you'll need about fifteen men. Say, five gendarmes, in case of trouble, and ten of those civilians.'

'That should be enough,' agreed Ruffy.

'Bring a couple of dozen sheets of corrugated iron back with you. We'll use them to make a shield to protect us from arrows while we're working.'

'Yeah, that's a good idea.'

They settled the details, picked men to go back, loaded the trucks, worked them out of the laager, and Bruce watched them disappear down the road towards Port Reprieve. An ache started deep behind his eyes and suddenly he was very tired, drained of energy by too little sleep, by the heat and by the emotional pace of the last four days. He made one last circuit of the laager, checking the defences, chatting for a few minutes with his gendarmes and then he stumbled to the Ford, slid onto the front seat, laid his helmet and rifle aside, lowered his head onto his arms and was instantly asleep.

CHAPTER 21

Shermaine woke him after dark with food unheated from the cans and a bottle of Ruffy's beer.

'I'm sorry, Bruce, we have no fire to cook upon. It is very unappetizing and the beer is warm.'

Bruce sat up and rubbed his eyes. Six hours' sleep had helped; they were less swollen and inflamed. The headache was still there.

'I'm not really hungry, thank you. It's this heat.'

'You must eat, Bruce. Try just a little,' and then she smiled. 'At least you are more gallant after having rested. It is "Thank you" now, instead of "Keep quiet and stay out of the way".'

Ruefully Bruce grimaced. 'You are one of those women with a built-in recording unit; every word remembered and used in evidence against a man later.' Then he touched her hand. 'I'm sorry.'

'I'm sorry,' she repeated. 'I like your apologies, mon capitaine. They are like the rest of you, completely masculine. There is nothing about you which is not male, sometimes almost overpoweringly so.' Impishly she watched his eyes; he knew she was talking about the little scene on the train that Wally Hendry had interrupted.

'Let's try this food,' he said, and then a little later, 'Not bad—you are an excellent cook.'

'This time the credit must go to M. Heinz and his fifty-seven children. But one day I shall make for you one of my tournedos au Prince. It is my special.'

'Speciality,' Bruce corrected her automatically.

The murmur of voices within the laager was punctuated occasionally by a burst of laughter. There was a feeling of relaxation. The canvas roof and the wall of vehicles gave security to them all. Men lay in dark huddles of sleep or talked quietly in small groups.

Bruce scraped the metal plate and filled his mouth with the last of the food.

'Now I must check the defences again.'

'Oh, Bonaparte. It is always duty.' Shermaine sighed with resignation.

'I will not be long.'

'And I'll wait here for you.'

Bruce picked up his rifle and helmet, and was half way out of the Ford when out in the jungle the drum started.

'Bruce!' whispered Shermaine and clutched his arm. The voices round them froze into a fearful silence, and the drum beat in the night. It had a depth and resonance that you could feel; the warm sluggish air quivered with it. Not fixed in space but filling it, beating monotonously, insistently, like the pulse of all creation.

'Bruce!' whispered Shermaine again; she was trembling and the fingers on his arm dug into his flesh with the strength of terror. It steadied his own leap of fear.

'Baby, baby,' he soothed her, taking her to his chest and holding her there. 'It's only the sound of two pieces of wood being knocked together by a naked savage. They can't tough us here, you know that.'

'Oh, Bruce, it's horrible—it's like bells, funeral bells.'

'That's silly talk.' Bruce held her at arms' length. 'Come with me. Help me calm down these others, they'll be terrified. You'll have to help me.'

And he pulled her gently across the seat out of the Ford, and with one arm round her waist walked her into the centre of the laager.

What will counteract the stupefying influence of the drum, the hypnotic beat of it, he asked himself. Noise, our own noise.

'Joseph, M'pophu—' he shouted cheerfully, picking out the two best singers among his men. 'I regret the drumming is of a low standard, but the Baluba are monkeys with no understanding of music. Let us show them how a Bambala can sing.'

They stirred; he could feel the tension diminish.

'Come, Joseph—' He filled his lungs and shouted the opening chorus of one of the planting songs, purposely off-key, singing so badly that it must sting them.

Someone laughed, then Joseph's voice hesitantly starting the chorus, gathering strength. M'pophu coming in with the bass to give a solid foundation to the vibrant, sweet-ringing tenor. Half-beat to the drum, hands clapped in the dark; around him Bruce could feel the rhythmic swinging of bodies begin.

Shermaine was no longer trembling; he squeezed her waist and felt her body cling to him.

Now we need light, thought Bruce. A night lamp for my children who fear the darkness and the drum.

With Shermaine beside him he crossed the laager.

'Sergeant Jacque.'

'Captain?'

'You can start sweeping with the searchlights.'

'Oui, Captain.' The answer was less subdued. There were two spare batteries for each light, Bruce knew. Eight hours' life in each, so they would last tonight and tomorrow night.

From each side of the laager the beams leapt out, solid white shafts through the darkness; they played along the edge of the jungle and reflected back, lighting the interior of the laager sufficiently to make out the features of each man. Bruce looked at their faces. They're all right now, he decided, the ghosts have gone away.

'Bravo, Bonaparte,' said Shermaine, and Bruce became aware of the grins on the faces of his men as they saw him embracing her. He was about to drop his arm, then stopped himself. The hell with it, he decided, give them something else to think about. He led her back to the Ford.

'Tired?' he asked.

'A little,' she nodded.

'I'll fold down the seat for you. A blanket over the windows will give you privacy.'

'You'll stay close?' she asked quickly.

'I'll be right outside.' He unbuckled the webbing belt that carried his pistol. 'You'd better wear this from now on.'

Even at its minimum adjustment the belt was too large for her and the pistol hung down almost to her knee.

'The Maid of Orleans.' Bruce revenged himself. She pulled a face at him and crawled into the back of the station wagon.

A long while later she called softly above the singing and the throb of the drum.

'Bruce.'

'Yes?'

'I wanted to make sure you were there. Good night.'

'Good night, Shermaine.'

Bruce lay on a single blanket and sweated. The singing had long ago ceased but the drum went on and on, never faltering, throb-throb-throbbing out of the jungle. The searchlights swept regularly back and forth, at times lighting the laager clearly and at others leaving it in shadow. Bruce could hear around him the soft sounds of sleep, the sawing of breath, a muted cough, a gabbled sentence, the stirring of dreamers.

But Bruce could not sleep. He lay on his back with one hand under his head, smoking, staring up at the canvas. The events of the preceding four days ran through his mind: snatches of conversation, André dying, Boussier standing with his wife, the bursting of grenades, blood sticky on his hands, the smell of dead, the violence and the horror.

He moved restlessly, flicked away his cigarette and covered his eyes with his hands as though to shut out the memories. But they went on flickering through his mind like the images of a gigantic movie projector, confused now, losing all meaning but retaining the horror.

He remembered the fly upon his arm, grinning at him, rubbing its legs together, gloating, repulsive. He rolled his head from side to side on the blanket.

I'm going mad, he thought, I must stop this.

He sat up quickly, hugging his knees to his chest and the memories faded. But now he was sad, and alone. So terribly alone, so lost, so without purpose.

He sat alone on the blanket and he felt himself shrinking, becoming small and frightened.

I'm going to cry, he thought, I can feel it there heavy in my throat. and like a hurt child crawling into its mother's lap, Bruce Curry groped his way over the tailboard of the station wagon to Shermaine.

'Shermaine!' he whispered, blindly searching for her.

'Bruce, what is it?' She sat up quickly. She had not been sleeping either.

'Where are you?' There was panic in Bruce's voice.

'Here I am—what's the matter?'

And he found her; clumsily he caught her to him.

'Hold me, Shermaine, please hold me.'

'Darling.' She was anxious. 'What is it? Tell me, my darling.'

'Just hold me, Shermaine. Don't talk.' He clung to her, pressing his face into her neck. 'I need you so much—oh, God! How I need you!'

'Bruce.' She understood, and her fingers were at the nape of his neck, stroking, soothing.

'My Bruce,' she said and held him. Instinctively her body began to rock, gentling him as though he were her child.

Slowly his body relaxed, and he sighed against her—a gusty broken sound.

'My Bruce, my Bruce.' She lifted the thin cotton vest that was all she wore and, instinctively in the ageless ritual of comfort, she gave him her breasts. Holding his mouth to them with both her arms clasped around his neck, her head bowed protectively over his, her hair falling forward and covering them both.

With the hard length of his body against hers, with the soft tugging at her bosom, and in the knowledge that she was giving strength to the man she loved, she realized she had never known happiness before this moment. Then his body was no longer quiescent; she felt her own mood change, a new urgency.

'Oh yes, Bruce, yes!' Speaking up into his mouth, his hungry hunting mouth and he above her, no longer child, but full man again.

'So beautiful, so warm.' His voice was strangely husky, she shuddered with the intensity of her own need.

'Quickly, Bruce, oh, Bruce.' His cruel loving hands, seeking, finding.

'Oh, Bruce—quickly,' and she reached up for him with her hips.

'I'll hurt you.'

'No—yes, I want the pain.' She felt the resistance to him within her and cried out impatiently against it.

'Go through!' and then, 'Ah! It burns.'

'I'll stop.'

'*No, No!*'

'Darling. It's too much.'

'Yes—I can't—oh, Bruce. My heart—you've touched my heart.'

Her clenched fists drumming on his back. And in to press against the taut, reluctantly yielding springiness, away, then back, away, and back to touch the core of all existence, leave it, and come long gliding back to it, nuzzle it, feel it tilt, then come away, then back one more. Welling slowly upwards, scalding, no longer to be contained, with pain almost— and gone, and gone, and gone.

'I'm falling. Oh, Bruce! Bruce! Bruce!'

Into the gulf together—gone, all gone. Nothing left, no time, no space, no bottom to the gulf.

Nothing and everything. Complete.

Out in the jungle the drum kept beating.

Afterwards, long afterwards, she slept with her head on his arm and her face against his chest. And he unsleeping listened to her sleep. The sound of it was soft, so gentle breathing soft that you could not hear it unless you listened very carefully— or unless you loved her, he thought.

Yes. I think I love this woman—but I must be certain. In fairness to her and to myself I must be entirely certain, for I cannot live through another time like the last, and because I love her I don't want her to take the terrible wounding of a bad marriage. Better, much better to leave it now, unless it has the strength to endure.

Bruce rolled his head slowly until his face was in her hair, and the girl nuzzled his chest in her sleep.

But it is so hard to tell, he thought. It is so hard to tell at the beginning. It is so easy to confuse pity or loneliness with love, but I cannot afford to do that now. So I must try to think clearly about my marriage to Joan. It will be difficult, but I must try.

Was it like this with Joan in the beginning? It was so long ago, seven years, that I do not know, he answered truthfully. All I have left from those days are the pictures of places and the small heaps of words that have struck where the wind and the pain could not blow them away.

A beach with the sea mist coming in across it, a whole tree of driftwood half buried in the sand and bleached white with the salt, a basket of strawberries bought along the road, so that when I kissed her I could taste the sweet tartness of the fruit on her lips.

I remember a tune that we sang together, 'The mission bells told me that I mustn't stay, South of the border, down Mexico way.' I have forgotten most of the words.

And I remember vaguely how her body was, and the shape of her breasts before the children were born.

But that is all I have left from the good times.

The other memories are clear; stinging, whiplash clear. Each ugly word, and the tone in which it was said. The sound of sobbing in the night, the way it dragged itself on for three long grey years after it was mortally wounded, and both of us using all our strength to keep it moving because of the children.

The children! Oh, God, I mustn't think about them now. It hurts too much. Without the children to complicate it, I must think about her for the last time; I must end this woman Joan. So now finally and for all to end this woman who made me cry. I do not hate her for the man with whom she went away. She deserved another try for happiness. But I hate her for my children and for making shabby the love that I could have given Shermaine as a new thing. Also, I pity her for her inability to find the happiness for which she hunts so fiercely. I pity her for her coldness of body and of mind, I pity her for her prettiness that is now almost gone (it goes round the eyes first, cracking like oil paint) and I pity her for her consuming selfishness which will lose her the love of her children.

My children—not hers! My children!

That is all, that is an end to Joan, and now I have Shermaine who is none of the things that Joan was. I also deserve another try.

'Shermaine,' he whispered and turned her head slightly to kiss her. Shermaine, wake up.'

She stirred and murmured against him.

'Wake up.' He took the lobe of her ear between his teeth and bit it gently. Her eyes opened.

'Bon matin, *madame*.' He smiled at her.

'Bonjour, *monsieur*,' she answered and closed her eyes to press her face once more against his chest.

'Wake up. I have something to tell you.'

'I am awake, but tell me first if I am still dreaming. I have a certainty that this cannot be reality.'

'You are not dreaming.'

She sighed softly, and held him closer.

'Now tell me the other thing.'

'I love you,' he said.

'No. Now I am dreaming.'

'In truth,' he said.

'No, do not wake me. I could not bear to wake now.'

'And you?' he asked.

'You know it—' she answered. 'I do not have to tell you.'

'It is almost morning,' he said. 'There is only a little time.'

'Then I will fill that little time with saying it—' He held her and listened to her whispering it to him.

No, he thought, now I am certain. I could not be that wrong. This is my woman.

CHAPTER 22

The drum stopped with the dawn. And after it the silence was very heavy, and it was no relief.

They had grown accustomed to that broken rhythm and now in some strange way they missed it.

As Bruce moved around the laager he could sense the uneasiness in his men. There was a feeling of dread anticipation on them all. They moved with restraint, as though they did not want to draw attention to themselves. The laughter with which they acknowledged his jokes was nervous, quickly cut off, as though they had laughed in a cathedral. And their eyes kept darting back towards the ring of jungle.

Bruce found himself wishing for an attack. His own nerves were rubbed sensitive by contact with the fear all around him.

If only they would come, he told himself. If only they would show themselves and we could see men not phantoms.

But the jungle was silent. It seemed to wait, it watched them. They could feel the gaze of hidden eyes. Its malignant presence pressed closer as the heat built up.

Bruce walked across the laager to the south side, trying to move casually. He smiled at Sergeant Jacque, squatted beside him and peered from under the truck across open ground at the remains of the bridge.

'Trucks will be back soon,' he said. 'Won't take long to repair that.'

Jacque did not answer. There was a worried frown on his high intelligent forehead and his face was shiny with perspiration.

'It's the waiting, Captain. It softens the stomach.'

'They will be back soon,' repeated Bruce. If this one is worried, and he is the best of them, then the others must be almost in a jelly of dread.

Bruce looked at the face of the man on the other side of Jacque. Its expression shrieked with fear.

If they attack now, God knows how it will turn out. An African can think himself to death, they just lie down and die. They are getting to that stage now; if an attack comes they will either go berserk or curl up and wail with fear. You can never tell.

Be honest with yourself—you're not entirely happy either, are you? No, Bruce agreed, it's the waiting does it.

It came from the edge of the clearing on the far side of the laager. A high-pitched inhuman sound, angry, savage.

Bruce felt his heart trip and he spun round to face it. For a second the whole laager seemed to cringe from it.

It came again. Like a whip across aching nerves. Immediately it was lost in the roar of twenty rifles.

Bruce laughed. Threw back his head and let it come from the belly. The gunfire stammered into silence and others were laughing also. The men who had fired grinned sheepishly and made a show of reloading.

It was not the first time that Bruce had been startled by the cry of a yellow hornbill. But now he recognized his laughter and the laughter of the men around him, a mild form of hysteria.

'Did you want the feathers for your hat?' someone shouted and the laughter swept round the laager.

The tension relaxed as the banter was tossed back and forth. Bruce stood up and brought his own laughter under control.

No harm done, he decided. For the price of fifty rounds of ammunition, a purchase of an hour's escape from tension. A good bargain.

He walked across to Shermaine. She was smiling also.

'How is the catering section?' He grinned at her. 'What miracle of the culinary art is there for lunch?'

'Bully beef.'

'And onions?'

'No, just bully beef. The onions are finished.'

Bruce stopped smiling.

'How much is left?' he asked.

'One case—enough to last till lunchtime tomorrow.'

It would take at least two days to complete the repairs to the bridge; another day's travel after that.

'Well,' he said, 'we should all have healthy appetites by the time we get home. You'll have to try and spread it out. Half rations from now on.'

He was so engrossed in the study of this new complication that he did not notice the faint hum from outside the laager.

'Captain,' called Jacque. 'Can you hear it?'

Bruce inclined his head and listened.

'The trucks!' His voice was loud with relief, and intantly there was an excited murmur around the laager.

The waiting was over.

They came growling out of the bush into the clearing. Heavily loaded, timber and sheet-iron protruding backwards from under the canopies, sitting low on their suspensions.

Ruffy leaned from the cab of the leading truck and shouted.

'Hello, boss. Where shall we dump?'

'Take it up to the bridge. Hang on a second and I'll come with you.'

Bruce slipped out of the laager and crossed quickly to Ruffy's truck.

He could feel his back tingling while he was in the open and he slammed the door behind him with relief.

'I don't relish stopping an arrow,' he said.

'You have any trouble while we were gone?'

'No,' Bruce told him. 'But they're here. They were drumming in the jungle all night.'

'Calling up their buddies,' grunted Ruffy and let out the clutch. 'We'll have some fun before we finish this bridge. Most probably take them a day or two to get brave, but in the end they'll have a go at us.'

'Pull over to the side of the bridge, Ruffy,' Bruce instructed and rolled down his window. 'I'll signal Hendry to pull in beside us. We'll off-load into the space between the two trucks and start building the corrugated iron shield there.'

While Hendry manoeuvred his truck alongside, Bruce forced himself to look down on the carnage of the beach.

'Crocodiles,' he exclaimed with relief. The paunching racks still stood as he had last seen them, but the reeking pile of human remains was gone. The smell and the flies, however, still lingered.

'During the night,' agreed Ruffy as he surveyed the long slither marks in the sand of the beach.

'Thank God for that.'

'Yeah, it wouldn't have made my boys too joyful having to clean up that lot.'

'We'll send someone down to tear out those racks. I don't want to look at them while we work.'

'No, they're not very pretty.' Ruffy ran his eyes over the two sets of gallows.

Bruce climbed down into the space between the trucks. 'Hendry.'

'That's my name.' Wally leaned out of the window.

'Sorry to disappoint you, but the crocs have done the chore for you.'

'I can see. I'm not blind.'

'Very well then. On the assumption that you are neither blind nor paralysed, how about getting your trucks unloaded?'

'Big deal,' muttered Hendry, but he climbed down and began shouting at the men under the canvas canopy.

'Get the lead out there, you lot. Start jumping about!'

'What were the thickest timbers you could find?' Bruce turned to Ruffy.

'Nine by threes, but we got plenty of them.'

'They'll do,' decided Bruce. 'We can lash a dozen of them together for each of the main supports.' Frowning with concentration, Bruce began the task of organizing the repairs.

'Hendry, I want the timber stacked by sizes. Put the sheet-iron over here.' He brushed the flies from his face. 'Ruffy, how many hammers have we got?'

'Ten, boss, and I found a couple of handsaws.'

'Good. What about nails and rope?'

'We got plenty. I got a barrel of six-inch and—'

Preoccupied, Bruce did not notice one of the coloured civilians leave the shelter of the trucks. He walked a dozen paces towards the bridge and stopped. Then unhurriedly he began to unbutton his trousers and Bruce looked up.

'What the hell are you doing?' he shouted and the man started guiltily. He did not understand the English words, but Bruce's tone was sufficiently clear.

'Monsieur,' he explained, 'I wish to—'

'Get back here!' roared Bruce. The man hesitated in confusion and then he began closing his fly.

'Hurry up—you bloody fool.'

Obediently the man hastened the closing of his trousers. Everyone had stopped work and they were all watching him. His face was dark with embarrassment and he fumbled clumsily.

'Leave that.' Bruce was frantic. 'Get back here.'

The first arrow rose lazily out of the undergrowth along the river in a silent parabola. Gathering speed in its descent, hissing softly, it dropped into the ground at the man's feet and stuck up jauntily. A thin reed, fletched with green leaves, it looked harmless as a child's plaything.

'Run,' screamed Bruce. The man stood and stared with detached disbelief at the arrow.

Bruce started forward to fetch him, but Ruffy's huge black hand closed on his arm and he was helpless in its grip. He struck out at Ruffy, struggling to free himself but he could not break that hold.

A swarm of them like locusts on the move, high arcing, fluting softly, dropping all around the man as he started to run.

Bruce stopped struggling and watched. He heard the metal heads clanking onto the bonnet of the truck, saw them falling wide of the man, some of the frail shafts snapping as they hit the ground.

Then between the shoulders, like a perfectly placed *banderilla*, one hit him. It flapped against his back as he ran and he twisted his arms behind him, vainly trying to reach it, his face twisted in horror and in pain.

'Hold him down,' shouted Bruce as the coloured man ran into the shelter. Two gendarmes jumped forward, took his arms and forced him face downwards onto the ground.

He was gabbling incoherently with horror as Bruce straddled his back and gripped the shaft. Only half the barbed head had buried itself—a penetration of less than an inch—but when Bruce pulled the shaft it snapped off in his hand leaving the steel twitching in the flesh.

'Knife,' shouted Bruce and someone thrust a bayonet into his hand.

'Watch those barbs, boss. Don't cut yourself on them.'

'Ruffy, get your boys ready to repel them if they rush us,' snapped Bruce and ripped away the shirt. For a moment he stared at the crudely hand-beaten iron arrow-head. The poison coated it thickly, packed in behind the barbs, looking like sticky black toffee.

'He's dead,' said Ruffy from where he leaned over the bonnet of the truck. 'He just ain't stopped breathing yet.'

The man screamed and twisted under Bruce as he made the first incision, cutting in deep beside the arrowhead with the point of the bayonet.

'Hendry, get those pliers out of the tool kit.'

'Here they are.'

Bruce gripped the arrow-head with the steel jaws and pulled. The flesh clung to it stubbornly, lifting in a pyramid. Bruce hacked at it with the bayonet, feeling it tear. It was like trying to get the hook out of the rubbery mouth of a cat-fish.

'You're wasting your time, boss!' grunted Ruffy with all the calm African acceptance of violent death. 'This boy's a goner. That's no horse! That's snake juice in him, fresh mixed. He's finished.'

'Are you sure, Ruffy?' Bruce looked up. 'Are you sure it's snake venom?'

'That's what they use. They mix it with kassava meal.'

'Hendry, where's the snake bite outfit?'

'It's in the medicine box back at the camp.'

Bruce tugged once more at the arrow-head and it came away, leaving a deep black hole between the man's shoulder-blades.

'Everybody into the trucks, we've got to get him back. Every second is vital.'

'Look at his eyes,' grunted Ruffy. 'That injection stuff ain't going to help him much.'

The pupils had contracted to the size of match heads and he was shaking uncontrollably as the poison spread through his body.

'Get him into the truck.'

They lifted him into the cab and everybody scrambled aboard. Ruffy started the engine, slammed into reverse and the motor roared as he shot backwards over the intervening thirty yards to the laager.

'Get him out,' instructed Bruce. 'Bring him into the shelter.'

The man was blubbering through slack lips and he had started to sweat. Little rivulets of it coursed down his face and naked upper body. There was hardly any blood from the wound, just a trickle of brownish fluid. The poison must be a coagulant, Bruce decided.

'Bruce, are you all right?' Shermaine ran to meet him.

'Nothing wrong with me.' Bruce remembered to check his tongue this time. 'But one of them has been hit.'

'Can I help you?'

'No, I don't want you to watch.' And he turned from her. 'Hendry, where's that bloody snake bite outfit?' he shouted.

They had dragged the man into the laager and laid him on a blanket in the shade. Bruce went to him and knelt beside him. He took the scarlet tin that Hendry handed him and opened it.

'Ruffy, get those two trucks worked into the circle and make sure your boys are on their toes. With this success they may get brave sooner than you expected.'

Bruce fitted the hypodermic needle onto the syringe as he spoke.

'Hendry, get them to rig some sort of screen round us. You can use blankets.'

With his thumb he snapped the top off the ampoule and filled the syringe with the pale yellow serum.

'Hold him,' he said to the two gendarmes, lifted a pinch of skin close beside the wound and ran the needle under it. The man's skin felt like that of a frog, damp and clammy.

As he expelled the serum Bruce was trying to calculate the time that had elapsed since the arrow had hit. Possibly seven or eight minutes; mamba venom kills in fourteen minutes.

'Roll him over,' he said.

The man's head lolled sideways, his breathing was quick and shallow and the saliva poured from the corners of his mouth, running down his cheeks.

'Get a load of that!' breathed Wally Hendry, and Bruce glanced up at his face. His expression was a glow of deep sensual pleasure and his breathing was as quick and shallow as that of the dying man.

'Go and help Ruffy,' snapped Bruce as his stomach heaved with disgust.

'Not on your Nelly. This I'm not going to miss.'

Bruce had no time to argue. He lifted the skin of the man's stomach and ran the needle in again. There was an explosive spitting sound as the bowels started to vent involuntarily.

'Jesus,' whispered Hendry.

'Get away,' snarled Bruce. 'Can't you let him die without gloating over it?'

Hopelessly he injected again, under the skin of the chest above the heart. As he emptied the syringe the man's body twisted violently in the first seizure and the needle snapped off under the skin.

'There he goes,' whispered Hendry, 'there he goes. Just look at him, man. That's really something.'

Bruce's hands were trembling and slowly a curtain descended across his mind.

'You filthy swine,' he screamed and hit Hendry across the face with his open hand, knocking him back against the side of the gasoline tanker. Then he went for his throat and found it with both hands. The wind pipe was ropy and elastic under his thumbs.

'Is nothing sacred to you, you unclean animal,' he yelled into Hendry's face. 'Can't you let a man die without—'

Then Ruffy was there, effortlessly plucking Bruce's hands from the throat, interposing the bulk of his body, holding them away from each other.

'Let it stand, boss.'

'For that—' gasped Hendry as he massaged his throat. 'For that I'm going to make you pay.'

Bruce turned away, sick and ashamed, to the man on the blanket.

'Cover him up.' His voice was shaky. 'Put him in the back of one of the trucks. We'll bury him tomorrow.'

CHAPTER 23

Before nightfall they had completed the corrugated iron screen. It was a simple four-walled structure with no roof to it. One end of it was detachable and all four walls were pierced at regular intervals with small loopholes for defence.

Long enough to accommodate a dozen men in comfort, high enough to reach above the heads of the tallest, and exactly the width of the bridge, it was not a thing of beauty.

'How you going to move it, boss?' Ruffy eyed the screen dubiously.

'I'll show you. We'll move it back to the camp now, so that in the morning we can commute to work in it.'

Bruce selected twelve men and they crowded through the open end into the shelter, and closed it behind them.

'Okay, Ruffy. Take the trucks away.'

Hendry and Ruffy reversed the two trucks back to the laager, leaving the shelter standing at the head of the bridge like a small Nissen hut. Inside it Bruce stationed his men at intervals along the walls.

'Use the bottom timber of the frame to lift on,' he shouted. 'Are you all ready? All right, lift!'

The shelter swayed and rose six inches above the ground. From the laager they could see only the boots of the men inside.

'All together,' ordered Bruce. 'Walk!'

Rocking and creaking over the uneven ground the structure moved ponderously back towards the laager. Below it the feet moved like those of a caterpillar.

The men in the laager started to cheer, and from inside the shelter they answered with whoops of laughter. It was fun. They were enjoying themselves enormously, completely distracted from the horror of poison arrows and the lurking phantoms in the jungle around them.

They reached the camp and lowered the shelter. Then one at a time the gendarmes slipped across the few feet of open into the safety of the laager to be met with laughter, and back-slapping and mutual congratulation.

'Well, it works, boss,' Ruffy greeted Bruce in the uproar.

'Yes.' Then he lifted his voice. 'That's enough. Quiet down all of you. Get back to your posts.'

The laughter subsided and the confusion became order again. Bruce walked to the centre of the laager and looked about him. There was complete quiet now. They were all watching him. I have read about this so often, he grinned inwardly, the heroic speech to the men on the eve of battle. Let's pray I don't make a hash of it.

'Are you hungry?' he asked loudly in French and received a chorus of hearty affirmatives.

'There is bully beef for dinner.' This time humorous groans.

'And bully beef for breakfast tomorrow,' he paused, 'and then it's finished.'

They were silent now.

'So you are going to be truly hungry by the time we cross this river. The sooner we repair the bridge the sooner you'll get your bellies filled again.'

I might as well rub it in, decided Bruce.

'You all saw what happened to the person who went into the open today, so I don't have to tell you to keep under cover. The sergeant major is making arrangements for sanitation—five-gallon drums. They won't be very comfortable, so you won't be tempted to sit too long.'

They laughed a little at that.

'Remember this. As long as you stay in the laager or the shelter they can't touch you. There is absolutely nothing to fear. They can beat their drums and wait as long as they like, but they can't harm us.'

A murmur of agreement.

'And the sooner we finish the bridge the sooner we will be on our way.'

Bruce looked round the circle of faces and was satisfied with what he saw. The completion of the shelter had given their morale a boost.

'All right, Sergeant Jacque. You can start sweeping with the searchlights as soon as it's dark.'

Bruce finished and went across to join Shermaine beside the Ford. He loosed the straps of his helmet and lifted it off his head. His hair was damp with perspiration and he ran his fingers through it.

'You are tired,' Shermaine said softly, examining the dark hollows under his eyes and the puckered marks of strain at the corners of his mouth.

'No. I'm all right,' he denied, but every muscle in his body ached with fatigue and nervous tension.

'Tonight you must sleep all night,' she ordered him. 'I will make the bed in the back of the car.'

Bruce looked at her quickly. 'With you?' he asked.

'Yes.'

'You do not mind that everyone should know?'

'I am not ashamed of us.' There was a fierceness in her tone.

'I know, but—'

'You said once that nothing between you and I could ever be dirty.'

'No, of course it couldn't be dirty. I just thought—'

'Well then, I love you and from now on we have only one bed between us.' She spoke with finality.

Yesterday she was a virgin, he thought with amazement, and now— well, now it's no holds barred. Once she is roused a woman is more reckless of consequences than any man. They are such wholesale creatures. But she's right, of course. She's my woman and she belongs in my bed. The hell with the rest of the world and what it thinks!

'Make the bed, wench.' He smiled at her tenderly.

Two hours after dark the drum started again. They lay together, holding close, and listened to it. It held no terror now, for they were warm and secure in the afterglow of passion. It was like lying and listening to the impotent fury of a rainstorm on the roof at night.

CHAPTER 24

They went out to the bridge at sunrise, the shelter moving across the open ground like the carapace of a multi-legged metallic turtle. The men chattered and joked loudly inside, still elated by the novelty of it.

'All right, everybody. That's enough talking,' Bruce shouted them down. 'There's work to do now.'

And they began.

Within an hour the sun had turned the metal box into an oven. They stripped to the waist and the sweat dripped from them as they worked. They worked in a frenzy, gripped by a new urgency, oblivious of everything but the rough-sawed timber that drove white splinters into their skin at the touch. The worked in the confined heat, amidst the racket of hammers and in the piney smell of sawdust. The labour fell into its own pattern with only an occasional grunted order from Bruce or Ruffy to direct it.

By midday the four main trusses that would span the gap in the bridge had been made up. Bruce tested their rigidity by propping one at both ends and standing all his men on the middle of it. It gave an inch under their combined weight.

'What do you think, boss?' Ruffy asked without conviction.

'Four of them might just do it. We'll put in king-posts underneath,' Bruce answered.

'Man, I don't know. That tanker weighs plenty.'

'It's no flyweight,' Bruce agreed. 'But we'll have to take the chance. We'll bring the Ford across first, then the trucks and the tanker last.'

Ruffy nodded and wiped his face on his forearm; the muscles below his armpits knotted as he moved and there was no flabbiness in the powerful bulge of his belly above his belt.

'Phew!' He blew his lips out. 'I got the feeling for a beer now. This thirst is really stalking me.'

'You've got some with you?' Bruce asked as he passed his thumbs across his eyebrows and squeezed the moisture from them so it ran down his cheeks.

'Two things I never travel without, my trousers and a stock of the brown and bubbly.' Ruffy picked up the small pack from the corner of the shelter and it clinked coyly. 'You hear that sound, boss?'

'I hear it, and it sounds like music,' grinned Bruce. 'All right, everybody.' He raised his voice. 'Take ten minutes.'

Ruffy opened the bottles and passed them out, issuing one to be shared between three gendarmes. 'These Arabs don't properly appreciate this stuff,' he explained to Bruce. 'It'd just be a waste.'

The liquor was lukewarm and gassy; it merely aggravated Bruce's thirst. He drained the bottle and tossed it out of the shelter.

'All right.' He stood up. 'Let's get these trusses into position.'

'That's the shortest ten minutes I ever lived,' commented Ruffy.

'Your watch is slow,' said Bruce.

Carrying the trusses within it, the shelter lumbered out onto the bridge. There was no laughter now, only laboured breathing and curses.

'Fix the ropes!' commanded Bruce. He tested the knots personally, then looked up at Ruffy and nodded.

'That'll do.'

'Come on, you mad bastards,' Ruffy growled. 'Lift it.'

The first truss rose to the perpendicular and swayed there like a grotesque maypole with the ropes hanging from its top.

'Two men on each rope,' ordered Bruce. 'Let it down gently.' He glanced round to ensure that they were all ready.

'Drop it over the edge, and I'll throw you bastards in after it,' warned Ruffy.

'Lower away!' shouted Bruce.

The truss leaned out over the gap towards the fire-blackened stump of bridge on the far side, slowly at first, then faster as gravity took it.

'Hold it, damn you. Hold it!' roared Ruffy with the muscles in his shoulders humped out under the strain. They lay back against the ropes, but the weight of the truss dragged them forward as it fell.

It crashed down across the gap, lifted a cloud of dead wood ash as it struck, and lay there quivering.

'Man, I thought we'd lost that one for sure,' growled Ruffy, then turned savagely on his men.

'You bastards better be sharper with the next one—if you don't want to swim this river.'

The repeated the process with the second truss, and again they could not hold its falling length, but this time they were not so lucky. The end of the truss hit the far side, bounced and slid sideways.

'It's going! Pull, you bastards, pull!' shouted Ruffy.

The truss toppled slowly sideways and over the edge. It hit the river below them with a splash, disappeared under the surface, then bobbed up and floated away downstream until checked by the ropes.

Both Bruce and Ruffy fumed and swore during the lengthy exasperating business of dragging it back against the current and manhandling its awkward bulk back onto the bridge. Half a dozen times it slipped at the crucial moment and splashed back into the river.

Despite his other virtues, Ruffy's vocabulary of cursing words was limited and it added to his frustration that he had to keep repeating himself. Bruce did much better—he remembered things that he had heard and he made up a few.

When finally they had the dripping baulk of timber back on the bridge and were resting, Ruffy turned to Bruce with honest admiration.

'You swear pretty good,' he said. 'Never heard you before, but no doubt about it, you're good! What's that one about the cow again?'

Bruce repeated it for him a little self-consciously.

'You make that up yourself?' asked Ruffy.

'Spur of the moment,' laughed Bruce.

'That's 'bout the dirtiest I ever heard.' Ruffy could not conceal his envy. 'Man, you should write a book.'

'Let's get this bridge finished first,' said Bruce. 'Then I'll think about it.'

Now the truss was almost servile in its efforts to please. It dropped neatly across the gap and lay beside its twin.

'You curse something good enough, and it works everytime,' Ruffy announced sagely. 'I think your one about the cow made all the difference, boss.'

With two trusses in position they had broken the back of the project. They carried the shelter out and set it on the trusses, straddling the gap. The third and fourth trusses were dragged into position and secured with ropes and nails before nightfall.

When the shelter waddled wearily back to the laager at dusk, the men within it were exhausted. Their hands were bleeding and bristled with wood splinters, but they were also mightily pleased with themselves.

'Sergeant Jacque, keep one of your searchlights trained on the bridge all night. We don't want our friends to come out and set fire to it again.'

'There are only a few hours' life left in each of the batteries.' Jacque kept his voice low.

'Use them one at a time then.' Bruce spoke without hesitation. 'We must have that bridge lit up all night.

'You think you could spare a beer for each of the boys that worked on the bridge today?'

'A whole one each!' Ruffy was shocked. 'I only got a coupla cases left.'

Bruce fixed him with a stern eye and Ruffy grinned.

'Okay, boss. Guess they've earned it.'

Bruce transferred his attention to Wally Hendry who sat on the running-board of one of the trucks cleaning his nails with the point of his bayonet.

'Everything under control here, Hendry?' he asked coolly.

'Sure, what'd you think would happen? We'd have a visit from the archbishop? The sky'd fall in? Your French thing'd have twins or something?' He looked up from his nails at Bruce. 'When are you jokers going to get that bridge finished, instead of wandering around asking damn-fool questions?'

Bruce was too tired to feel annoyed. 'You've got the night watch, Hendry,' he said, 'from now until dawn.'

'Is that right, hey? And you? What're you going to do all night, or does that question make your blush?'

'I'm going to sleep, that's what I'm going to do. I haven't been lolling round camp all day.'

Hendry pegged the bayonet into the earth between his feet and snorted.

'Well, give her a little bit of sleep for me too, Bucko.'

Bruce left him and crossed to the Ford.

'Hello, Bruce. How did it go today? I missed you,' Shermaine greeted him, and her face lit up as she looked at him. It is a good feeling to be loved, and some of Bruce's fatigue lifted.

'About half finished, another day's work.' Then he smiled back at her. 'I won't lie and say I missed you—I've been too damn busy.'

'Your hands!' she said with quick concern and lifted them to examine them. 'They're in a terrible state.'

'Not very pretty, are they?'

'Let me get a needle from my case. I'll get the splinters out.'

From across the laager Wally Hendry caught Bruce's eye and with one hand made a suggestive sign below his waist. Then, at Bruce's frown of anger, he threw back his head and laughed with huge delight.

CHAPTER 25

Bruce's stomach grumbled with hunger as he stood with Ruffy and Hendry beside the cooking fire. In the early morning light he could just make out the dark shape of the bridge at the end of the clearing. That drum was still beating in the jungle, but they hardly noticed it now. It was taken for granted like the mosquitoes. 'The batteries are finished,' grunted Ruffy. The feeble yellow beam of the searchlight reached out tiredly towards the bridge.

'Only just lasted the night,' agreed Bruce.

'Christ, I'm hungry,' complained Hendry. 'What could I do to a couple of fried eggs and a porterhouse steak.'

At the mention of food Bruce's mouth flooded with saliva. He shut his mind against the picture that Wally's words had evoked in his imagination.

'We won't be able to finish the bridge and get the trucks across today,' he said, and Ruffy agreed.

'There's a full day's work left on her, boss.'

'This is what we'll do then,' Bruce went on. 'I'll take the work party out to the bridge. Hendry, you will stay here in the laager and cover us the same as yesterday. And Ruffy, you take one of the trucks and a dozen of your boys. Go back ten miles or so to where the forest is open and they won't be able to creep up on you. Then cut us a mountain of firewood; thick logs that will burn all night. We will set a ring of watch fires round the camp tonight.'

'That makes sense,' Ruffy nodded. 'But what about the bridge?'

'We'll have to put a guard on it,' said Bruce, and the expressions on their faces changed as they thought about this.

'More pork chops for the boys in the bushes,' growled Hendry. 'You won't catch me sitting out on the bridge all night.'

'No one's asking you to,' snapped Bruce. 'All right, Ruffy. Go and fetch the wood, and plenty of it.'

Bruce completed the repairs to the bridge in the late afternoon. The most anxious period was in the middle of the day when he and four men had to leave the shelter and clamber down onto the supports a few feet above the surface of the river to set the king-posts in place. Here they were exposed at random range to arrows from the undergrowth along the banks. But no arrows came and they finished the job and climbed back to safety again with something of a sense of anticlimax.

They nailed the crossties over the trusses and then roped everything into a compact mass.

Bruce stood back and surveyed the fruit of two full days' labour.

'Functional,' he decided, speaking aloud. 'But we certainly aren't going to win any prizes for aesthetic beauty or engineering design.'

He picked up his jacket and thrust his arms into the sleeves; his sweaty upper body was cold now that the sun was almost down.

'Home, gentlemen,' he said, and his gendarmes scattered to their positions inside the shelter.

The metal shelter circled the laager, squatting every twenty or thirty paces like an old woman preparing to relieve herself. When it lifted and moved on it left a log fire behind it. The ring of fires was completed by dark and the shelter returned to the laager.

'Are you ready, Ruffy?' From inside the shelter Bruce called across to where Ruffy waited.

'All set, boss.'

Followed by six heavily armed gendarmes, Ruffy crossed quickly to join Bruce and they set off to begin their all-night vigil on the bridge.

Before midnight it was cold in the corrugated iron shelter, for the wind blew down the river and they were completely exposed to it, and there was no cloud cover to hold the day's warmth against the earth.

The men in the shelter huddled under their gas capes and waited. Bruce and Ruffy leaned together against the corrugated iron wall, their shoulders almost touching. There was sufficient light from the stars to light the interior of the shelter and allow them to make out the guard rails of the bridge through the open ends.

'Moon will be up in an hour,' murmured Ruffy.

'Only a quarter of it, but it will give us a little more light,' Bruce concurred, and peered down into the black hole between his feet where he had prised up one of the newly laid planks.

'How about taking a shine with the torch?' suggested Ruffy.

'No.' Bruce shook his head, and passed the flashlight into his other hand. 'Not until I hear them.'

'You might not hear them.'

'If they swim downstream and climb up the piles, which is what I expect, then we'll hear them all right. They'll be dripping water all over the place,' said Bruce.

'Kanaki and his boys didn't hear them,' Ruffy pointed out.

'Kanaki and his boys weren't listening for it,' said Bruce.

They were silent then for a while. One of the gendarmes started to snore softly and Ruffy shot out a huge booted foot that landed in the small of his back. The man cried out and scrambled to his knees, looking wildly about him.

'You have nice dreams?' Ruffy asked pleasantly.

'I wasn't sleeping,' the man protested, 'I was thinking.'

'Well, don't think so loudly,' Ruffy advised him. 'Sounds though you were sawing through the bridge with a cross cut.'

Another half hour dragged itself by like a cripple.

'Fires are burning well,' commented Ruffy, and Bruce turned his head and glanced through the loophole in the corrugated iron behind him at the little garden of orange flame-flowers in the darkness.

'Yes, they should last till morning.'

Silence again, with only the singing of the mosquitoes and the rustle of the river as it flowed by the piles of the bridge. Shermaine has my pistol, Bruce remembered with a small trip in his pulse, I should have taken it back from her. He unclipped the bayonet from the muzzle of his rifle, tested the edge of the blade with his thumb, and slid it into the scabbard on his web-belt. Could easily lose the rifle if we start mixing it in the dark, he decided.

'Christ, I'm hungry,' grunted Ruffy beside him.

'You're too fat,' said Bruce. 'The diet will do you good.' And they waited.

Bruce stared down into the hole in the floorboards. His eyes began weaving fantasies out of the darkness; he could see vague shapes that moved, like things seen below the surface of the sea. His stomach tightened and he fought the impulse to shine his flashlight into the hole. He closed his eyes to rest them. I will count slowly to ten, he decided, and then look again.

Ruffy's hand closed on his upper arm; the pressure of his fingers transmitted alarm like a current of electricity. Bruce's eyelids flew open.

'Listen,' breathed Ruffy.

Bruce heard it. The stealthy drip of water on water below them. Then something bumped the bridge, but so softly that he felt rather than heard the jar.

'Yes,' Bruce whispered back. He reached out and tapped the shoulder of the gendarme beside him and the man's body stiffened at his touch.

With his breath scratching his dry throat, Bruce waited until he was sure the warning had been passed to all his men. Then he shifted the weight of his rifle from across his knees and aimed down into the hole.

He drew in a deep breath and switched on the flashlight. The beam shot down and he looked along it over his rifle barrel.

The square aperture in the floorboards formed a frame for the picture that flashed into his eyes. Black bodies, naked, glossy with wetness, weird patterns of tattoo marks, a face staring up at him, broad sloped forehead above startlingly white eyes and flat nose. The long gleaming blade of a panga. Clusters of humanity clinging to the wooden piles like ticks on the legs of a beast. Legs and arms and shiny trunks merged into a single organism, horrible as some slimy sea-creature.

Bruce fired into it. His rifle shuddered against his shoulder and the long orange spurts from its muzzle gave the picture a new flickering horror. The mass of bodies heaved, and struggled like a pack of rats trapped in a dry well. They dropped splashing into the river, swarmed up the timber piles, twisting and writhing as the bullets hit them, screaming, babbling over the sound of the rifle.

Bruce's weapon clicked empty and he groped for a new magazine.

Ruffy and his gendarmes were hanging over the guard rails of the bridge, firing downwards, sweeping the piles below them with long bursts, the flashes lighting their faces and outlining their bodies against the sky.

'They're still coming!' roared Ruffy. 'Don't let them get over the side.'

Out of the hole at Bruce's feet thrust the head and naked upper body of a man. There was a panga in his hand; he slashed at Bruce's legs, his eyes glazed in the beam of the flashlight.

Bruce jumped back and the knife missed his knees by inches. The man wormed his way out of the hole towards Bruce. He was screaming shrilly, a high meaningless sound of fury.

Bruce lunged with the barrel of his empty rifle at the contorted black face. All his weight was behind that thrust and the muzzle went into the Baluba's eye. The foresight and four inches of the barrel disappeared into his head, stopping only when it hit bone. Colourless fluid from the burst eyeball gushed from round the protruding steel.

Tugging and twisting, Bruce tried to free the rifle, but the foresight had buried itself like the barb of a fish hook. The Baluba had dropped his panga and was clinging to the rifle barrel with both hands. He was wailing and rolling on his back upon the floorboards, his head jerking every time Bruce tried to pull the muzzle out of his head.

Beyond him the head and shoulders of another Baluba appeared through the aperture.

Bruce dropped his rifle and gathered up the fallen panga; he jumped over the writhing body of the first Baluba and lifted the heavy knife above his head with both hands.

Two-handed, as though he were chopping wood, Bruce swung his whole body into the stroke. The shock jarred his shoulders and he felt blood splatter his legs. The untempered blade snapped off at the hilt and stayed imbedded in the Baluba's skull.

Panting heavily, Bruce straightened up and looked wildly about him. Baluba were swarming over the guard rail on one side of the bridge. The starlight glinted on their wet skins. One of his gendarmes was lying in a dark huddle, his head twisted back and his rifle still in his hands. Ruffy and the other gendarmes were still firing down over the far side.

'Ruffy!' shouted Bruce. 'Behind you! They're coming over!' and he dropped the handle of the panga and ran towards the body of the gendarme. He needed that rifle.

Before he could reach it the naked body of a Baluba rushed at him. Bruce ducked under the sweep of the panga and grappled with him.

They fell locked together, the man's body slippery and sinuous against him, and the smell of him fetid as rancid butter.

Bruce found the pressure point below the elbow of his knife arm and dug in with his thumb. The Baluba yelled and his panga clattered on the floorboards. Bruce wrapped his arm round the man's neck while with his free hand he reached for his bayonet.

The Baluba was clawing for Bruce's eyes with his fingers, his nails scored the side of Bruce's nose, but Bruce had his bayonet out now. He placed the point against the man's chest and pressed it in. He felt the steel scrape against the bone of a rib and the man redoubled his struggles at the sting of it. Bruce twisted the blade, working it in with his wrist, forcing the man's head backwards with his other arm.

The point of the bayonet scraped over the bone and found the gap between. Like taking a virgin, suddenly the resistance to its entrance was gone and it slid home full length. The Baluba's body jerked mechanically and the bayonet twitched in Bruce's fist.

Bruce did not even wait for the man to die. He pulled the blade out against the sucking reluctance of tissue that clung to it and scrambled to his feet in time to see Ruffy pick another Baluba from his feet and hurl him bodily over the guard rail.

Bruce snatched the rifle from the gendarme's dead hands and stepped to the guard rail. They were coming over the side, those below shouting and pushing at the ones above.

Like shooting a row of sparrows from a fence with a shotgun, thought Bruce grimly, and with one long burst he cleared the rail. Then he leaned out and sprayed the piles below the bridge. The rifle was empty. He reloaded with a magazine from his pocket. But it was all over. They were dropping back into the river, the piles below the bridge were clear of men, their heads bobbed away downstream.

Bruce lowered his rifle and looked about him. Three of his gendarmes were killing the man that Bruce had wounded, standing over him and grunting as they thrust down with their bayonets. The man was still wailing.

Bruce looked away.

One horn of the crescent moon showed above the trees; it had a gauzy halo about it.

Bruce lit a cigarette and behind him those gruesome noises ceased.

'Are you okay, boss?'

'Yes, I'm fine. How about you, Ruffy?'

'I got me a terrible thirst now. Hope nobody trod on my pack.'

About four minutes from the first shot to the last, Bruce guessed. That's the way of war, seven hours of waiting and boredom, then four minutes of frantic endeavour. Not only of war either, he thought. The whole of life is like that.

Then he felt the trembling in his thighs and the first spasm of nausea as the reaction started.

'What's happening?' A shout floated across from the laager. Bruce recognized Hendry's voice. 'Is everything all right?'

'We've beaten them off,' Bruce shouted back. 'Everything under control. You can go to sleep again.'

And now I have got to sit down quickly, he told himself.

Except for the tattoos upon his cheeks and forehead the dead Baluba's features were little different from those of the Bambala and Bakuba men who made up the bulk of Bruce's command.

Bruce played the flashlight over the corpse. The arms and legs were thin but stringy with muscle, and the belly bulged out from years of malnutrition. It was an ugly body, gnarled and crabbed. With distaste Bruce moved the light back to the features. The bone of the skull formed harsh angular planes beneath the skin, the nose was flattened and the thick lips had about them a repellent brutality. They were drawn back slightly to reveal the teeth which had been filed to sharp points like those of a shark.

'This is the last one, boss. I'll toss him overboard.' Ruffy spoke in the darkness beside Bruce.

'Good.'

Ruffy heaved and grunted, the corpse splashed below them and Ruffy wiped his hands on the guard rail, then came to sit beside Bruce.

'Goddam apes.' Ruffy's voice was full of the bitter tribal antagonism of Africa. 'When we get shot of these U.N. people there'll be a bit of sorting out to do. They've got a few things to learn, these bloody Baluba.'

And so it goes, thought Bruce, Jew and Gentile, Catholic and Protestant, black and white, Bambala and Baluba.

He checked the time, another two hours till dawn. His nervous reaction from physical violence had abated now; the hand that held the cigarette no longer trembled.

'They won't come again,' said Ruffy. 'You can get some sleep now if you want. I'll keep an eye open, boss.'

'No, thanks. I'll wait with you.' His nerves had not settled down enough for sleep.

'How's it for a beer?'

'Thanks.'

Bruce sipped the beer and stared out at the watch fires round the laager. They had burned down to puddles of red ash but Bruce knew that Ruffy was right. The Baluba would not attack again that night.

'So how do you like freedom?'

'How's that, boss?' The question puzzled Ruffy and he turned to Bruce questioningly.

'How do you like it now the Belgians have gone?'

'It's pretty good, I reckon.'

'And if Tshombe has to give in to the Central Government?'

'Those mad Arabs!' snarled Ruffy. 'All they want is our copper. They're going to have to get up early in the morning to take it. We're in the saddle here.'

The great jousting tournament of the African continent. I'm in the saddle, try to unhorse me! As in all matters of survival it was not a question of ethics and political doctrine (except to the spectators in Whitehall, Moscow, Washington and Peking). There were big days coming, thought Bruce. My own country, when she blows, is going to make Algiers look like an old ladies' sewing circle.

CHAPTER 26

The sun was up, throwing long shadows out into the clearing, and Bruce stood beside the Ford and looked across the bridge at the corrugated iron shelter on the far bank.

He relaxed for a second and let his mind run unhurriedly over his preparations for the crossing. Was there something left undone, some disposition which could make it more secure?

Hendry and a dozen men were in the shelter across the bridge, ready to meet any attack on that side.

Shermaine would take the Ford across first. Then the lorries would follow her. They would cross empty to minimize the danger of the bridge collapsing, or being weakened for the passage of the tanker. After each lorry had crossed, Hendry would shuttle its load and passengers over in the shelter and deposit them under the safety of the canvas canopy.

The last lorry would go over fully loaded. That was regrettable but unavoidable.

Finally Bruce himself would drive the tanker across. Not as an act of heroism, although it was the most dangerous business of the morning, but because he would trust no one else to do it, not even Ruffy. The five hundred gallons of fuel it contained was their safe-conduct home. Bruce had taken the precaution of filling all the gasoline tanks in the convoy in case of accidents, but they would need replenishing before they reached Msapa Junction.

He looked down at Shermaine in the driver's seat of the Ford.

'Keep it in low gear, take her over slowly but steadily. Whatever else you do, don't stop.'

She nodded. She was composed and she smiled at him. Bruce felt a stirring of pride as he looked at her, so small and lovely, but today she was doing man's work. He went on. 'As soon as you are over, I will send one of the trucks after you. Hendry will put six of his men into it and then come back for the others.'

'Oui, Monsieur Bonaparte.'

'You'll pay for that tonight,' he threatened her. 'Off you go.'

Shermaine let out the clutch and the Ford bounced over rough ground to the road, then accelerated smoothly out onto the bridge.

Bruce held his breath, but there was only a slight check and sway as it crossed the repaired section.

'Thank God for that.' Bruce let out his breath and watched while Shermaine drew up alongside the shelter.

'Allez,' Bruce shouted at the coloured engine driver who was ready at the wheel of the first truck. The man smiled his cheerful chubby-faced smile, waved, and the truck rolled forward.

Watching anxiously as it went onto the bridge, Bruce saw the new timbers give perceptibly beneath the weight of the truck, and he heard them creak loudly in protest.

'Not so good,' he muttered.

'No—' agreed Ruffy. 'Boss, why don't you let someone else take the tanker over?'

'We've been over that already,' Bruce answered him without turning his head. Across the river Hendry was transferring his men from the shelter to the back of the truck. Then the shelter started its tedious way back towards them.

Bruce fretted impatiently during the four hours that it took to get four trucks across. The long business was the shuttling back and forth of the corrugated iron shelter, at least ten minutes for each trip.

Finally there was only the fifth truck and the tanker left on the north bank. Bruce started the engine of the tanker and put her into auxiliary low, then he blew a single blast on the horn. The driver of the truck ahead of him waved an acknowledgement and pulled forward.

The truck reached the bridge and went out into the middle. It was fully loaded, twenty men aboard. It came to the repaired section and slowed down, almost stopping.

'Go on! Keep it going, damn you,' Bruce shouted in impotent anger.

The fool of a driver was forgetting his orders. He crawled forward and the bridge gave alarmingly under the full weight, the high canopied roof rocked crazily, and even above the rumble of his own engine Bruce could hear the protesting groan of the bridge timbers.

'The fool, oh, the bloody fool,' whispered Bruce to himself. Suddenly he felt very much alone and unprotected here on the north bank with the bridge being mutilated by the incompetence of the truck driver. He started the tanker moving.

Ahead of him the other driver had panicked. He was racing his engine, the rear wheels spun viciously, blue smoke of scorched tyres, and one of the floorboards tore loose. Then the truck lurched forward and roared up the south bank.

Bruce hesitated, applying the brakes and bring the tanker to a standstill on the threshold of the bridge.

He thought quickly. The sensible thing would be to repair the damage to the bridge before chancing it with the weight of the tanker. But that would mean another day's delay. None of them had eaten since the previous morning. Was he justified in gambling against even odds, for that's what they were? A fifty-fifty chance, heads you get across, tails you dump the tanker in the middle of the river.

Then unexpectedly the decision was made for him.

From across the river a Bren gun started firing. Bruce jumped in his seat and looked up. Then a dozen other guns joined in and the tracer flew past the tanker. They were firing across towards him, close on each side of him. Bruce struggled to drag from his uncomprehending brain an explanation of this new development. Suddenly everything was moving too swiftly. Everything was confusion and chaos.

Movement in the rear-view mirror of the tanker caught his eye. He stared at it blankly. Then he twisted quickly in his seat and looked back.

'Christ!' he swore with fright.

From the edge of the jungle on both sides of the clearing Baluba were swarming into the open. Hundreds of them running towards him, the animal-skin kilts swirling about their legs, feather head-dresses fluttering, sun bright on the long blades of their pangas. An arrow rang dully against the metal body of the tanker.

Bruce revved the engine, gripped the wheel hard with both hands and took the tanker out onto the bridge. Above the sound of the guns he could hear the shrill ululation, the excited squealing of two hundred Baluba. It sounded very close, and he snatched a quick look in the mirror. What he saw nearly made him lose his head and give the tanker full throttle. The nearest Baluba, screened from the guns on the south bank by the tanker's bulk, was only ten paces away. So close that Bruce could see the tattoo marks on his face and chest.

With an effort Bruce restrained his right foot from pressing down too hard, and instead he bore down on the repaired section of the bridge at a sedate twenty miles an hour. He tried to close his mind to the squealing behind him and the thunder of gunfire ahead of him.

The front wheels hit the new timbers, and above the other sounds he heard them groan loudly, and felt them sag under him.

The tanker rolled on and the rear wheels brought their weight to bear. The groan of wood became a cracking, rending sound. The tanker slowed as the bridge subsided, its wheels spun without purchase, it tilted sideways, no longer moving forward.

A sharp report, as one of the main trusses broke, and Bruce felt the tanker drop sharply at the rear; its nose pointed upwards and it started to slide back.

'Get out!' his brain shrieked at him. 'Get out, it's falling!' He reached for the door handle beside him, but at that moment the bridge collapsed completely. The tanker rolled off the edge.

Bruce was hurled across the cab with a force that stunned him, his legs wedged under the passenger seat and his arms tangled in the strap of his rifle. The tanker fell free and Bruce felt his stomach swoop up and press against his chest as though he rode a giant roller coaster.

The sickening drop lasted only an instant, and then the tanker hit the river. Immediately the sounds of gunfire and the screaming of Baluba were drowned out as the tanker disappeared below the surface. Through the windscreen Bruce saw now the cool cloudy green of water, as though he looked into the windows of an aquarium. With a gentle rocking motion the tanker sank down through the green water.

'Oh, my God, not this!' He spoke aloud as he struggled up from the floor of the cab. His ears were filled with the hiss and belch of escaping air bubbles; they rose in silver clouds past the windows.

The truck was still sinking, and Bruce felt the pain in his eardrums as the pressure built up inside the cab. He opened his mouth and swallowed convulsively, and his eardrums squeaked as the pressure equalized and the apin abated. Water was squirting in through the floor of the cab and jets of it spurted out of the instrument panel of the dashboard. The cab was flooding.

Bruce twisted the handle of the door beside him and hit it with his shoulder. It would not budge an inch. He flung all his weight against it, anchoring his feet on the dashboard and straining until he felt his eyeballs starting out of their sockets. It was jammed solid by the immense pressure of water on the outside.

'The windscreen,' he shouted aloud. 'Break the windscreen.' He groped for his rifle. The cab had flooded to his waist as he sat in the passenger's seat. He found the rifle and brought it dripping to his shoulder. He touched the muzzle to the windscreen and almost fired. But his food sense warned him.

Clearly he saw the danger of firing. The concussion in the confined cab would burst his eardrums, and the avalanche of broken glass that would be thrown into his face by the water pressure outside would certainly blind and maim him.

He lowered the rifle despondently. He felt his panic being slowly replaced by the cold certainty of defeat. He was trapped fifty feet below the surface of the river. There was no way out.

He thought of turning the rifle on himself, ending the inevitable, but he rejected the idea almost as soon as it had formed. Not that way, never that way!

He flogged his mind, driving it out of the cold lethargic clutch of certain death. There must be something. Think! Damn you, think!

The tanker was still rocking; it had not yet settled into the ooze of the river bottom. How long had he been under? About twenty seconds. Surely it should have hit the bottom long ago.

Unless! Bruce felt hope surge into new life within him. The tank! By God, that was it.

The great, almost empty tank behind him! The five-thousand-gallon tank which now contained only four hundred gallons of gasoline—it would have a displacement of nearly eighteen tons! It would float.

As if in confirmation of his hope, he felt his eardrums creak and pop. The pressure was falling! He was rising.

Bruce stared out at green water through the glass. The silver clouds of bubbles no longer streamed upwards; they seemed to hang outside the cab. The tanker had overcome the initial impetus that had driven it far below the surface, and now it was floating upwards at the same rate of ascent as its bubbles.

The dark green of deep water paled slowly to the colour of Chartreuse. And Bruce laughed. It was a gasping hysterical giggle and the sound of it shocked him. He cut it off abruptly.

The tanker bobbed out onto the surface, water streamed from the windscreen and through it Bruce caught a misty distorted glimpse of the south bank.

He twisted the door handle and this time the door burst open readily, water poured into the cab and Bruce floundered out against its rush.

With one quick glance he took in his position. The tanker had floated down twenty yards below the bridge, the guns on the south bank had fallen silent, and he could see no Baluba on the north bank. They must have disappeared back into the jungle.

Bruce plunged into the river and struck out for the south bank. Vaguely he heard the thin high shouts of encouragement from his gendarmes.

Within a dozen strokes he knew he was in difficulties. The drag of his boots and his sodden uniform was enormous. Treading water he tore off his steel helmet and let it sink. Then he tried to struggle out of his battle-jacket. It clung to his arms and chest and he disappeared under the surface four times before he finally got rid of it. He had breathed water into his lungs and his legs were tired and heavy.

The south bank was too far away. He would never make it. Coughing painfully he changed his objective and struck upstream against the current towards the bridge.

He felt himself settling lower in the water; he had to force his arms to lift and fall forward into each stroke.

Something plopped into the water close beside him. He paid no attention to it; suddenly a sense of disinterest had come over him, the first stage of drowning. He mistimed a breath and sucked in more water. The pain of it goaded him into a fresh burst of coughing. He hung in the water, gasping and hacking painfully.

Again something plopped close by, and this time he lifted his head. An arrow floated past him—then they began dropping steadily about him.

Baluba hidden in the thick bush above the beach were shooting at him; a gentle pattering rain of arrows splashed around his head. Bruce started swimming again, clawing his way frantically upstream. He swam until he could no longer lift his arms clear of the surface and the weight of his boots dragged his feet down.

Again he lifted his head. The bridge was close, not thirty feet away, but he knew that those thirty feet were as good as thirty miles. He could not make it.

The arrows that fell about him were no longer a source of terror. He thought of them only with mild irritation.

Why the hell can't they leave me alone? I don't want to play any more. I just want to relax. I'm so tired, so terribly tired.

He stopped moving and felt the water rise up coolly over his mouth and nose.

'Hold on, boss. I'm coming.' The shout penetrated through the grey fog of Bruce's drowning brain. He kicked and his head rose once more above the surface. He looked up at the bridge.

Stark naked, big belly swinging with each pace, thick legs flying, the great dangling bunch of his genitals bouncing merrily, black as a charging hippopotamus, Sergeant Major Ruffararo galloped out along the bridge.

He reached the fallen section and hauled himself up onto the guard rail. The arrows were falling around him, hissing down like angry insects. One glanced off his shoulder without penetrating and Ruffy shrugged at it, then launched himself up and out, falling in an ungainly heap of arms and legs to hit the water with a splash.

'Where the hell are you, boss?'

Bruce croaked a water-strangled reply and Ruffy came ploughing down towards him with clumsy overarm strokes.

He reached Bruce.

'Always playing around,' he grunted. 'Guess some guys never learn!' He fist closed on a handful of Bruce's hair.

Struggling unavailingly Bruce felt his head tucked firmly under Ruffy's arm and he was dragged through the water. Occasionally his face came out long enough to suck a breath but mostly he was under water. Consciousness receded and he felt himself going, going.

His head bumped against something hard but he was too weak to reach out his hand.

'Wake up, boss. You can have a sleep later.' Ruffy's voice bellowed in his ear. He opened his eyes and saw beside him the pile of the bridge.

'Come on. I can't carry you up here.'

Ruffy had worked round the side of the pile, shielding them from arrows, but the current was strong here, tugging at their bodies. Without the strength to prevent it Bruce's head rolled sideways and his face flopped into the water.

'Come on, wake up.' With a stinging slap Ruffy's open hand hit Bruce across the cheek. The shock roused him, he coughed and a mixture of water and vomit shot up his throat and out of his mouth and nose. Then he belched painfully and retched again.

'How's it feel now?' Ruffy demanded.

Bruce lifted a hand from the water and wiped his mouth. He felt much better.

'Okay? Can you make it?'

Bruce nodded.

'Let's go then.'

With Ruffy dragging and pushing him, he worked his way up the pile. Water poured from his clothing as his body emerged, his hair was plastered across his forehead and he could feel each breath gurgle in his lungs.

'Listen, boss. When we get to the top we'll be in the open again. There'll be more arrows—no time to sit around and chat. We're going over the rail fast and then run like hell, okay?'

Bruce nodded again. Above him were the floorboards of the bridge. With one hand he reached up and caught an upright of the guard rail, and he hung there without strength to pull himself the rest of the way.

'Hold it there,' grunted Ruffy and wriggled his shiny wet bulk up and over.

The arrows started falling again; one pegged into the wood six inches from Bruce's face and stood there quivering. Slowly Bruce's grip relaxed. I can't hold on, he thought, I'm going.

Then Ruffy's hand closed on his wrist, he felt himself dragged up, his legs dangled. He hung suspended by one arm and the water swirled smoothly past twenty feet below.

Slowly he was drawn upwards, his chest scraped over the guard rail, tearing his shirt, then he tumbled over it into an untidy heap on the bridge.

Vaguely he heard the guns firing on the south bank, the flit and thump of the arrows, and Ruffy's voice.

'Come on, boss. Get up.'

He felt himself being lifted and dragged along. With his legs boneless soft under him, he staggered beside Ruffy. Then there were no more arrows; the timbers of the bridge became solid earth under his feet. Voices and hands on him. He was being lifted, then lowered face down onto the wooden floor of a truck. The rhythmic pressure on his chest as someone started artificial respiration above him, the warm gush of water up his throat, and Shermaine's voice. He could not understand what she was saying, but just the sound of it was enough to make him realize he was safe. Darkly through the fog he became aware that her voice was the most important sound in his life.

He vomited again.

Hesitantly at first, and then swiftly, Bruce came back from the edge of oblivion.

'That's enough,' he mumbled and rolled out from under Sergeant Jacque who was administering the artificial respiration. The movement started a fresh paroxysm of coughing and he felt Shermaine's hands on his shoulders restraining him.

'Bruce, you must rest.'

'No.' He struggled into a sitting position. 'We've got to get out into the open,' he gasped.

'No hurry, boss. We've left all the Baluba on the other bank. There's a river between us.'

'How do you know?' Bruce challenged him.

'Well—'

'You don't!' Bruce told him flatly. 'There could easily be another few hundred on this side.' He coughed again painfully and then went on. 'We're leaving in five minutes, get them ready.'

'Okay.' Ruffy turned to leave.

'Ruffy!'

'Boss?' He turned back expectantly.

'Thank you.'

Ruffy grinned self-consciously. ''At's all right. I needed a wash anyway.'

'I'll buy you a drink when we get home.'

'I won't forget,' Ruffy warned him, and climbed down out of the truck. Bruce heard him shouting to his boys.

'I thought I'd lost you.' Shermaine's arm was still round his shoulders and Bruce looked at her for the first time.

'My sweet girl, you won't get rid of me that easily,' he assured her. He was feeling much better now.

'Bruce, I want to—I can't explain—' Unable to find the words she leaned forward instead and kissed him, full on the mouth.

When they drew apart, Sergeant Jacque and the two gendarmes with him were grinning delightedly.

'There is nothing wrong with you now, Captain.'

'No, there isn't,' Bruce agreed. 'Make your preparations for departure.'

———————————

From the passenger seat of the Ford Bruce took one last look at the bridge.

The repaired section hung like a broken drawbridge into the water. Beyond it on the far bank were scattered a few dead Baluba, like celluloid dolls in the sunlight. Far downstream the gasoline tanker had been washed by the current against the beach. It lay on its side, half-submerged in the shallows and the white Shell insignia showed clearly.

And the river flowed on, green and inscrutable, with the jungle pressing close along its banks.

'Let's get away from here,' said Bruce.

Shermaine started the engine and the convoy of trucks followed them along the track through the belt of thick river bush and into the open forest again.

Bruce looked at his watch. The inside of the glass was dewed with moisture and he lifted it to his ear.

'Damn thing has stopped. What's your time?'

'Twenty minutes to one.'

'Half the day wasted,' Bruce grumbled.

'Will we reach Msapa Junction before dark?'

'No, we won't. For two good reasons. Firstly, it's too far, and secondly, we haven't enough gas.'

'What are you going to do?' Her voice was unruffled; already she had complete faith in him. I wonder how long it will last, he mused cynically. At first you're a god. You have not a single human weakness. They set a standard for you, and the standard is perfection. Then the first time you fall short of it, their whole world blows up.

'We'll think of something,' he assured her.

'I'm sure you will,' she agreed complacently and Bruce grinned. The big joke, of course, was that when she said it he also believed it. Damned if being in love doesn't make you feel one hell of a man.

He changed to English so as to exclude the two gendarmes in the back seat from the conversation.

'You are the best thing that has happened to me in thirty years.'

'Oh, Bruce.' She turned her face towards him and the expression of trusting love in it and the intensity of his own emotion struck Bruce like a physical blow.

I will keep this thing alive, he vowed. I must nourish it with care and protect it from the dangers of selfishness and familiarity.

'Oh, Bruce, I do love you so terribly much. This morning when— when I thought I had lost you, when I saw the tanker go over into the river—' She swallowed and now her eyes were full of tears. 'It was as though the light had gone—it was so dark, so dark and cold without you.'

Absorbed with him so that she had forgotten about the road, Shermaine let the Ford veer and the offside wheels pumped into the rough verge.

'Hey, watch it!' Bruce cautioned her. 'Dearly as I love you also, I have to admit that you're a lousy driver. Let me take her.'

'Do you feel up to it?'

'Yes, pull into the side.'

Slowly, held to the speed of the lumbering vehicles behind them, they drove on through the afternoon. Twice they passed deserted Baluba villages beside the road, the grass huts disintegrating and the small cultivated lands about them thickly overgrown.

'My God, I'm hungry. I've got a headache from it and my belly feels as though it's full of warm water,' complained Bruce.

'Don't think you're the only one. This is the strictest diet I've ever been on, must have lost four pounds! But I always lose in the wrong place, never on my bottom.'

'Good,' Bruce said. 'I like it just the way it is, never shed an ounce there.' He looked over his shoulder at the two gendarmes. 'Are you hungry?' he asked in French.

'Mon Dieu!' exclaimed the fat one. 'I will not be able to sleep tonight, if I must lie on an empty stomach.'

'Perhaps it will not be necessary.' Bruce let his eyes wander off the road into the surrounding bush. The character of the country had changed in the last hundred miles. 'This looks like game country. I've noticed plenty of spoor on the road. Keep your eyes open.'

The trees were tall and widely spaced with grass growing beneath them. Their branches did not interlock so that the sky showed through. At intervals there were open glades filled with green swamp grass and thickets of bamboo and ivory palms.

'We've got another half hour of daylight. We might run into something before then.'

In the rear-view mirror he watched the lumbering column of transports for a moment. They must be almost out of gasoline by now, hardly enough for another half-hour's driving. There were compensations however; at least they were in open country now and only eighty miles from Msapa Junction.

He glanced at the petrol gauge—half the tank. The Ranchero still had sufficient to get through even if the trucks were almost dry.

Of course! That was the answer. Find a good camp, leave the convoy, and go on in the Ford to find help. Without the trucks to slow him down he could get through to Msapa Junction in two hours. There was a telegraph in the station office, even if the junction was still deserted.

'We'll stop on the other side of this stream,' said Bruce and slowed the Ford, changed into second gear and let it idle down the steep bank.

The stream was shallow. The water hardly reached the hub-caps as they bumped across the rocky bottom. Bruce gunned the Ford up the far bank into the forest again.

'There!' shouted one of the gendarmes from the back seat and Bruce followed the direction of his arm.

Standing with humped shoulders, close beside the road, bunched together with mournfully drooping horns, heads held low beneath the massive bosses, bodies very big and black, were two old buffalo bulls.

Bruce hit the brakes, skidding the Ranchero to a stop, reaching for his rifle at the same instant. He twisted the door handle, hit the door with his shoulder and tumbled out onto his feet.

With a snort and a toss of their ungainly heads the buffalo started to run.

Bruce picked the leader and aimed for the neck in front of the plunging black shoulder. Leaning forward against the recoil of the rifle he fired and heard the bullet strike with a meaty thump. The bull slowed, breaking his run. The stubby forelegs settled and he slid forward on his nose, rolling as he fell, dust and legs kicking.

Turning smoothly without taking the butt from his shoulder, swinging with the run of the second bull, Bruce fired again, and again the thump of bullet striking.

The buffalo stumbled, giving in the legs, then he steadied and galloped on like a grotesque rocking horse, patches of baldness grey on his flanks, big-bellied, running heavily.

Bruce shifted the bead of the foresight onto his shoulder and fired twice in quick succession, aiming low for the heart, hitting each time, the bull so close he could see the bullet wounds appear on the dark skin.

The gallop broke into a trot, with head swinging low, mouth open, legs beginning to fold. Aiming carefully for the head Bruce fired again. The bull bellowed—a sad lonely sound—and collapsed into the grass.

The lorries had stopped in a line behind the Ford, and now from each of them swarmed black men. Jabbering happily, racing each other, they streamed past Bruce to where the buffalo had fallen in the grass beside the road.

'Nice shooting, boss,' applauded Ruffy. 'I'm going to have me a piece of tripe the size of a blanket.'

'Let's make camp first.' Bruce's ears were still singing with gunfire. 'Get the lorries into a ring.'

'I'll see to it.'

Bruce walked up to the nearest buffalo and watched for a while as a dozen men strained to roll it onto its back and begin butchering it. There were clusters of grape-blue ticks in the folds of skin between the legs and body.

A good head, he noted mechanically, forty inches at least.

'Plenty of meat, Captain. Tonight we eat thick!' grinned one of his gendarmes as he bent over the huge body to begin flensing.

'Plenty,' agreed Bruce and turned back to the Ranchero. In the heat of the kill it was a good feeling: the rifle's kick and your stomach screwed up with excitement. But afterwards you felt a little bit dirtied; sad and guilty as you do after lying with a woman you do not love.

He climbed into the car and Shermaine sat away from him, withdrawn.

'They were so big and ugly—beautiful,' she said softly.

'We needed the meat. I didn't kill them for fun.' But he thought with a little shame, I have killed many others for fun.

'Yes,' she agreed. 'We needed the meat.'

He turned the car off the road and signalled to the truck drivers to pull in behind him.

CHAPTER 27

Later it was all right again. The meat-rich smoke from a dozen cooking fires drifted across the camp. The dark treetops silhouetted against a sky full of stars, the friendly glow of the fires, and laughter, men's voices raised, someone singing, the night noises of the bush—insects and frogs in the near-by stream—a plate piled high with grilled fillets and slabs of liver, a bottle of beer from Ruffy's hoard, the air at last cooler, a small breeze to keep the mosquitoes away, and Shermaine sitting beside him on the blankets.

Ruffy drifted across to them, in one hand a stick loaded with meat from which the juice dripped and in the other hand a bottle held by the throat.

'How's it for another beer, boss?'

'Enough.' Bruce held up his hand. 'I'm full to the back teeth.'

'You're getting old, that's for sure. Me and the boys going to finish them buffalo or burst trying.' He squatted on his great haunches and his tone changed. 'The trucks are flat, boss. Reckon there's not a bucketful of gas in the lot of them.'

'I want you to drain all the tanks, Ruffy, and pour it into the Ford.'

Ruffy nodded and bit a hunk of meat off the end of the stick.

'Then first thing tomorrow morning you and I will go on to Msapa in the Ranchero and leave everyone else here. Lieutenant Hendry will be in charge.'

'You talking about me?' Wally came from one of the fires.

'Yes, I'm going to leave you in charge here while Ruffy and I go on to Msapa Junction to fetch help.' Bruce did not look at Hendry and he had difficulty keeping the loathing out of his voice. 'Ruffy, fetch the map will you?'

They spread it on the earth and huddled round it. Ruffy held the flashlight.

'I'd say we are about here.' Bruce touched the tiny black vein of the road. 'About seventy, eighty miles to Msapa.' He ran his finger along it. 'It will take us about five hours there and back. However, if the telegraph isn't working we might have to go on until we meet a patrol or find some other way of getting a message back to Elisabethville.'

Almost parallel to the road and only two inches from it on the large-scale map ran the thick red line that marked the Northern Rhodesian border. Wally Hendry's slitty eyes narrowed even further as he looked at it.

'Why not leave Ruffy here, and I'll go with you.' Hendry looked up at Bruce.

'I want Ruffy with me to translate if we meet any Africans along the way.' Also, thought Bruce, I don't want to be left on the side of the road with a bullet in my head while you drive on to Elisabethville.

'Suits me,' grunted Hendry. He dropped his eyes to the map. About forty miles to the border. A hard day's walk.

Bruce changed to French and spoke swiftly. 'Ruffy, hide the diamonds behind the dashboard of your truck. That way we are certain they will send a rescue party, even if we have to go to Elisabethville.'

'Talk English, Bucko,' growled Hendry, but Ruffy nodded and answered, also in French.

'I will leave Sergeant Jacque to guard them.'

'NO!' said Bruce. 'Tell no one.'

'Cut it out!' rasped Hendry. 'Anything you say I want to hear.'

'We'll leave at dawn tomorrow,' Bruce reverted to English.

'May I go with you?' Shermaine spoke for the first time.

'I don't see why not.' Bruce smiled quickly at her, but Ruffy coughed awkwardly.

'Reckon that's not such a good idea, boss.'

'Why?' Bruce turned on him with his temper starting to rise.

'Well, boss,' Ruffy hesitated, and then went on, 'you, me and the lady all shoving off towards Elisabethville might not look so good to the boys. They might get ideas, think we're not coming back or something.'

Bruce was silent, considering it.

'That's right,' Hendry cut in. 'You might just take it into your head to keep going. Let her stay, sort of guarantee for the rest of us.'

'I don't mind, Bruce. I didn't think about it that way. I'll stay.'

'She'll have forty good boys looking after her, she'll be all right,' Ruffy assured Bruce.

'All right then, that's settled. It won't be for long, Shermaine.'

'I'll go and see about draining the trucks.' Ruffy stood up. 'See you in the morning, boss.'

'I'm going to get some more of that meat.' Wally picked up the map carelessly. 'Try and get some sleep tonight, Curry. Not too much grumble and grunt.'

In his exasperation, Bruce did not notice that Hendry had taken the map.

CHAPTER 28

It rained in the early hours before the dawn and Bruce lay in the back of the Ranchero and listened to it drum on the metal roof. It was a lulling sound and a good feeling to lie warmly listening to the rain with the woman you love in your arms.

He felt her waking against him, the change in her breathing and the first slow movements of her body.

There were buffalo steaks for breakfast, but no coffee. They ate swiftly and then Bruce called across to Ruffy.

'Okay, Ruffy?'

'Let's go, boss.' They climbed into the Ford and Ruffy filled most of the seat beside Bruce. His helmet perched on the back of his head, rifle sticking out through the space where the windscreen should have been, and two large feet planted securely on top of the case of beer on the floor.

Bruce twisted the key and the engine fired. He warmed it at a fast idle and turned to Hendry who leaned against the roof of the Ford and peered through the window.

'We'll be back this afternoon. Don't let anybody wander away from camp.'

'Okay.' Hendry breathed his morning breath full into Bruce's face.

'Keep them busy, otherwise they'll get bored and start fighting.'

Before he answered Hendry let his eyes search the interior of the Ford carefully and then he stood back.

'Okay,' he said again. 'On your way!'

Bruce looked beyond him to where Shermaine sat on the tailboard of a truck and smiled at her.

'Bon voyage!' she called and Bruce let out the clutch. They bumped out onto the road amid a chorus of cheerful farewells from the gendarmes round the cooking fires and Bruce settled down to drive. In the rear-view mirror he watched the camp disappear round the curve in the road. There were puddles of rain water in the road, but above them the clouds had broken up and scattered across the sky.

'How's it for a beer, boss?'

'Instead of coffee?' asked Bruce.

'Nothing like it for the bowels,' grunted Ruffy and reached down to open the case

---

Wally Hendry lifted his helmet and scratched his scalp. His short red hair felt stiff and wiry with dried sweat and there was a spot above his right ear that itched. He fingered it tenderly.

The Ranchero disappeared round a bend in the road, the trees screening it abruptly, and the hum of its motor faded.

Okay, so they haven't taken the diamonds with them. I had a bloody good look around. I guessed they'd leave them. The girl knows where they are like as not. Perhaps—no, she'd squeal like a stuck pig if I asked.

Hendry looked sideways at Shermaine; she was staring after the Ranchero.

Silly bitch! Getting all broody now that Curry's giving her the rod. Funny how these educated Johnnies like their women to have small tits —nice piece of arse though. Wouldn't mind a bit of that myself. Jesus, that would really get to Mr High Class Bloody Curry, me giving his pretty the business. Not a chance though. These niggers think he's a god or something. They'd tear me to pieces if I touched her. Forget about it! Let's get the diamonds and take off for the border.

Hendry settled his helmet back on his head and strolled casually across to the truck that Ruffy had been driving the day before.

Got a map, compass, coupla spare clips of ammo—now all we need is the glass.

He climbed into the cab and opened the cubbyhole.

Bet a pound to a pinch of dung that they've hidden them somewhere in this truck. They're not worried—think they've got me tied up here. Never occurred to them that old Uncle Wally might up and walk away. Thought I'd just sit here and wait for them to come back and fetch me— take me in and hand me over to a bunch of nigger police aching to get their hands on a white man.

Well, I got news for you, Mr Fancy-talking Curry!

He rummaged in the cubbyhole and then slammed it shut.

Okay, they're not there. Let's try under the seats. The border is not guarded, might take me three or four days to get through to Fort Rosebery, but when I do I'll have me a pocket full of diamonds and there's a direct air service out to Ndola and the rest of the world. Then we start living!

There was nothing under the seats except a greasy dust-coated jack and wheel spanner. Hendry turned his attention to the floorboards.

Pity I'll have to leave that bastard Curry. I had plans for him. There's a guy who really gets to me. So goddam cocksure of himself. One of them. Makes you feel you're shit—fancy talk, pretty face, soft hands. Christ, I hate him.

Viciously he tore the rubber mats off the floor and the dust made him cough.

Been to university, makes him think he's something special. The bastard. I should have fixed him long ago—that night at the road bridge I nearly gave it to him in the dark. Nobody would have known, just a mistake. I shouda done it then. I shoulda done it at Port Reprieve when he ran out across the road to the office block. Big bloody hero. Big lover. Bet he had everything he ever wanted, bet his Daddy gave him all the money he could use. And he looks at you like that, like you crawled out of rotting meat.

Hendry straightened up and gripped the steering wheel, his jaws chewing with the strength of his hatred. He stared out ot the windscreen.

Shermaine Cartier walked past the front of the truck. She had a towel and a pink plastic toilet bag in her hand; the pistol swung against her leg as she moved.

Sergeant Jacque stood up from the cooking fire and moved to intercept her. They talked, arguing, then Shermaine touched the pistol at her side and laughed. A worried frown creased Jacque's black face and he shook his head dubiously. Shermaine laughed again, turned from him and set off down the road towards the stream. Her hair, caught carelessly at her neck with a ribbon, hung down her back onto the rose-coloured shirt she wore and the heavy canvas holster emphasized the unconsciously provocative swing of her hips. She went out of sight down the steep bank of the stream.

Wally Hendry chuckled and then licked his lips with the quick-darting tip of his tongue.

'This is going to make it perfect,' he whispered. 'They couldn't have done things to suit me better if they'd spent a week working it out.'

Eagerly he turned back to his search for the diamonds. Leaning forward he thrust his hand up behind the dashboard of the truck and it brushed against the bunch of canvas bags that hung from the mass of concealed wires.

'Come to Uncle Wally.' He jerked them loose and, holding them in his lap, began checking their contents. The third bag he opened contained the gem stones.

'Lovely, lovely grub,' he whispered at the dull glint and sparkle in the depths of the bag. Then he closed the draw string, stuffed the bag into the pocket of his battle-jacket and buttoned the flap. He dropped the bags of industrial diamonds on the floor and kicked them under the seat, picked up his rifle and stepped down out of the truck.

Three or four gendarmes looked up curiously at him as he passed the cooking fires. Hendry rubbed his stomach and pulled a face.

'Too much meat last night!'

The gendarme who understood English laughed and translated into French. They all laughed and one of them called something in a dialect that Hendry did not understand. They watched him walk away among the trees.

As soon as he was out of sight of the camp Hendry started to run, circling back towards the stream.

'This is going to be a pleasure!' He laughed aloud.

CHAPTER 29

Fifty yards below the drift where the road crossed the stream Shermaine found a shallow pool. There were reeds with fluffy heads around it and a small beach of white river sand, black boulders, polished round and glossy smooth, the water almost blood warm and so clear that she could see a shoal of fingerlings nibbling at the green algae that coated the boulders beneath the surface.

She stood barefooted in the sand and looked around carefully, but the reeds screened her, and she had asked Jacque not to let any of his men come down to the river while she was there.

She undressed, dropped her clothes across one of the black boulders and with a cake of soap in her hand waded out into the pool and lowered herself until she sat with the water up to her neck and the sand pleasantly rough under her naked behind.

She washed her hair first and then lay stretched out with the water moving gently over her, soft as the caress of silk. Growing bold the tiny fish darted in and nibbled at her skin, tickling, so that she gasped and splashed at them.

At last she ducked her head under the surface and, with the water streaming out of her hair into her eyes, she groped her way back to the bank.

As she stooped, still half blinded, for her towel, Wally Hendry's hand closed over her mouth and his other arm circled her waist from behind.

'One squeak out of you and I'll wring your bloody neck.' He spoke hoarsely into her ear. She could smell his breath, warm and sour in her face. 'Just pretend I'm old Bruce—then both of us will enjoy it.' And he chuckled.

Sliding quickly over her hip his hand moved downwards and the shock of it galvanized her into frantic struggles. Holding her easily Hendry kept on chuckling.

She opened her mouth suddenly and one of his fingers went in between her teeth. She bit with all her strength and felt the skin break and tasted blood in her mouth.

'You bitch!' Hendry jerked his hand away and she opened her mouth to scream, but the hand swung back, clenched, into the side of her face, knocking her head across. The scream never reached her lips for he hit her again and she felt herself falling.

Stunned by the blows, lying in the sand, she could not believe it was happening, until she felt his weight upon her and his knee forced cruelly between hers.

Then she started to struggle again, trying to twist away from his mouth and the smell of his breath.

'No, no, no.' She repeated it over and over, her eyes shut tightly so he did not have to see that face above her, and her head rolling from side to side in the sand. He was so strong, so immensely powerful.

'No,' she said, and then, 'Ooah!' at the pain, the tearing stinging pain within, and the thrusting heaviness above.

And through the pounding, grunting, thrusting nightmare she could smell him and feel the sweat drip from him and splash into her up-turned unprotected face.

It lasted forever, and then suddenly the weight was gone and she opened her eyes.

He stood over her, fumbling with his clothing, and there was a dull-ness in his expression. He wiped his mouth with the back of his hand and she saw the fingers were trembling. His voice when he spoke was tired and disinterested.

'I've had better.'

Swiftly Shermaine rolled over and reached for the pistol that lay on top of her clothes. Hendry stepped forward with all his weight on her wrist and she felt the bones bend under his boot and she moaned. But through pain she whispered, 'You pig, you filthy pig', and he hit her again, flat-handed across the face, knocking her onto her back once more.

He picked up the pistol and opened it, spilling the cartridges into the sand, then he unclipped the lanyard and threw the pistol far out into the reed bed.

'Tell Curry I say he can have my share of you,' he said and walked quickly away among the reeds.

The white sand coated her damp body like icing sugar. She sat up slowly, holding her wrist, the side of her face inflamed and starting to swell where he had hit her.

She started to cry, shaking silently, and the tears squeezed out between her eyelids and matted her long dark lashes.

CHAPTER 30

Ruffy held up the brown bottle and inspected it ruefully.

'Seems like one mouthful and it's empty.' He threw the bottle out of the side window. It hit a tree and burst with a small pop.

'We can always find our way back by following the empties,' smiled Bruce, once more marvelling at the man's capacity. But there was plenty of storage space. He watched Ruffy's stomach spread onto his lap as he reached down to the beer crate.

'How we doing, boss?'

Bruce glanced at the milometer.

'We've come eighty-seven miles,' and Ruffy nodded.

'Not bad going. Be there pretty soon now.'

They were silent. The wind blew in onto them through the open front. The grass that grew between the tracks brushed the bottom of the chassis with a continuous rushing sound.

'Boss—' Ruffy spoke at last.

'Yes?'

'Lieutenant Hendry—those diamonds. You reckon we did a good thing leaving him there?'

'He's stranded in the middle of the bush. Even if he did find them they wouldn't do him much good.'

'Suppose that's right.' Ruffy lifted the beer bottle to his lips and when he lowered it he went on. 'Mind you, that's one guy you can never be sure of.' He tapped his head with a finger as thick and as black as a blood-sausage. 'Something wrong with him—he's one of the maddest Arabs I've found in a long time of looking.'

Bruce grunted grimly.

'You want to be careful there, boss,' observed Ruffy. 'Any time now he's going to try for you. I've seen it coming. He's working himself up to it. He's a mad Arab.'

'I'll watch him,' said Bruce.

'Yeah, you do that.'

Again they were silent in the steady swish of the wind and the drone of the motor.

'There's the railway.' Ruffy pointed to the blue-gravelled embankment through the trees.

'Nearly there,' said Bruce.

They came out into another open glade and beyond it the water tank at Msapa Junction stuck up above the forest.

'Here we are,' said Ruffy and drained the bottle in his hand.

'Just say a prayer that the telegraph lines are still up and that there's an operator on the Elisabethville end.'

Bruce slowed the Ford past the row of cottages. They were exactly as he remembered them, deserted and forlorn. The corners of his mouth were compressed into a hard angle as he looked at the two small mounds of earth beneath the casia flora trees. Ruffy looked at them also but neither of them spoke.

Bruce stopped the Ford outside the station building and they climbed out stiffly and walked together onto the veranda. The wooden flooring echoed dully under their boots as they made for the door of the office.

Bruce pushed the door open and looked in. The walls were painted a depressing utility green, loose paper was scattered on the floor, the drawers of the single desk hung open, and a thin grey skin of dust coated everything.

'There she is,' said Ruffy and pointed to the brass and varnished wood complexity of the telegraph on a table against the far wall.

'Looks all right,' said Bruce. 'As long as the lines haven't been cut.'

As if to reassure him, the telegraph began to clatter like a typewriter.

'Thank God for that,' sighed Bruce.

They walked across to the table.

'You know how to work this thing?' asked Ruffy.

'Sort of,' Bruce answered and set his rifle against the wall. He was relieved to see a Morse table stuck with adhesive tape to the wall above the apparatus. It was a long time since he had memorized it as a boy scout.

He laid his hand on the transmission key and studied the table. The call sign for Elisabethville was 'EE'.

He tapped it out clumsily and then waited. Almost immediately the set clattered back at him, much too fast to be intelligible and the roll of paper in the repeater was exhausted. Bruce took off his helmet and laboriously spelled out, 'Transmit slower'.

It was a long business with requests for repetition. 'Not understood' was made nearly every second signal, but finally Bruce got the operator to understand that he had an urgent message for Colonel Franklyn of President Tschombe's staff.

'Wait,' came back the laconic signal.

And they waited. They waited an hour, then two.

'That mad bastard's forgotten about us,' grumbled Ruffy and went to the Ford to fetch the beer crate. Bruce fidgeted restlessly on the un-padded chair beside the telegraph table. He reconsidered anxiously all his previous arguments for leaving Wally Hendry in charge of the camp, but once again decided that it was safe. He couldn't do much harm. Unless, unless, Shermaine! No, it was impossible. Not with forty loyal gendarmes to protect her.

He started to think about Shermaine and the future. There was a year's mercenary captain's pay accumulated in the Crédit Banque Suisse at Zurich. He made the conversion from francs to pounds—about two and a half thousand. Two years' operating capital, so they could have a holiday before he started working again. They could take a chalet up in the mountains—there should be good snow this time of the year.

Bruce grinned. Snow that crunched like sugar, and a twelve-inch-thick eiderdown on the bed at night.

Life had purpose and direction again.

'What you laughing at, boss?' asked Ruffy.

'I was thinking about a bed.'

'Yeah? That's a good thing to think about. You start there, you're born there, you spend most of your life in it, you have plenty of fun in it, and if you're lucky you die there. How's it for a beer?'

The telegraph came to life at Bruce's elbow. He turned to it quickly.

'Curry—Franklyn,' it clattered. Bruce could imagine the wiry, red-faced little man at the other end. Ex-major in the third brigade of the Legion. A prime mover in the O.A.S., with a sizeable price still on his head from the De Gaulle assassination attempt.

'Franklyn—Curry,' Bruce tapped back. 'Train unserviceable. Motorized transport stranded without fuel. Port Reprieve road. Map reference approx—' He read the numbers off the sheet on which he had noted them.

There was a long pause, then:

'Is U.M.C. property in your hands?' The question was delicately phrased.

'Affirmative,' Bruce assured him.

'Await air-drop at your position soonest. Out.'

'Message understood. Out.' Bruce straightened from the telegraph and sighed with relief.

'That's that, Ruffy. They'll drop gas to us from one of the Dakotas. Probably tomorrow morning.' He looked at his wrist watch. 'Twenty to one, let's get back.'

Bruce hummed softly, watching the double tracks ahead of him, guiding the Ford with a light touch on the wheel.

He was contented. It was all over. Tomorrow the fuel would drop from the Dakota under those yellow parachutes. (He must lay out the smudge signals this evening.) And ten hours later they would be back in Elisabethville.

A few words with Carl Engelbrecht would fix seats for Shermaine and himself on one of the outward-bound Daks. Then Switzerland, and the chalet with icicles hanging from the eaves. A long rest while he decided where to start again. Louisiana was under Roman–Dutch Law, or was it Code Napoléon? He might even have to rewrite his bar examinations, but the prospect pleased rather than dismayed him. It was fun again.

'Never seen you so happy,' grunted Ruffy.

'Never had so much cause,' Bruce agreed.

'She's a swell lady. Young still—you can teach her.'

Bruce felt his hackles rise, and then he thought better of it and laughed.

'You going to sign her up, boss?'

'I might.'

Ruffy nodded wisely. 'Man should have plenty wives—I got three. Need a couple more.'

'One I could only just handle.'

'One's difficult. Two's easier. Three, you can relax. Four, they're so busy with each other they don't give you no trouble at all.'

'I might try it.'

'Yeah, you do that.'

And ahead of them through the trees they saw the ring of trucks.

'We're home,' grunted Ruffy, then he stirred uncomfortably in his seat. 'Something going on.'

Men stood in small groups. There was something in their attitude: strain, apprehension. Two men ran up the road to meet them. Bruce could see their mouths working, but could not hear the words.

Dread, heavy and cold, pushed down on the pit of Bruce's gut.

Gabbled, incoherent, Sergeant Jacque was trying to tell him something as he ran beside the Ford.

''Tenent Hendry—the river—the madame—gone.' French words like driftwood in the torrent of dialect.

'Your girl,' translated Ruffy. 'Hendry's done her.'

'Dead?' The question dropped from Bruce's mouth.

'No. He's hurt her. He's—you know!'

'Where is she?'

'They've got her in the back of the truck.'

Bruce climbed heavily out of the car. Now they were silent, grouped together, not looking at him, faces impassive, waiting.

Bruce walked slowly to the truck. He felt cold and numb. His legs moved automatically beneath him. He drew back the canvas and pulled himself up into the interior. It was an effort to move forward, to focus his eyes in the gloom.

Wrapped in a blanket she lay small and still.

'Shermaine.' It stuck in his throat.

'Shermaine,' he said again and knelt beside her. A great livid swelling distorted the side of her face. She did not turn her head to him, but lay staring up at the canvas roof.

He touched her face and the skin was cold, cold as the dread that gripped his stomach. The coldness of it shocked him so he jerked his hand away.

'Shermaine.' This time it was a sob. The eyes, her big haunted eyes, turned unseeing towards him and he felt the lift of escape from the certainty of her death.

'Oh, God,' he cried and took her to him, holding the unresisting frailty of her to his chest. He could feel the slow even thump of her heart beneath his hand. He drew back the blanket and there was no blood.

'Darling, are you hurt? Tell me, are you hurt?' She did not answer. She lay quietly in his arms, not seeing him.

'Shock,' he whispered. 'It's only shock,' and he opened her clothing. With tenderness he examined the smoothly pale body; the skin was clammy and damp, but there was no damage.

He wrapped her again and laid her gently back on the floor.

He stood and the thing within him changed shape. Cold still, but now burning cold as dry ice.

Ruffy and Jacque were waiting for him beside the tailboard.

'Where is he?' asked Bruce softly.

'He is gone.'

'Where?'

'That way.' Jacque pointed towards the south-east. 'I followed the spoor a short distance.'

Bruce walked to the Ford and picked up his rifle from the floor. He opened the cubbyhole and took two spare clips of ammunition from it.

Ruffy followed him. 'He's got the diamonds, boss.'

'Yes,' said Bruce and checked the load of his rifle. The diamonds were of no importance.

'Are you going after him, boss?'

Bruce did not answer. Instead he looked up at the sky. The sun was half way towards the horizon and there were clouds thickly massed around it.

'Ruffy, stay with her,' he said softly. 'Keep her warm.'

Ruffy nodded.

'Who is the best tracker we've got?'

'Jacque. Worked for a safari outfit before the war as a tracker boy.'

Bruce turned to Jacque. The thing was still icy cold inside him, with tentacles that spread out to every extremity of his body and his mind.

'When did this happen?'

'About an hour after you left,' answered Jacque.

Eight hours start. It was a long lead.

'Take the spoor,' said Bruce softly.

CHAPTER 31

The earth was soft from the night's rain and the spoor deep trodden, the heels had bitten in under Hendry's weight, so they followed fast.

Watching Sergeant Jacque work, Bruce felt his anxiety abating, for although the footprints were so easy to follow in these early stages that it was no test of his ability, yet from the way he moved swiftly along—half-crouched and wholly absorbed, occasionally glancing ahead to pick up the run of the spoor, stooping now and then to touch the earth and determine its texture—Bruce could tell that this man knew his business.

Through the open forest with tufted grass below, holding steadily south by east, Hendry led them straight towards the Rhodesian border. And after the first two hours Bruce knew they had not gained upon him. him. Hendry was still eight hours ahead, and at the pace he was setting eight hours' start was something like thirty miles in distance.

Bruce looked over his shoulder at the sun where it lay wedged between two vast piles of cumulus nimbus. There in the sky were the two elements which could defeat him.

Time. There were perhaps two more hours of daylight. With the onset of night they would be forced to halt.

Rain. The clouds were swollen and dark blue round the edges. As Bruce watched, the lightning lit them internally, and at a count of ten the thunder grumbled suddenly. If it rained again before morning there would be no spoor to follow.

'We must move faster,' said Bruce.

Sergeant Jacque straightened up and looked at Bruce as though he were a stranger. He had forgotten his existence.

'The earth hardens.' Jacque pointed at the spoor and Bruce saw that in the last half hour the soil had become gritty and compacted. Hendry's heels no longer broke the crust. 'It is unwise to run on such a lean trail.'

Again Bruce looked back at the menace of gathering clouds.

'We must take the chance,' he decided.

'As you wish,' grunted Jacque, and transferred his rifle to his other shoulder, hitched up his belt and settled the steel helmet more firmly on his head.

'Allez!'

They trotted on through the forest towards the south-east. Within a mile Bruce's body had settled into the automatic rhythm of his run, leaving his mind free.

He thought about Wally Hendry, saw again the little eyes and round them the puffy folded skin, and the mouth below, thin and merciless, the obscene ginger stubble of beard. He could almost smell him. His nostrils flared at the memory of the red-hand's rank body odour. Unclean, he thought, unclean mind and unclean body.

His hatred of Wally Hendry was a tangible thing. He could feel it sitting heavily at the base of his throat, tingling in his finger tips and giving strength to his legs.

And yet there was something else. Suddenly Bruce grinned: a wolfish baring of his teeth. That tingling in his finger tips was not all hatred, a little of it was excitement.

What a complex thing is a man, he thought. He can never hold one emotion—always there are others to confuse it. Here I am hunting the thing that I most loathe and hate, and I am enjoying it. Completely unrelated to the hatred is the thrill of hunting the most dangerous and cunning game of all, man.

I have always enjoyed the chase, he thought. It has been bred into me, for my blood is that of the men who hunted and fought with Africa as the prize.

The hunting of this man will give me pleasure. If ever a man deserved to die, it is Wally Hendry. I am the plaintiff, the judge and the executioner.

Sergeant Jacque stopped so suddenly that Bruce ran into him and they nearly fell.

'What is it?' panted Bruce, coming back to reality.

'Look!'

The earth ahead of them was churned and broken.

'Zebra,' groaned Bruce, recognizing the round uncloven hoof prints. 'God damn it to hell—of all the filthy luck!'

'A big herd,' Jacque agreed. 'Spread out. Feeding.'

As far ahead as they could see through the forest the herd had wiped out Hendry's tracks.

'We'll have to cast forward.' Bruce's voice was agonized by his impatience. He turned to the nearest tree and hacked at it with his bayonet, blazing it to mark the end of the trail, swearing softly, venting his disappointment on the trunk.

'Only another hour to sunset,' he whispered. 'Please let us pick him up again before dark.

Sergeant Jacque was already moving forward, following the approximate line of Hendry's travel, trying vainly to recognize a single footprint through the havoc created there by the passage of thousands of hooves. Bruce hurried to join him and then moved out on his flank. They zigzagged slowly ahead, almost meeting on the inward leg of each tack and then separating again to a distance of a hundred yards.

There it was! Bruce dropped to his knees to make sure. Just the outline of the toecap showing from under the spoor of an old zebra stallion. Bruce whistled, a windy sound through his dry lips, and Jacque came quickly. One quick look, then:

'Yes, he is holding more to the right now.' He raised his eyes and squinted ahead, marking a tree which was directly in line with the run of the spoor. They went forward.

'There's the herd.' Bruce pointed at the flicker of a grey body through the trees.

'They've got our wind.'

A zebra snorted and then there was a rumbling, a low blurred drumming of hooves as the herd ran. Through the trees Bruce caught glimpses of the animals on the near side of the herd. Too far off to show the stripes, looking like fat grey ponies as they galloped, ears up, blackmaned heads nodding. Then they were gone and the sound of their flight dwindled.

'At least they haven't run along the spoor,' muttered Bruce, and then bitterly: 'Damn them, the stupid little donkeys! They've cost us an hour. A whole priceless hour.'

Desperately searching, wild with haste, they worked back and forth. The sun was below the trees; already the air was cooling in the short African dusk. Another fifteen minutes and it would be dark.

Then abruptly the forest ended and they came out on the edge of a vlei. Open as wheatland, pastured with green waist-high grass, hemmed in by the forest, it stretched ahead of them for nearly two miles. Dotted along it were clumps of ivory palms with each graceful stem ending in an untidy cluster of leaves. Troops of guinea-fowls were scratching and chirruping along the edge of the clearing, and near the far end a herd of buffalo formed a dark mass as they grazed beneath a canopy of white egrets.

In the forest beyond the clearing, rising perhaps three hundred feet out of it, stood a kopje of tumbled granite. The great slabs of rock with their sheer sides and square tops looked like a ruined castle. The low sun struck it and gave the rock an orange warmth.

But Bruce had no time to admire the scene; his eyes were on the earth, searching for the prints of Hendry's jungle boots.

Out on his left Sergeant Jacque whistled sharply and Bruce felt the leap of excitement in his chest. He ran across to the crouching gendarme.

'It has come away.' Jacque pointed at the spoor that was strung ahead of them like beads on a string, skirting the edge of the vlei, each depression filled with shadow and standing out clearly on the sandy grey earth.

'Too late,' groaned Bruce. 'Damn those bloody zebra.' The light was fading so swiftly it seemed as though it were a stage effect.

'Follow it.' Bruce's voice was sharp with helpless frustration. 'Follow it as long as you can.'

It was not a quarter of a mile farther on that Jacque rose out of his and only the white of his teeth showed in the darkness as he spoke.

'We will lose it again if we go on.'

'All right.' Bruce unslung his rifle with weary resignation. He knew that Wally Hendry was at least forty miles ahead of them; more if he kept travelling after dark. The spoor was cold. If this had been an ordinary hunt he would long ago have broken off the chase.

He looked up at the sky. In the north the stars were fat and yellow, but above them and to the south it was black with cloud.

'Don't let it rain,' he whispered. 'Please God, don't let it rain.'

The night was long. Bruce slept once for perhaps two hours and then the strength of his hatred woke him. He lay flat upon his back and stared up at the sky. It was all dark with clouds; only occasionally they opened and let the stars shine briefly through.

'It must not rain. It must not rain.' He repeated it like a prayer, staring up at the dark sky, concentrating upon it as though by the force of his mind he could control the elements.

There were lions hunting in the forest. He heard the male roaring, moving up from the south, and once his two lionesses answered him. They killed a little before dawn and Bruce lay on the hard earth and listened to their jubilation over the kill. Then there was silence as they began to feed.

That I might have success as well, he thought. I do not often ask for favours, Lord, but grant me this one. I ask it not only for myself but for Shermaine and the others.

In his mind he saw again the two children lying where Hendry had shot them. The smear of mingled blood and chocolate across the boy's cheek.

He deserves to die, prayed Bruce, so please don't let it rain.

As long as the night had been, that quickly came the dawn. A grey dawn, gloomy with low cloud.

'Will it go?' Bruce asked for the twentieth time, and this time Jacque looked up from where he knelt beside the spoor.

'We can try now.'

They moved off slowly with Jacque leading, doubled over to peer short-sightedly at the earth and Bruce close behind him, bedevilled by his impatience and anxiety, lifting his head every dozen paces to the dirty grey roof of cloud.

The light strengthened and the circle of their vision opened from six feet to as many yards, to a hundred, so they could make out the tops of the ivory palms, shaggy against the grey cloud.

Jacque broke into a trot and ahead of them was the end of the clearing and the beginning of the forest. Two hundred yards beyond rose the massive pile of the kopje, in the early light looking more than ever like a castle, turreted and sheer. There was something formidable in its outline. It seemed to brood above them and Bruce looked away from it uneasily.

Cold and with enough weight behind it to sting, the first raindrop splashed against Bruce's cheek.

'Oh, no!' he protested, and stopped. Jacque straightened up from the spoor and he too looked at the sky.

'It is finished. In five minutes there will be nothing to follow.'

Another drop hit Bruce's upturned face and he blinked back the tears of anger and frustration that pricked the rims of his eyelids.

Faster now, tapping on his helmet, plopping onto his shoulders and face, the rain fell.

'Quickly,' cried Bruce. 'Follow as long as you can.'

Jacque opened his mouth to speak, but before a word came out he was flung backwards, punched over as though by an invisible fist, his helmet flying from his head as he fell and his rifle clattering on the earth.

Simultaneously Bruce felt the bullet pass him, disrupting the air, so the wind of it flattened his shirt against his chest, cracking viciously in his ears, leaving him dazedly looking down at Sergeant Jacque's body.

It lay with arms thrown wide, the jaw and the side of the head below the ear torn away, white bone and blood bubbling over it. The trunk twitched convulsively and the hands fluttered like trapped birds. Then flat-sounding through the rain he heard the report of the rifle.

The kopje, screamed Bruce's brain, *he's lying in the kopje!*

And Bruce moved, twisting sideways, starting to run.

CHAPTER 32

Wally Hendry lay on his stomach on the flat top of the turret. His body was stiff and chilled from the cold of the night and the rock was harsh under him, but the discomfort hardly penetrated the fringe of his mind. He had built a low parapet with loose flakes of granite, and he had screened the front of it with the thick bushy stems of broom bush.

His rifle was propped on the parapet in front of him and at his elbow were the spare ammunition clips.

He had lain in this ambush for a long time now—since early the preceding afternoon. Now it was dawn and the darkness was drawing back; in a few minutes he would be able to see the whole of the clearing below him.

I coulda been across the river already, he thought, *coulda been fifty miles away*. He did not attempt to analyse the impulse that had made him lie here unmoving for almost twenty hours.

Man, I knew old Curry would have to come. I knew he would only bring one nigger tracker with him. These educated Johnnies got their own rules—man to man stuff, and he chuckled as he remembered the two minute figures that he had seen come out of the forest in the fading light of the previous evening.

The bastard spent the night down there in the clearing. Saw him light a match and have himself a smoke in the night—well, I hope he enjoyed it, his last.

Wally peered anxiously out into the gradually gathering dawn.

They'll be moving now, coming up the clearing. Must get them before they reach the trees again. Below him the clearing showed as a paleness, a leprous blotch, on the dark forest.

The bastard! Without preliminaries Hendry's hatred returned to him. *This time he don't get to make no fancy speeches. This time he don't get no chance to be hoity-toity.*

The light was stronger now. He could see the clumps of ivory palms against the pale brown grass of the clearing.

'Ha!' Hendry exclaimed.

There they were, like two little ants, dark specks moving up the middle of the clearing. The tip of Hendry's tongue slipped out between his lips and he flattened down behind his rifle.

Man, I've waited for this. Six months now I've thought about this. And when it's finished I'll go down and take his ears. He slipped the safety catch; it made a satisfying mechanical click.

Nigger's leading, that's Curry behind him. Have to wait till they turn, don't want the nigger to get it first. Curry first, then the nigger.

He picked them up in his sights, breathing quicker, the thrill of it so intense that he had to swallow and it caught in his throat like dry bread.

A raindrop hit the back of his neck. It startled him. He looked up quickly at the sky and saw it coming.

'Goddam it,' he groaned, and looked back at the clearing. Curry and the nigger were standing together, a single dark blob in the half-light. There was no chance of separating them. The rain fell faster, and suddenly Hendry was overwhelmed by the old familiar feeling of inferiority; of knowing that everything, even the elements, conspired against him; the knowledge that he could never win, not even this once.

They, God and the rest of the world.

The ones who had given him a drunk for a father.

A squalid cottage for a home and a mother with cancer of the throat.

The ones who had sent him to reform school, had fired him from two dozen jobs, had pushed him, laughed at him, gaoled him twice—They, all of them (and Bruce Curry who was their figurehead), they were going to win again. Not even this once, not even ever.

'Goddam it,' he cursed in hopeless, wordless anger against them all.

'Goddam it, goddam it to hell,' and he fired at the dark blob in his sights.

CHAPTER 33

As he ran Bruce looked across a hundred yards of open ground to the edge of the forest.

He felt the wind of the next bullet as it cracked past him.

If he uses rapid fire he'll get me even at three hundred yards.

And Bruce jinked his run like a jack-rabbit, the blood roaring in his ears, fear driving his feet.

Then all around him the air burst asunder, buffeting him so he staggered; the vicious whip-whip-whip of bullets filled his head.

I can't make it.

Seventy yards to the shelter of the trees. Seventy yards of open meadow land, and above him the commanding mass of the kopje.

The next burst is for me—it must come, now!

And he flung himself to one side so violently that he nearly fell. Again the air was ripping to tatters close beside him.

I can't last! He must get me!

In his path was an ant-heap, a low pile of clay, a pimple on the open expanse of earth. Bruce dived for it, hitting the ground so hard that the wind was forced from his lungs out through his open mouth.

The next burst of gunfire kicked lumps of clay from the top of the ant-heap, showering Bruce's back.

He lay with his face pressed into the earth, wheezing with the agony of empty lungs, flattening his body behind the tiny heap of clay.

Will it cover me? Is there enough of it?

And the next hail of bullets thumped into the ant-heap, throwing fountains of earth, but leaving Bruce untouched.

I'm safe. The realization came with a surge that washed away his fear.

But I'm helpless, answered his hatred. *Pinned to the earth for as long as Hendry wants to keep me here.*

The rain fell on his back, soaking through his jacket, coldly caressing the nape of his neck and dribbling down over his jaws.

He rolled his head sideways, not daring to lift it an inch, and the rain beat onto the side of his face.

The rain! Falling faster. Thickening. Hanging from the clouds like the skirts of a woman's dress.

Curtains of rain. Greying out the edge of the forest, leaving no solid shapes in the mist of falling liquid mother-of-pearl.

Still gasping but with the pain slowly receding, Bruce lifted his head.

The kopje was a vague blue-green shape ahead of him, then it was gone, swallowed by the eddying columns of rain.

Bruce pushed himself up onto his knees and the pain in his chest made him dizzy.

Now! he thought. *Now, before it thins*, and he lumbered clumsily to his feet.

For a moment he stood clutching his chest, sucking for breath in the haze of water-filled air, and then he staggered towards the edge of the forest.

His feet steadied under him, his breathing eased, and he was into the trees.

They closed round him protectively. He leaned against the rough back of one of them and wiped the rain from his face with the palm of his hand. The strength came back to him and with it his hatred and his excitement.

He unslung the rifle from his shoulder and stood away from the tree with his feet planted wide apart.

'Now, my friend,' he whispered, 'we fight on equal terms.' He pumped a round into the chamber of the FN and moved towards the kopje, stepping daintily, the weight of the rifle in his hands, his mind suddenly sharp and clear, vision enhanced, feeling his strength and the absence of fear like a song within him, a battle hymn.

He made out the loom of the kopje through the dripping rain-heavy trees and he circled out to the right. *There is plenty of time*, he thought. *I can afford to case the joint thoroughly.* He completed his circuit of the rock pile.

The kopje, he found, was the shape of a galleon sinking by the head. At one end the high double castles of the poop, from which the main deck canted steeply forward as though the prow were already under water. This slope was scattered with boulders and densely covered with dwarf scrub, an interwoven mass of shoulder-high branches and leaves.

Bruce squatted on his haunches with the rifle in his lap and looked up the ramp at the twin turrets of the kopje. The rain had slackened to a drizzle.

Hendry was on top. Bruce knew he would go to the highest point. Strange how height makes a man feel invulnerable, makes him think he is a god.

And since he had fired upon them he must be in the turret nearest the vlei, which was slightly the higher of the two, its summit crowned by a patch of stunted broom bush.

So now I know exactly where he is and I will wait half an hour. He may become impatient and move; if he does I will get a shot at him from here.

Bruce narrowed his eyes, judging the distance. About two hundred yards.

He adjusted the rear-sight of the FN and then checked the load, felt in the side pocket of his jacket to make sure the two extra clips of ammunition were handy, and settled back comfortably to wait.

'Curry, you sonofabitch, where are you?' Hendry's shout floated down through the drizzling rain and Bruce stiffened. *I was right—he's on top of the left-hand turret.*

'Come on, Bucko. I've been waiting for you since yesterday afternoon.'

Bruce lifted the rifle and sighted experimentally at a dark patch on the wall of the rock. It would be difficult shooting in the rain, the rifle slippery with wet, the fine drizzle clinging to his eyebrows and dewing the sights of the rifle with little beads of moisture.

'Hey, Curry, how's your little French piece of pussy? Man, she's hot, that thing, isn't she?'

Bruce's hands tightened on the rifle.

'Did she tell you how I gave her the old business? Did she tell you how she loved it? You should have heard her panting like a steam engine. I'm telling you, Curry, she just couldn't get enough!'

Bruce felt himself start to tremble. He clenched his jaws, biting down until his teeth ached.

Steady, Bruce my boy, that's what he wants you to do.

The trees dripped steadily in the silence and a gust of wind stirred the scrub on the slope of the kopje. Bruce waited, straining his eyes for the first hint of movement on the left-hand turret.

'You yellow or something, Curry? You scared to come on up here? Is that what it is?'

Bruce shifted his position slightly, ready for a snap shot.

'Okay, Bucko. I can wait, I've got all day. I'll just sit here thinking about how I mucked your little bit of French. I'm telling you it was something to remember. Up and down, in and out, man it was something!'

Bruce came carefully up onto his feet behind the trunk of the tree and once more studied the layout of the kopje.

If I can move up the slope, keeping well over to the side, until I reach the right-hand turret, there's a ledge there that will take me to the top. I'll be twenty or thirty feet from him, and at that range it will all be over in a few seconds.

He drew a deep breath and left the shelter of the tree.

Wally Hendry spotted the movement in the forest below him; it was a flash of brown quickly gone, too fast to get a bead on it.

He wiped the rain off his face and wriggled a foot closer to the edge.

'Come on, Curry. Let's stop buggering about,' he shouted, and cuddled the butt of his rifle into his shoulder. The tip of his tongue kept darting out and touching his lips.

At the foot of the slope he saw a branch move slightly, stirring when there was no wind. He grinned and snuggled his hips down onto the rock. *Here he comes,* he gloated, *he's crawling up, under the scrub.*

'I know you're sitting down there. Okay, Curry, I can wait also.'

Half way up the slope the top leaves of another bush swayed gently, parting and closing.

'Yes!' whispered Wally, 'Yes!' and he clicked off the safety catch of the rifle. His tongue came out and moved slowly from one corner of his mouth to the other.

I've got him, for sure! There—he'll have to cross that piece of open ground. A couple of yards, that's all. But it'll be enough.

He moved again, wriggling a few inches to one side, settling his aim into the gap between two large grey boulders; he pushed the rate-of-fire selector onto rapid and his forefinger rested lightly on the trigger.

'Hey, Curry, I'm getting bored. If you are not going to come up, how about singing to me or cracking a few jokes?'

Bruce Curry crouched behind a large grey boulder. In front of him were three yards of open ground and then the shelter of another rock. He was almost at the top of the slope and Hendry had not spotted him. Across the patch of open ground was good cover to the foot of the right-hand turret.

It would take him two seconds to cross and the chances were that Hendry would be watching the forest at the foot of the slope.

He gathered himself like a sprinter on the starting blocks.

'Go!' he whispered and dived into the opening, and into a hell storm of bullets. One struck his rifle, tearing it out of his hand with such force that his arm was paralysed to the shoulder, another stung his chest, and then he was across. He lay behind the far boulder, gasping with the shock, and listened to Hendry's voice roaring triumphantly.

'Fooled you, you stupid bastard! Been watching you all the way up from the bottom.'

Bruce held his left arm against his stomach; the use of it was returning as the numbness subsided, but with it came the ache. The top joint of his thumb had caught in the trigger guard and been torn off; now the blood well out of the stump thickly and slowly, dark blood the colour of apple jelly. With his right hand he groped for his handkerchief.

'Hey, Curry, your rifle's lying there in the open. You might need it in a few minutes. Why don't you go out and fetch it?'

Bruce bound the handkerchief tightly round the stump of his thumb and the bleeding slowed. Then he looked at the rifle where it lay ten feet away. The foresight had been knocked off, and the same bullet that had amputated his thumb had smashed into the breech, buckled the loading handle and the slide. He knew that it was damaged beyond repair.

'Think I'll have me a little target practice,' shouted Hendry from above, and again there was a burst of automatic fire. Bruce's rifle disappeared in a cloud of dust and flying rock fragments and when it cleared the woodwork of the rifle was splintered and torn and there was further damage to the action.

Well, that's that, thought Bruce, *rifle's wrecked, Shermaine has the pistol, and I have only one good hand. This is going to be interesting.*

He unbuttoned the front of his jacket and examined the welt that the bullet had raised across his chest. It looked like a rope burn, painful and red, but not serious. He rebuttoned the jacket.

'Okay, Bruce Baby, the time for games is over. I'm coming down to get you.' Hendry's voice was harsh and loud, filled with confidence.

Bruce rallied under the goading of it. He looked round quickly. *Which way to go? Climb high so he must come up to get at you. Take the right-hand turret, work round the side of it and wait for him on the top.*

In haste now, spurred by the dread of being the hunted, he scrambled to his feet and dodged away up the slope, keeping his head down, using the thick screen of rock and vegetation.

He reached the wall of the right-hand turret and followed it round, found the spiral ledge that he had seen from below and went onto it, up along it like a fly on a wall, completely exposed, keeping his back to the cliff of granite, shuffling sideways up the eighteen-inch ledge with the drop below him growing deeper with each step.

Now he was three hundred feet above the forest and could look out across the dark green land to another row of kopjes on the horizon. The rain had ceased but the cloud was unbroken, covering the sky.

The ledge widened, became a platform and Bruce hurried across it round the far shoulder and came to a dead end. The ledge had petered out and there was only the drop below. He had trapped himself on the side of the turret—the summit was unattainable. If Hendry descended to the forest floor and circled the kopje he would find Bruce completely at his mercy, for there was no cover on the narrow ledge. Hendry could have a little more target practice.

Bruce leaned against the rock and struggled to control his breathing. His throat was clogged with the thick saliva of exhaustion and fear. He felt tired and helpless, his thumb throbbed painfully and he lifted it to examine it once more. Despite the tourniquet it was bleeding slowly, a wine-red drop at a time.

Bleeding! Bruce swallowed the thick gluey stuff in his throat and looked back along the way he had come. On the grey rock the bright red splashes stood out clearly. He had laid a blood spoor for Hendry to follow.

All right then, perhaps it is best this way. At least I may be able to come to grips with him. If I wait behind this shoulder until he starts to cross the platform, there's a three hundred foot drop on one side, I may be able to rush him and throw him off.

Bruce leaned against the shoulder of granite, hidden from the platform, and tuned his ears to catch the first sound of Hendry's approach.

The clouds parted in the eastern sector of the sky and the sun shone through, slanting across the side of the kopje.

It will be better to die in the sun, thought Bruce, *a sacrifice to the sun god thrown from the roof of the temple*, and he grinned without mirth, waiting with patience and with pain.

The minutes fell like drops into the pool of time, slowly measuring out the ration of life that had been allotted to him. The pulse in his ears counted also, and this breath that he drew and held and gently exhaled —how many more would there be?

I should pray, he thought, *but after this morning when I prayed that it should not rain, and the rains came and saved me, I will not presume again to tell the Old Man how to run things. Perhaps he knows best after all.*

Thy will be done, he thought instead, and suddenly his nerves jerked tight as a line hit by a marlin. The sound he had heard was that of cloth brushing against rough rock.

He held his breath and listened, but all he could discern was the pulse in his ears and the wind in the trees of the forest below. The wind was a lonely sound.

Thy will be done, he repeated without breathing, and heard Hendry breathe close behind the shoulder of rock.

He stood away from the wall and waited. Then he saw Hendry's shadow thrown by the early morning sun along the ledge. A great distorted shadow on the grey rock.

Thy will be done. And he went round the shoulder fast, his good hand held like a blade and the weight of his body behind it.

Hendry was three feet away, the rifle at high port across his chest, standing close in against the cliff, the cup-shaped steel helmet pulled low over the slitty eyes and little beads of sweat clinging in the red-gold stubble of his beard. He tried to drop the muzzle of the rifle but Bruce was too close.

Bruce lunged with stiff fingers at his throat and he felt the crackle and give of cartilage. Then he weight carried him on and Hendry sprawled backwards onto the stone platform with Bruce on top of him.

The rifle slithered across the rock and dropped over the edge, and they lay chest to chest with legs locked together in a horrible parody of the love act. But in *this* act we do not procreate, we destroy!

Hendry's face was purple and swollen above his damaged throat, his mouth open as he struggled for air, and his breath smelt old and sour in Bruce's face.

With a twist towards the thumb Bruce freed his right wrist from Hendry's grip and, lifting it like an axe, brought it down across the bridge of Hendry's nose. Twin jets of blood spouted from the nostrils and gushed into his open mouth.

With a wet strangling sound in his throat Hendry's body arched violently upwards and Bruce was thrown back against the side of the cliff with such force that for a second he lay there.

Wally was on his knees, facing Bruce, his eyes glazed and sightless, and the strangling rattling sound spraying from his throat in a pink cloud of blood. With both hands he was fumbling his pistol out of its canvas holster.

Bruce drew his knees up to his chest, then straightened his legs in a mule kick. His feet landed together in the centre of Hendry's stomach, throwing him backwards off the platform. Hendry made that strangled bellow all the way to the bottom, but at the end it was cut off abruptly, and afterwards there was only the sound of the wind in the forest below.

For a long time, drained of strength and the power to think, Bruce sat on the ledge with his back against the rock.

Above him the clouds had rolled aside and half the sky was blue. He looked out across the land and the forest was lush and clean from the rain. *And I am still alive.* The realization warmed Bruce's mind as comfortably as the early sun was warming his body. He wanted to shout it out across the forest. *I am still alive!*

At last he stood up, crossed to the edge of the cliff and looked down at the tiny crumpled figure on the rocks below. Then he turned away and dragged his beaten body down the side of the turret.

It took him twenty minutes to find Wally Hendry in the chaos of broken rock and scrub below the turret. He lay on his side with his legs drawn up as though he slept. Bruce knelt beside him and drew his pistol from the olive-green canvas holster; then he unbuttoned the flap of Hendry's bulging breast pocket and took out the white canvas bag.

He stood up, opened the mouth of the bag and stirred the diamonds with his forefinger. Satisfied, he jerked the draw string closed and dropped them into his own pocket.

In death he is even more repulsive than he was alive, thought Bruce without regret as he looked down at the corpse.

The flies were crawling into the bloody nostrils and clustering round the eyes.

Then he spoke aloud.

'So Mike Haig was right and I was wrong—you can destroy it.'

Without looking back he walked away. The tiredness left him.

CHAPTER 34

Carl Engelbrecht came through the doorway from the cockpit into the main cabin of the Dakota.

'Are you two happy?' he asked above the deep drone of the engines, and then grinning with his big brown face, 'I can see you are!'

Bruce grinned back at him and tightened his arm around Shermaine's shoulders.

'Go away! Can't you see we're busy?'

'You've got lots of cheek for a hitch-hiker—bloody good mind to make you get out and walk,' he grumbled as he sat down beside them on the bench that ran the full length of the fuselage. 'I've brought you some coffee and sandwiches.'

'Good. Good. I'm starving.' Shermaine sat up and reached for the Thermos flask and the greaseproof paper packet. The bruise on her cheek had faded to a shadow with yellow edges—it was almost ten

days old. With his mouth full of chicken sandwich Bruce kicked one of
the wooden cases that were roped securely to the floor of the aircraft.

'What have you got in these, Carl?'

'Dunno,' said Carl and poured coffee into three plastic mugs. 'In
this game you don't ask questions. You fly out, take your money, and
let it go.' He drained his mug and stood up. 'Well, I'll leave you two
alone now. We'll be in Nairobi in a couple of hours, so you can sleep or
something!' He winked. 'You'll have to stay aboard while we refuel.
But we'll be airborne again in an hour or so, and the day after tomorrow,
God and the weather permitting, we'll set you down in Zurich.'

'Thanks, old cock.'

'Think nothing of it—all in the day's work.'

He went forward and disappeared into the cockpit, closing the door
behind him.

Shermaine turned back to Bruce, studied him for a moment and
then laughed.

'You look so different—now you look like a lawyer!'

Self-consciously Bruce tightened the knot of his Old Michael-
house tie.

'I must admit it feels strange to wear a suit and tie again.' He looked
down at the well-cut blue suit—the only one he had left—and then up
again at Shermaine.

'And in a dress I hardly recognize you either.' She was wearing a
lime-green cotton frock, cool and crisp looking, white high-heeled
shoes and just a little make-up to cover the bruise. A damn fine woman,
Bruce decided with pleasure.

'How does your thumb feel?' she asked, and Bruce held up the stump
with its neat little turban of adhesive tape.

'I had almost forgotten about it.'

Suddenly Shermaine's expression changed, and she pointed excitedly
out of the perspex window behind Bruce's shoulder.

'Look, there's the sea!' It lay far below them, shaded from blue to
pale green in the shallows, with a rind of white beach and the wave
formation moving across it like ripples on a pond.

'That's Lake Tanganyika.' Bruce laughed. 'We've left the Congo
behind.'

'Forever?' she asked.

'Forever!' he assured her.

The aircraft banked slightly, throwing them closer together, as Carl
picked out his landmarks and altered course towards the north-east.

Four thousand feet below them the dark insect that was their shadow
flitted and hopped across the surface of the water.

THE EYE OF THE TIGER

'TIGER! TIGER! burning bright
In the forests of the night . . .
In what distant deeps or skies
Burnt the fire of thine eyes?'

William Blake

For my wife, Danielle, with love

It was one of those seasons when the fish came late. I worked my boat and crew hard, running far northwards each day, coming back into grand harbour long after dark each night, but it was November 6th when we picked up the first of the big ones riding down on the wine-purple swells of the Mozambique current.

By this time I was desperate for a fish. My charter was a party of one, an advertising wheel from New York named Chuck McGeorge, one of my regulars who made the annual six-thousand mile pilgrimage to St Mary's Island for the big marlin. He was a short wiry little man, bald as an ostrich egg and grey at the temples, with a wizened brown monkey face but the good hard legs that are necessary to take on the big fish.

When at last we saw the fish, he was riding high in the water, showing the full length of his fin, longer than a man's arm and with the scimitar curve that distinguishes it from shark or porpoise. Angelo spotted him at the instant that I did, and he hung out on the foredeck stay and yelled with excitement, his gipsy curls dangling on his dark cheeks and his teeth flashing in the brilliant tropical sunlight.

The fish crested and wallowed, the water opening about him so that he looked like a forest log, black and heavy and massive, his tail fin echoing the graceful curve of the dorsal, before he slid down into the next trough and the water closed over his broad glistening back.

I turned and glared down into the cockpit. Chubby was already helping Chuck into the big fighting chair, clinching the heavy harness and gloving him up, but he looked up and caught my eye.

Chubby scowled heavily and spat over the side, in complete contrast to the excitement that gripped the rest of us. Chubby is a huge man, as tall as I am but a lot heavier in the shoulder and gut. He is also one of the most staunch and consistent pessimists in the business.

'Shy fish!' grunted Chubby, and spat again. I grinned at him.

'Don't mind him, Chuck,' I called, 'old Harry is going to set you into that fish.'

'I've got a thousand bucks that says you don't.' Chuck shouted back, his face screwed up against the dazzle of the sun-flecked sea, but his eyes twinkling with excitement.

'You're on!' I accepted a bet I couldn't afford and turned my attention to the fish.

Chubby was right, of course. After me, he is the best billfish man in the entire world. The fish was big and shy and scary.

Five times I had the baits to him, working him with all the skill and cunning I could muster. Each time he turned away and sounded as I brought *Wave Dancer* in on a converging course to cross his beak.

'Chubby, there is a fresh dolphin bait in the ice box: haul in the teasers, and we'll run him with a single bait,' I shouted despairingly.

I put the dolphin to him. I had rigged the bait myself and it swam with a fine natural action in the water. I recognized the instant in which the marlin accepted the bait. He seemed to hunch his great shoulders and I caught the flash of his belly, like a mirror below the surface, as he turned.

'Follow!' screamed Angelo. 'He follows!'

I set Chuck into the fish at a little after ten o'clock in the morning, and I fought him close. Superfluous line in the water would place additional strain on the man at the rod. My job required infinitely more skill than gritting the teeth and hanging onto the heavy fibreglass rod. I kept *Wave Dancer* running hard on the fish through the first frenzied charges and frantic flashing leaps until Chuck could settle down in the fighting chair and lean on the marlin, using those fine fighting legs of his.

A few minutes after noon, Chuck had the fish beaten. He was on the surface, in the first of the wide circles which Chuck would narrow with each turn until we had him at the gaff.

'Hey, Harry!' Angelo called suddenly, breaking my concentration. 'We got a visitor, man!'

'What is it, Angelo?'

'Big Johnny coming up current.' He pointed. 'Fish is bleeding, he's smelt it.'

I looked and saw the shark coming. The blunt fin moving up steadily, drawn by the struggle and smell of blood. He was a big hammerhead, and I called to Angelo.

'Bridge, Angelo,' and I gave him the wheel.

'Harry, you let that bastard chew my fish and you can kiss your thousand bucks good-bye,' Chuck grunted sweatily at me from the fighting chair, and I dived into the main cabin.

Dropping to my knees I knocked open the toggles that held down the engine hatch and I slid it open.

Lying on my belly, I reached up under the decking and grasped the stock of the FN carbine hanging in its special concealed slings of inner tubing.

As I came out onto the deck I checked the loading of the rifle, and pushed the selector to automatic fire.

'Angelo, lay me alongside that old Johnny.'

Hanging over the rail in *Wave Dancer*'s bows, I looked down onto the shark as Angelo ran over him. He was a hammerhead all right, a big one, twelve feet from tip to tail, coppery bronze through the clear water.

I aimed carefully between the monstrous eyestalks which flattened and deformed the shark's head, and I fired a short burst.

The FN roared, the empty brass cases spewed from the weapon and the water erupted in quick stabbing splashes.

The shark shuddered convulsively as the bullets smashed into his head, shattering the gristly bone and bursting his tiny brain. He rolled over and began to sink.

'Thanks, Harry,' Chuck gasped, sweating and red-faced in the chair.

'All part of the service,' I grinned at him, and went to take the wheel from Angelo.

At ten minutes to one, Chuck brought the marlin up to the gaff, punishing him until the great fish came over on his side, the sickle tail beating feebly, and the long beak opening and shutting spasmodically. The glazed single eye was as big as a ripe apple, and the long body pulsed and shone with a thousand flowing shades of silver and gold and royal purple.

'Cleanly now, Chubby,' I shouted, as I got a gloved hand on the steel trace and drew the fish gently towards where Chubby waited with the stainless-steel hook at the gaff held ready.

Chubby withered me with a glance that told me clearly that he had been pulling the steel into billfish when I was still a gutter kid in a London slum.

'Wait for the roll,' I cautioned him again, just to plague him a little, and Chubby's lip curled at the unsolicited advice.

The swell rolled the fish up to us, opening the wide chest that glowed silver between the spread wings of the pectoral fins.

'Now!' I said, and Chubby sank the steel in deep. In a burst of bright crimson heart blood, the fish went into its death frenzy, beating the surface to flashing white and drenching us all under fifty gallons of thrown sea water.

I hung the fish on Admiralty Wharf from the derrick of the crane. Benjamin, the harbour-master, signed a certificate for a total weight of 817 lbs. Although the vivid fluorescent colours had faded in death to flat sooty black, yet it was impressive for its sheer bulk—fourteen feet six from the point of its bill to the tip of its flaring swallow tail.

'Mister Harry done hung a Moses on Admiralty,' the word was carried through the streets by running bare-footed urchins, and the islanders joyously snatched at the excuse to cease work and crowd the wharf in fiesta array.

The word travelled as far as old Government House on the bluff, and the presidential Landrover came buzzing down the twisting road with the gay little flag fluttering on the bonnet. It butted its way through the crowd and deposited the great man on the wharf. Before independence, Godfrey Biddle had been St Mary's only solicitor, island-born and London-trained.

'Mister Harry, what a magnificent specimen,' he cried delightedly. A fish like this would give impetus to St Mary's budding tourist trade, and he came to clasp my hand. As State Presidents go in this part of the world, he was top of the class.

'Thank you, Mr President, sir.' Even with the black homburg on his head, he reached to my armpit. He was a symphony in black, black wool suit and patent leather shoes, skin the colour of polished anthracite and only a fringe of startlingly white fluffy hair curling around his ears.

'You really are to be congratulated.' President Biddle was dancing with excitement, and I knew I'd be eating at Government House on guest nights again this season. It had taken a year or two—but the President had finally accepted me as though I were island-born. I was one of his children, with all the special privilege that this position carried with it.

Fred Coker arrived in his hearse, but armed with his photographic equipment, and while he set up his tripod and disappeared under the black cloth to focus the ancient camera, we posed for him beside the colossal carcass. Chuck in the middle holding the rod, with the rest of us grouped around him, arms folded like a football team. Angelo and I were grinning and Chubby was scowling horrifically into the lens. The picture would look good in my new advertising brochure—loyal crew and intrepid skipper, hair curling out from under his cap and from the vee of his shirt, all muscle and smiles—it would really pack them in next season.

I arranged for the fish to go into the cold room down at the pineapple export sheds. I would consign it out to Rowland Wards of London for

mounting on the next refrigerated shipment. Then I left Angelo and
Chubby to scrub down *Dancer*'s decks, refuel her across the harbour at
the Shell basin and take her out to moorings.

As Chuck and I climbed into the cab of my battered old Ford pick-
up, Chubby sidled across like a racecourse tipster, speaking out of the
corner of his mouth.

'Harry, about my billfish bonus—' I knew exactly what he was going
to ask, we went through this every time.

'Mrs Chubby doesn't have to know about it, right?' I finished for him.

'That's right,' he agreed lugubriously, and pushed his filthy deep-sea
cap to the back of his head.

I put Chuck on the plane at nine the next morning and I sang the
whole way down from the plateau, honking the horn of my battered old
Ford pick-up at the island girls working in the pineapple fields. They
straightened up with big flashing smiles under the brims of the wide
straw hats and waved.

At Coker's Travel Agency I changed Chuck's American Express
traveller's cheques, haggling the rate of exchange with Fred Coker.
He was in full fig, tailcoat and black tie. He had a funeral at noon.
The camera and tripod laid up for the present, photographer became
undertaker.

Coker's Funeral Parlour was in the back of the Travel Agency opening into the alley, and Fred used the hearse to pick up tourists at the
airport, first discreetly changing his advertising board on the vehicle
and putting the seats in over the rail for the coffins.

I booked all my charters through him, and he clouted his ten per
cent off my traveller's cheques. He had the insurance agency as well,
and he deducted the annual premium for *Dancer* before carefully counting out the balance. I recounted just as carefully, for although Fred
looks like a schoolmaster, tall and thin and prim, with just enough
island blood to give him a healthy all-over tan, he knows every trick in
the book and a few which have not been written down yet.

He waited patiently while I checked, taking no offence, and when I
stuffed the roll into my back pocket, his gold pince-nez sparkled and he
told me like a loving father, 'Don't forget you have a charter party
coming in tomorrow, Mister Harry.'

'That's all right, Mr Coker—don't you worry, my crew will be
just fine.'

'They are down at the Lord Nelson already,' he told me delicately.
Fred keeps his finger firmly on the island's pulse.

'Mr Coker, I'm running a charter boat, not a temperance society. Don't worry,' I repeated, and stood up. 'Nobody ever died of a hangover.'

I crossed Drake Street to Edward's Store and a hero's welcome. Ma Eddy herself came out from behind the counter and folded me into her warm pneumatic bosom.

'Mister Harry,' she cooed and bussed me, 'I went down to the wharf to see the fish you hung yesterday.' Then she turned, still holding me, and shouted at one of her counter girls, 'Shirley, you get Mister Harry a nice cold beer now, hear?'

I hauled out my roll. The pretty little island girls chittered like sparrows when they saw it, and Ma Eddy rolled her eyes and hugged me closer.

'What do I owe you, Missus Eddy?' From June to November is a long off-season, when the fish do not run, and Ma Eddy carries me through that lean time.

I propped myself against the counter with a can of beer in my hand, picking the goods I needed from the shelves and watching their legs as the girls in their mini-skirts clambered up the ladders to fetch them down—old Harry feeling pretty good and cocky with that hard lump of green stuff in his back pocket.

Then I went down to the Shell Company basin and the manager met me at the door of his office between the big silver fuel storage tanks.

'God, Harry, I've been waiting for you all morning. Head Office has been screaming at me about your bill.'

'Your waiting is over, brother,' I told him. But *Wave Dancer*, like most beautiful women, is an expensive mistress, and when I climbed back into the pick-up, the lump in my pocket was severely depleted.

They were waiting for me in the beer garden of the Lord Nelson. The island is very proud of its associations with the Royal Navy, despite the fact that it is no longer a British possession but revels in an independence of six years' standing; yet for two hundred years previously it had been a station of the British fleet. Old prints by long-dead artists decorated the public bar, depicting the great ships beating up the channel or lying in grand harbour alongside Admiralty Wharf—men-of-war and merchantmen of John Company victualled and refitted here before the long run south to the Cape of Good Hope and the Atlantic.

St Mary's has never forgotten her place in history, nor the admirals and mighty ships that made their landfall here. The Lord Nelson is a parody of its former grandeur, but I enjoy its decayed and seedy elegance and its associations with the past more than the tower of glass and concrete that Hilton has erected on the headland above the harbour.

Chubby and his wife sat side by side on the bench against the far wall, both of them in their Sunday clothes. This was the easiest way to tell them apart, the fact that Chubby wore the three-piece suit which he had bought for his wedding—the buttons straining and gaping, and the deep-sea cap stained with salt crystals and fish blood on his head—while his wife wore a full-length black dress of heavy wool, faded greenish with age, and black button-up boots beneath. Otherwise their dark mahogany faces were almost identical, though Chubby was freshly shaven and she did have a light moustache.

'Hello, Missus Chubby, how are you?' I asked.

'Thank you, Mister Harry.'

'Will you take a little something, then?'

'Perhaps just a little orange gin, Mister Harry, with a small bitter to chase it down.'

While she sipped the sweet liquor, I counted Chubby's wages into her hand, and her lips moved as she counted silently in chorus. Chubby watched anxiously, and I wondered once again how he had managed all these years to fool her on the billfish bonus.

Missus Chubby drained the beer and the froth emphasized her moustache.

'I'll be off then, Mister Harry.' She rose majestically, and sailed from the courtyard. I waited until she turned into Frobisher Street before I slipped Chubby the little sheath of notes under the table and we went into the private bar together.

Angelo had a girl on each side of him and one on his lap. His black silk shirt was open to the belt buckle, exposing gleaming chest muscles. His denim pants fitted skin-tight, leaving no doubt as to his gender, and his boots were hand-tooled and polished westerns. He had greased his hair and sleeked it back in the style of the young Presley. He flashed his grin like a stage lamp across the room and when I paid him he tucked a banknote into the front of each girl's blouse.

'Hey, Eleanor, you go sit on Harry's lap, but careful now. Harry's a virgin—you treat him right, hear?' He roared with delighted laughter and turned to Chubby.

'Hey, Chubby, you quit giggling like that all the time, man! That's stupid—all that giggling and grinning.' Chubby's frown deepened, his whole face crumpling into folds and wrinkles like that of a bulldog. 'Hey, Mister barman, you give old Chubby a drink now. Perhaps that will stop him cutting up stupid, giggling like that.'

At four that afternoon Angelo had driven his girls off, and he sat with his glass on the table top before him. Beside it lay his bait knife honed to a razor edge and glinting evilly in the overhead lights. He muttered darkly to himself, deep in alcoholic melancholy. Every few minutes he would test the edge of the knife with his thumb and scowl around the room. Nobody took any notice of him.

Chubby sat on the other side of me, grinning like a great brown toad —exposing a set of huge startlingly white teeth with pink plastic gums.

'Harry,' he told me expansively, one thick muscled arm around my neck. 'You are a good boy, Harry. You know what, Harry, I'm going to tell you now what I never told you before.' He nodded wisely as he gathered himself for the declaration he made every pay day. 'Harry, I love you, man. I love you better than my own brother.'

I lifted the stained cap and lightly caressed the bald brown dome of his head. 'And you are my favourite eggshell blond,' I told him.

He held me at arm's length for a moment, studying my face, then burst into a lion's roar of laughter. It was completely infectious and we were both still laughing when Fred Coker walked in and sat down at the table. He adjusted his pince-nez and said primly, 'Mister Harry, I have just received a special delivery from London. Your charter's cancelled.' I stopped laughing.

'What the hell!' I said. Two weeks without a charter in the middle of high season and only a lousy two-hundred-dollar reservation fee.

'Mr Coker, you have got to get me a party.' I had three hundred dollars left in my pocket from Chuck's charter.

'You got to get me a party,' I repeated, and Angelo picked up his knife and with a crash drove the point deeply into the table top. Nobody took any notice of him, and he scowled angrily around the room.

'I'll try,' said Fred Coker, 'but it's a bit late now.'

'Cable the parties we had to turn down.'

'Who will pay for the cables?' Fred asked delicately.

'The hell with it, I'll pay.' And he nodded and went out. I heard the hearse start up outside.

'Don't worry, Harry,' said Chubby. 'I still love you, man.'

Suddenly beside me Angelo went to sleep. He fell forward and his forehead hit the table top with a resounding crack. I rolled his head so that he would not drown in the puddle of spilled liquor, returned the knife to its sheath, and took charge of his bank roll to protect him from the girls who were hovering close.

Chubby ordered another round and began to sing a rambling, mumbling shanty in island patois, while I sat and worried.

Once again I was stretched out neatly on the financial rack. God how I hate money—or rather the lack of it. Those two weeks would make all the difference as to whether or not *Dancer* and I could survive the off-season, and still keep our good resolutions. I knew we couldn't. I knew we would have to go on the night run again.

The hell with it, if we had to do it, we might as well do it now. I would pass the word that Harry was ready to do a deal. Having made the decision, I felt again that pleasurable tightening of the nerves, the gut thing that goes with danger. The two weeks of cancelled time might not be wasted after all.

I joined Chubby in song, not entirely certain that we were singing the same number, for I seemed to reach the end of each chorus a long time before Chubby.

It was probably this musical feast that called up the law. On St Mary's this takes the form of an Inspector and four troopers, which is more than adequate for the island. Apart from a great deal of 'carnal knowledge under the age of consent' and a little wife-beating, there is no crime worthy of the name.

Inspector Peter Daly was a young man with a blond moustache, a high English colour on smooth cheeks and pale blue eyes set close together like those of a sewer rat. He wore the uniform of the British colonial police: the cap with the silver badge and shiny patent leather peak, the khaki drill starched and ironed until it crackled softly as he walked, the polished leather belt and Sam Browne cross-straps. He carried a malacca cane swagger stick which was also covered with polished leather. Except for the green and yellow St Mary's shoulder flashes, he looked like the Empire's pride, but like the Empire the men who wore the uniform had also crumbled.

'Mr Fletcher,' he said, standing over our table and slapping the swagger stick lightly against his palm. 'I hope we are not going to have any trouble tonight.'

'Sir,' I prompted him. Inspector Daly and I were never friends—I don't like bullies, or persons who in positions of trust supplement a perfectly adequate salary with bribes and kick-backs. He had taken a lot of my hard-won gold from me in the past, which was his most unforgivable sin.

His mouth hardened under the blond moustache and his colour came up quickly. 'Sir,' he repeated reluctantly.

Now it is true that once or twice in the remote past Chubby and I had given way to an excess of boyish high spirits when we had just hung a Moses fish—however, this did not give Inspector Daly any excuse for talking like that. He was, after all, a mere expatriate out on the island for a three-year contract—which I knew from the President himself would not be renewed.

'Inspector, am I correct in my belief that this is a public place—and that neither my friends nor I are committing a trespass?'

'That is so.'

'Am I also correct in thinking that singing of tuneful and decent songs in a public place does not constitute a criminal act?'

'Well, that is true, but—'

'Inspector, piss off,' I told him pleasantly. He hesitated, looking at Chubby and me. Between the two of us we make up a lot of muscle, and he could see the unholy battle gleam in our eyes. You could see he wished he had his troopers with him.

'I'll be keeping an eye on you,' he said and, clutching at his dignity like a beggar's rags, he left us.

'Chubby, you sing like an angel,' I said and he beamed at me.

'Harry, I'm going to buy you a drink.' And Fred Coker arrived in time to be included in the round. He drank lager and lime juice which turned my stomach a little, but his tidings were an effective antidote.

'Mister Harry, I got you a party.'

'Mister Coker, I love you.'

'I love you too,' said Chubby, but deep down I felt a twinge of disappointment. I had been looking forward to another night run.

'When are they arriving?' I asked.

'They are here already—they were waiting for me at my office when I got back.'

'No kidding.'

'They knew that your first party had cancelled, and they asked for you by name. They must have come in on the same plane as the special delivery.'

My thinking was a little muzzy right then or I might have pondered a moment how neatly one party had withdrawn and another had stepped in.

'They are staying up at the Hilton.'

'Do they want me to pick them up?'

'No, they'll meet you at Admiralty Wharf ten o'clock tomorrow morning.'

I was grateful that the party had asked for such a late starting time. That morning *Dancer* was crewed by zombies. Angelo groaned and turned a light chocolate colour every time he bent over to coil a rope or rig the rods and Chubby sweated neat alcohol and his expression was truly terrifying. He had not spoken a word all morning.

I wasn't feeling all that cheerful myself. *Dancer* was snugged up alongside the wharf and I leaned on the rail of the flying bridge with my darkest pair of Polaroids over my eyes, and although my scalp itched I was afraid to take off my cap in case the top of my skull came with it.

The island's single taxi, a '62 Citroën, came down Drake Street and stopped at the top end of the wharf to deposit my party. There were two of them, and I had expected three; Coker had definitely said a party of three.

They started down the long stone-paved wharf, walking side by side, and I straightened up slowly as I watched them. I felt my physical distress fade into the realms of the inconsequential, to be replaced by that gut thing again, the slow coiling and clenching within, and the little tickling feeling along the back of my arms and in the nape of the neck.

One was tall and walked with that loose easy gait of a professional athlete. He was bare-headed and his hair was pale gingery and combed carefully across a prematurely balding pate so the pink scalp showed through. However, he was lean around the belly and hips, and he was aware. It was the only word to describe the charged sense of readiness that emanated from him.

It takes one to recognize one. This was a man trained to live with and by violence. He was muscle, a *soldier*, in the jargon. It mattered not for which side of the law he exercised his skills—law enforcement or its frustration—he was very bad news. I had hoped never to see this kind of barracuda cruising St Mary's placid waters. It gave me a sick little slide in the guts to know that it had found me out again. Quickly I glanced at the other man; it wasn't so obvious in him, the edge was blunted a little, the outline blurred by time and flesh, but it was there also—more bad news.

'Nice going, Harry,' I told myself bitterly. 'All this, and a hangover thrown in.'

Clearly now I recognized that the older man was the leader. He walked half a pace ahead, the younger taller man paying him that respect. He was a few years my senior also, probably late thirties. There was the beginning of a paunch over the crocodile skin belt, and pouches of flesh along the line of his jawbone, but his hair had been styled in Bond Street and he wore his Sulka silk shirt and Gucci loafers like badges of rank. As he came on down the wharf he dabbed at his chin and upper lip with a white handkerchief and I guessed the diamond on his little finger at two carats. It was set in a plain gold ring and the wrist watch was gold also, probably by Lanvin or Piaget.

'Fletcher?' he asked, stopping below me on the jetty. His eyes were black and beady, like those of a ferret. A predator's eyes, bright without warmth. I saw he was older than I had guessed, for his hair was certainly tinted to conceal the grey. The skin of his cheeks was unnaturally tight and I could see the scars of plastic surgery in the hair line. He'd had a facelift—a vain man then, and I stored the knowledge.

He was an old soldier, risen from the ranks to a position of command. He was the brain, and the man that followed him was the muscle. Somebody had sent out their first team and, with a clairvoyant flash, I realized why my original party had cancelled.

A phone call followed by a visit from this pair would put the average citizen off marlin-fishing for life. They had probably done themselves a serious injury in their rush to cancel.

'Mr Materson? Come aboard—' One thing was certain, they had not come for the fishing, and I decided on a low and humble profile until I had figured out the percentages, so I threw in a belated '—sir.'

The muscle man jumped down to the deck, landing soft-footed like a cat and I saw from the way that the folded coat over his arm swung heavily there was something weighty in the pocket. He confronted my crew, thrusting out his jaw and running his eyes over them swiftly.

Angelo flashed a watered-down version of the celebrated smile and touched the brim of his cap. 'Welcome, sir.' And Chubby's scowl lightened momentarily and he muttered something that sounded like a curse, but was probably a warm greeting. The man ignored them and turned to hand Materson down to the deck where he waited while his bodyguard checked out *Dancer*'s main saloon. Then he went in and followed him.

Our accommodation is luxurious, at 125,000 nicker it should be. The air-conditioning had taken the bite out of the morning heat and Materson sighed with relief and dabbed again with his handkerchief as he sank into one of the padded seats.

'This is Mike Guthrie.' He indicated the muscle who was moving about the cabin checking at the ports, opening doors and generally over-playing his hand, coming on very tough and hard.

'My pleasure, Mr Guthrie.' I grinned with all my boyish charm and he waved airily without glancing at me.

'A drink, gentlemen?' I asked, as I opened the liquor cabinet. They took a Coke each, but I needed something medicinal for the shock and the hangover. The first swallow of cold beer from the can revitalized me.

'Well, gentlemen, I think I shall be able to offer you some sport. Only yesterday I hung a very good fish, and all the signs are for a big run—'

Mike Guthrie stepped in front of me and stared into my face. His yes were flecked with brown and pale green, like a hand-loomed tweed.

'Don't I know you?' he asked.

'I don't think I've ever had the pleasure.'

'You're a London boy, aren't you?' He had picked up the accent.

'I left Blighty a long time ago, mate,' I grinned, letting it come out broad. He did not smile, and dropped into the seat opposite me, placing his hands on the table top between us, spreading his fingers palm downwards. He continued to stare at me. A very tough baby, very hard.

'I'm afraid that it is too late for today,' I babbled on cheerfully. 'If we are going to fish the Mozambique, we have to clear harbour by six o'clock. However, we can make an early start tomorrow—'

Materson interrupted my chatter. 'Check that list out, Fletcher, and let us know what you are short.' He passed me a folded sheet of foolscap, and I glanced down the handwritten column. It was all scuba diving gear and salvage equipment.

'You gentlemen aren't interested in big game fishing then?' Old Harry showing surprise and amazement at such an unlikely eventuality.

'We have come out to do a little exploring—that's all.'

I shrugged. 'You're paying, we do what you want to do.'

'Have you got all that stuff?'

'Most of it.' In the off-season I run a cut-rate package deal for scuba buffs which helps pay expenses. I had a full range of diving sets and there was an air compressor built into *Dancer*'s engine room for recharging. 'I don't have the air bags or all that rope—'

'Can you get them?'

'Sure.' Ma Eddy had a pretty good selection of ships' stores, and Angelo's old man was a sail-maker. He could run up the air bags in a couple of hours.

'Right then, get it.'

I nodded. 'When do you want to start?'

'Tomorrow morning. There will be one other person with us.'

'Did Mr Coker tell you it's five hundred dollars a day—and I'll have to charge you for this extra equipment?'

Materson inclined his head and made as if to rise.

'Would it be okay to see a little of that out front?' I asked softly, and they froze. I grinned ingratiatingly.

'It's been a long lean winter, Mr Materson, and I've got to buy this stuff and fill my fuel tanks.'

Materson took out his wallet and counted out three hundred pounds in fivers. As he was doing so he said in his soft purry voice, 'We won't need your crew, Fletcher. The three of us will help you handle the boat.'

I was taken aback. I had not expected that. 'They'll have to draw full wages, if you lay them off. I can't reduce my rate.'

Mike Guthrie was still sitting opposite me, and now he leaned forward. 'You heard the man, Fletcher, just get your niggers off the boat,' he said softly.

Carefully I folded the bundle of five pound notes and buttoned them into my breast pocket, then I looked at him. He was very quick. I could see him tense up ready for me and for the first time he showed expression in those cold speckled eyes. It was anticipation. He knew he had reached me, and he thought I was going to try him. He wanted that, he wanted to take me apart. He left his hands on the table, palms downwards, fingers spread. I thought how I might take the little finger of each hand and snap them at the middle joint like a pair of cheese sticks. I knew I could do it before he had a chance to move, and the knowledge gave me a great deal of pleasure, for I was very angry. I haven't many friends, but I value the few I have.

'Did you hear me speak, boy?' Guthrie hissed at me, and I dredged up the boyish grin again and let it hang at a ridiculous angle on my face.

'Yes, sir, Mr Guthrie,' I said. 'You're paying the money, whatever you say.'

I nearly choked on the words. He leaned back in his seat, and I saw that he was disappointed. He was muscle, and he enjoyed his work. I think I knew then that I was going to kill him, and I took enough comfort from the thought to enable me to hold the grin.

Materson was watching us with those bright little eyes. His interest was detached and clinical, like a scientist studying a pair of laboratory specimens. He saw that the confrontation had been resolved for the present, and his voice was soft and purry again.

'Very well, Fletcher.' He moved towards the deck. 'Get that equipment together and be ready for us at eight tomorrow morning.'

I let them go, and I sat and finished the beer. It may have been just my hangover, but I was beginning to have a very ugly feeling about this whole charter and I realized that after all it might be best to leave Chubby and Angelo ashore. I went out to tell them.

'We've got a pair of freaks. I'm sorry, but they have got some big secret and they are dealing you out.' I put the aqualung bottles on the compressor to top up, and we left *Dancer* at the wharf while I went up to Ma Eddy's and Angelo and Chubby took my drawing of the air bags across to his father's workshop.

The bags were ready by four o'clock and I picked them up in the Ford and stowed them in the sail locker under the cockpit seats. Then I spent an hour stripping and reassembling the demand valves of the cubas and checking out all the other diving equipment.

At sundown I ran *Dancer* out to her moorings on my own, and was bout to leave her and row ashore in the dinghy when I had a good hought. I went back into the cabin and knocked back the toggles on he engine-room hatch.

I took the FN carbine from its hiding-place, pumped a cartridge into he breech, set her for automatic fire and clicked on the safety catch efore hanging her in the slings again.

Before it was dark, I took my old cast net and waded out across the lgoon towards the main reef. I saw the swirl and run beneath the sur-ace of the water which the setting sun had burnished to the colour of opper and flame, and I sent the net spinning high with a swing of houlders and arms. It ballooned like a parachute, and fell in a wide ircle over the shoal of striped mullet. When I pulled the drag line and losed the net over them, there were five of the big silvery fish as long as ny forearm kicking and thumping in the coarse wet folds.

I grilled two of them and ate them on the veranda of my shack. They asted better than trout from a mountain stream, and afterwards I oured a second whisky and sat on into the dark.

Usually this is the time of day when the island enfolds me in a great ense of peace, and I seem to understand what the whole business of ving is all about. However, this night was not like that. I was angry hat these people had come out to the island and brought with them heir special brand of poison to contaminate us. Five years ago I had un from that, believing I had found a place that was safe. Yet beneath he anger, when I was honest with myself, I recognized also an excite-nent, a pleasurable excitement. That gut thing again, knowing that I vas at risk once more. I was not sure yet what the stakes were, but I new they were high and that I was sitting in the game with the big oys once again.

I was on the left-hand path again. The path I had chosen at seven-een, when I had deliberately decided against the university bursary vhich I had been awarded and instead I bunked from St Stephen's rphanage in north London and lied about my age to join a whaling actory ship bound for the Antarctic. Down there on the edge of the reat ice I lost my last vestige of appetite for the academic life. When ne money I had made in the south ran out I enlisted in a special service attalion where I learned how violence and sudden death could be ractised as an art. I practised that art in Malaya and Vietnam, then tter in the Congo and Biafra—until suddenly one day in a remote jungle village while the thatched huts burned sending columns of tarry black smoke into an empty brazen sky and the flies came to the dead in humming blue clouds, I was sickened to the depths of my soul. I wanted out.

In the South Atlantic I had come to love the sea, and now I wanted a place beside it, with a boat and peace in the long quiet evenings.

First I needed money to buy those things—a great deal of money—so much that the only way I could earn it was in the practice of my art.

One last time, I thought, and I planned it with utmost care. I needed an assistant and I chose a man I had known in the Congo. Between us we lifted the complete collection of gold coins from the British Museum of Numismatology in Belgrave Square. Three thousand rare gold coins that fitted easily into a medium-sized briefcase, coins of the Roman Caesars and the Emperors of Byzantium, coins of the early states of America and of the English Kings—florins and leopards of Edward III, nobles of the Henrys and angels of Edward IV, treble sovereigns and unites, crowns of the rose from the reign of Henry VIII and five-pound pieces of George III and Victoria—three thousand coins, worth, even on a forced sale, not less than two million dollars.

Then I made my first mistake as a professional criminal. I trusted another criminal. When I caught up with my assistant in an Arab hotel in Beirut I reasoned with him in fairly strong terms, and when finally I put the question to him of just what he had done with the briefcase of coins, he snatched a .38 Beretta from under his mattress. In the ensuing scuffle he had his neck broken. It had been a mistake. I didn't mean to kill the man—but even more I didn't mean him to kill me. I hung a 'DON'T DISTURB' sign on his door and I caught the next plane out. Ten days later the police found the briefcase with the coins in the left-luggage department at Paddington Station. It made the front page of all the national newspapers.

I tried again at an exhibition of cut diamonds in Amsterdam, but I had done faulty research on the electronic alarm system and I tripped a beam that I had overlooked.

The plain clothes security guards who had been hired by the organizers of the exhibition rushed headlong into the uniformed police coming in through the main entrance and a spectacular shoot-out ensued, while a completely unarmed Harry Fletcher slunk away into the night to the sound of loud cries and gunfire.

I was half way to Schipol airport by the time a cease-fire was called between the opposing forces of the law—but not before a sergeant of the Dutch police received a critical chest wound.

I sat anxiously chewing my nails and drinking innumerable beers in my room in the Holiday Inn near Zürich Airport, as I followed the gallant sergeant's fight for life on the TV set. I would have hated like all hell to have another fatality on my conscience, and I made a solemn vow that if the policeman died I would forget for ever about my place in the sun.

However, the Dutch sergeant rallied strongly and I felt an immense proprietary pride in him when he was finally declared out of danger. And when he was promoted to assistant inspector and awarded a bonus of five thousand crowns I persuaded myself that I was his fairy godfather and that the man owed me eternal gratitude.

Still, I had been shaken by two failures and I took a job as an instructor at an Outward Bound School for six months while I considered my future. At the end of six months, I decided for one more try.

This time I laid the ground-work with meticulous care. I emigrated to South Africa, where I was able with my qualifications to obtain a post as an operator with the security firm responsible for bullion shipments from the South African Reserve Bank in Pretoria to overseas destinations. For a year I worked with the transportation of hundreds of millions of dollars worth of gold bars, and I studied the system in every minute detail. The weak spot, when I found it, was at Rome— but again I needed help.

This time I went to the professionals, but I set my price at a level that made it easier for them to pay me out than put me down and I covered myself a hundred times against treachery.

It went as smoothly as I had planned it, and this time there were no victims. Nobody came out with a bullet or a cracked skull. We merely switched part of a cargo and substituted leaded cases. Then we moved two and a half tons of gold bars across the Swiss border in a furniture removals van.

In Basle, sitting in a banker's private rooms furnished with priceless antiques, above the wide swift waters of the Rhine on which the stately white swans rode in majesty, they paid me out. Manny Resnick signed the transfer into my numbered account of £150,000 sterling and he laughed a fat hungry little laugh.

'You'll be back, Harry—you've tasted blood now and you'll be back. Have a nice holiday, then come to me again when you've thought up another deal like this one.'

He was wrong, I never went back. I rode up to Zürich in a hire car and flew to Paris Orly. In the men's room there, I shaved off the beard and picked up the briefcase from the pay locker that contained the passport in the name of Harold Delville Fletcher. Then I flew out Pan Am for Sydney, Australia.

Wave Dancer cost me £125,000 sterling and I took her under a deck load of fuel drums across to St Mary's, two thousand miles, a voyage on which we learned to love each other.

On St Mary's I purchased twenty-five acres of peace, and built the shack with my own hands—four rooms, a thatched roof and a wide veranda, set amongst the palms above the white beach. Except for the occasions when a night run had been forced upon me, I had walked the right-hand path since then.

It was late when I had done my reminiscences and the tide was push-ing high up the beach in the moonlight before I went into the shack, but then I slept like an innocent.

They were on time the following morning. Charly Materson ran a tight outfit. The taxi deposited them at the head of the wharf while I had *Dancer* singled up at stem and stern and both engines burbling sweetly.

I watched them come, concentrating on the third member of the group. He was not what I had expected. He was tall and lean with a wide friendly face and dark soft hair. Unlike the others, his face and arms were darkly suntanned, and his teeth were large and very white. He wore denim shorts and a white sweatshirt and he had a swimmer's wide rangy shoulders and powerful arms. I knew instantly who was to use the diving equipment.

He carried a big green canvas kit bag over one shoulder. He carried it easily, though I could see that it was weighty, and he chatted gaily with his two companions who answered him in monosyllables. They flanked him like a pair of guards.

He looked up at me as they came level and I saw that he was young and eager. There was an excitement, an anticipation, about him, that reminded me sharply of myself ten years previously.

'Hi,' he grinned at me, an easy friendly grin and I realized that he was an extremely good-looking youngster.

'Greetings,' I replied, liking him from the first and intrigued as to how he had found a place with the wolf pack. Under my direction they took in the mooring lines and, from this brief exercise, I learned that the youngster was the only one of them familiar with small boats.

As we cleared the harbour, he and Materson came up on to the flying bridge. Materson had coloured slightly and his breathing was raggedy from the mild exertion. He introduced the newcomer.

'This is Jimmy,' he told me, when he had caught his breath. We shook hands and I put his age at not much over twenty. Close up I had no cause to revise my first impressions. He had a level and innocent gaze from sea-grey eyes, and his grip was firm and dry.

'She's a darling boat, skipper,' he told me, which was rather like telling a mother that her baby is beautiful.

'She's not a bad old girl.'

'What is she, forty-four, forty-five feet?'

'Forty-five,' I said, liking him a little more.

'Jimmy will give you your directions,' Materson told me. 'You will follow his orders.'

'Fine,' I said, and Jimmy coloured a little under his tan.

'Not orders, Mr Fletcher, I'll just tell you where we want to go.'

'Fine, Jim, I'll take you there.'

'Once we are clear of the island, you will turn due west.'

'Just how far in that direction do you intend going?' I asked.

'We want to cruise along the coast of the African mainland,' Materson cut in.

'Lovely,' I said, 'that's great. Did anybody tell you that they don't hang out the welcome mat for strangers there?'

'We will stay well offshore.'

I thought a moment, hestitating before turning back to Admiralty Wharf and packing the whole bunch ashore.

'Where do you want to go—north or south of the river-mouth?'

'North,' said Jimmy, and that altered the proposition for the good. South of the river they patrolled with helicopters and were very touchy about their territorial waters. I would not go in there during daylight.

In the north there was little coastal activity. There was a single crash boat at Zinballa, but when its engines were in running order, which was a few days a week, then its crew were mostly blown out of their minds with the virulent palm liquor brewed locally along the coast. When crew and engines were functioning simultaneously, they could raise fifteen knots, and *Dancer* could turn on twenty-two any time I asked her.

The final trick in my favour was that I could run *Dancer* through the maze of off-shore reefs and islands on a dark night in a roaring monsoon, while it was my experience that the crash boat commander avoided this sort of extravagance. Even on a bright sunny day and in a flat calm, he preferred the quiet and peace of Zinballa Bay. I had heard that he suffered acutely from sea sickness, and held his present appointment only because it was far away from the capital, where as a minister of the government the commander had been involved in a little unpleasantness regarding the disappearance of large amounts of foreign aid.

From my point of view he was the ideal man for the job.

'All right,' I agreed, turning to Materson. 'But I'm afraid what you're asking is going to cost you another two-fifty dollars a day— danger money.'

'I was afraid it might,' he said softly.

I brought the *Dancer* around, close to the light on Oyster Point.

It was a bright morning with a high clear sky into which the stationary clouds that marked the position of each group of islands towered in soft columns of blinding white.

The solemn progress of the trade winds across the ocean was interrupted by the bulwark of the African continent on which they broke. We were getting the backlash here in the inshore channel, and random squalls and gusts of it spread darkly across the pale green waters and flecked the surface chop with white. *Dancer* loved it, it gave her an excuse to flounce and swish her bottom.

'You looking for anything special—or just looking?' I asked casually, and Jimmy turned to tell me all about it. He was itchy with excitement, and the grey eyes sparkled as he opened his mouth.

'Just looking,' Materson interrupted with a ring in his voice and a sharp warning in his expression, and Jimmy's mouth closed.

'I know these waters. I know every island, every reef. I might be able to save you a lot of time—and a bit of money.'

'That's very kind of you,' Materson thanked me with heavy irony. 'However, I believe we can manage.'

'You're paying,' I shrugged, and Materson glanced at Jimmy, inclined his head in a command to follow and led him down into the cockpit. They stood together beside the stern rail and Materson spoke to him quietly but earnestly for two minutes. I saw Jimmy flush darkly, his expression changing from dismay to boyish sulks and I guessed that he was having his ear chewed to ribbons on the subject of secrecy and security.

When he came back onto the flying bridge he was seething with anger, and for the first time I noticed the strong hard line of his jaw. He wasn't just a pretty boy, I decided.

Evidently on Materson's orders, Guthrie, the muscle, came out of the cabin and swung the big padded fighting chair to face the bridge. He lounged in it, even in his relaxation charged with the promise of violence like a resting leopard, and he watched us, one leg draped over the arm rest and the linen jacket with the heavy weight in its pocket folded in his lap.

A happy ship, I chuckled, and ran *Dancer* out through the islands, threading a fine course through the clear green waters where the reefs lurked darkly below the surface like malevolent monsters and the islands were fringed with coral sand as dazzling white as a snowdrift, and crowned with dark thick vegetation over which the palm stems curved gracefully, their tops shaking in the feeble remnants of the trade.

It was a long day as we cruised at random and I tried to get some hint of the object of the expedition. However, still smarting from Materson's reprimand, Jimmy was tight mouthed and grim. He asked for changes of course at intervals, after I had pointed out our position on the large scale admiralty chart which he produced from his bag.

Although there were no extraneous markings on his chart, when I examined it surreptitiously I was able to figure that we were interested in an area fifteen to thirty miles north of the multiple mouths of the Rovuma River, and up to sixteen miles offshore. An area containing perhaps three hundred islands varying in size from a few acres to many square miles—a very big haystack in which to find his needle.

I was content enough to perch up on *Dancer*'s bridge and run quietly along the seaways, enjoying the feel of my darling under me and watching the activity of the sea animals, and birds.

In the fighting chair Mike Guthrie's scalp started to show through the thin cover of hair like strips of scarlet neon lighting.

'Cook, you bastard,' I thought happily, and neglected to warn him about the tropical sun until we were running home in the dusk. The next day he was in agony with white goo smeared over his bloated and incarnadined features and a wide cloth hat covering his head, but his face flashed like the port light of an ocean-goer.

By noon on the second day I was bored. Jimmy was poor company for although he had recovered a little of his good humour he was so conscious of security that he even thought for thirty seconds before accepting an offer of coffee.

It was more for something to do than because I wanted fish for my dinner that when I saw a squadron of small kingfish charging a big shoal of sardine ahead of us, I gave the wheel to Jimmy.

'Just keep her on that heading,' I told him and dropped down into the cockpit. Guthrie watched me warily from his swollen crimson face as I glanced into the cabin and saw that Materson had my bar open and was mixing himself a gin and tonic. At $750 a day I didn't grudge it to him. He hadn't emerged from the cabin in two days.

I went back to the small tackle locker and selected a pair of feather jigs and tossed them out. As we crossed the track of the shoal I hit a kingfish and brought him out kicking, flashing golden in the sun.

Then I recoiled the lines and stowed them, wiped the blade of my heavy bait-knife across the oil stone to brighten up the edge and split the kingfish's belly from anal vent to gills and pulled out a handful of bloody gut to throw it into the wake.

Immediately a pair of gulls that had been weaving and hovering over us screeched with greed and plunged for the scraps. Their excitement summoned others and within minutes there was a shrieking flapping host of them astern of us.

Their din was not so loud that it covered the metallic snicker close behind me, the unmistakable sound of the slide on an automatic pistol being drawn back and released to load and cock. I moved entirely from instinct. Without thought, the big bait-knife spun in my right hand as I changed smoothly to a throwing grip and I turned and dropped to the deck in a single movement, breaking fall with heels and left arm as the knife went back over my right shoulder and I began the throw at the instant that I lined up the target.

Mike Guthrie had a big automatic in his right hand. An old-fashioned naval .45, a killer's weapon, one which would blow a hole in a man's chest through which you could drive a London cab.

Two things saved Guthrie from being pinned to the back of the fighting chair by the long heavy blade of the bait-knife. Firstly, the fact that the .45 was not pointed at me and, secondly, the expression of comical amazement on the man's scarlet face.

I prevented myself from throwing the knife, breaking the instinctive action by a major effort of will, and we stared at each other. He knew then how close he had come, and the grin he forced to his swollen sun burned lips was shaky and unconvincing. I stood up and pegged the knife into the bait chopping board.

'Do yourself a favour,' I told him quietly. 'Don't play with that thing behind my back.'

He laughed then, blustering and tough again. He swivelled the seat and aimed out over the stern. He fired twice, the shots crashing out loudly above the run of *Dancer*'s engines and the brief smell of cordite was whipped away on the wind.

Two of the milling gulls exploded into grotesque bursts of blood and feathers blown to shreds by the heavy bullets, and the rest of the flock scattered with shrieks of panic. The manner in which the birds were torn up told me that Guthrie had loaded with explosive bullets, a more savage weapon than a sawn-off shotgun.

He swivelled the chair back to face me and blew into the muzzle of the pistol like John Wayne. It was fancy shooting with that heavy calibre weapon.

'Tough cooky,' I applauded him, and turned to the bridge ladder, but Materson was standing in the doorway of the cabin with the gin in his hand and as I stepped past him he spoke quietly.

'Now I know who you are,' he said, in that soft purry voice. 'It's been worrying us, we thought we knew you.'

I stared at him, and he called past me to Guthrie.

'You know who he is now, don't you?' and Guthrie shook his head. I don't think he could trust his voice. 'He had a beard then, think about it—a mug shot photograph.'

'Jesus,' said Guthrie. 'Harry Bruce!' I felt a little shock at hearing the name spoken out loud again after all these years. I had hoped it was forgotten for ever.

'Rome,' said Materson. 'The gold heist.'

'He set it up.' Guthrie snapped his fingers. 'I was sure I knew him. It was the beard that fooled me.'

'I think you gentlemen have the wrong address,' I said with a desperate attempt at a cool tone, but was thinking quickly, trying to weigh this fresh knowledge. They had seen a mug-shot—where? When? Were they law men or from the other side of the fence? I needed time to think—and I clambered up to the bridge.

'Sorry,' muttered Jimmy, as I took the wheel from him. 'I should have told you he had a gun.'

'Yeah,' I said. 'It might have helped.' My mind was racing, and the first turning it took was along the left-hand path. They would have to go. They had blown my elaborate cover, they had sniffed me out and there was only one sure way. I looked back into the cockpit but both Materson and Guthrie had gone below.

An accident, take them both out at once stroke, aboard a small boat there were plenty of ways a greenhorn could get hurt in the worst possible way. They had to go.

Then I looked at Jimmy, and he grinned at me.

'You move fast,' he said. 'Mike nearly wet himself, he thought he was going to get that knife through his gizzard.'

The kid also? I asked myself—if I took out the other two, he would have to go as well. Then suddenly I felt the same physical nausea that I had first known long ago in the Biafran village.

'You okay, skipper?' Jimmy asked quickly, it had shown on my face.

'I'm okay, Jim,' I said. 'Why don't you go fetch us a can of beer.'

While he was below I reached my decision. I would do a deal. I was certain that they didn't want their business shouted in the streets. I'd trade secrecy for secrecy. Probably they were coming to the same conclusion in the cabin below.

I locked the wheel and crossed quietly to the corner of the bridge, making sure my footsteps were not picked up in the cabin below.

The ventilator there funnels fresh air into the inlet above the saloon table. I had found that the ventilator made a reasonably effective voice tube, that sound was carried through it to the bridge.

However, the effectiveness of this listening device depends on a number of factors, chief of these being the direction and strength of the wind and the precise position of the speaker in the cabin below.

The wind was on our beam, gusting into the opening of the ventilator and blotting out patches of the conversation in the cabin. However, Jimmy must have been standing directly below the vent for his voice came through strongly when the wind roar did not smother it.

'Why don't you ask him now?' and the reply was confused, then the wind gusted and when it cleared, Jimmy was speaking again.

'If you do it tonight, where will you—' and the wind roared, '—to get the dawn light then we will have to—' The entire discussion seemed to be on times and places, and as I wondered briefly what they hoped to gain by leaving harbour at dawn, he said it again. 'If the dawn light is where—' I strained for the next words but the wind killed them for ten seconds, then '—I don't see why we can't—' Jimmy was protesting and suddenly Mike Guthrie's voice came through sharp and hard. He must have gone to stand close beside Jimmy, probably in a threatening attitude.

'Listen, Jimmy boy, you let us handle that side of it. Your job is to find the bloody thing, and you aren't doing so good this far.'

They must have moved again for their voices became indistinct and I heard the sliding door into the cockpit opening and I turned quickly to the wheel and freed the retaining handle just as Jimmy's head appeared over the edge of the deck as he came up the ladder.

He handed me the beer and he seemed to be more relaxed now. The reserve was gone from his manner. He smiled at me, friendly and trusting.

'Mr Materson says that's enough for today. We are to head for home.'

I swung *Dancer* across the current and we came in from the west, past the mouth of Turtle Bay and I could see my shack standing amongst the palms. I felt a sudden chilling premonition of loss. The fates had called for a new deck of cards, and the game was bigger; the stakes were too rich for my blood but there was no way I could pull out now.

However, I suppressed the chill of despair, and turned to Jimmy. I would take advantage of his new attitude of trust and try for what information I could glean.

We chatted lightly on the run down the channel into grand harbour.

They had obviously told him that I was off the leper list. Strangely the fact that I had a criminal past made me more acceptable to the wolf-pack. They could reckon the angles now. They had found a lever, so now they could handle me—though I was pretty sure they had not explained the whole proposition to young James.

It was obviously a relief for him to act naturally with me. He was a friendly and open person, completely lacking in guile. An example of this was the way that his surname had been guarded like a military secret from me, and yet around his neck he wore a silver chain and a Medic-alert tag that warned that J. A. NORTH, the wearer, was allergic to penicillin.

Now he forgot all his former reserve, and gently I drew small snippets of information from him that I might have use for in the future. In my experience it's what you don't know that can really hurt you.

I chose the subject that I guessed would open him up completely.

'See that reef across the channel, there where she's breaking now? That's Devil Fish Reef and there is twenty fathoms sheer under the sea side of her. It's a hangout of some real big old bull grouper. I shot one there last year that weighed in at over two hundred kilos.'

'Two hundred—' he exclaimed. 'My God, that's almost 450 lbs.'

'Right, you could put your head and shoulders in his mouth.'

The last of his reserves disappeared. He had been reading history and philosophy at Cambridge but spent too much time in the sea, and had to drop out. Now he ran a small diving equipment supply company and underwater salvage outfit, that gave him a living and allowed him to dive most days of the week. He did private work and had contracted to the Government and the Navy on some jobs.

More than once he mentioned the name 'Sherry' and I probed carefully.

'Girl friend or wife?' and he grinned.

'Sister, big sister, but she's a doll—she does the books and minds the shop, all that stuff,' in a tone that left no doubt as to what James thought about book-keeping and counter-jumping. 'She's a red-hot conchologist and she makes two thousand a year out of her sea shells.' But he didn't explain how he had got into the dubious company he was now keeping, nor what he was doing half way around the world from his sports shop. I left them on Admiralty Wharf, and took *Dancer* over to the Shell Basin for refuelling before dark.

That evening I grilled the kingfish over the coals, roasted a couple of big sweet yams in their jackets and was washing it down with a cold beer sitting on the veranda of the shack and listening to the surf when I saw the headlights coming down through the palm trees.

The taxi parked beside my pick-up, and the driver stayed at the wheel while his passengers came up the steps on to the stoep. They had left James at the Hilton, and there were just the two of them now— Materson and Guthrie.

'Drink?' I indicated the bottles and ice on the side table. Guthrie poured gin for both of them and Materson sat opposite me and watched me finish the last of the fish.

'I made a few phone calls,' he said when I pushed my plate away. 'And they tell me that Harry Bruce disappeared in June five years ago and hasn't been heard of since. I asked around and found out that Harry Fletcher sailed into Grand Harbour here three months' later— inward bound from Sydney, Australia.'

'Is that the truth?' I picked a little fish bone out of my tooth, and lit a long black island cheroot.

'One other thing, someone who knew him well tells me Harry Bruce had a knife scar across his left arm,' he purred, and I involuntarily glanced at the thin line of scar tissue that laced the muscle of my forearm. It had shrunk and flattened with the years, but was still very white against the dark sun-bronzed skin.

'Now that's a hell of a coincidence,' I said, and drew on the cheroot. It was strong and aromatic, tasting of sea and sun and spices. I wasn't worried now—they were going to make a deal.

'Yeah, isn't it,' Materson agreed, and he looked around him elaborately. 'You got a nice set-up here, Fletcher. Cosy, isn't it, really nice and cosy.'

'It beats hell out of working for a living,' I admitted.

'—Or out of breaking rocks, or sewing mail bags.'

'I should imagine it does.'

'The kid is going to ask you some questions tomorrow. Be nice to him, Fletcher. When we go you can forget you ever saw us, and we'll forget to tell anybody about that funny coincidence.'

'Mr Materson, sir, I've got a terrible memory,' I assured him.

After the conversation I had overheard in *Dancer*'s cabin, I expected them to ask for an early start time the following morning, for the dawn light seemed important to their plans. However, neither of them mentioned it, and when they had gone I knew I wouldn't sleep so I walked out along the sand around the curve of the bay to Mutton Point to watch the moon come up through the palm trees. I sat there until after midnight.

The dinghy was gone from the jetty but Hambone, the ferry man, rowed me out to *Dancer*'s moorings before sun-up the following morning and as we came alongside I saw the familiar shape shambling around the cockpit, and the dinghy tied alongside.

'Hey, Chubby.' I jumped aborad. 'Your Missus kick you out of bed, then?'

Dancer's deck was gleaming white even in the bad light, and all the metal work was brightly burnished. He must have been at it for a couple of hours; Chubby loves *Dancer* almost as much as I do.

'She looked like a public shit-house, Harry,' he grumbled. 'That's a sloppy bunch you got aboard,' and he spat noisily over the side. 'No respect for a boat, that's what.'

He had coffee ready for me, as strong and as pungent as only he can make it, and we drank it sitting in the saloon. Chubby frowned heavily into his mug and blew on the steaming black liquid. He wanted to tell me something.

'How's Angelo?'

'Pleasuring the Rawano widows,' he growled. The island does not provide sufficient employment for all its able-bodied young men—so most of them ship out on three-year labour contracts to the American satellite tracking station and airforce base on Rawano island. They leave their young wives behind, the Rawano widows, and the island girls are justly celebrated for the high temperature of their blood and their friendly dispositions.

'That Angelo going to shag his brain loose, he's been at it night and day since Monday.'

I detected more than a trace of envy in his growl. Missus Chubby kept him on a pretty tight lead—he sipped noisily at the coffee.

'How's your party, Harry?'

'Their money is good.'

'You not fishing, Harry.' He looked at me. I watch you from Coolie Peak, man, you don't go near the channel—you are working inshore.'

'That's right, Chubby.' He returned his attention to his coffee.

'Hey, Harry. You watch them. You be good and careful, hear. They bad men, those two. I don't know the young one—but the others they are bad.'

'I'll be careful, Chubby.'

'You know the new girl at the hotel, Marion? The one over for the season?' I nodded, she was a pretty slim little wisp of a girl with lovely long legs, about nineteen with glossy black hair, freckled skin, bold eyes and an impish smile. 'Well, last night she went with the blond one, the one with the red face.' I knew that Marion sometimes combined business with pleasure and provided for selected hotel guests services beyond the call of duty. On the island this sort of activity drew no social stigma.

'Yes,' I encouraged Chubby.

'He hurt her, Harry. Hurt her bad.' Chubby took another mouthful of coffee. 'Then he paid her so much money she couldn't go to the police.'

I liked Mike Guthrie a little less now. Only an animal would take advantage of a girl like Marion. I knew her well. She had an innocence, a child-like acceptance of life that made her promiscuity strangely appealing. I remembered how I had thought I might have to kill Guthrie one day—and tried not to let the thought perish.

'They are bad men, Harry. I thought it best you know that.'

'Thanks, Chubby.'

'And don't you let them dirty up *Dancer* like that,' he added accusingly. 'The saloon and deck—they were like a pigsty, man.'

He helped me run *Dancer* across to Admiralty Wharf and then he set off homewards, grumbling and muttering blackly. He passed Jimmy coming in the opposite direction and shot him a single malevolent glance that should have shrivelled him in his tracks.

Jimmy was on his own, fresh-faced and jaunty.

'Hi, skipper,' he called, as he jumped down onto *Dancer*'s deck, and I went into the saloon with him and poured coffee for us.

'Mr Materson says you have some questions for me, is that right?'

'Look, Mr Fletcher, I want you to know that I didn't mean offence by not talking to you before. It wasn't me—but the others.'

'Sure,' I said. 'That's fine, Jimmy.'

'It would have been the sensible thing to ask your help long ago, instead of blundering around the way we have been. Anyway, now the others have suddenly decided it's okay.'

He had just told me much more than he imagined, and I adjusted my opinion of Master James. It was clear that he possessed information, and he had not shared it with the others. It was his insurance, and he had probably insisted on seeing me alone to keep his insurance policy intact.

'Skipper, we are looking for an island, a specific island. I can't tell you why, I'm sorry.'

'Forget it, Jimmy. That's all right.' What will there be for you, James North, I wondered suddenly. What will the wolf pack have for you once you have led them to this special island of yours? Will it be something a lot less pleasant than penicillin allergy?

I looked at that handsome young face, and felt an unaccustomed flood of affection for him—perhaps it was his youth and innocence, the sense of excitement with which he viewed this tired and wicked old world. I envied and liked him for that, and I did not relish seeing him pulled down and rolled in the dirt.

'Jim, how well do you know your friends?' I asked him quietly, and he was taken by surprise, then almost immediately he was wary.

'Well enough,' he replied carefully. 'Why?'

'You have known them less than a month,' I said as though I knew, and saw the confirmation in his expression. 'And I have known men like that all my life.'

'I don't see what this has to do with it, Mr Fletcher.' He was stiffening up now; I was treating him like a child and he didn't like that.

'Listen, Jim. Forget this business, whatever it is. Drop it, and go back to your shop and your salvage company.'

'That's crazy,' he said. 'You don't understand.'

'I understand, Jim. I really do. I travelled the same road, and I know it well.'

'I can look after myself. Don't worry about me.' He had flushed up under his tan, and the grey eyes snapped with defiance. We stared at each other for a few moments, and I knew I was wasting time and emotion. If anyone had spoken like this to me at the same age I would have thought him senile.

'All right, Jim,' I said. 'I'll drop it, but you know the score. Just play it cool and loose, that's all.'

'Okay, Mr Fletcher.' He relaxed slowly, and then grinned a charming and engaging grin. 'Thanks anyway.'

'Let's hear about this island,' I suggested and he glanced about the cabin.

'Let's go up on the bridge,' he suggested, and out in the open air he took a stub of pencil and a scrap pad from the map bin above the chart table.

'I reckon it lies off the African shore about six to ten miles, and ten to thirty miles north of the mouth of the Rovuma River—'

'That covers a hell of a lot of ground, Jim—as you may have noticed during the last few days. What else do you know about it?'

He hesitated a little longer, before grudgingly doling out a few more coins from his hoard. He took the pencil and drew a horizontal line across the pad.

'Sea level—' he said, and then above the line he raised an irregular profile that started low, and then climbed steeply into three distinct peaks before ending abruptly, '—and that's the silhouette that it shows from the sea. The three hills are volcanic basalt, sheer rock with little vegetation.'

'The Old Men—' I recognized it immediately, '—but you are a long way out in your other calculations, it's more like twenty miles offshore—'

'But within sight of the mainland?' he asked quickly. 'It has to be within sight.'

'Sure, you could see a long way from the tops of the hills,' I pointed out as he tore the sheet from the pad and carefully ripped it to shreds, and dropped them into the harbour.

'How far north of the river?' He turned back to face me.

'Offhand I'd say sixty or seventy miles,' and he looked thoughtful.

'Yes, it could be that far north. It could fit, it depends on how long it would take—' He did not finish, he was taking my advice about playing it cool. 'Can you take us there, skip?'

I nodded. 'But it's a long run and best come prepared to sleep on the boat overnight.'

'I'll fetch the others,' he said, eager and excited once more. But on the wharf he looked back at the bridge.

'About the island, what it looks like and all that, don't discuss it with the others, okay?'

'Okay, Jim,' I smiled back at him. 'Off you go.' I went down to have a look at the admiralty chart. The Old Men were the highest point on a ridge of basalt, a long hard reef that ran parallel to the mainland for two hundred miles. It disappeared below the water, but reappeared at intervals, forming a regular feature amongst the haphazard sprinkling of coral and sand islands and shoals.

It was marked as uninhabited and waterless, and the soundings showed a number of deep channels through the reefs around it. Although it was far north of my regular grounds, yet I had visited the area the previous year as host to a marine biology expedition from UCLA who were studying the breeding habits of the green turtles that abound there.

We had camped for three days on another island across the tide channel from the Old Men, where there was an all-weather anchorage in an enclosed lagoon, and brackish but just drinkable water in a fisherman's well amongst the palms. Looking across from the anchorage, the Old Men showed exactly the outline that Jimmy had sketched for me, that was how I had recognized it so readily.

Half an hour later, the whole party arrived; strapped on the roof of the taxi was a bulky piece of equipment covered with a green canvas dust sheet. They hired a couple of lounging islanders to carry this, and the overnight bags they had with them, down the wharf to where I was waiting.

They stowed the canvas package on the foredeck without unwrapping it and I asked no questions. Guthrie's face was starting to fall off in layers of sun-scorched skin, leaving wet red flesh exposed. He had smeared white cream over it. I thought of him slapping little Marion around his suite at the Hilton, and I smiled at him.

'You look so good, have you ever thought of running for Miss Universe?' and he glowered at me from beneath the brim of his hat as he took his seat in the fighting chair. During the run northwards he drank beer straight from the can and used the empties as targets. Firing the big pistol at them as they tumbled and bobbed in *Dancer*'s wake.

A little before noon, I gave Jimmy the wheel and went down to use the heads below deck. I found that Materson had the bar open and the gin bottle out.

'How much longer?' he asked, sweaty and flushed despite the air-conditioning.

'Another hour or so,' I told him, and thought that Materson was going to find himself with a drinking problem the way he handled spirits at midday. However, the gin had mellowed him a little and—always the opportunist—I loosened another three hundred pounds from his wallet as an advance against my fees before going up to take *Dancer* in on the last leg through the northern tide channel that led to the Old Men.

The triple peaks came up through the heat haze, ghostly grey and ominous, seeming to hang disembodied above the channel.

Jimmy was examining the peaks through his binoculars, and then he lowered them and turned delightedly to me.

'That looks like it, skipper,' and he clambered down into the cockpit. The three of them went up on to the foredeck, passed the canvas-wrapped deck cargo, and stood shoulder to shoulder at the rail staring through the sea fret at the island as I crept cautiously up the channel.

We had a rising tide pushing us up the channel, and I agreed to use it to approach the eastern tip of the Old Men, and make a landing on the beach below the nearest peak. This coast has a tidal fall of seventeen feet at full springs, and it is unwise to go into shallow water on the ebb. It is easy to find yourself stranded high and dry as the water falls away beneath your keel.

Jimmy borrowed my hand-bearing compass and packed it with his chart, a Thermos of iced water and a bottle of salt tablets from the medicine chest into his haversack. While I crept cautiously in towards the beach, Jimmy and Materson stripped off their footwear and trousers.

When *Dancer* bumped her keel softly on the hard white sand of the beach I shouted to them.

'Okay—over you go,' and with Jimmy leading, they went down the ladder I had rigged from *Dancer*'s side. The water came to their armpits, and James held the haversack above his head as they waded towards the beach.

'Two hours!' I called after them. 'If you're longer than that you can sleep ashore. I'm not coming in to pick you up on the ebb.'

Jimmy waved and grinned. I put *Dancer* into reverse and backed off cautiously, while the two of them reached the beach and hopped around awkwardly as they donned their trousers and shoes and then set off into the palm groves and disappeared from view.

After circling for ten minutes and peering down through the water that was clear as a trout stream, I picked up the dark shadow across the bottom that I was seeking and dropped a light head anchor.

While Guthrie watched with interest I put on a face-plate and gloves and went over the side with a small oyster net and a heavy tyre lever. There was forty feet of water under us, and I was pleased to find my wind was still sufficient to allow me to go down and prise loose a netful of the big double-shelled sun clams in one dive. I shucked them on the foredeck, and then, mindful of Chubby's admonitions, I threw the empty shells overboard and swabbed the deck carefully before taking a pailful of the sweet flesh down to the galley. They went into a casserole pot with wine and garlic, salt and ground pepper and just a bite of chilli. I set the gas-plate to simmer and put the lid on the pot.

When I went back on deck, Guthrie was still in the fighting chair.

'What's wrong, big shot, are you bored?' I asked solicitously. 'No little girls to kick around?' His eyes narrowed thoughtfully. I could see him checking out my source of information.

'You've got a big mouth, Bruce. Somebody is going to close it for you one day.' We exchanged a few more pleasantries, none of them much above this level, but it served to pass the time until the two distant figures appeared on the beach and waved and hallooed. I pulled up the hook, and went in to pick them up.

Immediately they were aboard, they called Guthrie to them and assembled on the foredeck for one of their group sessions. They were all excited, Jimmy the most so, and he gesticulated and pointed out into the channel, talking quietly but vehemently. For once they seemed all to be in agreement, but by the time they had finished talking there was an hour of sunlight left and I refused to agree to Materson's demands that I should continue our explorations that evening. I had no wish to creep around in the darkness on an ebb tide.

Firmly I took *Dancer* across to the safe anchorage in the lagoon across the channel, and by the time the sun went down below a blazing horizon I had *Dancer* riding peacefully on two heavy anchors, and I was sitting upon the bridge enjoying the last of day and the first Scotch of the evening. In the saloon below me there was the interminable murmur of discussion and speculation. I ignored it, not even bothering to use the ventilator, until the first mosquitoes found their way across the lagoon and began whining around my ears. I went below and the conversation dried up at my entry.

I thickened the juice and served my clam casserole with baked yams and pineapple salad and they ate in dedicated silence.

'My God, that's even better than my sister's cooking,' Jimmy gasped finally. I grinned at him. I am rather vain about my culinary skills and young James was clearly a gourmet.

I woke after midnight and went up on deck to check *Dancer*'s moorings. She was all secure and I paused to enjoy the moonlight.

A great stillness lay upon the night, disturbed only by the soft chuckle of the tide against *Dancer*'s side—and far off the boom of the surf on the outer reef. It was coming in big and tall from the open ocean, and breaking in thunder and white upon the coral of Gunfire Reef. The name was well chosen, and the deep belly-shaking thump of it sounded exactly like the regular salute of a minute gun.

The moonlight washed the channel with shimmering silver and highlighted the bald domes of the peaks of the Old Men so they shone like ivory. Below them the night mists rising from the lagoon writhed and twisted like tormented souls.

Suddenly I caught the whisper of movement behind me and I whirled to face it. Guthrie had followed me as silently as a hunting leopard. He wore only a pair of jockey shorts and his body was white and muscled and lean in the moonlight. He carried the big black .45, dangling at arm's length by his right thigh. We stared at each other for a moment before I relaxed.

'You know, luv, you've just got to give up now. You really aren't my type at all,' I told him, but there was adrenalin in my blood and my voice rasped.

'When the time comes to rim you, Fletcher, I'll be using this,' he said, and lifted the automatic, 'all the way up, boy,' and he grinned.

We ate breakfast before sun-up and I took my mug of coffee to the bridge to drink as we ran up the channel towards the open sea. Materson was below, and Guthrie lolled in the fighting chair. Jimmy stood beside me and explained his requirements for the day.

He was tense with excitement, seeming to quiver with it like a young gun dog with the first scent of the bird in his nostrils.

'I want to get some shots off the peaks of the Old Men,' he explained. 'I want to use your hand-bearing compass, and I'll call you in.'

'Give me your bearings, Jim, and I'll plot it and put you on the spot,' I suggested.

'Let's do it my way, skipper,' he replied awkwardly, and I could not prevent a flare of irritation in my reply.

'All right, then, eagle scout.' He flushed and went to the port rail to sight the peaks through the lens of the compass. It was ten minutes or so before he spoke again.

'Can we turn about two points to port now, skipper?'

'Sure we can,' I grinned at him, 'but, of course, that would pile us on to the end of Gunfire Reef—and we'd tear her belly out.'

It took another two hours of groping about through the maze of reefs before I had worked *Dancer* out through the channel into the open sea and circled back to approach Gunfire Reef from the east.

It was like the child's game of hunt the thimble; Jimmy called 'hotter' and 'colder' without supplying me with the two references that would enable me to place *Dancer* on the precise spot he was seeking.

Out here the swells marched in majestic procession towards the land, growing taller and more powerful as they felt the shelving bottom. *Dancer* rolled and swung to them as we edged in towards the outer reef.

Where the swells met the barrier of coral their dignity turned to sudden fury, and they boiled up and burst in leviathan spouts of spray, pouring wildly over the coral with the explosive shock of impact. Then they sucked back, exposing the evil black fangs, white water cascading and creaming from the barrier, while the next swell moved up, humping its great slick back for the next assault.

Jimmy was directing me steadily southwards in a gradual converging course with the reef, and I could tell we were very close to his marks. Through the compass he squinted eagerly, first at one and then the other peak of the Old Men.

'Steady as you go, skipper,' he called. 'Just ease her down on that heading.'

I looked ahead, tearing my eyes away from the menacing coral for a few seconds, and I watched the next swell charge in and break—except at a narrow point five hundred yards ahead. Here the swell kept its shape and ran on uninterrupted towards the land. On each side, the swell broke on coral, but just at that one point it was open.

Suddenly I remembered Chubby's boast.

'I was just nineteen when I pulled my first jewfish out of the hole at

Gunfire Break. Weren't no other would fish with me—don't say as I blame them. Wouldn't go into the Break again—got a little more brains now.'

Gunfire Break, suddenly I knew that was where we were heading. I tried to remember exactly what Chubby had told me about it.

'If you come in from the sea about two hours before high water, steer for the centre of the gap until you come up level with a big old head of brain coral on your starboard side, you'll know it when you see it; pass it close as you can and then come roundhard to starboard and you'll be sitting in a big hole tucked in neatly behind the main reef. Closer you are on the back of the reef the better, man—' I remembered it clearly then, Chubby in his talkative phase in the public bar of the Lord Nelson, boastful as one of the very few men who had been through the Gunfire Break. 'No anchor going to hold you there, you got to lean on the oars to hold station in the gap—the hole at Gunfire Break is deep, man, deep, but the jewfish in there are big, man, big. One day I took four fish, and the smallest was three hundred pounds. Could have took more—but time was up. You can't stay in Gunfire Break more than an hour after high water—she sucks out through the Break like they pulled the chain on the whole damned sea. You come out the same way you went in, only you pray just a little harder on the way out—'cos you got a ton of fish on board, and ten feet less water under your keel. There is another way out through a channel in the back of the reef. But I don't even like to talk about that one. Only tried it once.'

Now we were bearing down directly on the Break; Jimmy was going to run us right into the eye of it.

'Okay, Jim,' I called. 'That's as far as we go.' I opened the throttle and sheered off, making a good offing before turning back to face Jimmy's wrath.

'We were almost there, damn you,' he blustered. 'We could have gone in a little closer.'

'You have trouble up there, boy?' Guthrie shouted up from the cockpit.

'No, it's all right,' Jimmy called back, and then turned furiously to me. 'You are under contract, Mr Fletcher—'

'I want to show you something, James—' and I took him to the chart table. The Break was marked on the admiralty chart by a single laconic sounding of thirty fathoms; there was no name or sailing instruction for it. Quickly I pencilled in the bearings of the two extreme peaks of the Old Men from the break, and then used the protractor to measure the angle they subtended.

'That right?' I asked him, and he stared at my figures.

'It's right, isn't it?' I insisted and then reluctantly he nodded.

'Yes, that's the spot,' he agreed, and I went on to tell him about Gunfire Break in every detail.

'But we have to get in there,' he said at the end of my speech, as though he had not heard a word of it.

'No way,' I told him. 'The only place I'm interested in now is grand Harbour, St Mary's Island,' and I laid *Dancer* on that course. As far as I was concerned the charter was over.

Jimmy disappeared down the ladder, and returned within minutes with reinforcements—Materson and Guthrie, both of them looking angry and outraged.

'Say the word, and I'll tear the bastard's arm off and beat him to death with the wet end,' Mike Guthrie said with relish.

'The kid says you're pulling out?' Materson wanted to know. 'Now that's not right—is it?'

I explained once more about the hazards of Gunfire Break and they sobered immediately.

'Take me close as you can—I'll swim in the rest of the way,' Jimmy said to me, but I replied directly to Materson.

'You'd lose him, for certain sure. Do you want to risk that?'

He didn't answer, but I could see that Jimmy was much too valuable for them to take the chance.

'Let me try,' Jimmy insisted, but Materson shook his head irritably.

'If we can't get into the Break, at least let me take a run along the reef with the sledge,' Jimmy went on, and I knew then what we were carrying under the canvas wrapping on the foredeck.

'Just a couple of passes along the front edge of the reef, past the entrance to the Break.' He was pleading now, and Materson looked questioningly at me. You don't often have opportunities like this offered you on a silver tray. I knew I could run *Dancer* within spitting distance of the coral without risk, but I frowned worriedly.

'I'd be taking a hell of a chance—but if we could agree on a bit of old danger money—'

I had Materson over the arm of the chair and I caned him for an extra day's hire—five hundred dollars, payable in advance.

While we did the business, Guthrie helped Jimmy unwrap the sledge and carry it back to the cockpit.

I tucked the sheath of bank notes away and went back to rig the tow lines. The sledge was a beautifully constructed toboggan of stainless steel and plastic. In place of snow runners, it had stubby fin controls, rudder and hydrofoils, operated by a short joystick below the perspex pilot's shield.

There was a ring bolt in the nose to take the tow line by which I would drag the sledge in *Dancer*'s wake. Jimmy would lie on his belly behind the transparent shield, breathing compressed air from the twin tanks that were built into the chassis of the sledge. On the dashboard were depth and pressure gauges, directional compass and time elapse clock. With the joystick Jimmy could control the depth of the sledge's dive, and yaw left or right across *Dancer*'s stern.

'Lovely piece of work,' I remarked, and he flushed with pleasure.

'Thanks, skipper, built it myself.' He was pulling on the wet suit of thick black neoprene rubber and while his head was in the clinging hood I stooped and examined the maker's plate that was riveted to the sledge's chassis, memorizing the legend.

'BUILT BY NORTH'S UNDERWATER WORLD.
5, PAVILION ARCADE.
BRIGHTON, SUSSEX.'

I straightened up as his face appeared in the opening of the hood.

'Five knots is a good tow speed, skipper. If you keep a hundred yards off the reef, I'll be able to deflect outwards and follow the contour of the coral.'

'Fine, Jim.'

'If I put up a yellow marker, ignore it, it's only a find, and we will go back to it later—but if I send up a red, it's trouble, try and get me off the reef and haul me in.'

I nodded. 'You have three hours,' I warned him. 'Then she will begin the ebb up through the break and we'll have to haul off.'

'That should be long enough,' he agreed.

Guthrie and I lifted the sledge over the side, and it wallowed low in the water. Jimmy clambered down to it and settled himself behind the screen, testing the controls, adjusting his face-plate and cramming the mouth-piece of the breathing device into his mouth. He breathed noisily and then gave me the thumbs up.

I climbed quickly to the bridge and opened the throttles. *Dancer* picked up speed and Guthrie paid out the thick nylon rope over the stern as the sledge fell away behind us. One hundred and fifty yards of rope went over, before the sledge jerked up and began to tow.

Jimmy waved, and I pushed *Dancer* up to a steady five knots. I circled wide, then edged in towards the reef, taking the big swells on *Dancer*'s beam so she rolled appellingly.

Again Jimmy waved, and I saw him push the control column of the sledge forwards. There was a turmoil of white water along her control fins and then suddenly she put her nose down and ducked below the surface. The angle of the nylon rope altered rapidly as the sledge went down, and then swung away towards the reef.

The strain on the rope made it quiver like an arrow as it strikes, and the water squirted from the fibres.

Slowly we ran parallel to the reef, closing the Break. I watched the coral respectfully, taking no chances, and I imagined Jimmy far below the surface flying silently along the bottom, cutting in to skim the tall wall of underwater coral. It must have been an exhilarating sensation, and I envied him, deciding to hitch a ride on the sledge when I got the opportunity.

We came opposite the Break, passed it and just then I heard Guthrie shout. I glanced quickly over the stern and saw the big yellow balloon bobbing in our wake.

'He found something,' Guthrie shouted.

Jimmy had dropped a light leaded line, and a sparklet bulb had automatically inflated the yellow balloon with carbon dioxide gas to mark the spot.

I kept going steadily along the reef, and a quarter of a mile farther on the angle of the tow line flattened and the sledge popped to the surface in a welter of water.

I swung away from the reef to a safe distance, and then went down to help Guthrie recover the sledge.

Jimmy clambered into the cockpit, and when he pulled off his faceplate his lips were trembling and his grey eyes blazed. He took Materson's arm and dragged him into the cabin, splashing sea water all over Chubby's beloved deck.

Guthrie and I coiled the rope then lifted the sledge into the cockpit. I went back to the bridge, and took *Dancer* on a slow return to the entrance of Gunfire Break.

Materson and Jimmy came up onto the bridge before we reached it. Materson was affected by Jimmy's excitement.

'The kid wants to try for a pick up.' I knew better than to ask what it was.

'What size?' I asked instead, and glanced at my wristwatch. We had and hour and a half before the rip tide began to run out through the Break.

'Not very big—' Jimmy assured me. 'Fifty pounds maximum.'

'You sure, James? Not bigger?' I didn't trust his enthusiasm not to minimize the effort involved.

'I swear it.'

'You want to put an airbag on it?'

'Yes, I'll lift it with an airbag and then tow it away from the reef.'

I reversed *Dancer* in gingerly towards the yellow balloon that played lightly in the angry coral jaws of the Break.

'That's as close as I'll go,' I shouted down into the cockpit, and Jimmy acknowledged with a wave.

He waddled duck-footed to the stern and adjusted his equipment. He had taken two airbags as well as the canvas cover from the sledge, and was roped up to the coil of nylon rope.

I saw him take a bearing on the yellow marker with the compass on his wrist, then once again he glanced up at me on the bridge before he flipped backwards over the stern and disappeared.

His regular breathing burst in a white rash below the stern, then began to move off towards the reef. Guthrie paid out the bodyline after him.

I kept *Dancer* on station by using bursts of forward and reverse, holding her a hundred yards from the southern tip of the Break.

Slowly Jimmy's bubbles approached the yellow marker, and then broke steadily beside it. He was working below it, and I imagined him fixing the empty airbags to the object with the nylon slings. It would be hard work with the suck and drag of the current worrying the bulky bags. Once he had fitted the slings he could begin to fill the bags with compressed air from his scuba bottles.

If Jimmy's estimate of size was correct it would need very little inflation to pull the mysterious object off the bottom, and once it dangled free we could tow it into a safer area before bringing it aboard.

For forty minutes I held *Dancer* steady, then quite suddenly two swollen green shiny mounds broke the surface astern. The airbags were up—Jimmy had lifted his prize.

Immediately his hooded head surfaced beside the filled bags, and he held his right arm straight up. The signal to begin the tow.

'Ready?' I shouted at Guthrie in the cockpit.

'Ready!' He had secured the line, and I crept away from the reef, slowly and carefully to avoid up-ending the bags and spilling out the air that gave them lift.

Five hundred yards off the reef, I kicked *Dancer* into neutral and went to help haul in the swimmer and his fat green airbags.

'Stay where you are,' Materson snarled at me as I approached the ladder and I shrugged and went back to the wheel.

The hell with them all, I thought, and lit a cheroot—but I couldn't prevent the tickle of excitement as they worked the bags alongside, and then walked them forward to the bows.

They helped Jimmy aboard, and he shrugged off the heavy compressed air bottles, dropping them to the deck while he pushed his face-plate onto his forehead.

His voice, ragged and high-pitched, carried clearly to me as I leaned on the bridge rail.

'Jackpot!' he cried. 'It's the—'

'Watch it!' Materson cautioned him, and James cut himself off and they all looked at me, lifting their faces to the bridge.

'Don't mind me, boys,' I grinned and waved the cheroot cheerily. They turned away and huddled. Jimmy whispered, and Guthrie said, 'Jesus Christ!' loudly and slapped Materson's back, and then they were all exclaiming and laughing as they crowded to the rail and began to lift the airbags and their burden aboard. They were clumsy with it. *Dancer* was rolling heavily, and I leaned forward with curiosity eating a hole in my belly.

My disappointment and chagrin were intense when I realized that Jimmy had taken the precaution of wrapping his prize in the canvas sledge cover. It came aboard as a sodden, untidy bundle of canvas, swathed in coils of nylon rope.

It was heavy, I could see by the manner in which they handled it— but it was not bulky, the size of a small suitcase.

They laid it on the deck and stood around it happily. Materson smiled up at me.

'Okay, Fletcher. Come take a look.'

It was beautifully done; he played like a concert pianist on my curiosity. Suddenly I wanted very badly to know what they had pulled from the sea. I clamped the cheroot in my teeth as I swarmed down the ladder, and hurried towards the group in the bows. I was half way across the foredeck, right out in the open, and Materson was still smiling as he said softly, 'Now!'

Only then did I know it was a set-up, and my mind began to move so fast that it all seemed to go by in extreme slow motion.

I saw the evil black bulk of the .45 in Guthrie's fist, and it came up slowly to aim into my belly. Mike Guthrie was in the marksman's crouch, right arm fully extended, and he was grinning as he screwed up those speckled eyes and sighted along the thick-jacketed barrel.

I saw Jimmy North's handsome young face contort with horror, saw him reach out to grip the pistol arm but Materson, still grinning, shoved him roughly aside and he staggered away with *Dancer's* next roll.

I was thinking quite clearly and rapidly; it was not a procession of thought but a set of simultaneous images. I thought how neatly they had dropped the boom on me, a really professional hit.

I thought how presumptuous I had been in trying to make a deal with the wolf pack. For them it was easier to hit than to negotiate.

I thought that they would take out Jimmy now that he had watched his. That must have been their intention from the start. I was sorry for hat. I had come to like the kid.

I thought about the heavy soft explosive lead slug that the .45 threw, about how it would tear up the target, hitting with the shock of two thousand foot pounds.

Guthrie's forefinger curled on the trigger and I began to throw myelf at the rail beside me with the cheroot still in my mouth, but I knew it was too late.

The pistol in Guthrie's hand kicked up head high, and I saw the muzzle flash palely in the sunlight. The cannon roar of the blast and the heavy lead bullet hit me together. The din deafened me and snapped my head back and the cheroot flipped up high in the air leaving a trail of sparks. Then the impact of the bullet doubled me over, driving the air from my lungs, and lifted me off my feet, hurling me backwards until the deck rail caught me in the small of the back.

There was no pain, just that huge numbing shock. It was in the chest, I was sure of that, and I knew that it must have blown me open. It was a mortal wound, I was sure of that also and I expected my mind to go now. I expected to fade, going out into blackness.

Instead the rail caught me in the back and I somersaulted, going over the side head-first and the quick cold embrace of the sea covered me. It steadied me, and I opened my eyes to the silver clouds of bubbles and the soft green of sunlight through the surface.

My lungs were empty, the air driven out by the impact of the bullet, and my instinct told me to claw to the surface for air, but surprisingly my mind was still clear and I knew that Mike Guthrie would blow the top off my skull the moment I surfaced. I rolled and dived, kicking clumsily, and went down under *Dancer*'s hull.

On empty lungs it was a long journey. *Dancer*'s smooth white belly passed slowly above me, and I drove on desperately, amazed that there was strength in my legs still.

Suddenly darkness engulfed me, a soft dark red cloud, and I nearly panicked, thinking my vision had gone—until suddenly I realized it was my own blood. Huge billowing clouds of my own blood staining the water. Tiny zebra-striped fish darted wildly through the cloud, gulping greedily at it.

I struck out, but my left arm would not respond. It trailed limply at my side, and blood blew like smoke about me.

There was strength in my right arm and I forged on under *Dancer*, passed under her keel and rose thankfully towards her far waterline

As I came up I saw the nylon tow rope trailing over her stern, a bight of it hanging down below the surface and I snatched at it thankfully

I broke the surface under *Dancer's* stern, and I sucked painfully for air; my lungs felt bruised and numb, the air tasted like old copper in my mouth but I gulped it down.

My mind was still clear. I was under the stern, the wolf pack was in the bows, the carbine was under the engine hatch in the main cabin

I reached up as high as I could and took a twist of the nylon rope around my right wrist, lifted my knees and got my toes on to the rubbing strake along *Dancer's* waterline.

I knew I had enough strength for one attempt, no more. It would have to be good. I heard their voices from up in the bows, raised angrily, shouting at each other, but I ignored them and gathered all my reserve.

I heaved upwards, with both legs and the one good arm. My vision starred with the effort, and my chest was a numbed mass, but I came clear of the water and fell half across the stern rail, hanging there like an empty sack on a barbed-wire fence.

For seconds I lay there, while my vision cleared and I felt the slick warm outpouring of blood along my flank and belly. The flow of blood galvanized me. I realized how little time I had before the loss of it sent me plunging into blackness. I kicked wildly and tumbled headlong on to the cockpit floor, striking my head on the edge of the fighting chair, and grunting with the new pain of it.

I lay on my side and glanced down at my body. What I saw terrified me. I was streaming great gouts of thick blood—it was forming a puddle under me.

I clawed at the deck, dragging myself towards the cabin, and reached the combing beside the entrance. With another wild effort I pulled myself upright, hanging on one arm, supported by legs already weak and rubbery.

I glanced quickly around the angle of the cabin, down along the foredeck to where the three men were still grouped in the bows.

Jimmy North was struggling to strap his compressed air bottles onto his back again, his face was a mask of horror and outrage and his voice was strident as he screamed at Materson.

'You filthy bloody murderers. I'm going down to find him. I'm going to get his body—and, so help me Christ, I'll see you both hanged—'

Even in my own distress I felt a sudden flare of admiration for the kid's courage. I don't think it ever occurred to him that he was also on the list.

'It was murder, cold-blooded murder,' he shouted, and turned to the rail, settling the face-plate over his eyes and nose.

Materson looked across at Guthrie, the kid's back was turned to them, and Materson nodded.

I tried to shout a warning, but it croaked hollowly in my throat, and Guthrie stepped up behind Jimmy. This time he made no mistake. He touched the muzzle of the big .45 to the base of Jimmy's skull, and the shot was muffled by the neoprene rubber hood of the diving-suit.

Jimmy's skull collapsed, shattered by the passage of the heavy bullet. It came out through the glass plate of the diving mask in a cloud of glass fragments. The force of it clubbed him over the side, and his body splashed alongside. Then there was silence in which the memory of gunfire seemed to echo with the sound of wind and water.

'He'll sink,' said Materson calmly. 'He had on a weight belt—but we had better try and find Fletcher. We don't want him washed up with that bullet hole in his chest.'

'He ducked—the bastard ducked—I didn't hit him squarely—' Guthrie protested, and I heard no more. My legs collapsed and I sprawled on the deck of the cockpit. I was sick with shock and horror and the quick flooding flow of my blood.

I have seen violent death in many guises, but Jimmy's had moved me as never before. Suddenly there was only one thing I wanted to do before my own violent death overwhelmed me.

I began to crawl towards the engine-room hatch. The white deck seemed to stretch before me like the Sahara desert, and I was beginning to feel the leaden hand of a great weariness upon my shoulder.

I heard their footsteps on the deck above me, and the murmur of their voices. They were coming back to the cockpit.

'Ten seconds, please God,' I whispered. 'That's all I need,' but I knew it was futile. They would be into the cabin long before I reached the hatch—but I dragged myself desperately towards it.

Then suddenly their footsteps paused, but the voices continued. They had stopped to talk out on the deck, and I felt a lift of relief for I had reached the engine hatch.

Now I struggled with the toggles. They seemed to have jammed immovably, and I realized how weak I was, but I felt the revitalizing stir of anger through the weariness.

I wriggled around and kicked at the toggles and they flew back. I fought my weakness aside and got on to my knees. As I leaned over the hatch a fresh splattering of bright blood fell on the white deck.

'Eat your liver, Chubby,' I thought irrelevantly, and prised up the hatch. It came up achingly slowly, heavy as all the earth, and now I felt the first lances of pain in my chest as bruised tissue tore.

The hatch fell back with a heavy thump, and instantly the voices on deck were silent, and I could imagine them listening.

I fell on my belly and groped desperately under the decking and my right hand close on the stock of the carbine.

'Come on!' There was a loud exclamation, and I recognized Materson's voice, and immediately the pounding of running footsteps along the deck towards the cockpit.

I tugged wearily at the carbine, but it seemed to be caught in the slings and resisted my efforts.

'Christ! There's blood all over the deck.' Materson shouted.

'It's Fletcher,' Guthrie yelled. 'He came in over the stern.'

Just then the carbine came free and I almost dropped it down into the engine-room, but managed to hold it long enough to roll clear.

I sat up with the carbine in my lap, and pushed the safety catch across with my thumb. Sweat and salt water streamed into my eyes blurring my vision as I peered up at the entrance to the cabin.

Materson ran into the cabin three paces before he saw me, then he stopped and gaped at me. His face was red with effort and agitation and he lifted his hands, spreading them in a protective gesture before him as I brought up the carbine. The diamond on his little finger winked merrily at me.

I lifted the carbine one-handed from my lap, and its immense weight appalled me. When the muzzle was pointed at Materson's knees I pressed the trigger.

With a continuous shattering roar the carbine spewed out a solid blast of bullets, and the recoil flung the barrel upwards, riding the stream of fire from Materson's crotch up across his belly and chest. It flung him backwards against the cabin bulkhead, and split him like the knife-stroke that guts a fish while he danced a grotesque and jerky little death jig.

I knew that I should not empty the carbine, there was still Mike Guthrie to deal with, but somehow I seemed unable to release my grip on the trigger and the bullets tore through Materson's body, smashing and splintering the woodwork of the bulkhead.

Then suddenly I lifted my finger. The torrent of bullets ceased and Materson fell heavily forward.

The cabin stank with burned cordite and the sweet heavy smell of blood.

Guthrie ducked into the companionway of the cabin, crouching with right arm outflung and he snapped off a single shot at me as I sat in the centre of the cabin.

He had all the time he needed for a clean shot at me, but he hurried it, panicky and off-balance. The blast slapped against my ear drums, and the heavy bullet disrupted the air against my cheek as it flew wide. The recoil kicked the pistol high, and as it dropped for his next shot I fell sideways and pulled up the carbine.

There must have been a single round left in the breech, but it was a lucky one. I did not aim it, but merely jerked at the trigger as the barrel came up.

It hit Guthrie in the crook of his right elbow, shattering the joint and the pistol flew backwards over his shoulder, skidded across the deck and thudded into the stern scuppers.

Guthrie spun aside, the arm twisting grotesquely and hanging from the broken joint and at the same instant the firing pin of the carbine fell on an empty chamber.

We stared at each other, both of us badly hit, but the old antagonism was still there between us. It gave me strength to come up on my knees and start towards him, the empty carbine falling from my hand.

Guthrie grunted and turned away, gripping the shattered arm with his good hand. He staggered towards the .45 lying in the scuppers.

I saw there was no way I could stop him. He was not mortally hit, and I knew he could shoot probably as well with his good left hand. Still I made my last try and dragged myself over Materson's body and out into the cockpit, reaching it just as Guthrie stooped to pick the pistol out of the scuppers.

Then *Dancer* came to my aid, and she reared like a wild horse as a freak swell hit her. She threw Guthrie off balance, and the pistol went skidding away across the deck. He turned to chase it, his feet slipped in the blood which I had splashed across the cockpit and he went down.

He fell heavily, pinning his shattered arm under him. He cried out, and rolled onto his knees and began crawling swiftly after the glistening black pistol.

Against the outer bulkhead of the cockpit the long flying gaffs stood in their rack like a set of billiard cues. Ten feet long, with the great stainless steel hooks uppermost.

Chubby had filed the points as cruelly as stilettos. They were designed to be buried deep into a game fish's body, and the shock of the blow would detach the head from the stock. The fish could then be dragged on board with the length of heavy nylon rope that was spliced onto the hook.

Guthrie had almost reached the pistol as I knocked upon the clamp on the rack and lifted down one of the gaffs.

Guthrie scooped up the pistol left-handed, juggling it to get a grip on it, concentrating his whole attention on the weapon and while he was busy I came up on my knees again and lifted the gaff with one hand, throwing it up high and reaching out over Guthrie's bowed back. As the hook flashed down over him I hit the steel in hard, driving it full length through his ribs, burying the gleaming steel to the curve. The shock of it pulled him down onto the deck and once again the pistol dropped from his hand and the roll of the boat pushed it away from him.

Now he was screaming, a high-pitched wail of agony with the steel deep in him. I tugged harder, single-handed, trying to work it into heart or lung and the hook broke from the stock. Guthrie rolled across the deck towards the pistol. He groped frantically for it, and I dropped the gaff stock and groped just as frantically for the rope to restrain him.

I have seen two women wrestlers fighting in a bath of black mud, in a nightclub in the St Pauli district of Hamburg—and now Guthrie and I performed the same act, only in place of mud we fought in a bath of our own blood. We slithered and rolled about the deck, thrown about mercilessly by *Dancer*'s action in the swell.

Guthrie was weakening at last, clawing with his good hand at the great hook buried in his body, and with the next roll of the sea I was able to throw a coil of the rope around his neck and get a firm purchase against the base of the fighting chair with one foot. Then I pulled with all the remains of my strength and resolve.

Suddenly, with a single explosive expulsion of breath, his tongue fell out of his mouth and he relaxed, his limbs stretched out limply and his head lolled loosely back and forth with *Dancer*'s roll.

I was tired beyond caring now. My hand opened of its own accord and the rope fell from it. I lay back and closed my eyes. Darkness fell over me like a shroud.

———————

When I regained consciousness my face felt as though it had been scalded with acid, my lips were swollen and my thirst raged like a forest fire. I had lain face up under a tropical sun for six hours, and it had burned me mercilessly.

Slowly I rolled onto my side, and cried out weakly at the immensity of pain that was my chest. I lay still for a while to let it subside and then I began to explore the wound.

The bullet had angled in through the bicep of my left arm, missing bone, and come out through the tricep, tearing a big exit hole. Immediately it had ploughed into the side of my chest.

Sobbing with the effort I traced and probed the wound with my finger. It had glanced over a rib, I could feel the exposed bone was cracked and rough ended where the slug had struck and been deflected and left slivers of lead and bone chips in the churned flesh. It had gone through the thick muscle of my back—and torn out below the shoulder blade, leaving a hole the size of a *demi-tasse* coffee cup.

I fell back onto the deck, panting and fighting back waves of giddy nausea. My exploration had induced fresh bleeding, but I knew at least that the bullet had not entered the chest cavity. I still had some sort of a chance.

While I rested I looked blearily about me. My hair and clothing were stiff with dried blood, blood was coated over the cockpit, dried black and shiny or congealed.

Guthrie lay on his back with the gaff hook still in him and the rope around his neck. The gases in his belly had already blown, giving him a pregnant swollen look.

I got up onto my knees and began to crawl. Materson's body half-blocked the entrance to the cabin, shredded by gunfire as though he had been mauled by a savage predator.

I crawled over him, and found I was whimpering aloud as I saw the icebox behind the bar.

I drank three cans of Coca Cola, gasping and choking in my eagerness, spilling the icy liquid down my chest, and moaning and snuffling through each mouthful. Then I lay and rested again. I closed my eyes and just wanted to sleep for ever.

'Where the hell are we?' The question hit me with a shock of awareness. *Dancer* was adrift on a treacherous coast, strewn with reefs and shoals.

I dragged myself to my feet and reached the blood-caked cockpit.

Beneath us flowed the deep purple blue of the Mozambique, and a clear horizon circled us, above which the massive cloud ranges climbed to a tall blue sky. The ebb and the wind had pushed us far out to the east, we had plenty of sea room.

My legs collapsed under me, and I may have slept for a while. When I woke my head felt clearer, but the wound had stiffened horribly. Each movement was agony. On my hand and knees I reached the shower room where the medicine chest was kept. I ripped away my shirt and poured undiluted acriflavine solution into the cavernous wounds. Then I plugged them roughly with surgical dressing and strapped the whole as best I could, but the effort was too much.

The dizziness overwhelmed me again and I crashed down onto the linoleum floor unconscious.

I awoke light-headed, and feeble as a new-born infant.

It was a major effort to fashion a sling for the wounded arm, and the journey to the bridge was an endless procession of dizziness and pain and nausea.

Dancer's engines started with the first kick, sweet as ever she was.

'Take me home, me darling,' I whispered, and set the automatic pilot. I gave her an approximate heading. *Dancer* settled on course, and the darkness caught me again. I went down sprawling on the deck, welcoming oblivion as it washed over me.

It may have been the altered action of *Dancer*'s passage that roused me. She no longer swooped and rolled with the big swell of the Mozambique, but ambled quietly along over a sheltered sea. Dusk was falling swiftly.

Stiffly I dragged myself up to the wheel. I was only just in time, for dead ahead lay the loom of land in the fading light. I slammed *Dancer*'s throttle closed, and kicked her into neutral. She came up and rocked gently in a low sea. I recognized the shape of the land—it was Big Gull Island.

We had missed the channel of Grand Harbour, my heading had been a little southerly and we had run into the southernmost straggle of tiny atolls that made up the St Mary's group.

Hanging on to the wheel for support I craned forward. The canvas-wrapped bundle still lay on the foredeck—and suddenly I knew that I must get rid of it. My reasons were not clear then. Dimly I realized that it was a high card in the game into which I had been drawn. I knew I dare not ferry it back into Grand Harbour in broad daylight. Three men had been killed for it already—and I'd had half my chest shot away. There was some strong medicine wrapped up in that sheet of canvas.

It took me fifteen minutes to reach the foredeck, and I blacked out twice on the way. When I crawled to the bundle of canvas I was sobbing aloud with each movement.

For another half-hour I tried feebly to unwrap the stiff canvas and untie the thick nylon knots. With only one hand and my fingers so numb and weak that they could not close properly it was a hopeless task, and the blackness kept filling my head. I was afraid I would go out with the bundle still aboard.

Lying on my side I used the last rays of the setting sun to take a bearing off the point of the island, lining up a clump of palms and the point of the high ground—marking the spot with care.

Then I opened the swinging section of the foredeck railing through which we usually pulled big fish aboard, and I wriggled around the canvas bundle, got both feet onto it and shoved it over the side. It fell with a heavy splash and droplets splattered in my face.

My exertions had re-opened the wounds and fresh blood was soaking my clumsy dressing. I started back across the deck but I did not make it. I went out for the last time as I reached the break of the cockpit.

The morning sun and a raucous barnyard squawking woke me, but when I opened my eyes the sun seemed shaded, darkened as though in eclipse. My vision was fading, and when I tried to move there was no strength for it. I lay crushed beneath the weight of weakness and pain. *Dancer* was canted at an absurd angle, probably stranded high and dry on the beach.

I stared up into the rigging above me. There were three black-backed gulls as big as turkeys sitting in a row on the cross stay. They twisted their heads sideways to look down at me, and their beaks were clear yellow and powerful. The upper part of the beak ended in a curved point that was a bright cherry red. They watched me with glistening black eyes, and fluffed out their feathers impatiently.

I tried to shout at them, to drive them away but my lips would not move. I was completely helpless, and I knew that soon they would begin on my eyes. They always went for the eyes.

One of the gulls above me grew bold and, spreading his wings, planed down to the deck near me. He folded his wings and waddled a few steps closer, and we stared at each other. Again I tried to scream, but no sound came and the gull waddled forward again, then stretched out his neck, opened that wicked beak and let out a hoarse screech of menace. I felt the whole of my dreadfully abused body cringing away from the bird.

Suddenly the tone of the screeching gulls altered, and the air was filled with their wing beats. The bird that I was watching screeched again, but this time in disappointment and it launched itself into flight, the draught from its wings striking my face as it rose.

There was a long silence then, as I lay on the heavily listing deck, fighting off the waves of darkness that tried to overwhelm me. Then suddenly there was a scrabbling sound alongside.

I rolled my head again to face it, and at that moment a dark chocolate face rose above deck level and stared at me from a range of two feet.

'Lordy!' said a familiar voice. 'Is that you, Mister Harry?'

I learned later that Henry Wallace, one of St Mary's turtle hunters, had been camped out on the atolls and had risen from his bed of straw to find *Wave Dancer* stranded by the ebb on the sand bar of the lagoon with a cloud of gulls squabbling over her. He had waded out across the bar, and climbed the side to peer into the slaughterhouse that was *Dancer*'s cockpit.

I wanted to tell him how thankful I was to see him, I wanted to promise him free beer for the rest of his life—but instead I started to weep, just a slow welling up of tears from deep down. I didn't even have the strength to sob.

———————

'Little scratch like that,' marvelled MacNab. 'What's all the fussing about?' and he probed determinedly.

I gasped as he did something else to my back; if I had had the strength I would have got up off the hospital bed and pushed that probe up the most convenient opening of his body. Instead I moaned weakly.

'Come on, Doc. Didn't they teach you about morphine and that stuff back in the time when you should have failed your degree?'

MacNab came around to look in my face. He was plump and scarlet-faced, fiftyish and greying in hair and moustache. His breath should have anaesthetized me.

'Harry, my boy, that stuff costs money—what are you, anyway, National Health or a private patient?'

'I just changed my status—I'm private.'

'Quite right, too,' MacNab agreed. 'Man of your standing in the community,' and he nodded to the sister. 'Very well then, my dear, give Mister Harry a grain of morphine before we proceed,' and while he waited for her to prepare the shot he went on to cheer me up. 'We put six whole pints of blood into you last night, you were just about dry. Soaked it up like a sponge.'

Well, you wouldn't expect one of the giants of the medical profession to be practising on St Mary's. I could almost believe the island rumour that he was in partnership with Fred Coker's mortician parlour.

'How long you going to keep me in here anyway, Doc?'

'Not more than a month.'

'A month!' I struggled to sit up and two nurses pounced on me to restrain me, which required no great effort. I could still hardly raise my head. 'I can't afford a month. My God, it's right in the middle of the season. I've got a new party coming next week—'

The sister hurried across with the syringe.

'—You trying to break me? I can't afford to miss a single party—'

The sister hit me with the needle.

'Harry old boy, you can forget about this season. You won't be fishing again,' and he began picking bits of bone and flakes of lead out of me while he hummed cheerily to himself. The morphine dulled the pain—but not my despair. If *Dancer* and I missed half a season we just couldn't keep going. Once again they had me stretched out on the financial rack. God, how I hated money.

MacNab strapped me up in clean white bandages, and spread a little more sunshine.

'You going to lose some function in your left arm there, Harry boy. Probably always be a little stiff and weak, and you going to have some pretty scars to show the girls.' He finished winding the bandage and turned to the sister. 'Change the dressings every six hours, swab out with Eusol and give hin his usual dose of Aureo Mycytin every four hours. Three Mogadon tonight and I'll see him on my rounds tomorrow.' He turned back to grin at me with bad teeth under the untidy grey moustache. 'The entire police force is waiting outside this very room. I'll have to let them in now.' He started towards the door, then paused to chuckle again. 'You did a hell of a job on those two guys, spread them over the scenery with a spade. Nice shooting, Harry boy.'

Inspector Daly was dressed in impeccable khaki drill, starched and pristine, and his leather belts and straps glowed with a high polish.

'Good afternoon, Mr Fletcher. I have come to take a statement from you. I hope you feel strong enough.'

'I feel wonderful, Inspector. Nothing like a bullet through the chest to set you up.'

Daly turned to the constable who followed him and motioned him to take the chair beside the bed, and as he sat and prepared his shorthand pad the constable told me softly, 'Sorry you got hurt, Mister Harry.'

'Thanks, Wally, but you should have seen the other guys.'

Wally was one of Chubby's nephews, and his mother did my laundry. He was a big, strong, darkly good-looking youngster.

'I saw them,' he grinned. 'Wow!'

'If you are ready, Mr Fletcher,' Daly cut in primly, annoyed by the exchange. 'We can get on.'

'Shoot,' I said, and I had my story well prepared. Like all good stories, it was the exact and literal truth, with omissions. I made no mention of the prize that James North had lifted, and which I had dumped again off Big Gull Island—nor did I tell Daly in which area we had conducted our search. He wanted to know, of course. He kept coming back to that.

'What were they searching for?'

'I have no idea. They were very careful not to let me know.'

'Where did all this happen?' he persisted.

'In the area beyond Herring Bone Reef, south of Rastafa Point.' This was fifty miles from the break at Gunfire Reef.

'Could you recognize the exact point where they dived?'

'I don't think so, not within a few miles. I was merely following instructions.'

Daly chewed his silky moustache in frustration.

'All right, you say they attacked you without warning,' and I nodded. 'Why did they do that—why would they try to kill you?'

'We never really discussed it. I didn't have a chance to ask them.' I was beginning to feel very tired and feeble again, I didn't want to go on talking in case I made a mistake. 'When Guthrie started shooting at me with that cannon of his I didn't think he wanted to chat.'

'This isn't a joke, Fletcher,' he told me stiffly, and I rang the bell beside me. The sister must have been waiting just outside the door.

'Sister, I'm feeling pretty bad.'

'You'll have to go now, Inspector.' She turned on the two policemen like a mother hen, and drove them from the ward. Then she came back to rearrange my pillows.

She was a pretty little thing with huge dark eyes, and her tiny waist was belted in firmly to accentuate her big nicely shaped bosom on which she wore her badges and medals. Lustrous chestnut curls peeled from under the saucy little uniform cap.

'What is your name, then?' I whispered hoarsely.

'May.'

'Sister May, how come I haven't seen you around before?' I asked, as she leaned across me to tuck in my sheet.

'Guess you just weren't looking, Mister Harry.'

'Well, I'm looking now.' The front of her crisp white uniform blouse was only a few inches from my nose. She stood up quickly.

'They say here you're a devil man,' she said. 'I know now they didn't tell me lies.' But she was smiling. 'Now you go to sleep. You've got to get strong again.'

'Yeah, we'll talk again then,' I said, and she laughed out loud.

The next three days I had a lot of time to think for I was allowed no visitors until the official inquest had been conducted. Daly had a constable on guard outside my room, and I was left in no doubt that I stood accused of murder most vile.

My room was cool and airy with a good view down across the lawns to the tall dark-leafed banyan trees, and beyond them the massive stone walls of the fort with the cannons upon the battlements. The food was good, plenty of fish and fruit, and Sister May and I were becoming good, if not intimate, friends. She even smuggled in a bottle of Chivas Regal which we kept in the bedpan. From her I heard how the whole island was agog with the cargo that *Wave Dancer* had brought into Grand Harbour. She told me they buried Materson and Guthrie on the second day in the old cemetery. A corpse doesn't keep so well in those latitudes.

In those three days I decided that the bundle I had dropped off Big Gull Island would stay there. I guessed that from now on there would be a lot of eyes watching me, and I was at a complete disadvantage. I didn't know who the watchers were and I didn't know why. I would keep down off the sky-line until I worked out where the next bullet was likely to come from. I didn't like the game. They could deal me out and I would stick to the action I could call and handle.

I thought a lot about Jimmy North also, and every time I felt myself grieving unnecessarily I tried to tell myself that he was a stranger, that he had meant nothing to me, but it didn't work. This is a weakness of mine which I must always guard against. I become too readily emotionally bound up with other people. I try to walk alone, avoiding involvement, and after years of practice I have achieved some success. It is seldom these days that anyone can penetrate my armour the way Jimmy North did.

By the third day I was feeling much stronger. I could lift myself into a sitting position without assistance and with only a moderate degree of pain.

They held the official inquest in my hospital room. It was a closed session, attended only by the heads of the legislative, judicial and executive branches of St Mary's government.

The President himself, dressed as always in black with a crisp white shirt and a halo of snowy wool around his bald pate, chaired the meeting. Judge Harkness, tall and thin and sunburned to dark brown, assisted him—while Inspector Daly represented the executive.

The President's first concern was for my comfort and well-being. I was one of his boys.

'You be sure you don't tire yourself now, Mister Harry. Anything you want you just ask, hear? We have only come here to hear your version, but I want to tell you now not to worry. There is nothing going to happen to you.'

Inspector Daly looked pained, seeing his prisoner declared innocent before his trial began.

So I told my story again, with the President making helpful or admiring comments whenever I paused for breath, and when I finished he shook his head with wonder.

'All I can say, Mister Harry, is there are not many men would have had the strength and courage to do what you did against those gangsters, is that right, gentlemen?'

Judge Harkness agreed heartily, but Inspector Daly said nothing.

'And they were gangsters too,' he went on. 'We sent their finger-prints to London and we heard today that those men came here under false names, and that both of them have got police records at Scotland Yard. Gangsters, both of them.' The President looked at Judge Harkness. 'Any questions, Judge?'

'I don't think so, Mr President.'

'Good.' The President nodded happily. 'What about you, Inspector?' And Daly produced a typewritten list. The President made no effort to hide his irritation.

'Mister Fletcher is still a very sick man, Inspector. I hope your questions are really important.'

Inspector Daly hesitated and the President went on brusquely, 'Good, well then we are all agreed. The verdict is death by misadventure. Mister Fletcher acted in self-defence, and is hereby discharged from any guilt. No criminal charges will be brought against him.' He turned to the shorthand recorder in the corner. 'Have you got that? Type it out and send a copy to my office for signature.' He stood up and came to my bedside. 'Now you get better soon, Mister Harry. I expect you for dinner at Government House soon as you are well enough. My secretary will send you a formal invitation. I want to hear the whole story again.'

Next time I appear before a judicial body, as I surely shall, I hope for the same consideration. Having been officially declared innocent I was allowed visitors.

Chubby and Mrs Chubby came together dressed in their standard number one rig. Mrs Chubby had baked one of her splendid banana cakes, knowing my weakness for them.

Chubby was torn by relief at seeing me still alive and outrage at what I had done to *Wave Dancer*. He scowled at me fiercely as he started giving me a large slice of his mind.

'Ain't never going to get that deck clean again. It soaked right in, man. That damned old carbine of yours really chewed up the cabin bulkhead. Me and Angelo been working three days at it now, and it still needs a few more days.'

'Sorry, Chubby, next time I shoot somebody I'm going to make them stand by the rail first.' I knew that when Chubby had finished repairing the woodwork the damage would not be detectable.

'When you coming out anyway? Plenty of big fish working out there on the stream, Harry.'

'I'll be out pretty soon, Chubby. One week tops.'

Chubby sniffed. 'Did hear that Fred Coker wired all your parties for the rest of the season—told them you were hurt bad and switched their bookings to Mister Coleman.'

I lost my temper than. 'You tell Fred Coker to get his black arse up here soonest,' I shouted.

Dick Coleman had a deal with the Hilton Hotel. They had financed the purchase of two big game fishing boats, which Coleman crewed with a pair of imported skippers. Neither of his boats caught much fish, they didn't have the feel of it. He had a lot of difficulty getting charters, and I guessed Fred Coker had been handsomely compensated to switch my bookings to him. Coker arrived the following morning.

'Mister Harry, Dr MacNab told me you wouldn't be able to fish again this season. I couldn't let my parties down, they fly six thousand miles to find you in a hospital bed. I couldn't do that—I got my reputation to think of.'

'Mr Coker, your reputation smells like one of those stiffs you got tucked away in the back room.' I told him, and he smiled at me blandly from behind his gold-rimmed spectacles, but he was right of course—it would be a long time still before I could take *Dancer* out after the big billfish.

'Now don't you fuss yourself, Mister Harry. Soon as you better I will arrange a few lucrative charters for you.'

He was talking about the night run again; his commission on a single run could go as high as $750. I could handle that even in my present beaten-up condition, it involved merely conning *Dancer* in and out again—just as long as we didn't run into trouble.

'Forget it, Mr Coker. I told you from now on I fish, that's all,' and he nodded and smiled and went on as though I had not spoken.

'Had persistent enquiries from one of your old clients.'

'Body? Box?' I demanded. Body was the illegal carrying to or from the African mainland of human beings, fleeing politicians with the goon squad after them—or on the other hand aspiring politicians trying for radical change in the régime. Boxes usually contained lethal hardware and it was a one-way traffic. In the old days they called it gun-running.

Coker shook his head and said, 'Five, six,'—from the old nursery rhyme: 'Five, six. Pick up sticks.' In this context sticks were tusks of ivory. A massive, highly organized poaching operation was systematically wiping out the African elephant from the game reserves and tribal lands of East Africa. The Orient was an insatiable and high-priced market for the ivory. A fast boat and a good skipper were needed to get the valuable cargo out of an estuary mouth, through the dangerous inshore waters, out to where one of the big ocean-going dhows waited on the stream of the Mozambique.

'Mr Coker,' I told him wearily. 'I'm sure your mother never even knew your father's name.'

'It was Edward, Mister Harry,' he smiled carefully. 'I told the client that the going rate was up. What with inflation and the price of diesel fuel.'

'How much?'

'Seven thousand dollars a trip,' which was not as much as it sounds after Coker had clouted fifteen per cent, then Inspector Peter Daly had to be slipped the same again to dim his eyesight and cloud his hearing. On top of that Chubby and Angelo always earned a danger money bonus of five hundred each for a night run.

'Forget it, Mr Coker,' I said unconvincingly. 'You just fix a couple of fishing parties.' But he knew I couldn't fight it.

'Just as soon as you fit enough to fish, we'll fix that. Meantime, when do you want to do the first night run? Shall I tell them ten days from today? That will be high spring tide and a good moon.'

'All right,' I agreed with resignation. 'Ten days' time.'

With a positive decision made, it seemed that my recovery from the wounds was hastened. I had been in peak physical condition which contributed, and the gaping holes in my arm and back began to shrink miraculously.

I reached a milestone in my convalescence on the sixth day. Sister May was giving me a bed bath, with a basin of suds and a face cloth, when there was a monumental demonstration of my physical well-being. Even I, who was no stranger to the phenomenon, was impressed, while Sister May was so overcome that her voice became a husky little whisper.

'Lord!' she said. 'You've sure got your strength back.'

'Sister May, do you think we should waste that?' I asked, and she shook her head vehemently.

From then onwards I began to take a more cheerful view of my circumstances, and not surprisingly the canvas-wrapped secret off Big Gull Island began to nag me. I felt my good resolutions weakening.

'I'll just take a look,' I told myself. 'When I am sure the dust has really settled.'

They were allowing me up for a few hours at a time now, and I felt restless and anxious to get on with it. Not even Sister May's devoted efforts could blunt the edge of my awakening energy. MacNab was impressed.

'You heal well, Harry old chap. Closing up nicely—another week.'

'A week, hell!' I told him determinedly. Seven days from now I was making the night run. Coker had set it up without trouble—and I was just about stony broke. I needed that run pretty badly.

My crew came up to visit me every evening, and to report progress on the repairs to *Dancer*. One evening Angelo arrived earlier than usual; he was dressed in his courting gear—rodeo boots and all—but he was strangely subdued and not alone.

The lass with him was the young nursery grade teacher from the government school down near the fort. I knew her well enough to exchange smiles on the street. Missus Eddy had summed up her character for me once.

'She's a good girl, that Judith. Not all flighty and flirty like some others. Going to make some lucky fellow a good wife.'

She was also good-looking with a tall willowy figure, neatly and conservatively dressed, and she greeted me shyly.

'How do, Mister Harry.'

'Hello, Judith. Good of you to come,' and I looked at Angelo, unable to hide my grin. He couldn't meet my eye, colouring up as he hunted for words.

'Me and Judith planning to marry up,' he blurted at last. 'Wanted you to know that, boss.'

'Think you can keep him under control, Judith?' I laughed delightedly.

'You just watch me,' she said with a flash of dark eyes that made the question superfluous.

'That's great—I'll make a speech at your wedding,' I assured them. 'You going to let Angelo go on crewing for me?'

'Wouldn't ever try to stop him,' she assured me. 'It's good work he's got with you.'

They stayed for another hour and when they left I felt a small prickle of envy. It must be a good feeling to have someone—apart from yourself. I thought some day if I ever found the right person I might try it. Then I dismissed the thought, raising my guard again. There were a hell of a lot of women—and no guarantee you will pick right.

MacNab discharged me with two days to spare. My clothes hung on my bony frame, I had lost nearly two stone in weight and my tan had faded to a dirty yellow brown, there were big blue smears under my eyes and I still felt weak as a baby. The arm was in a sling and the wounds were still open, but I could change the dressing myself.

Angelo brought the pick-up to the hospital and waited while I said good-bye to Sister May on the steps.

'Nice getting to know you, Mister Harry.'

'Come out to the shack some time soon. I'll grill you a mess of cray-fish, and we'll drink a little wine.'

'My contract ends next week. I'll be going home to England then.'

'You be happy, hear,' I told her.

Angelo drove me down to Admiralty, and with Chubby we spent an hour going over *Dancer*'s repairs.

Her decks were snowy white, and they had replaced all the wood-work in the saloon bulkhead, a beautiful piece of joinery with which even I could find no fault.

We took her down the channel as far as Mutton Point and it was good to feel her riding lightly under my feet and hear the sweet burble of her engines. We came home in the dusk to tie up at moorings and sit out on the bridge in the dark, drinking beer out of the can and talking.

I told them that we had a run set for the following night, and they asked where to and what the cargo was. That was all—it was set, there was no argument.

'Time to go,' Angelo said at last. 'Going to pick up Judith from night school,' and we rowed ashore in the dinghy.

There was a police Landrover parked beside my old pick-up at the back of the pineapple sheds and Wally, the young constable, climbed out as we approached. He greeted his uncle, and then turned to me.

'Sorry to worry you, Mister Harry, but Inspector Daly wants to see you up at the fort. He says it's urgent.'

'God,' I growled. 'It can wait until tomorrow.'

'He says it can't, Mister Harry.' Wally was apologetic, and for his sake I went along.

'Okay, I'll follow you in the pick-up—but we got to drop Chubby and Angelo off first.'

I thought it was probably that Daly wanted to haggle about his pay off. Usually Fred Coker fixed that, but I guessed that Daly was raising the price of his honour.

Driving one-handed and holding the steering wheel with a knee while I shifted gear with my good hand, I followed the red tail lights of Wally's Landrover rattling over the drawbridge and parked beside it in the courtyard of the fort.

The massive stone walls had been built by slave labour in the mid-eighteenth century and from the wide ramparts the long thirty-six pounder cannon ranged the channel and the entrance to Grand Harbour.

One wing was used as the island police headquarters, gaol and armoury—the rest of it was government offices and the Presidential and State apartments.

We climbed the front steps to the charge office and Wally led me through a side door, and along a corridor, down steps, another corridor, more stone steps.

I had never been down here before and I was intrigued. The stone walls here must have been twenty feet thick, the old powder store probably. I half expected the Frankenstein monster to be lurking behind the thick oak door, iron studded and weathered, at the end of the last passage. We went through.

It wasn't Frankenstein, but next best. Inspector Daly waited for us with another of his constables. I noticed immediately they both wore sidearms. The room was empty except for a wooden table and four P.W.D. type chairs. The walls were unpainted stonework and the floor was paved.

At the back of the room an arched doorway led to a row of cells. The lights were bare hundred-watt bulbs hanging on black electrical cable that ran exposed across the beamed roof. They cast hard black shadows in the angles of the irregularly shaped room.

On the table lay my FN carbine. I stared at it uncomprehendingly. Behind me Wally closed the oak door.

'Mr Fletcher, is this your firearm?'

'You know damn well it is,' I said angrily. 'Just what the hell are you playing at, Daly?'

'Harold Delville Fletcher, I am placing you under arrest for the unlawful possession of Category A firearms. To wit, one unlicensed automatic rifle type Fabrique Nationale Serial No. 4163215.'

'You're off your head,' I said, and laughed. He didn't like that laugh. The weak little lips below his moustache puckered up like those of a sulky child and he nodded at his constables. They had been briefed, and they went out through the oak door.

I heard the bolts shoot home, and Daly and I were alone. He was standing well away from me across the room—and the flap of his holster was unbuttoned.

'Does his excellency know about this, Daly?' I asked, still smiling.

'His excellency left St Mary's at four o'clock this afternoon to attend the conference of Commonwealth heads in London. He won't be back for two weeks.'

I stopped smiling. I knew it was true. 'In the meantime I have reason to believe the security of the State is endangered.'

He smiled now, thinly and with the mouth only. 'Before we go any further I want you to be sure I am serious.'

'I believe you.' I said.

'I have two weeks with you alone, here, Fletcher. These walls are pretty thick, you can make as much noise as you like.'

'You are a monstrous little turd, you really are.'

'There is only one of two ways you are going to leave here. Either you and I come to an arrangement—or I'll get Fred Coker to come and fetch you in a box.'

'Let's hear your deal, little man.'

'I want to know exactly—and I mean exactly—where your charter carried out their diving operations before the shoot out.'

'I told you—somewhere off Rastafa Point. I couldn't give you the exact spot.'

'Fletcher, you know the spot to within inches. I'm willing to stake *your* life on that. You wouldn't miss a chance like that. You know it. I know it—and they knew it. That's why they tried to sign you off.'

'Inspector, go screw,' I said.

'What is more it was nowhere near Rastafa Point. You were working north of here, towards the mainland. I was interested—I had some reports of your movements.'

'It was somewhere off Rastafa Point,' I repeated doggedly.

'Very well,' he nodded. 'I hope you aren't as tough as you put out, Fletcher, otherwise this is going to be a long messy business. Before we start though, don't waste our time with false data. I'm going to keep you here while I check it out—I've got two weeks.'

We stared at each other, and my flesh began to crawl. Peter Daly was going to enjoy this, I realized. There was a gloating expression on those thin lips and a smoky glaze to his eyes.

'I had a great deal of experience in interrogation in Malaya, you know. Fascinating subject. So many aspects to it. So often it's the tough, strong ones that pop first—and the little runts that hang on for ever—'

This was for kicks, I saw clearly that he was aroused by the prospect of inflicting pain. His breathing had changed, faster and deeper, there was fresh colour in his cheeks.

'—of course, you are at a physical low ebb right now, Fletcher. Probably your threshold of pain is much lowered after your recent misadventures. I don't think it will take long—'

He seemed to regret that. I gathered myself, tightening up for an attempt.

'No,' he snapped. 'Don't do it, Fletcher.' He placed his hand on the butt of the pistol. He was fifteen feet away. I was one-armed, weak, there was a locked door behind me, two armed constables—my shoulders sagged as I relaxed.

'That's better.' He smiled again. 'Now I think we will handcuff you to the bars of a cell, and we can get to work. When you have had enough you have merely to say so. I think you will find my little electrical set up simple but effective. It's merely a twelve-volt car battery—and I clip the terminals on to interesting parts of the body—'

He reached behind him—and for the first time I noticed the button of an electric bell set on the wall. He pressed it and I heard the bell ring faintly beyond the oaken door.

The bolts shot back and the two constables came back in.

'Take him through to the cells,' Daly ordered, and the constables hesitated. I guessed they were strangers to this type of operation.

'Come on,' snapped Daly, and they stepped up on either side of me. Wally laid a hand lightly on my injured arm, and I allowed myself to be led forward towards the cells—and Daly.

I wanted to have a chance at him, just one chance.

'How's your mom, Wally?' I asked casually.

'She's all right, Mister Harry,' he muttered embarrassedly.

'She get the present I sent up for her birthday?'

'Yeah, she got it.' He was distracted as I intended.

We had come level with Daly, he was standing by the doorway to the cells, waiting for us to go through, slapping the malacca swagger stick against his thigh.

The constables were holding me respectfully, loosely, unsure of themselves, and I stepped to one side pushing Wally slightly off balance —then I spun back, breaking free.

Not one of them was ready for it, and I covered the three paces to Daly before they had realized what I was doing—and I put my right knee into him with my full body weight behind it. It thumped into the crotch of his legs, a marvellously solid blow. Whatever the price I was going to have to pay for the pleasure, it was cheap.

Daly was lifted off his feet, a full eighteen inches in the air, and he flew backwards to crash against the bars. Then he doubled up, both hands pressed into his lower body, screaming thinly—a sound like steam from a boiling kettle. As he went over I lined up for another shot at his face. I wanted to take his teeth out with a kick in the mouth—but the constables recovered their wits and leaped forward to drag me away. They were rough now, twisting the arm.

'You didn't ought to do that, Mister Harry,' Wally shouted angrily. His fingers bit into my bicep and I gritted my teeth.

'The President himself cleared me, Wally. You know that,' I shouted back at him, and Daly straightened up, his face twisted with agony, still holding himself.

'This is a frame up.' I knew I had only a few seconds to talk, Daly was reeling towards me, brandishing the swagger stick, his mouth wide open as he tried to find his voice.

'If he gets me in that cell he's going to kill me, Wally—'

'Shut up!' screeched Daly.

'He wouldn't dare try this if the President—'

'Shut up! Shut up!' He swung the swagger stick, a side-arm cut, that hissed like a cobra. He had gone for my wounds deliberately, and the supple cane snapped around me like a pistol shot.

The pain of it was beyond belief, and I convulsed, bucking involuntarily in their grip. They held me.

'Shut up!' Daly was hysterical with pain and rage. He swung again, and the cane cut deeply into half-healed flesh. This time I screamed.

'I'll kill you, you bastard.' Daly staggered back, still hunched with pain, and he fumbled with his holstered pistol.

What I had hoped for now happened. Wally released me and jumped forward.

'No,' he shouted. 'Not that.'

He towered over Daly's slim crouching form and with one massive brown hand he blocked Daly's draw.

'Get out of my way. That's an order,' shouted Daly, but Wally unclipped the lanyard from the pistol's butt and disarmed him, stepping back with the pistol in his hand.

'I'll break you for this,' snarled Daly. 'It's your duty—'

'I know my duty, Inspector,' Wally spoke with a simple dignity, 'and it's not to murder prisoners.' Then he turned to me. 'Mister Harry, you'd best get out of here.'

'You're freeing a prisoner—' Daly gasped. 'Man, I'm going to break you.'

'Didn't see no warrant,' Wally cut in. 'Soon as the President signs a warrant, we'll fetch Mister Harry right back in again.'

'You black bastard,' Daly panted at him, and Wally turned to me.

'Get!' he said. 'Quickly.'

It was a long ride out to the shack, every bump in the track hit me in the chest. One thing I had learned from the evening's jollifications was that my original thoughts were correct—whatever that bundle off Big Gull Island contained, it could get a peace-loving gentleman like myself into plenty of trouble.

I was not so trusting as to believe that Inspector Daly had made his last attempt at interrogating me. Just as soon as he recovered from the kick in his multiplication machinery which I had given him, he was going to make another attempt to connect me up to the lighting system. I wondered if Daly was acting on his own, or if he had partners—and I guessed he was alone, taking opportunity as it presented itself.

I parked the pick-up in the yard and went through onto the veranda of my shack. Missus Chubby had been out to sweep and tidy while I was away. There were fresh flowers in a jam-jar on the dining-room table—but more important there were eggs and bacon, bread and butter in the icebox.

I stripped off my blood-stained shirt and dressing. There were thick raised welts around my chest that the cane had left, and the wounds were a mess.

I showered and strapped on a fresh dressing, then, standing naked over the stove, I scrambled a pan full of eggs with bacon and while it cooked, I poured a very dark whisky and took it like medicine.

I was too tired to climb between the sheets, and as I fell across the bed I wondered if I would be fit enough to work the night run on schedule. It was my last thought before sun-up.

After I had showered again and swallowed two Doloxene pain-killers with a glass of cold pineapple juice and eaten another panful of eggs for breakfast, I thought the answer was yes. I was stiff and sore, but I could work. At noon I drove into town, stopped off at Missus Eddy's store for supplies and then went on down to Admiralty.

Chubby and Angelo were on board already, and *Dancer* lay against the wharf.

'I filled the auxiliary tanks, Harry,' Chubby told me. 'She's good for a thousand miles.'

'Did you break out the cargo nets?' I asked, and he nodded.

'They are stowed in the main sail locker.' We would use the nets to deck load the bulky ivory cargo.

'Don't forget to bring a coat—it will be cold out on the stream with this wind blowing.'

'Don't worry, Harry. You the one should watch it. Man, you look bad as you were ten days ago. You look real sick.'

'I feel beautiful, Chubby.'

'Yeah,' he grunted, 'like my mother-in-law,' then he changed the subject. 'What happened to your carbine, man?'

'The police are holding it.'

'You mean we going out there without a piece on board?'

'We never needed it yet.'

'There is always a first time,' he grunted. 'I'm going to feel mighty naked without it.'

Chubby's obsession with armaments always amused me.

Despite all the evidence that I presented to the contrary, Chubby could never quite shake off the belief that the velocity and range of a bullet depended upon how hard one pulled the trigger—and Chubby intended that his bullets go very fast and very far indeed.

The savage strength with which he sent them on their way would have buckled a less robust weapon than the FN. He also suffered from a complete inability to keep his eyes open at the moment of firing.

I have seen him miss a fifteen-foot tiger shark at a range of ten feet with a full magazine of twenty rounds. Chubby Andrews was never going to make it to Bisley, but he just naturally loved firearms and things that went bang.

'It will be a milk run, a ruddy pleasure cruise, Chubby, you'll see,' and he crossed his fingers to avert the hex, and shuffled off to work on *Dancer*'s already brilliant brasswork, while I went ashore.

The front office of Fred Coker's travel agency was deserted and I rang the bell on the desk. He stuck his head through from the back room.

'Welcome, Mister Harry.' He had removed his coat and tie and had rolled up his shirt sleeves; about his waist he wore a red rubber apron. 'Lock the front door, please, and come through.'

The back room was in contrast to the front office with its gaudy wallpaper and bright travel posters. It was a long, gloomy barn. Along one wall were piled cheap pine coffins. The hearse was parked inside the double doors at the far end. Behind a grimy canvas screen in one corner was a marble slab table with guttering around the edges and a spout to direct fluid from the guttering into a bucket on the floor.

'Come in, sit down. There is a chair. Excuse me if I carry on working while we talk. I have to have this ready for four o'clock this afternoon.'

I took one look at the frail naked corpse on the slab. It was a little girl of about six years of age with long dark hair. One look was enough and I moved the chair behind the screen so I could see only Fred Coker's bald head, and I lit a cheroot. There was a heavy smell of embalming fluid in the room, and it caught in my throat.

'You get used to it, Mister Harry.' Fred Coker had noticed my distaste.

'Did you set it up?' I didn't want to discuss his gruesome trade.

'It's fixed,' he assured me.

'Did you square our friend at the fort?'

'It's all fixed.'

'When did you see him?' I persisted, I wanted to know about Daly.

was very interested in how Daly felt.

'I saw him this morning, Mister Harry.'

'How was he?'

'He seemed all right.' Coker paused in his grisly task and looked at me questioningly.

'Was he standing up, walking around, dancing a jig, singing, tying the dog loose?'

'No. He was sitting down, and he was not in a very good mood.'

'It figures.' I laughed and my own injuries felt better. 'But he took the pay off?'

'Yes, he took it.'

'Good, then we have still got a deal.'

'Like I told you, it's all fixed.'

'Lay it on me, Mr Coker.'

'The pick up is at the mouth of the Salsa stream where it enters the south channel of the main Duza estuary.' I nodded, that was acceptable. There was a good channel and the holding ground off the Salsa was satisfactory.

'The recognition signal will be two lanterns—one over the other, placed on the bank nearest the mouth. You will flash twice, repeated at thirty-second intervals and when the lower lantern is extinguished you can anchor. Got that?'

'Good.' It was all satisfactory.

'They will provide labour to load from the lighters.'

I nodded, then asked. 'They know that slack water is three o'clock—and I must be out of the channel before that?'

'Yes, Mister Harry. I told them they must finish loading before two hundred hours.'

'All right then—what about the drop off?'

'Your drop off will be twenty-five miles due east of Rastafa Point.'

'Fine.' I could check my bearings off the lighthouse at Rastafa. It was good and simple.

'You will drop off to a dhow-rigged schooner, a big one. Your recognition signal will be the same. Two lanterns on the mast, you will flash twice at thirty seconds, and the lower lamp will extinguish. You can then offload. They will provide labour and will put down an oil slick for you to ride in. I think that is all.'

'Except for the money.'

'Except for the money, of course.' He produced an envelope from the front pocket of his apron. I took it gingerly between thumb and forefinger and glanced at his calculations scribbled in ballpoint on the envelope.

'Half up front, as usual, the rest on delivery.' he pointed out.

That was thirty-five hundred, less twenty-one hundred for Coker's commission and Daly's pay off. It left fourteen hundred, out of which I had to find bonus for Chubby and Angelo—a thousand dollars—not much over.

I grimaced. 'I'll be waiting outside your office at nine o'clock tomorrow morning, Mr Coker.'

'I'll have a cup of coffee ready for you, Mister Harry.'

'That had better not be all,' I told him, and he laughed and stooped once more over the marble slab.

We cleared Grand Harbour in the late afternoon, and I made a fake run down the channel towards Mutton Point for the benefit of a possible watcher with binoculars on Coolie Peak. As darkness fell, I came around onto my true heading, and we went in through the inshore channel and the islands towards the wide tidal mouth of the Duva River.

There was no moon but the stars were big and the break of surf flared with phosphorescence, ghostly green in the afterglow of the setting sun.

I ran *Dancer* in fast, picking up my marks successively—the loom of an atoll in the starlight, the break of a reef, the very run and chop of the water guided me through the channels and warned of shoals and shallows.

Angelo and Chubby huddled beside me at the bridge rail. Occasionally one of them would go below to brew more of the powerful black coffee, and we sipped at the steaming mugs, staring out into the night watching for a flash of paleness that was not breaking water but the hull of a patrol boat.

Once Chubby broke the silence. 'Hear from Wally you had some trouble up at the fort last night.'

'Some,' I agreed.

'Wally had to take him up to the hospital afterwards.'

'Wally still got his job?' I asked.

'Only just. The man wanted to lock him up but Wally was too big.'

Angelo joined in. 'Judith was up at the airport at lunch time. Went up to fetch a crate of school books, and she saw him going out on the plane to the mainland.'

'Who?' I asked.

'Inspector Daly, he went across on the noon plane.'

'Why didn't you tell me before?'

'Didn't think it was important, Harry.'

'No,' I agreed. 'Perhaps it isn't.'

There were a dozen reasons why Daly might go out to the mainland, none of them remotely connected with my business. Yet it made me feel uneasy—I didn't like that kind of animal prowling around in the undergrowth when I was taking a risk.

'Wish you'd brought that piece of yours, Harry,' Chubby repeated mournfully, and I said nothing but wished the same.

The flow of the tide had smoothed the usual turmoil at the entrance to the southern channel of the Duza and I groped blindly for it in the dark. The mud banks on each side were latticed with standing fish traps laid by the tribal fishermen, and they helped to define the channel at last.

When I was sure we were in the correct entrance, I killed both engines and we drifted silently on the incoming tide. All of us listened with complete concentration for the engine beat of a patrol boat, but there was only the cry of a night heron and the splash of mullet leaping in the shallows.

Ghost silent, we were swept up the channel; on each side the dark masses of mangrove trees hedged us in and the smell of the mud swamps was rank and fetid on the moisture-laden air.

The starlight danced in spots of light on the dark agitated surface of the channel, and once a long narrow dugout canoe slid past us like a crocodile, the phosphorescence gleaming on the paddles of the two fishermen returning from the mouth. They paused to watch us for a moment and then drove on without calling a greeting, disappearing swiftly into the gloom.

'That was bad,' said Angelo.

'We will be drinking a lager in the Lord Nelson before they could tell anyone who matters.' I knew that most of the fishermen on this coast kept their own secrets, close with words like most of their kind. I was not purturbed by the sighting.

Looking ahead I saw the first bend coming up, and the current began to push *Dancer* out towards the far bank. I hit the starter buttons, the engines murmured into life, and I edged back into the deep water.

We worked our way up the snaking channel, coming out at last into the broad placid reach where the mangroves ended and firm ground rose gently on each side.

A mile ahead I saw the tributary mouth of the Salsa as a dark break in the bank, screened by tall stands of fluffy headed reeds. Beyond it the twin signal lanterns glowed yellow and soft, one upon the other.

'What did I tell you, Chubby, a milk run.'

'We aren't home yet.' Chubby the eternal optimist.

'Okay, Angelo. Get up on the bows. I'll tell you when to drop the hook.'

We crept on down the channel and I found the words of the nursery rhyme running through my mind as I locked the wheel and took the hand spotlight from the locker below the rail.

'Three, Four, knock at the door, Five, Six, pick up sticks.'

I thought briefly of the hundreds of great grey beasts that had died for the sake of their tusks—and I felt a draught of guilt blow coldly along my spine at my complicity in the slaughter. But I turned my mind away from it by lifting the spotlight and aiming the agreed signal upstream at the burning lanterns.

Three times I flashed the recognition code but I was level with the signal lanterns before the bottom one was abruptly extinguished.

'Okay, Angelo. Let her go,' I called softly as I killed the engines. The anchor splashed over and the chain ran noisily in the silence. *Dancer* snubbed up, and swung around at the restraint of the anchor, facing back down the channel.

Chubby went to break out the cargo nets for loading, but I paused by the rail, peering across at the signal lantern. The silence was complete, except for the clink and croak of the swamp frogs in the reed banks of the Salsa.

In that silence I felt more than heard the beat like that of a giant's heart. It came in through the soles of my feet rather than my ears.

There is no mistaking the beat of an Allison marine diesel. I knew that the old Second World War Rolls-Royce marines had been stripped out of the Zinballa crash boats and replaced by Allisons, and right now the sound I was feeling was the idling note of an Allison marine.

'Angelo,' I tried to keep my voice low, but at the same time transmit my urgency. 'Slip the anchor. For Christ's sake! Quick as you can.'

For just such an emergency I had a shackle pin in the chain, and I thanked the Lord for that as I dived for the controls.

As I started engines, I heard the thump of the four-pound hammer as Angelo drove out the pin. Three times he struck, and then I heard the end of the chain splash overboard.

'She's gone, Harry,' Angelo called, and I threw *Dancer* into drive and pushed open the throttles. She bellowed angrily and the wash of her propellers spewed whitely from below her counter as she sprang forward.

Although we were facing downstream, *Dancer* had a five-knot current running into her teeth and she did not jump away handily enough.

Even above our own engines I heard the Allisons give tongue, and from out of the reed-screened mouth of the Salsa tore a long deadly shape.

Even by starlight, I recognized her immediately, the widely flared bows, and the lovely thrusting lines, greyhound waisted and the square chopped-off stern—one of the Royal Navy crash boats who had spent her best days in the Channel and now was mouldering into senility on this fever coast.

The darkness was kind to her, covering the rust stains and the streaky paintwork, but she was an old woman now. Stripped of her marvellous Rolls marines—and underpowered with the more economical Allisons. In a fair run *Dancer* would toy with her—but this was no fair run and she had all the speed and power she needed as she charged into the channel to cut us off, and when she switched on her battle lights they hit us like something solid. Two glaring white beams, blinding in their intensity so I had to throw up my hand to protect my eyes.

She was dead ahead now, blocking the channel, and on her foredeck I could see the shadowy figures of the gun crew crouching around the three-pounder on its wide traversing plate. The muzzle seemed to be looking directly into my left nostril—and I felt a wild and desperate despair.

It was a meticulously planned and executed ambush. I thought of ramming her; she had a marine ply wooden hull, probably badly rotted, and *Dancer*'s fibreglass bows might stand the shock—but with the current against her *Dancer* was not making sufficient speed through the water.

Then suddenly a bull-horn bellowed electronically from the dark behind the dazzling battle lights.

'Heave to, Mr Fletcher. Or I shall be forced to fire upon you.'

One shell from the three-pounder would chop us down, and she was a quick firer. At this range they would smash us into a blazing wreck within ten seconds.

I closed down the throttles.

'A wise decision, Mr Fletcher—now kindly anchor where you are,' the bull-horn squawked.

'Okay, Angelo,' I called wearily, and waited while he rigged and dropped the spare anchor. Suddenly my arm was very painful again—for the last few hours I had forgotten about it.

'I said we should have brought that piece,' Chubby muttered beside me.

'Yeah, I'd love to see you shooting it out with that dirty great cannon, Chubby. That would be a lot of laughs.'

The crash boat manoeuvred alongside inexpertly, with gun and lights still trained on us. We stood helplessly in the blinding illumination of the battle lights and waited. I didn't want to think, I tried to feel nothing—but a spiteful inner voice sneered at me.

'Say good-bye to *Dancer*, Harry old sport, this is where the two of you part company.'

There was more than a good chance that I would be facing a firing squad in the near future—but that didn't worry me as much as the thought of losing my boat. With *Dancer* I was Mister Harry, the damnedest fellow on St Mary's and one of the top billfish men in the whole cock-eyed world. Without her, I was just another punk trying to scratch his next meal together. I'd prefer to be dead.

The crash boat careered into our side, bending the rail and scraping off a yard of our paint before they could hook onto us.

'Motherless bastards,' growled Chubby, as half a dozen armed and uniformed figures poured over our side, in a chattering undisciplined rabble. They wore navy blue bell bottoms and bum-freezers with white flaps down the back of the neck, white and blue striped vests, and white berets with red pompons on the top—but the cut of the uniform was Chinese and they brandished long AK.47 automatic assault rifles with forward-curved magazines and wooden butts.

Fighting among themselves for a chance to get in a kick or a shove with a gun butt, they drove the three of us down into the saloon, and knocked us into the bench seat against the for'ard bulkhead. We sat there shoulder to shoulder while two guards stood over us with machine-guns a few inches from our noses, and fingers curved hopefully around the triggers.

'Now I know why you paid me that five hundred dollars, boss,' Angelo tried to make a joke of it, and a guard screamed at him and hit him in the face with the gun butt. He wiped his mouth, smearing blood across his chin, and none of us joked again.

The other armed seamen began to tear *Dancer* to pieces. I suppose it was meant to be a search, but they raged through her accommodation wantonly smashing open lockers or shattering the panelling.

One of them discovered the liquor cabinet, and although there were only one or two bottles, there was a roar of approval. They squabbled noisily as seagulls over a scrap of offal, then went on to loot the galley stores with appropriate hilarity and abandon. Even when their commanding officer was assisted by four of his crew to make the hazardous journey across the six inches of open space that separated the crash boat from *Dancer*, there was no diminution in the volume of shouting and laughter and the crash of shattering woodwork and breaking glass.

The commander wheezed heavily across the cockpit and stooped to enter the saloon. He paused there to regain his breath.

He was one of the biggest men I had ever seen, not less than six foot six tall and enormously gross—a huge swollen body with a belly like a barrage balloon beneath the white uniform jacket. The jacket strained at its brass buttons and sweat had soaked through at the armpits. Across his breast he wore a glittering burst of stars and medals, and among them I recognized the American Naval Cross and the 1918 Victory Star.

His head was the shape and colour of a polished black iron pot, the type they traditionally use for cooking missionaries, and a naval cap, thick with gold braid, rode at a jaunty angle upon it. His face ran with rivers of glistening sweat, as he struggled noisily with his breathing and mopped at the sweat, staring at me with bulging eyes.

Slowly his body began to inflate, swelling even larger, like a great bullfrog, until I grew alarmed—expecting him to burst.

The purple-black lips, thick as tractor tyres, parted and an un-believable volume of sound issued from the pink cavern of his mouth.

'Shut up!' he roared. Instantly his crew of wreckers froze into silence, one of them with his gun butt still raised to attack the panelling behind the bar.

The huge officer trundled forward, seeming to fill the entire saloon with his bulk. Slowly he sank into the padded leather seat. Once more he mopped at his face, then he looked at me again and slowly his whole face lit up into the most wonderfully friendly smile, like an enormous chubby and lovable baby; his teeth were big and flawlessly white and his eyes nearly disappeared in the rolls of smiling black flesh.

'Mr Fletcher, I can't tell you what a great pleasure this is for me.' His voice was deep and soft and friendly, the accent was British upper class—almost certainly acquired at some higher seat of learning. His English was better than mine.

'I have looked forward to meeting you for a number of years.'

'That's very decent of you to say so, Admiral.' With that uniform he could not rank less.

'Admiral,' he repeated with delight, 'I like that,' and he laughed. It began with a vast shaking of belly and ended with a gasping and strain-ing for breath. 'Alas, Mr Fletcher, you are deceived by appearances,' and he preened a little, touching the medals and adjusting the peak of his cap. 'I am only a humble Lieutenant Commander.'

'That's really tough, Commander.'

'No. No, Mr Fletcher—do not waste your sympathy on me. I wield all the authority I could wish for.' He paused for deep breathing exer-cises and to wipe away the fresh ooze of sweat. 'I hold the powers of life and death, believe me.'

'I believe you, sir,' I told him earnestly. 'Please don't feel you have to prove your point.'

He shouted with laughter again, nearly choked, coughed up something large and yellow, spat it onto the floor and then told me, 'I like you, Mr Fletcher, I really do. I think a sense of humour is very important. I think you and I could become very close friends.' I doubted it, but I smiled encouragingly.

'As a mark of my esteem you may use the familiar form when addressing me—Suleiman Dada.'

'I appreciate that—I really do, Suleiman Dada, and you may call me Harry.'

'Harry,' he said. 'Let's have a dram of whisky together.' At that moment another man entered the saloon. A slim boyish figure, dressed not in his usual colonial police uniform but in a lightweight silk suit and lemon-coloured silk shirt and matching tie, with alligator-skin shoes on his feet.

The light blond hair was carefully combed forward into a cow's lick, and the fluffy moustache was trim as ever, but he walked carefully, seeming to favour an injury. I grinned at him.

'So, how does the old ball-bag feel now, Daly?' I asked kindly, but he did not answer and went to sit across from Lieutenant Commander Suleiman Dada.

Dada reached out a huge black paw and relieved one of his men of the Scotch whisky bottle he carried, part of my previous stock, and he gestured to another to bring glasses from the shattered liquor cabinet.

When we all had half a tumbler of Scotch in our hands, Dada gave us the toast.

'To lasting friendship, and mutual prosperity.' We drank, Daly and I cautiously, Dada deeply and with evident pleasure. While his head was tilted back and his eyes closed, the crew man attempted to retrieve the bottle of Scotch from the table in front of him.

Without lowering the glass Dada hit him a mighty open-handed clout across the side of the head, a blow that snapped his head back and hurled him across the saloon to crash into the shattered liquor cabinet. He slid down the bulkhead and sat stunned on the deck, shaking his head dazedly. Suleiman Dada, despite his bulk, was a quick and fearsomely powerful man, I realized.

He emptied the glass, set it down, and refilled it. He looked at me now, and his expression changed. The clown had disappeared, despite the ballooning rolls of flesh; I was confronting a shrewd, dangerous and utterly ruthless opponent.

'Harry, I understand that you and Inspector Daly were interrupted in the course of a recent discussion,' and I shrugged.

'All of us here are reasonable men, Harry, of that I am certain.' I said nothing, but studied the whisky in my glass with deep attention. 'This is very fortunate—for let us consider what might happen to an unreasonable man in your position.' He paused, gargled a little with a sip of whisky. Sweat had formed like a rash of little white blisters on his nose and chin. He wiped it away. 'First of all, an unreasonable man might watch while his crew were taken out one at a time and executed. We use pick-axe handles here. It is a gruelling business, and Inspector Daly assures me that you have a special relationship with these two men.' Beside me Chubby and Angelo shifted uneasily in their seats. 'Then an unreasonable man would have his boat taken into Zinballa Bay. Once that happened there would be no way in which it would ever be returned to him. It would be officially confiscated, out of my humble hands.' He paused, and showed me the humble hands, stretching them towards me. They would have fitted a bull gorilla. We both stared at them for a moment. 'Then the unreasonable man might find himself in Zinballa gaol—which, as you are probably aware, is a maximum security political prison.'

I had heard of Zinballa prison, as had everyone on the coast. Those who came out of it were either dead or broken in body and spirit. They called it the 'Lion Cage'.

'Suleiman Dada, I want you to know that I am one of nature's original reasonable men,' I assured him, and he laughed again.

'I was certain of it,' he said. 'I can tell one a mile off,' then again he was serious. 'If we leave here immediately, before the turn of the tide we can be out of the inshore channel before midnight.'

'Yes,' I agreed, 'that we could.'

'Then you could lead us to this place of interest, wait while we satisfy ourselves as to your good faith—which I for one do not doubt one moment—you and your crew will then be free to sail way in your magnificent boat and you could sleep tomorrow night in your own bed.'

'Suleiman Dada—you are a generous and cultivated man. I also have no reason to doubt your good faith,'—no more than that of Materson and Guthrie, I silently qualified the statement—'and I have a peculiarly intense desire to sleep tomorrow night in my own bed.'

Daly spoke for the first time, snarling quietly under his little moustache. 'I think you should know that a turtle fisherman saw your boat anchored in the lagoon across the channel from the Old Men and Gunfire Reef on the night before the shooting incident—we will expect to be taken that way.'

'I have nothing against a man who takes a bribe, Daly—God knows I have done so myself—but then where is the honour among thieves that the poet sings of?' I was very disappointed in Daly, but he ignored my recriminations.

'Don't try any more of your tricks,' he warned me.

'You really are a champion turd, Daly. I could win prizes with you.'

'Please, gentlemen.' Dada held up his hands to halt my flow of rhetoric. 'Let us all be friends. Another small glass of whisky—and then Harry will take us all on a tour of interest.' Dada topped up our glasses, and paused before drinking again. 'I think I should warn you, Harry—I do not like rough water. It does not agree with me. If you take me into rough water I shall be very very angry. Do we understand each other?'

'Just for you I shall command the waters to stand still, Suleiman Dada,' I assured him, and he nodded solemnly, as though it were the very least he expected.

The dawn was like a lovely woman rising from the couch of the sea, soft flesh tones and pearly light, the cloud strands like her hair tresses flowing and tousled, gilded blonde by the early sunlight.

We ran northwards, hugging the quieter waters of the inshore channel. Our order of sailing placed *Wave Dancer* in the van, she ambled along like a blood filly mouthing the snaffle, while half a mile astern the crash boat waddled and wallowed, as the Allisons tried to push her up onto the plane. We were headed for the Old Man and Gunfire Reef.

On board *Dancer* I had the con, standing alone at the wheel upon the open bridge. Behind me stood Peter Daly, and an armed seaman from the crash boat.

In the saloon below us, Chubby and Angelo still sat on the bench seat and three more seamen, armed with assault rifles, kept them there.

Dancer had been looted of all her galley stores, so none of us had breakfasted, not even a cup of coffee.

The first paralysing despair of capture had passed—and I was now thinking frenetically, trying to plot my way out of the maze in which I was trapped.

I knew that if I showed Daly and Dada the break at Gunfire Reef they would either explore it and find nothihg—which was the most likely for whatever had been there was now packaged and deposited at Big Gull Island—or they would find some other evidence at the Break. In both cases I was in for unpleasantness—if they found nothing Daly would have the very great pleasure of connecting me up to the electrical system in an attempt to make me talk. If they found something definite my presence would become superfluous—and a dozen eager seamen would vie for job of executioner. I didn't like the sound of pick-handles—it promised to be a messy business.

Yet the chances of escape seemed remote. Although she was half a mile astern the three-pounder on the foredeck of Dada's crash boat kept us on an effective leash, and we had aboard Daly and four members of the goon squad.

I lit my first cheroot of the day and its effect was miraculous; almost immediately I seemed to see a pin-prick of light at the end of the long dark tunnel. I thought about it a little longer, puffing quietly on the black tobacco, and it seemed worth a try—but first I had to talk to Chubby.

'Daly,' I turned to speak over my shoulder. 'You had better get Chubby up here to take the wheel, I have got to go below.'

'Why?' he demanded suspiciously. 'What are you going to do?'

'Let's just say that whatever it is happens every morning at this time, and nobody else can do it for me. If you make me say more, I shall blush.'

'You should have been on the stage, Fletcher. You really slay me.'

'Funny you should mention that. It had crossed my mind.'

He sent the guard to fetch Chubby from the saloon, and I handed the con to him.

'Stick around, I want to talk to you later,' I muttered out of the side of my mouth and clambered down into the cockpit. Angelo brightened a little when I entered the saloon, and flashed a good imitation of the old bright grin, but the three guards, clearly bored, turned their weapons on me enthusiastically and I raised my hands hurriedly.

'Easy, boys, easy,' I soothed them and sidled past them down the companionway. However, two of them followed me. When I reached the heads they would have entered with me and kept me company. 'Gentlemen,' I protested, 'if you continue to point those things at me during the next few critical moments you will probably pioneer the sovereign cure for constipation.' They scowled at me uncertainly and as I closed the door firmly upon then I added, 'But you really don't want a Nobel prize—do you?'

When I opened it again they were waiting in exactly the same attitudes, as though they had not moved. With a conspiratory gesture I beckoned them to follow. Immediately they showed interest, and I led them to the master cabin. Below the big double bunk I had spent many hours building in a concealed locker. It was about the size of a coffin, and was ventilated. It would accommodate a man lying prone. During the time when I was running human cargo it had been a hidey hole in case of a search—but now I used it as a store for valuables and illicit or dangerous cargo. It contained at the present time five hundred rounds of ammunition for the F.N., a wooden crate of hand grenades, and two cases of Chivas Regal Scotch whisky.

With exclamations of delight the two guards slung their machine-guns on their shoulder straps and dragged out the whisky cases. They had forgotten about me and I slipped away and returned to the bridge. I stood next to Chubby, delaying the moment of take-over.

'You took your time,' growled Daly.

'Never rush a good thing,' I explained, and he lost interest and strolled back to stare across our wake at the following gunboat.

'Chubby,' I whispered. 'Gunfire Break. You told me once there was a passage through the reef from the landward side.'

'At high springs, for a whaleboat and a good man with a steady nerve,' he agreed. 'I did it when I was a crazy kid.'

'It's high spring in three hours. Could I run *Dancer* through?' I asked.

Chubby's expression changed. 'Jesus!' he whispered, and turned to stare at me in disbelief.

'Could I do it?' I insisted quietly, and he sucked his teeth noisily, looking away at the sunrise, scratching the bristles of his chin.

Then suddenly he reached an opinion, and spat over the side. 'You might, Harry—but nobody else I know could.'

'Give me the bearings, Chubby, quickly.'

'It was a long time ago, but,' sketchily he described the approach, and the passage of the Break, 'there are three turns in the passage, left, right then left again, then there is a narrow neck, brain coral on each hand—*Dancer* might just get through but she'll leave some paint behind. Then you are into the big pool at the back of the main reef. There is room to circle there and wait for the right sea before you shoot the gap out into the open water.'

'Thanks, Chubby,' I whispered. 'Now go below. I let the guards have the spare whisky. By the time I start my run for the Break they will be blasted right out through the top of their skulls. I will signal three stamps on the deck, then it will be up to you and Angelo to get those pieces away from them and wrap them up tightly.'

The sun was well up, and the triple-peaked silhouette of the Old Men was rising only a few miles dead ahead when I heard the first raucous shout of laughter and crash of breaking furniture below. Daly ignored it and we ran on over the quiet inshore waters towards the reverse side of Gunfire Reef. Already I could see the jagged line of the Reef, like the black teeth of an ancient shark. Beyond it the tall oceanic surf flashed whitely as it burst, and beyond that lay the open sea.

I edged in towards the reef, and eased open the throttles a fraction. *Dancer*'s engine beat changed, but not enough to alert Daly. He lounged against the rail, bored and unshaven and probably missing his breakfast. I could distinctly hear the boom of the surf on coral now, and from below, the sounds of revelry became continuous. Daly noticed at last, frowned and told the other guard to go below and investigate. The guard, also bored, disappeared below with alacrity and never returned.

I glanced astern. My increase in speed was slowly opening the gap between *Dancer* and the crash boat, and steadily we edged in closer to the reef.

I was looking ahead anxiously, trying to pick up the marks and bearings that Chubby had described to me. Gently I touched the throttles, opening them another notch. The crash boat fell a little farther astern.

Suddenly I saw the entrance to Gunfire Break a thousand yards ahead. Two pinnacles of old weathered coral marked it, and I could see the colour difference of clear sea water pouring through the gap in the coral barrier.

Below there was another screech of wild laughter, and one of the guards reeled drunkenly into the cockpit. He reached the rail only just in time and vomited copiously into the wake. Then his legs gave way and he collapsed onto the deck and lay in an abandoned huddle.

Daly let out an angry exclamation and raced down the ladder. I took the opportunity to push the throttles open another two notches.

I stared ahead, gathering myself for the effort. I must try and open the gap between *Dancer* and her escort a little more, every inch would help to confound her gunners.

I planned to come up level with the channel, and then commit *Dancer* to it under full power, risking the submerged coral fangs rather than test the aim of the gunners aboard the crash boat. It was half a mile of narrow, tortuous channel through the coral before we reached the open sea. For most of it, *Dancer* would be partially screened by coral outcrops, and the weaving of the channel would help to confuse the range of the three-pounder. I was hoping also that the surf working through the gap would give *Dancer* plenty of up-and-down movement, so that she would heave and weave unpredictably like one of those little ducks in a shooting gallery.

One thing was certain: that intrepid mariner, Lieutenant Commander Suleiman Dada, would not risk pursuit through the channel, so I could give his gun layer a rapidly increasing range to contend with.

I ignored the alcoholic din from below, and I watched the mouth of the channel approach rapidly. I found myself hoping that the seamanship of the crash boat's crew and commander was a faithful indication of their marksmanship.

Suddenly Peter Daly flew up the ladder to confront me. His face was pink with anger and his moustache tried to bristle its silky hairs. His mouth worked for a moment before he could speak.

'You gave them the liquor, Fletcher. Oh, you crafty bastard.'

'Me?' I asked indignantly. 'I wouldn't do a thing like that.'

'They're drunk as pigs—all of them,' he shouted, then he turned and looked over the stern. The crash boat was a mile behind us, and the distance was increasing.

'You are up to something,' he shrilled at me, and groped in the side pocket of his silk jacket. At that moment we came level with the entrance to the channel.

I hit both throttles wide open, and *Dancer* bellowed and hurled herself forward.

Still groping in his pocket, Daly was thrown off balance. He staggered backwards, still shouting.

I spun the wheel to full right lock, and *Dancer* whirled like a ballet dancer. Daly changed the direction of his stagger; thrown wildly across the deck he came up hard against the side rail as *Dancer* leaned over steeply in her turn. At that moment Daly dragged a small nickelled-silver automatic from his side pocket. It looked like a .25, the type ladies carry in their handbags.

I left *Dancer*'s wheel for an instant. Stooping, I got my hand on Daly's ankles and lifted sharply. 'Leave us now, comrade,' I said as he went backwards over the rail, falling twelve feet, striking the lower deck rail a glancing blow and then splashing untidily into the water alongside.

I darted back to the wheel, catching *Dancer*'s head before she could pay off, and at the same time stamping three times on the deck.

As I lined *Dancer* up for the entrance I heard the shouts of conflict in the saloon below, and winced as a machine-gun fired with a sound like ripping cloth—barrapp—and bullets exploded out through the deck behind me, leaving a jagged hole edged with white splinters. At least they were fired at the roof, and were unlikely to have hit either Angelo or Chubby.

Just before I entered the coral portals, I glanced back once more. The crash boat still lumbered along a mile behind, while Daly's head bobbed in the churning white wake. I wondered if they would reach him before the sharks did.

Then there was no more time for idle speculation. As *Dancer* dashed headlong into the channel I was appalled by the task I had set her.

I could have leant over and touched coral outcrops on each hand

and I could see the sinister shape of more coral lurking below the shallow turbulent waters ahead. The waters had expended most of their savagery on the long twisting run through the channel, but the farther in we went the wilder they would become, making *Dancer*'s response to the helm just that much more unpredictable.

The first bend in the channel showed ahead, and I put *Dancer* to it. She came around willingly, swishing her bottom, and with only a trifling yaw that pushed her outwards towards the menacing coral.

As I straightened her into the next stretch, Chubby came swarming up the ladder. He was grinning hugely. Only two things put him into that sort of mood—and one of them was a good punch up. He had skinned his right knuckle.

'All quiet below, Harry. Angelo's looking after them.' He glanced around. 'Where's the policeman?'

'He went for a swim.' I did not take my attention from the channel. 'Where is the crash boat? What are they doing?'

Chubby peered across at her. 'No change. It doesn't seem to have sunk in yet—hold on, though—' his voice changed, '—yes; there they go. They are manning the deck gun.'

We drove on swiftly down the channel, and I risked a quick glance backwards. At that instant I saw the long streak of white cordite smoke blow like a feather from the three-pounder, and an instant later there was the sharp crack of shot passing high overhead, followed immediately by the flat report of the shot.

'Ready for it now, Harry. Left-hander coming up.'

We swept into the next turn, and the next round fell short, bursting in a shower of fragments and blue smoke on one of the coral heads fifty yards off our beam.

I coaxed *Dancer* smoothly into the turn, and as we went into it another shell fell in our wake, lifting a tall and graceful column of white water high above the bridge. The following wind blew the spray over us.

We were half way through now, and the waves that rushed to meet us were six feet high and angry with the restraint enforced upon them by the walls of coral.

The guncrew of the crash boat were making alarmingly erratic practice. A round burst five hundred yards astern, then the next went between Chubby and me, a stunning blaze of passing shot that sent me reeling in the backwash of disrupted air.

'Here's the neck now,' Chubby called anxiously and my spirit quailed as I saw how the channel narrowed and how bridge-high buttresses of coral guarded it.

It seemed impossible that *Dancer* would pass through so narrow an opening.

'Here we go, Chubby, cross your fingers,' and, still under full throttle, I put *Dancer* at the neck. I could see him grasping the rail with both hands, and I expected the stainless steel to bend with the strength of his grip.

We were halfway through when we hit, with a jarring, rending crash. *Dancer* lurched and hesitated.

At the same moment another shell burst alongside. It showered the bridge with coral chips and humming steel fragments, but I hardly noticed it as I tried to ease *Dancer* through the gap.

I sheered off the wall, and the tearing scraping sound ran along our starboard side. For a moment we jammed solidly, then another big green wave raced down on us, lifting us free of the coral teeth and we were through the neck. *Dancer* lunged ahead.

'Go below, Chubby,' I shouted. 'Check if we holed the hull.' Blood was dripping from a fragment scratch on his chin, but he dived down the ladder.

With another stretch of open water ahead, I could glance back at the crash boat. She was almost obscured by an intervening block of coral, but she was still firing rapidly and wildly. She seemed to have heaved to at the entrance to the channel, probably to pick up Daly—but I knew she would not attempt to follow us now. It would take her four hours to work her way round to the main channel beyond the Old Man.

The last turn in the channel came up ahead, and again *Dancer*'s hull touched coral; the sound of it seemed to tear into my own soul. Then at last we burst out into the deep pool in the back of the main reef, a circular arena of deep water three hundred yards across, fenced in by coral walls and open only through the Gunfire Reef to the wild surf of the Indian Ocean.

Chubby appeared at my shoulder once more. 'Tight as a mouse's ear, Harry. Not taking on a drop.' Silently I applauded my darling.

Now for the first time we were in full view of the gun crew half a mile away across the reef, and my turn into the pool presented *Dancer* to them broadside. As though they sensed that this was their last chance they poured shot after shot at us.

It fell about us in great leaping spouts, too close to allow me any latitude of decision. I swung *Dancer* again, aimed her at the narrow break, and let her race for the gap in Gunfire Reef.

I committed her and when we had passed the point of no return, I felt my belly cramp up with horror as I looked ahead through the gap to the open sea. It seemed as though the whole ocean was rearing up ahead of me, gathering itself to hurl down upon the frail little vessel like some rampaging monster.

'Chubby,' I called hollowly. 'Will you look at that.'

'Harry,' he whispered, 'this a good time to pray.'

And *Dancer* ran out bravely to meet this freak Goliath of the sea.

It came up, humping monstrous shoulders as it charged, higher and higher still it rose, a glassy green wall and I could hear it rustling—like wildfire in dry grass.

Another shot passed close overhead but I hardly noticed it, as *Dancer* threw up her head and began to climb that mountainous wave.

It was turning pale green along the crest high above, beginning to curl, and *Dancer* went up as though she were on an elevator.

The deck canted steeply, and we clung helplessly to the rail.

'She's going over backwards,' Chubby shouted, as she began to stand on her tail. 'She's turtling, man!'

'Go through her,' I called to *Dancer*. 'Cut through the green!' and as though she heard me she lunged with her sharp prow into the curl of the wave an instant before it could fall upon us and crush the hull.

It came aboard us in a roaring green horror, solid sheets of it swept *Dancer* from bows to stern, six feet deep, and she lurched as though to a mortal blow.

Then suddenly we burst out through the back of the wave, and below us was a gaping valley, a yawning abyss into which *Dancer* hurled herself, falling free, gut-swooping drop down into the trough.

We hit with a sickening crash that seemed to stun her, and which threw Chubby and me to the deck. But as I dragged myself up again, *Dancer* shook herself free of the tons of water that had come aboard, and she ran on to meet the next wave.

It was smaller, and *Dancer* beat the curl and porpoised over her.

'That's my darling,' I shouted to her and she picked up speed, taking the third wave like a steeple-chaser.

Somewhere close another three-pound shell cracked the sky, but then we were out and running for the long horizon of the ocean and I never heard another shot.

The guard who had passed out in the cockpit from an excess of Scotch whisky must have been washed overboard by the giant wave, for we never saw him again. The other three we left on a small island thirty miles north of St Mary's where I knew there was water in a brackish well, and which would certainly be visited by fishermen from the mainland.

They had sobered by that time, and were all inflicted with nasty hangovers. They made three forlorn figures on the beach as we ran southwards into the dusk. It was dark when we crept into Grand Harbour. I picked up moorings, not tying up to the wharf at Admiralty. I did not want *Dancer*'s glaring injuries to become a subject of speculation around the island.

Chubby and Angelo went ashore in the dinghy—but I was too exhausted to make the effort, and dinnerless I collapsed across the double bunk in the master cabin and slept without moving until Judith woke me after nine in the morning. Angelo had sent her down with a dinner pail of fish cakes and bacon.

'Chubby and Angelo gone up to Missus Eddy's to buy some stores they need to repair the boat,' she told me. 'They'll be down soon now.'

I wolfed the breakfast and went to shave and shower. When I returned she was still there, sitting on the edge of the bunk. She clearly had something to discuss.

She brushed away my clumsy efforts at dressing my wound, and had me sit while she worked on it.

'Mister Harry, you aren't going to get my Angelo killed or gaoled, are you?' she demanded. 'If you go on like this, I'm going to make him come ashore.'

'That's great, Judith.' I laughed at her concern. 'Why don't you send him across to Rawano for three years, while you sit here.'

'That's not kind, Mister Harry.'

'Life is not very kind, Judith,' I told her more gently. 'Angelo and I are both doing the best we can. Just to keep my boat afloat, I've got to take a few chances. Some with Angelo. He told me that he's saved enough to buy you a nice little house up near the church. He got the money by running with me.'

She was silent while she finished the dressing, and when she would have turned to go I took her hand and drew her back. She would not look at me, until I took her chin and lifted her face. She was a lovely child, with great smoky eyes and a smoothly silken skin.

'Don't fuss yourself, Judith. Angelo is like a kid brother to me. I'll look after him.'

She studied my face a long moment. 'You really mean that, don't you?' she asked.

'I really do.'

'I believe you,' she said at last, and she smiled. Her teeth were very white against the golden amber skin. 'I trust you.'

Women are always saying that to me. 'I trust you.' So much for feminine intuition.

'You name one of the kids for me, hear?'

'The first one, Mister Harry.' Her smile blazed and her dark eyes flashed. 'That's a promise.'

'They do say that when you fall from a horse you should immediately ride him again—so as not to lose your nerve, Mister Harry.' Fred Coker sat at his desk in the travel agency, behind him a poster of a beef-eater and Big Ben—'England Swings', it said. We had just discussed at great length our mutual concern at Inspector Peter Daly's perfidious conduct, though I suspected that Fred Coker's concern was considerably less than mine. He had collected his commission in advance and nobody had put his head in a noose, nor had they almost wrecked his boat. We were now discussing the subject of whether or not our business arrangement should continue.

'They also say, Mr Coker, that a man with his buttocks hanging out of the holes in his trousers should not be too fussy,' I said, and Coker's spectacles glittered with satisfaction. He nodded his head.

'And that, Mister Harry, is probably the wiser of the two sayings,' he agreed.

'I'll take anything, Mr Coker. Body, box or sticks. Just one thing, the cost of dying has gone up to ten thousand dollars a run—all in advance.'

'Even at that price, we'll find work for you,' he promised, and I realized I had been working cheaply before.

'Soon,' I insisted.

'Very soon,' he agreed. 'You are fortunate. I do not think that Inspector Daly will be returning to St Mary's now. You will save the commission usually payable there.'

'He owes me that at least,' I agreed.

I made three night runs in the next six weeks. Two body carries, and a box job—all below the river into Portuguese waters. The bodies were both singles, silent black men dressed in jungle fatigues, and I took them far south, deep penetrations. They waded ashore on remote beaches and I wondered briefly upon what unholy missions they travelled—how much pain and death would arise from those secret landings.

The box job involved eighteen long wooden crates with Chinese markings. We picked up from a submarine out in the channel, and dropped off in a river-mouth, unloading into pairs of dug-out canoes lashed together for stability. We spoke to no one and nobody challenged us.

They were milk runs and I cleared eighteen thousand dollars—
enough to carry me and my crew through the off-season in the style to
which we were accustomed. More important, the intervals of quiet
and rest were sufficient to heal my wounds and give me back my
strength. At first I lay for hours in the hammock under the palms,
reading or sleeping. Then as it came back to me, I swam and fished and
sun-baked, went for oysters and crayfish—until I was hard and lean
and sunbrowned again.

The wound healed into a thickened and irregular cicatrice, tribute
to MacNab's surgical skills; it curled around my chest and onto my
back like an angry purple dragon. In one thing he had been correct,
the massive damage to my upper left arm left it stiff and weakened. I
could not lift my elbow above shoulder-level, and I lost my title in
Indian wrestling to Chubby in the bar of the Lord Nelson. However, I
hoped that swimming and regular exercise would strengthen it.

As my strength returned so did my curiosity and sense of adventure.
I began dreaming about the canvas-wrapped package off Big Gull
Island. In one dream I swam down and opened the package—it contained a tiny feminine figure, the size of a Dresden doll, a golden mermaid with Sister May's lovely face and a truly startling bosom; the
tail was the graceful sickle shape of a marlin's. The little mermaid
smiled shyly and held out her hand to me. On her palm lay a shiny
silver shilling.

'Sex, money and billfish—' I thought when I woke, '—good old un-
complicated Harry, real Freud food.' I knew then that pretty soon I
would be going for Big Gull Island.

It was very late in the season before I could prevail on Fred Coker
to arrange a straight fishing charter for me, and it turned sour as cheap
wine. The party consisted of two overweight, flabby German indus-
trialists with fat bejewelled wives. I worked hard for them, and put
both men into fish.

The first was a good black marlin, but the party screwed down on his
stardrag, freezing the reel while the fish was still green and crazy to run.
It lifted the German's huge backside out of the seat, and before I could
release the stardrag for him, it had my three hundred dollar rod down
on the gunwale. The fibreglass rod snapped like a matchstick.

The other member of the party, after losing two decent fish, panted
and sweated three hours over a baby blue marlin. When he finally
brought it to the gaff, I could hardly bring myself to put the steel in,
and I was too ashamed to hang it on Admiralty. We took the photographs on board *Dancer* and I smuggled it ashore wrapped in a tarpaulin. Like Fred Coker I also have a reputation to preserve. The

German industrialist, however, was so delighted by his prowess that he slipped an extra five hundred dollars into my avaricious little paw. I told him it was a truly magnificent fish, which was a thousand-dollar lie. I always give good value. Then the wind backed into the south, the temperature of the water in the channel dropped four degrees and the fish were gone. For ten days we hunted far north but it was over, another season was past.

We stripped and cleaned all the billfish equipment and laid it away in thick yellow grease. I pulled *Dancer* up onto the slip at the fuelling basin and we went over her hull, cleaning it down, re-working the temporary patches I had put on the injuries she had received at Gunfire Reef.

Then we painted her until she glistened, sleek and lovely, before we refloated her and took her out to moorings. There we worked lackadaisically on her upper works, stripping varnish, sand-papering, re-varnishing, checking out the electrical system, re-soldering a connection here, replacing wiring there.

I was in no hurry. It would be three weeks before my next charter arrived—an expedition of marine biologists from a Canadian university.

In the meantime the days were cooler, and I was feeling the old glow of good health and bodily well-being again. I dined at Government House, sometimes as often as once a week, and each time I had to tell the full story of the shoot-out with Guthrie and Materson. President Biddle knew the story by heart and corrected me if I omitted a single detail. It always ended with the President crying excitedly, 'Show them your scar, Mister Harry,' and I had to open the starched front of my dress shirt at the dinner table.

They were good lazy days. The island life drifted placidly by. Peter Daly never returned to St Mary's—and at the end of six weeks, Wally Andrews was promoted to acting Inspector and commanding officer of the police force. One of his first acts was to return to me my FN carbine.

This quiet time was spiced by the secret tingle of anticipation which I felt. I knew that one day soon I was going back to Big Gull Island and the piece of unfinished business that lay there in the shallow limpid waters—and I teased myself with the knowledge.

Then one Friday evening I was rounding out the week with my crew in the bar of the Lord Nelson. Judith was with us, having replaced the flock that had previously gathered around Angelo on Friday nights. She was good for him, he no longer drank to the morbid stage.

Chubby and I had just begun the first duet of the evening and were keeping within a few beats of each other when Marion slipped into the seat beside me.

I put one arm around her shoulders and held my tankard to her lips while she drank thirstily, but the distraction caused me to forge even further ahead of Chubby in the song.

Marion worked on the switchboard at the Hilton Hotel. She was a pretty little thing with a sexy pugface and long straight black hair. It was she whom Mike Guthrie had used for a punch-bag so long ago.

When Chubby and I straggled to the end of the chorus, Marion told me, 'There is a lady asking for you, Mister Harry.'

'What lady?'

'At the hotel, one of the guests. She came in on this morning's plane. She knew your name and everything. She wants to see you. I told her I would see you tonight and give you the message.'

'What is she like?' I asked Marion with interest.

'She's beautiful, Mister Harry. Such a lady too.'

'Sounds like my type,' I agreed, and ordered a pint for Marion.

'Aren't you going to see her now?'

'With you beside me, Marion, all the beautiful ladies of the world can wait until tomorrow.'

'Oh, Mister Harry, you are a real devil man,' she giggled, and snuggled a little closer.

'Harry,' said Chubby on my other side, 'I'm going to tell you now what I never told you before.' He took a long swallow from his tankard, then went on with sentimental tears swimming in his eyes. 'Harry, I love you, man. I love you better than my own brother.'

I went up to the Hilton a few minutes before midday. Marion came through from her cubicle behind the reception desk. She still had her earphones around her neck.

'She's waiting for you on the terrace.' She pointed across the vast reception area with its *ersatz* Hawaiian décor. 'The blonde lady in the yellow bikini.'

She was reading a magazine, lying on her belly on one of the reclining sun couches, and she had her back to me so my first impression was of masses of blonde hair, thick and shiny, teased up like the mane of a lion, then falling in a slick golden cascade.

She heard my footsteps on the paving. She glanced around, pushed her sunglasses up on top of her head, then she stood up to face me, and I realized that she was tiny, seeming to reach not much higher than my chest. The bikini also was tiny and showed a flat smooth belly with a deep navel, firm shoulders lightly tanned, small breasts, and a trim

waist. Her legs had lovely lines and her neat little feet were thrust into
open sandals, the nails painted clear red to match her long fingernails.
Her hands as she pushed at her hair were small and shapely.

She wore heavy make-up, but wore it with rare skill, so that her skin
had a soft pearly lustre and colour glowed subtly on her cheeks and lips.
Her eyes had long dark artificial lashes, and the eyelids were touched
with colour and line to give them an exotic oriental cast.

'Duck, Harry!' Something deep inside me shouted a warning, and I
almost obeyed. I knew this type well, there had been others like her—
small and purringly feline—I had scars to prove it, scars both physical
and spiritual. However, one thing nobody can say about old Harry is
that he runs for cover when the knickers are down.

Courageously I stepped forward, crinkling my eyes and twisting my
mouth into the naughty small boy grin that usually dynamites them.

'Hello,' I said, 'I'm Harry Fletcher.'

She looked at me, starting at my feet and going up six feet four to the
top where her gaze lingered speculatively and she pouted her lower lip.

'Hello,' she answered, her voice was husky, breathless-sounding—
and carefully rehearsed. 'I'm Sherry North, Jimmy North's sister.'

We were on the veranda of the shack in the evening. It was cool and
the sunset was a spectacular display of pyrotechnics that flamed and
faded above the palms.

She was drinking a Pimms No. 1 filled with fruit and ice—one of my
seduction specials—and she wore a kaftan of light floating stuff through
which her body showed in shadowy outline as she stood against the rail
backlit by the sunset. I could not be certain as to whether or not she
wore anything beneath the kaftan—this and the tinkle of ice in her
glass distracted me from the letter I was reading. She had showed it to
me as part of her credentials. It was a letter from Jimmy North written
a few days before his death. I recognized the handwriting and the turn
of phrase was typical of that bright and eager lad. As I read on, I forgot
the sister's presence in the memory of the past. It was a long bubbling
letter, written as though to a loving friend, with veiled references to the
mission and its successful outcome, the promise of a future in which
there would be wealth and laughter and all good things.

I felt a pang of regret and personal loss for the boy in his lonely sea
grave, for the lost dreams that drifted with him like rotting seaweed.

Then suddenly my own name leapt from that page at me, '—you
can't help liking him, Sherry. He's big and tough-looking, all scarred

and beat up like an old tom cat that's been out alley-fighting every night. But under it, I swear he is really a softy. He seems to have taken a shine to me. Even gives me fatherly advice!—'

There was more in the same vein that embarrassed me so that my throat closed up and I took a swallow of whisky, which made my eyes water and the words swim, while I finished the letter and refolded it.

I handed it to Sherry, and walked away to the end of the veranda. I stood there for a while looking out over the bay. The sun slid below the horizon and suddenly it was dark and chill.

I went back and lit the lamp, setting it up high so the glare did not fall in our eyes. She watched me in silence until I had poured another Scotch and settled in my cane-backed chair.

'Okay,' I said, 'you're Jimmy's sister. You've come to St Mary's to see me. Why?'

'You liked him, didn't you?' she asked, as she left the rail and came to sit beside me.

'I like a lot of people. It's a weakness of mine.'

'Did he die—I mean, was it like they said in the newspapers?'

'Yes,' I said. 'It was like that.'

'Did he ever tell you what they were doing out here?'

I shook my head. 'They were very cagey—and I don't ask questions.'

She was silent then, dipping long tapered fingers into her glass to pick out a slice of pineapple, nibbling at the fruit with small white teeth, dabbing at her lips with a pink pointed tongue like that of a cat.

'Because Jimmy liked and trusted you, and because I think you know more than you've told anyone, also because I need your help. I am going to tell you a story—okay?'

'I love stories,' I said.

'Have you heard of the "pogo stick"?' she asked.

'Sure, it's a child's toy.'

'It's also the code name for an American naval experimental vertical take-off all-weather strike aircraft.'

'Oh yea, I remember, I saw an article in *Time Magazine*. Questions in the Senate. I forget the details.'

'There was opposition to the fifty million development allocation.'

'Yes, I remember.'

'Two years ago, on August 16th to be precise, a prototype "pogo stick" took off from Rawano airforce base in the Indian Ocean. It was armed with four air-to-surface "killer whale" missiles, each of them equipped with tactical nuclear warheads—'

'That must have been a fairly lethal package.'

She nodded. 'The "killer whale" is designed as an entirely new concept in missiles. It is an anti-submarine device which will seek and track
surfaced or submerged naval craft. It can kill an aircraft carrier or it
can change its element—air for water—and go down a thousand
fathoms to destroy enemy submarines.'

'Wow,' I said, and took a little more whisky. We were talking heady
stuff now.

'Do you recall August 16th that year—were you here?'

'I was here, but that's a long time ago. Refresh my memory.'

'Cyclone Cynthia,' she said.

'God, of course.' It had come roaring across the islands, winds of 150
miles an hour, taking away the roof of the shack and almost swamping
Dancer at her moorings in Grand Harbour. These cyclones were not un-
common in this area.

'The "pogo stick" took off from Rawano a few minutes before the
typhoon struck. Twelve minutes later the pilot ejected and the aircraft
went into the sea with her four nuclear missiles and her flight recorder
still aboard. Rawano radar was blanked out by the typhoon. They
were not tracking.'

It was starting to make some sort of sense at last.

'How does Jimmy fit into this?'

She made an impatient gesture. 'Wait,' she said, then went on. 'Do
you have any idea what the value of that cargo might be in the open
market?'

'I should imagine you could write your own cheque—give or take a
couple of million dollars.' And old bad Harry came to attention, he
had been getting exercise lately and growing stronger.

Sherry nodded. 'The test pilot of the "pogo stick" was a Commander
in the U.S. Navy named William Bryce. The aircraft developed a fault
at fifty thousand feet, just before he came out through the top of the
weather. He fought her all the way down, he was a conscientious
officer, but at five hundred feet he knew he wasn't going to make it. He
ejected and watched the aircraft go in.'

She was speaking carefully, and her choice of words was odd, too
technical for a woman. She had learned all this, I was certain—from
Jimmy? Or from somebody else?

Listen and learn, Harry, I told myself.

'Billy Bryce was three days on a rubber raft on the ocean in a typhoon
before the rescue helicopter from Rawano found him. He had time to
do some thinking. One of the things he thought about was the value of
that cargo—and he compared it to the salary of a Commander. His
evidence at the court of enquiry omitted the fact that the "pogo stick"

had gone down within sight of land, and that Bryce had been able to take a fix on a recognizable land feature before he was blown out to sea by the typhoon.'

I could not see any weakness in her story—it looked all right—and very interesting.

'The court of enquiry gave a verdict of "pilot error" and Bryce resigned his commission. His career was destroyed by that verdict. He decided to earn his own retirement annuity and also to clear his reputation. He was going to force the U.S. Navy to buy back its "killer whale" missiles and to accept the evidence of the flight recorder.'

I was going to ask a question, but again Sherry stopped me with a gesture. She did not want her recital interrupted.

'Jimmy had done some work for the U.S. Navy—a hull inspection of one of their carriers—and he had met Bryce at that time. They had become friends, and so Billy Bryce naturally came to Jimmy. Between them they had not sufficient capital for the expedition they needed to mount, so they planned to find financial backers. It isn't the kind of thing you can advertise in *The Times*, and they were working on it when Billy Bryce was killed in his Thunderbird on the M4 near the Heathrow turn-off.'

'There seems to be some sort of curse on this thing,' I said.

'Are you superstitious, Harry?' she asked, looking at me through those slanted tiger eyes.

'I don't knock it,' I admitted, and she nodded, seeming to file the information away before she went on.

'After Billy was dead, Jimmy went on with the project. He found backers. He wouldn't tell me who, but I guessed they were unsavoury. He came out here with them—and you know the rest.'

'I know the rest,' I agreed, and instinctively massaged the thickened scar tissue through the silk of my shirt. 'Except of course the site of the crash.'

We stared at each other.

'Did he tell you?' I asked, and she shook her head.

'Well, it was an interesting story.' I grinned at her. 'It's a pity we can't check out the truth of it.'

She stood up abruptly and went to the veranda rail. She hugged her arms and she was so angry that if she'd had a tail she would have switched it like a lioness.

I waited for her to recover, and the moment came when she shrugged her shoulders and turned back to me. Her smile was light.

'Well, that's that! I thought I was entitled to some of the rewards. Jimmy was my brother—and I came a long way to find you because he

liked and trusted you. I thought we could work together—but I guess
if you want it all, there's not much I can do about it.'

She shook out her hair, and it rippled and shone in the lamplight. I
stood up.

'I'll take you home now,' I said, and touched her arm. She reached
up with both arms, and her fingers locked in the thick curly hair at the
back of my neck.

'It's a long way home,' she whispered, and pulled my head down,
standing on her tiptoes.

Her lips were very soft and moist, and her tongue was thrusting and
restless. After a while she drew back and smiled up at me, her eyes were
unfocused and her breath was short and fast.

'Perhaps it wasn't a wasted journey, after all?'

I picked her up, and she was light as a child, hugging my neck,
pressing her cheek to mine as I carried her into the shack. I learned long
ago to eat hearty whenever there was food, because you never know
when the famine is going to hit.

Even the soft light of dawn was cruel to her as she lay sprawled in
sleep beneath the mosquito net on the big double bed. Her make-up
had smeared and caked, and she slept with her mouth open. The mane
of blonde hair was a tangled bush and it did not match the triangle of
thick dark curls at the base of her belly. I felt repelled by her this morning, for I had learned during the night that Miss Sherry was a raving
sadist.

I slipped out of the bed and stood over her a few moments, searching
her sleeping face in vain for a resemblance to Jimmy North. I left her
and, still naked, walked out of the shack and down to the beach.

The tide was in and I plunged into the cool clear water and swam
out to the entrance to the bay. I swam fast, driving hard in an Australian
crawl, and the salt water stung the deep scratches in my back.

It was one of my lucky mornings, old friends were waiting for me
beyond the reef—a school of big bottle-nosed dolphin, who came flashing to meet me, their tall fins cutting the dark surface as they steeple-
chased over the swells. They circled me, whistling and snorting, the
blowholes in the tops of their heads gulping like tiny mouths and their
own huge mouths fixed in idiotic grins of pleasure.

They teased me for ten minutes before one of the big old bulls allowed
me to get a grip on his dorsal fin and gave me a tow. It was a thrilling
sleigh ride that had the water creaming wildly about my chest and
head. He took me half a mile offshore before the force of water tore me
from his back.

It was a long swim back, with the bull dolphin circling me and giving me an occasional friendly prod in the backside, inviting me aboard for another ride. At the reef they whistled farewell and slid gracefully away, and I was happy when I waded ashore. The arm ached a little, but it was the healthy ache of healing and growing strength.

The bed was empty, and the bathroom door was locked. She was probably shaving her armpits with my razor, I thought. I felt a flare of annoyance, an old dog like me doesn't like his routine disturbed. I used the guest shower to sluice off the salt and my annoyance receded under the rush of hot water. Then fresh but unshaven and hungry as a python, I went through to the kitchen. I was frying gammon with pineapple and buttering thick cuts of toast when Sherry came into the kitchen.

She was once more immaculate. She must have carried a complete cosmetic counter in the Gucci handbag, and her hair was dressed and lacquered into its mane and fall.

Her smile was brilliant. 'Good morning, lover,' she said and came to kiss me lingeringly. I was now well disposed towards the world and all its creatures. I no longer felt repelled by this glittering woman. The fine mood of the dolphins had returned and my gaiety must have been infectious. We laughed a lot over the meal and afterwards I took the coffee pot out onto the veranda.

'When are we going to find the "pogo stick"?' she asked suddenly, and I poured another mug of strong black coffee without answering. Sherry North had evidently decided that a night of her company had made me her slave for life. Now I may not be a connoisseur of women, but on the other hand I have had some little experience—I mean I'm not exactly a virgin—and I didn't rate Sherry North's charms as worth four killer whale missiles and the flight recorder of a secret strike aircraft.

'Just as soon as you show me the way,' I answered carefully. It is an old-fashioned feminine conceit that if a man pleasures them with skill and aplomb, then he must be made to pay for it. I have long believed that it should be the other way around.

She reached across and held my wrist; the tiger's eyes were suddenly big and soulful.

'After last night,' she whispered huskily, 'I know that there is a lot ahead of us, Harry. You and I, together.'

I had lain awake for hours during the night and reached my decision. Whatever lay in the package was not an entire aircraft, but probably some small part of it—something that identified it clearly. It was almost certainly neither the flight recorder nor one of the missiles. Jimmy North would not have had sufficient time to remove the recorder from the fuselage, even if he had known where it was situated and had the proper tools. On the other hand the package was the wrong shape and size for a missile—it was a squat round object, not aerodynamically designed.

It was almost certainly some fairly innocuous object. If I took Sherry North with me to recover it, I would be playing only a minor card from my hand—although it would look like a major trump.

I would be giving nothing away, not the site of the crash at Gunfire Reef, nor any of the valuable objects associated with it.

On the other hand, I would be beating the tall grass for tigers. It would be very instructive to see exactly how Mademoiselle North reacted, once she thought she knew the site of the crash.

'Harry,' she whispered again. 'Please,' and she leaned closer. 'You must believe me. I have never felt like this before. From the first moment I saw you—I just knew—'

I roused myself from my calculations and leaned towards her, assuming an expression of simple-minded passion and lust.

'Darling—' I began but my voice choked up, and I enfolded her in a bear hug, feeling her stiffen irritably as I smeared her lipstick and ruffled the meticulously dressed hairstyle. I could sense the effort it required for her to respond with equal passion.

'Do you feel the same way?' she asked from the depths of my embrace, smothered against my chest, and for the fun of watching her play the role she had assigned herself, I picked her up again and carried her through to the frowsy rumpled bed.

'I will show you how I feel for you,' I muttered hoarsely.

'Darling,' she protested desperately, 'not now.'

'Why not?'

'We have so much to do. There will be time later—all the time in the world.' With a show of reluctance I set her down, although truthfully I was thankful for I knew that on top of a huge breakfast of gammon and three cups of coffee, it would have given me heartburn.

It was a few minutes after noon when I cleared Grand Harbour and swung away south and east. I had told my crew to take a day ashore, I would not be fishing.

Chubby looked down at Sherry North, sprawled bikini-clad on the cockpit deck, and scowled noncommittally, but Angelo rolled his eyes expressively and asked, 'Pleasure cruise?' with a certain inflection.

'You've got a filthy mind,' I scolded him and he laughed delightedly, as though I had paid him the nicest compliment, and the two of them walked away up the wharf.

Dancer romped down the necklace of atolls and islands until, a little after three o'clock, I ran the deep-water passage between Little Gull Island and Big Gull Island, and rounded into the shallow open water between the east shore of Big Gull and the blue water of the Mozambique.

There was enough breeze to make the day pleasantly cool, and to kick up a white flecky chop off the surface.

I manoeuvred carefully, squinting over at Big Gull as I put *Dancer* in position. When I hit the marks I pushed a little upwind to allow for *Dancer*'s fall-back. Then I cut the engines and hurried down to the foredeck to drop the hook.

Dancer came around and settled down like a well-behaved lady.

'Is this the place?' Sherry had watched everything I did with her disconcerting feline stare.

'This is it,' and I risked overplaying my part as the besotted lover by pointing out the marks to her.

'I lined up those two palms, the ones leaning over, with that single palm right up on the skyline, see it?'

She nodded silently; again I caught that look as though the information were being carefully filed and remembered.

'Now what do we do?' she asked.

'This is where Jimmy dived,' I explained. 'When he came back on board he was very excited. He spoke secretly with the others—Materson and Guthrie—and they seemed to catch his excitement. Jimmy went down again with rope and a tarpaulin. He was down a long time—and when he came up again, it started, the shooting.'

'Yes,' she nodded eagerly, the reference to her brother's death seemed to leave her unmoved. 'We should go now, before someone else sees us here.'

'Go?' I asked, looking at her. 'I thought we were going to have a look?'

She recognized her mistake. 'We should organize it properly, come back when we are prepared, when we have made arrangements to pick up and transport—'

'Lover,' I grinned, 'I didn't come all this way not to take at least one quick look.'

'I don't think you should, Harry,' she called after me, but already I was opening the engine-room hatch.

'Let's come back another time,' she persisted, but I went down the ladder to the rack which held the air bottles and took down a Draeger twin set. I fitted the breathing valve and tested the seal, sucking air out of the rubber mouth-piece.

Glancing quickly up at the hatch to make sure she was not watching me, I reached across and threw the concealed cut-out switch on the electrical system. Now nobody could start *Dancer*'s engines while I was overboard.

I swung the diving ladder over the stern and then dressed in the cockpit—short-sleeved neoprene wet suit and hood, weight belt and knife, Nemrod wrap-around face-plate and fins.

I slung the scuba set on my back, picked up a coil of light nylon rope and hooked it onto my belt.

'What happens if you don't come back?' Sherry asked, showing apprehension for the first time. 'I mean, what happens to me?'

'You'll pine to death,' I told her, and went over the side, not in a showy back flip but a simple use of the steps, more in keeping with my age and dignity.

The water was transparent as mountain air, and as I went head down I could see every detail of the bottom fifty feet below.

It was a coral landscape, lit with dappled light and wondrous colour. I drifted down to it, and the sculptured shapes of the coral were softened and blurred with sea growth and restless with the sparkling jewels of myriad tropical fish. There were deep gullies and standing towers of coral, fields of eel grass between, and open stretches of blinding white coral sand.

My marks had been remarkably accurate, considering the fact that I had been only just conscious from blood loss. I had dropped the anchor almost directly on top of the canvas package. It lay on one of the open spaces of coral sand, looking like some horrible sea monster, green and squat with the loose ropes floating about it like tentacles.

I crouched beside it, and shoals of tiny fish, zebra-striped in gold and black, gathered around me in such numbers that I had to blow bubbles at them and shoo them off, before I could get on with the job.

I unclipped the nylon rope from my belt, and lashed one end securely to the package with a series of half-hitches. Then I rose to the surface slowly paying out the line. I surfaced thirty feet astern of *Dancer*, swam to the ladder, and clambered into the cockpit. I made the end of the line fast to the arm of the fighting chair.

'What did you find?' Sherry demanded anxiously.

'I don't know yet,' I told her. I had resisted the temptation to open the package on the bottom. I hoped it might be worth the sacrifice to watch her expression as I opened the canvas.

I stripped my diving gear and washed it off with fresh water before stowing it all carefully away. I wanted the tension to eat into her a little longer.

'Damn you, Harry. Let's get it up,' she burst out at last.

I remembered the package as being as heavy as all creation, but the my strength had been almost gone. Now I braced myself against th gunwale and began recovering line. It was heavy, but not impossibl so, and I coiled the wet line as it came in with the old tunny fisherman wrist action.

The green canvas broke the surface alongside, sodden and gushin water. I reached over and got a purchase on the knotted rope; with single heave I lifted it over the side and it clunked weightily onto th deck of the cockpit—metal against wood.

'Open it,' ordered Sherry impatiently.

'Right away, madam,' I said, and drew the bait-knife from th sheath on my belt. It was razor sharp, and I cut the ropes with a singl stroke for each.

Sherry was leaning forward eagerly as I drew the stiff wet folds c canvas aside, and I was watching her face.

The greedy, anticipatory expression flared suddenly into triumph a she recognized the object. She recognized it before I did, and then in stantly she dropped a curtain of uncertainty over her eyes and face.

It was nicely done, she was an actress of skill. Had I not been watch ing carefully for it, I would have missed the quick play of emotion.

I looked down at the humble object for which already so many mer had been killed or mutilated, and I was torn with surprise and puzzle ment—and disappointment. It was not what I had expected.

Half of it was badly eaten away as though by a sand-blasting machin —the bronze was raw and shiny and deeply etched. The upper half o it was intact, though tarnished heavily with a thick skin of greenisl verdigris, but the lug for the shackle was intact and the ornamentatio1 was still clear through the corrosion—a heraldic crest—or part of it— and lettering in a flowery antique style. The lettering was fragmentary most of it had been etched away in an irregular flowing line, leavin₢ the bright worn metal.

It was a ship's bell, cast in massive bronze. It must have weighec close to a hundred pounds, with a domed and lugged top and a wid flared mouth.

Curiously I rolled it over. The clapper had corroded solidly, anc barnacle and other shellfish had encrusted the interior. I was intriguec by the pattern of wear and corrosion on the outside, until suddenly the solution occurred to me. I had seen other metal objects marked like this after long submersion. The bell had been half buried on the sandy bottom, the exposed portion had been subjected to the tidal rush o Gunfire Break, and the fine grains of coral sand had abrased away a quarter of an inch of the outer skin of the metal.

However, the portion that had been buried was protected, and now I examined the remaining lettering more closely.

'VV N   L'

There was an extended 'V' or a broken 'W' followed immediately by a perfect 'N'—then a gap and a whole 'L'; beyond that the lettering had been obliterated again.

The coat of arms worked into the metal on the opposite side of the barrel was an intricate design with two rampart beasts—probably lions—supporting a shield and a mailed head. It seemed vaguely familiar, and I wondered where I had seen it before.

I rocked back on my heels and looked at Sherry North. She was unable to meet my gaze.

'Funny thing,' I mused. 'A jet aircraft with a bloody great brass bell hanging on its nose.'

'I don't understand it,' she said.

'No more do I.' I stood up and went to get a cheroot from the saloon. I lit it and sat back in the fighting chair.

'Okay. Let's hear your theory.'

'I don't know, Harry. Truly I don't.'

'Let's try some guesses,' I suggested. 'I'll begin.'

She turned away to the rail.

'The jet aircraft turned into a pumpkin,' I hazarded. 'How about that one?'

She turned back to me. 'Harry, I don't feel well. I think I'm going to be sick.'

'So, what must I do?'

'Let's go back now.'

'I was thinking of another dive—look around a bit more.'

'No,' she said quickly. 'Please, not now. I don't feel up to it. Let's go. We can come back if we have to.'

I studied her face for evidence of her sickness: she looked like an advert for health food.

'All right,' I agreed; there was not really much point in another dive, but only I knew that. 'Let's go home and try and work it out.'

I stood up and began rewrapping the brass bell.

'What are you going to do with that?' she asked anxiously.

'Redeposit it,' I told her. 'I am certainly not going to take it back to St Mary's and display it in the market place. Like you said, we can always come back.'

'Yes,' she agreed immediately. 'You are right, of course.'

I dropped the package over the side once more and went to haul the hook.

On the homeward run I found Sherry North's presence on the bridge irritated me. There was a lot of hard thinking I had to do. I sent her down to make coffee.

'Strong,' I told her, 'and with four spoons of sugar. It will be good for your seasickness.'

She reappeared on the bridge within two minutes.

'The stove won't light,' she complained.

'You have to open the main gas cylinders first.' I explained where to find the taps. 'And don't forget to close them when you finish, or you'll turn the boat into a bomb.'

She made lousy coffee.

It was late evening when I picked up moorings in Grand Harbour, and dark by the time I dropped Sherry at the entrance of the hotel. She didn't even invite me in for a drink, but kissed me on the cheek and said, 'Darling, let me be alone tonight. I am exhausted. I'm going to bed now. Let me think about all this, and when I feel better we can plan more clearly.'

'I'll pick you up here—what time?'

'No,' she said. 'I'll meet you at the boat. Early. Eight o'clock. Wait for me there—we can talk in private. Just the two of us, no one else—all right?'

'I'll bring *Dancer* to the wharf at eight,' I promised her.

It had been a thirsty day, and on the way home I stopped off at the Lord Nelson.

Angelo and Judith were with a noisy party of their own age in one of the booths. They called me over and made room for me between two of the girls.

I brought them each a pint, and Angelo leaned over confidentially. 'Hey, skipper, are you using the pick-up tonight?'

'Yes,' I said. 'To get me home.' I knew what was coming, of course. Angelo acted as though he had shares in the vehicle.

'There's a big party down at South Point tonight, boss,' suddenly he was very free with the 'boss' and 'skipper', 'I thought if I run you out to Turtle Bay, then you'd let us have the truck. I'd pick you up early tomorrow, promise.'

I took a swallow at my tankard and they were all watching me with eager hopeful faces.

'It's a big party, Mister Harry,' said Judith. 'Please.'

'You pick me up seven o'clock sharp, Angelo, hear?' and there was a spontaneous burst of relieved laughter. They clubbed in to buy me another pint.

I had a disturbed night, with restless sleep interspersed with periods of wakefulness. I had the dream again, when I dived to the canvas package. Once more it contained a tiny Dresden mermaid, but this time she had Sherry North's face and she offered me the model of a jet fighter aircraft that changed into a golden pumpkin as I reached for it. The pumpkin was etched with the letters:

'VV N   L'

It rained after midnight, solid sheets of water, that poured off the eaves, and the lightning silhouetted the palm fronds against the night sky.

It was still raining when I went down to the beach, and the heavy drops exploded in minute bomb bursts of spray upon my naked body. The sea was black in the bad light, and the rain squalls reached to the horizon. I swam alone, far out beyond the reef, but when I came back to the beach the excursion had not provided the usual lift to my spirits. My body was blue and shivering with the cold, and a vague but pervading sense of trouble and depression pressed heavily upon me.

I had finished breakfast when the pick-up came down the track through the palm plantation, splashing through the puddles, splattered with mud and with headlights still burning.

In the yard Angelo hooted and shouted, 'You ready, Harry?' and I ran out with a sou'-wester held over my head.

Angelo smelled of beer and he was garrulous and slightly bleary of eye.

'I'll drive,' I told him, and as we crossed the island he gave me a blow-by-blow description of the great party—from what he told me it seemed there might be an epidemic of births on St Mary's in nine months' time.

I was only half listening to him, for as we approached the town so my sense of disquiet mounted.

'Hey, Harry, the kids said to thank you for the loan of the pick-up.'

'That's okay, Angelo.'

'I sent Judith out to the boat—she's going to tidy up, Harry, and get the coffee going for you.'

'She shouldn't have worried,' I said.

'She wanted to do that specially—sort of thank you, you know.'

'She's a good girl.'

'Sure is, Harry. I love that girl,' and Angelo burst into song, 'Devil Woman' in the style of Mick Jagger.

When we crossed the ridge and started down into the valley I had a sudden impulse. Instead of continuing straight down Frobisher Street to the harbour, I swung left onto the circular drive above the fort and hospital and went up the avenue of banyan trees to the Hilton Hotel. I parked the pick-up under the canopy and went through to the reception lobby.

There was nobody behind the desk this early in the morning, but I leaned across the counter and peered into Marion's cubicle. She was at her switchboard and when she saw me her face lit up in a wide grin and she lifted off her earphones.

'Hello, Mister Harry.'

'Hello, Marion, love,' I returned the grin. 'Is Miss North in her room?'

Her expression changed. 'Oh no,' she said, 'she left over an hour ago.'

'Left?' I stared at her.

'Yes. She went out to the airport with the hotel bus. She was catching the seven-thirty plane.' Marion glanced at the cheap Japanese watch on her wrist. 'They would have taken off ten minutes ago.'

I was taken completely off-balance, of all things I had least expected this. It didn't make sense for many seconds—and then suddenly and sickeningly it did.

'Oh Jesus Christ,' I said. 'Judith!' and I ran for the pick-up. Angelo saw my face as I came and he sat up straight in the seat and stopped singing.

I jumped into the driver's seat and started the engine, thrusting the pedal down hard and swinging in a roaring two-wheeled turn.

'What is it, Harry?' Angelo demanded.

'Judith?' I asked grimly. 'You sent her down to the boat, when?'

'When I left to fetch you.'

'Did she go right away?'

'No, she'd have to bath and dress first.' He was telling it straight, not hiding the fact they had slept together. He sensed the urgency of the situation. 'Then she'd have to walk down the valley from the farm.' Angelo had lodgings with a peasant family up near the spring; it was a three-mile walk.

'God, let us be in time,' I whispered. The truck was bellowing down the avenue, and I hit the gears in a racing change as we went out

through the gates in a screaming broadside, and I slammed down hard
again on the accelerator, pulling her out of the skid by main strength.

'What the hell is it, Harry?' he demanded once again.

'We've got to stop her going aboard *Dancer*,' I told him grimly as we
roared down the circular drive above the town. Past the fort a vista of
Grand Harbour opened beneath us. He did not waste time with inane
questions. We had worked together too long for that and if I said so
then he accepted it as so.

Dancer was still at her moorings among the other island craft, and
half way out to her from the wharf Judith was rowing the dinghy. Even
at this distance I could make out the tiny feminine figure on the thwart,
and recognize the short businesslike oar-strokes. She was an island girl,
and rowed like a man.

'We aren't going to make it,' said Angelo. 'She'll get there before
we reach Admiralty.'

At the top of Frobisher Street I put the heel of my left hand on the
horn ring, and blowing a continuous blast I tried to clear the road. But
it was a Saturday morning, market day, and already the streets were
filling. The country folk had come to town in their bullocks, carts and
ancient jalopies. Cursing with a terrible frustration, I hooted and
forced my way through them.

It took us three minutes to cover the half mile from the top of the
street down to Admiralty Wharf.

'Oh God,' I said, leaning forward in the seat as I shot through the
mesh gates, and crossed the railway tracks.

The dinghy was tied up alongside *Wave Dancer*, and Judith was
climbing over the side. She wore an emerald green shirt and short
denim pants. Her hair was in a long braid down her back.

I skidded the truck to a halt beside the pineapple sheds, and both
Angelo and I hit the wharf at a run.

'Judith!' I yelled, but my voice did not carry out across the harbour.

Without looking back, Judith disappeared into the saloon. Angelo
and I raced down to the end of the jetty. Both of us were screaming
wildly, but the wind was in our faces and *Dancer* was five hundred yards
out across the water.

'There's a dinghy!' Angelo caught my arm. It was an ancient clinker-
built mackerel boat, but it was chained to a ring in the stone wharf.

We jumped into it, leaping the eight foot drop and falling in a heap
together over the thwart. I scrambled to the mooring chain. It had
quarter-inch galvanized steel links, and a heavy brass padlock secured
it to the ring.

I took two twists of chain around my wrist, braced one foot against the wharf and heaved. The padlock exploded, and I fell backwards into the bottom of the dinghy.

Angelo already had the oars in the rowlocks.

'Row,' I shouted at him. 'Row like a mad bastard.'

I was in the bows cupping my hands to my mouth as I hailed Judith, trying to make my voice carry above the wind.

Angelo was rowing in a dedicated frenzy, swinging the oar blades flat and low on the back reach and then throwing his weight upon them when they bit. His breathing exploded in a harsh grunt at each stroke.

Half way out to *Dancer* another rain squall enveloped us, shrouding the whole of Grand Harbour in eddying sheets of grey water. It stung my face, so I had to screw up my eyes.

Dancer's outline was blurred by grey rain, but we were coming close now. I was beginning to hope that Judith would sweep and tidy the cabins before she struck a match to the gas ring in the galley. I was also beginning to hope that I was wrong—that Sherry North had not left a farewell present for me.

Yet still I could hear my own voice speaking to Sherry North the previous day. 'You have to open the main gas cylinders first—and don't forget to close them when you finish, or you'll turn the boat into a bomb.'

Closer still we came to *Dancer* and she seemed to hang on tendrils of rain, ghostly white and insubstantial in the swirling mist.

'Judith,' I shouted, she must hear me now—we were that close. There were two fifty-pound cylinders of Butane gas on board, enough to destroy a large brickbuilt house. The gas was heavier than air, once it escaped it would slump down, filling *Dancer*'s hull with a murderously explosive mixture of gas and air. It needed just one spark from battery or match.

I prayed that I was wrong and yelled again. Then suddenly *Dancer* blew.

It was flash explosion, a fearsome blue light that shot through her. It split her hull with a mighty hammer stroke, and blew her superstructure open, lifting it like a lid.

Dancer reared to the mortal blow, and the blast hit us like a storm wind. Immediately I smelled the electric stench of the blast, acrid as an air-sizzling strike of lightning against ironstone.

Dancer died as I watched, a terrible violent death, and then her torn and lifeless hull fell back and the cold grey waters rushed into her. The heavy engines pulled her swiftly down, and she was gone into the grey waters of Grand Harbour.

Angelo and I were frozen with horror, crouching in the violently rocking dinghy, staring at the agitated water that was strewn with loose wreckage—all that remained of a beautiful boat and a lovely young girl. I felt a vast desolation descend upon me. I wanted to cry aloud in my anguish, but I was paralysed.

Angelo moved first. He leapt upright with a sound in his throat like a wounded beast. He tried to throw himself over the side, but I caught and held him.

'Leave me,' he screamed. 'I must go to her.'

'No.' I fought with him in the crazily rocking dinghy. 'It's no good, Angelo.'

Even if he could get down through the forty feet of water in which *Dancer*'s torn hull now lay, what he would find might drive him mad. Judith had stood at the centre of that blast, and she would have been subjected to all the terrible trauma of massive flash explosion at close range.

'Leave me, damn you.' Angelo got one arm free and hit me in the face, but I saw it coming and rolled my head. It grazed the skin from my cheek, and I knew I had to get him quieted down.

The dinghy was on the point of capsizing. Though he was forty pounds lighter than me, Angelo fought with maniac strength. He was calling her name now.

'Judith, Judith,' on an hysterical rising inflection. I released my grip on his shoulder with my right hand, and swung him slightly away from me, lining him up carefully. I hit him with a right chop, my fist moving not more than four inches. I hit him cleanly on the point below his left ear, and he dropped instantly, gone cold. I lowered him to the floor-boards and laid him out comfortably. I rowed back to the wharf without looking back. I felt completely numbed and drained.

I carried Angelo down the wharf and I hardly felt his weight in my arms. I drove him up to the hospital and MacNab was on duty.

'Give him something to keep him muzzy and in bed for the next twenty-four hours,' I told MacNab, and he began to argue.

'Listen, you broken-down old whisky vat,' I told him quietly, 'I'd love an excuse to beat your head in.'

He paled until the broken veins in his nose and cheeks stood out boldly.

'Now listen—Harry old man,' he began. I took a step towards him, and he sent the duty sister to the drug cupboard.

I found Chubby at breakfast and it took only a minute to explain what had happened. We went up to the fort in the pick-up, and Wally Andrews responded quickly. He waived the filing of statements and other police procedure and instead we piled the police diving equipment into the truck and by the time we reached the harbour, half of St Mary's had formed a silent worried crowd along the wharf. Some had seen it and all of them had heard the explosion.

An occasional voice called condolences to me as we carried the diving equipment to the mackerel boat.

'Somebody find Fred Coker,' I told them. 'Tell him to get down here with a bag and basket,' and there was a buzz of comment.

'Hey, Mister Harry, was there somebody aboard?'

'Just get Fred Coker,' I told them, and we rowed out to *Dancer*'s moorings.

While Wally kept the dinghy on station above us, Chubby and I went down through the murky harbour water.

Dancer lay on her back in forty-five feet, she must have rolled as she sank—but there was no need to worry about access to her interior, for her hull had been torn open along the keel. She was far past any hope of refloating.

Chubby waited at the hole in the hull while I went in.

What remained of the galley was filled with swirling excited shoals of fish. They were in a feeding frenzy and I choked and gagged into the mouthpiece of my scuba when I saw what they were feeding upon.

The only way I knew it was Judith was the tatters of green cloth clinging to the fragments of flesh. We got her out in three main pieces, and placed her in the canvas bag that Fred Coker provided.

I dived again immediately, and worked my way through the shattered hull to the compartment below the galley where the two long iron gas cylinders were still bolted to their beds. Both taps were wide open, and somebody had disconnected the hoses to allow the gas to escape freely.

I have never experienced anger so intense as I felt then. It was that strong for it fed upon my loss. *Dancer* was gone—and *Dancer* had been half my life. I closed the taps and reconnected the gas hose. It was a private thing—I would deal with it personally.

When I walked back along the wharf to the pick-up, all that gave me comfort was the knowledge that *Dancer* had been insured. There would be another boat—not as beautiful or as well beloved as *Dancer*—but a boat nevertheless.

In the crowd I noticed the shiny black face of Hambone Williams—the harbour ferryman. For forty years he had plied his old dinghy back and forth at threepence a hire.

'Hambone,' I called him over. 'Did you take anybody out to *Dancer* last night?'

'No, sir, Mister Harry.'

'Nobody at all?'

'Only your party. She left her watch in the cabin. I took her out to fetch it.'

'The lady?'

'Yes, the lady with the yellow hair.'

'What time, Hambone?'

'About nine o'clock—did I do wrong, Mister Harry?'

'No, it's all right. Just forget it.'

We buried Judith next day before noon. I managed to get the plot beside her mother and father for her. Angelo liked that. He said he did not want her to be lonely up there on the hill. Angelo was still half doped, and he was quiet and dreamy eyed at the graveside.

The next morning the three of us began salvage work on *Dancer*. We worked hard for ten days and we stripped her completely of anything that had a possible value—from the big-game fishing reels and the FN carbine to the twin bronze propellers. The hull and superstructure were so badly broken up as to be of no value.

At the end of that time *Wave Dancer* had become a memory only. I have had many women, and now they are just a pleasant thought when I hear a certain song or smell a particular perfume. Like them, already *Dancer* was beginning to recede into the past.

On the tenth day I went up to see Fred Coker—and the moment I entered his office I knew there was something very wrong. He was shiny with nervous sweat, his eyes moved shiftily behind the glittering spectacles and his hands scampered about like frightened mice—running over his blotter or leaping up to adjust the knot of his necktie or smooth down the thin strands of hair on his polished cranium. He knew I'd come to talk insurance.

'Now don't get excited please, Mister Harry,' he advised me. Whenever people tell me that, I become very excited indeed.

'What is it, Coker? Come on! Come on!' I slammed one fist on the desk top, and he leapt in his chair so the gold-rimmed spectacles slid down his nose.

'Mister Harry, please—'

'Come on! You miserable little grave worm—'

'Mister Harry—it's about the premiums on *Dancer*.' I stared at him.

'You see—you had never made a claim before—it seemed such a waste to—'

I found words. 'You pocketed the premiums,' I whispered, my voice failing me suddenly. 'You didn't pay them over to the company.'

'You understand,' Fred Coker nodded. 'I knew you'd understand.'

I tried to go over the desk to save time, but I tripped and fell. Fred Coker leapt from his chair, slipping through my outstretched groping fingers. He ran through the back door, slamming it behind him.

I ran straight through the door, tearing off the lock, and leaving it hanging on broken hinges.

Fred Coker ran as though all the dark angels pursued him, which would have been better for him. I caught him at the big doors into the alley and lifted him by the throat, holding him with one hand, pressing his back against a pile of cheap pine coffins.

He had lost his spectacles, and he was weeping with fright, big slow tears welling out of the helpless short-sighted eyes.

'You know I'm going to kill you,' I whispered, and he moaned, his feet dancing six inches above the floor.

I pulled back my right fist and braced myself solidly on the balls of my feet. It would have taken my head off. I couldn't do it—but I had to hit something. I drove my fist into the coffin beside his right ear. The panelling shattered, stove in along its full length. Fred Coker shrieked like an hysterical girl at a pop festival, and I let him drop. His legs could not hold him and he sank to the concrete floor.

I left him lying there moaning and blubbering with terror—and I walked out into the street as near to bankrupt as I'd been in the last ten years.

Mister Harry transformed in a single stroke into Fletcher, wharf rat and land-bound bum. It was a classic case of reversion to type—before I reached the Lord Nelson I was thinking the same way I had ten years before. Already I was calculating the percentages, seeking the main chance once more.

Chubby and Angelo were the only customers in the public bar so early in the afternoon. I told them, and they were quiet. There wasn't anything to say.

We drank the first one in silence, then I asked Chubby, 'What will you do now?' and he shrugged.

'I've still got the old whaleboat—' It was a twenty-footer, admiralty design, open-decked, but sea-kindly. 'I'll go for stump again, I reckon.' Stump were the big reef crayfish. There was good money in the frozen tails. It was how Chubby had earned his bread before *Dancer* and I came to St Mary's.

'You'll need new engines, those old Sea Gulls of yours are shot.' We drank another pint, while I worked out my finances—what the hell, a couple of thousand dollars was not going to make much difference to me. 'I'll buy two new twenty horse Evinrudes for the boat, Chubby,' I volunteered.

'Won't let you do it, Harry.' He frowned indignantly and shook his head. 'I got enough saved up working for you,' and he was adamant.

'What about you, Angelo?' I asked.

'Guess I'll go sell my soul on a Rawano contract.'

'No,' Chubby scowled at the thought. 'I'll need crew for the stump-boat.'

They were all settled then. I was relieved, for I felt responsible for them both. I was particularly glad that Chubby would be there to care for Angelo. The boy had taken Judith's death very badly. He was quiet and withdrawn, no longer the flashing Romeo. I had kept him working hard on the salvage of *Dancer*, that alone seemed to have given him the time he needed to recover from the wound.

Nevertheless he began drinking hard now, chasing tots of cheap brandy with pints of bitter. This is the most destroying way to take in alcohol, short of drinking meths, that I know of.

Chubby and I took it nice and slow, lingering over our tankards, yet under our jocularity was a knowledge that we had reached a crossroads and from tomorrow we would no longer be travelling together. It gave the evening the fine poignancy of impending loss.

There was a South African trawler in harbour that night that had come in for bunkers and repairs. When at last Angelo passed out cold, Chubby and I began our singing. Six of the trawler's beefy crew members voiced their disapproval in the most slanderous terms. Chubby and I could not allow insults of that nature to pass unchallenged. We all went out to discuss it in the backyard.

It was a glorious discussion, and when Wally Andrews arrived with the riot squad he arrested all of us, even those who had fallen in the fray.

'My own flesh and blood—' Chubby kept repeating as he and I staggered arm and arm into the cells. 'He turned on me. My own sister's son—'

Wally was human enough to send one of his constables down to the Lord Nelson for something to make our durance less vile. Chubby and I became very friendly with the trawlermen in the next cell, passing the bottle back and forth between the bars.

When we were released next morning, Wally Andrews declining to press charges, I drove out to Turtle Bay to begin closing up the shack. I made sure the crockery was clean, threw a few handfuls of mothballs in the cupboards and did not bother to lock the doors. There is no such thing as burglary on St Mary's.

For the last time I swam out beyond the reef, and for half an hour hoped that the dolphins might come. They did not and I swam back, showered and changed, picked up my old canvas and leather campaign bag from the bed and went out to where the pick-up was parked in the yard. I didn't look back as I drove up through the palm plantation, but I made myself a promise that I'd be coming this way again.

I parked in the front lot of the hotel and lit a cheroot. When Marion finished her shift at noon she came out the front entrance and set off down the drive with her cheeky little bottom swinging under the mini skirt.

I whistled and she saw me. She slipped into the passenger's seat beside me.

'Mister Harry, I'm so sorry about your boat—' We talked for a few minutes until I could ask the question.

'Miss North, while she was staying at the hotel, did she make any phone calls or send a cable?'

'I don't remember, Mister Harry, but I could check for you.'

'Now?'

'Sure,' she agreed.

'One other thing, could you also check with Dicky if he got a shot of her?' Dicky was the roving hotel photographer; it was a good chance that he had a print of Sherry North in his file.

Marion was gone for nearly three-quarters of an hour, but she returned with a triumphant smile.

'She sent a cable on the night before she left.' Marion handed me a flimsy copy. 'You can keep this copy,' she told me as I read the message.

It was addressed to: 'MANSON FLAT 5 CURZON STREET 97 LONDON W.1.' and the message read: 'CONTRACT SIGNED RETURNING HEATHROW BOAC FLIGHT 316 SATURDAY.' There was no signature.

'Dicky had to go through all his files—but he found one.' She handed me a six-by-four glossy print. It was of Sherry North reclining on a sun couch on the hotel terrace. She wore her bikini and sunglasses, but it was a good likeness.

'Thanks, Marion.' I gave her a five-pound note.

'Gee, Mister Harry,' she grinned at me as she tucked it into the front of her bra. 'For that price you can take what you fancy.'

'I've got a plane to catch, love.' I kissed her on the little snub nose, and slapped her bottom as she climbed out of the cab.

Chubby and Angelo came out to the airport. Chubby was to take care of the pick-up for me. We were all subdued, and shook hands awkwardly at the departure gate. There wasn't much to say, we had said it all the night before.

As the piston-engined aircraft took off for the mainland, I glimpsed the two of them standing together at the perimeter fence.

I stopped over three hours at Nairobi before catching the BOAC
flight on to London. I did not sleep during the long night flight. It was
many years since I had returned to my native land—and I was coming
back now on a grim mission of vengeance. I wanted very much to talk
to Sherry North.

When you are flat broke, that is the time to buy a new car and a
hundred-guinea suit. Look brave and prosperous, and people will
believe you are.

I shaved and changed at the airport and instead of a Hillman I hired
a Chrysler from the Hertz Depot at Heathrow, slung my bag in the boot
and drove to the nearest Courage pub.

I had a double portion of ham and egg pie, washed down with a pint
of Courage while I studied the road map. It was all so long ago that I
was unsure of my directions.

The lush and cultivated English countryside was too tame and green
after Malaya and Africa, and the autumn sunshine was pale gold when
I was used to a brighter fiercer sun—but it was a pleasant drive over the
downs and into Brighton.

I parked the Chrysler on the promenade opposite the Grand Hotel
and dived into the warren of The Lanes. They were filled with tourists
even this late in the season.

Pavilion Arcade was the address I had read so long ago on Jimmy
North's underwater sledge, and it took me nearly an hour to find it. It
was tucked away at the back of a cobbled yard, and most of the windows
and doors were shuttered and closed.

'North's Underwater World' had a ten-foot frontage onto the lane.
It was also closed, and a blind was drawn across the single window. I
tried without success to peer round the edge of the blind, but the interior was darkened, so I hammered on the door. There was no sound
from within, and I was about to turn away when I noticed a square
piece of cardboard that had once been stuck onto the bottom of the
window but had fallen to the floor inside. By twisting my head acro-
batically, I could read the handwritten message which had fortunately
fallen face up: Enquiries to Seaview, Downers Lane, Falmer, Sussex.
I went back to the car and took the road map out of the glove compartment.

It began to rain as I pushed the Chrysler through narrow lanes. The windscreen wipers flogged sullenly at the spattering drops and I peered into the premature gloom of early evening.

Twice I lost my way but finally I pulled up outside a gate in a thick hedge. The sign nailed to the gate read: NORTH SEAVIEW, and I believed that it might be possible to look southwards on a clear day and see the Atlantic.

I drove down between hedges, and came into the paved yard of an old double-storied red-brick farmhouse, with oak beams set into the walls and green moss growing on the wood-shingle roof. There was a light burning downstairs.

I parked the Chrysler and crossed the yard to the kitchen door, turning up my collar against the wind and rain. I beat on the door, and heard somebody moving around inside. The bolts were shot back and the top half of the stable door opened on a chain. A girl looked out at me.

I was not immediately impressed by her for she wore a baggy blue fisherman's jersey and she was a tall girl with a swimmer's shoulders. I thought her plain—in a striking manner.

Her brow was pale and broad, her nose was large but not bony or beaked, and below it her mouth was wide and friendly. She wore no make-up at all, so her lips were pale pink and there was a peppering of fine freckles on her nose and cheeks.

Her hair was drawn back severely from her face into a thick braid behind her neck. Her hair was black, shimmering iridescent black in the lamplight, and her eyebrows were black also, black and boldly arched over eyes that seemed also to be black until the light caught them and I realized they were the same dark haunted blue as the Mozambique current when the noon sun strikes directly into it.

Despite the pallor of her skin, there was an aura of good and glowing health about her. The pale skin had a lustre and plasticity to it, a quality that was somehow luminous so that when you studied her closely—as I was now doing—it seemed that you could see down through the surface to the flush of clean blood rising warmly to her cheeks and neck. She touched the tendril of silky dark hair that escaped the braid and floated lightly on her temple. It was an appealing gesture, that betrayed her nervousness and belied the serene expression in the dark blue eyes.

Suddenly I realized that she was an unusually handsome woman, for, although she was only in her mid-twenties, I knew she was no longer girl—but full woman. There was a strength and maturity about her, a deep sense of calm that I found intriguing.

Usually the women I choose are more obvious, I do not like to tie up too much of my energy in the pursuit. This was something beyond my experience and for the first time in years I felt unsure of myself.

We had been staring at each other for many seconds, neither of us speaking or moving.

'You're Harry Fletcher,' she said at last, and her voice was low and gently modulated, a cultivated and educated voice. I gaped at her.

'How the hell did you know that?' I demanded.

'Come in.' She slipped the chain and opened the bottom of the stable door, and I obeyed. The kitchen was warm and welcoming and filled with the smell of good food cooking.

'How did you know my name?' I asked again.

'Your picture was in the newspaper—with Jimmy's,' she explained. We were silent again, once more studying each other.

She was taller even than I had thought at first, reaching to my shoulder, with long legs clad in dark blue pants and the tops thrust into black leather boots. Now I could see the narrow waist and the promise of good breasts beneath the thick jersey.

At first I had thought her plain, ten seconds later I had reckoned her handsome, now I doubted I had ever seen a more beautiful woman. It took time for the full effect to sink in.

'You have me at a disadvantage,' I said at last. 'I don't know your name.'

'I'm Sherry North,' she answered, and I stared at her for a moment before I recovered from the shock. She was a very different person from the other Sherry North I had known.

'Did you know that there is a whole tribe of you?' I asked at last.

'I don't understand.' She frowned at me. Her eyes were enchantingly blue under the lowered brows.

'It's a long story.'

'I'm sorry.' For the first time she seemed to become aware that we were standing facing each other in the centre of the kitchen. 'Won't you sit down. Can I get you a beer?'

Sherry took a couple of cans of Carlsberg lager from the cupboard and sat opposite me across the kitchen table.

'You were going to tell me a long story.' She popped the tabs on the cans, and slid one across to me, then looked at me expectantly.

I began to tell her the carefully edited version of my experiences since Jimmy North arrived at St Mary's. She was very easy to talk to, like being with an old and interested friend. Suddenly I wanted to tell her everything, the entire unblemished truth. It was important that from the very beginning it should be right, with no reservations.

She was a complete stranger, and yet I was placing trust in her beyond any person I had ever known. I told her everything exactly as it had happened.

She fed me after dark had fallen, a savoury casserole out of an earthenware pot which we ate with homemade bread and farm butter. I was still talking but no longer about the recent events on St Mary's, and she listened quietly. At last I had found another human being with whom I could talk without reserve.

I went back in my life. In a complete catharsis I told her of the early days, even of the dubious manner in which I had earned the money to buy *Wave Dancer*, and how my good resolutions since then had wavered.

It was after midnight when at last she said: 'I can hardly believe all you've told me. You don't look like that—you look so,' she seemed to search for the word, 'wholesome.' But you could see it was not the word she wanted.

'I work hard at being that. But sometimes my halo falls over my eyes. You see, appearances are deceptive,' I said, and she nodded.

'Yes, they are,' and there was a significance in the way she said it, a warning perhaps. 'Why have you told me all this? It is not really very wise, you know.'

'It was just time that somebody knew about me, I suppose. Sorry, you were elected.'

She smiled. 'You can sleep in Jimmy's room tonight,' she said. 'I can't risk you rushing out and telling anybody else.'

I hadn't slept the night before and suddenly I was exhausted. I felt as though I did not have the strength to climb the stairs to the bedroom—but I had one question still to ask.

'Why did Jimmy come to St Mary's? What was he looking for?' I asked. 'Do you know who he was working with, who they were?'

'I don't know.' She shook her head, and I knew it was the truth. She wouldn't lie to me now, not after I had placed such trust in her.

'Will you help me find out? Will you help me find them?'

'Yes, I'll help you,' she said, and stood up from the table. 'We'll talk again in the morning.'

Jimmy's room was under the eaves, the pitch of the roof giving it an irregular shape. The walls were lined with photographs and packed bookshelves, silver sporting trophies and the treasured *bric-à-brac* of boyhood.

The bed was high and the mattress soft.

I went to fetch my bag from the Chrysler while Sherry put clean sheets upon the bed. Then she showed me the bathroom and left me.

I lay and listened to the rain on the roof for only a few minutes before I slept. I woke in the night and heard the soft whisper of her voice somewhere in the quiet house.

Barefooted and in my underpants I opened the bedroom door and crept silently down the passage to the stairs. I looked down into the hall. There was a light burning and Sherry North stood at the wall-hung telephone. She was speaking so quietly into the receiver, cupping her hands to her mouth, that I could not catch the words. The light was behind her. She wore a flimsy nightdress, and her body showed through the thin stuff as though she were naked.

I found myself staring like a peeping Tom. The lamplight glowed on the ivory sheen of her skin, and there were intriguing secret hollows and shadows beneath the transparent cloth.

With an effort I pulled my eyes off her and went back to my bed. I thought about Sherry's telephone call and felt a vague disquiet, but soon sleep overtook me once more.

In the morning the rain had stopped but the ground was slushy and the grass heavy and wet when I went out for a breath of cold morning air.

I expected to feel awkward with Sherry after the previous night's outpourings of the soul, but it was not so. We talked easily at breakfast, and afterwards she said, 'I promised I'd help you; what can I do?'

'Answer a few questions.'

'All right, ask me.'

Jimmy North had been very secretive, she did not know he was going to St Mary's. He had told her he had a contract to install some electronic underwater equipment at the Cabora-Bassa Dam in Portuguese Mozambique. She had taken him up to the airport with all his equipment. As far as she knew he was travelling alone. The police had come to the shop in Brighton to tell her of his murder. She had read the newspaper reports, and that was all.

'No letters from Jimmy?'

'No, nothing,' I nodded, the wolf-pack must have intercepted his mail. The letter I had been shown by Sherry's impostor was certainly genuine.

'I don't understand anything about this. Am I being stupid?'

'No.' I took out a cheroot, and almost lit it before I stopped myself. 'Okay if I smoke one of these?'

'It doesn't bother me,' she said, and I was glad, for it would have been hell giving them up. I lit it and drew in the fragrant smoke.

'It looks as though Jimmy stumbled on something big. He needed backing and he went to the wrong people. As soon as they thought they knew where it was, they killed him and tried to kill me. When that didn't work they sent out someone impersonating you. When she thought she knew the location of this object, she set a trap for me and went home. Their next move will be a return to the area off Big Gull Island, where they are due for another disappointment.'

She refilled the coffee cups, and I noticed that she had applied make-up this morning—but so lightly that the freckles still showed. I reconsidered the previous night's judgement—and confirmed that she was one of the most beautiful women I had ever met, even in the early morning.

She was frowning thoughtfully, staring into her coffee cup and I wanted to touch one of her slim strong-looking hands that lay on the tablecloth near my own.

'What were they after, Harry? And who are these people who killed him?' she asked at last.

'Two excellent questions. I have leads to both—but we will tackle the questions in the order you asked them. Firstly, what was Jimmy after? When we know that we can go after his murderers.'

'I have no idea at all what it could be.' She looked up at me. The blue of her eyes was lighter than it had been last night, it was the colour of a good sapphire. 'What clues have you?'

'The ship's bell. The design upon it.'

'What does it signify?'

'I don't know, but it shouldn't be too hard to find out.' I could no longer resist the temptation. I placed my hand over hers. It felt as firm and strong as it looked and her flesh was warm. 'But first I should like to check the shop in Brighton and Jimmy's room here. There might be something we can use.'

She had not withdrawn her hand. 'All right, shall we go to the shop first? The police have already been through it all, but they might have overlooked something.'

'Fine. I'll buy you lunch.' I squeezed her hand, and she turned it in my grasp and squeezed back.

'I'll take you up on that,' she said, and I was too astonished by my own reaction to her grip to find a light reply. My throat was dry and my pulse beat as though I'd run a mile. Gently she removed her hand and stood up.

'Let's do the breakfast dishes.'

If the girls of St Mary's could only have seen Mister Harry drying dishes, my reputation would have shattered into a thousand pieces.

She let us into the shop the back way, through a tiny enclosed yard which was almost filled with unusual objects, all of them associated with diving and the underwater world—discarded air bottles and a portable compressor, brass portholes and other salvage from wrecked ships, even the jawbone of a killer whale with all its teeth intact.

'I haven't been in for a long time,' Sherry apologized as she unlocked the back door of the shop. 'Without Jimmy—' she shrugged and then went on, '—I must really get down to selling up all this junk and closing the shop down. I could re-sell the lease, I suppose.'

'I'm going to look round, okay?'

'Fine, I'll get the kettle going.'

I started in the yard, searching quickly but thoroughly through the piles of junk. There was nothing that had significance as far as I could see. I went into the shop and poked around among the sea shells and sharks' teeth on the shelves and in the display case. Finally I saw a desk in the corner and began going through the drawers.

Sherry brought me a cup of tea and perched on the corner of the desk while I piled old invoices, rubber bands and paper clips on the top. I read every scrap of paper and even rifled through the ready reckoner.

'Nothing?' Sherry asked.

'Nothing,' I agreed and glanced at my watch. 'Lunchtime,' I told her.

She locked up the shop and by good fortune we stumbled on English's restaurant. They gave us a secluded table in the back room and I ordered a bottle of Pouilly Fuissé to go with the lobster. Once I recovered from the shock of the price, we laughed a lot during the meal, and it wasn't just the wine. The feeling between us was good and growing stronger.

After lunch we drove back to Seaview and we went up to Jimmy's room.

'This is our best bet,' I guessed. 'If he was keeping secrets, this is where they would be.' But I knew I had a long job ahead of me. There were hundreds of books and piles of magazines—mostly *American Argosy*, *Trident*, *The Diver* and other diving publications. There was also a complete shelf of springback files at the foot of the bed.

'I'll leave you to it,' Sherry said, and went.

I took down the contents of a shelf, sat at the reading table and began to skim through the publications. Immediately I saw it was an even bigger task than I had thought. Jimmy had been one of those people who read with a pencil in one hand. There were notes pencilled in the margin, comments, queries and exclamation marks, and anything that interested him was underlined.

I read doggedly, looking for something that could remotely be linked to St Mary's.

Around eight o'clock I began on the shelf that held the springback files. The first two were filled with newspaper clippings on shipwrecks or other marine phenomena. The third of them had an unlabelled, black imitation leather cover. It held a thin sheath of papers, and I saw immediately that they were out of the ordinary.

They were a series of letters filed with their envelopes and stamps still attached. There were sixteen of them in all, addressed to Messrs Parker and Wilton in Fenchurch Street.

Every letter was in a different hand, but all were executed in the elegant penmanship of the last century.

The envelopes were sent from different parts of the old Empire— Canada, South Africa, India—and the nineteenth century postage stamps lone must have been of considerable value.

After I had read the first two letters, it was clear that Messrs Parker and Wilton were agents and factors, and they had acted for a number of distinguished clients in the service of Queen Victoria. The letters were instructions to deal with estates, moneys and securities.

All the letters were dated during the period from August 1857 to July 1858 and must have been offered by a dealer or an antique auctioneer as a lot.

I glanced through them quickly, but the contents were really very dull. However, something on the single page of the tenth letter caught my eye and I felt my nerves jump.

Two words had been underlined in pencil and in the margin was a notation in Jimmy North's handwriting.

'B. Mus. E.6914(8).'

However, it was the words themselves that held me.

'Dawn Light.'

I had heard those words before. I wasn't sure when, but they were significant.

Quickly I began at the top of the page. The sender's address was a laconic 'Bombay', and it was dated September 16th 1857.

My Dear Wilton,

I charge you most strictly with the proper care and safe storage of five pieces of luggage consigned in my name to your London address aboard the Hon. Company's ship Dawn Light. *Due out of this port before the 25th instant and bound for the Company's wharf in the Port of London.*

Please acknowledge safe receipt of same with all despatch.

I remain yours faithfully,

Colonel Sir Roger Goodchild.
Officer Commanding 101st Regiment
  Queens Own India Rifles.
Delivery by kind favour of Captain commanding Her Majesty's Frigate Panther.

The paper rustled and I realized that my hand was shaking with excitement. I knew I was on to it now. This was the key. I laid the letter carefully on the reading table and placed a silver paper knife upon it to weight it down.

I began to read it again slowly, but there was a distraction. I heard the engine noise of an automobile coming down the lane from the gate. Headlights flashed across the window and then rounded the corner of the house.

I sat up straight, listening. The engine noise died, and car doors slammed shut.

There was a long silence then before I heard the murmur and growl of voices—men's voices. I began to stand up from the table.

Then Sherry screamed. It rang clearly through the old house, and cut into my brain like a lance. It aroused in me a protective instinct so fierce that I was down the stairs and into the hall before I realized I had moved.

The door to the kitchen was open and I paused in the doorway. There were two men with Sherry. The heavier and elder of the two wore a beige camelhair topcoat and a tweed cap. He had a greyish, heavy lined face and deep-sunk eyes. His lips were thin and colourless.

He had Sherry's left hand twisted up between her shoulder-blades, and was holding her jammed against the wall beside the gas stove.

The other man was younger, and he was slim and pale, bare-headed with long straw-yellow hair falling to the shoulders of his leather jacket. He was grinning gleefully as he held Sherry's other hand over the blue flames of the gas ring, bringing it down slowly.

She was struggling desperately, but they held her and her hair had come loose as she fought.

'Slowly, lad,' the man in the cap spoke in a thick strangled voice. 'Give her time to think about it.'

Sherry screamed again as her fingers were forced down remorselessly towards the hissing blue flames.

'Go ahead, luv, shout your head off,' laughed the blond. 'There isn't anybody to hear you.'

'Only me,' I said, and they spun to face me, with expressions of comical amazement.

'Who—' asked the blond, releasing Sherry's arm and reaching quickly for his back pocket.

I hit him twice, left in the body and right in the head, and although neither shot pleased me particularly—there was not the right solidness at impact—the man went down, falling heavily over a chair and crashing into the cupboard. I had no more time for him, and I went for the one in the cloth cap.

He was still holding Sherry in front of him, and as I started forward he hurled her at me. It took me off-balance and I was forced to grab her, to save both of us from falling.

The man turned and darted out of the door behind him. It took me a few seconds to disentangle myself from Sherry and cross the kitchen. As I barged out into the yard he was half way to an elderly Triumph sports car, and he glanced over his shoulder.

I could almost see him make the calculation. He wasn't going to be able to get into the car and turn it to face the lane before I caught him. He swerved to the left and sprinted into the dark mouth of the lane with the skirts of the camelhair coat billowing behind him. I raced after him.

The surface was greasy with wet clay, and he was making heavy going of it. He slid and almost fell, and I was right behind him, coming up swiftly when he turned and I heard the snap of the knife and saw the flash of the blade as it jumped out. He dropped into a crouch with the knife extended and I ran straight in without a check.

He didn't expect that, the glint of steel will stop most men dead. He went for my belly, a low underhand stroke, but he was shaky and breathless and it lacked fire. I blocked on the wrist and at the same time hit the pressure point in his forearm. The knife dropped out of his hand and I threw him over my hip. He fell heavily on his back, and although the mud softened the impact I dropped on one knee into his belly. It had 210 lbs of body weight behind it and it drove the air out of his lungs in a loud whoosh. He doubled up like a foetus in the womb, wheezing for breath, and I flipped him over onto his face. The cloth cap fell off his head and I found that he had a thick shock of dark hair shot through with strands of silver. I took a good handful of it, sat on his shoulders and pushed his face deep into the yellow mud.

'I don't like little boys who bully girls,' I told him conversationally, and behind me the engine of the Triumph roared into life. The head-lights blazed out and then swung in a wide arc until they burned directly up the narrow lane.

I knew I hadn't taken the blond out properly, it had been a hurried botchy job. I left the man in the mud and ran back down the lane. The wheels of the Triumph spun on the paving of the yard and, with its headlights blazing dazzlingly into my eyes, it jumped forward, slewing and skidding as it left the paving and entered the muddy lane. The driver met the skid and came straight at me.

I fell flat and rolled into the cold ooze of a narrow open drain that carried run-off water through the tall hedge.

The Triumph hit the side a glancing blow and the hedge pushed it slightly off its line. The nearside wheels spun viciously on the edge of the stone coping of the drain inches from my face, and mud and a shower of twigs fell on me. Then it was past.

It checked as it came level with the man in the muddy camelhair coat. He was kneeling on the verge of the road and now he dragged himself into the passenger seat of the Triumph. Just as I crawled out of the drain and ran up behind the sports car it pulled away again, mud spraying from the spinning rear wheels. In vain I raced after it, but it gathered speed and tore away up the slope.

I gave up, turned and ran back down the lane, groping for the keys of the Chrysler in my sodden trouser pockets, and realized I had left them on the table in Jimmy's room.

Sherry was leaning in the open doorway of the kitchen. She held her burned hand to her chest and her hair was in tangled disarray. The sleeve of her jersey was torn loose from the shoulder.

'I couldn't stop him, Harry,' she gasped. 'I tried.'

'How bad is it?' I asked her, abandoning all thought of chasing the sports car when I saw her distress.

'Slightly singed.'

'I'll take you to a doctor.'

'No. It doesn't need it,' but her smile was lopsided with pain. I went up to Jimmy's room and from my travelling medicine kit I took a Doloxene for the pain and Mogadon to let her sleep.

'I don't need it,' she protested.

'Do I have to hold your nose and force them down?' I asked, and she grinned, shook her head and swallowed them.

'You'd better take a bath,' she said, 'you're soaked,' and suddenly I realized I was sodden and cold. When I came back to the kitchen, glowing from the bath, she was already whoozy with the pills, but she had made coffee for us and strengthened it with a tot of whisky. We drank it sitting opposite each other.

'What did they want?' I asked. 'What did they say?'

'They thought I knew why Jimmy had gone to St Mary's. They wanted to know.'

I thought about that. Something didn't make sense, it worried me.

'I think—' Sherry's voice was unsteady and she staggered slightly as she tried to stand. 'Wow! What did you give me?'

I picked her up and she protested weakly, but I carried her up to her room. It was chintzy and girlish, with rose-patterned wallpaper. I laid her on the bed, pulled off her shoes and covered her with the quilt.

She sighed and closed her eyes. 'I think I'll keep you around,' she whispered. 'You're very useful.'

Thus encouraged, I sat on the edge of the bed and gentled her to sleep, smoothing her hair off her temples and stroking the broad forehead; her skin felt like warm velvet. She was asleep within a minute. I switched off the light, and was about to leave when I thought better of it.

I slipped off my own shoes and crept in under the quilt. In her sleep she rolled quite naturally into my arms, and I held her close.

It was a good feeling and soon I slept also. I woke in the dawn. Her face was pressed into my neck, one leg and arm were thrown over me and her hair was soft and tickling against my cheek.

Without waking her, I gently disengaged myself, kissed her forehead, picked up my shoes and went back to my own room. It was the first time I had spent an entire night with a beautiful woman in my arms, and done nothing but sleep. I felt puffed up with virtue.

The letter lay upon the reading table in Jimmy's room where I had left it and I read it through again before I went to the bathroom. The pencilled note in the margin 'B. Mus. E.6914(8)' puzzled me and I fretted over it while I shaved.

The rain had stopped and the clouds were breaking up when I went down into the yard to examine the scene of the previous night's encounter. The knife lay in the mud and I picked it up and tossed it over the hedge. I went into the kitchen, stamping my feet and rubbing my hands in the cold.

Sherry had started breakfast.

'How's the hand?'

'Sore,' she admitted.

'We'll find a doctor on the way up to London.'

'What makes you think I'm going to London?' she asked carefully, as she buttered toast.

'Two things. You can't stay here. The wolf pack will be back.' She looked up at me quickly but was silent. 'The other is that you promised to help me—and the trail leads to London.'

She was unconvinced, so while we ate I showed her the letter I had found in Jimmy's file.

'I don't see the connection,' she said at last, and I admitted frankly, 'It's not clear to me even.' I lit my first cheroot of the day as I spoke, and the effect was almost magical. 'But as soon as I saw the words *Dawn Light* something went click—' I stopped. 'My God!' I breathed. 'That's it. The *Dawn Light*!' I remembered the scraps of conversation carried to the bridge of *Wave Dancer* through the ventilator from the cabin below.

'To get the dawn light then we will have to—' Jimmy's voice, clear and tight with anticipation. 'If the dawn light is where—' Again the words repeated had puzzled me at the time. They had stuck like burrs in my memory.

I began to explain to Sherry, but I was so excited that it came tumbling out in a rush of words. She laughed, catching my excitement but not understanding the explanations.

'Hey!' she protested. 'You're not making sense.'

I began again, but half way through I stopped and stared at her silently.

'Now what is it?' She was half amused, half exasperated. 'This is driving me crazy, also.'

I snatched up my fork. 'The bell. You remember the bell I told you about. The one Jimmy pulled up at Gunfire Reef?'

'Yes, of course.'

'I told you it had lettering on it, half eaten away by sand.'

'Yes, go on.'

With the fork I scratched on the butter, using it as a slate.

'—VV N   L—'

I drew in the lettering that had been chased into the bronze.

'That was it,' I said. 'It didn't mean anything then—but now—' Quickly I completed the letters, 'DAWN LIGHT.'

And she stared at it, nodding slowly as it fitted together.

'We have to find out about this ship, the *Dawn Light*.'

'How?'

'It should be easy. We know she was an East Indiaman—there must be records—Lloyd's—the Board of Trade?'

She took the letter from my hand and read it again. 'The gallant colonel's luggage probably contained dirty socks and old shirts.' She pulled a face and handed it back to me.

'I'm short of socks,' I said.

Sherry packed a case, and I was relieved to see that she had the rare virtue of being able to travel light. She went down to speak to the tenant farmer while I packed the bags into the Chrysler. He would keep an eye on the cottage during her absence, and when she came back she merely locked the kitchen door and climbed into the Chrysler beside me.

'Funny,' she said. 'This feels like the beginning of a long journey.'

'I have my plans,' I warned and leered at her.

'Once I thought you looked wholesome,' she said sorrowfully, 'but when you do that—'

'Sexy, isn't it?' I agreed, and took the Chrysler up the lane.

I found a doctor in Haywards Heath. Sherry's hand had now blistered badly, fat white bags of fluid hung from her fingers like sickly grapes. He drained them, and rebandaged the hand.

'Feels worse now,' she murmured as we drove on northwards, and she was pale and silent with the pain of it. I respected her silence, until we were into the suburbs of the city.

'We had better find some place to stay,' I suggested. 'Something comfortable and central.'

She looked across at me quizzically.

'It would probably be a lot more comfortable and cheaper if we got a double room somewhere, wouldn't it?'

I felt something turn over in my belly, something warm and exciting. 'Funny you should say that, I was just about to suggest the same.'

'I know you were,' she laughed for the first time in two hours. 'I saved you the trouble.' She shook her head, still laughing. 'I'll stay with my uncle. He's got a spare room in his apartment in Pimlico, and there is a little pub around the corner. It's friendly and clean—you could do worse.'

'I am crazy about your sense of humour,' I muttered.

She phoned the uncle from a call box, while I waited in the car.

'It's fixed up,' she told me, as she climbed into the passenger seat. 'He's at home.'

It was a ground-floor apartment in a quiet street near the river. I carried Sherry's bag for her as she led the way, and rang the doorbell.

The man that opened the door was small and lightly built. He was sixtyish and he wore a grey cardigan, darned at the elbows. His feet were thrust into carpet slippers. The homely attire was somehow incongruous, for his iron-grey hair was neatly cropped as was the short stiff moustache. His skin was clear and ruddy, but it was the fierce predatory glint of the eye and the military set of the shoulders that warned me. This man was aware.

'My uncle, Dan Wheeler.' Sherry stood aside to introduce us. 'Uncle Dan this is Harry Fletcher.'

'The young man you were telling me about,' he nodded abruptly. His hand was bony and dry and his gaze stung like nettles. 'Come in. Come in, both of you.'

'I won't bother you, sir—' it was quite natural to call him that, an echo of my military training from so long ago, 'I want to find digs myself.'

Uncle Dan and Sherry exchanged glances and I thought she shook her head almost imperceptibly, but I was looking beyond them into the apartment. It was monastic, completely masculine in the severity and economy of furniture and ornaments. Somehow that room seemed to confirm my first impressions of the man. I wanted as little to do with him as I could arrange while seeing as much of Sherry as I possibly could.

'I'll pick you up in an hour for lunch, Sherry,' and when she agreed I left them and returned to the Chrysler. The pub that Sherry recommended was the Windsor Arms, and when I mentioned the uncle's name as she suggested, they put me in a quiet back room with a fine view of sky and television aerials. I lay on the bed fully clothed, and considered the North family and its relatives while I waited for the hour to run by. Of one thing only was I certain—that Sherry North the Second was not going to pass me silently in the night. I was going to keep pretty close station upon her, and yet there was much about her that still puzzled me. I suspected that she was a more complicated person than her serene and lovely face suggested. It was going to be interesting finding out. I put the thought aside, sat up and reached for the telephone. I made three phone calls in the next twenty minutes. One to Lloyd's Register of Shipping in Fenchurch Street, another to the National Maritime Museum at Greenwich and the last to the India Office Library in Blackfriars Road. I left the Chrysler in the private parking lot behind the pub—a car is more trouble than it is worth in London—and I walked back to the uncle's apartment. Sherry answered the door herself, and she was ready to leave. I liked that about her, she was punctual.

'You didn't like Uncle Dan, did you?' she challenged me over the lunch table and I ducked.

'I made some phone calls. The place that we are looking for is in Blackfriars Road. It's in Westminster. The India Office Library. We will go down there after we've eaten.'

'He really is very sweet when you get to know him.'

'Look, darling girl, he's your uncle. You keep him.'

'But why, Harry? It interests me.'

'What does he do for a living—Army, Navy?'

She stared at me. 'How did you know that?'

'I can pick them out of a crowd.'

'He's Army, but retired—why should that make a difference?'

'What are you going to try?' I waved the menu at her. 'If you take the roast beef, I'll go for the duck,' and she accepted the decoy, and concentrated on the food.

The India Office Archives were housed in one of those square modern blocks of greenish glass and airforce-blue steel panels.

Sherry and I armed ourselves with visitor's passes and signed the book. We made our way first to the Catalogue Room and thence to the marine section of the archives. These were presided over by a neatly dressed but stern-faced lady with greying hair and steel-rimmed spectacles.

I handed her a requisition slip for the dossier which would include material on the Honourable Company's ship *Dawn Light* and she disappeared among the laden ceiling-high tiers of steel shelving.

It was twenty minutes before she returned and placed a bulky dossier on the counter top before me.

'You'll have to sign here,' she told me, indicating a column on the stiff cardboard folder. 'Funny!' she remarked. 'You are the second one who has asked for this file in less than a year.'

I stared at the signature J. A. North in the last space. We were following closely in Jimmy's footsteps, I thought, as I signed 'RICHARD SMITH' below his name.

'You can use one of the desks over there, dear.' She pointed across the room. 'Please try and keep the file tidy, won't you, then.'

Sherry and I sat down at the desk shoulder to shoulder, and I untied the tape that secured the file.

The *Dawn Light* was of the type known as the Blackwall Frigate, characteristically built at the Blackwall yards in the early nineteenth century. The type was very similar to the naval frigates of that period.

She had been built at Sunderland for the Honourable English East India Company, and she was of 1,330 net register tons. At the waterline her dimensions were 226 feet with a beam of twenty-six feet. Such a narrow beam would have made her very fast but uncomfortable in a stiff blow.

She had been launched in 1832, just the year before the Company lost its China monopoly, and this stroke of ill-fortune seemed to have dogged her whole career.

Also in the file were a whole series of reports of the proceedings of various courts of enquiry. Her first master gloried in the name of Hogge and on her maiden voyage he piled the *Dawn Light* onto the bank at Diamond Harbour in Hooghly River. He was found by the court of enquiry to be under the influence of strong drink at the time and stripped of his command.

'Made a pig of himself,' I observed to Sherry, and she groaned softly and rolled her eyes at my wit.

The trail of misfortune continued. In 1840 while making passage in the South Atlantic the elderly mate who had the dog watch let her come up, and away went her masts. Wallowing helpless with her top hamper dragging alongside, she was found by a Dutchman. They cut away the wreckage and she was dragged into Table Bay. The Salvage Court made an award of £12,000.

In 1846 while half her crew was ashore on the wild coast of New Guinea they were set upon by the cannibals and slaughtered to a man. Sixty-three of her crew died.

Then on September 23rd 1857, she sailed from Bombay, outward bound for St Mary's, the Cape of Good Hope, St Helena and the Pool of London.

'The date.' I placed my finger on the line. 'This is the voyage that Goodchild talks of in the letter.'

Sherry nodded without reply; I had learned in the last few minutes that she read faster than I did. I had to restrain her from turning each page when I was only three-quarters finished. Now her eyes darted across each line, her colour was up, a soft flush upon her pale cheeks, and she was biting her underlip.

'Come on,' she urged me. 'Hurry up!' and I had to hold her wrist.

The *Dawn Light* never reached St Mary's—she disappeared. Three months later, she was considered lost at sea with all hands and the underwriters were ordered by Lloyd's to make good their assurances to the owners and shippers.

The manifest of her cargo was impressive for such a small ship for she had loaded out of China and India a cargo that consisted of:

364 chests of tea	72 tons on behalf of
494 half-chests of tea	Messrs Dunbar and Green.
101 chests of tea	65 tons on behalf of
618 half-chests of tea	Messrs Simpson, Wyllie & Livingstone.
577 bales of silk	82 tons on behalf of
	Messrs Elder and Company.
5 cases goods	4 tons on behalf of
	Col. Sir Roger Goodchild.

16 cases goods	6 tons on behalf of Major John Cotton.
10 cases goods	2 tons on behalf of Lord Elton.
26 boxes various spices	2 tons on behalf of Messrs Paulson and Company.

Wordlessly I laid my finger on the fourth item of the manifest, and again Sherry nodded, with her eyes shining like sapphires. The claim had been settled and the matter appeared closed until, four months later in April, 1858, the East Indiaman *Walmer Castle* arrived in England, carrying aboard the survivors from the *Dawn Light*.

There were six of them. The first mate, Andrew Barlow, a boatswain's mate, and three topmast men. There was also a young woman of twenty-two years, a Miss Charlotte Cotton, who had been a passenger making the homeward passage with her father, a Major in the 40th Foot.

The mate, Andrew Barlow, gave his evidence to the Court of Enquiry, and beneath the dry narrative and the ponderous questions and guarded replies lay an exciting and romantic story of the sea, an epic of shipwreck and survival.

As we read I saw the meagre scraps of knowledge I had scraped together fit neatly into the story.

Fourteen days out from Bombay, the *Dawn Light* was set upon by a furious storm out of the south-east. For seven days the savagery of the storm raged unabated, driving the ship before her. I could imagine it clearly, one of those great cyclones that had torn the roof from my own shack at Turtle Bay.

Once again *Dawn Light* was dismasted, no spars were left standing except the fore lower mast, mizzen lower mast, and bowsprit. The rest had been carried away on the tempest and there was no opportunity to set up a jury mainmast or send yards aloft in the mountainous seas.

Thus when land was sighted to leeward, there was no chance that the ship might avoid her fate. A conspiracy of wind and current hurled her down into the throat of a funnel-shaped reef upon which the storm burst like the thunder of the heavens.

The ship struck and held, and Andrew Barlow was able with the help of twelve members of his crew to launch one of the boats. Four passengers, including Miss Charlotte Cotton, left the stricken ship with them, and Barlow, with an unlikely combination of good fortune and seamanship, was able to find a passage through the wild sea and murderous reefs into the quieter waters of the inshore channel.

Finally they ran the boat ashore on the spindrift-smothered beach of an island. Here the survivors huddled for four days while the cyclone blew itself out.

Barlow alone climbed to the summit of the southernmost of the treble peaks of the island. The description was completely clear. It was the Old Man and Gunfire Reef. There was no doubt of it. This then was how Jimmy North had known what he was looking for—the island with three peaks and a barrier of coral reef.

Barlow took bearings off the sea-battered hull of the *Dawn Light* as she lay in the jaws of the reef, swept by each successive wave. On the second day the ship's hull began to break up, and while Barlow watched from the peak, the front half of her was carried up over the reef to disappear into a dark gaping hole in the coral. The stern fell back into the sea and was smashed to matchwood.

When at last the skies cleared and the wind dropped, Andrew Barlow discovered that his small party were all that survived from a ship's company of 149 souls. The others had perished in the wild sea.

To the west, low against the horizon, he descried a low land mass which he hoped was the African mainland. He embarked his party in the ship's boat once more and they made the crossing of the inshore channel. His hopes were fulfilled, it was Africa—but as always she was hostile and cruel.

The seventeen lost beings began a long and dangerous journey southwards, and three months later only Barlow, four seamen and Miss Charlotte Cotton reached the island port of Zanzibar. Fever, wild animals, wild men and misfortune had whittled away their numbers—and even those who survived were starved to gaunt living skeletons, yellowed with fever and riddled with dysentery from foul water.

The court of enquiry had highly commended Andrew Barlow, and the Hon. Company had made him an award of £500 for meritorious service.

When I finished reading, I looked up at Sherry. She was watching me.

'Wow!' she said, and I also felt drained by the magnitude of the old drama.

'It all fits, Sherry,' I said. 'It's all there.'

'Yes,' she said.

'We must see if they have the drawings here.'

The Prints and Drawings Room was on the third floor and a quick search by an earnest assistant soon revealed the *Dawn Light* in all her splendour.

She was a graceful three-masted ship with a long low profile. She had no crossjack or mizzen course. Instead she carried a large spanker and a full set of studding sails. The long poop gave space for several passenger cabins, and she carried her boats on top of her deck-house aft.

She was heavily armed, with thirteen black-painted gunports aside from which she could run out her long eighteen-pounder cannon to defend herself in those hostile seas east of the Cape of Good Hope across which she plied to China and India.

'I need a drink,' I said, and picked up the drawings of the *Dawn Light*. 'I'll get them to make copies of these for us.'

'What for?' Sherry wanted to know.

The assistant emerged from her lair among the piled trays of old prints and sucked in her cheeks at my request for copies.

'I'll have to charge you seventy-five pence,' she tried to discourage me.

'That's reasonable,' I said.

'And we won't have them ready until next week,' she added inexorably.

'Oh dear,' said I, and gave her the smile. 'I did need them tomorrow afternoon.'

The smile crushed her, she lost the air of purpose and tried to tuck her straying wisps of hair into the side frames of her glasses.

'Well, I'll see what I can do then,' she relented.

'That's very sweet of you, really it is,' and we left her looking confused, but pleased.

My sense of direction was returning and I found my way to El Vino's without trouble. The evening flood of journalists from Fleet Street had not yet swamped it and we found a table at the back. I ordered two Vermouths and we saluted each other over the glasses.

'You know, Harry, Jimmy had a hundred schemes. His whole life was one great treasure hunt. Every week he had found, almost found the location of a treasure ship from the Armada or a sunken Aztec city a buccaneer wreck—' she shrugged. 'I have a built-in resistance to believing any of it. But this one—' She sipped the wine.

'Let's go over what we have,' I suggested. 'We know that Goodchild was very concerned that his agent receive five cases of luggage and put it into safe keeping. We know that he was going to ship it aboard *Dawn Light* and he sent advance notice, probably through a personal friend the captain of the naval frigate *Panther*.'

'Good,' she agreed.

'We know that those cases were listed on the ship's manifest. That the ship was lost, presumably with them still on board. We know the exact location of the wreck. We have had it confirmed by the ship's bell.'

'Still good.'

'We only do not know what those cases contained.'

'Dirty socks,' she said.

'Four tons of dirty socks?' I asked, and her expression changed. The weight of the cargo had not meant anything to her.

'Ah,' I grinned at her, 'it went over your head. I thought so. You read so fast you only take in half of it.'

She pulled a face at me.

'Four tons, my darling girl, is a great deal of something—whatever it is.'

'All right,' she agreed. 'Figures don't mean much to me, I admit. But it sounds a lot.'

'Say the same weight as a new Rolls Royce—to put it in terms you might understand,' and her eyes widened and turned a darker blue.

'That *is* a lot.'

'Jimmy obviously knew what it was, and had sufficient proof to convince some very hard-headed backers. They took it seriously.'

'Seriously enough to—' and she stopped herself. For an instant I saw the old grief for Jimmy's death in her eyes. I was embarrassed by it, and I looked away, making a show of taking the letter out of my inner pocket.

Carefully I spread it on the table top between us. When I looked at her, she had recovered her composure once more.

The pencilled note in the margin engaged my attention again.

'B. Mus. E.6914(8).' I read it aloud. 'Any ideas?'

'Bachelor of Music.'

'Oh, that's great,' I applauded.

'You do better,' she challenged, and I folded the letter away with dignity and ordered two more drinks.

'Well, that was a good run on that scent,' I said when I had paid the waiter. 'We have an idea what it was all about. Now, we can go on to my other lead.'

She sat forward and encouraged me silently.

'I told you about your impostor, the blonde Sherry North?' and she nodded. 'On the night before she left the island she sent a cable to London.' I produced the flimsy copy from my wallet and handed it to Sherry. While she read it, I went on, 'This was clearly an okay to her principal, Manson. He must be the big man behind this. I am going to start moving in on him now.' I finished my Vermouth. 'I'll drop you back with your martial uncle, and contact you again tomorrow.'

Her lips set in a line of stubbornness which I had not seen before and there was a glint in her eyes like the blue of gunmetal.

'Harry Fletcher, if you think you are going to ditch me just when things start livening up, you must be off your tiny head.'

The cab dropped us in Berkeley Square and I led her into Curzon Street.

'Take my arm quickly,' I muttered, glancing over my shoulder in a secretive manner. Instantly she obeyed, and we had gone fifty yards before she whispered, 'Why?'

'Because I like the feel of it,' I grinned at her and spoke in a natural voice.

'Oh, you!' She made as if to pull away, but I held her and she capitulated. We sauntered up the street towards Shepherd Market, stopping now and then to window-shop like a pair of tourists.

No. 97 Curzon Street was one of those astronomically expensive apartment blocks, six storeys of brick facing, and an ornate street door of bronze and glass beyond which was a marbled foyer guarded by a uniformed doorman. We went on past it, up as far as the White Elephant Club and there we crossed the street and wandered back on the opposite pavement.

'I could go and ask the doorman if Mr Manson occupied Flat No. 5,' Sherry volunteered.

'Great,' I said, 'When he says "yes", what do you do then? Tell him Harry Fletcher says hello?'

'You are really very droll,' she said, and once more she tried to take her hand away.

'There is a restaurant diagonally opposite No. 97.' I prevented her withdrawal. 'Let's get a table in the front window, drink some coffee, and watch for a while.'

It was a little past three o'clock when we settled at the window seat with a good view across the street, and the next hour passed pleasantly. I found it not a difficult task to keep Sherry amused; we shared a similar sense of humour and I liked to hear her laugh.

I was in the middle of a long, complicated story when I was interrupted by the arrival outside No. 97 of a Silver Wraith Rolls Royce. It pulled to the kerb and a chauffeur in a smart dove-grey uniform left the car and entered the foyer. He and the doorman fell into conversation, and I resumed my story.

Ten minutes later, there was sudden activity opposite. The elevator began a series of rapid ascents and descents, each time discharging a load of matching crocodile-skin luggage. This was carried out by the doorman and chauffeur and packed into the Rolls. It seemed endless, and Sherry remarked, 'Somebody is off on a long holiday.' She sighed wistfully.

'How do you fancy a tropical island with blue water and white sands, a thatched shack amongst the palms—'

'Stop it,' she said. 'On an autumn day in old London, I just can't bear the thought.'

I was about to move into a stronger position when the footman and chauffeur stood to attention and once more the glass doors of the lift opened and a man and woman stepped out of it.

The woman wore a full-length honey mink and her blonde hair was piled high on her head in an elaborate lacquered Grecian style. Anger struck me like a fist in the guts as I recognized her.

It was Sherry North, the First. The nice lady who had blown Judith and *Wave Dancer* to the bottom of Grand Harbour.

With her was a man of medium height with soft brown hair fashionably long and curly over his ears. He had a light tan, probably from a sun lamp, and he was dressed too well. Very expensively, but as flamboyantly as an entertainment personality. He had a heavy jaw and a long fleshy nose with soft gazelle eyes, but his mouth was pinched and hungry. A greedy mouth that I remembered so well.

'Manson!' I said. 'Jesus! Manson Resnick—Manny Resnick.' He would be just the one Jimmy North would find his way to with his outrageous proposition. In exactly the same way that so long ago I had gone to him with my plans for the gold heist at Rome Airport. Manny was an underworld entrepreneur, and he had clearly climbed a long way up the ladder since our last meeting.

He was keeping great style now, I thought, as he crossed the pavement and entered the back seat of the Rolls, settling down next to the mink-clad blonde.

'Wait here,' I told Sherry urgently, as the Rolls pulled away towards Park Lane.

I ran out onto the pavement and searched wildly for a cab to follow them. There were none and I ran after the Rolls praying desperately for the sight of a big black cab with its top light burning, but ahead of me the Rolls swung right into South Audley Street and accelerated smoothly away.

I stopped at the corner and it was already far ahead, infiltrating the traffic towards Grosvenor Square.

I turned and ambled disappointedly back to where Sherry waited. I knew that Sherry had been correct. Manny and the blonde were off on a long journey. There was no point in hanging around No. 97 Curzon Street any longer.

Sherry was waiting for me outside the restaurant.

'What was that all about?' she demanded and I took her arm. As we walked back towards Berkeley Square, I told her.

'That man is probably the one who ordered Jimmy murdered, who was responsible for having half my chest shot away, who had them to roast your lovely pinkies—in short, the big man.'

'You know him?'

'I did business with him a long time ago.'

'Nice friends you have.'

'I'm trying for a better class lately,' I said, and squeezed her arm. She ignored my gallantry.

'And the woman. Is she the one from St Mary's, the one who blew up your boat and the young girl?'

I experienced a violent return of the anger which had gripped me a few minutes earlier when I had seen that sleek, meticulously polished predator dressed in mink.

Beside me Sherry gasped, 'Harry, you are hurting me!'

'Sorry.' I relaxed my grip on her arm.

'I guess that answers my question,' she muttered ruefully, and massaged her upper arm.

The private bar of the Windsor Arms was all dark oak panels and antique mirrors. It was crowded by the time Sherry and I returned. Outside darkness had fallen and there was an icy wind stirring the fallen leaves in the gutters.

The warmth of the pub was welcome. We found seats in a corner, but the crowd pushed us together, forcing me to place an arm around Sherry's shoulders, and our heads were close so we could hold a very private conversation in this public place.

'I can guess where Manny Resnick and his friend are headed,' I said.

'Big Gull Island?' Sherry asked, and when I nodded she went on, 'He'll need a boat and divers.'

'Don't worry, Manny will get them.'

'And what will we do?'

'We?' I asked.

'A form of speech,' she corrected herself primly. 'What will you do?'

'I have a choice. I can forget about it all—or I can go back to Gunfire Reef and try to find out what the hell was in Colonel Goodchild's five cases.'

'You'll need equipment.'

'It might not be as elaborate as Manny Resnick's will be, but I could get enough together.'

'How are you for money, or is that a rude question?'

'The answer is the same. I could get enough together.'

'Blue water and white sand,' she murmured dreamily.

'—and the palm fronds clattering in the trade winds.'

'Stop it, Harry.'

'Fat crayfish grilling on the coals, and me beside you singing in the wilderness,' I went on remorselessly.

'Pig,' she said.

'If you stay here, you'll never know if it was dirty socks,' I pressed her.

'You'd write and tell me,' she pleaded.

'No, I wouldn't.'

'I'll have to come with you,' she said at last.

'Good girl.' I squeezed her shoulder.

'But I insist on paying my own way, I refuse to become a kept woman.' She had guessed how hard pressed I was financially.

'I should hate to erode your principles,' I told her happily, and my wallet sighed with relief. It was going to be a near-run thing to mount an expedition to Gunfire Reef on what I had left. There was much we had to discuss now that the decision had been made. It seemed only minutes later that the landlord was calling, 'Time, gentlemen.'

'The streets are dangerous at night,' I warned Sherry. 'I don't think we should chance it. Upstairs I have a very comfortable room with a fine view—'

'Come on, Fletcher.' Sherry stood up. 'You had better walk me home, or I shall set my uncle on you.'

As we walked the half block to her uncle's apartment, we agreed to meet for lunch next day. I had a list of errands to perform in the morning, including making the airline reservations, while Sherry had to have her passport renewed and pick up the photostat drawings of the *Dawn Light*.

At the door of the apartment we faced each other; suddenly both of us were shy. It was so terribly corny that I almost laughed. We were like a pair of old-fashioned teenagers at the end of our first date—but sometimes corny feels good.

'Good night, Harry,' she said, and with the age-old artistry of womankind she showed me in some indefinable manner that she was ready for kissing.

Her lips were soft and warm, and the kiss went on for a long time.

'My goodness,' she whispered throatily, and drew away at last.

'Are you sure you won't change your mind—it is a beautiful room, hot and cold water, carpets on the floor, T.V.—'

She laughed shakily and pushed me gently backwards. 'Good night, dear Harry,' she repeated, and left me.

I went out into the street and strolled back towards my pub. The wind had dropped but I could smell the damp emanating from the river close by. The street was deserted but the kerb was lined with parked vehicles, bumper to bumper they reached to the corner.

I sauntered along the pavement, in no hurry for bed, even toying with the idea of a stroll down the Embankment first. My hands were thrust deep into the pockets of my car coat, and I was feeling relaxed and happy as I thought about this woman.

There was a lot to think about Sherry North, much that was unclear or not yet explained, but mainly I cherished the thought that perhaps here at last was something that might last longer than a night, a week, or a month—something that was already strong and that would not be like the others, diminishing with the passage of time, but instead would grow every stronger.

Suddenly a voice beside me said, 'Harry!' It was a man's voice, a strange voice, and I turned instinctively towards it. As I did so I knew that it was a mistake.

The speaker was sitting in the back seat of one of the parked cars. It was a black Rover. The window was open and his face was merely a pale blob in the darkness of the interior.

Desperately I tried to pull my hands out of my pockets and turn to face the direction from which I knew the attack would come. As I turned I ducked and twisted, and something whirred past my ear and struck my shoulder a numbing blow.

I struck backwards with both elbows, connecting solidly and hearing the gasp of pain. Then my hands were clear and I was around, moving fast, weaving, for I knew they would use the cosh again.

They were just midnight shapes, menacing and huge, dressed in dark clothing. It seemed there were a legion of them, but there were only four—and one in the car. They were all big men, and the one had the cosh up to strike again. I hit him under the chin with the palm of my hand, snapping his head backwards and I thought I might have broken his neck, for he went down hard on the pavement.

A knee drove for my groin, but I turned and caught it on the thigh, using the impetus of the turn to counter-punch. It was a good one, jolting me to the shoulder, and the man took it in the chest and was thrown backwards, but immediately one of them was hugging the arm, smothering it and a fist caught me in the cheek under the eye. I felt the skin tear open.

Another one was on my back, an arm around my throat throttling me, but I heaved and pushed. In a tight knot, locked together, we surged around the pavement.

'Hold him still,' another voice called, low and urgent. 'Let me get a shot at him.'

'What the bloody hell you think we are trying to do?' panted another, and we fell against the side of the Rover. I was pinned there, and I saw the one with the cosh was on his feet. He swung again, and I tried to roll my head, but it caught me in the temple. It did not put me out completely, but it knocked all the fight out of me. I was instantly weak as a child, hardly able to support my own weight.

'That's it, get him into the back.' They hustled me into the centre seat in the back of the Rover and one of them crowded in on each side of me. The doors slammed, the engine whirred and caught and we pulled away swiftly.

My brain cleared, but the side of my head was numb and felt like a balloon. There were three of them in the front seat, one on each side of me in the back. All of them were breathing heavily, and the one next to the driver was massaging his neck and jaw tenderly. The one on my right had been eating garlic, and he panted heavily as he searched me for weapons.

'I think you should know that something died in your mouth a long time ago, and it's still there,' I told him, with a thickened tongue and an ache in my head, but the effort was not worth it. He showed no sign of having heard, but continued doggedly with his task. At last he was satisfied and I readjusted my clothing.

We drove in silence for five minutes, following the river towards Hammersmith, before they had all recovered their breath and tended their wounds, then the driver spoke.

'Listen, Manny wants to talk to you, but he said it's no big thing. He was merely curious. He said also that if you gave us a hard time, not to go to no trouble, just to sign you off and toss you in the river.'

'Charming chap, Manny,' I said.

'Shut up!' said the driver. 'So you see, it's up to you. Behave yourself and you get to live a little longer. I heard you used to be a sharp operator, Harry. We been expecting you to show up, ever since Lorna missed you on the island—but sure as hell we didn't expect you to parade up and down Curzon Street like a brass band. Manny couldn't believe it. He said, "That can't be Harry. He must have gone soft." It made him sad. "How are the mighty fallen. Tell it not in the streets of Ashkelon", he said.'

'That's Shakespeare,' said the one with the garlic breath.

'Shut up,' said the driver and then went on, 'Manny was sad but not that sad that he cried or anything, you understand.'

'I understand,' I mumbled.

'Shut up,' said the driver. 'Manny said, "Don't do it here. Just follow him to a nice quiet place and pick him up. If he comes quietly you bring him to talk to me—if he cuts up rough then toss him in the river".'

'That sounds like my boy, Manny. He always was a soft-hearted little devil.'

'Shut up,' said the driver.

'I look forward to seeing him again.'

'You just stay good and quiet and you might get lucky.'

I stayed that way through the night as we picked up the M4 and rushed westwards. It was two in the morning when we entered Bristol, skirting the city centre as we followed the A4 down to Avonmouth.

Among the other craft in the yacht basin was a big motor yacht. She was moored to the wharf and she had her gangplank down. Her name painted on the stern and bows was *Mandrake*. She was an ocean-goer, steel-hulled painted blue and white, with pleasing lines. I judged her fast and sea-kindly, probably with sufficient range to take her anywhere in the world. A rich man's toy. There were figures on her bridge, light burning in most of her portholes, and she seemed ready for sea.

They crowded me as we crossed the narrow space to the gangplank. The Rover backed and turned and drove away as we climbed to the *Mandrake*'s deck.

The saloon was too tastefully fitted out for Manny Resnick's style— it had either been done by the previous owners or a professional decorator. There were forest-green wall-to-wall carpets and matching velvet curtains, the furniture was dark teak and polished leather and the pictures were choice oils toned to the general décor.

This was half a million pounds worth of vessel, and I guessed it was a charter. Manny had probably taken her for six months and put in his own crew—for Manny Resnick had never struck me as a blue water man.

As we waited in the centre of the wall-to-wall carpeting, a grimly silent group, I heard the unmistakable sounds of the gangplank being taken in, and the moorings cast off. The tremble of her engines became a steady beat, and the harbour lights slid past the saloon portholes as we left the entrance and thrust out into the tidal waters of the River Severn.

I recognized the lighthouses at Portishead Point and Red Cliff Bay as *Mandrake* came around for the run down-river past Weston-super-Mare and Berry for the open sea.

Manny came at last. He wore a blue silk gown and his face was still crumpled from sleep, but his curls were neatly combed and his smile was white and hungry.

'Harry,' he said, 'I told you that you would be back.'

'Hello, Manny. I can't say it's any great pleasure.'

He laughed lightly and turned to the woman as she followed him into the saloon. She was carefully made up and every hair of the elaborate hairstyle was in its place. She wore a long white house-gown with lace at throat and cuffs.

'You have met Lorna, I believe, Lorna Page.'

'Next time you send somebody to hustle me, Manny, try for a little better class. I'm getting fussy in my old age.'

Her eyes slanted wickedly, but she smiled.

'How's your boat, Harry? Your lovely boat?'

'It makes a lousy coffin.' I turned back to Manny. 'What's it going to be, Manny, can we work out a deal?'

He shook his head sorrowfully. 'I don't think so, Harry. I would like to —truly I would, if just for old times' sake. But I can't see it. Firstly, you haven't anything to trade—and that makes for a lousy deal. Secondly, I know you are too sentimental. You'd louse up any deal we did make for purely emotional reasons. I couldn't trust you, Harry, all the time you'd be thinking about Jimmy North and your boat, you'd be thinking about the little island girl that got in the way, and about Jimmy North's sister who we had to get rid of—' I took a mild pleasure in the fact that Manny had obviously not heard what had happened to the goon squad he had sent to take care of Sherry North, and that she was still very much alive. I tried to make my voice sincere and my manner convincing.

'Listen, Manny, I'm a survivor. I can forget anything, if I have to.'

He laughed again. 'If I didn't know you better, I'd believe you, Harry.' He shook his head again. 'Sorry, Harry, no deal.'

'Why did you go to all the trouble to bring me down here, then?'

'I sent others to do the job twice before, Harry. Both times they missed you. This time I want to make sure. We will be cruising over some deep water on the way to Cape Town, and I'm going to hang some really heavy weights onto you.'

'Cape Town?' I asked. 'So you are going after the *Dawn Light* in person. What is so fascinating about that old wreck?'

'Come on, Harry. If you didn't know, you wouldn't be giving me such a hard time.' He laughed, and I thought it best not to let them know my ignorance.

'You think you can find your way back?' I asked the blonde. 'It's a big sea and a lot of islands look the same. I think you should keep me as insurance,' I insisted.

'Sorry, Harry.' Manny crossed to the teak and brass bar. 'Drink?' he asked.

'Scotch,' I said, and he half filled a glass with the liquor and brought it to me.

'To be entirely truthful with you, part of this is for Lorna's benefit. You made the girl bitter, Harry, I don't know why—but she wanted especially to be there when we say goodbye. She enjoys that sort of thing, don't you, darling, it turns her on.'

I drained the glass. 'She needs turning on—as you and I both know, she's a lousy lay without it,' I observed, and Manny hit me in the mouth, crushing my lips and the whisky stung the raw flesh.

'Lock him up,' he said softly. As they hustled me out of the saloon, and along the deck towards the bows, I took pleasure in knowing that Lorna would have painful questions to answer. On either hand the shore lights moved steadily past us in the night, and the river was black and wide.

———————————

Forward of the bridge there was a low deckhouse above the fore-castle, and a louvred companionway opened onto a deck ladder that descended to a small lobby. This was obviously the crew's quarters—doors opened off the lobby into cabins and a communal mess.

In the bows was a steel door and a stencilled sign upon it read 'FORECASTLE STORE'. They shoved me through the doorway and slammed the heavy door. The lock turned and I was alone in a steel cubicle probably six by four. Both bulkheads were lined with storage lockers, and the air was damp and musty.

My first concern was to find some sort of weapon. The cupboards were all of them locked and I saw that the planking was inch-thick oak. I would need an axe to hack them open, nevertheless I tried. I attempted to break in the doors using my shoulder as a ram, but the space was too confined and I could not work up sufficient momentum.

However, the noise attracted attention. The door swung open and one of the crew stood well back with a big ugly .41 Rueger Magnum in his hand.

'Cut it out,' he said. 'There ain't anything in there,' and he gestured to the pile of old life-jackets against the far wall. 'You just sit there nice and quiet or I'll call some of the boys to help me work you over.' He slammed the door and I sank down onto the life-jackets.

There was clearly a guard posted at the door full-time. The others would be within easy call. I hadn't expected him to open the door and I had been off-balance. I had to get him to do it again—but this time I would have a go. It was a poor chance, I realized. All he had to do was point that cannon into the storeroom and pull the trigger. He could hardly miss.

I needed some sort of distraction, some sort of cover to get close enough. I looked longingly at the lockers again, then turned my attention to my own pockets. They had cleaned me out, my lighter and cheroots, car keys, penknife were all gone. But they had left my handkerchief, three five-pound notes folded into my hip pocket they had overlooked and I had my wrist watch.

I looked down at the pile of life-jackets, and stood again to pull them aside. Beneath them was a small wooden fruit box. It contained discarded cleaning materials: a nylon floorbrush, cleaning rags, a tin of Brasso, half a cake of yellow soap, and a brandy bottle half filled with clear fluid. I unscrewed the cap and sniffed it. It was benzine.

I sat down again and reassessed my position, trying to find a percentage in it without much success.

The light switch was outside the doorway and the light overhead was in a thick glass cover. I stood up and climbed half way up the lockers, wedging myself there while I unscrewed the light cover and examined the bulb. It gave me a little hope.

I climbed down again and selected one of the heavy canvas life-jackets. The clasp of the steel strap on my wrist watch made a blunt blade and I sawed and hacked at the canvas, tearing a hole large enough to get my forefinger in. I ripped the canvas open and pulled out handfuls of the white kapok stuffing. I piled it on the floor, tearing open more life-jackets until I had a considerable heap.

I soaked the cotton waste with benzine from the bottle and took a handful of it with me when I climbed again to the light fitting. I removed the bulb and was plunged instantly into darkness. Working by sense of touch alone, I pressed the benzine-soaked stuffing close to the electricity terminals. I had nothing to use as insulation so I held the steel strap of my wristwatch in my bare hands and used it to dead-short the terminals.

There was a sizzling blue flash, the benzine ignited instantly and 180 volts hit me like a charge of buckshot, knocking me off my perch. I fell in a heap onto the deck with a ball of flaming kapok in my hands.

Outside I heard faint shouts of annoyance and anger. I had succeeded in shorting the entire lighting system of the forecastle. Quickly I tossed the burning kapok onto the prepared pile, and it burned up fiercely. I brushed the sparks from my hands, wrapped the handkerchief around my mouth and nose, snatched up one of the undamaged life-belts and went to stand against the steel door.

In seconds the benzine burned away and the cotton began to

smoulder, fiercely pouring out thick black smoke that smelled vile. It filled the store, and my eyes began to stream with tears. I tried to breathe shallowly but the smoke tore my lungs and I coughed violently.

There was another shout beyond the door.

'Something is burning.' And it was answered, 'For Chrissake, get those lights on.'

It was my cue, I began beating on the steel door and screaming at the top of my voice. 'Fire! The ship is on fire!' It was not all acting. The smoke in my prison was thick and solid, and more boiled off the burning cotton kapok. I realized that if nobody opened that door within the next sixty seconds I would suffocate and my screams must have carried conviction. The guard swung the door open; he carried the big Rueger revolver and shone a flashlight into the storeroom.

I had time only to notice those details and to see that the ship's lights were still dead; shadowy figures milled about in the gloom, some with flashlights—then a solid black cloud of smoke boiled out of the storeroom.

I came out with the smoke like a fighting bull from its pen, desperate for clean air and terrified at how close I had come to suffocating. It gave strength to my efforts.

The guard went sprawling under my rush and the Rueger fired as he went down. The muzzle flame was bright as a flashbulb, lighting the whole area and allowing me to get my bearings on the companion ladder to the deck.

The blast of the shot was so deafening in the confined space that it seemed to paralyse the other shadowy figures. I was half way to the ladder before one of them leaped to intercept me. I drove my shoulder into his chest and heard the wind go out of him like a punctured football.

There were shouts of concern now, and another big dark figure blocked the foot of the ladder. I had gathered speed across the lobby and I put that and all my weight into a kick that slogged into his belly, doubling him over and dropping him to his knees. As he went over a flashlight lit his face and I saw it was my friend with the garlicky breath. It gave me a lift of pleasure to light me on my way, and I put one foot on his shoulder and used it as a springboard to leap half way up the ladder.

Hands clutched at my ankle but I kicked them away, and dragged myself to the deck level. I had only one foot on the rungs, and I was clinging with one hand to the life-jacket and with the other to the brass handrail. In that helpless moment, the doorway to the deck was blocked by yet another dark figure—and the lights went on. A sudden blinding blaze of light.

The man above me was the lad with the cosh, and I saw his savage delight as he raised it over my helpless head. The only way to avoid it was to let go the handrail and drop back into the forecastle, which was filled with surging angry goons.

I looked back and was actually opening my grip when behind me, the gunman with the Rueger Magnum sat up groggily, lifted the weapon, tried to brace himself against the ship's movement and fired at me. The heavy bullet cracked past my ear, almost splitting my ear drum and it hit the coshman in the centre of his chest. It picked him up and hurled him backwards across the deck. He hung in the rigging of the foremast with his arms spread like those of a derelict scarecrow, and with a desperate lunge I followed him out onto the deck and rolled to my feet still clutching the life-jacket.

Behind me the Rueger roared again and I heard the bullet splinter the coping of the hatch. Three running strides carried me to the rail and I dived over the side in a gut-swooping drop until I hit the black water flat, but I was dragged deep as the boil of the propellers caught me and swirled me under.

The water was shockingly cold; it seemed to drive in the walls of my lungs and probe with icy lances into the marrow of my bones.

The life-jacket helped pull me to the surface at last and I looked wildly about me. The lights of the coast seemed clear and very bright, twinkling whitely across the black water. Out here in the seaway there was a chop and swell to the surface, alternately lifting and dropping me.

Mandrake slid steadily onwards towards the black void of the open sea. With all her lights blazing she looked as festive as a cruise ship as she sailed away from me.

Awkwardly I rid myself of my shoes and jacket, then I managed to get my arms into the sleeves of the life-jacket. When I looked again *Mandrake* was a mile away, but suddenly she began to turn and from her bridge the long white beam of a spotlight leaped out and began to probe lightly and dance across the surface of the dark sea.

Quickly I looked again towards the land, seeking and finding the riding lights of the buoy at English Ground and relating it to the lighthouse on Flatholm. Within seconds the relative bearing of the two lights had altered slightly, the tide was ebbing and the current was setting westerly. I turned with it and began to swim.

The *Mandrake* had slowed and was creeping back towards me. The spotlight turned and flared, swept and searched, and steadily it came down towards me.

I pushed with the current, using a long side stroke so as not to break the surface and show white water, restraining myself from going into an overarm stroke as the brightly lit ship crept closer. The beam of the spotlight was searching the open water on the far side of *Mandrake* as she drew level with me.

The current had pushed me out of her track, and the *Mandrake* was as close as she would come on this leg—about 150 yards off—but I could see the men on her bridge. Manny Resnick's blue silk gown glowed like a butterfly's wing in the bridge lights and I could hear his voice raised angrily, but could not make out the words.

The beam reached towards me like the long cold white finger of an accuser. It quartered the sea in a tight search pattern, back and across, back and across, the next pass must catch me. It reached the end of its traverse, swung out and came back. I lay full in the path of the swinging beam, but at the instant it swept over me, a chance push of the sea lifted a swell of dark water and I dropped into the trough. The light washed over me, diffused by the crest of the swell, and it did not check. It swept onwards in the relentless search pattern.

They had missed me. They were going on, back towards the mouth of the Severn. I lay in the harsh embrace of the canvas life-jacket and watched them bear away and I felt sick and nauseated with relief and the reaction from violence. But I was free. All I had to worry about now was how long it would take to freeze to death.

I began swimming again, watching *Mandrake*'s lights dwindle and lose themselves against the spangled backdrop of the shore.

I had left my wrist watch in the forecastle so I did not know how long it was before I lost all sense of feeling in my arms and legs. I tried to keep swimming but I was not sure if my limbs were responding.

I began to feel a wonderful floating sense of release. The lights of the land faded out, and I seemed to be wrapped in warmth and soft white clouds. I thought that if this was dying it wasn't as bad as its propaganda, and I giggled, lying sodden and helpless in the life-jacket.

I wondered with interest why my vision had gone, it wasn't the way I had heard it told. Then suddenly I realized that the sea fog had come down in the dawn, and it was this that had blinded me. However, the morning light was growing in strength, I could see clearly twenty feet into the eddying fog banks.

I closed my eyes and fell asleep; my last thought was that this was probably my last thought. It made me giggle again as darkness swept over me.

Voices woke me, voices very clear and close in the fog, the rich and lovely Welsh accents roused me. I tried to shout, and with a sense of great achievement it came out like the squawk of a gull.

Out of the fog loomed the dark ungainly shape of an ancient lobster boat. It was on the drift, setting pots, and two men hung over the side, intent on their labours.

I squawked again and one of the men looked up. I had an impression of pale blue eyes in a weathered and heavily lined ruddy face, cloth cap and an old briar pipe gripped in broken yellow teeth.

'Good morning,' I croaked.

'Jesus!' said the lobster man around the stem of his pipe.

I sat in the tiny wheelhouse wrapped in a filthy old blanket, and drank steaming unsweetened tea from a chipped enamel mug— shivering so violently that the mug leaped and twitched in my cupped hands.

My whole body was a lovely shade of blue, and returning circulation was excruciating agony in my joints. My two rescuers were taciturn men, with a marvellous sense of other people's privacy, probably bred into them by a long line of buccaneers and smugglers.

By the time they had set their pots and cleared for the homeward run it was after noon and I had thawed out. My clothes had dried over the stove in the miniature galley and I had a belly full of brown bread and smoked mackerel sandwiches.

We went into Port Talbot, and when I tried to pay them with my rumpled fivers for their help, the older of the two lobster men turned a blue and frosty eye upon me.

'Any time I win a man back from the sea, I'm paid in full, mister. Keep your money.'

———————————

The journey back to London was a nightmare of country buses and night trains. When I stumbled out of Paddington Station at ten o'clock the next morning I understood why a pair of bobbies paused in their majestic pacing to study my face. I must have looked like an escaped convict.

The cabby ran a world-weary eye over my two days' growth of dark stiff beard, the swollen lip and the bruised eye. 'Did her husband come home early, mate?' he asked, and I groaned weakly.

Sherry North opened the door to her uncle's apartment and stared at me with huge startled blue eyes.

'Oh my God, Harry! What on earth happened to you? You look terrible.'

'Thanks,' I said. 'That really cheers me up.'

She caught my arm and drew me into the apartment. 'I've been going out of my mind. Two days. I've even called the police, the hospitals—everywhere I could think of.'

The uncle was hovering in the background and his presence set my nerves on edge. I refused the offer of a bath and clean clothes—and instead I took Sherry back with me to the Windsor Arms.

I left the door to the bathroom open while I shaved and bathed so that we could talk, and although she kept out of direct line of sight while I was in the tub, I thought it was developing a useful sense of intimacy between us.

I told her in detail of my abduction by Manny Resnick's trained gorillas, and of my escape—making no attempt to play down my own heroic role—and she listened in a silence that I could only believe was fascinated admiration.

I emerged from the bath with a towel wound round my waist and sat on the bed to finish the tale while Sherry doctored my cuts and abrasions.

'You'll have to go to the police now, Harry,' she said at last. 'They tried to murder you.'

'Sherry, my darling girl, please don't keep talking about the police. You make me nervous.'

'But, Harry—'

'Forget about the police, and order some food for us. I haven't eaten since I can remember.'

The hotel kitchen sent up a fine grilling of bacon and tomatoes, fried eggs, toast and tea. While I ate, I tried to relate the recent rapid turn of events to our previous knowledge, and alter our plans to fit in.

'By the way, you were on the list of expendables. They didn't intend merely holding a barbecue with your fingers. Manny Resnick was convinced that his boys had killed you—' and a queasy expression passed over her lovely face. 'They were apparently getting rid of anyone who knew anything at all about the *Dawn Light*.'

I took another mouthful of egg and bacon and chewed in silence.

'At least we have a timetable now. Manny's charter—which is incidentally called *Mandrake*—looks very fast and powerful, but it's still going to take him three or four weeks to get out to the islands. It gives us time.'

She poured tea for me, milk last the way I like it.

'Thanks, Sherry, you are an angel of mercy.' She stuck out her tongue at me, and I went on, 'Whatever it is we are looking for, it just has to be something extraordinary. That motor yacht Manny has hired himself looks like the Royal Yacht. He must be laying out close to a hundred thousand pounds on this little lark. God, I wish we knew what those five cases contain. I tried to sound Manny out—but he laughed at me. Told me I knew or I wouldn't be taking so much trouble—'

'Oh, Harry.' Sherry's face lit up. 'You've given us the bad news— now stand by for the good.'

'I could stand a little.'

'You know Jimmy's note on the letter—B. Mus?'

I nodded. 'Bachelor of Music?'

'No, idiot—British Museum.'

'I'm afraid you just lost me.'

'I was discussing it with Uncle Dan. He recognized it immediately. It's a reference to a work in the library of the British Museum. He holds a reader's card. He's researching a book, and works there often.'

'Could we get in there?'

'We'll give it a college try.'

I waited almost two hours beneath the vast golden and blue dome of the Reading Room at the British Museum, and the craving for a cheroot was like a vice around my chest.

I did not know what to expect—I had simply filled in the withdrawals form with Jimmy North's reference number—so when at last the attendant laid a thick volume before me, I seized it eagerly.

It was a Secker and Warburg edition, first published in 1963. The author was a Doctor P. A. Ready and the title was printed in gold on the spine: LEGENDARY AND LOST TREASURES OF THE WORLD.

I lingered over the closed book, teasing myself a little, and I wondered what chain of coincidence and luck had allowed Jimmy North to follow this paperchase of ancient clues. Had he read this book first in his burning obsession with wrecks and sea treasure and he had then stumbled on the batch of old letters? I would never know.

There were forty-nine chapters, each listing a separate item. I read carefully down the list.

There were Aztec treasures of gold, the plate and bullion of Panama, buccaneer hoards, a lost gold mine in the Rockies of North America, a valley of diamonds in South Africa, treasure ships of the Armada, the *Lutine* bullion ship from which the famous *Lutine* Bell at Lloyd's had been recovered, Alexandra the Great's chariot of gold, more treasure ships—both ancient and modern—from the Second World War to the sack of Troy, treasures of Mussolini, Prester John, Darius, Roman generals, privateers and pirates of Barbary and Coromandel. It was a vast profusion of fact and fancy, history and conjecture. The treasures of lost cities and forgotten civilizations, from Atlantis to the fabulous golden city of the Kalahari Desert—there was so much of it, and I did not know where to look.

With a sigh I turned to the first page, ducking the introduction and preface. I began to read.

By five o'clock I had skimmed through sixteen chapters which could not possibly relate to the *Dawn Light* and had read five others in depth and by this time I understood how Jimmy North could have been bitten by the romance and excitement of the treasure hunter. It was making me itchy also—these stories of great riches, abandoned, waiting merely to get gathered up by someone with the luck and fortitude to ferret them out.

I glanced at the new Japanese watch with which I'd replaced my Omega, and hurried out of the massive stone portals of the museum and crossed Great Russell Street to my rendezvous with Sherry. She was waiting in the crowded saloon bar of the Running Stag.

'Sorry,' I said, 'I forgot the time.'

'Come on.' She grabbed my arm. 'I'm dying of thirst and curiosity.'

I gave her a pint of bitter for her thirst, but could only inflame her curiosity with the title of the book. She wanted to send me back to the library, before I had finished my supper of ham and turkey from the carvery behind the bar, but I held out and managed to smoke half a cheroot before she drove me out into the cold.

I gave her the key to my room at the Windsor Arms, placed her in a cab and told her to wait for me there. Then I hurried back to the Reading Room.

The next chapter of the book was entitled 'THE GREAT MOGUL AND THE TIGER THRONE OF INDIA.'

It began with a brief historical introduction describing how Babur, descendant of Timur and Genghis Khan, the two infamous scourges of the ancient world, crossed the mountains into northern India and established the Mogul Empire. I recognized immediately that this fell within the area of my interest, the *Dawn Light* had been outward bound from that ancient continent.

The history covered the period of Babur's illustrious successors, Muslim rulers who rose to great power and influence, who built mighty cities and left behind such monuments to man's sense of beauty as the Taj Mahal. Finally it described the decline of the dynasty, and its destruction in the first year of the Indian mutiny when the avenging

British forces stormed and sacked the ancient citadel and fortress at Delhi—shooting the Mogul princes out of hand and throwing the old emperor Bahadur Shah into captivity.

Then abuptly the author switched his attention from the vast sweep of history.

In 1665 Jean Baptiste Tavernier, a French traveller and jeweller, visited the court of the Mogul Emperor Aurangzeb. Five years later he published in Paris his celebrated *Travels in the Orient*. He seems to have won special favour from the Muslim Emperor, for he was allowed to enter the fabled treasure chambers of the citadel and to catalogue various items of special interest. Among these was a diamond which he named the 'Great Mogul'. Tavernier weighed this stone and listed its bulk at 280 carats. He described this paragon as possessing extraordinary fire and a colour as clear and white 'as the great North Star of the heavens'.

Tavernier's host informed him that the stone had been recovered from the famed Golconda Mines in about 1650 and that the rough stone had been a monstrous 787 carats.

The cut of the stone was a distinctive rounded rose, but was not symmetrical—being proud on the one side. The stone has been unrecorded since that time and many believe that Tavernier actually saw the Koh-i-noor or the Orloff. However, it is highly improbable that such a trained observer and craftsman as Tavernier could have erred so widely in his weights and descriptions. The Koh-i-noor before it was recut in London weighed a mere 191 carats, and was certainly not a rose cut. The Orloff, although rose cut, was and is a symmetrical gem stone and weighs 199 carats. The descriptions simply cannot be mated with that of Tavernier, and all the evidence points to the existence of a huge white diamond that has dropped out of the known world.

In 1739 when Nadir Shah of Persia entered India and captured Delhi, he made no attempt to hold his conquest, but contented himself with vast booty, which included the Koh-i-noor diamond and the peacock throne of Shah Jehan. It seems probable that the Great Mogul diamond was overlooked by the rapacious Persian and that after his withdrawal, Mohammed Shah the incumbent Mogul Emperor, deprived of his traditional throne, ordered the construction of a substitute. However, the existence of this new treasure was veiled in secrecy and although there are references to its existence in the native accounts, only one European reference can be cited.

The journal of the English Ambassador to the Court of Delhi during the year of 1747, Sir Thomas Jenning, describes an audience granted by the Mogul Emperor at which he was 'clad in precious silks and bedecked with flowers and jewels, seated upon a great throne of gold. The shape of the throne was as of a fierce tiger, with gaping jaws and a single glittering cyclopean eye. The body of the tiger was amazingly worked with all manner of precious stones. His majesty was gracious enough to allow me to approach the throne closely and to examine the eye of the tiger which he assured me was a great diamond descended from the reign of his ancestor Aurangzeb.'

Was this Tavernier's 'Great Mogul' now incorporated into the 'Tiger Throne of India'? If it was, then credence is given to a strange set of circumstances which must end our study of this lost treasure.

In 1857 on September 16th, desperate street fighting filled the streets of Delhi with heaps of dead and wounded, and the outcome of the struggle hung in the balance as the British forces and loyal native troops fought to clear the city of the mutinous sepoys and seize the ancient fortress that dominated the city.

While the fighting raged within, a force of loyal native troops from 101st regiment under two European officers was ordered to cross the river and encircle the walls to seize the road to the north. This was in order to prevent members of the Mogul royal family or rebel leaders from escaping the doomed city.

The two European officers were Captain Matthew Long and Colonel Sir Roger Goodchild—

The name leapt out of the page at me not only because someone had underlined it in pencil. In the margin, also in pencil, was one of Jimmy North's characteristic exclamation marks. Master James's disrespect for books included those belonging to such a venerable institution as the British Museum. I found I was shaking again, and my cheeks felt hot with excitement. This was the last fragment missing from the puzzle. It was all here now and my eyes raced on across the page.

No one will ever know now what happened on that night on a lonely road through the Indian jungle—but six months later, Captain Long and the Indian Subahdar, Ram Panat, gave evidence at the court martial of Colonel Goodchild.

They described how they had intercepted a party of Indian nobles fleeing the burning city. The party included three Muslim priests and two princes of the royal blood. In the presence of Captain Long one of the princes attempted to buy their freedom by offering to lead the British officers to a great treasure, a golden throne shaped like a tiger and with a single diamond eye.

The officers agreed, and the princes led them into the forest to a jungle mosque. In the courtyard of the mosque were six bullock carts. The drivers had deserted, and when the British officers dismounted and examined the contents of these vehicles they proved indeed to contain a golden throne statue of a tiger. The throne had been broken down into four separate parts to facilitate transportation—hindquarters, trunk, forequarters and head. In the light of the lanterns these fragments nestled in beds of straw, blazing with gold and encrusted with precious and semi-precious stones.

Colonel Roger Goodchild then ordered that the princes and priests should be executed out of hand. They were lined up against the outer wall of the mosque and despatched with a volley of musketry. The Colonel himself walked among the fallen noblemen administering the *coup-de-grâce* with his service revolver. The corpses were afterwards thrown into a well outside the walls of the mosque.

The two officers now separated, Captain Long with most of the native troops returning to the patrol of the city walls, while the Colonel, Subahdar Ram Panat and fifteen sepoys rode off with the bullock carts.

The Indian Subahdar's evidence at the court martial described how they had taken the precious cargo westwards, passing through the British lines by the Colonel's authority. They camped three days at a small native village. Here the local carpenter and his two sons laboured under the Colonel's direction to manufacture four sturdy wooden crates to hold the four parts of the throne. The Colonel in the meantime set about removing from the statue the stones and jewels that were set into the metal. The position of each was carefully noted on a diagram prepared by Goodchild and the stones were numbered and packed into an iron chest of the type used by army paymasters for the safekeeping of coin and specie in the field.

Once the throne and the stones had been packed into the four crates and iron chest, they were loaded once more onto the bullock carts and the journey towards the railhead at Allahabad was continued.

The luckless carpenter and his sons were obliged to join the convoy. The Subahdar recalled that when the road entered an area of dense forest, the Colonel dismounted and led the three craftsmen among the trees. Six pistol shots rang out and the Colonel returned alone.

I broke off my reading for a few moments to reflect on the character of the gallant Colonel. I should have liked to introduce him to Manny Resnick, they would have had much in common. I grinned at the thought and read on.

The convoy reached Allahabad on the sixth day and the Colonel claimed military priority to place his five crates upon a troop train returning to Bombay. Having done this he and his small command rejoined the regiment at Delhi.

Six months later, Captain Long supported by the Indian Petty Officer, Ram Panat, brought charges against the commanding officer. We can believe that thieves had fallen out; Colonel Goodchild had perhaps decided that one share was better than three. Be that as it may, nothing has since given a clue to the whereabouts of the treasure.

The trial conducted in Bombay was a *cause célèbre* and was widely reported in India and at home. However, the weakness of the prosecution's case was that there was no booty to show, and dead men tell no tales.

The Colonel was found not guilty. However, the pressure of the scandal left him no choice but to resign his commission and return to London. If he managed somehow to take with him the Great Mogul diamond and the golden tiger throne, his subsequent career gave no evidence of his possessing great wealth. In partnership with a notorious lady of the town he opened a gaming house in the Bayswater Road which soon acquired an unsavoury reputation. Colonel Sir Roger Goodchild died in 1871, probably from tertiary syphilis contracted during his remarkable career in India. His death revived stories of the fabulous throne, but these soon subsided for lack of hard facts and the secret passed on with that sporting gentleman.

Perhaps we should have headed this chapter—'The Treasure That Never Was'.

'Not on, cock,' I thought happily. 'It was—and is.' And I began once more at the beginning of the story, but this time I made careful notes for Sherry's benefit.

She was waiting for me when I returned, sitting wakefully in the armchair by the window, and she flew at me when I entered.

'Where have you been?' she demanded, 'I've been sitting here all evening eating my heart out with curiosity.'

'You are not going to believe it,' I told her, and I thought she might do me a violence.

'Harry Fletcher, you've got ten seconds to cut out the introductory speeches and give me the goodies—after that I scratch your eyes out.'

We talked until long after midnight, and by then we had the floor strewn with papers over which we pored on knees and elbows. There was an Admiralty Chart of the St Mary's Archipelago, the copies of the drawings of the *Dawn Light*, the notes I had made of the mate's description of the wreck, and those I had made in the Reading Room of the British Museum.

I had out my silver travelling flask and we drank Chivas Regal from the plastic tooth mug as we argued and schemed—trying to guess in what section of the *Dawn Light*'s hull the five crates had been stowed, guessing also how she had broken up on the reef, what part of her had been washed into the break and what part had fallen to the seaward side.

I had made sketches of a dozen eventualities, and I had opened a running list of my minimum equipment requirements for an expedition, to which I added, as various items came to mind, or as Sherry made intelligent suggestions.

I had forgotten that she must be a first rate scuba diver, but I was reminded of this as we talked. I was aware now that she would not be a passenger on this expedition; my feelings towards her were becoming tinged with professional respect, and the mood of exhilaration mixed with camaraderie was building to a crescendo of physical tension.

Sherry's pale smooth cheeks were flushed with excitement, and we were shoulder to shoulder as we knelt on the carpeted floor. She turned to say something, she was chuckling and the blue lights in her eyes were teasing and inviting, only inches from mine.

Suddenly all the golden thrones and legendary diamonds in this world must wait their turn. We both recognized the moment, and we turned to each other with unashamed eagerness. We were in a consuming fever of urgency, and we became lovers without rising from the floor, right on top of the drawings of the *Dawn Light*—which was probably the happiest thing that had ever happened to that ill-starred vessel.

When at last I lifted her to the bed and we twined our bodies together beneath the quilt, I knew that all the brief amorous acrobatics that had preceded my meeting with this woman were meaningless. What I had just experienced transcended the flesh and became a thing of the spirit —and if it was not loving, then it was the nearest thing to it that I would ever know.

My voice was husky and unsteady with wonder as I tried to explain it to her. She lay quietly against my chest, listening to the words I had never spoken to another woman, and she squeezed me when I stopped talking—which was clearly a command to continue. I think I was still talking when we both fell asleep.

From the air, St Mary's has the shape of one of those strange fish from the ocean's abysmal depths, a squat mis-shapen body with stubby body fins and tailfins in unusual places, and a huge mouth many sizes too big for the rest of it.

The mouth was Grand Harbour and the town nestled in the hinge of the jaws. The iron roofs flashed like signal mirrors from the dark green cloak of vegetation. The aircraft circled the island, treating the passengers to a vista of snowy white beaches and water so clear that each detail of the reefs and deeps was whorled and smeared below the surface like some vast surrealistic painting.

Sherry pressed her face to the round perspex window and exclaimed with delight as the Fokker Friendship sank down over the pineapple fields where the women paused in their labours to look up at us. We touched down and taxied to the single tiny airport building on which a billboard announced 'St Mary's Island—Pearl of the Indian Ocean' and below the sign stood two other pearls of great price.

I had cabled Chubby and he had brought Angelo with him to welcome us. Angelo rushed to the barrier to embrace me and grab my bag, and I introduced him to Sherry.

Angelo's whole manner underwent a profound change. On the island there is one mark of beauty that is esteemed above all else. A girl might have buck teeth and a squint, but if she possessed a 'clear' complexion she would have suitors forming squadrons around her. A clear complexion did not mean that she was free of acne, it was rather a gauge of the colour of the skin—and Sherry must have had one of the clearest complexions ever to land on the island.

Angelo stared at her in a semi-catatonic state as she shook his hand. Then he roused himself, handed me back my bag and instead took hers from her hand. He then fell in a few paces behind her, like a faithful hound, staring at her solemnly and only breaking into his flashing smile whenever she glanced in his direction. He was her slave from the first moment.

Chubby trundled forward to meet us with more dignity, as big and timeless as a cliff of dark granite, and his face was contorted in a frown of even greater ferocity than usual as he took my hand in a huge horny fist and muttered something to the effect that it was good to see me back.

He stared at Sherry and she quailed a little beneath the ferocity of his gaze, but then something happened that I had never seen before. Chubby lifted his battered old sea cap from his head, exposing the gleaming polished brown dome of his pate in an unheard-of display of gallantry, and he smiled so widely that we could see the pink plastic gums of his artificial teeth. He pushed Angelo aside when Sherry's bags were brought out of the hold, picked up one in each hand and led her to the pick-up. Angelo followed her devotedly and I struggled along in the rear under the weight of my own luggage. It was fairly obvious that my crew approved of my choice, for once.

We sat in the kitchen of Chubby's house and Mrs Chubby fed us on banana cake and coffee while Chubby and I worked out a business deal. For a hard-bargained fee, he would charter his stump boat with its two spanking new Evinrude motors for an indefinite period. He and Angelo would crew it at the old wages, and there would be a large 'bill-fish bonus' at the end of the charter, if it were successful. I went into no detail as to the object of the expedition, but merely let them know that we would be camping on the outer islands of the group and that Sherry and I would be working underwater.

By the time we had agreed and slapped hands on the bargain, the traditional island rite of agreement, it was mid-afternoon and the island fever had already started to reassert its hold on my constitution. Island fever prevents the sufferer from doing today what can reasonably be put off until the morrow, so we left Chubby and Angelo to begin their preparations while Sherry and I stopped only briefly at Missus Eddy's for provisions before pushing the pick-up over the ridge and down through the palms to Turtle Bay.

'It's story book,' murmured Sherry, as she stood under the thatch on the wide veranda of the shack. 'It's make-believe.' She shook her head at the sway-boled palm trees and the aching white sands beyond.

I went to stand behind her, placing my arms around her middle and drawing her to me. She leaned back against me, crossing her own arms over mine and squeezing my hands.

'Oh, Harry, I didn't think it would be like this.' There was a change taking place within her, I could sense it clearly. She was like a winter plant, too long denied the sun, but there were reserves in her that I could not fathom and they troubled me. She was not a simple person, nor easily understood. There were barriers, conflicts within her that showed only as dark shadows in the depths of her ocean-blue eyes, shadows like those of killer sharks swimming deep. More than once when she believed herself unobserved I had caught her looking at me in a manner which seemed at once calculating and hostile—as though she hated me.

That had been before we came to the island, and now it seemed that, like the winter plant, she was blooming in the sun; as though here she could cast aside some restraint of the soul which had curbed her spirit before.

She kicked off her shoes, and barefooted turned within my encircling arms to stand upon tiptoe to kiss me.

'Thank you, Harry. Thank you for bringing me here.'

Mrs Chubby had swept the floors and aired the linen, placed flowers in the jars and charged the refrigerator. We walked through the shack hand in hand—and though Sherry murmured admiration for the utilitarian décor and solid masculine furnishings, yet I thought I detected that gleam in her eye which a woman gets just before she starts pushing the furniture around and throwing out the lovingly accumulated but humble treasures of a man's lifetime.

As she paused to rearrange the bowl of flowers that Mrs Chubby had placed upon the broad camphor-wood refectory table, I knew we were going to see some changes at Turtle Bay—but strangely the thought did not perturb me. I realized suddenly that I was sick to death of being my own cook and housekeeper.

We changed into swimsuits in the main bedroom—for I had found in the very few hours since we had become lovers that Sherry had an overdeveloped sense of personal modesty, and I knew it would take time before I could wean her to the standard casual Turtle Bay swimming attire. However, it was some compensation for my temporary overdress to see Sherry North in a bikini.

It was the first time I had really had an opportunity to look at her openly. The most striking single thing about her was the texture and lustre of her skin. She was tall, and if her shoulders were too wide and her hips a little too narrow, her waist was tiny and her belly was flat with a small delicately chiselled navel. I have always thought that the Turks were right in considering the navel as a highly erotic portion of a woman's anatomy—Sherry's would have launched a thousand ships.

She didn't like me staring at it. 'Oh, Grandma—what big eyes you've got,' she said, and wrapped a towel around her waist like a sarong. But she walked barefooted through the sand with an unconscious push and sway of buttock and breast that I watched with uninhibited pleasure.

We left our towels above the high water mark and ran down over the hard wet sand to the edge of the clear warm sea. She swam with a deceptively slow and easy stroke, that drove her through the water so swiftly that I had to reach out myself and drive hard to catch and hold her.

Beyond the reef we trod water and she was puffing a little. 'Out of training,' she panted.

While we rested I looked out to sea and at that moment a line of black fins broke the surface together in line abreast, bearing down on us swiftly and I could not restrain my delight.

'You are an honoured guest,' I told her. 'This is a special welcome.' The dolphins circled us, like a pack of excited puppies, gambolling and squeaking while they looked Sherry over carefully. I have known them sheer away from most stranger, and it was a rarity for them to allow themselves to be touched on a first meeting and then only after assiduous wooing. However, with Sherry it was love at first sight, almost of the calibre that Chubby and Angelo had demonstrated.

Within fifteen minutes they were dragging her on the Nantucket sleigh ride while she squealed with glee. The instant she fell off the back of one, there was another prodding her with his snout, competing fiercely for her attention.

When at last they had exhausted us both and we swam in wearily to the beach, one of the big bull dolphins followed Sherry into water so shallow it reached to her waist. There he rolled on his back while she scratched his belly with handfuls of coarse white sand and he grinned that fixed idiotic dolphin grin.

After dark, while we sat on the veranda and drank whisky together, we could still hear the old bull whistling and slapping the water with his tail, in an attempt to seduce her into the sea again.

The next morning I gamely fought off a fresh onslaught of island fever, and the temptation to linger in bed, especially as Sherry awoke beside me with the pink glossy look of a little girl, and her eyes were clear, her breath sweet and her lips languorous.

We had to check through the equipment we had salvaged from *Wave Dancer*, and we needed an engine to drive the compressor. Chubby was sent off with a fistfull of banknotes and returned with a motor that required much loving attention. As that occupied me for the rest of the day, Sherry was sent off to Missus Eddy's for camping equipment and provisions. We had set a three-day deadline for our departure and our schedule was tight.

It was still dark when we took our places in the boat, Chubby and Angelo at the motors in the stern and Sherry and I perched like sparrows on top of the load.

The dawn was a flaming glory of gold and hot red, promise of another fiery day, as Chubby took us northwards on a course possible only for a small boat and a good skipper. We ran close in on island and reef, sometimes with only eighteen inches of water between our keel and the fierce coral fangs.

All of us were in a mood of anticipation. I truly do not believe it was the prospect of vast wealth that excited me then—all I really needed in my life was another good boat like *Wave Dancer*—rather it was the thought of rare and exquisite treasure, and the chance to win it back from the sea. If what we sought had been merely bullion in bars or coin I do not think it would have intrigued me half as much. The sea was the adversary and once more we were pitted against each other.

The blazing colours of the dawn faded into the hard hot blue of the sky as the sun rose out of the sea, and Sherry North stood up in the bows to strip off her denim jacket and jeans. Under them she wore her bikini and now she folded the clothes away into her canvas duffle bag and produced a tube of sun lotion with which she began to anoint her fine pale body.

Chubby and Angelo reacted with undisguised horror. They held a hurried and scandalized consultation after which Angelo was sent forward with a sheet of canvas to rig a sun shelter for Sherry. There followed a heated exchange between Angelo and Sherry.

'You will damage your skin, Miss Sherry,' Angelo protested, but she drove him in defeat back to the stern.

There the two of them sat like mourners at a wake, Chubby's whole face creased into a huge brown scowl and Angelo openly wringing his hands in anxiety. Finally, they could stand it no longer and after another whispered discussion Angelo was elected as emissary once more and he crawled forward over the cargo to enlist my support.

'You can't let her do it, Mister Harry,' Angelo pleaded. 'She will go *dark*.'

'I think that's the idea, Angelo,' I told him. However, I did warn Sherry to take care of the sun at noon. Obediently she covered herself when we ran ashore on a sandy beach to eat our midday meal.

It was the middle of the afternoon when we raised the triple peaks of the Old Men and Sherry exclaimed, 'Just as the old mate described them.'

We approached the island from the sea side, through the narrow stretch of calm water between the island and the reef. When we passed the entrance to the channel through which I had taken *Wave Dancer* to escape from the Zinballa crash boat, Chubby and I grinned at each other in fond recollection, then I turned to Sherry and pointed it out to her.

'I plan to set up our base camp on the island, and we will use the gap to reach the area of the wreck.'

'It looks a little risky.' She eyed the narrow channel with reserve.

'It will save us a round journey of nearly twenty miles each day—and it isn't as bad as it looks. Once I took my big fifty-foot cruiser through there at full throttle.'

'You must be crazy.' She pushed her dark glasses up on top of her head to look at me.

'By now you should be a good judge of that.' I grinned at her, and she grinned back.

'I am an expert already,' she boasted. The sun had darkened the freckles on her nose and cheeks and given her skin a glow. She had one of those rare skins that do not redden and become angry when exposed to sunlight. Instead, it was the kind that quickly turned a golden honey brown.

It was high tide when we rounded the northern tip of the island into a protected cove and Chubby ran the whaleboat onto the sand only twenty yards from the first line of palm trees.

We off-loaded the cargo, carrying it up among the palms well above the high-water mark and once again covered it with tarpaulins to protect it from the ubiquitous sea salt.

It was late by the time we had finished. The heat had gone out of the sun, and the long shadows of the palms barred the earth as we trudged inland, carrying only our personal gear and a five-gallon container of fresh water. In the back of the most northerly peak, generations of visiting fishermen had scratched out a series of shallow caves in the steep slope.

I selected a large cave to act as our equipment store, and a smaller one as living quarters for Sherry and me. Chubby and Angelo chose another for themselves, about a hundred yards along the slope and screened from us by a patch of scrub.

I left Sherry to sweep out our new quarters with a brush improvised from a palm frond, and to lay out our sleeping bags on the inflatable mattress while I took my cast net and went back to the cove.

It was dark when I returned with a string of a dozen big striped mullet. Angelo had the fire burning and the kettle bubbling. We ate in contented silence, and afterwards Sherry and I lay together in our cave and listened to the big fiddler crabs clicking and scratching among the palms.

'It's primeval,' Sherry whispered, 'as though we are the first man and woman in the world.'

'Me Tarzan, you Jane,' I agreed, and she chuckled and drew closer to me.

———————————

In the dawn Chubby set off alone in the whaleboat on the long return journey to St Mary's. He would return next day with a full load of petrol and fresh water in jerry cans. Sufficient to last us for two weeks or so.

While we waited for him to return, Angelo and I took on the wearying task of carrying all the equipment and stores up to the caves. I set up the compressor, charged the empty air bottles and checked the diving gear, and Sherry arranged hanging space for our clothes and generally made our quarters comfortable.

The next day, she and I roamed the island, climbing the peaks and exploring the valleys and beaches between. I had hoped to find water, a spring or well overlooked by the other visitors—but naturally there was none. Those canny old fishermen overlooked nothing.

The south end of the island, farthest from our camp, was impenetrable with salt marsh between the peak and the sea. We skirted the acres of evil-smelling mud and thick swamp grass. The air was rank and heavy with rotted vegetation and dead fish.

Colonies of red and purple crabs had covered the mudflats with their holes from which they peered stalk-eyed as we passed. In the mangroves, the herons were breeding, perched long-legged upon their huge shaggy nests, and once I heard a splash and saw the swirl of something in one of the swamp pools that could only have been a crocodile. We left the fever swamps and we climbed to the higher ground, then we picked our way through the thickets of shrub growth towards the southernmost peak.

Sherry decided we must climb this one also. I tried to dissuade her for it was the tallest and steepest. My protests went completely unnoticed, and even after we had made our way onto a narrow ledge below the southern cliff of the peak, she pressed on determinedly.

'If the mate of the *Dawn Light* found a way to the top—then I'm going up there too,' she announced.

'You'll get the same view from there as from the other peaks,' I pointed out.

'That's not the point.'

'What is the point, then?' I asked, and she gave me the pitying look usually reserved for small children and half-wits, refused to dignify the question with an answer, and continued her cautious sideways shuffle along the ledge.

There was a drop of at least two hundred feet below us, and if there is one deficiency in my formidable arsenal of talent and courage, it is that I have no head for heights. However, I would rather have balanced on one leg atop St Paul's Cathedral than admit this to Miss North, and so with great reluctance I followed her.

Fortunately it was only a few paces farther that she uttered a cry of triumph and turned off the ledge into a narrow vertical crack that split the cliff-face. The fracturing of the rock had formed a stepped and readily climable chimney to the summit, into which I followed her with relief. Almost immediately Sherry cried out again.

'Oh dear God, Harry, look!' and she pointed to a protected area of the wall, in the back of the dark recess. Somebody long ago had patiently chipped an inscription into the flat stone surface.

A. BARLOW.
WRECKED ON THIS PLACE
14th OCT. 1858.

As we stared at it, I felt her hand grope for mine and squeeze for comfort. No longer the intrepid mountaineer, her expression was half fearful as she studied the writing.

'It's creepy,' she whispered. 'It looks as though it was written yesterday—not all those years ago.'

Indeed, the letters had been protected from weathering so that they seemed fresh cut and I glanced around almost as though I expected to see the old seaman watching us.

When at last we climbed the steep chimney to the summit we were still subdued by that message from the remote past. We sat there for almost two hours watching the surf break in long white lines upon Gunfire Reef. The gap in the reef and the great dark pool of the Break showed very clearly from our vantage point, while it was just possible to make out the course of the narrow channel through the coral. From here Arthur Barlow had watched the *Dawn Light* in her death throes, watched her broken up by the high surf.

'Time is running against us now, Sherry,' I told her, as the holiday mood of the last few days evaporated. 'It's fourteen days since Manny Resnick sailed in the *Mandrake*. He will not be far from Cape Town by now. We will know when he reaches there.'

'How?'

'I have an old friend who lives there. He is a member of the Yacht Club—and he will watch the traffic and cable me the moment *Mandrake* docks.'

I looked down the back slope of the peak, and for the first time noticed the blue haze of smoke spreading through the tops of the palms from Angelo's cooking fire.

'I have been a little half-arsed on this trip,' I muttered, 'we have been behaving like a group of school kids on a picnic. From now on we will have to tighten up the security—just across the channel there is my old friend Suleiman Dada, and *Mandrake* will be in these waters sooner than I'd like. We will have to keep a nice low silhouette from now on.'

'How long will we need, do you think?' Sherry asked.

'I don't know, my sweeting—but be sure that it will be longer than we think possible. We are shackled by the need to ferry all our water and petrol from St Mary's—we will only be able to work in the pool during a few hours of each tide when the condition and the height of the water will let us. Who knows what we are going to find in there once we start, and finally we may discover that the Colonel's parcels were stowed in the rear hold of the *Dawn Light*—that part of the ship that was carried out into the open water. If it was, then you can kiss it all goodbye.'

'We've been over that part of it before, you dreadful old pessimist,' Sherry rebuked me. 'Think happy thoughts.'

So we thought happy thoughts and did happy things until at last I made out the tiny dark speck, like a water beetle on the brazen surface of the sea, as Chubby returned from St Mary's in the whaleboat.

We climbed down the peak and hurried back through the palm groves to meet him. He was just rounding the point and entering the cove as we came out on the beach. The whaleboat was low in the water under her heavy cargo of fuel and drinking water. And Chubby stood in the stern as big and solid and as eternal as a great rock. When we waved and shouted he inclined his head gravely in acknowledgement. Mrs Chubby had sent a banana cake for me and for Sherry a large sunhat of woven palm fronds. Chubby had obviously reported Sherry's behaviour, and his expression was more than normally lugubrious when he saw that the damage was already being done. Sherry was toasted to an edible medium rare.

It was after dark by the time we had carried fifty jerry-cans up to the cave. Then we gathered about the fire where Angelo was cooking an island chowder of clams that he had gathered from the lagoon that afternoon. It was time to tell my crew the true reason for our expedition. Chubby I could trust to say nothing, even under torture—but I had waited to get Angelo into the isolation of the island before telling him. He has been known to commit the most monstrous indiscretions— usually in an attempt to impress one of his young ladies.

They listened in silence to my explanation, and remained silent after I had finished. Angelo was waiting for a lead from Chubby—and that gentleman was not one to charge his fences. He sat scowling into the fire, and his face looked like one of those copper masks from an Aztec temple. When he had created the correct atmosphere of theatrical suspense he reached into his back pocket and produced a purse, so old and well handled that the leather was almost worn through.

'When I was a boy and fished the pool at Gunfire Break, I took a big old Daddy grouper fish. When I open his belly pouch I found this in him.' From the purse he took out a round disc. 'I kept it since then, like a good luck charm, even though I was offered ten pounds for it by an officer on one of my ships.'

He handed me the disc and I examined it in the firelight. It was a gold coin, the size of a shilling. The reverse side was covered with oriental characters which I could not read—but the obverse face bore a crest of two rampant lions supporting a shield and an armoured head. The same design as I had last seen on the bronze ship's bell at Big Gull Island. The legend below the shield read: 'AUS: REGIS & SENAT: ANGLIA.' while the rim was struck with the bold title 'ENGLISH EAST INDIA COMPANY'.

'I always promised me that I would go back to Gunfire Break— looks like this is the time,' Chubby went on, as I examined the coin minutely. There was no date on it, but I had no doubt that it was a gold mohur of the company. I had read of the coin but never seen one before.

'You got this out of a fish's gut, Chubby?' I asked, and he nodded.

'Guess that old grouper seen it shine and took a snap at it. Must have stuck in his belly until I pulled him out.'

I handed the coin back to him. 'Well then, Chubby, that goes to show there is some truth in my story.'

'Guess it does, Harry,' he admitted, and I went to the cave to fetch the drawings of the *Dawn Light* and a gas lantern. We pored over the drawings. Chubby's grandfather had sailed as a topmastman in an East Indiaman, which made Chubby something of an expert. He was of the opinion that all passengers' luggage and other small pieces would be stowed in the fore-hold beside the forecastle—I wasn't going to argue with him. Never hex yourself, as Chubby had warned me so often.

When I produced my tide tables and began calculating the time differences for our latitude, Chubby actually smiled, although it was hard to recognize it as such. It looked much more like a sneer, for Chubby had no faith in rows of printed figures in pamphlets. He preferred to judge the tides by the sea clock in his own head. I have known him to call the tides accurately for a week ahead without reference to any other source.

'I reckon we will have a high tide at one-forty tomorrow,' I announced.

'Man, you got it right for once,' Chubby agreed.

Without the enormous loads that had been forced on her recently, the whaleboat seemed to run with a new lightness and eagerness. The twin Evinrudes put her up on the plane, and she flew at the narrow channel through the reef like a ferret into a rabbit-hole.

Angelo stood in the bows, using hand signals to indicate underwater snags to Chubby in the stern. We had picked good water to come in on, and Chubby met the dying surf with confidence. The little whaleboat tossed up her head and kicked her heels over the swells, splattering us with spray.

The passage was more exhilarating than dangerous, and Sherry whooped and laughed with the thrill of it.

Chubby shot us through the narrow neck between the coral cliffs with feet to spare on each side, for the whaleboat had half of *Wave Dancer*'s beam, then we zigzagged through the twisted gut of the channel beyond and at last burst out into the pool.

'No good trying to anchor,' Chubby growled, 'it's deep here. The reef goes down sheer. We got twenty fathoms under us here and the bottom is foul.'

'How you going to hold?' I asked.

'Somebody got to sit at the motor and keep her there with power.'

'That's going to chew fuel, Chubby.'

'Don't I know it,' he growled.

With a tide only half made, the occasional wave was coming in over the reef. Not yet with much force, just a frothing spill that cascaded into the pool, turning the surface to ginger beer with bubbles. However, as the tide mounted so the surf would come over stronger. Soon it would be unsafe in the pool and we would have to run for it. We had about two hours in which to work, depending on the stage of neap and spring tides. It was a cycle of too little or too much. At low tide there was insufficient water to negotiate the entrance channel—and at high tide the surf breaking over the reef might overwhelm the open whaleboat. Each of our moves had to be finely judged.

Now every minute was precious. Sherry and I were already dressed in our wet suits with face-plates on our foreheads, and it was necessary only for Angelo to lift the heavy scuba sets onto our backs and to clinch the webbing harness.

'Ready, Sherry?' I asked, and she nodded, the ungainly mouthpiece already stuffed into her pretty mouth.

'Let's go.'

We dropped over the side, and sank down together beneath the cigar-shaped hull of the whaleboat. The surface was a moving sheet of quicksilver above us, and the spill over the reef charged the upper layer of water with a rash of champagne bubbles.

I checked with Sherry. She was comfortable, and breathing in the slow rhythm of the experienced diver that conserves air and ventilates the body effectively. She grinned at me, her lips distorted by the mouthpiece and her eyes enormously enlarged by the glass face-plate, and she gave me the high sign with both thumbs.

I pointed my head straight for the bottom and began pedalling with my swimming fins, going down fast, reluctant to waste air on a slow descent.

The pool was a dark hole below us. The surrounding walls of coral shut out much of the light, and gave it an ominous appearance. The water was cold and gloomy. I felt a prickle of almost superstitious awe. There was something sinister about this place, as though some evil and malignant force lurked in the sombre depths.

I crossed my fingers at my sides, and went on down, following the sheer coral cliff. The coral was riddled with dark caves and ledges that overhung the lower walls. Coral of a hundred different sorts, outcropped in weird and lovely shapes, tinted with the complete spectrum of colour. Weeds and marine growth waved and tossed in the movement of water, like the hands of supplicating beggars, or the dark manes of wild horses.

I looked back at Sherry. She was close behind me and she smiled again. Clearly she felt nothing of my own sense of awe. We went on down.

From secret ledges protruded the long yellow antennae of giant crayfish, gently they moved, sensing our presence in the disturbed water. Clouds of multi-coloured coral fish floated along the cliff-face; they sparkled like gemstones in the fading blue light that penetrated into the depths of the pool.

Sherry tapped my shoulder and we paused to peer into a deep black cave. Two great owl eyes peered back at us, and as my eyes became accustomed to the light I made out the gargantuan head of a grouper. It was speckled like a plover's egg, splotches of brown and black on a beige-grey ground and the mouth was a wide slash between thick rubbery lips. As we watched, the huge fish assumed a defensive attitude. It blew itself out, increasing its already impressive girth, spread the gill covers, enlarged the head and finally it opened its mouth in a gape that could have swallowed a man whole—a cavernous maw, lined with spiked teeth. Sherry seized my hand. We drew away from the cave, and the fish closed its mouth and subsided. Any time I wanted to claim a world record grouper I knew where to come looking. Even allowing for the magnifying effect of water I judged that he was close to a thousand pounds in weight.

We went on down the coral wall, and all around us was the wondrous marine world seething with life and beauty, death and danger. Lovely little damsel fish nestled in the venomous arms of giant sea anemone, immune to the deadly darts; a moray eel slid like a long black battle pennant along the coral wall, reached its lair and turned to threaten us with dreadful ragged teeth and glittering snake-like eyes.

Down we went, pedalling with our fins, and now at last I saw the bottom. It was a dark jungle of sea growth, dense stands of sea bamboo and petrified coral trees thrust out of the smothering marine foliage, while mounds and hillocks of coral were worked and riven into shapes that teased the imagination and covered I knew not what.

We hung above this impenetrable jungle and I checked my time-elapse wrist watch and depth gauge. I had 128 feet, and time elapsed was five minutes forty seconds.

I gave Sherry the hand signal to remain where she was and I sank down to the tops of the marine jungle and gingerly parted the cold slimy foliage. I worked my way down through it and emerged into a relatively open area below. It was a twilight area roofed in by the bamboo and people with strange new tribes of fish and marine animals.

I knew at once that it would not be a simple task to search the floor of the pool. Visibility here was ten feet or less, and the total area we must cover was two or three acres in extent.

I decided to bring Sherry down with me and for a start we would make a sweep along the base of the cliff, keeping in line abreast and within sight of each other.

I inflated my lungs and used the buoyancy to rise from the bottom, out through the thick belt of foliage into the clear.

I did not see Sherry at first, and I felt a quick dart of concern stab me. Then I saw the silver stream of her bubbles rising against the black wall of coral. She had moved away, ignoring my instruction, and I was annoyed. I finned towards her and was twenty feet from her when I saw what she was doing. My annoyance gave way instantly to shock and horror.

The long series of accidents and mishaps that were to haunt us in Gunfire Break had begun.

Growing out of the coral cliff was a lovely fern-like structure, graceful sweeps, branching and rebranching, pale pink shading to crimson. Sherry had broken off a large branch of it. She held it in her bare hands and even as I raced towards her I saw her legs brush lightly against the red arms of the dreaded fire coral.

I seized her wrists and dragged her off the cruel and beautiful plant. I dug my thumbs into her flesh, shaking her hands viciously, forcing her to drop her fearsome burden. I was frantic in the knowledge that from their cells in the coral branches tens of thousands of minute polyps were firing their barbed poison darts into her flesh.

She was staring at me with great stricken eyes, aware that something bad had happened, but not yet sure what it was. I held her and began the ascent immediately. Even in my anxiety I was careful to obey the elementary rules of ascent, never overtaking my own bubbles but rising steadily with them.

I checked my watch—eight minutes thirty seconds elapsed. That was three minutes at 130 feet. Quickly I calculated my decompression stops, but I was caught between the devil of diver's bends and the deep blue sea of Sherry's coming agony.

It hit her before we were half way to the surface; her face contorted and her breathing went into the shallow ragged panting of deep distress until I feared she might beat the mechanical efficiency of her demand valve, jamming it so that it could no longer feed her with air.

She began to writhe in my grip and the palms of her hands blushed angrily, the livid red weals rose like whiplashes across her thighs— and I thanked God for the protection her suit had given to her torso.

When I held her at a decompression stop fifteen feet below the surface she fought me wildly, kicking and twisting in my grip. I cut the stop fine as I dared, and took her to the surface.

The instant our heads broke clear I spat out my mouthpiece and yelled: 'Chubby! Quick!'

The whaleboat was fifty yards away, but the motor was ticking over steadily and Chubby spun her on her own tail. The instant she was pointed at us, he gave the con to Angelo and scrambled up into the bows, coming down on us like a great brown colossus.

'It's fire coral, Chubby,' I shouted. 'She's hit hard. Get her out!'

Chubby leaned out, took hold of the webbing harness at the back of her neck and lifted her bodily from the water; she dangled from his big brown fists like a drowning kitten.

I ditched my scuba set in the water for Angelo to recover, shrugging out of the harness, and when I scrambled over the side, Chubby had laid her on the floorboards and was leaning over her, folding her in his arms to quieten her struggles and still her moans and sobs of agony.

I found my medical kit under a pile of loose equipment in the bows, and my fingers were clumsy with haste as I heard Sherry's sobs behind me. I snapped the head of an ampoule of morphine and filled a disposable syringe with the clear fluid. Now I was angry as well as concerned.

'You stupid broad,' I snarled at her. 'What made you do a crazy, half-witted thing like that?'

She could not answer me, her lips were shaking and blue, flecked with spittle. I took a pinch of skin on her thigh and thrust the needle into it as I expelled the fluid into her flesh. I went on angrily.

'Fire coral—my God, you aren't an effing conchologist's backside. Isn't a kid on the island that stupid.'

'I didn't think, Harry,' she panted wildly.

'Didn't think—' I repeated, her pain was goading me to new excesses of anger. 'I don't think you've got anything in your head to think with, you stupid little bird-brain.'

I withdrew the needle, and ransacked the medicine box for the antihistamine spray.

'I should put you over my knee, you—'

Chubby looked up at me. 'Harry, you talk to Miss Sherry just one more word like that and, man—I'm going to have to break your head, hear?'

With only mild surprise I realized that he meant it. I had seen him break heads before, and knew it was something to avoid, so I told him, 'Instead of making speeches—how about you get us the hell out of here and back to the island.'

'You just treat her gentle, man, otherwise I'm going to roast your arse so you wish you'd been the one that sat on a bunch of fire coral instead of her, hear?'

I ignored this mutinous outburst and sprayed the ugly scarlet weals, coating them with a protective and soothing skin, and then I lifted her into my arms and held her like that while the morphine smoothed out the fearful burning agony of the stings and Chubby ran us back to the island.

When I carried Sherry up to the cave she was already half comatose from the drug. All that night I stayed by her side, helping her through the shivering and sweating fever produced by the virulent poison. Once she moaned and whispered half in delirium, 'I'm sorry, Harry. I didn't know. It's the first time I've dived in coral water. I didn't recognize it.'

Chubby and Angelo did not sleep either. I heard the murmur of their voices from the fireside and every hour one of them would cough outside the cave entrance and then inquire anxiously, 'How's she doing, Harry?'

By the morning Sherry had fought off the worst effects of the poisoning, and the stings had subsided into an ugly rash of blisters. However, it was another thirty-six hours before any of us could raise the enthusiasm to tackle the pool again, then the tides were wrong. We had to wait another day.

The precious hours were slipping away. I could imagine the *Mandrake* making fair passage; she had looked a fast and powerful vessel and each day wasted whittled away the lead I had counted upon.

On the third day, we ran out again to the pool. It was mid-afternoon and we took a chance with the water in the channel, scraping through early in the flood with inches to spare over the sharp coral snags.

Sherry was still in mild disgrace and, with her hands wrapped in acriflavine bandages, she was left in the whaleboat to keep Angelo company. Chubby and I dived together, going down fast and pausing above the swaying bamboo tops only long enough to drop the first marker buoy. I had decided it was necessary to search the pool bottom systematically. I was marking off the whole area into squares, anchoring inflatable buoys above the marine forest on thin nylon line.

We worked for an hour and found nothing that was obviously wreckage, although there were masses of coral covered with marine growth that would bear closer investigation. I marked these on the underwater slate attached to my thigh.

At the end of that hour, our air reserves in the double ninety-cubic-foot bottles were uncomfortably low. Chubby used more air than I did, for he was a much bigger man and his technique lacked finesse, so I regularly checked his pressure gauge.

I took him up and was especially carefully on the decompression periods, although Chubby showed his usual impatience. He had never seen, as I had, a diver come up too fast so the blood in his veins starts fizzing like champagne. The resultant agonies can cripple a man and an air bubble lodged in the brain can do permanent damage.

'Any luck?' Sherry called as soon as we surfaced, and I gave her the thumbs down as we swam to the whaleboat. We drank a cup of coffee from the Thermos and I smoked an island cheroot while we rested and chatted. I think we were all mildly disappointed that success had not been immediate, but I kept their spirits up by anticipating the first find.

Chubby and I changed our demand valves onto freshly charged bottles and down we went again. This time I would only allow forty-five minutes working at 130 feet, for the effects of gas absorption into the blood are cumulative, and repeated deep diving greatly increases the danger.

We worked carefully through the forests of bamboo stems and over the tumbled coral blocks, exploring the gullies and cracks between them, pausing every few minutes to map the locations of interesting features, then going on, back and forth on the legs of a search pattern between my marker buoys.

Time elapse was forty-three minutes, and I glanced across at Chubby. None of our wet suits would fit him, so he dived naked except for an ancient black woollen bathing costume. He looked like one of my friendly dolphins—only not as graceful—as he forced his way through the thickets. I grinned at the thought and was about to turn away when a chance ray of light pierced the canopy above us and glinted upon something white on the floor below Chubby. I finned in quickly, and examined the white object. At first I thought it was a piece of clam shell, but then I noticed that it was too thick and regular in shape. I sank down closer to it and saw that it was embedded in a decaying sheet of coelentrate coral. I groped for the small jenny bar on my webbing belt, drew it from its sheath and prised off the lump of coral containing the white object. The lump weighed about five pounds and I slipped it into my netting carrybag.

Chubby was watching me and I gave him the signal for the ascent.

'Anything?' Sherry called immediately we surfaced. Her confinement to the whaleboat was obviously playing the devil with her nerves. She was irritable and impatient—but I was not letting her dive until the ugly, suppurating lesions on her hands and thighs had healed. I knew how easily secondary infection could attack those open sores under these conditions, and I was feeding her antibiotics and trying to keep her quiet.

'I don't know,' I answered, as we swam to the boat and I handed the net bag up to her. She took it eagerly, and while we climbed aboard and stripped our equipment she was examining it closely, turning it over in her hands.

Already the surf was breaking heavily on the reef, boiling into the pool, and the whaleboat was swinging and bobbing in the disturbance. Angelo was having difficulty holding her on station—and it was time to go. We had spent as much time underwater as I considered safe for one day, and soon now the heavy oceanic surf would begin leaping the coral barrier and sweeping the pool.

'Take us home, Chubby,' I called and he went to the motors. All our attention was focused on the wild ride back through the channel. With the flood of the tide the swells came up under our stern, surfing us,

coming through under our hull so fast that our relative speed was reversed and the whaleboat's steering was inverted so we threatened to
broach to and tumble broadside onto the coral walls of the channel.
However, Chubby's seamanship never faltered, and at last we shot out
into the protected waters behind the reef and turned for the island.

Now I could give my attention to the object I had recovered from the
pool. With Sherry giving me a great deal of advice that I did not really
need, and cautioning me to exercise care, I placed the lump of dead
coral on the thwart and gave it a smart crack with the jenny bar. It
split into three pieces and revealed a number of articles that had been
ingested and protected by the living coral polyps.

There were three round grey objects the size of marbles and I picked
one out of the coral bed and weighed it in my hand. It was heavy. I
handed it to Sherry.

'Guesses?' I asked.

'Musket balls,' she said without hesitation.

'Of course,' I agreed. I should have recognized it and I made
amends by identifying the next object.

'A small brass key.'

'Genius!' she said with irony, and I ignored her as I worked delicately to free the white object which had first caught my attention. It
came away at last and I turned it over to examine the blue design
worked on one side.

It was a segment of white glazed porcelain, a chip from the rim of a
plate which had been ornamented by a coat of arms. Half of the design
was missing but I recognized the rampant lion immediately, and the
words 'Senat. ANGLIA.' It was the device of John Company again, part
of a set of ship's plate.

I passed it to Sherry and suddenly I saw how it must have been. I
told her my vision and she listened quietly, fondling the chip of porcelain. 'When at last the surf broke her back and the coral tore her in half,
she would have gone down by the middle, and all her heavy cargo and
gear would have shifted—tearing out her inner bulkhead. It would all
have poured out of her, cannon and shot, plate and silver, flash and cup,
coin and pistol—it would have littered the floor of the pool, a rich
sowing of man-made articles and the coral has sucked it up and
absorbed it.'

'The treasure crates?' Sherry demanded. 'Would they have fallen
out of the hull?'

'I don't know,' I admitted, and Chubby, who had been listening
intently, spat over the side and growled.

'The forehold was always double-skinned, three-inch oak planks, to hold the cargo from shifting in a storm. Anything was in there then, is still in there now.'

'And that opinion would have cost you ten guineas in Harley Street,' I told Sherry, and winked at her. She laughed and turned to Chubby.

'I don't know what we would do without you, Chubby dear,' and Chubby scowled murderously and suddenly found something of engrossing interest out on the distant horizon.

It was only later, after Sherry and I had taken our swim on one of the secluded beaches and had changed into fresh clothes and were sitting around the fire drinking Chivas Regal and eating fresh prawns netted in the lagoon, that the elation of our first minor finds wore off—and I began soberly to consider the implications of the *Dawn Light* broken up and scattered across the marine hothouse of the pool.

If Chubby were wrong and the treasure crates, with their enormous weight of gold, had smashed through the sides of the hold and fallen free, then it would be an endless task searching for them. I had seen two hundred blocks and mounds of coral that day—any one of which could have concealed a part of the tiger throne of India.

If he were correct and the hold had retained its cargo, then the coral polyps would have spread over the entire front section of the vessel as it lay on the bottom, covering the woodwork with layer upon layer of calcified stone, until it had become an armoured repository for the treasure, disguised with a growth of marine plants.

We discussed it in detail, all of us beginning to appreciate the magnitude of the task we had set ourselves, and we agreed that it fell into two separate parts.

First we had to locate and identify the treasure cases, and then we had to wrest them from the stubborn embrace of the coral.

'You know what we are going to need, don't you, Chubby?' I asked, and he nodded.

'You still got those two cases?' I felt ashamed to mention the word gelignite in front of Sherry. It reminded me too vividly of the project for which Chubby and I had found it necessary to lay in large stocks of high explosive. That had been three years ago, during a lean season when I had been desperate for ready cash to keep myself and *Wave Dancer* aloft. Not even by stretching the letter of the law could our project have been considered legal, and I would rather have closed that chapter and forgotten it—but we needed gelignite now.

Chubby shook his head. 'Man, that stuff began sweating like a stevedore in a heatwave. If you belched within fifty feet of it—it would have blown the top off the island.'

'What did you do with it?'

'Angelo and I took it out into the Mozambique Channel and gave it a deep six.'

'We will need at least a couple of cases. It will take a full shot to break up those big chunks down there.'

'I'll speak to Mister Coker again—he should be able to fix it.'

'Do that, Chubby. Next time you go back to St Mary's you tell Fred Coker to get us three cases.'

'What about the pineapples we saved from *Wave Dancer*?' Chubby asked.

'No good,' I told him; I did not want my obituary to read, 'The man who tried to fuse MK VII hand-grenades in 130 feet of water.'

I was wakened the next morning by the unnatural hush, and the static charged heat of the air. I lay awake listening, but even the fiddler crabs were silent and the perpetual rattle of the palm fronds was stilled. The only sound was the low and gentle breathing of the woman beside me. I kissed her lightly on the cheek and managed to withdraw my bad arm from under her head without waking her. Sherry boasted that she never used a pillow, it was bad for the spine she told me with an air of rectitude, but this didn't prevent her from using any convenient portion of my anatomy as a substitute.

I ambled out of the cave trying to restore the circulation to my limb by massage, and while I made a libation to my favourite palm tree I studied the sky.

It was a sickly dawn, smeared with a dark haze that dimmed the stars. The heated air lay heavy and languorous against the earth, with no breeze to stir it, and my skin prickled in the charged atmosphere.

Chubby was feeding twigs to the fire and blowing life into it when I returned. He looked up at me and confirmed my diagnosis.

'Weather going to break.'

'What is coming, Chubby?' and he shrugged. 'Glass is down to 28.2, but we'll know by noon,' and he went back to huffing and puffing over the fire.

The weather had affected Sherry also. The hair at her temples was damp with perspiration and she snapped at me peevishly as I changed her dressings, but minutes later she came up behind me as I dressed, and laid her cheek against my naked back.

'Sorry, Harry, it's just so sticky and close this morning,' and she ran her lips across my back, touching the thick raised cicatrice of the bullet scar with her tongue.

'Forgive?' she asked.

Chubby and I dived into the pool at eleven o'clock that morning. We had been down thirty-eight minutes without making any further significant discovery when I heard the tinny clink! clink! clink!— transmitted through the water. I paused and listened, noticing that Chubby had stopped also. It came again, thrice repeated.

On the surface, Angelo had immersed half of a three-foot length of iron rail into the water and was beating out the recall signal upon it with a hammer from the tool kit.

I gave Chubby the open-handed 'wash out' sign and we began the ascent at once.

As we climbed into the boat I asked impatiently, 'What is it, Angelo?' and in reply he pointed out to seaward over the jagged and irregular back of the reef.

I pulled off my mask and blinked my eyes, refocusing after the limited horizons of the marine world.

It lay low and black against the sea, a thin dark smear as though some playful god had drawn a charcoal line across the horizon—but even as I watched, it seemed to grow—spreading wider into the paler blue of the sky, darker and still darker it rose out of the sea. Chubby whistled softly and shook his head.

'Here comes Lady C. and, man, she is in a big hurry.'

The speed of that low dark front was uncanny. It lifted up, drawing a funereal curtain across the sky and as Chubby gunned the motors and ran for the channel the first racing streamers of cloud spread across the sun.

Sherry came to sit beside me on the thwart and help me strip the clinging wet rubber suit.

'What is it, Harry?' she asked.

'Lady C,' I told her. 'It's the cyclone, the same one that killed the *Dawn Light*. She's out hunting again,' and Angelo fetched the lifebelts from the forepeak and handed one to each of us. We tied them on and sat close together and watched it come on in awesome grandeur, overwhelming the sun, changing the sky from a high pure blue dome into a low grey roof of filthy scudding cloud.

We were running hard before her, leaving the channel and flying across the inner waters to the shelter of the cove. All our faces were turned to watch it, all our hearts quailed at the sense of our own frailty before such force and power.

The cloud front passed over our heads as we ran into the bay, and immediately we were plunged into a twilight world, fraught with the fury to come. The cloud dragged a skirt of cold damp air beneath it. It passed over us, and we shivered in the sudden drop in temperature. With a shriek, the wind was upon us, turning the air into a mixture of sand and driven spray.

'The motors,' Chubby bellowed at me, as the whaleboat touched the beath. Those two new Evinrudes represented half the savings of a lifetime and I understood his concern.

'We'll take them with us.'

'And the boat?' Chubby persisted.

'Sink it. There's a firm bottom of sand for it to lie on.'

As Chubby and I freed the motors, Angelo and Sherry lashed the folds of the tarpaulin over the open deck to secure the equipment, and then used the nylon diving lines to tie down the irreplaceable scuba sets and the waterproof cases that contained my medical kit and tools.

Then, while Chubby and I hefted the two heavy Evinrudes, Angelo allowed the wind to push the whaleboat out into the bay where he pulled the drainplugs and she filled immediately with water. The steep wind-maddened sea poured in over the side, and she went down swiftly in twenty feet of water.

Angelo returned to the beach using a dogged sidestroke with the waves breaking over his head. By this time, Sherry and I had almost reached the line of palm trees.

Doubled under my load, I glanced back. Chubby was lumbering after us. He was similarly burdened by the second motor, doubled also under the dead weight of metal and wading through the waist-high torrent of blown white sand. Angelo emerged from the water and followed him.

They were close behind us as we ran into the trees. If I had hoped to find shelter here, then I was a fool, for we found ourselves transferred from an exposed position of acute discomfort into one of real and deadly danger.

The great winds of the cyclone had thrashed the palms into a lunatic frenzy. The sound of it was a deafening clattering roar that was stunning in its intensity. The long graceful stems of the palms whipped about wildly, and the wind clawed loose the fronds and sent them flying off into the haze of sand and spray like huge mis-shapen birds.

We ran in single file along one of the ill-defined footpaths, Sherry leading us, covering her head with both hands, while I was for the first time grateful for the scanty cover given me by the big white motor on my shoulder, for all of us were exposed to the double threat of danger.

The whipping of the tall palms flung from the fifty-foot-high heads their clusters of iron-hard nuts. Big as a cannon-ball and almost as dangerous, these projectiles bombarded as as we ran. One of them struck the motor I carried, a blow that made me stagger, another fell beside the path and on the second bounce hit Sherry on the lower leg. Even though most of its power was spent, still it knocked her down and rolled her in the sand like a running springbok hit by a high-powered rifle. When she regained her feet she was limping heavily—but she ran on through the lethal hail of coconuts.

We had almost reached the saddle of the hills when the wind increased the power of its assault. I heard it shrieking overhead on a higher angrier note, and coming in across the treetops roaring like a wild beast.

It hurled a new curtain of sand at us, and as I glanced ahead I saw the first palm tree begin to go.

I saw it lean out wearily, exhausted by its efforts to resist the wind, the earth around its base heaved upwards as the root system was torn from the sandy soil. As it came down so it gathered speed; swinging in a terrible arc, like the axe of the headsman, it fell towards us. Sherry was fifteen paces ahead of me, just beginning the ascent of the saddle and she had her face turned downwards, watching her own feet, her hands still held to her head.

She was running into the path of the falling tree, and she seemed so small and fragile beneath that solid bole of descending timber. It would crush her with a single gargantuan blow.

I screamed at her, but although she was so close she could not hear me. The roaring of the wind seemed to swamp all our senses. Down swung the long limber stem of the palm tree, and Sherry ran on into its path. I dropped the motor, shrugging it from my shoulder and I ran forward. Even then I saw I could not reach her in time, and I dived belly down, reaching out to the full stretch of my right arm and I hit Sherry's back foot, slapping it across the other as she swung it forward. The ankle tap of the football field, and it tripped her. She fell flat on her face in the sand. As the two of us lay outstretched the palm tree descended. The fury of its stroke rushed through the air even above the sound of the wind and it struck with a blow that was transmitted through the earth into my body, jarring me and rattling the teeth in my skull.

Instantly I was up and dragging Sherry to her feet. The palm tree had missed her by eighteen inches and she was stunned and terrified. I hugged her for a few moments, trying to give her comfort and strength. Then I lifted her over the palm stem that blocked the path, pointed her at the saddle and gave her a shove.

'Run!' I shouted and she staggered onwards. Angelo helped me lift the motor onto my shoulder once more. We clambered over the tree and toiled on up the slope after Sherry's running figure.

All around us in the palm groves I could hear the thud and crash of other trees falling and I tried to run with my face upturned to catch the next threat before it developed, but another flying coconut hit me a glancing blow on the temple, dimming my vision for a moment and I staggered on blindly, taking my chances among the monstrous guillotines of the falling palms.

I reached the crest of the saddle without realizing it, and I was unprepared for the full unbroken force of the wind in my back. It hurled me forward, the ground fell away from under my feet as I was thrown over the saddle, my knees gave way and the motor and I rolled headlong down the reverse slope. On the way down we caught up with Sherry North, taking her in the back of the legs. She collapsed on top of me and joined the motor and me on our hurried descent.

One moment I was on top and the next Miss North was seated between my shoulder blades, then the motor was on top of both of us.

When we reached the bottom of the steepest pitch and lay together in a battered and weary heap, we were protected by the saddle from the direct fury of the wind so it was possible to hear what Sherry was saying. It was immediately obvious that she bitterly resented what she considered to be an unprovoked assault, and she was loudly casting doubt on my parentage, character and breeding. Even in my own desperate straits her anger was suddenly terribly comical, and I began to laugh. I saw that she was trying to find sufficient strength to hit me so I decided to distract her.

> '—*Jack and Jill went up the hill*
> *They each had a dollar and a quarter*—'

I croaked at her,

> '—*Jill came down with half a crown*
> *They didn't go up for water.*'

She stared at me for a moment as though I had started frothing at the mouth, then she started to laugh also, but the laughter had a wild hysterical note to it.

'Oh you swine!' she sobbed with laughter, tears streaming down her cheeks and her sodden sand-caked hair dangling in thick dark snakes about her face.

Angelo thought she was weeping when he reached us and he drew her tenderly to her feet and helped her down the last few hundred yards to the caves, leaving me to hoist the motor once more to my bruised shoulder and follow them.

Our cave was well placed to weather the cyclone winds, probably chosen by the old fishermen with that in mind. I retrieved the canvas fly leaf from where it was wrapped around the bole of a palm tree and used it to screen the entrance, piling stones upon the trailing end to hold it down and we had a dimly lit haven into which we crept like two wounded animals.

I had left my motor with Chubby in his cave. I felt at that moment that if I never saw it again it would be too soon, but I knew Chubby would treat it with all the loving care of a mother for her sickly infant and that when the cyclone passed on, it would once more be ready for sea.

Once I had rigged the tarpaulin to screen the cave and keep out the wind, Sherry and I could strip and clean ourselves of the salt and sand. We used a basinful of the precious fresh water for this purpose, each of us taking it in turn to stand in the basin and be sponged down by the other.

I was a mass of scratches and bruises from my long battle with the motor, and although my medical kit was still in the boat at the bottom of the bay, I found a large bottle of mercurochrome in my bag. Sherry began a convincing imitation of Florence Nightingale; with the anti-septic and a roll of cotton wool she anointed my wounds, murmuring condolences and sympathetic sounds.

I rather enjoy being fussed over, and I stood there in a semi-hypnotic state lifting an arm or moving a leg as I was bidden. The first hint that I received that Miss North was not treating my crippling injuries with the true gravity they deserved was when she suddenly emitted a hoot of glee and daubed my most delicate extremity with a scarlet splash of mercurochrome.

'Rudolph the red-nosed reindeer,' she chortled, and I roused myself to protest bitterly.

'Hey! That stuff doesn't wash off.'

'Good!' she cried. 'I'll be able to find you now if you ever get lost in a crowd.' I was shocked by such unseeming levity. I gathered about me my dignity and went to find a pair of dry pants.

Sherry reclined on the mattress and watched me scratching in my bag.

'How long is this going to last?' she asked.

'Five days,' I told her, as I paused to listen to the unabated roar of the wind.

'How do you know?'

'It always lasts five days,' I explained, as I stepped into my shorts and hoisted them.

'That's going to give us a little time to get to know each other.'

We were caged by the cyclone, locked together in the confined few square feet of the cave, and it was a strange experience.

Any venture out into the open forced upon us by nature, or to check how Chubby and Angelo were faring, was fraught with discomfort and danger. Although the trees were stripped of most of their fruit during the first twelve hours and the weaker trees fell during that period also— yet there was still the occasional tree that came crashing down, and the loose trash and fronds flew like arrows on the wind with sufficient force to blind a person or inflict other injury.

Chubby and Angelo worked away quietly on the motors, stripping them down and cleaning them of salt water. They had something to keep them busy.

In our cave, once the initial novelty had passed there developed some crisis of will and decision which I did not properly understand, but which I sensed was critical.

I had never pretended to understand Sherry North in any depth; there were too many unanswered questions, too many areas of reserve, barriers of privacy beyond which I was not allowed to pass. She had not to this time made any declaration of her feelings, there was never any discussion of the future. This was strange, for any other woman I had ever known expected—nay demanded—declarations of love and passion. I sensed also that this indecision was causing her as much distress as it was me. She was caught up in something against which she struggled, and in the process her emotions were being badly mauled.

However, with Sherry there was nothing spoken of—for I had accepted the tacit agreement and we did not discuss any of our feelings for each other. I found this restricting, for I am a lover with a florid turn of speech. If I have not yet succeeded in talking a bird down out of a tree—it is probably because I have never seriously made the attempt. I could make this adjustment without too much pain, however; it was the lack of a future that chafed at me.

It seemed that Sherry did not look for our relationship to last longer than the setting of the sun, yet I knew that she could not feel this way, for in the moments of warmth that interspersed those of gloom, there could be no doubts.

Once when I started to speak of my plans for when we had raised the treasure—how I would have another boat built to my design, a boat that incorporated all the best features of the beloved *Wave Dancer*— how I would build a new dwelling at Turtle Bay that would not deserve the title of shack—how I would furnish it and people it—she took no part in the discussion. When I ran out of words, she turned away from me on the mattress and pretended to sleep although I could feel the tension in her body without touching her.

At another time I found her watching me with that hostile, hating look. While an hour later she was in a frenzy of physical passion which was in diametric contrast.

She sorted and mended my clothing from the bag, sitting cross-legged on the mattress and working with neat businesslike stitches. When I thanked her, she became caustic and derisive, and we ended up in a blazing row until she flung herself out of the cave and ran through the raging wind to Chubby's cave. She did not return until after dark, with Chubby escorting her and holding a lantern to light her way.

Chubby regarded me with an expression that would have melted a lesser man and frostily refused my invitation to drink whisky, which meant that he was either very sick or very disapproving, then he disappeared again into the storm muttering darkly.

By the fourth day my nerves were in a jangling mess, but I had considered the problem of Sherry's strange behaviour from every angle and I reached my conclusions.

Cooped up with me in that tiny cave she was being forced at last to consider her feelings for me. She was falling in love, probably for the first time in her life, and her fiercely independent spirit was hating the experience. I cannot say in truthfulness that I was enjoying it very much either—or rather I enjoyed the short periods of repentance and loving between each new tantrum—but I looked forward fervently to the moment when she accepted the inevitable and succumbed completely.

I was still awaiting that happy moment when I awoke in the dawn of the fifth day. The island was in a grip of a stillness that was almost numbing after the uproar of the cyclone. I lay and listened to the silence without opening my eyes, but when I felt movement beside me I rolled my head and looked into her face.

'The storm is over,' she said softly, and rose from the bed.

We walked out side by side into the early morning sunlight, blinking around us at the devastation which the storm had created. The island looked like the photographs of a World War I battlefield. The palms were stripped of their foliage, the bare masts pointed pathetically at the sky and the earth below was littered thickly with palm fronds and coconuts. The stillness hung over it all, no breath of wind, and the sky was pale milky blue, still filled with a haze of sand and sea.

From their cave Chubby and Angelo emerged, like big bear and little bear at the end of winter. They stood and looked about them uncertainly.

Suddenly Angelo let out a Commanche whoop and leaped four feet in the air. After five days of forced confinement his animal spirits could no longer be suppressed. He took off through the palm trees like a greyhound.

'Last one in the water is a fascist,' he shouted, and Sherry was the first to accept the challenge. She was ten paces behind him when they hit the beach but they dived simultaneously into the lagoon, fully clad, and began immediately pelting each other with handfuls of wet sand. Chubby and I followed at a sedate pace more in keeping with our years. Still wearing his vividly striped pyjamas, Chubby lowered his massive hams into the sea.

'I got to tell you, man, that feels good,' he admitted gravely. I drew deeply on my cheroot as I sat beside him waist deep, then I handed him the butt.

'We lost five days, Chubby,' I said, and immediately he scowled.

'Let's get busy,' he growled, sitting in the lagoon in yellow and purple striped pyjamas, cheroot in his mouth, like a big brown bullfrog.

From the peak we looked down into the shallow waters of the lagoon and although they were still a little murky with spindrift and churned sand, yet the whaleboat was clearly visible. She had drifted sideways in the bay and was lying on the bottom in twenty feet of water with the yellow tarpaulin still covering her deck.

We raised the whaleboat with air bags and once her gunwales broke the surface we were able to bale her out and row her into the beach. The rest of that day was needed to unload the waterlogged cargo, clean and dry it, pump the air bottles, get the motors aboard and prepare for the next visit to Gunfire Reef.

I was beginning to become seriously concerned by the delays which had left us sitting on the island, day after day, while Manny Resnick and his merry men cut away the lead we have started with.

That evening we discussed it around the campfire, and agreed that we also had made no progress in ten days other than to confirm that part of the *Dawn Light*'s wreckage had fallen into the pool.

However, the tides were set fair for an early start in the morning and Chubby ran us through the channel with hardly sufficient light to recognize the coral snags, and when we took up our station in the back of the reef the sun was only just showing its blazing upper rim above the horizon.

During the five days we had lain ashore, Sherry's hands had almost entirely healed, and although I suggested tactfully that she should allow Chubby to accompany me for the next few days, my tact and concern were wasted. Sherry North was suited and finned and Chubby sat in the stern beside the motors holding us on station.

Sherry and I went down fast and entered the forest of sea bamboo, picking up position from the markers that Chubby and I had left on our last dive.

We were working in close to the base of the coral cliff and I placed Sherry on the inside berth where it would be easier to hold position in the search pattern while she orientated herself.

We had hardly begun the first leg and had swum fifty feet from the last marker when Sherry tapped urgently on her bottles to attract my attention and I pushed my way through the bamboo to her.

She was hanging against the side of the coral cliff upside down like a bat, closely examining a fall of coral and debris that had slid down to the floor of the pool. She was in deep shade under the loom of dark coral so I was at her side before I saw what had attracted her.

Propped against the cliff, its bottom end lying in the mound of debris and weed, was a long cylindrical object which itself was heavily infested with marine growth and had already been partially ingested by the living coral.

Yet its size and regular shape indicated that it was manmade—for it was nine feet long and twenty inches thick, perfectly rounded and slightly tapered.

Sherry was studying it with interest and when I came up she turned to meet me and made signs of incomprehension.

I had recognized what it was immediately and the skin of my forearms and at the nape of my neck felt prickly with excitement. I made a pistol of my thumb and forefinger and mimed the act of firing it, but she did not understand and shook her head so I scribbled quickly on the underwater slate and showed it to her.

'Cannon.'

She nodded vigorously, rolled her eyes and blew bubbles to register triumph before turning back to the cannon.

It was about the correct size to be one of the long nine-pounders that had formed part of the *Dawn Light*'s armament but there was no chance that I would be able to read any inscription upon it, for the surface was crocodile-skinned with growth and corrosion. Unlike the bronze bell that Jimmy North had recovered, it had not been buried in the sand to protect it.

I floated down along the massive barrel examining it closely and almost immediately found another cannon in the deeper gloom nearer the cliff. However, three-quarters of this weapon had been incorporated into the cliff, built into it by the living coral polyps.

I swam in closer, ducking under the first barrel, and went into the jumble of debris and fallen coral blocks. I was within two feet of this amorphous mass when with a shock which constricted my breathing and flushed warmly through my blood I recognized what I was looking at.

Quickly and excitedly I finned over the mound of debris, finding where it ended and the unbroken coral began, forcing my way up through the sea bamboo to estimate its size, and pausing to examine any opening or irregularity in it.

The total mass of debris was the size of a couple of railway pullman coaches, but it was only when I pushed aside a larger floating clump of weed and peered into the squared opening of a gun port, from which the muzzle of a cannon still protruded and which had not been completely altered in shape by the encroaching coral, that I was certain that what we had discovered was the entire forward section of the frigate *Dawn Light*, broken off just behind the main mast.

I looked around wildly for Sherry and saw her finned feet protruding from another portion of the wreckage. I pulled her out, removed her mouthpiece and kissed her lustily before replacing it. She was laughing with excitement and when I signalled her that we were ascending, she shook her head vehemently and shot away from me to continue her explorations. It was fully fifteen minutes later that I was able to drag her away and take her up to the whaleboat.

We both began talking at once the moment we had the rubber mouthpieces out of the way. My voice is louder than hers, but she is more persistent. It took me some minutes to assert my rights as expedition leader and I could begin to describe it to Chubby.

'It's the *Dawn Light* sure enough. The weight of her armament and cargo must have pulled her down the instant she was clear of the reef. She went down like a stone, and she is lying against the foot of the cliff. Some of her cannons have fallen out of the hull, and they're lying jumbled around it—'

'We didn't recognize it at first,' Sherry chimed in again, just when I had her quietened down. 'It's like a rubbish dump. Just an enormous heap.'

'From what I could judge she must have broken her back abaft the main mast, but she's been smashed up badly for most of her length. The cannon must have torn up her gundeck and it's only the two ports nearest the bows that are intact—'

'How does she lie?' Chubby demanded, coming immediately to the pith of the matter.

'She's bottom up,' I admitted. 'She must have rolled as she went down.'

'That makes it a real problem, unless you can get in at a gun port or under the waist,' Chubby growled.

'I had a good look,' I told him, 'but I couldn't find a point at which we could penetrate the hull. Even the gunports are solid with growth.'

Chubby shook his head mournfully. 'Man, looks like this place is badly hexed,' and immediately all three of us made the cross-fingered sign against it.

Angelo told him primly, 'You talking up a storm. Shouldn't say that, hear?' but Chubby shook his head again, and his face collapsed into pessimistic folds.

I slapped him on his back and asked him, 'Is it true that you pass iced water—even in hot weather?' and my attempt at humour made him look as cheerful as an unemployed undertaker.

'Oh, leave Chubby alone,' Sherry came to his rescue. 'Let's go down again and try and find a break in the hull.'

'We'll take half an hour's rest,' I said, 'a smoke and a mug of coffee— then we'll go take another look.'

We stayed down so long on the second dive that Chubby had to sound the triple recall signal—and when we surfaced the pool was boiling. The cyclone had left a legacy of high surf, and on the rising tide it was coming in heavily across the reef and pounding in through the gap, higher in the channel than we had ever known it.

We clung to the thwarts in silence as Chubby took us home on a wild ride, and it was only when we entered the quieter waters of the lagoon that we could continue the discussion.

'She's as tight as the Chatwood lock on the national safe deposit,' I told them. 'The one gun port is blocked by the cannon, and I got into the other about four feet before I ran into part of the bulkhead which must have collapsed. It's the den of a big old moray eel that looks like a python—he's got teeth on him like a bulldog and he and I aren't friends.'

'What about the waist?' Chubby demanded.

'No,' I said, 'she's settled down heavily, and the coral has closed her up.'

Chubby put on an expression which meant that he had told us so. I could have beaten him over the head with a spanner, he was so smug— but I ignored him and showed them the piece of woodwork that I had prised off the hull with a crowbar.

'The coral has closed everything up solid. It's like those old forests that have been petrified into stone. The *Dawn Light* is a ship of stone,

armour-plated with coral. There is only one way we will get into her—
and that is to pop her open.'

Chubby nodded, 'That's the way to do it,' and Sherry wanted to
know, 'But if you use explosive, won't it just blow everything to
bits?'

'We won't use an atomic bomb,' I told her. 'We'll start with half a
stick in the forward gunport. Just enough to kick out a chunk of that
coral plating,' and I turned back to Chubby. 'We need that gelignite
right away, every hour is precious now, Chubby. We've got a good
moon. Can you take us back to St Mary's tonight?' and Chubby did
not bother to answer such a superfluous question. It was an indirect slur
on his seamanship.

There was a horned moon, with a pale halo round it. The atmosphere
was still full of dust from the big winds. The stars also were misty and
very far away, but the cyclone had blown great masses of oceanic
plankton into the channel so that the sea was a glowing phosphorescent
mass wherever it was disturbed.

Our wake glowed green and long, spread behind us like a peacock's
tail, and the movement of fish beneath the surface shone like meteors.
Sherry dipped her hand over the side and brought it out burning with
a weird and liquid flame, and she cooed with wonder.

Later when she was sleepy she lay against my chest under the tarpaulin I had spread to keep off the damp and we listened to the booming
of the giant manta rays out in the open water as they leaped high and
fell to smack the surface of the sea with their flat bellies and tons of
dead weight.

It was long after midnight when we raised the lights of St Mary's
like a diamond necklace around the throat of the island.

The streets were utterly deserted as we left the whaleboat at her
moorings and walked up to Chubby's house. Missus Chubby opened
to us in a dressing-gown that made Chubby's pyjamas look conserva-
tive. She had her hair in large pink plastic curlers. I had never seen her
without a hat before and I was surprised that she was not as bald as her
spouse. They looked so alike in every other way.

She gave us coffee before Sherry and I climbed into the pick-up and
drove to Turtle Bay. The bedclothes were damp and needed airing but
neither of us complained.

I stopped at the Post Office in the early morning and my box was
half filled, mostly with fishing equipment catalogues and junk mail,
but there were a few letters from old clients inquiring for charter—that
gave me a pang—and one of the buff cable envelopes which I opened
last. Cables have always borne bad news for me. Whenever I see one

of those envelopes with my name peering out of the window like a long-term prisoner I have this queasy feeling in my stomach.

The message read: 'MANDRAKE SAILED CAPE TOWN OUTWARD BOUND ZANZIBAR 12.00 HOURS FRIDAY 16TH. STEVE.'

My premonitions of evil were confirmed. *Mandrake* had left Cape Town six days ago. She had made a faster passage than I would have believed possible. I felt like rushing to the top of Coolie Peak to search the horizon. Instead I passed the cable to Sherry and drove down to Frobisher Street.

Fred Coker was just opening the street door of his travel agency as I parked outside Missus Eddy's store and sent Sherry in with a shopping list while I walked on down the street to the Agency.

Fred Coker had not seen me since I had dropped him moaning on the floor of his own morgue, and now he was sitting at his desk in a white shark-skin suit and wearing a necktie which depicted a Hula girl on a palm-lined beach and the legend 'Welcome to St Mary's! Pearl of the Indian Ocean.'

He looked up with a smile that went well with the tie, but the moment he recognized me his expression changed to utter dismay. He let out a bleat like an orphan lamb and shot out of his chair, heading for the back room.

I blocked his escape and he backed away before me, his gold-rimmed glasses glittering like the sheen of nervous sweat that covered his face until the chair caught him in the back of his knees and he collapsed into it. Only then did I give him my big friendly grin—and I thought he would faint with relief.

'How are you, Mister Coker?' He tried to answer but his voice failed him. Instead he nodded his head so rapidly that I understood he was very well. 'I want you to do me a favour.'

'Anything,' he gabbled, suddenly recovering the power of speech. 'Anything, Mister Harry, you have only to ask.'

Despite his protestations it took him only a few minutes to recover his courage and wits. He listened to my very reasonable request for three cases of high explosive, and went into a pantomime to impress me with the utter impossibility of compliance. He rolled his eyes, sucked in his cheeks and made clucking noises with his tongue.

'I want it by noon tomorrow—latest,' and he clasped his forehead as if in agony.

'And if it's not here by twelve o'clock precisely, you and I will continue our discussion on the insurance premiums—'

He dropped his hand and sat upright, his expression once more willing and intelligent.

'That's not necessary, Mister Harry. I can get what you ask—but it will cost a great deal of money. Three hundred dollars a case.'

'Put it on the slate,' I told him.

'Mister Harry!' he cried, 'you know I cannot extend credit.'

I was silent, but I slitted my eyes, clenched my jaws and began to breathe deeply.

'Very well,' he said hurriedly. 'Until the end of the month, then.'

'That's very decent of you, Mister Coker.'

'It's a pleasure, Mister Harry,' he assured me. 'A very great pleasure.'

'There is just one other thing, Mr Coker,' and I could see him mentally quail at my next request, but he braced himself like a hero.

'In the near future I expect to be exporting a small consignment to Zürich in Switzerland.' He sat a little forward in his seat. 'I do not wish to be bothered with customs formalities—you understand?'

'I understand, Mister Harry.'

'Do you ever have requests to send the body of one of your customers back to the near and dear?'

'I beg your pardon?' He looked confused.

'If a tourist were to pass away on the island—say of a heart attack—you would be called on to embalm his corpse for posterity and to ship it out in a casket. Am I correct?'

'It has happened before,' he agreed. 'On three occasions.'

'Good, so you are familiar with the procedure?'

'I am, Mister Harry.'

'Mister Coker, lay in a casket and get yourself a pile of the correct forms. I'll be shipping soon.'

'May I ask what you intend to export—in lieu of a cadaver?' He phrased the question delicately.

'You may well ask, Mister Coker.'

I drove down to the fort and spoke to the President's secretary. He was in a meeting, but he would see me at one o'clock if I would care to lunch with him in his office. I accepted the invitation and, to pass the hours until then, I drove up the track to Coolie Peak as far as the pick-up would take me. There I parked it and walked onto the ruins of the old lookout and signal station. I sat on the parapet looking out across a vista of sea and green islands while I smoked a cheroot and did my last bit of careful planning and decision-making, glad of this opportunity to make certain of my plans before committing myself to them.

I thought of what I wanted from life, and decided it was three things—Turtle Bay, *Wave Dancer II* and Sherry North, not necessarily in that order of preference.

To stay on at Turtle Bay, I had to keep a clean pair of hands in St Mary's, to have *Wave Dancer II* I needed cash and plenty of it, and Sherry North—well, that took plenty of hard thought, and at the end of it my cheroot had burned to a stub and I ground it out on the stone parapet. I took a deep breath and squared my shoulders.

'Courage, Harry me lad,' I said and drove down to the fort.

The President was delighted to see me, coming out into the reception room to welcome me and rising on tip-toe to place an arm around my shoulders and lead me into his office.

It was a room like a baronial hall with a beamed ceiling, panelled walls and English landscapes in massive ornate frames and dark smoky looking oils. The diamond-paned window rose from the floor to the ceiling and looked out over the harbour, and the floor was lush with oriental carpets.

Luncheon was spread on the oaken conference table below the windows—smoked fish, cheese and fruit with a bottle of Château Lafite '62 from which the cork had been drawn.

The President poured two crystal glasses of the deep red wine, offered one to me and then plopped two cubes of ice into his own glass. He grinned impishly as he saw my startled expression. 'Sacrilege, isn't it?' He raised the glass of rare wine and ice cubes to me. 'But, Harry, I know what I like. What is suitable on the Rue Royale isn't necessarily suitable on St Mary's.'

'Right on, sir!' I grinned back at him and we drank.

'Now, my boy, what did you want to talk to me about?'

I found a message that Sherry had gone to visit Missus Chubby when I arrived back at the shack, so I went out onto the veranda with a cold beer. I went over my meeting with President Bingle, reviewing it word for word, and found myself satisfied. I thought I had covered all the openings—except the ones I might need to escape through.

Three wooden cases marked 'Canned Fish. Produce of Norway' arrived on the ten o'clock plane from the mainland addressed to Coker's Travel Agency.

'Eat your liver, Alfred Nobel,' I thought when I saw the legend as Fred Coker unloaded them from the hearse at Turtle Bay and I placed them in the rear of the pick-up under the canvas cover.

'Until the end of the month then, Mister Harry,' said Fred Coker, like the leading man from a Shakespearian tragedy.

'Depend upon it, Mister Coker,' I assured him and he drove away through the palms.

Sherry had finished packing away the stores. She looked so different from yesterday's siren, with her hair scraped back, dressed in one of my old shirts, which fitted her like a nightdress, and a pair of faded jeans with raggedy legs cut off below the knees.

I helped her carry the cases out to the pick-up, and we climbed into the cab.

'Next time we come back here we'll be rich,' I said, and started the motor, forgetting to make the sign against the hex.

We ground up through the palm grove, hit the main road below the pineapple fields and climbed up the ridge.

We came out on the crest above the town and the harbour.

'God damn it!' I shouted angrily, and hit the brakes hard, swinging off the road onto the verge so violently that the pineapple truck following us swerved to avoid running into our rear, and the driver hung out of his window to shout abuse as he passed.

'What is it?' Sherry pulled herself off the dashboard where my manoeuvre had thrown her. 'Are you crazy?'

It was a bright and cloudless day, the air so clear that every detail of the lovely white and blue ship stood out like a drawing. She lay at the entrance to Grand Harbour on the moorings usually reserved for visiting cruise ships, or the regular mail ship.

She was flying a festival burst of signal flags and I could see her crew in tropical whites lining the rail and staring at the shore. The harbour tender was running out to her, carrying the harbour master, the customs inspector and Dr MacNab.

'*Mandrake*?' Sherry asked.

Mandrake and Manny Resnick,' I agreed, and swung the truck into a U-turn across the road.

'What are you going to do?' she asked.

'One thing I'm not going to do is show myself in St Mary's while Manny and his fly lads are ashore. I've met most of them before in circumstances which are likely to have burned my lovely features clearly into even their rudimentary brains.'

Down the hill at the first bus stop beyond the turn off to Turtle Bay was the small General Dealers' Store which supplied me with eggs, milk, butter and other perishables. The proprietor was delighted to see me and he flourished my outstanding bill like a winning lottery ticket. I paid him, and then closed the door of his back office while I used the telephone.

Chubby did not have a phone, but his next-door neighbour called him to speak to me.

'Chubby,' I told him, 'that big white floating brothel at the mail ship mooring is no friend of ours.'

'What you want me to do, Harry?'

'Move fast. Cover the water cans with stump nets and make like you are going fishing. Get out to sea and come around to Turtle Bay. We'll load from the beach and run for Gunfire Reef as soon as it's dark.'

'I'll be in the bay in two hours,' he said and hung up.

He was there in one hour forty-five minutes. One of the reasons I liked working with him is that you can put money on his promises.

As soon as the sun set and visibility was down to a hundred yards we slipped out of Turtle Bay, and we were well clear of the island by the time the moon came up.

Huddled under the tarpaulin, sitting on a case of gelignite, Sherry and I discussed the arrival of *Mandrake* in Grand Harbour.

'First thing Manny will do, he will send his lads out with a pocketful of bread to ask a few questions around the shops and bars. "Anyone seen Harry Fletcher?" and they'll be queueing up to tell him all about it. How Mister Harry chartered Chubby Andrews' stump boat, and how they been diving looking for sea shells. If he gets really lucky somebody will point him in the direction of Frederick Coker Esquire—and Fred will fall over himself to tell all, as long as the price is right.'

'Then what will he do?'

'He will have an attack of the vapours when he hears that I didn't drown in the Severn. When he recovers from that, he will send a team out to ransack and search the shack at Turtle Bay. He will draw a dud card there. Then the lovely Miss Lorna Page will lead them all to the alleged site of the wreck off Big Gull. That will keep them happy and busy for two or three days—until they find they have nothing but the ship's bell.'

'Then?'

'Well, then Manny is going to get mad. I think Lorna is in line for some unpleasantness—but after that I don't know what will happen. All we can do is try to keep out of sight and work like a tribe of beavers to get the Colonel's goodies out of the wreck.'

The next day the state of the tides was such that we could not navigate the channel before the late morning. It gave us time to make preparations. I opened one of the cases of gelignite and took out ten of the waxy yellow sticks. I reclosed the case and buried it with the other two in the sandy soil of the palm grove, well away from the camp.

Then Chubby and I assembled and checked the blasting equipment. It was a home-made contraption, but it had proved its efficiency before. It consisted of two nine-volt transistor batteries in a simple switchbox. We had four reels of light insulated copper wire, and a cigar-box of detonators. Each of the lethal silver tubes was carefully wrapped in cotton wool. There was also a selection of time-delayed detonators of the pencil type in the box.

Chubby and I isolated ourselves while we worked with them, clamping the electric detonators to the hand-made terminals that I had soldered for the purpose.

The use of high explosives is simple in theory, and nerve-racking in practice. Even an idiot can wire it up and hit the button, but in its refined form it becomes an art.

I have seen a medium-sized tree survive a blast of half a case, losing only its leaves and some of its bark—but with half a stick I can drop the same tree neatly across a road to block it effectively, without removing a single leaf. I consider myself something of an artist, and I had taught Chubby all I knew. He was a natural, although he could never be termed an artist—his glee in the proceedings was too frankly childlike. Chubby just naturally loved to blow things up. He hummed happily to himself as he worked with the detonators.

We took up position in the pool a few minutes before noon and I went down alone, armed only with a Nemrod captive air spear gun with a barbed crucifix head I had designed and made myself. The point was needle-sharp, and it was multi-barbed for the first six inches; twenty-four small sharp barbs, like those used by Batonka tribesmen when they spear catfish in the Zambesi River. Behind the barbs was the crucifix, a four-inch cross-piece which would prevent the victim slipping down the shaft close enough to attack me when I held the reverse end. The line was five hundred pound blue nylon and there was a twenty foot loop of it under the barrel of the spear gun.

I finned down onto the overgrown heap of wreckage and I settled myself comfortably beside the gunport and closed my eyes for a few seconds to accustom them to the gloom, then I peered cautiously into the dark square opening, pushing the barrel of the spear gun ahead of me.

The dark slimy coils of the Moray eel slithered and unwound as it sensed my presence, and it reared threateningly, displaying the fearsome irregular yellow fangs. In the gloom the eyes were black and bright, catching the feeble light like those of a cat.

He was a huge old mugger, thick as my calf and longer than the stretch of both my arms. The waving mane of his dorsal fin was angrily erected as he threatened me.

I lined him up carefully, waiting for him to turn his head and offer a better target. It was a scary few moments, I had one shot and if that was badly placed he would fly at me. I had seen a captive Moray chew mouthfuls out of the woodwork of a dinghy. Those fangs would tear easily through rubber suit and flesh, right down to the bone.

He was weaving slowly, like a flaring cobra, watching me and the range was extreme for accurate shooting. I waited for the moment, and at last he went into the second stage of aggression. He blew up his throat and turned slightly to offer me a profile.

'My God,' I thought, 'I once used to do this for fun,' and I took up the slack in the trigger. The gas hissed viciously and the plunger thudded to the end of its travel as it threw the spear. It flew in a long blur with the line whipping out behind it.

I had aimed for the dark earlike marking at the back of the skull, and I was an inch and a half high and two inches right. The Moray exploded into a spinning, whipping ball of coils that seemed to fill the whole gunport. I dropped the gun and with a push of my fins I shot forward and got a grip of the hilt of the spear. It kicked and thumped in my hands as the eel wound its thick dark body around the shaft. I drew him out of his lair, pinned by a thick bite of skin and rubbery muscle to the barbed head.

His mouth was opened in a silent screech of fury, and he unwound his body and let it fly and writhe like a pennant in a high wind.

The tail slapped into my face, dislodging my mask. Water flooded into my nose and eyes and I had to blow it clear before I could begin the ascent.

Now the eel twisted its head back at an impossible angle and closed the dreadfully gaping jaws on the metal shaft of the spear. I could hear the fangs grinding and squeaking in the steel, and there were bright silver scratches where it had bitten.

I came out through the surface holding aloft my prize. I heard Sherry squeal with horror at the writhing snake-like monster, and Chubby grunted, 'Come to papa, you beauty,' and he leaned out to grasp the spear and lift the eel aboard. He was showing his plastic gums in a happy grin for Moray eel was Chubby's favourite food. He held the neck against the gunwale and, with an expert sweep of his bait-knife, lopped the monstrous head cleanly away, letting it fall into the pool.

'Miss Sherry,' he said, 'you going to love the taste of him.'

'Never!' Sherry shuddered, and drew herself farther away from the bleeding, wriggling carcass.

'Okay, my children, let's have the gelly.' Angelo had the underwater carry-net ready to pass to me, and Sherry slid in over the side prepared to dive. She had the reel of insulated wire and she paid it out smoothly as we went down.

Once again I went directly to the now untenanted gunport and crept into it. The breech of the cannon was jammed solidly against the mass of debris beyond.

I chose two sites to place my shots. I wanted to kick the cannon aside, using it like a giant lever to tear out a slab of the petrified planking. The second shot fired simultaneously would blow into the wall of debris that barred entry to the gundeck.

I wired the shots firmly into place. Sherry passed the end of the line in to me and I snipped and bared the copper wire with the side-cutters before connecting it up to the terminals.

I checked the job once it was finished and then backed out of the port. Sherry was sitting cross-legged on the hull with the reel on her lap and I grinned at her around my mouthpiece and gave her the thumbs up before I retrieved my spear gun from where I had dropped it.

When we climbed over the side of the whaleboat Chubby had the battery switchbox beside him on the thwart and it was wired up. He was scowling with anticipation, as he crouched possessively over the blaster. It would have taken physical force to deprive him of the pleasure of hitting the button.

'Ready to shoot, skipper,' he growled.

'Shoot her then, Chubby.' He fussed with the box a little longer, drawing out the pleasure, then he turned the switch.

The surface of the pool bounced and shivered and we felt the bump come up through the bottom of the boat. Many seconds later there was a surge and frothing of bubbles, as though somebody had dropped a ton of Alka Seltzer into the pool. Slowly it cleared.

'I want you to put the trousers of your suit on, my sweeting,' I told Sherry, and predictably she took the order as an invitation to debate its correctness.

'Why, the water is warm?'

'Gloves and bootees also,' I said, as I began to pull on my own rubber full-length pants. 'If the hull is open we may penetrate her on this dive. You'll need protection against snags.'

Convinced at last, she did what she should have done without question. I still had a lot of work to do before she was properly trained, I thought, as I assembled the other equipment I needed for this descent.

I took the sealed unit underwater torch, the jenny bar and a coil of light nylon line and waited while Sherry completed the major task of wiggling her bottom into the tight rubber pants, assisted faithfully by Angelo. Once she had them hoisted and had buttoned the crotch piece, we were set to go.

When we were half way down, we came upon the first dead fish floating belly up in the misty blue depths. There were hundreds of them that the explosions had killed or maimed, and they ranged in size from fingerlings to big striped snapper and reef bass as long as my arm. I felt a pang of remorse at the massacre I had perpetrated, but consoled myself with the thought I had killed less than a bluefin tunny would in a single day's feeding.

We went down through this killing ground, and the light caught the eddying and drifting carcasses so they blinked and shone like dying stars in a smoky azure sky.

The bottom of the pool was murky with particles of sand and other material stirred up by the shock of the blast. There was a hole torn in the cover of sea bamboo and we went down into it.

I saw at once that I had achieved my purpose. The explosion had kicked the massive cannon out of the hull, tearing it like a rotten tooth from the black and ancient maw of the gunport. It had fallen to the bed of the pool surrounded by the debris that it had brought away with it.

The upper lip of the gunport had been knocked out, enlarging the opening so that a man might stand almost upright in it. When I flashed the torch into the darkness beyond, I saw that it was a turgid fog of suspended dirt and particles which would take time to settle. My impatience would not allow that, however, and as we settled on the hull I checked my time elapse and air reserves. Quickly I calculated our working time, allowing for my two previous descents which would necessitate additional decompression. I reckoned we had seventeen minutes' safe time before beginning the ascent and I set the swivel ring on my wrist watch before preparing for the penetration.

I used the jettisoned cannon as a convenient anchor point on which to fix the end of the nylon line and then rose again to the opening, paying it out behind me as I went.

I had to remove Sherry North from the gunport; in the few seconds while I was busy with the line she had almost disappeared into the hole in the hull. I made angry signs at her to keep clear, and in return she made an unladylike gesture with two fingers which I pretended not to see.

Gingerly I entered the gunport and found that the visibility was down to about three feet in the murky soup.

The shots had only partially moved the blockage beyond the spot where the cannon had lain. There seemed to be a gap beyond but it needed to be enlarged before I could get through. I used the jenny bar to prise a lump of the wreckage away and discovered that it was the heavy gun carriage that was causing most of the blockage.

Working in freshly blasted wreckage is a delicate business, for it is impossible to know how critically balanced the mass may be. Even the slightest disturbance can bring the whole weight of it sliding and crashing down upon the trespasser, pinning and crushing him beneath it.

I worked slowly and deliberately, ignoring the regular thumps on my rump with which Sherry signalled her burning impatience. Once when I emerged with a section of shattered planking, she took my slate and wrote on it 'I am smaller!!' and underlined the 'smaller' twice in case the double exclamation mark was not noticed when she thrust the slate two inches from my nose. I returned her Churchillian salute and went back to my burrowing.

I had now cleared the area sufficiently to see that my only remaining obstacle was the heavy timber bulk of the gun carriage which was hanging at a drunken angle across the entry to the gundeck. The jenny bar was totally ineffective against this mass, and I could abandon the effort and return with another charge of gelignite tomorrow or I could take a chance.

I glanced at my time elapse and saw that I had been busy for twelve minutes. I reckoned that I had probably been using air more wastefully than usual during my recent exertions. Nevertheless, I decided to take a flier.

I passed the torch and jenny bar out to Sherry, and worked my way carefully back into the opening. I got my shoulder under the upper end of the gun carriage, and moved my feet around until I had a firm stance. When I was solidly placed, I took a good breath of air and began to lift.

Slowly I increased the strain until I was thrusting upwards with all the strength of my legs and back. I felt my face and throat swelling with pumping blood and my eyes felt ready to jump out of their sockets. Nothing moved, and I took another lungful of air and tried again, but this time throwing all my weight on the timber beam in a single explosive effort.

It gave way, and I felt like Samson who had pulled the temple down on his own head. I lost my balance and tumbled backwards in a storm of falling debris that groaned and grated as it fell, thudding and bumping around me.

When silence had settled, I found myself in utter darkness, a thick pea soup of swirling filth that blotted out the light. I tried to move, and

found my leg pinned. Panic rushed through me in an icy wave and I
fought frantically to free my leg. It took only half-a-dozen terrified
kicks before I realized that I had escaped with great good luck. The
gun carriage had missed my foot by a quarter of an inch, and had fallen
across the rubber swimming fin. I pulled my foot out of the shoe,
abandoning it, and groped my way out into the open.

Sherry was waiting eagerly for news, and I wiped the slate and wrote
'OPEN!!' underlining the word twice. She pointed into the gunport,
demanding permission to enter and I checked my time elapse. We had
two minutes, So I nodded and led the way in.

Flashing the beam of the torch ahead I had visibility of eighteen
inches, enough to find the opening I had cleared. There was just
sufficient clearance to allow me through without fouling my air bottles
or breathing hose.

I paid out the nylon line behind me, like Theseus in the labyrinth of
the Minotaur so as not to lose my direction in the *Dawn Light*'s warren
of decks and companionways.

Sherry followed me along the line. I could feel her hand touch my
foot and brush my leg as she groped after me.

Beyond the blockage, the water cleared a little, and we found ourselves in the low wide chamber of the gundeck. It was murky and
mysterious, with strange shapes strewn about us in profusion. I saw
other gun carriages, cannonballs strewn loosely or in heaps against
angles and corners, and other equipment so altered by long immersion
as to be unrecognizable.

We moved slowly forward, our fins stirring up fresh whirlpools of
dirt and mud. Here also there were dead fish floating about us, although
I noticed some of the red reef crayfish scrambling away like monstrous
spiders into the depths of the ship. They at least had survived the blast
in their armoured carapaces.

I played the beam of the torch on the deck above our heads, looking
for the entry point to the lower decks and the holds. With the ship lying
upside down, I had to keep trying to relate the existing geography of the
wreck to the drawing I had studied.

About fifteen feet from our entry point I found the forecastle ladder,
another dark square opening above my head, and I rose into it, my
bubbles blowing upwards in a silver shower and running like liquid
mercury across the bulkheads and decking. The ladder was rotted so
that it fell to pieces at my touch, the pieces hanging suspended in the
water around my head as I went on into the lower deck.

This was a narrow and crowded alleyway, probably serving the
passenger cabins and officers' mess. The claustrophobic atmosphere

reminded me of the appalling conditions in which the crew of the frigate must have lived.

I ventured gingerly along this passage, attracted powerfully to the doorways on either hand which promised all manner of fascinating discoveries. I resisted their temptation and finned on down the long deck until it ended abruptly against a heavy timber bulkhead.

This would be the outer wall of the well of the forward hold, where it pierced the deck and went down into the ship's belly.

Satisfied with what we had achieved, I turned the beam of the torch onto my wrist and realized with a guilty thrill that we had overrun our working time by four minutes. Every second was taking us closer to the dreaded danger of empty air bottles and uncompleted decompression stops.

I grabbed Sherry's wrist and gave her the cut-throat hand signal for danger before tapping my wrist watch. She understood immediately, and followed me meekly on the long slow journey back through the hull along the guiding line. Already I could feel the stiffening of the demand valve, as it gave me air more reluctantly now that the bottles were almost exhausted.

We came out into the open and I made certain that Sherry was by my side before I looked upwards. What I saw above me made my breathing choke in my throat, and the horror I felt turned to a warm oily liquid sensation in my bowels.

The pool of Gunfire Break had been transformed into a bloody arena. Attracted by the tons of dead fish that had been killed by the blast, the deep-water killer sharks had arrived in their scores. The scent of flesh and blood, together with the excited movements of their fellows transmitted to them through the water, had driven them into that mindless savagery known as the feeding frenzy.

Quickly I drew Sherry back into the gunport and we cowered there, looking up at the huge gliding shapes so clearly silhouetted against the light source of the surface.

Among the shoals of smaller sharks there were at least two dozen of the ugly beasts that the islanders called Albacore shark. They were barrel-bodied and swing-bodied, big powerful fish with rounded snouts and wide grinning jaws. They swirled about the pool like some grotesque carousel, with their tails waggling and their mouths opening mechanically to gulp down shreds of flesh. I knew them for greedy but stupid animals, easily discouraged by any aggressive display when not in feeding frenzy. Now they were in intense excitation they would be dangerous, yet I would have accepted the risk of a decompression ascent if it had been for them alone.

What truly appalled me were two other long lithe shapes that sped silently about the pool, turning with a single powerful flick of the long swallow tail, so that the pointed nose almost touched the tip of the tail, then gliding away again with all the power and grace of an eagle in flight.

When either one of these terrible fish paused to feed, the sickle-moon mouth opened and the multiple rows of teeth came erect like the quills of a porcupine and flared outwards.

They were a matched pair, each about twelve feet in length from nose to tail-tip, with the standing blade of the dorsal fin as long as a man's arm; they were slaty blue across the back and with snowy white bellies and dark tips to tail and fins, they could bite a man in half and swallow the pieces whole.

One of them saw us crouching in the mouth of the gunport, and it turned sharply and came down over us, planing a few feet above us as we cowered back into the gloom so that I could clearly see the long trailing spikes of the male reproductive organs.

These were the dreaded white death sharks, the most vicious fish of all the seas, and I knew that to attempt to ascend in the clear and decompress adequately with limited air and no protection would be certain death.

If I were to get Sherry out alive I would have to take risks that in any other circumstances would be unthinkable.

Quickly I scribbled on the slate: 'STAY!! I am free ascending for air and gun.'

She read the message and immediately shook her head in refusal and made urgent signs to prevent me, but already I had pulled the pin out of the quick release buckle of my harness and I took the last deep, chest-swelling breath before I thrust my scuba set into her hands. I dropped my weight belt to give myself buoyancy and slid down the side of the hull, using the tumble home to cover me as I finned swiftly for the cover of the cliff.

I had left Sherry what remained of my air supplies, perhaps five or six minutes' breathing if she used it sparingly, and now with only the air that I held in my lungs I had to run the gauntlet of the pool and try for the surface.

I reached the cliff and began to go up, close in against the coral, hoping that my dark suit would blend with the shades. I went up with my back to the coral, facing out into the open pool where the great sinister shapes still swirled and milled.

Twenty feet from the bottom and the air in my lungs was expanding rapidly as the pressure of water decreased. I could not hold it in or it would rupture the tissue of my lungs. I let it trickle from my lips, a silver beacon of bubbles that one of the white death sharks noticed immediately.

He rolled and turned, dashing across the pool with slashing strokes of his tail, bearing down upon me.

Desperately I glanced up the cliff and found six feet above me one of the small caves in the rotten coral. I dived into it just as the shark flashed past me, turned and sped back for a second pass as I shrank into my shallow shelter. The shark lost interest and swirled away to pick up the falling-leaf body of a dead snapper, gulping it down convulsively.

My lungs were throbbing and pumping now for the oxygen had been all absorbed from the air I held, and the carbon-dioxide was building up in my blood. Soon I would begin to black out into anoxia.

I left the shelter of the cave, but, still following the cliff, I drove upwards as hard as I could with the single swimming fin, wishing bitterly for the use of the other still trapped under the gun carriage.

Again I had to release expanding air as I rose, and I knew that in my veins nitrogen was also decompressing too rapidly and soon it would turn to gas and bubble like champagne in my blood.

Above me I saw the silvery moving mirror of the surface and the black cigar shape of the whaleboat's hull suspended upon it. I was coming up fast and I glanced down again. Far below me I could see the shark pack still milling and turning. It looked as though I had escaped their notice.

My lungs burned with the craving for air, and the blood pounded in my temples as I decided that the time had arrived when I must forsake the shelter of the cliff and cross the open pool to the whaleboat.

I kicked out and shot towards the whaleboat where it lay a hundred feet from the reef. Half way across I glanced down and saw one of the white death's had seen me and was chasing. It came up from the blue depths with incredible speed, and terror gave me new strength as I drove for the surface and the boat.

I was looking down, watching the shark come. I seemed to swell up in size as it rushed towards me. Every detail was burned into my mind in those frantic seconds. I saw the hog's snout with the two slitted nostrils, the golden eyes with the black pupils like arrowheads, the broad blue back from which stood the tall executioner's blade of the dorsal fin.

I came out through the surface so fast that I broke clear to my waist, and I turned in the air and got my good arm over the gunwale of the boat. With all my strength I swung my body forward and jack-knifed my legs up under my chin.

In that instant the white death struck, the water exploded about me as he burst through the surface, I felt the harsh gritty skin tear across the legs of my suit as he brushed against me, then there was a shuddering crash as he struck the hull of the whaleboat.

I saw Chubby and Angelo's startled faces as the boat heeled over and rocked wildly. My violent contortion had thrown the shark off his run, and he had missed my legs and collided with the hull.

Now with one more desperate kick and heave I tumbled over the gunwale and fell into the bottom of the whaleboat. Again the shark crashed into the hull as I went over, missing me again by inches.

I lay there pumping air into my aching lungs, great sweet gulps of it that made me light-headed and giddy as on strong wine.

Chubby was yelling at me, 'Where is Miss Sherry? That big Johnny Uptail get Miss Sherry?'

I rolled onto my back, panting and sobbing for the precious air.

'Spare lungs,' I gasped. 'Sherry waiting in the wreck. She needs air.'

Chubby leaped into the bows and dragged the canvas sheet off the extra scuba sets stacked there. In a crisis he is the kind of man I like to have covering for me.

'Angelo,' he growled, 'get them Johnny pills.' They were a pack of copper acetate shark repellent pills which I had ordered from an American sports good catalogue and for which Chubby had professed a deep and abiding scorn. 'Let's see if those fancy things are any bloody good.'

I had breathed enough to drag myself off the floorboards and to tell Chubby: 'We've got problems. The pool is full of big Johnnys, and there are two really mean uptails with them. That one that charged me and another.'

Chubby scowled as he fitted the demand valves to the new sets.

'Did you come straight up, Harry?'

I nodded. 'I left my bottles for Sherry. She's waiting down there.'

'You going to bend, Harry?' He looked up at me and I saw the worry in his eyes.

'Yes,' I nodded, as I dragged myself to my tackle box and lifted the lid. 'I've got to get down again fast—got to put pressure on my blood again before she fizzes.'

I picked out the bandolier of explosive heads for my hand spear. There were twelve of them, and I wished for more as I strapped the bandolier around my thigh. Each head was hand-tapped to screw onto the shaft of a ten foot stainless steel spear. It contained explosive charge equivalent to that of a 12-gauge shotgun shell and I could fire the charge with a trigger on the handle. It was an effective shark-killer.

Chubby hoisted one of the scuba sets onto my back and clinched the harness, and Angelo knelt before me to strap the shark repellent tablets in their perforated plastic containers to my ankles.

'I'll need another weight belt,' I said, 'and I lost a fin. There is a spare set in —' I did not finish the sentence. Blinding burning agony struck me in the elbow of my bad arm. Agony so fierce that I cried aloud, and my arm snapped closed like the blade of a clasp knife. It was an involuntary reaction, the joint doubling as the pressure of bubbles in the blood pressed on nerve and tendons.

'He's bending,' snarled Chubby. 'Sweet Mary, he's bending.' He leapt to the motors and gunned them, taking me in close to the reef. 'Work fast, Angelo,' Chubby shouted, 'we got to get him down again.'

The pain struck again, a fiery cramping agony in my right leg. The knee doubled under me and I whimpered like an infant. Angelo strapped the weight belt around my waist, and thrust the swimming fin onto my crippled leg.

Chubby cut the motors and we coasted in under the lee of the reef, while Chubby scrambled back to where I crouched on the thwart. He stooped over me to thrust the mouthpiece between my lips and open the cocks on the air bottles.

'Okay?' he asked, and I sucked from the set and nodded.

Chubby leaned over the side and peered down into the pool. 'Okay,' he grunted, 'Johnny Uptail gone somewhere else.'

He lifted me like a child, for I had lost the use of arm and leg, and he lowered me into the water between boat and reef.

Angelo hooked the harness of the extra scuba set for Sherry onto my belt, then he passed me the ten-foot spear and I prayed that I would not drop it.

'You go get Miss Sherry out of there,' said Chubby, and I rolled over in a clumsy one-legged duck dive and went down.

Even in the cramping agony of the bends my first concern was to search for the sinister gliding shapes of the white deaths. I saw one of them, but he was deep down, among the pack of lumbering Albacore sharks. Clinging to the shelter of the reef, I kicked and wriggled downwards like a maimed water beetle. Thirty feet under the surface the pain began to recede. Renewed pressure of water was reducing the size of the bubbles in my bloodstream, my limbs straightened and I had use of them.

I went down faster, and the relief was swift and blessed. I felt new courage and confidence flooding away my earlier despair. I had air and a weapon. I had a fighting chance now.

I was ninety feet down, in clear sight of the bottom. I could see

Sherry's bubbles rising from the smoky blue depths, and the sight cheered me. She was still breathing, and I had a fully charged extra scuba set for her. All I had to do was get it to her.

One of the fat ugly Albacore sharks saw me as I slid down the dark cliff face, and he swerved towards me. Already gorged with food, but endlessly hungry, he came in at me grinning horribly and paddling his wide tail.

I backed up and hung in the water against the cliff, facing him. I had the spear with its explosive head extended towards him, and as I finned gently to hold myself ready the streamers of bright blue dye from the shark repellent tablets smoked out in a cloud around me.

The shark came on in, and I lined up to hit him fairly on the snout, but the instant his head and gills encountered clouds of blue dye he spun away, flapping his tail in shock and dismay. The copper acetate had burned his gills and eyes, and he retreated hurriedly.

'Eat your liver, Chubby Andrews,' I thought. 'They work!'

Down again I went, almost to the tops of the bamboo forest, seeing Sherry still crouched in the gunport thirty feet away watching me. She had exhausted her own air bottles and was using mine—but I could tell by the volume and scanty rate of flow of bubbles that she had only seconds of breathing time left to her.

I started towards her, leaving the cliff—and only her frantic hand signals alerted me. I turned and saw the white death coming like a long blue torpedo. He was skimming the tops of the bamboo, and from one corner of his jaws hung a tattered streamer of flesh. He opened that wide maw to gulp down the morsel, and the rows of fangs gleamed whitely, like the petals of some obscene flower.

I faced him as he charged, but at the same time I fell back kicking my fins in his direction and laying a thick smoke-screen of blue dye between us.

With hard slashing strokes of his tail, he arrowed in the last few yards, but then he hit the blue dye and swirled, altering the direction of his charge as he sheered away.

He passed me so close that his tail struck me a heavy blow on the shoulder, sending me tumbling end over end. For seconds I lost my bearings, but as I recovered my balance and looked wildly about me I found the great shark circling.

He swept around me, forty feet away, and in his full length he seemed to my heated eye as long as a battleship and as blue and as vast as a summer sky. It seemed impossible to believe that these fish grew to almost twice this size. This one was still a baby—I was thankful for that.

Suddenly the slim steel spear in which I had placed so much faith seemed futile, and the shark regarded me with a cold yellow eye across which the pale nictitating membrane flicked occasionally in a sardonic wink, and once he opened his jaws in a convulsive gulp, as though in anticipation of the taste of my flesh.

He continued in those wide racing circles, with myself always at the centre, turning with him and paddling frantically with my fins to match his smooth unforced speed.

As I turned, I unhooked the spare lung from my belt and slung it by the harness on my left shoulder like the shield of a Roman legionary, and I tucked the hilt of the spear under my arm and kept the head pointed at the circling monster.

My whole body tingled with the warm flush of adrenalin in the blood-stream, and my senses were enhanced and sharpened by the arednalin high—the intensely pleasurable sensation of acute fear to which a man can become an addict.

Each detail of the deadly fish was etched indelibly on my memory, from the gentle pulsing of the multiple gill behind the head to the long trailing ribbons of the remora fish holding by their suckers to the smooth snowy expanse of his belly. With a fish of this size, it would only infuriate him further if I went for a hit with the explosive spear on his snout. My only chance was for a hit on the brain.

I recognized the moment when the shark's distaste for the blue mist of repellent was overcome by his hunger and his anger. His tail seemed to stiffen and it gave a series of rapid strokes, driving his speed up sharply.

I braced myself, lifting the spare scuba protectively, and the shark turned hard and fast, breaking the wide circle and coming in directly at me.

I saw the jaws open like a pit, lined with the wedge-shaped fangs, and at the moment of strike I thrust the twin steel bottles of the scuba into it.

The shark closed its jaws on the decoy and it was torn from my grasp, while the impact of the attack tossed me aside like a floating leaf. When I had gathered myself again I looked around frantically and found the white death was twenty feet away, moving only slowly but worrying the steel bottles the way a puppy chews a slipper.

It was shaking its head in the instinctive reaction which tears lumps of flesh from a victim—but which was now inflicting only deep scratches on the painted metal of the scuba.

This was my chance, my one and only chance. Kicking hard, I spurted above the broad blue back, brushing the tall dorsal fin and I sank down over him, coming in on his blind spot like an attacking fighter pilot from high astern.

I reached out with the steel spear and pressed the tip of it firmly onto the curved blue skull, directly between those cold and deadly yellow eyes—and I squeezed the spring-loaded trigger on the hilt of the spear.

The shot fired with a crack that beat in upon my eardrums, and the spear jumped heavily in my grip.

The white death shark reared on its tail like a startled horse, and once again I was tossed lightly aside by his careless bulk, but I recovered to watch him go into a terrible frenzy. The muscles beneath the smooth skin twitched and rippled at random impulse from the damaged brain, and the shark spun and dived, rolling wildly on its back, arrowing downwards to crash snout first into the rocky bottom of the pool, then it stood on its tail and scooted in aimless parabolas through the pale blue waters.

Still watching it, and keeping a respectful distance, I unscrewed the exploded head off the spear and replaced it with a fresh charge.

The white death still had Sherry's air supply clamped in his jaws. I could not leave it. I trailed his violent, unpredictable manoeuvres warily, and when at last he hung stationary for a moment nose down, suspended on the wide flukes of his tail, I shot in again and once more pressed the explosive charge to his skull, holding it firmly against the cartilaginous dome, so that the full shock of the charge would be transmitted directly to the tiny brain.

I fired the shot, cracking painfully in my own ears, and the shark froze rigidly. It never moved again but still in that frozen rigour it rolled over slowly and began to sink towards the floor of the pool. I darted in and wrested the damaged scuba from his jaws.

I saw immediately the air hoses had been torn and shredded by the shark's teeth, but the bottles were only extensively scratched.

Carrying the lung with me I sprinted across the tops of the bamboo towards the wreck. There were no longer air bubbles rising from the gunport, and as I came in sight of her I saw that Sherry had discarded the last empty scuba set. They were empty, and she was dying slowly.

Yet even in the extremes of slow suffocation she had not made the suicidal attempt to rise to the surface. She was waiting for me, dying slowly, but trusting me.

As I came down beside her, I pulled out my own mouthpiece and offered it to her. Her movements were slow and un-coordinated. The mouthpiece slipped from her grasp and floated upwards, spewing out a torrent of air. I grabbed it and forced it into her mouth, holding it there while lowering myself slightly below her level to induce a readier flow of air.

She began to breathe. Her chest rose and fell in long deep draughts of the precious stuff, and almost immediately I saw her regaining strength and purpose. Satisfied I turned my attention to removing a demand valve from one of the abandoned lungs from which the air supply was exhausted and using it to replace the one damaged by the shark.

I breathed off it for half a minute, before strapping it onto Sherry's back and retrieving my own mouthpiece.

We had air now, enough to take us through the long period of slow decompression ahead of us. I knelt facing Sherry in the gunport and she grinned lopsidedly around the mouthpiece and lifted her thumb in a high sign and I returned it. You okay, me okay, I thought, and unscrewed the expended head from the spear and renewed it from the bandolier on my thigh.

Then once more I peered from the safety of the gunport out into the open waters of the pool.

As the supply of dead fish was depleted so the shark pack seemed to have dispersed. I saw one or two of the ungainly dark shapes still searching and sniffing the tainted waters, but their frenzy was reduced. They moved in a more leisurely fashion, and I felt happier about taking Sherry out now.

I reached for her hand and was surprised at how small and cold it felt in mine, but she answered my gesture with a squeeze of her fingers.

I pointed to the surface and she nodded. I led her out of the gunport and we slid down the hull and under cover of the bamboo crossed quickly to the shelter of the reef.

Side by side, still holding hands and with our backs to the cliff, we rose slowly up out of the pool.

The light strengthened and when I looked up I could see the whaleboat high above. My spirits rose.

At sixty feet I stopped for a minute to begin decompressing. A fat old Albacore shark swam past us, blotched and piebald like a pig, but he paid us no attention and I lowered the spear as he drifted away into the hazy distance.

Slowly we rose to the next decompression stop at forty feet, where we stayed for two minutes, allowing the nitrogen in our blood to evaporate out through our lungs gradually. Then up to twenty feet for the next stop.

I peered into Sherry's face-mask and she rolled her eyes at me— clearly she was regaining her courage and cheek. It was all going smoothly now. We were as good as home, and drinking whisky—just another twelve minutes.

The whaleboat was so close it seemed that I could touch it with the spear. I could quite clearly see Chubby's and Angelo's brown faces hanging over the side as they waited anxiously for us to emerge.

I looked away from them, making another careful search of the water about us. At the extreme range of my vision, where the haze of water shaded away to solid blue, I saw something move. It was just a suspicion of a shadow that had come and gone before I had really seen it, but I felt the returning prickle of fear and apprehension.

I hung in the water, completely alert once more, searching and waiting while the last few slow minutes dragged by like crippled insects.

The shadow passed again, this time clearly seen, a swift and deadly movement that left me in no doubt that it was not an Albacore shark. It was the difference between the shape of the prowling hyena in the shadows around the campfire to that of the lion when he hunts.

Suddenly, through the misty blue curtains of water, came the second white death shark. He came swiftly and silently, passing fifty feet away, seeming to ignore us and going on almost to the range of our vision and then turning steeply and returning to pass us again, like a caged animal back and forth along the bars.

Sherry cowered close to me and I disengaged my hand from the death grip in which she had it. I needed both hands now.

On the next pass the shark broke the pattern of its movements and went into the great sweeping circles which always precede attack. Around and around it went, with that pale yellow eye fastened hungrily upon us.

Suddenly my attention was distracted by the slow descent from above of a dozen of the blue plastic shark-repellent containers. Seeing our predicament Chubby must have emptied the entire boxfull over the side. One of them passed closely enough for me to snatch it up and hand it to Sherry.

It smoked blue dye in her hand, and I transferred my attention back to the shark. It had sheered off a little from the blue dye, but it was still circling swiftly and grinning loathsomely at us.

I glanced at my watch, three minutes more to be safe, but I could risk sending Sherry out ahead of me. Unlike myself she had not already had a nitrogen fizz in her blood, she would probably be safe in another minute.

The shark tightened its circle, boring in relentlessly on us. Close—so very close that I looked deep into the black spearheaded pupil of his eye, and read his intention there.

I glanced at the watch. It was cutting it fine—very fine, but I decided to send Sherry up. I slapped her shoulder and pointed urgently to the surface. She hesitated, but I slapped her again and repeated my instruction.

She began to rise, going up slowly, the right way, but her legs dangled invitingly. The shark left me and rose slowly in time with her, following her.

She saw it and began to rise faster; smoothly the shark closed in on her. Now I was under them both, and I finned out fast to one side just as the shark went into the stiff-tailed attitude which signalled the instant of his attack.

I was directly under him, as he turned to maul Sherry. I reached up and pressed the spear-head into the softly obscene throat, and I hit the trigger.

I saw the shock kick into the bloated white flesh, and the shark reared away with a convulsive beat of its tail. It shot upwards and went out through the surface, leaping out high and clear, and falling back heavily in a creaming froth of bubbles.

Immediately it began to spin and fly in maddened, crazy circles, as though beset by a swarm of bees. Repeatedly its jaws opened and snapped closed.

Torn with terrible anxiety, I watched Sherry maintain her mental discipline and rise leisurely towards the whaleboat. A pair of huge brown paws were thrust down through the surface to welcome her. As I watched, she came within reach of them. The brown fingers closed on her like steel grab-hooks and she was plucked with miraculous strength from the water.

I could now employ all my attention on the problem of staying alive through the next few minutes before I could follow her. The shark seemed to recover from the shock of the charge, and it exchanged its mindless crazy gyrations for the terrible familiar circling.

It began again on the wide circumference, closing in steadily with each circuit. I glanced at my wrist watch and saw that at last I could begin to rise through the final stage.

I drifted upwards slowly. The agony of the bends was fresh in my memory—but the white death shark was pressing closer and closer.

Ten feet below the whaleboat, I paused again and the shark was suspicious, probably remembering the recent violent explosion in its throat. It ceased its circling and hung motionless in the pale water on the wide pointed wings of his pectoral fins. We stared at each other across a distance of fifteen feet, and I could sense that the great blue beast was gathering himself for the final rush.

I extended the spear to the full reach of my arm, and gently, so as not to trigger him, I finned towards him until the explosive charge was an inch from the nostril slits below the snout.

I hit the trigger and he reared back in shock as the explosive cracked.

He whirled away in a wide angry turn and I dropped the spear and shot for the surface.

He was angry as a wounded lion, goaded by the hurts he had received, and he charged for me with his humped back large as a blue mountain and his wide jaws gaping open. I knew there was no turning him this time, nothing short of death would stop him.

As I shot for the surface I saw Chubby's hands waiting for me, the fingers like a bunch of brown bananas, and I loved him at that moment. I lifted my right arm above my head, offering it to Chubby and as the shark flashed across the last few feet that separated us I felt Chubby's fingers close on my wrist.

Then the water exploded about me. I felt the enormous drag on my arm and the powerful disruption of the water as the shark's bulk tore it apart. Then I was lying on my back upon the deck of the whaleboat, dragged from the very jaws of that dreadful animal.

'You got some nice pets, Harry,' said Chubby in a disinterested tone that I knew was forced, and I looked about quickly for Sherry.

'You okay?' I called, as I saw her wet and pale-faced in the stern. She nodded; I doubted she could speak.

I jerked out the quick release pin on my harness, freeing myself of the weight of the scuba.

'Chubby, set up a stick of gelly ready to shoot,' I called, as I rid myself of mask and fins and peered over the side of the whaleboat.

The shark was still with us, circling the whaleboat in a fury of hurt and frustration. He came up to show the full length of his dorsal fin above the surface. I knew he could easily attack and stove in the planking of the whaleboat.

'Oh God, Harry, he's horrible.' Sherry found her voice at last, and I knew how she felt. I hated that loathsome fish with the full force of my recent terror—but I had to distract it from direct attack.

'Angelo, give me that Moray and a bait-knife,' I shouted and he handed me the cold slimy body. I hacked off a ten-pound lump of the dead eel and tossed it into the pool.

The shark swirled and raced for the scrap, gulping it down and scraping the hull of the whaleboat as it passed so close. We rocked violently at its passing.

'Hurry up, Chubby,' I shouted, and fed the shark another lump. It took it as readily as a hungry dog, dashing past under the hull and again bumping the boat so that it swayed unpleasantly and Sherry squeaked and grabbed the gunwale.

'Ready,' said Chubby, and I passed him a two-foot section of the eel with its empty belly cavity hanging open like a pouch.

'Put the stick in there, and tie it up,' I instructed him, and he began to grin.

'Hey, Harry,' he chortled, 'I like it.'

While I fed the monster with scraps of eel, Chubby trussed up the stick of gelignite in a neat parcel of eel flesh, with the insulated copper wire protruding from it. He passed it to me.

'Connect her up,' I instructed, as I coiled a dozen loops of the wire into my left hand.

'Ready to shoot,' grinned Chubby, and I threw the bundle of meat and explosive into the path of the circling shark.

It raced for it, and its glistening blue back broke the surface as it swallowed the offering. Immediately the wire began to stream away over the side and I paid out more from the reel.

'Let him eat it down,' I said and Chubby nodded happily.

'Okay, Chubby, blow the bastard to hell,' I snarled as the fish came to the surface, fin up, and swung around us in another circle, with the copper wire trailing from the corner of the sickle-moon mouth.

Chubby hit the switch, and the shark erupted in a tall burst of pink spray, like a bursting water melon, as his pale blood mingled with the paler flesh and purple contents of the belly cavity, spurting fifty feet into the air and splattering the pool and whaleboat. The shattered carcass wallowed like a bleeding log upon the surface, then rolled over and began to sink.

'Goodbye, Johnny Uptail,' hooted Angelo, and Chubby grinned like a cherub.

'Let's go home,' I said, for already the oceanic surf was breaking over the reef, and I thought I was going to throw up.

However, my indisposition responded miraculously to a treatment of Chivas Regal whisky, even though taken from an enamel mug, and much later in the cave Sherry said: 'I suppose you want me to thank you for saving my life, and all that crap?'

I grinned at her and opened my arms. 'No, my sweeting, just show me how grateful you are,' which she did, and afterwards there were no ugly dreams to spoil my sleep for I was exhausted in body and spirit.

———————

I think all of us were coming to regard the pool at Gunfire Break with a superstitious dread. The series of accidents and mishaps to which we had been subject appeared to be the result of some deliberate malevolent scheme.

It seemed as though each time we returned to the pool it had grown more sinister in its aspect and that an aura of menace was growing about it.

'You know what I think,' Sherry said laughingly, but not completely as a joke. 'I think the spirits of the murdered Mogul princes have followed the treasure to act as guardians—' Even in the bright sunshine of a glorious morning I saw the expressions on the faces of Angelo and Chubby. 'I think the spirits were in those two big Johnny Uptails that we killed yesterday.' Chubby looked as though he had breakfasted off a dozen rotten oysters, he blanched to a waxy golden brown and I saw him make the sign with his right hand.

'Miss Sherry,' said Angelo severely, 'you must never talk like that.' I could see gooseflesh on his forearms. Both he and Chubby had an attack of the ghostlies.

'Yes, cut it out,' I agreed.

'I was joking,' protested Sherry.

'Good joke,' I said, 'you really slayed us.' And we were all silent during the passage of the channel and until we had taken station in the shelter of the reef.

I was sitting in the bows, and when all three of them looked at me I saw by the expressions on their faces that I had a crisis of morale on my hands.

'I will go down alone,' I announced, and there was a small stir of relief.

'I'll go with you,' Sherry volunteered half-heartedly.

'Later,' I agreed, 'but first I want to check for Johnnies, and recover the equipment we lost yesterday.'

I went down cautiously, hanging just under the boat for five minutes while I scrutinized the depths of the pool for those evil dark shapes, and then finning down quietly.

It was cold and eerie in the deeper shades, but I saw that the night tide had scoured the pool and sucked out to sea all the carrion and blood that had attracted the shark pack the previous day.

There was no sign of the huge white death carcasses, and the only fish I saw were the multitudinous shoals of brilliant coral dwellers. A glint of silver from below led me to the spear I had abandoned in my rush for the boat, and I found the empty scubas and the damaged demand valve where we had left them in the gunport.

I surfaced with my load, and there were smiles among my crew for the first time that day when I reported the pool clear.

'All right,' I capitalized on the rise of their spirits, 'today we are going to open up the hold.'

'You going in through the hull?' Chubby asked.

'I thought about that, Chubby, but I reckoned that it would need a couple of heavy charges to get in that way. I've decided to go in through the passenger deck into the well.' I sketched it on my slate for them as I explained. 'The cargo will have shifted, it will be lying in a jumble just beyond that bulkhead and once we pop her open here, we can drag it out item by item into the companionway.'

'It's a long haul from there to the gunport.' Chubby lifted his cap and massaged his bald dome thoughtfully.

'I'll rig a light block and tackle at the gundeck ladder and another at the gunport.'

'A lot of work,' Chubby looked sad.

'The first time you agree with me—I'm going to begin worrying that I may be wrong.'

'I didn't say you were wrong,' said Chubby stiffly, 'I just said it was a lot of work. You can't let Miss Sherry haul on a block and tackle, can you now?'

'No,' I agreed. 'We need somebody with beef,' and I prodded his bulging rock-hard gut.

'That's what I thought,' said Chubby mournfully. 'You want me to get geared up?'

'No.' I stopped him. 'Sherry can come down with me to set the charges now.' I wanted her to test her nerves after the previous day's horrors. 'We will blast the well open and then go home. We aren't going to work again immediately after blasting. We are going to let the tide clean the pool of dead fish before going down. I don't want an action replay of yesterday.'

We crept in through the gunport and followed the nylon guide line we had placed on our first visit, along the gundeck, up through the companion ladder to the passenger deck, and then along the dark forbidding tunnel to the dead-end bulkhead of the forward well.

While Sherry held the torch for me, I began to drill a hole through the partition with the brace and bit that I had brought from the surface. It was awkward working without a really firm stance on which to anchor myself, but the first inch and a half was easy going. This layer of wood had rotted to a soft corky consistency, but beyond that I encountered iron-hard oak planking and I had to abandon my efforts. I would have been a week at the task.

Unable to place my explosive in prepared shot holes, I would now have to use a larger charge than I really wanted and rely on the tunnel effect of the passageway for a secondary shock to drive the panel inwards. I used six half sticks of gelignite, placed on the corners and in the centre of the bulkhead, and I secured them to bolts driven into the woodwork with a slap hammer.

It took almost half an hour to set up the blast, and afterwards it was a relief to leave the claustrophobic confines of the ancient hull and to rise up through clean clear water to the silver surface, trailing the insulated wires behind us.

Chubby fired the shots while we stripped off our equipment. The shock was cushioned by the hull of the wreck so that it was hardly noticeable to us on the surface.

We left the pool immediately afterwards and ran home with rising spirits to the prospect of a lazy day while we waited for the tide to clean the pool of carrion.

In the afternoon Sherry and I went on a picnic down to the south tip of the island. For provisions we took a wicker-covered two-litre bottle of Portuguese *vinos verde*, but to supplement this we dug out a batch of big sand clams which I wrapped in seaweed and reburied in the sand. Over them I built an open fire of driftwood.

By the time we had almost finished the wine, the sun was setting and the clams were ready to eat. The wine and the food and the glorious sunset had a softening effect on Sherry North. She became doe-eyed and melting, and when the sunset faded at last and made way for a fat yellow lovers' moon, we walked home barefooted on the wet sand.

The next morning Chubby and I worked for half an hour bringing down the equipment we needed from the whaleboat and stacking it on the gundeck of the wreck before we were able to penetrate deeper into the hull.

The heavy charges I had set against the well had wrought the sort of havoc I feared. They had torn out the decking and smashed in the bulkheads of the passenger cabins, blocking the passage for a quarter of its length.

We found a good anchor point for our block and tackle and while Chubby rigged it, I left him and floated back to the nearest cabin. I played my torch through the shattered panelling. The interior was, like everything else, smothered in a thick furring of marine growth but I could make out the shape of the simple furniture beneath it.

I eased myself through the gap, and moved slowly across the cluttered deck, fascinated by the objects which I found scattered and heaped about the cabin. There were items of porcelain and china, a shattered washbasin and a magnificent chamber pot with a pink floral design showing through the film of accumulated sediment. There were cosmetic pots and scent bottles, smaller indefinable metal objects and mounds of rotted and amorphous material which may have been clothing, curtaining or mattresses and bed-clothing.

I glanced at my watch and saw that it was time to leave and surface for a change of air bottles. As I turned, a small square object caught my attention and I played the torchbeam upon it while I gently brushed it clear of the thick layer of muddy filth. It was a wooden box, the size of a portable transistor radio, but the lid was beautifully inlaid with mother-of-pearl and tortoiseshell. I picked it up and tucked it under my arm. Chubby had finished rigging the block and tackle and he was waiting for me beside the gundeck ladder. When we surfaced beside the whaleboat I passed the box up to Angelo before climbing aboard.

While Sherry poured coffee for us and Angelo charged the demand valves to the fresh scuba bottles, I lit a cheroot and examined the box.

It was in a sorry state of deterioration, I saw at once. The inlay was rotten and falling out of its seating, the rosewood was swollen and distorted and the lock and hinges half eaten away.

Sherry came to sit beside me on the thwart and examined my prize with me. She recognized it immediately.

'It's a lady's jewel box,' she exclaimed. 'Open it, Harry. Let's see what's inside.'

I slipped the blade of a screw-driver under the lock and at the first pressure the hinges snapped and the lid flew off.

'Oh, Harry!' Sherry was first into it, and she came out with a thick gold chain and a heavy locket of the same material. 'This stuff is so in fashion, you'd never believe it.'

Everyone was dipping into the box now. Angelo ripped off a pair of gold and sapphire earrings which immediately replaced the brass pair he habitually wore, while Chubby picked an enormous necklace of garnets which he hung around his neck and preened like a teenage girl.

'For my missus,' he explained.

It was the personal jewellery of a middle-class wife, probably some minor official or civil servant—none of it of great value, but in its context it was a fascinating collection. Inevitably Miss North acquired the lion's share—but I managed to snatch away a thick plain gold wedding band.

'What do you want with that?' she challenged me, reluctant to yield a single item.

'I'll find a use for it,' I told her, and gave her one of my looks of deep significance, which was completely wasted for she had returned to ransacking the jewel box.

Nevertheless I tucked the ring safely away in the small zip pocket of my canvas gear bag. Chubby by this stage was bedecked with chunky jewellery like a Hindu bride.

'My God, Chubby, you're a dead ringer for Liz Taylor,' I told him and he accepted the compliment with a graceful inclination of his head.

I had a difficult job getting him interested in a return to the wreck, but once we were in the passenger deck again, he worked like a giant among the shattered wreckage.

We hauled out the panelling and timber baulks that blocked the passage by use of the block and tackle and our combined strength, and we dragged it down to the gundeck and stacked it out of the way in the recesses of that gloomy gallery.

We had reached the well of the forward hold by the time our air supplies were almost exhausted. The heavy planking had broken up in the explosion and beyond the opening we could make out what appeared to be a solid dark mass of material. I guessed that this was a conglomerate formed by the cargo out of its own weight and pressure.

However, it was afternoon the following day before I found that I was correct. We were at last into the hold, but I had not expected such a Herculean task as awaited us there.

The contents of the hold had been impregnated with sea water for over a century. Ninety per cent of the containers had rotten and collapsed, and the perishable contents had coalesced into a friable dark mass.

Within this solid heap of marine compost, the metal objects, the containers of stronger and impervious material and other imperishable objects, both large and small, were studded like lucky coins in a Christmas pudding. We would have to dig for them.

At this point we encountered our next problem. At the slightest disturbance of this rotted mass the water was immediately filled with a swirling storm of dark particles that blotted out the beams of the torches and plunged us into clouds of blinding darkness.

We were forced to work by sense of touch alone. It was painfully slow progress. When we encountered some solid body in the softness we had to drag it clear, manoeuvre it down the passage, lower it to the gundeck and there try to identify it. Sometimes we were obliged to break open what remained of the container, to get at the contents.

If they were of little value or interest, we tucked them away in the depths of the gundeck to keep our working field clear.

At the end of the first day's work we had salvaged only one item which we decided was worth raising. It was a sturdy case of hard wood, covered with what appeared to be leather and with the corners bound in heavy brass. It was the size of a large cabin trunk.

It was so heavy that Chubby and I could not lift it between us. The weight alone gave me high hopes. I believed it could very readily contain part of the golden throne. Although the container did not look like one that had been manufactured by an Indian village carpenter and his sons in the middle of the nineteenth century, yet there was a chance that the throne had been repacked before it was shipped from Bombay.

If it did contain part of the throne, then our task would be simplified. We would know what type of container to look for in the future. Using the block and tackle Chubby and I dragged the case down the gundeck to the gunport and there we shrouded it in a nylon cargo net to prevent it bursting open or breaking during the ascent. To the eyes spliced into the circumference of the net we attached the canvas flotation bags and inflated them from our air bottles.

We went up with the case, controlling its ascent by either spilling air from the bags, or adding more from our bottles. We came out beside the whaleboat and Angelo passed us half a dozen nylon slings with which we secured the case before climbing aboard.

The weight of the case defeated our efforts to lift it over the side, for the whaleboat heeled dangerously when the three of us made the attempt. We had to step the mast and use it as a derrick, only then did our combined efforts suffice and the case swung on board, spouting water from its seams. The moment that it sank to the deck Chubby scrambled back to the motors and ran for the channel. The tide pressed closely on our heels as we went.

The case was too weighty and our curiosity too strong to allow us to carry it up to the caves. We opened it on the beach, prising the lid open with a pair of jenny bars. The elaborate locking device in the lid was of brass and had withstood the ravages of salt sea water. It resisted our efforts bravely, but at last with a rending of woodwork the lid flew back and creaked against the heavily corroded hinges.

My disappointment was immediate, for it was clear that this was no tiger throne. It was only when Sherry lifted out one of the large gleaming discs and turned it curiously in her hands that I began to suspect that we had been awarded an enormous bonus.

It was an entrée plate she held, and my first thought was that it was of solid gold. However, when I snatched a mate from its slot in the cunningly designed rack and turned it to examine the hallmarks, I realized that it was silver and gold gilt.

The gold plating had protected it from the sea so that it was perfectly preserved, a masterpiece of the silversmith's art with a raised coat of arms in the centre and the rim wondrously chased with scenes of woods and deer, of huntsmen and birds.

The plate I held weighed almost two pounds and as I set it aside and examined the rest of the set I saw the weight of the chest fully accounted for.

There were servings for thirty-six guests in the set; soup bowls, fish plates, entrée plates, dessert bowls, side plates and all the cutlery to go with it. There were serving dishes, a magnificent chafing dish, wine coolers, dish covers and a carving dish almost the size of a baby's bath.

Every piece was wrought with the same coat of arms, and the ornamental scenes of wild animals and huntsmen, and the case had been designed to hold this array of plate.

'Ladies and gentlemen,' I said, 'as your chairman, it behoves me to assure you, one and all, that our little venture is now in profit.'

'It's just plates and things,' said Angelo, and I winced theatrically.

'My dear Angelo, this is probably one of the few complete sets of Georgian banquet silverware remaining anywhere in the world—it's priceless.'

'How much?' asked Chubby, doubtfully.

'Good Lord, I don't know. It would depend of course on the maker and the original owner—this coat of arms probably belongs to some noble house. A wealthy nobleman on service in India, an earl, a duke perhaps, even a viceroy.'

Chubby looked at me as though I were trying to sell him a spavined horse.

'How much?' he repeated.

'At Messrs Sothebys on a good day,' I hesitated, 'I don't know, say, a hundred thousand pounds.'

Chubby spat into the sand and shook his head. You couldn't fool old Chubby.

'This fellow Sotheby, does he run a loony house?'

'It's true, Chubby,' Sherry cut in. 'This stuff is worth a fortune. It could be more than that.'

Chubby was now torn between natural scepticism and chivalry. It would be an ungentlemanly act to call Sherry a liar. He compromised by lifting his hat and rubbing his head, spitting once more and saying nothing.

However, he handled the case with new respect when we dragged it up through the palms to the caves. We stored it behind the stack of jerrycans, and I went to fetch a new bottle of whisky.

'Even if there is no tiger throne in the wreck, we aren't going to do too badly out of this,' I told them.

Chubby sipped at his whisky mug and muttered, 'A hundred thousand—they've got to be crazy.'

'We've got to go through that hold and the cabins more carefully. We are going to leave a fortune down there if we don't.'

'Even the little items, less spectacular than the silver plate, they have enormous antique value,' Sherry agreed.

'Trouble is when you touch anything down there it stirs up such a fog you can't see the tip of your nose,' gloomed Chubby, and I refilled his mug with good cheer.

'Listen, Chubby, you know the centrifugal water pump that Arnie Andrews has got out at Monkey Bay?' I asked, and Chubby nodded.

'Will he lend it to us?' Arnie was Chubby's uncle. He owned a small market garden on the southern side of St Mary's island.

'He might,' Chubby answered warily. 'Why?'

'I want to try and rig a dredge pump,' I explained and sketched it for them in the sand between my feet. 'We set the pump up in the whale-boat, and we use a length of steam hose to reach the wreck— like this.' I roughed it out with my finger. 'Then we used it like a vacuum cleaner in the hold, suck out all that muck and pump it to the surface—'

'Hey, that's right,' Angelo burst out enthusiastically. 'When it spills out of the pump we run it through a sieve, and we will be able to pick up all the small stuff.'

'That's right. Only muck and small light items will go up the spout— anything large or heavy will be left behind.'

We discussed it for an hour working out details and refinements on the basic idea. During that time Chubby tried manfully to show no signs of enthusiasm, but finally he could contain himself no longer.

'It might work,' he muttered, which from him was a high accolade.

'Well, you better go fetch that pump then, hadn't you?' I asked.

'I think I will have one more drink,' he procrastinated, and I handed him the bottle.

'Take it with you,' I suggested. 'It will save time.'

He grunted, and went to fetch his overcoat.

———————

Sherry and I slept late, gloating on the lazy day ahead and at the feeling of having the island entirely to ourselves. We did not expect Chubby and Angelo to return before noon.

After breakfast we crossed the saddle between the hills and went down to the beach. We were playing in the shallows, and the rumble of the surf on the outer reef and our own splashing and laughter blanketed any other sounds. It was only by chance that I looked up and saw the light aircraft sweeping in from the landward channel.

'Run!' I shouted at Sherry, and she thought I was joking until I pointed urgently at the approaching aircraft.

'Run! Don't let him see us,' and this time she responded quickly. We floundered naked from the water, and went up the beach at the top of our speed.

Now I could hear the buzz of the aircraft engines and I glanced over my shoulder. It was banking low over the southernmost peak of the island and levelling over the long straight beach towards us.

'Faster!' I yelled at Sherry, as she ran long-legged and full-bottomed ahead of me with the wet tresses of her sable hair dangling down her darkly tanned back.

I looked back and the aircraft was headed directly at us, still about a mile distant, but I could see that it was twin-engined. As I watched, it sank lower towards the snowy expanse of coral sands.

We snatched up our discarded clothing at full run, and sprinted the last few yards into the palm grove. There was a mound formed by a fallen palm tree and the fronds torn off the trees by the storm. It was a convenient shelter and I grabbed Sherry's arm and dragged her down.

We rolled under the shelter of the dead fronds and lay side by side, panting wildly from the run up the beach.

It saw now that it was a twin-engined Cessna. It came down the beach and swept past our hideaway only twenty feet above the water's edge.

The fuselage was painted a distinctive daisy yellow and was blazoned with the name 'Africair'. I recognized the aircraft. I had seen it before at St Mary's Airport on half a dozen occasions, usually discharging or picking up groups of wealthy tourists. I knew that Africair was a charter company based on the mainland, and that its aircraft were for hire on a mileage tariff. I wondered who was paying for the hire on this trip.

There were two persons in the forward seats of the aircraft, the pilot and a passenger, and their faces were turned towards us as it roared past. However, they were too far from us to make out the features and I could not be sure if I knew either of them. They were both white men, that was all that was certain.

The Cessna turned steeply out over the lagoon and, one wing pointed directly down into the crystal water, it swept around and then levelled for another run down the beach.

This time it passed so closely that for an instant I looked up into the face of the passenger as he peered down into the palm grove. I thought I recognized him, but I could not be certain.

The Cessna then turned away, rising slowly, and set a new course for the mainland. There was something about her going that was complacent, the air of someone having achieved his purpose, a job well done.

Sherry and I crawled from our hiding-place and stood up to brush the sand from our damp bodies.

'Do you think they saw us?' she asked timidly.

'With that bottom of yours flashing like a mirror in the sunlight, they could hardly miss.'

'They might have mistaken us for a couple of native fishermen.'

I looked at her, not at her face, and I grinned. 'Fishermen? With those great beautiful boobs?'

'Harry Fletcher, you are a disgusting beast,' she said. 'But seriously, Harry, what is going to happen now?'

'I wish I knew, my sweeting, I wish I knew,' I answered, but I was glad that Chubby had taken the case of silverware back to St Mary's with him. By now it was probably buried behind the shack at Turtle Bay. We were still in profit—even if we had to run for it soon.

The visit by the aircraft instilled in us all a new sense of urgency. We knew now that our time was strictly rationed, and Chubby brought news with him when he returned that was equally disturbing.

'The *Mandrake* cruised for five days in the south islands. They saw her nearly every day from Coolie Peak, and she was messing about like she didn't know what she was doing,' he reported. 'Then on Monday she anchored again in Grand Harbour. Wally says that the owner and his wife went up to the hotel for lunch, then afterwards they took a taxi and went down to Frobisher Street. They spent an hour with Fred Coker in his office, then he drove them down to Admiralty Wharf and they went back on board *Mandrake*. She weighed and sailed almost immediately.'

'Is that all?'

'Yes,' Chubby nodded, 'except that Fred Coker went straight up to the bank afterwards and put fifteen hundred dollars into his savings account.'

'How do you know that?'

'My sister's third daughter works at the bank.'

I tried to show a cheerful face, although I felt ugly little insects crawling around in my stomach. 'Well,' I said, 'no use moping around. Let's try and get the pump assembled so we can catch tomorrow's tide.'

Later, after we had carried the water pump up to the caves, Chubby returned alone to the whaleboat and when he came back he carried a long canvas-wrapped bundle.

'What have you got there, Chubby?' I demanded, and shyly he opened the canvas cover. It was my FN carbine and a dozen spare magazines of ammunition packed into a small haversack.

'Thought it might come in useful,' he muttered.

I took the weapon down into the grove and buried it beside the cases of gelignite in a shallow grave. Its proximity gave me a little comfort when I returned to assist in assembling the water pump.

We worked on into the night by the light of the gas lanterns, and it was after midnight when we carried the pump and its engine down to the whaleboat and bolted it to a makeshift mounting of heavy timber which we placed squarely amidship, Angelo and I were still working on the pump when we ran out towards the reef in the morning. We had been on station for half an hour before we had it assembled and ready to test.

Three of us dived on the wreck—Chubby, Sherry and myself—and we manhandled the stiff black snake of the hose through the gunport and up into the breach through the well of the hold.

Once it was in position, I slapped Chubby on the shoulder and pointed to the surface. He replied with a high sign and finned away, leaving Sherry and me in the passenger deck.

We had planned this part of the operation carefully and we waited impatiently while Chubby went up, decompressing on his way, and climbed into the whaleboat to prime the pump and start the motor.

We knew he had done so by the faint hum and vibration that was transmitted to us down the hose.

I braced myself in the ragged entrance to the hold, and grasped the end of the hose with both hands. Sherry trained the torchbeam onto the dark heap of cargo, and I swung the open end of the hose slowly over the rotted cargo.

I saw immediately that it was going to work, small pieces of debris vanished miraculously into the hose, and it caused a small whirlpool as it sucked in water and floating motes of rubbish.

At this depth and with the RPM provided by the petrol engine, the pump was rated to move thirty thousand gallons of water an hour, which was a considerable volume. Within seconds I had cleared the working area and we still had good visibility. I could start probing into the heap with a jenny bar, breaking out larger pieces and pushing them back into the passage behind us.

Once or twice I had to resort to the block and tackle to clear some bulky case or object, but mostly I was able to advance with only the hose and the jenny bar.

We had moved almost fifty cubic feet of cargo before it was time to ascend for a change of air bottles. We left the end of the hose firmly anchored in the passenger deck, and went up to a hero's welcome. Angelo was in transports of delight and even Chubby was smiling.

The water around the whaleboat was clouded and filthy with the thick soup of rubbish we had pumped out of the hold, and Angelo had retrieved almost a bucketful of small items that had come through the outlet of the pump and fallen into the sieve—it was a collection of buttons, nails, small ornaments from women's dresses, brass military insignia, some small copper and silver coins of the period, and odds and ends of metal and glass and bone.

Even I was impatient to return to the task, and Sherry was so insistent that I had to donate my half-smoked cheroot to Chubby and we went down again.

We had been working for fifteen minutes when I came upon the corner of an up-ended crate similar to others that we had already cleared. Although the wood was soft as cork, the seams had been reinforced with strips of hoop iron and iron nails so I struggled with it for some time before I prised out a plank and pushed it back between us. The next plank came free more readily, and the contents seemed to be a mattress of decomposed and matted vegetable fibre.

I pulled out a large hunk of this and it almost jammed the opening of the hose, but eventually disappeared on its way to the surface. I almost lost interest in this box and was about to begin working in another area—but Sherry showed strong signs of disapproval, shaking her head, thumping my shoulder and refusing to direct the beam of the torch anywhere but at the unappetizing mess of fibre.

Afterwards I asked her why she had insisted and she fluttered her eyelashes and looked important.

'Female intuition, my dear. You wouldn't understand.'

At her urging, I once more attacked the opening in the case, but scratching smaller chunks of the fibre loose so as not to block the hose opening.

I had removed about six inches of this material when I saw the gleam of metal in the depths of the excavation. I felt the first deep throb of certainty in my belly then, and I tore out another plank with furious impatience. It enlarged the opening so I could work in it more easily.

Slowly I removed the layers of compacted fibre which I realized must have been straw originally used as packing. Like a face materializing in a dream, it was revealed.

The first tiny gleam opened to a golden glory of intricately worked metal and I felt Sherry's grip on my shoulder as she crowded down close beside me.

There was a snout, and lips below that were drawn up in a savage snarl, revealing great golden fangs and an arched tongue. There was a broad deep forehead as wide as my shoulders, and ears flattened down close upon the burnished skull—and there was a single empty eye-socket set fairly in the centre of the wide brow. The lack of an eye gave the animal a blind and tragic expression, like some maimed god from mythology.

I felt an almost religious awe as I stared at the huge, wonderfully fashioned tiger's head we had exposed. Something cold and frightening slithered up my spine, and involuntarily I glanced about me into the dark and forbidding recesses of the hold, almost as if I expected the spirits of the Mogul prince guardians to be lurking there.

Sherry squeezed my shoulder again and I returned my attention to the golden idol, but the sense of awe was so strong upon me that I had to force myself to return to the task of clearing the packing from around it. I worked very carefully for I was fully aware that the slightest scratch or damage would greatly reduce the value and the beauty of this image.

When our working time was exhausted we drew back and stared at the exposed head and shoulders, and the torch beam was reflected from the brilliant surface in arrows of golden light that lit the hold like some holy shrine. We turned then and left it to the silence and the dark, while we went up into the sunlight.

Chubby was aware immediately that something significant had happened, but he said nothing until we had climbed aboard and in silence shed our equipment. I lit a cheroot and drew deeply upon it, not bothering to mop the droplets of sea water that ran from my sodden hair down my cheeks. Chubby was watching me but Sherry was withdrawn from us, wrapped in secret thoughts, turned inward upon herself.

'You found it?' Chubby asked at last, and I nodded.

'Yes, Chubby, it's there.' I was surprised to hear that my own voice was husky and unsteady.

Angelo who had not sensed the mood looked up quickly from where he was stacking our equipment. He opened his mouth to say something, but then slowly closed it as he became aware of the charged atmosphere.

We were all silent, moved beyond speech. I had not expected it would be like this, and I looked at Sherry. She met my gaze at last and her dark eyes were haunted.

'Let's go home, Harry,' she said and I nodded at Chubby. He buoyed the hose and dropped it overboard to be retrieved on the following day. Then he threw the motors into gear and swung our bows to face the channel.

Sherry moved across the whaleboat and came to sit beside me on the thwart. I placed my arm about her shoulders but neither of us spoke until the whaleboat slid silently up onto the white beach of the island.

In the sunset Sherry and I climbed to the peak above the camp and we sat close together staring out across the reef, and watching the light fade on the sea and plunge the pool at Gunfire Reef into deeper shadow.

'I feel guilty in a way,' Sherry whispered, 'as though I have committed some dreadful sacrilege.'

'Yes,' I agreed, 'I know what you mean.'

'That thing—it seemed to have a life of its own. It was strange that we should have exposed its head, before any other part of it. Just suddenly to have that face glaring out at one,' she shuddered and was silent for a few moments, 'and yet I felt also a deep satisfaction, a good quiet feeling inside myself. I don't know if I can explain it properly— for the two feelings were so opposite, and yet mingled.'

'I understand. I had the same feelings.'

'What are we going to do with it, Harry, what are we going to do with that fantastic animal?'

Somehow I did not want to talk about money and buyers at that moment—which in itself was a measure of how profound was my involvement with the golden idol.

'Let's go down,' I suggested instead. 'Angelo will be waiting dinner for us.'

Sitting in the firelight with a good meal filling and warming the cold empty place in my belly, and with a mug of whisky in one hand and a cheroot in the other, I felt at last able to tell the others about it.

I explained how we had come upon it, and I described the fearsome golden head. They listened in complete and intent silence.

'We have cleared the head down to the shoulder. I think that is where it ends. It is notched there, probably to fit into the next section. Tomorrow we should be able to lift it clear, but it's going to be ticklish work. We can't just haul it out with the block and tackle. It has to be protected from damage before we can move it.'

Chubby made a suggestion, and for a while we discussed in detail how the head should be handled to minimize the risk of damage.

'We can expect that all five cases containing the treasure were loaded together. I hope to find them in the same part of the hold, probably similarly packed in wooden crates and reinforced with hoop iron—'

'Except for the stones,' Sherry interrupted. 'In the court-martial evidence, the Subahdar described how they were packed in a paymaster's chest.'

'Yes, of course,' I agreed.

'What would that look like?' Sherry asked.

'I saw one on display in the arsenal at Copenhagen which would probably be very similar. It's like a small iron safe—the size of a large biscuit bin.' I sketched the size with the spread of my hands like a fisherman boasting of his catch. 'It is ribbed with iron bands and has a locking rod and a pair of head padlocks at each corner.'

'It sounds formidable.'

'After a hundred-odd years in the pool it will probably be soft as chalk—even if it's still in one piece.'

'We'll find out tomorrow,' Sherry announced with confidence.

We tramped down to the beach in the morning with rain drumming on our oilskins and cascading from them in sheets. The cloud was right down on the peaks, oily dark banks that rolled steadily in from the sea to loose their bomb loads of moisture upon the island.

The force of the rain lifted a fine pearly spray from the surface of the sea, and the moving grey curtains reduced visibility to a few hundred yards so that the island disappeared in a grey haze as we ran out to the reef.

Everything in the whaleboat was cold and clammy and running with water. Angelo had to bale regularly and we huddled miserably in our oilskins while Chubby stood in the stern and slitted his eyes against the slanting, driving rain as he negotiated the channel.

The fluorescent orange buoy still bobbed close in beside the reef and we picked it up and dragged in the end of the hose and connected it to the pump head. It served as an anchor cable and Chubby could cut the motors.

It was a relief to leave the boat, escape from the cold needle lances of the rain and go down into the quiet blue mists of the pool.

After withstanding considerable pressure from Chubby and me, Angelo had at last succumbed to veiled threats and open bribes, and relinquished his ticking mattress stuffed with coconut-fibre. Once the mattress was thoroughly soaked with seawater, it sank readily, and I took it down with me in a neat roll, tied with line.

Only when I had manoeuvred it through the gunport, down the gundeck and into the passenger deck did I cut the line and spread the mattress.

Then Sherry and I returned to the hold where the tiger's head still snarled blindly into the torchlight.

Ten minutes' work was all that was necessary to free the head from its nest. As I suspected, this section ended at shoulder level, and the junction area was neatly flanged—clearly it would mate with the trunk section of the throne, and the flange would engage the female slot to form a joint that would be strong and barely perceivable.

When I rolled the head carefully onto its side I made another discovery. Somehow I had taken it for granted that the idol was made from solid gold, but now I saw that in fact it was a hollow casting.

The actual thickness of metal was only about an inch, and the interior was rough and knobbly to the touch. I realized immediately that a solid idol would have weighed hundreds of tons, and that the cost of such a construction would have been prohibitive even to an emperor who could support the construction of a temple as vast as the Taj Mahal.

The thinness of the metal skin had naturally weakened the structure, and I saw immediately when I turned it that the head had already suffered damage.

The rim of the neck cavity was flattened and distorted, probably during its secret journey through the Indian forests in an unsprung cart—or possibly during the wild death struggles of the *Dawn Light* during the cyclone.

Bracing myself in the entrance to the hold, I stooped over it to test its weight, and I cradled the head in my arms like the body of a child. Gradually I increased the strength of my lift and was pleased, but not surprised, when it came up in my arms.

It was, of course, tremendously weighty, and it required all of my strength from a carefully selected stance—but I could lift it. It weighed not much more than three hundred pounds, I thought, as I turned awkwardly under the oppressive load of gleaming gold and laid it gently on the coir mattress that Sherry was holding ready to receive it. Then I straightened up to rest and massage those parts where the sharp edges of metal had bitten into my flesh. While I did so I tried a little mental arithmetic. 300 pounds avoirdupois at 16 ounces to the pound was 4,800 ounces, at 150 to the ounce was almost three-quarters of a million dollars. That was the intrinsic value of the head alone. There were three other sections to the throne, all were probably heavier and larger—then there was the value of the stones. It was an astronomic total, but could be doubled or even trebled if the artistic and historical value of the hoard were taken into account.

I abandoned my calculations. They were meaningless at this time, and instead I helped Sherry to fold the mattress around the tiger's head and to rope it all into a secure bundle. Then I could use the block and tackle to drag it down to the companion ladder and lower it to the gundeck.

Laboriously we dragged it to the gunport and there we struggled to pass it through the restricted opening, but at last it was accomplished and we could place the nylon cargo net around it and inflate the airbags. Again we had to step the mast to lift it aboard.

But there was no suggestion that the head should remain covered once we had it safely in the whaleboat, and with what ceremony and aplomb I could muster in the streaming tropical rain, I unveiled it for Chubby and Angelo. They were an appreciative audience. Their excitement superseded even the miserable sodden conditions, and they crowded about the head to fondle and examine it amid shouted comment and giddy laughter. It was the festive gaiety which our first discovery of the treasure had lacked. I had taken the precaution of slipping my silver travelling flask into my gearbag, and now I laced the steaming mugs of black coffee with liberal portions of Scotch whisky and we toasted each other and the golden tiger in the steaming liquor, laughing while the rain gushed down upon us and rattled on the fabulous treasure at our feet.

At last I swilled out my mug over the side and checked my watch.

'We'll do another dive,' I decided. 'You can start the pump again, Chubby.'

Now we knew where to continue the search, and after I had broken out the remains of the case that had contained the head, I saw, in the opening beyond, the side of a similar crate and I pressed the hose into the area to clear it of dirt before proceeding.

My excavations must have unbalanced the rotting heap of ancient cargo, and it needed only the further disturbance caused by suction of the hose to dislodge a part of it. With a groaning and rumbling it collapsed around us and instantly the swirling clouds of muck defeated the efforts of the hose to clear them and we were plunged into darkness once more.

I groped quickly for Sherry through the darkness, and she must have been searching for me, for our hands met and held. With a squeeze she reassured me that she had not been hit by the sliding cargo, and I could begin to clear out the fouled water with the suction hose.

Within five minutes I could make out the yellow glow of Sherry's torch through the murk, and then her shape and the vague jumble of freshly revealed cargo.

With Sherry beside me, we moved farther into the hold again.

The slide had covered the wooden crate on which I had been working, but in exchange it had exposed something else that I recognized instantly, despite its sorry condition, for it was almost exactly as I had described it to Sherry the previous evening, even down to the detail of the rod that ran through the locking device and the double padlocks. The paymaster's chest was, however, almost eaten through with rust and when I touched it my hand came away smeared with the chalky red of iron oxide.

In each end of the case were heavy iron carrying rings, which had most likely swivelled at one time but were now solidly rusted into the metal side—but still they enabled me to get a firm grip and gently to work the chest out of the clutching bed of muck. It came free in a minor storm of debris, and I was able to lift it fairly easily. I doubt that the total weight exceeded 150 lbs, and I felt certain that most of that was made up by the massive iron construction.

After the enormously heavy head in its soft bulky mattress, it was a minor labour to get the smaller lighter chest out of the wreck, and it needed only a single airbag to lift it dangling out of the gunport.

Once again the tide and surf were pouring alarmingly into the pool, and the whaleboat tossed and kicked impatiently as we lifted the chest on board and laid it on the canvas-covered heap of scuba bottles in the bows.

Then at last Chubby could start the motors and take us out through the channel. We were still all high with excitement, and the silver flask passed from hand to hand.

'What's it feel like to be rich, Chubby?' I called, and he took a swallow from the flask, screwing up his eyes and then coughing at the sting of the liquor before he grinned at me.

'Just like before, man. No change yet.'

'What you going to do with your share?' Sherry insisted.

'It's a little late in the day, Miss Sherry—if only I had it twenty years ago, then I have use for it—and how.' He took another swallow. 'That's the trouble—you never have it when you're young, and when you're old, it's just too damned late.'

'What about you, Angelo?' Sherry turned to him as he perched on the rusted pay-chest, with his gipsy curls heavy with rain dangling onto his cheeks and the droplets clinging in the long dark eyelashes. 'You're still young, what will you do?'

'Miss Sherry, I've been sitting here thinking about it—and already I've got a list from here to St Mary's and back.'

It took two trips from the beach to the camp before we had both the head and the chest out of the rain and into the cave we were using as the store room.

Chubby lit two gas lanterns, for the lowering sky had brought on the evening prematurely, and we gathered around the chest, while the golden head snarled down upon us from a place of honour, an earthen ledge hewn into the back of the cave.

With a hacksaw and jenny bar, Chubby and I began work on the locking device and found immediately that the decrepit appearance of the metal was deceptive; clearly it had been hardened and alloyed. We broke three hacksaw blades in the first half-hour and Sherry professed to be severely shocked by my language. I sent her to fetch a bottle of Chivas Regal from our cave to keep the workers in good cheer and Chubby and I took the Scottish equivalent of a tea-break.

With renewed vigour we resumed our assault on the case, but it was another twenty minutes before he had sawn through the rod. By that time it was dark outside the cave. The rain was still hissing down steadily, but the soft clatter of the palm fronds heralded the rising westerly wind that would disperse the storm clouds by morning.

With the locking rod sawn through, we started it from its ringbolts with a two-pound hammer from the toolbox. Each blow loosened a soft patter of rust scales from the surface of the metal, and it required a number of goodly blows to drive the rod from the clutching fist of corrosion.

Even when it was cleared, the lid would not lift. Although we hammered it from a dozen different directions and I treated it with a further laying-on of abuse, it would not yield.

I called another whisky break to discuss the problem.

'What about a stick of gelly?' Chubby suggested with a gleam in his eye, but reluctantly I had to restrain him.

'We need a welding torch,' Angelo announced.

'Brilliant,' I applauded him ironically, for I was fast losing my patience. 'The nearest welding set is fifty miles away—and you make a remark like that.'

It was Sherry who discovered the secondary locking device, a secret pinning through the lid that hooked into recesses in the body of the chest. It obviously needed a key to release this, but for lack of it I selected a half-inch punch and drove it into the keyhole and by luck I caught the locking arm and snapped it.

Chubby started on the lid again, and this time it came up stiffly on corroded hinges with some of the rotting evil-smelling contents sticking to the inside of it and tearing away from the main body of aged brown cloth. It was woven cotton fabric, a wet solid brick of it, and I guessed that it had been cheap native robes or bolts of cloth used as packing.

I was about to explore further, but suddenly found myself in the second row looking over Sherry North's shoulder.

'You'd better let me do this,' she said. 'You might break something.'

'Come on!' I protested.

'Why don't you get yourself another drink?' she suggested placatingly, as she began lifting off layers of sodden fabric. The suggestion had some merit, I thought, so I refilled my mug and watched Sherry expose a layer of cloth-wrapped parcels.

Each was tied with twine that fell apart at the touch, and the first parcel also disintegrated as she tried to lift it out. Sherry cupped her hand around the decaying mass and scooped it onto a folded tarpaulin placed beside the chest. The parcel contained scores of small nutty objects, varying in size from slightly larger than a match-head to a ripe grape and each had been folded in a wisp of paper which, like the cotton, had completely rotted away.

Sherry picked out one of these lumpy objects and rubbed away the remnants of paper between thumb and forefinger to reveal a large shiny blue stone, cut square and polished on one face.

'Sapphire?' she guessed, and I took it from her and examined it quickly in the lantern light. It was opaque and I contradicted her.

'No, I think it's probably lapis lazuli.' The scrap of paper still adhering to it was faintly discoloured with a blue dye. 'Ink, I should say.' I crumpled it between my fingers. 'At least Roger, the Colonel, took the trouble to identify each stone. He probably wrapped each piece in a numbered slip of paper which related to a master sketch of the throne to enable it to be reassembled.'

'There is no hope of that now,' said Sherry.

'I don't know,' I said. 'It would be a hell of a job, but it would still be possible to put it all together again.'

Among our stores was a roll of plastic packets, and I sent Angelo to ferret it out. As we opened each parcel of rotted fabric we superficially cleaned the stones it contained and packed each lot in a separate plastic packet.

It was slow work even though we all contributed and after almost two hours of it we had filled dozens of packets with thousands of semi-precious stones—lapis lazuli, beryl, tiger's eye, garnets, verdite, amethyst, and half a dozen others of whose identity I was uncertain. Each stone had clearly been lovingly cut and exactingly polished to fit into its own niche in the golden throne.

It was only when we had unpacked the chest to its last layer that we came upon the stones of greater value. The old Colonel had obviously selected these first and they had gone into the lowest layer of the chest.

I held a transparent plastic packet of emeralds to the lantern light, and they burned like a bursting green star. We all stared at it as if mesmerized while I turned it slowly to catch the fierce white light.

I laid it aside and Sherry dipped once more into the chest and after a moment's hesitation brought out a smaller parcel. She rubbed away the damp crumbling material that was wound thick about the single stone it contained.

Then she held up the Great Mogul diamond in the cupped palm of her hand. It was the size of a pullet's egg, cut into a faceted cushion shape, just as Jean Baptiste Tavernier had described it so many hundred years ago.

The glittering away of treasure we had handled before in no way dimmed the glory of this stone, as all the stars of the firmament cannot dull the rising of the sun. They paled and faded away before the brilliance and lustre of the great diamond.

Sherry slowing extended her cupped hand towards Angelo, offering it to him to hold and examine, but he snatched his hands away and clasped them behind his back, still staring at the stone in superstitious awe.

Sherry turned and offered it to Chubby, but with gravity he declined also.

'Give it to Mister Harry. Guess he deserves to be the one.'

I took it from her, and was surprised that such unearthly fire could be so cold to touch. I stood up and I carried it to where the golden tiger's head stood snarling angrily in the unwavering light of the lanterns and I pressed the diamond into the empty eye socket.

It fitted perfectly, and I used my bait-knife to close the golden clasps that held it firmly in place, and which the old Colonel had probably opened with a bayonet a century and a quarter ago.

I stood back then, and I heard the small gasps of wonder. With the eye returned to its socket the golden beast had come to life. It seemed now to survey us with an imperial mien, and at any instant we expected the cave to resound to its crackling wicked snarl of anger.

I went back and took my place in the squatting circle around the rusted chest, and we all stared up at the golden tiger head. We seemed like worshippers in some ancient heathen rite, crouched in awe before the fearsome idol.

'Chubby, my old well beloved and trusted buddy, you will earn yourself an entry on the title page of the book of mercy if you pass me that bottle,' I said, and that broke the spell. They all recovered their voices, competing fiercely for a turn to speak—and it wasn't long before I had to send Sherry to fetch another bottle to lubricate dry throats.

We all got more than a little drunk that night, even Sherry North, and she leaned against me for support as we finally made a riotous way through the rain to our own cave.

'You really are corrupting me, Fletcher.' She stumbled into a puddle, and nearly brought me down. 'This is the first time ever I have been stoned.'

'Be of good cheer, my pretty sweeting, your next lesson in corruption follows immediately.'

When I woke it was still dark and I rose from our bed, careful not to disturb Sherry who was breathing lightly and evenly in the darkness. It was cool so I pulled on shorts and a woollen jersey.

Outside the cave the west wind had broken up the cloud banks. It had stopped raining and the stars were showing in the breaks of the heavens, giving me enough light to read the luminous dial of my wrist watch. It was a little after three o'clock.

As I sought my favourite palm tree, I saw that we had left the lantern burning in the storage cave. I finished what I had to do and went up to the lighted entrance.

The open chest stood where we had left it, as did the priceless golden head with its glittering eye—and suddenly I was struck with the consuming terror that the miser must feel for his hoard. It was so vulnerable.

'—where thieves break in—' I thought, and it was not as though there were any shortage of them in the immediate vicinity.

I had to get it all stowed away safely, and tomorrow would be too late. Despite the pain in my head and the taste of stale whisky in the back of my throat, it must be done now—but I needed help.

Chubby roused to my first soft call at the entrance of his cave, and came out into the starlight, resplendent in his striped pyjamas and as wide awake as if he had drunk nothing more noxious than mother's milk before retiring.

I explained my fears and misgivings. Chubby grunted in agreement and went with me back to the storage cave. The plastic bags of gem stones we repacked casually into the iron chest and I secured the lid with a length of nylon line. The golden head we shrouded carefully in a length of green canvas tarpaulin and we carried both down into the palm grove, before returning for spades and the gas lantern.

By the flat white glare of the lantern we worked side by side, digging two shallow graves in the sandy soil within a few feet of where the gelignite and the FN rifle with its spare ammunition were already buried.

We laid the chest and the golden head away and covered them. Afterwards I brushed the soil over them with a palm frond to wipe out all trace of our labours.

'You happy now, Harry?' Chubby asked at last.

'Yeah, I'm happier, Chubby. You go and get some sleep, hear.'

He went away among the palms carrying the lantern and not looking back. I knew I would not be able to sleep again, for the spadework had cleared my head and roused my blood. It would be senseless to return to the cave and try to lie quietly beside Sherry until dawn.

I wanted to find some quiet and secret place where I could think out my next moves in this intricate game of chance in which I was involved. I chose the path that led to the saddle between the lesser peaks and as I climbed it, the last of the clouds were blown aside and revealed a pale yellow moon still a week from full. Its light was strong enough to show me the way to the nearest peak and I left the path and toiled upwards to the summit.

I found a place protected from the wind and settled into it. I wished that I had a cheroot with me for I think better with one of them in my mouth. I also think better without a hangover—but there was nothing I could do about either.

After half an hour I had firmly decided that we must consolidate what we had gained to this point. The miser's fears, which had assailed me earlier, still persisted and I had been given clear warning that the wolf pack was out hunting. As soon as it was light we would take what we had salvaged so far—the head and the chest—and run down the islands to St Mary's to dispose of them in the manner which I had already so carefully planned.

There would be time later to return to Gunfire Reef and recover what remained in the misty depths of the pool. Once the decision had been made I felt a lift of relief, a new lightness of spirit, and I looked forward to the solution of the other major puzzle that had troubled me for so long.

Very soon I would be in a position to call Sherry North's hand and have a sight of those cards which she concealed so carefully from me. I wanted to know what caused those shadows in the blue depths of her eyes, and the answers to many other mysteries that surrounded her. That time would soon come.

There was a paling of the sky at last; dawn's first pearling light spread across from the east and softened the harsh dark plain of the ocean. I rose stiffly from my seat among the rocks, and picked my way around the peak into the wicked eye of the west wind. I stood there on the exposed face above the camp with the wind raising a rash of goose bumps along my arms and ruffling my hair.

I looked down into the sheltering arms of the lagoon, and in the feeble glimmer of dawn, the darkened ship that was creeping stealthily into the open arms of the bay looked like some pale phantom.

Even as I stared I saw the splash at her bows as she let go her anchor, and she rounded up into the wind showing her full silhouette so that I could not doubt that she was the *Mandrake*.

Before I had recovered my wits, she had dropped a boat which sped in swiftly towards the beach.

I started to run.

———————

I fell once on the path, but the force of my headlong descent from the peak carried me on and with a single roll I was on my feet again, still running.

I was panting wildly as I burst into Chubby's cave, and I shouted, 'Move, man, move! They are on the beach already.'

The two of them tumbled from their sleeping bags. Angelo was tousle-haired and blank-eyed from sleep, but Chubby was quick and alert.

'Chubby,' I snapped, 'go get that piece out of the ground. Jump, man, they'll be coming up through the grove in a few minutes.' He had changed while I spoke, pulling on a shirt and belting his denim breeches. He grunted an acknowledgement. 'I'll follow you in a minute,' I called as he ran out into the feeble light of dawn.

'Angelo, snap out of it!' I grabbed his shoulder and shook him. 'I want you to look after Miss Sherry, hear?'

He was dressed now and he nodded owlishly at me.

'Come on.' I half dragged him as we ran across to my cave. I dragged her out of bed and while she dressed I told her.

'Angelo will go with you. I want you to take a can of drinking water and the two of you get the hell down to the south of the island—cross the saddle first though and keep out of sight. Climb the peak and hide out in the chimney where we found the inscription. You know where I mean.'

'Yes, Harry,' she nodded.

'Stay there. Don't go out or show yourself under any circumstances. Understand?'

She nodded as she tucked the tail of her shirt into her breeches.

'Remember, these people are killers. The time for games is over, this is a pack of wolves that we are dealing with.'

'Yes, Harry, I know.'

'Okay then,' I embraced and kissed her quickly. 'Off you go then.' And they went out of the cave, Angelo lugging a five-gallon can of drinking water, and they trotted away into the palm grove.

Quickly I threw a few items into a light haversack: a box of cheroots, matches, binoculars, water bottle and a heavy jersey, a tin of chocolate and of survival rations, a torch—and I buckled my belt around my waist with the heavy bait-knife in the sheath. Slinging the strap of the haversack over my shoulder, I also ran from the cave and followed Chubby down into the palm grove towards the beach.

I had run fifty yards when there was the thud, thudding of small-arms fire, a shout and another burst of firing. It was directly ahead of me and very close.

I paused and slipped behind the bole of a palm tree while I peered into the lightening shades of the grove. I saw movement, a figure running towards me and I loosened the bait-knife in its sheath and waited until I was sure, before I called softly, 'Chubby!'

The running figure swerved towards me. He was carrying the FN rifle and the canvas bandolier with spare magazines of ammunition, and he was breathing quickly but lightly as he saw me.

'They spotted me,' he grunted. 'There are hundreds of the bastards.'

At that moment I saw more movement among the trees.

'Here they come,' I said. 'Let's go.'

I wanted to give Sherry a clear run, so I did not take the path across the saddle, but turned directly southwards to lead the pursuit off her scent. We headed for the swamps at the southern end of the island.

They saw us as we ran obliquely across their front. I heard a shout, answered immediately by others, and then there were five scattered shots and I saw the muzzle flashes bloom among the dark trees. A bullet struck a palm trunk high above our heads, a woody thunk, but we were going fast and within minutes the shouts of pursuit were fading behind us.

I reached the edge of the saltmarsh, and swung away inland to avoid the stinking mudflats. On the first gentle slope of the hills I halted to listen and to regain our breath. The light was strengthening swiftly now. Within a short while it would be sunrise and I wanted to be under cover before then.

Suddenly there were distant cries of dismay from the direction of the swamps and I guessed that the pursuit had blundered into the glutinous mud. That would discourage them fairly persuasively, I thought, and grinned.

'Okay, Chubby, let's get on,' I whispered, and as we stood there was a new sound from a different direction.

The sound was muted by distance and by the intervening heights of the ridge, for it came from the seaward side of the island, but it was the unmistakable ripping sound of automatic gunfire.

Chubby and I froze into listening attitudes and the sound was repeated, another long tearing burst of machine-gun fire. Then there was silence, though we listened for three or four minutes.

'Come on,' I said quietly; we could delay no longer and we ran on up the slope towards the southernmost peak.

We climbed quickly in the fast-growing morning light, and I was too preoccupied to feel any qualms as we negotiated the narrow ledge and stepped at last into the deep rock crack where I had arranged to meet Sherry.

The shelter was silent and deserted but I called without hope, 'Sherry! Are you there, love?'

There was no reply from the shadows, and I turned back to Chubby.

'They had a good lead on us. They should have been here,' and only then did that burst of machine-gun fire we had heard earlier take on new meaning.

I removed the binoculars from the haversack and then thrust it away into a crack in the rock.

'They've run into trouble, Chubby,' I told him. 'Come on. Let's go and find out what happened.'

Once we were off the ledge we struck out through the jumble of broken rock towards the seaward side of the island, but even in my haste and dreadful anxiety for Sherry's safety, I moved with stealth and we were careful not to show ourselves to a watcher in the groves or on the beaches below us.

As we crossed the divide of the ridge a new vista opened before us, the curve of the beach and the jagged black sweep of Gunfire Reef.

I halted instantly and pulled Chubby down beside me as we crouched into cover.

Anchored in a position to command the mouth of the channel through Gunfire Reef was the armed crash boat from Zinballa Bay, flagship of my old friend Suleiman Dada. Returning to it from the beach was a small motor-boat, crowded with tiny figures.

'God damn it,' I muttered, 'they really had it planned. Manny Resnick has teamed up with Suleiman Dada. That's what took him so long to get here. While Manny hit the beach, Dada was covering the channel, so we couldn't make a bolt for it like we did before.

'And he had men on the beach—that was the machine-gun fire. Manny Resnick sailed *Mandrake* into the bay to flush us, and Dada had the back door covered.'

'What about Miss Sherry and Angelo? Do you think they got away? Did Dada's men catch them when they crossed the saddle?'

'Oh God!' I groaned, and cursed myself for not having stayed with her. I stood up and focused the binoculars on the motor-boat as it crawled across the clear waters of the outer lagoon to the anchored crash boat.

'I can't see them.' Even with the aid of the binoculars, the occupants of the dinghy were merely a dark mass, for the morning sun was rising beyond them and the glare off the water dazzled me. I could not make out separate figures, let alone recognize individuals.

'They may have them in the boat—but I can't see.' In my agitation I had left the cover of the rocks, and was seeking a better vantage point, moving about on the sky-line. Out in the open I must have been highlighted by the same sun rays that were blinding me.

I saw the familiar flash, and the long white feather of gunsmoke blow from the mounted quick-firer on the bows of the crash boat, and I heard the shell coming with a rushing sound like eagles' wings.

'Get down!' I shouted at Chubby, and threw myself flat among the rocks.

The shell burst in very close, with the bright hot glare like the brief opening of a furnace door. Shrapnel and rock fragments trilled and whined around us, and I jumped to my feet.

'Run!' I yelled at Chubby, and we jinked back over the skyline just as the next shell passed over us, making us both flinch our heads at the mighty crack of passing shot.

Chubby was wiping a smear of blood from his forearm as we crouched behind the ridge.

'Okay?' I asked.

'A scratch, that's all. Bit of a rock fragment,' he growled.

'Chubby, I'm going down to find out what happened to the others. No point both of us taking a chance. You wait here.'

'You're wasting time, Harry, I'm coming with you. Let's go.' He hefted the rifle and led the way down the peak. I thought of taking the FN away from him. In his hands it was about as lethal as a slingshot when fired with his closed-eyes technique. Then I left it. It made him feel good.

We moved slowly, hugging any cover there was and searching ahead before moving forward. However, the island was silent except for the sough and clatter of the west wind in the tops of the palms and we saw nobody as we moved up the seaward side of the island.

I cut the spoor left by Angelo and Sherry as they crossed the saddle, above the camp. Their running footsteps had bitten deep into the fluffy soil; Sherry's small slim prints were overlapped by Angelo's broad bare feet.

We followed them down the slope, and suddenly they shied off the track. They had dropped the water-can here and, turning abruptly, had separated slightly, as though they had run side by side for sixty yards.

There we found Angelo, and he was never going to enjoy his share of the spoils. He had been hit by three of the soft heavy-calibre slugs. They had torn through the thin fabric of his shirt, and opened huge dark wounds in his back and chest.

He had bled copiously but the sandy soil had absorbed most of it, and already what was left was drying into a thick black crust. The flies were assembled, crawling gleefully into the bullet holes and swarming on the long dark lashes around his wide open and startled eyes.

Following her tracks I saw where Sherry had run on for twenty paces, and then the little idiot had turned back and gone to kneel beside where Angelo lay. I cursed her for that. She might have been able to escape if she had not indulged in that useless and extravagant gesture.

They had caught her as she knelt beside the body and dragged her down through the palms to the beach. I could see the long slide marks in the sand where she had dug her feet in and tried to resist.

Without leaving the shelter of the trees, I looked down the smooth white sand, following their tracks to where the marks of the motor-boat's keel still showed in the sand of the water's edge.

They had taken her out to the crash boat, and I crouched behind a pile of driftwood and dried palm fronds to stare out at the graceful little ship.

Even as I watched she weighed anchor, picked up speed and passed slowly down the length of the island to round the point and enter the inner lagoon where *Mandrake* was still lying at anchor.

I straightened up and slipped back through the grove to where I had left Chubby. He had laid the carbine aside and he sat with Angelo's body in his arms, cradling the head against his shoulder. Chubby was weeping; fat glistening tears slid wearily down the seamed brown cheeks and fell from his jaw to wet the thick dark curls of the boy in his arms.

I picked up the rifle and stood guard over them while Chubby wept for both of us. I envied him the relief of tears, the outpouring of pain that would bring surcease. My own grief was as fierce as Chubby's, for I had loved Angelo as much, but it was down deep inside where it hurt more.

'All right, Chubby,' I said at last. 'Let's go, man.' He stood up with the boy still in his arms and we moved back along the ridge.

In a gully that was choked with rank vegetation we laid Angelo in a shallow grave that we scraped with our hands, and we covered him with a blanket of branches and leaves that I cut with my bait-knife before filling the grave. I could not bring myself to throw sand onto his unprotected face, and the leaves made a gentler shroud.

Chubby wiped away his tears with the open palm of his hand and he stood up.

'They got Sherry,' I told him quietly. 'She is aboard the crash boat.'

'Is she hurt?' he asked.

'I don't think so, not yet.'

'What do you want to do now, Harry?' he asked, and the question was answered for me.

Somewhere far off towards the camp, we heard a whistle shrill, and we moved up the ridge to a point where we could see down into the inner lagoon and landward side of the island.

Mandrake lay where I had last seen her and the Zinballa crash boat was anchored a hundred yards closer to the shore. They had seized the whaleboat and were using her to land men on the beach. They were all armed, and uniformed. They set off immediately into the palm trees and the whaleboat ran back to *Mandrake*.

I put the binoculars onto *Mandrake* and saw that there were developments taking place there also. In the field of the glasses I recognized Manny Resnick in a white open-neck shirt and blue slacks as he climbed down into the whaleboat. He was followed by Lorna Page. She wore dark glasses, a yellow scarf around her pale blonde hair and an emerald green slack suit. I felt hatred seethe in my guts as I recognized them.

Now something happened that puzzled me. The luggage that I had seen loaded into the Rolls at Curzon Street was brought out onto the deck by two of Manny's thugs and it also was passed down into the whaleboat.

A uniform crew member of *Mandrake* saluted from the deck, and Manny waved at him in a gesture of airy dismissal.

The whaleboat left *Mandrake*'s side and moved in towards the crash boat. As Manny, his lady friend, bodyguards and luggage were disembarked onto the deck of the crash boat, *Mandrake* weighed anchor, turned for the entrance of the bay, and set out in a determined fashion for the deep-water channel.

'She's leaving,' muttered Chubby. 'Why is she doing that?'

'Yes, she's leaving,' I agreed. 'Manny Resnick has finished with her. He's got a new ally now, and he doesn't need his own ship. She's probably costing him a thousand nicker a day—and Manny always was a shy man with a buck.'

I turned my glasses onto the crash boat again and saw Manny and his entourage enter the cabin.

'There is probably another reason,' I muttered.

'What's that, Harry?'

'Manny Resnick and Suleiman Dada will want as few witnesses as possible to what they intend doing now.'

'Yeah, I see what you mean,' grunted Chubby.

'I think, my friend, that we are about to be treated to the kind of nastiness that will make what they did to Angelo seem kind, by comparison.'

'We've got to get Miss Sherry off that boat, Harry.' Chubby was coming out of the daze of grief into which Angelo's killing had thrown him. 'We've got to do something, Harry.'

'It's a nice thought, Chubby, I agree. But we aren't going to help her much by getting ourselves killed. My guess is that she will be safe until they get their hands on the treasure.'

His huge brown face creased up like that of a worried bulldog.

'What we going to do, Harry?'

'Right now we are going to run again.'

'What do you mean?'

'Listen,' I told him, and he cocked his head. There was the shrill of the whistle again and then faintly we heard voices carried up to us on the wind.

'Looks like their first effort will be brute strength. They've landed the entire goon squad, and they are going to drive the island and put us up like a brace of cock pheasant.'

'Let's go down and have a go,' Chubby growled, and cocked the FN. 'I got a message for them from Angelo.'

'Don't be a fool, Chubby,' I snapped at him angrily. 'Now listen to me. I want to count how many men they have. Then, if we get a good chance, I want to try and get one of them alone and take his piece off him. Watch for an opportunity, Chubby, but don't have a go yet. Play it very cautious, hear?' I didn't want to refer to his marksmanship in derogatory tones.

'Okay,' Chubby nodded.

'You stay this side of the ridge. Count how many of them come down this side of the island. I'll cross over and do the same on the other side.' He nodded. 'I'll meet you at the spot where the crash boat shelled us in two hours.'

'What about you, Harry?' He made a gesture of handing me the FN but I didn't have the heart to deprive him.

'I'll be okay,' I told him. 'Off you go, man.'

It was a simple task to keep ahead of the line of beaters for they called to each other loudly to keep their spirits up, and they made no pretence at concealment or stealth, but advanced slowly and cautiously in an extended line.

There were nine of them on my side of the ridge, seven of them were blacks in naval uniform, armed with AK47 assault rifles and two of them were Manny Resnick's men. They were dressed in casual tropical gear and carried side-arms. One of them I recognized as the driver of the Rover that night so long ago, and the passenger in the twin-engined Cessna that had spotted Sherry and me on the beach.

Once I had made my head count, I turned my back on them and ran ahead to the curve of the salt marsh. I knew that when the line of beaters ran into this obstacle, it would lose its cohesion and that it was likely that some of its members would become isolated.

I found an advanced neck of swampland with stands of young mangrove and coarse swamp grass in dense shades of fever green. I followed the edge of this thicket and came upon a spot where a fallen palm tree lay across the neck like a bridge—offering escape in two directions. It had collected a dense covering of blown palm fronds and swamp grass which provided a good hide from which to mount an ambush.

I lay in the back of this shaggy mound of dead vegetation and I had the heavy bait-knife in my right hand ready to throw.

The line of beaters came on steadily, their voices growing louder as they approached the swamp. Soon I could hear the rustle and scrape of branches as one of them came directly down to where I lay.

He paused and called when he was about twenty feet from me, and I pressed my face close to the damp earth and peered under the pile of dead branches. There was an opening there and I saw his feet and his legs below the knees. His trousers were thick blue serge and he wore grubby white sneakers without socks. At each step his naked ankles showed very black African skin.

It was one of the sailors from the crash boat then, and I was pleased. He would be carrying an automatic weapon. I preferred that to a pistol, which was what Manny's boys were armed with.

Slowly I rolled onto my side and cleared my knife arm. The sailor called again so close and so loud that my nerves jumped and I felt the tingling flush of adrenalin in my blood. His call was answered from farther off, and the sailor came on.

I could hear his soft footfalls on the sand, padding towards me.

Suddenly he came into full view, as he rounded the fall of brushwood. He was ten paces from me.

He was in naval uniform, a blue cap on his head with its gay little red pompon on the top, but he carried the vicious and brutal-looking machine-gun on his hip. He was a tall lean youngster in his early twenties, smooth faced and sweating nervously so there was a purple black sheen on his skin, against which his eyes were very white.

He saw me and tried to swing the machine-gun onto me, but it was on his right hip and he blocked himself awkwardly in the turn. I aimed for the notch where the two collarbones meet, that was framed by the opening of his uniform at the base of his throat. I threw overhand, snapping my wrist into it at the moment of release so the knife leapt in a silvery blur and thudded precisely into the mark I had chosen. The blade was completely buried and only the dark walnut handle protruded from his throat.

He tried to cry out, but no sound came, for the blade had severed all his vocal chords as I intended. He sank slowly to his knees facing me in a prayerful attitude with his hands dangling at his sides and the machine-gun hanging on its strap.

We stared at each other for a moment that seemed to last for ever. Then he shuddered violently and a thick burst of bubbling blood poured from his mouth and nose, and he pitched face forward to the ground.

Crouched low, I flipped him onto his back and withdrew the knife against the clinging drag of wet flesh, and I cleaned the blade on his sleeve.

Working swiftly I stripped him of his weapon and the spare magazines in the bandolier on his webbing belt, then, still crouching low, I dragged him by his heels into the gluey mud of the creek and knelt on his chest to force him below the surface. The mud flowed over his face as slowly and thickly as molten chocolate, and when he was totally submerged I buckled the webbing belt around my waist, picked up the machine-gun and slipped back quietly through the breach that I had made in the line of beaters.

As I ran doubled over and using all the cover there was, I checked the load on the AK47. I was familiar with the weapon. I had used it in Biafra and I made sure that the magazine was full and that the breech was loaded before I slipped the strap over my right shoulder and held it ready on my hip.

When I had moved back about five hundred yards I paused and took shelter against the trunk of a palm while I listened. Behind me, the line of beaters seemed to have run into trouble against the swamp, and they were trying to sort themselves out. I listened to the shouts and the angry shrill of the whistle. It sounded like a cup final, I thought, and grinned queasily, for the memory of the man I had killed was still nauseatingly fresh.

Now that I had broken through their line I turned and struck directly across the island towards my rendezvous with Chubby on the south peak. Once I was out of the palm groves onto the lower slopes, the vegetation was thicker, and I moved more swiftly through the better cover.

Half way to the crest I was startled by a fresh burst of gunfire. This time it was the distinctive whipcracking lash of the FN, a sharper slower beat than the storm of AK47 machine-gun fire that answered it immediately.

I judged by the volume and duration of the outburst that all the weapons involved had emptied magazines in a continuous burst. A heavy silence followed.

Chubby was having a go, after all my warnings. Although I was bitterly angry, I was also thoroughly alarmed by what trouble he had gotten himself into. One thing was certain—Chubby had missed whatever he had aimed at.

I broke from a trot into a run, and angled upwards towards the crest, aiming to reach the area from which the gunfire had sounded.

I burst out of a patch of goosebush into a narrow overgrown path that followed the direction I wanted, and I turned into it and went into a full run.

I topped the rise and almost ran into the arms of one of the uniformed seamen coming in the opposite direction, also at a headlong run.

There were six of his comrades with him in Indian file, all making the best possible speed on his heels. Thirty yards farther back was another who had lost his weapon and whose uniform jacket was sodden with fresh blood.

On all their faces were expressions of abandoned terror, and they ran with the single-minded determination of men pursued closely by all the legions of hell.

I knew instantly that this rabble were the survivors of an encounter with Chubby Andrews, and that it had been too much for their nerves. They were hell-bent and homeward-bound—Chubby's shooting must have improved miraculously, and I made him a silent apology.

So much were the seamen involved with the devil behind them that they seemed not to notice me for the fleeting instant which it took for me to slip the safety-catch on the machine-gun on my hip, brace myself with knees bent and feet spread.

I swung the weapon in a short kicking traverse aimed low at their knees. With a rate of fire like that of an AK47, you must go for the legs, and rely on another three or four hits in the body as the man drops through the sheet of fire. It also defeats the efforts of the short barrel to ride up under the thrust of the recoil.

They went down in a sprawling shrieking mass, punched backwards into each other by the savage strike of the soft heavy-calibre slugs.

I held the trigger down for the count of four, and then I turned and plunged off the path into the thick wall of goosebush. It hid me instantly and I doubled over as I jinked and dodged under the branches.

Behind me, a machine-gun was firing, and the bullets tore and snapped through the thick foliage. None came near me and I settled back into a quick trot.

I guessed that my sudden and completely unexpected attack would have permanently accounted for two or three of the seamen, and may have wounded one or two others.

However, the effect on their morale would be disastrous—especially coming so soon after Chubby's onslaught. Once they reached the safety of the crash boat, I guessed that the forces of evil would debate long and hard before setting foot on the island again. We had won the second round decisively, but they still had Sherry North. That was the major trump in their hands. As long as they held her they could dictate the course of the game.

Chubby was waiting for me among the rocks on the saddle of the peak. The man was indestructible.

'Jesus, Harry, where the hell you been?' he growled. 'I've been waiting here all morning.'

I saw that he had retrieved my haversack from the cleft in the rocks where I had left it. It lay with two captured AK47 rifles and bandoliers of ammunition at his feet.

He handed me the water bottle, and only then did I realize how thirsty I was. The heavily chlorinated water tasted like Veuve Clicquot, but I rationed myself to three swallows.

'I got to apologize to you, Harry. I had a go. Just couldn't help it, man. They were bunched up and standing out in the open like a Sunday-school picnic. Just couldn't help myself, gave them a good old squirt. Dropped two of them and the others run like hens, shooting their pieces straight up in the air as they go.'

'Yeah,' I nodded. 'I met them as they crossed the ridge.'

'Heard the shooting. Just about to come and look for you.'

I sat down on the rock beside him, and found my cheroots in the haversack. We each lit one and smoked in grateful silence for a moment which Chubby spoiled.

'Well, we lit a fire under their tails—don't reckon they'll come back for more. But they have still got Miss Sherry, man. Long as they got her, they are winning.'

'How many were there, Chubby?'

'Ten.' He spat out a scrap of tobacco and inspected the glowing tip of the cheroot. 'But I took out two—and I think I winged another.'

'Yeah,' I agreed. 'I met seven on the ridge. I had a go at them also. Aren't more than four left now—and there are eight more out of my bunch. Say a dozen, plus those left on board—another six or seven. About twenty guns still against us, Chubby.'

'Pretty odds, Harry.'

'Let's work on it, Chubby.'

'Let's do that, Harry.'

I selected the newest and least abused of the three machine-guns and there were five full magazines of ammunition for it. I cached the discarded weapons under a slab of flat rock and loaded and checked the other.

We each had another short drink from the water bottle and then I led the way cautiously along the ridge, keeping off the sky-line, back towards the deserted camp.

From the spot at which I had first spotted the approach of the *Mandrake* we surveyed the whole northern end of the island.

As we guessed they would, Manny and Suleiman Dada had taken all their men off the island. Both the whaleboat and the smaller motor-boat were moored alongside the crash boat. There was much confused and meaningless activity on board, and as I watched the scurrying figures I imagined the scenes of terrible wrath and retribution which were taking place in the main cabin.

Suleiman Dada and his new protégé were certainly wreaking a fearful vengeance on their already badly beaten and demoralized troops.

'I want to go down to the camp, Chubby. See what they left for us,' I said at last, and handed him the binoculars. 'Keep watch for me. Three quick shots as a warning signal.'

'Okay, Harry,' he agreed, but as I stood up there was a renewed outbreak of feverish activity on board the crash boat. I took the glasses back from Chubby and watched Suleiman Dada emerge from the cabin and make a laborious ascent to the open bridge. In his white uniform, bedecked with medals that glittered in the sunlight and attended by a host of helpers, he reminded me of a fat white queen termite being moved from its royal cell by swarming worker ants.

The transfer was effected at last and as I watched through the binoculars I saw an electronic bullhorn handed to Suleiman. He faced the shore, lifted the hailer to his mouth and through the powerful lens I saw his lips moving. Seconds later the sound reached us clearly, magnified by the instrument and carried by the wind.

'Harry Fletcher. I hope you can hear me.' The deep well-modulated voice was given a harsher sound by the amplifier. 'I plan to put on a demonstration this evening which will convince you of the necessity of cooperating with me. Please be in a position where you can watch. You will find it fascinating. Nine o'clock this evening on the afterdeck of this ship. It's a date, Harry. Don't miss it.'

He handed the bullhorn to one of his officers and went below.

'They're going to do something to Sherry,' muttered Chubby and fiddled disconsolately with the rifle in his lap.

'We'll know at nine,' I said, and watched the officer with the bullhorn climb from the deck into the motor-boat. They set off on a slow circuit of the island, stopping every half mile to shout a repetition of Suleiman Dada's invitation to me at the silent tree-lined shore. He was very anxious for me to attend.

'All right, Chubby,' I glanced at my watch. 'We have hours yet. I'm going down to the camp. Watch out for me.'

The camp had been ransacked and plundered of most items of value, equipment and stores had been smashed and scattered about the caves—but still some of it had been overlooked.

I found five cans of fuel and hid them along with much other equipment that might be of value. Then I crept cautiously down into the grove, and learned with relief that the hiding-place of the chest and the golden tiger's head and the other stores was undisturbed.

Carrying a five-gallon can of drinking water and three cans of corned beef and mixed vegetables I climbed again to the ridge where Chubby waited. We ate and drank and I said to Chubby: 'Get some sleep if you can. It's going to be a long hard night.'

He grunted and curled up in the grass like a great brown bear. Soon he was snoring softly and regularly.

I smoked three cheroots slowly and thoughtfully, but it was only as the sun was setting that I had my first real stroke of genius. It was so simple, and so delightfully apt that it was immediately suspect and I re-examined it carefully.

The wind had dropped and it was completely dark by the time I was certain of my idea and I sat smiling and nodding contentedly as I thought about it.

The crash boat was brightly lit, all her ports glowed and a pair of floods glared whitely down upon the afterdeck, so it looked like an empty stage.

I woke Chubby and we ate and drank again. 'Let's go down to the beach,' I said. 'We'll have a better view from there.'

'It might be a trap,' Chubby warned me morosely.

'I don't think so. They are all on board, and they are playing from strength. They've still got Sherry. They don't have to try any fancy tricks.'

'Man, if they do anything to that girl—' he stopped himself, and stood up. 'All right, let's go.'

We moved silently and cautiously down through the grove with our weapons cocked and our fingers on the triggers, but the night was still and the grove deserted.

We halted among the trees at the top of the beach. The crash boat was only two hundred yards away and I leaned my shoulder against the trunk of a palm and focused my glasses on her. It was so clear and close that I could read the writing on the lid of a packet from which one of the sentries took and lit a cigarette.

We had a front row seat for whatever entertainment Suleiman Dada was planning, and I felt the stir of apprehension and knowledge of coming horror blow like a cold breeze across my skin.

I lowered the glasses and whispered softly to Chubby, 'Change your piece for mine,' and he passed me the long-barrelled FN and took the AK47.

I wanted the accuracy of the FN to command the deck of the crash boat. Naturally there was nothing I could do to intervene while Sherry was unharmed, but if they did anything to her—I would make sure she didn't suffer alone.

I squatted down beside the palm tree, adjusted the peep sights of the rifle, and drew a careful bead on the head of the deck guard. I knew I could put a bullet through his temple from where I sat and when I was satisfied I laid the rifle across my lap and settled down to wait.

The mosquitoes from the swamp whined around our ears but both Chubby and I ignored them and sat quietly. I longed for a cheroot to soothe the tension of my nerves, but I was forced to forgo that comfort.

Time passed very slowly, and new fears came to plague me and make the waiting seem even longer than it was—but finally, a few minutes before the promised hour, there was a renewed stirring and bustle on board the crash boat and once more Suleiman Dada was helped up the ladder by his men and took his place at the bridge rail looking down over the after-deck. He was sweating heavily and it had soaked the area around the armpits and across the back of his white uniform jacket. I guessed that he had passed his own period of waiting by frequent recourse to the whisky bottle, probably from my own stock that had been plundered from the cave.

He laughed and joked with the men around him, his vast belly shaking with mirth, and his men echoed the laughter slavishly. The sound of it carried across the water to the beach.

Suleiman was followed by Manny Resnick and his blonde lady friend. Manny was well groomed and cool-looking in his expensive casual clothing. He stood slightly apart from the others, his expression aloof and disinterested. He reminded me of an adult at a children's party, seeing out a boring and mildly unpleasant duty.

In contrast, Lorna Page was excited and shiny-eyed as a girl on her first date. She laughed with Suleiman Dada and leaned expectantly over the rail above the deserted deck. Through the powerful glasses I could see the flush on her cheeks which was not rouge.

I was concentrating on her so that it was only when I felt Chubby move suddenly and restlessly, and heard his grunt of alarm that I swung the glasses downwards onto the deck.

Sherry was there, standing between two of the uniformed sailors. They held her arms and she looked small and frail between them.

She still wore the clothes she had thrown on so hurriedly that morning and her hair was dishevelled. Her face was gaunt and her expression strained—but it was only when I studied her carefully that I saw that what looked like sleepless dark rings below her eyes were in fact bruises. With a cold chill of anger, I realized that her lips were swollen and puffed up as though they had been stung by bees. One of her cheeks was also fatly distorted and bruised.

They had beaten her and knocked her about badly. Now that I looked for it I could see dark splotches of dried blood on her blue shirt, and when one of the guards dragged her around roughly to face the shore I saw that one of her hands was bandaged roughly—and that either blood or disinfectant had stained the bandages.

She looked tired and ill, nearly at the end of her strength. My anger threatened to wipe out my reason. I wanted to inflict hurt upon those that had treated Sherry like this, and I had already begun to lift the rifle with hands that shook with the force of my hatred before I could control myself. I closed my eyes tightly and took a long deep breath to steady myself. The time would come—but it was not now.

When I opened my eyes again and refocused the binoculars, Suleiman Dada had the bullhorn to his lips.

'Good evening, Harry, my dear friend. I am sure you recognize this young lady.' He made a wide gesture towards Sherry and she looked up at him wearily. 'After questioning her closely, a procedure which alas caused her a little discomfort, I am at last convinced that she does not know the whereabouts of the property in which friends and I are interested. She tells me that you have hidden it.' He paused and mopped his streaming face with a towel handed to him by one of his men before he went on.

'She is no longer of any interest to me—except possibly as a medium of exchange.'

He made a gesture, and Sherry was hustled away below. Something cold and slimy moved in my guts at her going. I wondered if I would ever see her again—alive.

Onto the deserted deck filed four of Suleiman's men. Each of them had stripped to the waist and the floodlights rippled on their smooth darkly muscled bodies.

Each of them carried the hickory wooden handles of a pick-axe, and silently they formed up at the points of a star about the open deck. Next a man was led into the open centre by two guards. His hands were tied behind his back. They stood on each side of him and slowly forced him to turn in a circle and show himself while Suleiman Dada's voice boomed through the bullhorn.

'I wonder if you recognize him?' I stared at the stooped creature in canvas prison overalls that hung in filthy grey tatters from his gaunt frame. His skin was pale and waxy with deep-set dark eyes, long scraggly blond hair hung in greasy snakes about his face and his half-grown beard was thin and wispy.

He had lost teeth, probably knocked from his mouth with a careless blow.

'Yes, Harry?' Suleiman laughed fruitily over the loud hailer. 'A sojourn in Zinballa prison does wonders for a man, does it not— but the regulation garb is not as smart as that of an Inspector of Police.'

Only then did I recognize ex-Inspector Peter Daly—the man who I had pitched from the deck of *Wave Dancer* into the waters of the outer lagoon just before I had escaped from Suleiman Dada by running the channel at Gunfire Reef.

'Inspector Peter Daly,' Suleiman confirmed with a chuckle, 'a man who let me down badly. I do not like men who let me down, Harry. I really take it very hard. I brought him along for just such an eventuality. It was a wise precaution, for I believe that a graphic demonstration is so much more convincing than mere words.'

Once again he paused to mop his face and to drink deeply from a glass offered him by one of his men. Daly fell to his knees and looked up at the man on the bridge. His expression was of abject terror, and his mouth dribbled saliva as he pleaded for mercy.

'Very well, we can proceed if you are ready, Harry,' he boomed, and one of the guards produced a large black cloth bag which he pulled over Peter Daly's head and secured with a drawn string around his neck. They dragged him roughly to his feet again.

'It's our own variation on the game of blind man's bluff.'

Through the glasses I saw the liquid flood soak through the front of Peter Daly's canvas trousers, as his bladder emptied in anguished terror. Obviously he had seen this game played before during his stay in Zinballa prison.

'Harry, I want you to use your imagination. Do not see this snivelling filthy creature—but in his place imagine your lovely young lady friend.' He breathed heavily, but when the man beside him offered him the towel again Suleiman struck him a passionless back-handed blow that sent him sprawling across the bridge, and he continued evenly, 'Imagine her lovely young body, imagine her delicious fear as she stands in darkness not knowing what to expect.'

The two guards began to spin Daly between them, as they do in the children's game, around and around he went and now I could faintly hear his muffled shrieks and cries of fear.

Suddenly the two guards stepped away from him, and left the circle of half-naked men with their pick handles. One of them placed the butt of his weapon in the small of Daly's back and shoved him, reeling and staggering across the circle and the man opposite was waiting to drive the end of his club into Daly's belly.

Back and forth he staggered, driven by the thrust of the clubs. Slowly his tormentors increased the savagery of their attack, until one of them hefted his club and swung it like an axe at a tree. It smashed into Daly's ribs.

It was the signal to end it, and as Peter Daly fell to the deck they crowded about him, the clubs rising and falling in a fearsome rhythm and the blows sounding clearly across the lagoon to where we watched in disgust and revulsion.

One after the other they tired, and stepped back to rest from their grim work and Peter Daly's crumpled and broken body lay in the centre of the deck.

'Crude, you will say, Harry—but then you will not deny that it is effective.'

I was sickened by the barbaric cruelty of it, and Chubby muttered beside me, 'He's a monster—I've never heard of nothing like that before.'

'You have until noon tomorrow, Harry, to come to me unarmed and reasonable. We will talk, we will agree on certain matters, we will make an exchange of assets and we will part friends.'

He stopped speaking to watch while one of his men secured a line to Peter Daly's ankle, and they hoisted him to the mast-head of the crash boat where he dangled grotesquely, like some obscene pennant. Lorna Page was looking up at him, her head thrown back so the blonde hair hung down her back and her lips were slightly parted.

'If you refuse to be reasonable, Harry, then at noon tomorrow I shall sail around this island with your lady friend hanging like that—' He pointed up to the corpse whose masked head swung slowly back and forth only a few feet above the deck, '—from the mast. Think about it, Harry. Take your time. Think about it well.'

Suddenly the floodlights were switched off, and Suleiman Dada began his laborious descent to the cabin. Manny Resnick and Lorna Page followed him. Manny was frowning slightly, as though he were pondering a business deal, but I could see that Lorna was enjoying herself.

'I think I'm going to throw up,' muttered Chubby.

'Get it over then,' I said, 'because we have a lot of work to do.'

I stood up and quietly led the way back into the palm grove. We took it in turns to dig while the other stood guard among the trees. I would not use a light for fear of attracting attention from the crash boat and we were both exaggeratedly careful to maintain silence and not to let the clank of metal on metal sound through the grove.

We lifted the remaining cases of gelignite and blasting equipment, then we did the same with the rusted pay chest and carried it to a carefully chosen site below the steeply sloping ground of the peak. Fifty yards up the slope was a fold in the ground thickly screened with goosebush and salt grass.

We dug another hole for the chest, going deep into the soft soil until we struck water. Then we repacked the pay chest and reburied it. Chubby climbed up to the hidden fold above us and made his arrangements there.

In the meantime I reloaded the machine-gun and wrapped it lightly in one of my old shirts, the five full magazines placed with it, and I buried the lot under an inch of sand, next to the stem of the nearest palm tree where the recent rain waters had cut a shallow dry runnel down from the slope.

The water-torn trench and the tree were forty paces from the spot where the chest was buried, and I hoped it was far enough. The trench was little more than two feet deep and would provide scanty cover.

The moon came out after midnight and it gave us enough light to check our arrangements. Chubby made sure I was in full view from his hideaway up the slope when I stood beside the shallow runnel. Then I climbed up to him and double-checked him. We lit a cheroot each, sheltering the match and screening the glowing tips with cupped hands, while we went over our planning once again.

I was particularly anxious that there should be no misunderstanding in our timing and signals, and I made Chubby repeat them twice. He did so with long-suffering and theatrical patience, but at last I was satisfied. We dumped the cheroot butts and scraped sand over them and when we went down the slope we both carried palm-frond brooms to sweep out all signs of activity.

The first part of my planning was complete, and we returned to where the golden tiger and the rest of the gelignite was cached. We reburied the tiger and then I prepared a full case of gelignite. It was a massive overdose of explosive, sufficient for a tenfold over-kill—but I have never been a man to stint myself when I have the means to indulge.

I would not be able to use the electric blaster and insulated wire, and I must rely on one of the time-pencil detonators. I have a strong distaste for these temperamental little gadgets. They operate on the principle of acid eating through a thin wire which holds the hammer on a powder cap. When the acid cuts the wire the cap explodes, and the delay in the detonation is governed by the strength of the acid and the thickness of the wire.

There can be a large latitude of error in this timing which on one occasion caused me a nearly fatal embarrassment. However, in this case I had no choice in the matter—and I selected a pencil with a six-hour delay and prepared it for use with the gelignite.

Among the equipment overlooked by the looters was my old oxygen rebreathing underwater set. This diving set is almost as dangerous to use as the time pencils. Unlike the aqualung which uses compressed air, the rebreather employs pure oxygen which is filtered and cleansed of carbon dioxide after each breath and then cycled back to the user.

Oxygen breathed at pressures in excess of twice atmospheric becomes as poisonous as carbon monoxide. In other words, if you rebreathe pure oxygen below underwater depths of thirty-three feet, it will kill you. You have to have all your wits together to play around with the stuff— but it has one enormous advantage. It does not blow bubbles on the surface to alarm a sentry and give away your position to him.

Chubby carried the prepared case of gelignite and the rifle when we went back to the beach. It was after three o'clock when I had donned and tested the oxygen set, and then I carried the gelignite down to the water and tested that for buoyancy. It needed a few pounds of lead weights to give it a neutral buoyancy and make it easier to handle in the water.

We had reached the water from the beach around the horn of the bay from the anchored crash boat. The point of sand and palm trees covered us as we worked, and at last I was ready.

It was a long tiring swim. I had to round the point and enter the bay —a distance of almost a mile—and I had to tow the case of explosive with me. It dragged heavily through the water and it took me almost an hour before I could see the lights of the crash boat glimmering above me through the clear water.

Hugging the bottom I crept forward slowly, terribly aware that the moonlight would silhouette me clearly against the white sand of the lagoon bed, for the water was clear as gin and only twenty-five feet deep.

It was a relief to move slowly into the dark shadow cast by the crash boat's hull and to know that I was safe from discovery. I rested for a few minutes, then I unrolled the nylon slings that I had on my belt and secured them to the case of gelignite.

Now I checked the time on my wrist watch, and the luminous hands showed ten minutes past four o'clock.

I crushed the glass ampoule of the time pencil, releasing the acid to begin its slow eroding attack on the wire, and I returned it to its pre-pared slot in the case of explosive. In six hours, more or less, the whole lot would go up with the force of a two hundred pound aerial bomb.

Now I left the floor of the lagoon and rose slowly to the hull of the crash boat. It was foul with a hanging slimy beard of weed and the hull itself was thick with a rough scale of shellfish and goose-neck mussels.

I moved slowly along the keel, searching for an anchor point—but there was none and at last I was forced to use the shank of the rudder. I bound the case in position with all the nylon rope I had—and when I was finished I was certain that it would resist even the drag of water when the crash boat was travelling at the top of her speed.

Satisfied at last, I sank once more to the bed of the lagoon and moved off quietly on my return. I made much better speed through the water now without the burden of the gelignite case and Chubby was waiting for me on the beach.

'Fixed up?' he asked quietly, as he helped me shed the oxygen set.

'Just as long as that pencil does its job.'

I was so tired now that the walk back through the grove seemed like an eternity and my feet dragged in the loose footing. I had slept little the previous night, and not at all since then.

This time Chubby watched over me while I slept, and when he shook me gently awake it was after seven o'clock and the daylight was growing swiftly.

We ate a breakfast cold from the can, and I finished it with a handful of high-energy glucose tablets from the survival kit and washed them down with a mug of chlorinated water.

I drew the knife from the sheath on my belt and threw it underhand to pin into the trunk of the nearest palm. It stood there shivering with the force of the impact.

'Show off!' muttered Chubby, and I grinned at him, trying to look relaxed and easy.

'Look, just like the man said—no weapons,' and I spread my empty hands.

'You ready?' he asked, and we both stood up and looked at each other awkwardly. Chubby would never wish me good luck—which was the worst of all possible hex to put on someone.

'See you later,' he said.

'Okay, Chubby.' I held out my hand. He took it and squeezed it hard, then he turned away, picked up the FN rifle and plodded off through the grove.

I watched him out of sight, but he never looked back and I turned away myself and walked down unarmed to the beach.

I walked out from among the trees and stood at the water's edge, staring across the narrow strip of water at the crash boat. The dangling corpse had been removed from the masthead, I saw with relief.

For many seconds none of the sentries on deck noticed me, so I raised both hands above my head and gave them a loud 'Halloo'. Instantly there was a boil of activity and clamour of shouted orders on board the crash boat. Manny Resnick and Lorna appeared at the rail and stared across at me, while half a dozen armed seamen dropped into the whaleboat and headed for the beach.

As the boat touched, they leaped out onto the sand and surrounded me with the muzzles of the AK47s pressed eagerly into my back and belly. I kept my hands hoisted at half-mast and tried to maintain an expression of disinterest as a petty officer searched me with deliberate thoroughness for any weapon. When he was at last satisfied, he placed his hand between my shoulderblades and gave me a hearty shove towards the whaleboat. One of the more eager of his men took this as a licence and he tried to rupture my kidneys with the butt of his AK47— but the blow landed six inches high.

I made briskly for the whaleboat to forestall any further martial displays and they crowded into the boat around me, pressing the muzzles of their fully loaded weapons painfully into various parts of my anatomy.

Manny Resnick watched me come in over the side of the crash boat.

'Hallo again, Harry,' he smiled without mirth.

'The pleasure is all yours, Manny,' I returned the death's head grin, and another blow caught me between the shoulder-blades and drove me across the deck. I ground my teeth together to control my anger, and I thought about Sherry North. That helped.

Commander Suleiman Dada was sprawled on a low couch covered with plain canvas cushions. He had removed his uniform jacket and it hung heavy with all the braid and medals from a hook on the bulkhead beside him. He wore only a sweat-soaked and greyish sleeveless vest, and even this early in the morning he held a glass of pale brown liquid in his right hand.

'Ah, Harry Fletcher—or should it be Harry Bruce?' he grinned at me like an enormous coal-black baby.

'You take your pick, Suleiman,' I invited him, but I didn't feel like playing word games with him now. I had no illusions about how dangerous was the position in which Sherry and I were placed, and my nerves were painfully tight and fear growled like a caged animal in my belly.

'I have learned so much more about you from my good friends,' he indicated Manny and the blonde Lorna who had followed me into the main cabin. 'Fascinating, Harry. I never dreamed you were a man of such vast talent and formidable achievement.'

'Thanks, Suleiman, you really are a brick, but let's not get carried away with compliments. We have important business—don't we?'

'True, Harry, very true.'

'You have raised the tiger throne, Harry, we know that,' Manny cut in, but I shook my head.

'Only part of it. The rest has gone—but we salvaged what there was.'

'All right, I'll buy that,' Manny agreed. 'Just tell us what there is.'

'There is the head of the tiger, about three hundred pounds weight in gold—' Suleiman and Manny glanced at each other.

'Is that all?' Manny asked, and I knew instinctively that Sherry had told them everything she knew during the beating they had given her. I did not hold that against her. I had expected it.

'There is also the jewel chest. The stones removed from the throne were placed in an iron pay chest.'

'The diamond—the Great Mogul?' demanded Manny.

'We've got it,' I said, and they murmured and smiled and nodded at each other. 'But I'm the only one who knows where it is—' I added softly, and immediately they were tense and quiet again.

'This time I've got something to trade, Manny. Are you interested?'

'We are interested, Harry, very interested,' Suleiman Dada spoke for him, and I was aware of the tension growing between my two enemies now that the loot was almost in view.

'I want Sherry North,' I said.

'Sherry North?' Manny stared at me for a moment, and then let out a brief cough of amusement. 'You're a bigger fool than I thought you were, Harry.'

'The girl is of no further interest to us.' Suleiman took a swallow from his glass, and I could smell his sweat in the rising warmth of the cabin. 'You can have her.'

'I want my boat, fuel and water to get me off the island.'

'Reasonable, Harry, very reasonable,' Manny smiled again as if at a secret joke.

'And I want the tiger's head,' and both Manny and Suleiman laughed out loud.

'Harry! Harry!' Suleiman chided me, still laughing.

'Greedy Harry,' Manny stopped laughing.

'You can have the diamond and about fifty pounds weight of other gem stones—' I tried to sell the idea with all the persuasion I could muster. It was the understandable thing to do for a man in my position, '—in comparison the head is nothing. The diamond is worth a million —the head would just cover my expenses.'

'You are a hard man, Harry,' Suleiman chuckled. 'Too hard.'

'What will I get out of it, then?' I demanded.

'Your life, and be grateful for it,' Manny said softly, and I stared at him. I saw the coldness in his eyes, like those of a reptile, and I knew beyond all doubt what his intentions were for me, once I had led them to the treasure.

'How can I trust you?' I went through the motions, however, and Manny shrugged indifferently.

'Harry, how can you not trust us?' Suleiman intervened. 'What could we possibly gain by killing you and your young lady?'

'And what could you possibly lose,' I thought, but I nodded and said, 'Okay. I don't have much choice.'

They relaxed again, smiling at each other and Suleiman lifted his glass in a silent salute.

'Drink, Harry?' he asked.

'It's a little early for me, Suleiman,' I declined, 'but I would like to have the girl with me now.'

Suleiman motioned one of his men to fetch her.

'I want the whaleboat loaded with fuel and water and left on the beach,' I went on doggedly, and Suleiman gave the orders.

'The girl goes with me when we go ashore and after I have shown you the chest and the head, you'll take it and go.' I stared from one to the other. 'You'll leave us on the island unharmed, do we agree?'

'Of course, Harry.' Suleiman spread his hands disarmingly. 'We are all agreed.' I was afraid that they would see the disbelief in my expression—so I turned with relief to Sherry as she was led into the cabin.

My relief faded swiftly as I stared at her.

'Harry,' she whispered through her swollen purple lips. 'You came— oh God, you came.' She took a faltering step towards me.

Her cheek was bruised and swollen horribly, and from the extent of the oedema I thought perhaps the bone was cracked. The bruising under her eyes made her look sick and consumptive, and blood had dried in a black crust on the rims of her nostrils. I didn't want to look at her injuries, so I took her in my arms and held her to my chest.

They were watching the pair of us with amusement and interest. I felt their eyes upon us, but I did not want to face them and let them see the murderous hatred that must show in my eyes.

'All right,' I said, 'let's get it over with.' When at last I turned to face them, I hoped that my expression was under control.

'Unfortunately, I shall not be going with you,' Suleiman made no effort to rise from the couch. 'Climbing in and out of small boats, walking great distances in the sun and through the sand are not my particular pleasures. I shall say farewell to you here, Harry, and my friends—' again he indicated Manny and Lorna, '—will go with you as my representatives. Of course, you will also be accompanied by a dozen of my men—all of them armed and operating under my instructions.' I thought that this warning was not entirely for my benefit alone.

'Goodbye, Suleiman. Perhaps we'll meet again.'

'I doubt it, Harry,' he chuckled. 'But God speed and my blessings go with you.' He dismissed me with one great pink-palmed paw and with the other he raised his glass and drained the last half-inch of liquor.

Sherry sat close beside me in the motor-boat. She leaned against me, and her body seemed to have shrivelled with the pain of her ordeal. I put my arm about her shoulders, and she whispered wearily, 'They are going to kill us, Harry, you know that, don't you?'

I ignored the question and asked softly, 'Your hand,' it was still wrapped in the rough bandage, 'what happened?'

Sherry looked up at the blonde girl beside Manny Resnick, and I felt her shiver briefly against me.

'She did it, Harry.' Lorna Page was chatting animatedly to Manny Resnick. Her carefully lacquered hairstyle resisted the efforts of the breeze to ruffle it, and her face was meticulously made up with expensive cosmetics. Her lipstick was moist and glossy and her eyelids were silvery green, with long mascaraed lashes around the cat's eyes.

'They held me—and she pulled out my fingernails.' She shuddered again, and Lorna Page laughed lightly. Manny cupped his hands around a gold Dunhill lighter for her while she lit a cigarette. 'They kept asking me where the treasure was—and each time I couldn't answer she pulled out a nail with the pliers. They made a tearing sound as they came out.' Sherry broke off and held her injured hand protectively against her stomach. I knew how near she was to breaking completely and I held her close, trying to transmit strength to her by physical contact.

'Gently, baby, gently now,' I whispered, and she pressed a little closer to me. I stroked her hair, and tried once again to control my anger, bearing down hard upon it before it clouded my wits.

The motor-boat ran in and grounded on the beach. We climbed out and stood on the white sands while the guards ringed us with levelled weapons.

'Okay, Harry,' Manny pointed. 'There's your boat all ready for you.' The whaleboat was drawn up on the beach. 'The tanks are full and when you've shown us the goods—you can take off.'

He spoke easily, but the girl beside him looked at us with hot predatory eyes—the way a mongoose looks at a chicken. I wondered what way she had chosen for us. I guessed that Manny had promised us to her for her pleasure without reservations—just as soon as he was through with us.

'I hope we aren't going to play games, Harry. I hope you're going to be sensible—and not waste our time.'

I had noticed that Manny had surrounded himself with his own men. Four of them, all armed with pistols, one of them my old acquaintance who had driven the Rover on our first meeting. To balance them there were ten black seamen under a petty officer, and already I sensed that the opposition was divided into two increasingly hostile parties. Manny further reduced the number of seamen in the party by detailing two of them to stay with the motor-boat. Then he turned to me, 'If you are ready, Harry, you may lead the way.'

I had to help Sherry, holding her elbow and guiding her up through the grove. She was so weak that she stumbled repeatedly and her breathing was distressed and ragged before we reached the caves.

With the mob of armed men following us closely, we went on along the edge of the slope. Surreptitiously I glanced at my watch. It was nine o'clock. One hour to go before the case of gelignite under the crash boat blew. The timing was still within the limits I had set.

I made a small show out of locating the precise spot where the chest was buried, and it was with difficulty that I refrained from glancing up the slope to where the fold of ground was screened by vegetation.

'Tell them to dig here,' I said to Manny, and stepped back. Four seamen handed their weapons to a comrade and assembled the small folding army-type shovels they had brought with them.

The soil was soft and freshly turned so they went down at an alarming speed. They would expose the chest within minutes.

'The girl's hurt,' I said to Manny, 'she must sit down.' He glanced at me, and I saw his mind work swiftly. He knew Sherry could not run far and I think he welcomed the opportunity to distract some of the seamen—for he spoke briefly to the petty officer and I led Sherry to the palm tree and sat her down against the stem.

She sighed with weary relief, and two of the seamen came to stand over us with cocked weapons.

I glanced up the slope, but there was no sign of anything suspicious there, although I knew Chubby must be watching us intently. Apart from the two guards, everyone else was gathered expectantly around the four men who were already knee-deep in the freshly dug hole.

Even our two guards were consumed with curiosity; their attention kept wandering and they glanced repeatedly at the group forty yards away.

I heard quite clearly the clang as a spade struck the metal of the chest —and there was a shout of excitement. They all crowded around the excavation with a babble of rising voices, beginning to pull and elbow each other for the opportunity to look down into it. Our two guards turned their backs on us, and took a step or two in the same direction. It was more than I could have hoped for.

Manny Resnick shoved two seamen aside roughly, and jumped down into the hole beside the diggers. I heard him shouting, 'All right then, bring those ropes and let's lift it out. Carefully, don't damage anything.'

Lorna Page was leaning out over the hole also. It was perfect.

I lifted my right hand and wiped my forehead slowly in the signal I had arranged with Chubby, and as I dropped my hand again, I seized Sherry and rolled swiftly backwards into the shallow rain-washed runnel.

It caught Sherry by surprise, and I had handled her roughly in my anxiety to get under cover. She cried out as I hurt her already painful injuries.

The two guards whirled at the cry, lifting their machine-guns and I knew that they were going to fire—and that the shallow trench provided no cover.

'Now, Chubby, now!' I prayed and threw myself on top of Sherry to shield her from the blast of machine-gun fire and I clapped both hands over her ears to protect them.

At that instant Chubby switched the knob on the electric battery blaster, and the impulse ran down the insulated wire that we had concealed so carefully the night before. There was half a case of gelignite crammed into the iron pay chest—as much explosive as I dared use without destroying Sherry and myself in the blast.

I imagined Chubby's fiendish glee as the case blew. It blew upwards, deflected by the sides of the excavation—but I had packed the sticks of gelignite with sand and handfuls of semi-precious stones to serve as primitive shrapnel and to contain the blast and make it even more vicious.

The group of men around the hole were lifted high in the air, spinning and somersaulting like a troupe of insane acrobats, and a column of sand and dust shot a hundred feet into the air.

The earth jarred under us, slamming into our prone bodies—then the shock wave tore across us. It knocked sprawling the two guards who had been about to fire down on us, ripping their clothing from their bodies.

I thought my eardrums had both burst, I was completely deafened but I knew that I had saved Sherry's ears from damage. Deafened and half blinded by dust, I rolled off Sherry and scratched frantically in the sandy bottom of the trench. My fingers hit the machine-gun buried there and I dragged it out, pulling off the protective rags and coming swiftly to my knees.

Both the guards nearest me were alive, one crawling to his knees and the other sitting up dazedly with blood from a burst eardrum trickling down his cheek.

I killed them with two short bursts that knocked them down in the sand. Then I looked towards the broken heap of humanity around the excavation.

There was small, convulsive movement there and soft moans and whimpering sounds. I stood up shakily from the trench—and I saw Chubby standing up on the slope. He was shouting, but I heard nothing for the ringing buzzing din in my ears.

I stood there, swaying slightly, peering stupidly around me and Sherry rose to her feet beside me. She touched my shoulder, saying something, and with relief I heard her voice as the ringing in my ears subsided slightly.

I looked again towards the area of the explosion and saw a strange and frightening sight. A half-human figure, stripped of clothing and most of its skin, a raw bleeding thing with one arm half torn loose at the shoulder socket and dangling at its side by a shred of flesh rose slowly from beside the excavation like some horrible phantom from the grave.

It stood like that for the long moment which it took me to recognize Manny Resnick. It seemed impossible that he should have survived that holocaust, but more than that he began walking towards me.

He tottered step after step, closer and closer, and I stood frozen, unable to move myself. I saw then that he was blinded, the flying sand had scorched his eyeballs and flayed the skin from his face.

'Oh God! Oh God!' Sherry whispered beside me, and it broke the spell. I lifted the machine-gun and the stream of bullets that tore into Manny Resnick's chest were a mercy.

I was still dazed, staring about me at the shambles we had created when Chubby reached me. He took my arm and I could hear his voice as he shouted, 'Are you okay, Harry?' I nodded and he went on, 'The whaleboat! We have got to make sure of the whaleboat.'

I turned to Sherry. 'Go to the cave. Wait for me there,' and she turned away obediently.

'Make sure of these first,' I mumbled to Chubby, and we went to the heap of bodies about the shattered iron chest. All of them were dead or would soon be so.

Lorna Page lay upon her back. The blast had torn off her outer clothing and the slim pale body was clad only in lacy underwear, with shreds of the green slack suit hanging from her wrists and draped about her torn and still bleeding legs.

Defying even the explosion, her hairstyle retained its lacquered elegance except for the powdering of fine white sand. Death had played a macabre joke upon her—for a lump of blue lapis lazuli from the jewel chest had been driven by the force of the explosion deep into her forehead. It had embedded itself in the bone of her skull like the eye of the tiger from the golden throne.

Her own eyes were closed while the third precious eye of the stone glared up at me accusingly.

'They are all dead,' grunted Chubby.

'Yes, they're dead,' I agreed, and tore my eyes away from the mutilated girl. I was surprised that I felt no triumph or satisfaction at her death, nor at the manner of it. Vengeance, far from being sweet, is entirely tasteless, I thought, as I followed Chubby down to the beach.

I was still unsteady from the effects of the explosion, and although my ears had recovered almost entirely, I was hard-pressed to keep up with Chubby. He was light on his feet for such a big man.

I was ten paces behind him as we came out of the trees and stopped at the head of the beach.

The whaleboat lay where we had left her, but the two seamen detailed to guard the motor-boat must have heard the explosion and decided to take no chances.

They were half way back to the crash boat already, and when they saw Chubby and me, one of them fired his machine-gun in our direction. The range was far beyond the accurate limits of the weapon, and we did not bother to take cover. However, the firing attracted the attention of the crew remaining aboard the crash boat—and I saw three of them run forward to man the quick-firer in the bows.

'Here comes trouble,' I murmured.

The first round was high and wide, cracking into the palms behind us and pitting their stems with the burst of shrapnel.

Chubby and I moved quickly back into the grove and lay flat behind the sandy crest of the beach.

'What now?' Chubby asked.

'Stalemate,' I told him, and the next two round from the quick-firer burst in futile fury in the trees above and behind us—but then there was a delay of a few seconds and I saw them training the gun around.

The next shot lifted a tall graceful spout of water from the shallows alongside the whaleboat. Chubby let out a roar of anger, like a lioness whose cub is threatened.

'They are trying to take out the whaleboat!' he bellowed, as the next round tore into the beach in a brief spurt of soft sand.

'Give it to me,' I snapped, and took the FN from him, thrusting the short-barrelled AK47 at him and lifting the strap of the haversack off Chubby's shoulder. His marksmanship was not equal to the finer work that was now necessary.

'Stay here,' I told him, and I jumped up and doubled away around the curve of the bay. I had almost entirely recovered from the effects of the blast now—and as I reached the horn of the bay nearest the anchored crash boat I fell flat on my belly in the sand and pushed forward the long barrel of the FN.

The gun crew were still blazing away at the whaleboat, and spouts of sand and water rose in rapid succession about it. The plate of frontal armour of the gun was aimed diagonally away from me, and the backs and flanks of the gun crew were exposed.

I pushed the rate of fire selector of the FN onto single shot, and drew a few long deep breaths to steady my aim after the long run through the soft sand.

The gun-layer was pedalling the traversing and elevating handles of the gun and had his forehead pressed hard against the pad above the eye-piece of the gunsight.

I picked him up in the peepsight and squeezed off a single shot. It knocked him off his seat and flung him sideways across the breech of the gun. The untended aiming handles spiralled idly and the barrel of the gun lifted lazily towards the sky.

The two gun-loaders looked around in amazement and I squeezed off two more snap shots at them.

Their amazement was altered instantly to panic, and they deserted their posts and sprinted back along the deck, diving into an open hatchway.

I swung my aim across and up to the open bridge of the crash boat. Three shots into the assembled officers and seamen produced a gratifying chorus of yells and the bridge cleared miraculously.

The motor-boat from the beach came alongside, and I hastened the two seamen up the side and into the deckhouse with three more rounds. They neglected to make the boat fast and it drifted away from the side of the crash boat.

I changed the magazine of the FN and then carefully and deliberately I put a single bullet through each porthole on the near side of the boat. I could hear clearly the shattering crack of glass at each shot.

This proved too much provocation for Commander Suleiman Dada. I heard the donkey winch clatter to life and the anchor chain streamed in over the bows, glistening with sea-water, and the moment the fluked anchor broke out through the surface, the crash boat's propellers churned a white wash of water under her stern and she swung round towards the opening of the lagoon.

I kept her under fire as she moved slowly past my hiding-place lest she change her mind about leaving. The bridge was screened by a wind shield of dirty white canvas, and I knew the helmsman was lying behind this with his head well down. I fired shot after shot through the canvas, trying to guess his position.

There was no apparent effect so I turned my attention to the portholes again, hoping for a lucky ricochet within the hull.

The crash boat picked up speed rapidly until she was waddling along like an old lady hurrying to catch a bus. She rounded the horn of the bay, and I stood up and brushed off the sand. Then I reloaded the rifle and broke into a trot through the palm grove.

By the time I reached the north tip of the island, and climbed high enough up the slope to look out over the deep-water channel, the crash boat was a mile away, heading resolutely for the distant mainland of Africa, a small white shape against the shaded greens of the sea and the higher harsher blue of the sky.

I tucked the FN under my arm and found a seat from where I could watch her further progress. My wrist watch showed seven minutes past ten o'clock, and I began to wonder if the case of gelignite below the crash boat's stern had, after all, been torn loose by the drag of the water and the wash of the propellers.

The crash boat was now passing between the submerged outer reefs before entering the open inshore waters. The reefs blew regularly, breathing white foam at each surge of the sea as though a monster lay beneath the surface.

The small white speck of the crash boat seemed ethereal and insubstantial in that wilderness of sea and sky; soon she would merge with the wind-flecked and current-chopped waters of the open sea.

The explosion when it came was without passion, its violence muted by distance and its sound toned by the wind. There was a sudden soft waterspout that enveloped the tiny white boat. It looked like an ostrich feather, soft and blowing on the wind, bending when it reached its full height and then losing its shape and smearing away across the choppy surface.

The sound reached me many seconds later, a single un-warlike thud against my still-tender eardrums, and I thought I felt the flap of the blast like the puff of the wind against my face.

When the spray had blown into nothingness the channel was empty; no sign remained of the tiny vessel and there was no mark of her going upon the wind-blown waters.

I knew that with the tide the big evil-looking albacore sharks hunted inshore upon the flood. They would be quick to the taint of blood and torn flesh in the water, and I doubted that any of those aboard the crash boat who had survived the blast would long avoid the attentions of those single-minded and voracious killers. Those that found Commander Suleiman Dada would fare well, I thought, unless they recognized a kindred spirit and accorded him professional privilege. It was a grim little joke, and it gave me only fleeting amusement. I stood up and walked down to the caves.

I found my medical kit had been broken open and scattered during the previous day's looting, but I retrieved sufficient material to clean and dress Sherry's mutilated fingers. Three of the nails had been torn out. I feared that the roots had been destroyed, and that they would never grow again—but when Sherry expressed the same fears, I denied them stoutly.

Once her injuries were taken care of I made her swallow a couple of Codeine for the pain and made a bed for her in the darkness of the back of the cave.

'Rest,' I told her, kneeling to kiss her tenderly. 'Try and sleep. I will fetch you when we are ready to leave.'

Chubby was already busy with the necessary tasks. He had checked the whaleboat and, apart from a few shrapnel holes, found her in good condition.

We filled the holes with Pratleys putty from the toolchest, and left her on the beach.

The hole in which the chest had been buried served as a communal grave for the dead men and the woman lying about it. We laid them in it like sardines, and covered them with the soft sand.

We exhumed the golden head from its own grave with its glittering eye still in the broad forehead, and staggering under its weight we carried it down to the whaleboat and padded it with the polythene cushions in the bottom of the boat. The plastic packets of sapphires and emeralds I packed into my haversack and laid it beside the head.

Then we returned to the caves and salvaged all the undamaged stores and equipment—the jerrycans of water and petrol, the scuba bottles and the compressor. It was late afternoon before we had packed it all into the whaleboat and I was tired. I laid the FN rifle on top of the load and stood back.

'Okay, Chubby?' I asked, as I lit our cheroots and we took our first break. 'Reckon we can take off now.'

Chubby drew on the cheroot and blew a long flag of blue smoke before he spat on the sand. 'I just want to go up and fetch Angelo,' he muttered, and when I stared at him he went on. 'I'm not going to leave the kid up there. It's too lonely here, he'll want to be with his own people in a Christian grave.'

So while I went back to the caves to fetch Sherry, Chubby selected a bolt of canvas and went off into the gathering darkness.

I woke Sherry and made sure she was warmly dressed in one of my jerseys, then I gave her two more Codeine and took her down towards the beach. It was dark now, and I held the flashlight in one hand and helped Sherry with the other. We reached the beach and I paused uncertainly. There was something wrong, I knew, and I played the torch over the loaded vessel.

Then I realized what it was, and I felt a sick little jolt in my belly. The FN rifle was no longer where I had left it in the whaleboat.

'Sherry,' I whispered urgently, 'get down and stay there until I tell you.'

She sank swiftly to the sand beside the beached hull, and I looked around frantically for a weapon. I thought of the spear-gun, but it was under the jerrycans; my bait-knife was still pegged into a palm tree in the grove—I had forgotten about it until this moment. A spanner from the toolbox, perhaps—but the thought was as far as I got.

'All right, Harry, I've got the gun.' The deep throaty voice spoke out of the darkness close behind me. 'Don't turn around or do anything stupid.'

He must have been lying up in the grove after he had taken the rifle, and now he had come up silently behind me. I froze.

'Without turning around—just toss that flashlight back here. Over your shoulder.'

I did as he ordered and I heard the sand crunch under his feet as he stooped to pick it up.

'All right, turn around—slowly.' As I turned, he shone the powerful beam into my eyes, dazzling me. However, I could still vaguely make out the huge hulking shape of the man beyond the beam.

'Have a good swim, Suleiman?' I asked. I could see that he wore only a pair of short white underpants, and his enormous belly and thick shapeless legs gleamed wetly in the reflected torchlight.

'I am beginning to develop an allergy to your jokes, Harry,' he spoke again in that deep beautifully modulated voice, and I remembered too late how a grossly overweight man becomes light and strong in the supporting salt water of the sea. However, even with the turn of the tide to help him, Suleiman Dada had performed a formidable feat in surviving the explosion and swimming back through almost two miles of choppy water. I doubted any of his men had done as well.

'I think it should be in the belly first,' he spoke again, and I saw that he held the stock of the rifle across his left elbow. With the same hand he aimed the torch beam into my face. 'They tell me that is the most painful place to get it.'

We were silent for moments then, Suleiman Dada breathing with his deep asthmatic wheeze and I trying desperately to think of some way in which to distract him long enough to give me a chance to grab the barrel of the FN.

'I don't suppose you'd like to go down on your knees and plead with me?' he asked.

'Go screw, Suleiman,' I answered.

'No, I didn't really think you would. A pity, I would have enjoyed that. But what about the girl, Harry, surely it would be worth a little of your pride—'

We both heard Chubby. He had known there was no way he could cross the open beach undetected, even in the dark. He had tried to rush Suleiman Dada, but I am sure he knew that he would not make it. What he was really doing was giving me the distraction I so desperately needed.

He came fast out of the darkness, running in silently with only the squeak of the treacherous sand beneath his feet to betray him. Even when Suleiman Dada turned the rifle onto him, he did not falter in his charge.

There was the crack of the shot and the long lightning flash of the muzzle blast, but even before that, I was half way across the distance that separated me from the huge black man. From the corner of my eye I saw Chubby fall, and then Suleiman Dada began to swing the rifle back towards me.

I brushed past the barrel of the FN and crashed shoulder first into his chest. It should have staved his ribs in like the victim of a car smash —instead I found the power of my rush absorbed in the thick padding of dark flesh. It was like running into a feather mattress, and although he reeled back a few paces and lost the rifle, Suleiman Dada remained upright on those two thick tree-trunks of his legs, and before I could recover my own balance I was enfolded in a vast bear hug.

He picked me up off my feet, and pulled me to his mountainously soft chest, trapping both my arms and lifting me so that I could not brace my legs to resist his weight and strength. I experienced a chill of disbelief when I felt the strength of the man, not a hard brutal strength —but something so massive and weighty that there seemed no end to it, almost like the irresistible push and surge of the sea.

I tried with my elbows and knees, kicking and striking to break his hold, but the blows found nothing solid and made no impression upon the man. Instead, the enfolding grip of his arms began to tighten with the slow pulsing power of a giant python. I realized instantly that he was quite capable of literally crushing me to death—and I experienced a sense of panic. I twisted and struggled frantically and unavailingly in his arms, but as he brought more of his immense power to bear upon me, so his breathing wheezed more harshly and he leaned forward, hunching his great shoulders over me and forcing my back into an arc that must soon snap my spine.

I bent back my head, reached up with an open mouth and locked my teeth into the broad flattened nose. I bit in hard, with all my desperation, and quite clearly I felt my teeth slice through the flesh and gristle of his nose and instantly my mouth filled with the warm salty metallic flood of his blood. Like a dog at a bull-baiting, I worried and tugged at his nose.

The man bellowed a rear of agony and anger and he released his crushing grip from around my body to try and tear my teeth from his face. The instant my arms were free I twisted convulsively and got a purchase with both feet in the firm wet sand, so I could put my hip into him for the throw. He was so busy attempting to dislodge the grip of my teeth from his nose that he could not resist the throw and as he went over backwards my teeth tore loose, cutting away a lump of his living flesh.

I spat out the horrid mouthful but the warm blood streamed down my chin and I resisted the temptation to pause and wipe it clean.

Suleiman Dada was down on his back, stranded like some massive crippled black frog, but he would not remain helpless much longer. I had to take him out cleanly now and there was only one place where he might be vulnerable.

I jumped up high over him and came down to knee-drop into his throat, to drive my one knee with the full weight and momentum of my body into his larynx and crush it.

He was swift as a cobra, throwing up both arms to shield his throat and to catch me as I descended onto him. Once again, I was enmeshed by those thick black arms, and we rolled down the beach, locked chest to chest, into the warm shallow water of the lagoon.

In a direct contrast of weight for weight like this, I was outmatched, and he came up over me with blood streaming from his injured nose, still bellowing with anger, and he pinned me into the shallows forcing my head below the surface and bearing down upon my chest and lungs with all his vast weight.

I began to drown. My lungs caught fire, and the need to breathe laced my vision with sparks and whorls of fire. I could feel the strength going out of me and my consciousness receding into blackness.

The shot when it sounded was muted and dull. I did not recognize it for what it was, until I felt Suleiman Dada jerk and stiffen, felt the strength go out of him and his weight slip and fall from me.

I sat up coughing and gasping for air, with water cascading from my hair and streaming into my eyes. In the light of the fallen torch I saw Sherry North kneeling on the sand at the edge of the water. She had the rifle still clutched in her bandaged hand and her face was pale and frightened.

Beside me, Suleiman Dada floated face down in the shallow water, his half-naked body glistening blackly like a stranded porpoise. I stood up slowly, water pouring from my clothing and she stared at me, horrified with what she had done.

'Oh God,' she whispered, 'I've killed him. Oh God!'

'Baby,' I gasped. 'That was the best day's work you've ever done,' and I staggered past her to where Chubby lay.

He was trying to sit up, struggling feebly.

'Take it easy, Chubby,' I snapped at him, and picked up the torch.

There was fresh blood on his shirt and I unbuttoned it and pulled it open around the broad brown chest.

It was low and left, but it was a lung hit. I saw the bubbles frothing from the dark hole at each breath. I have seen enough gonshot wounds to be something of an authority and I knew that this was a bad one.

He watched my face. 'How does it look?' he grunted. 'It's not sore.'

'Lovely,' I answered grimly. 'Every time you drink a beer it will run out of the hole.' He grinned crookedly, and I helped him to sit up. The exit hole was clean and neat, the FN had been loaded with solid ammunition, and it was only slightly larger than the entry hole. The bullet had not mushroomed against bone.

I found a pair of field dressings in the medical chest and bound up the wounds before I helped him into the boat. Sherry had prepared one of the mattresses and we covered him with blankets.

'Don't forget Angelo,' he whispered. I found the long heart-breaking canvas bundle where Chubby had dropped it, and I carried Angelo down and laid him in the bows.

I shoved the whaleboat out until I was waist-deep, then I scrambled over the side and started the engines. My one concern now was to get proper medical attention for Chubby, but it was a long cold run down the islands to St Mary's.

Sherry sat beside Chubby on the floorboards, doing what little she could for his comfort—while I stood in the stern between the motors and negotiated the deep-water channel before turning southwards under a sky full of cold white stars, bearing my cargo of wounded, and dying and dead.

We had been going for almost five hours when Sherry stood up from beside the blanketed form in the bottom of the boat and made her way back to me.

'Chubby wants to talk to you,' she said quietly, and then impulsively she leaned forward and touched my cheek with the cold fingers of her uninjured hand. 'I think he is going, Harry.' And I heard the desolation in her voice.

I passed the con to her. 'You see those two bright stars,' I showed her the pointers of the Southern Cross, 'steer straight for them,' and I went forward to where Chubby lay.

For a while he did not seem to know me, and I knelt beside him and listened to the soft liquid sound of his breathing. Then at last he became aware. I saw the starlight catch his eyes and he looked up at me, and I leaned closer to that our faces were only inches apart.

'We took some good fish together, Harry,' he whispered.

'We are going to take a lot more,' I answered. 'With what we've got

aboard now we will be able to buy a really good boat. You and I will
be going for billfish again next season—that's for sure.'

Then we were silent for a long time, until at last I felt his hand grope
for mine and I took it and held it hard. I could feel the callouses and the
ancient line burns from handling heavy fish.

'Harry,' his voice was so faint I could just hear it over the sound of the
motors when I laid my ear to his lips, 'Harry, I'm going to tell you
something I never told you before. I love you, man,' he whispered. 'I
love you better than my own brother.'

'I love you too, Chubby,' I said, and for a little longer his grip was
strong again, and then it relaxed. I sat on beside him while slowly that
big horny paw turned cold in my hands, and dawn began to pale the
sky above the dark and brooding sea.

During the next three weeks, Sherry and I seldom left the sanctuary
of Turtle Bay. We went together to stand awkwardly in the graveyard
while they buried our friends, and once I drove alone to the fort and
spent two hours with President Godfrey Biddle and Inspector Wally
Andrews—but the rest of that time we were alone while the wounds
healed.

Our bodies healed more quickly than did our minds. One morning
as I dressed Sherry's hand, I noticed the pearly white seeds in the healing flesh of her fingertips and I realized that they were the nail roots
regrowing. She would have fingernails once more to grace those long
narrow hands—I was thankful for that.

They were not happy days, the memories were too fresh and the days
were dark with mourning for Chubby and Angelo and both of us knew
that the crisis of our relationship was at hand. I guessed what agonies
of decision she must be facing, and I forgave her the quick flares of
temper, the long sullen silences—and her sudden disappearances from
the shack when for hours at a time she walked the long deserted beaches
or made a remote and lonely figure sitting out on the headland of
the bay.

At last I knew that she was strong enough to face what lay ahead for
both of us. One evening I raised the subject of the treasure for the first
time since our return to St Mary's.

It lay now buried beneath the raised foundations of the shack. Sherry
listened quietly as we sat together upon the veranda, drinking whisky
and listening to the sound of the night surf upon the beach.

'I want you to go ahead to make the arrangements for the arrival of the coffin. Hire a car in Zürich and drive down to Basle. I have arranged a room for you at the Red Ox Hotel there. I have picked that hotel because they have an underground parking garage and I know the head porter there. His name is Max.' I explained my plans to her. 'He will arrange a hearse to meet the plane. You will play the part of the bereaved widow and bring the coffin down to Basle. We will make the exchange in the garage, and you will arrange for my banker to have an armoured car to take the tiger's head to his own premises from there.'

'You've got it all worked out, haven't you?'

'I hope so.' I poured another whisky. 'My bank is Falle et Fils and the man to ask for is M. Challon. When you meet him you will give him my name and the number of my account—ten sixty-six, the same as the battle of Hastings. You must arrange with M. Challon for a private room to which we can invite dealers to view the head—' I went on explaining in detail the arrangements I had made, and she listened intently. Now and then she asked a question but mostly she was silent, and at last I produced the air ticket and a thin sheaf of traveller's cheques to carry her through.

'You have made the reservations already?' she looked startled, and when I nodded she thumbed open the booklet of the air ticket. 'When do I leave?'

'On the noon plane tomorrow.'

'And when will you follow?'

'On the same plane as the coffin, three days later—on Friday. I will come in on the BOAC flight at 1.30. That will give you time to make the arrangements and be there to meet me.'

That night was as tender and loving as it had ever been, but even so I sensed a deeper mood of melancholia in Sherry—as at the time of leave-taking and farewell.

In the dawn, the dolphins met us at the entrance of the bay, and we romped with them for half the morning and then swam in slowly to the beach.

I drove her out to the airport in the old pick-up. For most of the ride she was silent and then she tried to tell me something, but she was confused and she did not make sense. She ended lamely, '—if anything ever happens to us, well, I mean nothing lasts for ever, does it—'

'Go on,' I said.

'No, it's nothing. Just that we should try to forgive each other—if anything does happen.' That was all she would say, and at the airport barrier she kissed me briefly and clung for a second with both arms about my neck, then she turned and walked quickly to the waiting aircraft. She did not look back or wave as she climbed the boarding ladder.

I watched the aircraft climb swiftly and head out across the inshore channel for the mainland, then I drove slowly back to Turtle Bay.

It was a lonely place without her, and that night as I lay alone under the mosquito net on the wide bed, I knew that the risk I was about to take was necessary. Highly dangerous, but necessary. I knew I must have her back here. Without her, it would all be tasteless. I must gamble on the pull I would be able to exert over her outweighing the other forces that governed her. I must let her make the choice herself, but I must try to influence it with every play in my power.

In the morning I drove into St Mary's and after Fred Coker and I had argued and consulted and passed money and promises back and forth, he opened the double doors to his warehouse and I drove the pick-up in beside the hearse. We loaded one of his best coffins, teak with silver-gilt handles, and red velvet-lined interior, into the back of the truck. I covered it with a sheet of canvas and drove back to Turtle Bay. When I had packed the coffin and screwed down the lid it weighed almost five hundred pounds.

When it was dark, I drove back into town and it was almost closing time at the Lord Nelson before I had completed my arrangements. I just had time for a quick drink and then I drove back to Turtle Bay to pack my battered old canvas campaign bag.

At noon on the next day, twenty-four hours earlier than I had arranged with Sherry North, I boarded the aircraft for the mainland and that evening caught the BOAC connection onwards from Nairobi.

There was no one to meet me at Zürich airport, for I was a full day early, and I passed quickly through customs and immigration and went out into the vast arrivals hall.

I checked my luggage before I went about tidying up the final loose threads of my plan. I found a flight outwards leaving at 1.20 the following day which suited my timing admirably. I made a single reservation, then I drifted over to the enquiries desk and waited until the pretty little blonde girl in the Swissair uniform was not busy, before engaging her in a long explanation. At first she was adamant, but I gave her the old crinkled eyes and smiled that way, until at last she became intrigued with it all—and giggled in anticipation.

'You sure you'll be on duty tomorrow?' I asked anxiously.

'Yes, Monsieur, don't worry, I will be here.'

We parted as friends and I retrieved my bag and caught a cab to the Zürich Holiday Inn just down the road. The same hotel where I had sweated out the survival of the Dutch policeman so long ago. I ordered a drink, took a bath and then settled down in front of the television set. It brought back memories.

A little before noon the following day I sat at the airport café pretending to read a copy of the *Frankfurter Allgemeine Zeitung* and watching the arrivals hall over the top of the page. I had already checked my baggage and my ticket. All I had to do was to go through into the final departure lounge.

I was wearing a new suit purchased that morning of such a bizarre cut and mousy shade of grey, that no one who knew him could believe that Harry Fletcher would be seen in public wearing it. It was two sizes too large for me, and I had padded myself with hotel towels to alter my shape entirely. I had also self-barbered my hair into a short and ragged style and dusted it with talcum powder to put fifteen years on my age. When I peered at my image through gold-rimmed spectacles in the mirror of the men's room, I did not even recognize myself.

At seven minutes past one, Sherry North walked in through the main doors of the terminal. She wore a suit of grey checked wool, a full length black leather coat and a small matching leather hat with a narrow businesslike brim. Her eyes were screened by a pair of dark glasses, but her expression was set and determined as she strode through the crowd of tourists.

I felt the sick slide and churn of my guts as I saw all my suspicions and fears confirmed and the newspaper shook in my hands. Following a pace behind and to her side was the small neatly dressed figure of the man she had introduced to me as Uncle Dan. He wore a tweed cap and carried an overcoat across his arm. More than ever he exuded an air of awareness, the hunter's alert and confident tread as he followed the girl.

He had four of his men with him. They moved quietly after him, quiet, soberly dressed men with closed watchful faces.

'Oh, you little bitch,' I whispered, but I wondered why I should feel so bitter. I had known for long enough now.

The group of girl and five men stopped in the centre of the hall and I watched dear Uncle Dan issuing his orders. He was a professional, you could see that in the way he staked out the hall for me. He placed his men to cover the arrivals gate and every exit.

Sherry North stood listening quietly, her face neutral and her eyes hidden by the glasses. Once Uncle Dan spoke to her and she nodded abruptly, then when the four strong-arm men had been placed, the two of them stood together facing the arrivals gate.

'Get out now, Harry,' the little warning voice urged me. 'Don't play fancy games. This is the wolf pack all over again. Run, Harry, run.'

Just then the public address system called the outward flight on which I had made a reservation the previous day. I stood up from the table in my cheap baggy suit and shuffled across to the enquiries desk. The little blonde Swissair hostess did not recognize me at first, then her mouth dropped open and her eyes flew wide. She covered her mouth with her hand and her eyes sparkled with conspiratory glee.

'The end booth,' she whispered, 'the end nearest the departures gate.' I winked at her and shuffled away. In the telephone booth I lifted the receiver and pretended to be speaking, but I broke the connection with a finger on the bar and I watched the hall through the glass door.

I heard my accomplice paging.

'Miss Sherry North, will Miss North please report to the enquiries desk.'

Through the glass I saw Sherry approach the desk and speak with the hostess. The blonde girl pointed to the booth beside mine and Sherry turned and walked directly towards me. She was screened from Uncle Dan and his merry men by the row of booths.

The leather coat swung gracefully about her long legs, and her hair was glossy black and bounding on her shoulders at each stride. I saw she wore black leather gloves to hide her injured hand, and I thought she had never looked so beautiful as in this moment of my betrayal.

She entered the booth beside me and lifted the receiver. Swiftly I replaced my own telephone and stepped out of the booth. As I opened her door she looked around with impatient annoyance.

'Okay, you dumb cop—give me a good reason why I shouldn't break your head,' I said.

'You!' Her expression crumpled, and her hand flew to her mouth. We stared at each other.

'What happened to the real Sherry North?' I demanded, and the question seemed to steady her.

'She was killed. We found her body—almost unrecognizable—in a quarry outside Ascot.'

'Manny Resnick told me he had killed her—' I said. 'I didn't believe him. He also laughed at me when I went on board to do a deal with him and Suleiman Dada for your life. I called you Sherry North and he laughed at me and called me a fool.' I grinned at her lopsidedly. 'He was right—wasn't he? I was a fool.'

She was silent then, unable to meet my eyes. I went on talking, confirming what I had guessed.

'So after Sherry North was killed, they decided not to announce her identity—but to stake out the North cottage. Hoping that the killers would return to investigate the new arrival—or that some other patsy would be sucked in and lead them home. They chose you for the stakeout, because you were a trained police diver. That's right, isn't it?'

She nodded, still not looking at me.

'They should have made sure you knew something about conchology as well. Then you wouldn't have grabbed that piece of fire coral—and saved me a lot of trouble.'

She was over the first shock of my appearance. Now was the time to whistle for Uncle Dan and his men, if she was going to. She remained silent, her face half-turned away, her cheek flushed with bright blood beneath the dark golden tan.

'That first night, you telephoned when you thought I was asleep. You were reporting to your superior officer that a sucker had walked in. They told you to play along. And—oh baby—how you played me.'

She looked at me at last, dark blue eyes snapping with defiance. Words seemed to boil behind her closed lips, but she held them back and I went on.

'That's why you used the back entrance to Jimmy's shop, to avoid the neighbours who knew Sherry. That's why those two goons of Manny's arrived to roast your fingers on the gas-ring. They wanted to find out who you were—because you sure as hell weren't Sherry North. They had killed her.'

I wanted her to speak now. Her silence was wearing my nerves.

'What rank is Uncle Dan—Inspector?'

'Chief Inspector,' she said.

'I had him tabbed the moment I laid eyes on him.'

'If you knew all this, then why did you go through with it?' she demanded.

'I was suspicious at first—but by the time I knew for certain I was crazy stupid in love with you.'

She braced herself, as though I had struck her, and I went on remorselessly.

'I thought by some of the things we did together that you felt pretty good about me. In my book when you love someone, you don't sell them down the river.'

'I'm a policewoman,' she flashed at me, 'and you're a killer.'

'I never killed a man who wasn't trying to kill me first,' I flashed back, 'just the way you hit Suleiman Dada.'

That caught her off-balance. She stammered and looked about her as if she were in a trap.

'You're a thief,' she attacked again.

'Yes,' I agreed. 'I was once—but that was a long time ago, and since then I worked hard on it. With a bit of help, I'd have made it.'

'The throne—' she went on, 'you are stealing the throne.'

'No, ma'am,' I grinned at her.

'What is in the coffin then?'

'Three hundred pounds of beach sand from Turtle Bay. When you see it, think of the times we had there.'

'The throne—where is it?'

'With its rightful owner, the representative of the people of St Mary's, President Godfrey Biddle.'

'You gave it up?' she stared at me with disbelief that faded slowly as something else began to dawn in her eyes. 'Why, Harry, why?'

'Like I said, I'm working hard on it.' Again we were staring hard at each other, and suddenly I saw the clear liquid flooding her dark blue eyes.

'And you came here—knowing what I had to do?' she asked, her voice choking.

'I wanted you to make a choice,' I said, and she let the tears cling like dewdrops in the thick dark eyelashes. I went on deliberately, 'I'm going to walk out of this booth and go out through that gate. If nobody blows the whistle I will be on the next flight out of here and the day after tomorrow, I will swim out through the reef to look for the dolphins.'

'They'll come after you, Harry,' she said, and I shook my head.

'President Biddle has just altered his extradition agreements. Nobody will be able to touch me on St Mary's. I have his word for it.'

I turned and opened the door of the booth. 'I'm going to be lonely as all hell out there at Turtle Bay.'

I turned my back on her then and walked slowly and deliberately to the departures gate, just as they called my flight for the second time. It was the longest and scariest walk of my entire life, and my heart thumped in time to my footsteps. Nobody challenged me and I dared not look back.

As I settled into the seat of the Swissair Caravelle and fastened my seat-belt, I wondered how long it would take her to screw up her nerve enough to follow me out to St Mary's, and I reflected that there was much I still had to tell her.

I had to tell her that I had contracted to raise the rest of the golden throne from Gunfire Break for the benefit of the people of St Mary's. In return President Godfrey Biddle had undertaken to buy me a new deep-sea boat from the proceeds—just like *Wave Dancer*—a token of the people's gratitude.

I would be able to keep my lady in the style to which I was accustomed, and of course there was always the case of Georgian silver gilt plate buried behind the shack at Turtle Bay for the lean and hungry off season. I hadn't reformed *that* much. There would be no more night runs, however.

As the Caravelle took off and climbed steeply up over the blue lakes and forested mountains, I realized that I did not even know her real name.

That would be the first thing I would ask her when I met her at the airport of St Mary's Island—Pearl of the Indian Ocean.